LIFELINE

LIFELINE

CATHERINE MCGUIRE

FHP
FOUNDERS HOUSE PUBLISHING

LIFELINE

Published by Founders House Publishing, LLC
Cover Art by Matt Forsyth

Paperback Edition: March 2017
ISBN-13: 978-1-945810-04-6
ISBN-10: 1-945810-04-1

For more information please visit www.foundershousepublishing.com

Published in the United States Of America

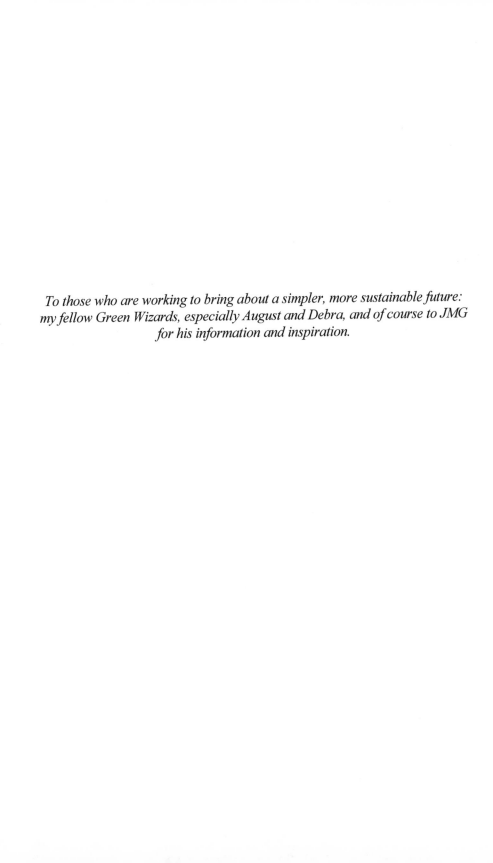

To those who are working to bring about a simpler, more sustainable future: my fellow Green Wizards, especially August and Debra, and of course to JMG for his information and inspiration.

LIFELINE

1

The old man was wearing an antique suit: a baggy navy blue zip jacket, bright red T-shirt printed with *Chairman Meow* and a cat wearing a cap, shredded jeans that sagged below his hips, revealing the edge of a back tattoo. His white hair, mustache and beard were groomed; black, blue and red tattoos snaked up his neck into his sideburns; a scuffed plastic Avengers backpack leaned at his ankle. At least 80, he was standing like a gnarled tree on the corner of Main and First, grinning manically, waving a small box.

"This is one of the original IPODs; still in its case; never opened."

He said it to the air, repeating it after a pause. He was as excited as if he held a bushel of fresh apples, or two tickets to the doctor.

"Adjustment Shock," Geoff muttered, "harmless. Come on, Martin."

I had heard of those who had lost their minds in the Adjustment, but I'd never seen one close up. The stories were legend. How one man had hoarded unusable power tools, starving to death in his garage. How others had climbed the high voltage towers, leaving wreaths and sacrifices to whatever god would send power surging again. Another walked around trying to sell his Playoff tickets (the sport varied with the telling) for hundreds of dollars, swearing there was just a delay of game for weather, until he'd finally dropped on the street and died. During the initial chaos, few had time or energy to cope with the deniers, so most of them died off. But here was one who must have been cared for by family; he looked healthy enough, except for the mad glint in his eyes. I wondered who claimed him. But Geoff was moving on, so—with a last glance at the madman—I followed.

Madison was in the wilds of Ohio; we were four days beyond the Pittsburgh railroad terminus, and just getting *out* to this first possible client town had been like a cheap mescal mu-vid. The "Ohio safari" planned in

New York already looked insanely naïve. It had seemed so simple, even fun, when they explained it: New York needed non-satellite-based relay towers. Commco sent me to find towns along the needed pathway, to offer to restore some of the boons of civilization in return for an agreement to build, power and guard the towers. After all, it had only been fifty years. I would never have believed that the countryside would have turned barbaric so fast.

But this town was as filthy as New York's infamous ancient sewers—the stink of shit mingled with the sweat of horses and oxen, and other things I didn't want to know about. Oddly, they'd saved some street trees as decoration, not that it helped. In a thin May drizzle, rivulets of grime crawled down the crumbling brick and stucco buildings of this ten-block wart on the landscape. A street of two-story wooden storefronts, their elaborately molded windows retrofitted with wood or metal shutters—a few of them opened to reveal plank counters—looked like a life-size Holiday Display from Hell. No window glass—just stretched cloth (or skin? one heard jokes) or the ubiquitous shutter. Had there been riots, like New York? This looked like decay, not destruction. Where were the reclamation agency buildings, the state standards offices? There were only walls layered with cryptic, peeling messages, like the graffittied subway cars in Brooklyn's old Transit Museum. From the days of wasted paint. Parked in front of a BurgerMan shop—now a shoemaker's—a flat plank cart with truck-tire wheels and a bony black horse, unwatched. Of course to steal that, you might have to carry the horse. Other horse and mule carts picked their way around hulks of half-dissected cars and trucks that lined, and sometimes blocked, the streets. Like the Nightmare of Sleepy Hollow they told us as kids.

The farther we'd traveled from New York, the smaller and weirder the towns had become. Along the railroad corridor, most places had managed about a thousand townies and maybe a couple hundred beyond the Wall. The corridor towns were neat and well-organized, with the usual amenities in the usual places; enough undamaged circuitry and lighting had been salvaged to give a semblance of civilization. I'd even seen an old gas-driven Model T automobile, so some silver spoon had gone feudal. But last night, outside the walls, we'd slept in a church basement hostel because hotels and restaurants had already disappeared. And here, I saw no more than twenty people, and modern tunics and pants were conspicuously absent.

They were dressed like they'd raided a landfill without paying attention; size and fit optional. One fortyish woman wore a long-tailed blue denim shirt over a green wool skirt plus black pants and yellow plastic boots. A pink straw hat with a wide brim hid her eyes, so I couldn't see if she was stunned. An old man wore a Day-Glo orange jacket over royal blue trousers. Was this Adjustment Shock, too? Now I understood why Geoff had made me wear antique jeans, a button-down shirt, denim jacket—which had cost the company some dinero. They were topped by my favorite gutta percha rain jacket—not antique but pleasingly retro.

This was not how the sales trip was supposed to go. *Ah, Martin, you've landed yourself in it again!* And to think I was even sober at the time. I'd figured, as a former guttersnipe, that a trip to the countryside would be cinchy. Ten years of desk frankly had me bored and nostalgic for my young punk days. And Melinda in Sales had been so impressed. Meh.

"I don't see PoPo loitering, at least," I commented.

"What?"

"Pissed off police—don't you get into the City?"

I caught sight of a couple of bent bicycles lying in an alley, alongside black fragments of what looked like a large-screen TV.

"You'd think they'd at least repair their damn bikes," I murmured, pulling my rain jacket tighter, "no circuitry needed there." Damn rain, damn natives, damn me for a stupid ass. The office staff would be having lunch about now—uptown hydroponic salads and barbecued pink. I could be chatting up Melinda or Dimalya, or easing with *Whack a Troll*. Safe. Relaxed. Well, as relaxed as I ever was. I hadn't seen pink vat-meat since lunch on our first day. And the real stuff had all kinds of nasty gristle and…bits. Too much like slum stew.

"Repair? What with?" Geoff asked. He was, as usual, scanning the surroundings. A thin 21-year-old, he somehow managed to blend into any background. Ebony hair spilled under a battered fedora from some Halloween costume, but his beard was trimmed short. He slouched like a side street fastfinger, hands in overall pockets. He was impatient with my continual surprise, I knew. But after 36 hours "past the Wall," I still struggled to grasp this surreal existence. No electricity, no running water, no currency. And silent—how could they live with this infernal silence? Even the Wall towns had lacked music...almost a week without songs floating in the air, weaving around the noise of traffic...I was off-balance. Nothing, including my first few City years fighting uphill had prepared me for this. I'd heard horror stories—everyone had. But none of us really believed them. Even the favelas of Long Island had jerry-rigged power! All the negotiating tricks I had planned to use—all the diplomacy, body language, social cues—would any of them work out here? How weird had it gotten??

A kid on a wheeled board shot around the corner behind me, and I leaped sideways, still torqued from our first encounter with bandits yesterday. Four slim, silent figures on speed bikes and skateboards had nimbly swerved around cracked pavement, chasing our e-bikes. Not slum sharks by any means, but they might have caught us if Geoff hadn't thrown a concussion grenade. That was outside of Middletown, and the roads had deteriorated a lot since then. We could have walked here faster.

"Why wouldn't they sell the bikes, at least?"

He shrugged. "Some towns care and some don't."

"It doesn't look promising. You were supposed to bring me to good-lead towns."

"The towns were picked by your company. Blame them."

His lack of concern was insolent. But he was bodyguard, guide and "smoother"; anything else was extra. A professional tracker, Geoff was apparently used to traveling alone. He'd been as silent as a dead vidscreen for most of the train trip, no matter how I pumped him for info. When I got back to the office, I would be talking to Cheyenne, oh yes. Maybe she was 'venging me for snagging the supervisor job; maybe this was her way of becoming the next one in that position. *Just trust him.* Yeah, right.

We ambled down Main Street, searching for any official-looking building. Finally, next to a salvage shop in a sandstone walk-up with actual glass windows, we found the Chamber of Commerce. Stepping adroitly around some fly-encrusted horse dung, I followed Geoff up worn stone steps into a surprisingly clean hallway. The gray tile floor had been washed, the mahogany hall table had been dusted recently and the walls were lined with framed pictures minus their glass—had those become the windows? The first door on the left was marked *Information.* I hesitated. I had planned to go in first, as a NYC rep with "protection", but I now wondered if the threat of Army retribution would keep me safe. After a moment, I waved Geoff in.

"Morning, sir. Could we speak to the manager?"

Geoff's voice was so oily smooth my head snapped around. What happened to his raspy growl? His slouch? This guy leaning over the counter was smiling, his granite-sharp customs officer expression morphing into something human. He removed his rain-spattered leather jacket and fished in the pocket of his red/black plaid overshirt, all the while smiling at the plump young man sitting at a desk behind the oak counter. He could have been a nearby farmer come to pay back taxes. The clerk barely glanced at me; his gaze was on Geoff, waiting to see what came out of the pocket. "Is he in? I know we don't have an appointment, but Mr.—oh, what was his name?"

"Jerolds," supplied the fascinated clerk.

"Jerolds, yes. Mr. Jerolds wants to be informed of these things." Probably truth, as far as it went. I stifled a grin.

Geoff finally pulled a folded paper from the pocket and placed it carefully on the counter. I had no idea what it was; could be a blank, a ploy. He brushed back his coal-black forelock and nodded brightly. The clerk stood, hesitant, pulled between counter and the door behind him. His dilemma was solved as the door opened and a wiry gray-haired man with a long, scraggly beard strode out. "Noam, I wanted that account book—" he stopped and stared at us.

"Mr. Jerolds," Geoff nodded at him and waved me forward. "Let me introduce you to Martin Forrester, an official representative from the city of New York, in the state of New York."

The astonishment in Jerold's eyes was a treat. Here was a man old enough to remember New York City—maybe he'd even visited it as a child. It was clear he was awed. A possible wedge.

"May we go into your office and discuss some important matters?" I looked for a way around the counter. Noam leaned over his desk and reached for a hinged section; I lifted it and went through. Geoff followed; our proximity made Jerolds back up toward his door, and I took that as an invite. He gave way before us and closed the door as I chose the cushioned leather chair, leaving Geoff the straightback.

"Mr. Jerolds, you are the person in charge of this town?" I tried to sound like my Uncle Rory, whose voice caused any daydreaming worker to pee his pants.

"What? I—well, I am President of the Chamber. The Mayor, well—the Mayor lives outside of town, and only comes in for Assembly Days. I take care of the details in between, I guess."

"I need to know if you can be trusted with this important task." I was troweling it, but this clearly wasn't a tech town. Authority might work better than geeks bearing gifts.

"Sirs, you have me at a disadvantage. I—we haven't heard from New York in several decades…didn't know it still existed," he finished, half to himself.

"It does, and it has tasked me with bringing Madison back into the 21st century," I said, with just a tinge of hauteur and vatloads of enthusiasm.

He shook his head, frowning. "New York? New York is…on the other side of Pennsylvania. That's… that's *days* away."

"Two days by train, Pittsburgh to the Apple—you do know we still have trains? No? Then that's the first pleasant surprise. The second is that we can still communicate by phone with Chicago, Los Angeles, Houston and the capital of the United States, Washington D.C."

His eyebrows shot up, then he peered at me, looking perhaps for the scam. I needed to make this as convincing as possible. Reaching into my raincoat pocket, I pulled out the phone, smiled at him, and keyed my office number, omitting mention that phones were for the elite—this Company beauty was only temporarily mine. I prayed to whatever god made little gray circuits that the battery was behaving today, and that I remembered my hasty training. But even a live plastic gizmo was enough to impress—or perhaps disturb—Jerolds. He leaned forward, mouth-breathing and blinking rapidly. *Come on, battery.* I tilted it so he couldn't see the phone bars raise and lower like a digital rollercoaster. Then the annoying little searchlight. Then bars again. Finally, the "no deal" exclamation point and beep. I grinned, assuming he didn't know it was out of range.

"The circuits are busy right now," I lied. "But I'll call again once I've filled you in." Jerolds nodded. He was staring at the phone and picking at the lint on his jacket cuff. "We are inviting Madison to be a part of our communications network." Stretching the truth like taffy. "Basically, for your cooperation in—" I revised the offer from *building*—they weren't capable—"in maintaining security of a communications tower, we will give you access—" once a year, as I understood it, "to the network we supervise." I sat back as if I'd bequeathed him the Brooklyn Bridge. Which I had, in a way.

He let his breath out slowly, then took another deep breath. His expression layered determination over confusion. "But we—but we can talk to everyone we know already."

Had it been that long, even for him? "But think of all the other people you could trade with. All the other towns who could provide you with information—"

"About what? About what, sir? I don't—I don't..." He paused; started again. "Your network offer is very generous, and no mistake, sir. It's just that I—" he looked around frantically, as if other townsfolk might appear to assist him. A committee complicated things. I raised my hands.

"It's alright, I understand, Mr. Jerolds. You have, I'm sure, made excellent use of the local area for trade and for survival. And there aren't many today who remember the vast trading networks that existed before the Adjustment."

This whole time, Geoff had been sitting silent, his posture and expression one of rapt attention. Now he cut in.

"Mr. Jerolds—do you know you are sitting on a middentrove of salvage?"

I remembered the bikes and grinned. "That's right—you could make a sizeable profit just by trading the machine parts that are sitting idle in your streets. Other towns would happily buy or trade for the unused bikes or cars—" An angry whinny from the street punctuated my sentence.

He sighed. "That's unclean. Can't do it."

I glanced over at Geoff, who was frowning. Unclean? Radioactivity? Frantically, I reviewed my mental list of nuclear plants. None for eighty miles. But there were other kinds of toxins. Geoff was getting out of his chair, smiling but tense.

"Well, thank you for your time, Mr. Jerolds," he said. "We won't keep you."

I stood. We'd failed, obviously. *Why??*

Outside, as he led me rapidly down the street, Geoff explained.

"They're *really* no-tech. Neo-Luddites, I'll bet."

We retraced our steps down a muddy side alley, along a noisy street of craftsmen and down another alley toward the creek. It was hard to keep up a full stride when I was gagged by the noxious odors and smoke from tannery, smithy and tar recycling as we passed them. Geoff had grudgingly told me a bit about NLs during our long train ride. They were against technology—with a vengeance.

"We were lucky Jerolds was such a rag-rug. By the time he spreads the word, we need to be out of town," Geoff said, dodging a small boy pulling a lopsided wooden cart.

"What about the old man?? The one with the iPod?"

"Probably the father of the mayor or some other honcho—you'd be amazed at the exceptions that are allowed if somebody knows somebody important."

No I wouldn't, I thought as we ducked into a rickety storage shed and uncovered our e-bikes. There were so many "exceptions" in the City that they should have been embarrassed to call them that. Just say there was one rule for the silver spoons and one for the others, and have done with it.

In five minutes we were on the gravel road that took us the ten miles back to Geoff's friends. Had Geoff really not known? He'd *seemed* surprised. Who had picked this town? *Someone* hadn't done their research. My stomach growled and I had a sudden craving for a Coney Island synthdog. Dinner was probably potatoes, and if we were really lucky, a chicken leg. With veins and stuff. Yum.

* * *

The farm consisted of about 15 acres with a three-bedroom woodframe house, four wheel-less RVs and a large sheet metal barn arranged in a cattywompus rectangle around a large mud patch where sawdust floated or sank but never helped. As we pulled up, a few wary chickens—yellow, white, speckled—were nosing out of the barn like little tug toys with bobbing heads, stopping to peck whatever rotten morsel they happened upon. They squawked and scattered as our e-bikes got closer. Just beyond the barn, two men and a teenage boy and girl were struggling to drag a plow through one of the mucky fields. They were horse-less—the group of them in rope harness dragging the plow as a skinny eight-year-old tried to steer. The resulting rows looked like a blind man's drawing. There was much shouting and arguing, and stopping to debate. My guess was that they'd been at this all day, although the acre was only half plowed. Geoff had said the twelve adults and eight kids who lived here relied on their corn-whiskey still and fields of marijuana to get them grains and meat. Pot and booze were the local anesthetics, according to Davis, the guy who had shown us around this morning, and with whom Geoff had slapped hands on an evening's accommodation. There were goats for milk and a couple acres of bug-nibbled veggies, but he'd said they lived mostly on eggs and on the flour and beans they traded for. Subsistence potheads, they were at least willing to share their space with Geoff and me—I shouldn't complain. And we would be moving on tomorrow.

We locked up our bikes and went into the main house. The smell of mildew and dog hair was almost tolerable, but the straw-flecked chaos of the living room—the sagging green sofa, taped-up narrow chairs that looked like old airplane seats and the crippled end tables with their wild assorted junk—*that* just made my skin crawl. Too close to the grungy communal gang quarters that I'd put up with for five long years. Not to mention their regal hospitality—they tolerated us, barely. More like Tramp Towers than Trump Towers. From the moment we had arrived this morning to arrange the overnight, I'd had a sense of being underfoot. Their attitude seemed to be "fend for yourself," but even sitting in the "wrong" chair got someone pissed off. A weird philosophical conundrum: it's okay to stay here in theory, but not be any particular physical *here*. And now there was nothing to do until dinner and then a long boring stretch until bedtime. Another thing to "discuss" with Cheyenne. But maybe there *was* no other option out here.

Rosie, the alpha female, was a small bony woman with still-black hair but wrinkled as a Shar-pei. She was sprawled along the couch with a joint dangling from her lips, halfheartedly knitting, and droning some complaint to a thin pregnant blonde of about 18 who was standing in the kitchen doorway, clutching her swollen belly under a greasy pink floral tent of a blouse.

"…So the bitch didn't even weigh the goddamn potatoes—she handed me a bag, and said 'five pounds' like I'm supposed to believe her…"

They glanced up as we walked in, but kept talking as if we weren't there. Geoff walked across into the back hallway and I heard the thump of his knapsack in the large communal bedroom. Actually, Davis and Rosie got their own room, but we shared ours with three almost identical thin, wiry men in their 20s who had some relationship to the family. They didn't speak when we were introduced, and I immediately forgot their names.

Twin boys of eight—Lyle and Lucky, I think—also shared the room according to Rosie, but I hadn't seen them this morning. "Bed" room was a misnomer—there were mattresses on the floor, and in some cases piles of clothing. No furniture (probably burned for heat long ago); barely room to step between piles; backpacks went on the piles. I had no intention of leaving my knapsack anywhere I couldn't see it, so I was forced to lug it around. The women glared at me silently as I strode toward the kitchen, and the blonde stepped aside to let me through.

The kitchen had been stripped of all electrical fixtures—fridge, stove, microwave, appliances—so either the appliances had died during the flare, or they'd found it more economical to sell them to someone who had electricity to run them. In their places were an iron woodstove, a pedal-powered grain grinder and some large wooden bins that held the bulk foods. Two black-chimneyed corn oil lamps were placed on a central table and counter—this was going to be a *dark* boring evening. Muddy boots were kicked aside by the back door; dirt and straw had been tracked through the room like a fetid slum river snaking over worn gray tiles. There was nothing like ready-made food, but I was hungry, and my annoyance suddenly spilled over. As silently as a snake, I went through wooden cupboards whose flaking beige paint resembled some kind of skin disease. Keeping a half eye on the doorway, I picked my way through almost-clean plates, bowls, chipped glasses. Should I go out and demand a snack, even if it cost extra? Hunger always made me savage—had been that way since childhood, worsened by my teen slum years. I thought of the nutrition bars in my knapsack, but I was damned if I was going to eat my emergency supplies because these barbarians couldn't be bothered. In one cupboard, I found a box of what looked like cookies, grabbed four and went out the back door. Thank you, Hotel Davis.

The small covered porch was deserted and with a sigh I eased into a rickety metal and wood-slat chair. There was still a light drizzle, but the clouds were breaking up and light in dramatic shafts were angling toward the wooded hills. As if in celebration, a trill of bird song erupted from a nearby grove, and my spirits lifted. I was not much for nature generally, but perhaps such things are built into us. The sudden beauty and peace was soothing after the craziness of the day that I was only now able to replay and consider.

Should I contact the office and tell them how bad it was? How could I describe it without seeming like a limp loonie? They would never believe me. Neither the empty wilderness of some stories, nor the “mini cities”—tiny mirror images of New York—that other stories described, it had fallen back into a *Little House in the Prayeree* existence. Looked like no one out here had figured out how to rework blasted circuits or, like today, could care less. Of course, the whispers could really be true: that government and the rich had made pre-emergency preps, the only thing allowing the City to survive the Adjustment. I nibbled the stale cookies, oatmeal with what I hoped were raisins. What if my *basics* suddenly dried up out here? I was vaguely aware of things I had taken for granted even at my lowest point, a 14-year-old non-entity in a low-level gang in a slum that fed off the City. There was always someone there who knew how to rig up a rooftop windmill or passive solar water heater. And water still came through guarded pipes down from the Catskills, stealthily tapped for local cisterns. Having to physically carry and filter your own river water, grind wheat to bake your own bread, and somehow make a decent shelter left nothing for what *I* called living: listening to good music, partying with friends, cheering sports teams, finding romance. Might as well be a chicken, spend my whole day pecking for food until was time for bed. Might as well take myself out.

I pulled out the cell phone and checked, but the bars were just as low as in Jerold’s office. Had the satellite gotten worse, or was it always this bad out here? And more to the point, what did I do next? Was there any other way to get messages back? Was there any way to tell where the connection was better? I was aware that I’d started scrambling frantically in my mind, and I took a couple deep breaths. Okay—this was more like sewer-sludging than windsurfing. But I still had a guide, and I could check the phone constantly as we rode tomorrow, and stop wherever the signal was strongest—let them know things were not looking good...and find out who picked these towns and whether the next few were worth it.

A gaggle of grubby barefoot kids ran into the backyard, screaming and laughing, as wild as any feral dog horde. They chased around and threw mud balls at a large gnarled tree, missing and splattering each other. I was about to push myself up and find a quieter seat when one of the men came around the house and yelled at them to start weeding. Without dropping the volume, they raced to the back of the half-acre yard. Walking down rows of early greens, they threw the mud-rooted weeds at each other as they pulled. I was torn between contempt and vicarious elation—I'd have been beaten raw for such behavior. And this ramshackle farm was proof that my parents' way was better—but I'd still escaped as soon as I could.

I winced, remembering long days at Astoria Farm putting in my child-labor until I was old enough to flee. Endless backbreaking hours: spring was clod busting after the plow had gone through; summer was hoeing rows of beans; autumn was picking apples and nuts; winter was shelling and sorting and fixing. Running off to play meant a beating and often a lost meal. The Commune took its work seriously and children were produced as labor, not as pets like in the GoodOlDays. My parents, relatives and the other current and retired Guard families really bought into the "loyal citizen" crap, and their military dictatorship was the model for other Long Island farms. At eighteen I'd made it into the Big City, and my heart almost broke when I saw how they'd been played. At least in New York it was damn clear that every one worked for themselves.

The shafts of sunlight brightened and the drizzle stopped. Perfume from apple blossoms wafted on a slight breeze. Diamond-glint raindrops shimmied like LEDs on tree limbs, weeds, fence posts, smashed plastic chairs, an old blue bicycle, three suspicious compost heaps, the edges of upturned machines—I made out a four-tined tiller and a multi-disc sod thingie, but the rest was a tangle of rusty steel. Were these potheads also neo-Luddite, or just too stupid to fix and use good tools? But of course it wasn't that simple: I remembered an uncle cursing a blue streak because some bolt or spring had been impossible to get—local blacksmiths were good, but many of these pre-collapse machines required *other* machines to make the parts! It seemed halfbrained, but apparently was common before the Adjustment. Uncle Bob had been certain the vendors were refusing him parts in order to be able to buy back his useless machine cheaply, and sell it to silver spoons who had "hook". He'd stubbornly refused, taking the tiller or thresher apart and reusing or selling the pieces. *It was dog eat dog*, he'd said with a nasty grin, and he liked eating dog.

As the sun slid down behind me, the eastern sky faded to a dark denim blue. Somewhere beyond the low hills, the City was lighting up like a star-studded sky. Nightfall was so much worse here—no streetlights, shop lights—no light at all! Just flickering tallow candles and oil lamps that managed to make it even darker. Last night at the church I'd sat in semi-darkness for three hours after a sparse dinner of corn pancakes, salt beef and thin beer, hearing the churchmen drone their prayers. Without an ear plug, I couldn't even listen to my jazz. By bedtime I'd been ready to stuff their prayer books down their throats. At least these potheads weren't likely to pray all night.

I wished Teg were here to puzzle over this with me. He would have really enjoyed this weirdness—he was constantly quoting old books, and wondering how the outside world had survived. A tall blond with a long Polish name, he was one of the more intelligent gang members, someone like me who wanted to get past the primitive and the petty squabbles, into the big City for a *real* life, where you weren't always watching your back. *If only he had known*, I thought wryly. "Marty," he used to say, "it's just our luck that we're living through the decline of the Roman Empire." He seemed mostly amused by how much worse we were after the Adjustment. Teg came from way far out on the Island, was six years older than me, and strong enough to smash a door in one blow of his axe. Given that guns were nonexistent, it helped to have a lot of muscle, and my habit of avoiding strenuous farm work had come back to haunt me. Teg demonstrated exercises to strengthen my arms so I could at least defend myself with the staves, knives and ax handles that were weapons of choice. And he told wonderful stories about other civilizations, how they rose and fell—the Romans were just one, apparently, and he said it was in the nature of things that no civilization lasted much longer than a couple hundred years. I probably learned more from him than I'd learned from any of the winter school I'd been forced to attend. Of course, the town school was more about teaching us to be good citizens, to do basic sums and read and write enough to follow orders. It was boring except when they showed us books with pictures—the only images my family owned were tractor diagrams and one or two ghostly-pale family photos. When the teacher brought photos of old times, strange animals or faraway places, I drank it in. But unless you passed a bunch of tests and proved you could be a scientist or engineer, it wasn't "need to know". So Teg was always zazzing me on being ignorant of my heritage, as if heritage had any useful survival value.

Still, I was the one who explained to him why there were no guns—my grandparents said the government had grabbed a lot in the first confusion, and then bought up most of the rest for food when things started to fall apart. Then it quickly became a serious crime to own one, and when I saw that bus-size pistol at the United Nations Plaza, its barrel twisted like a pretzel, I knew they weren't kidding. So at least within the reach of the City, fighting required close combat. I'd figured Teg would ace once he got inside, but he'd died during a turf battle, one that I wasn't part of. I was glad I never saw his body, but wished I'd gotten to say goodbye. It still hurt, and now I really wished I'd asked him more questions—he'd have some good explanation for why this place had fallen apart.

There was a groan and clank, and I looked around, but dusk obscured the yard. Sounds were louder out here, with no music or machines to soften them. I caught myself tensing and straining to decipher every new noise. The children returned from the garden, bickering and shoving each other as they crossed the yard. They bounded up the back stairs and passed me on the way to the kitchen.

Potatoes with gray tasteless gravy, dry biscuits, small bits of what I hoped was chicken in an onion gravy—dinner was filling but not guaranteed to stay down. I noticed the adults—dulled out on pot and "the evening sherry", which is how they described their shot of moonshine—ate less than the kids, who shoveled it away and grabbed for more until they got their hands slapped. I counted myself lucky that I hadn't chosen the "dope not dinner" route that had slowly killed many gang members. They'd get so spiffed they didn't notice they were starving. Growing up without any of that probably helped. Geoff smoked with them but not enough to lose his wits. He was being just as silent and unhelpful, but tonight I'd insist on some info—I was tired of being led around like a prize pig. He left the room twice during dinner, and both times one of the kids cleared his plate, something he ignored.

"You're dressed fancy, Willis," Davis commented to one of the men who lived in the RVs. The man's green flannel shirt was rubbed shiny at the elbows and neck—if *that* was fancy…! Willis shrugged and said he was going to listen to troubadours in the next town.

"It's Troobie Doobie Do," he said. "I heard them last year and they was pretty good."

"Heard them and made it home again?" Rosie laughed. "They're the *worst* kind of press gang—you'd never get *me* in the audience!"

"Boss Markham gave 'em permission to come back," Willis replied sullenly.

"Maybe he gets a percentage," Davis said.

"They're singers, not slavers," Troy insisted. Then everyone had to weigh in, and the room was a babble of voices: "...official passage through the county"...."where do they *go* then—when they disappear?".... "used to call it running away with the circus"..."not running if they're in shackles"....

I tried to follow the sense of the arguments—possibly there were something like slumlords out here, who had say-so about travelers, especially salesman, musicians and repairman—all the itinerant jobbers. The rest of the speculation bordered on absurd. Willis ended it by standing up suddenly and leaving the room.

"I'll be happy to comfort your widow!" Davis called after him. Rosie thumped him on a bony shoulder and he chuckled.

After the meal, the dishes were piled in the sink and the group moved into the living room, where the fireplace was lit with old scrap wood that stank of tar and rot. I sat as far upwind as I could manage, on a torn cube hassock with stuffing splayed like a squished maggot. The living room was crowded and no one seemed to value personal space—those few but distinct inches that was an insult or challenge to invade. I tried to keep my legs from touching the sprawled residents. Geoff had commandeered a chair from the kitchen despite disgruntled glares that he ignored.

There was a general rush toward the fireplace, but Davis kicked and elbowed his way to the lopsided upholstered armchair nearest it and sat, hollering, "Hey—work or move!" The kids on the floor made faces, but scrambled for some peeled twigs and knives. They started whittling, making who knows what, but that apparently granted them firelight and more importantly, warmth. Men and women in chairs were knitting or mending clothes, while those farther back in the darkness seemed too stoned to do much.

"Tell Corn Maze!" one of the younger kids piped up. Murmurs both pro and con sounded like a flock of crows. "No—Don Old Duck!" Another young voice cried, and they argued until Davis yelled at them to shut up.

"Corn Maze first, then the adults get to pick," he growled, settling back in the chair and toking deeply. "The Corn Maze was to honor the God of Corn," he began, "and every year, in the most worthy cornfield, the cornfield with the biggest heads—" laughter from the adults was quickly muffled, "...the God would lay down the stalks in a magical pattern that could only be seen by UFOs and birds, 'cause nothin' else could fly. Every year they held a contest to map the maze and figure out the message of the Corn God. This one particular year, Zak the Brave decided to enter the contest, even though his mother wept and pleaded with him."

"'Cause if you lose, you died!" one kid shouted.

"Shut up. Because whoever tried and failed to discover the true pattern, they would be sacrificed to the Corn God." Smirking and murmuring suggested strong approval for this.

Davis waved his joint. "Pipe down, you buggers... But Zak was determined. He showed up at the field with his big slate board and several pieces of chalk in his pockets, and paid his finder's fee of two chickens. That was almost all his family had to eat. But the prize—a year's worth of free food for his family—that was worth the risk."

As he droned on, talking almost in a trance, I pulled my thoughts back to my own problems. I leaned over to Geoff and whispered, "Where are we heading tomorrow?" He shrugged and I leaned closer and almost gripped his shoulder—a declaration of feud—and hissed, "*Tell* me! Where next, how far, and what kind of town, dammit?"

He glared at me, shrugged again, and muttered, "East Plains, a half day, mill town on a river." The bastard was enjoying 'shrooming me. I fought my fury. As soon as the connection was good, I'd request permission for him to lead me back to the City—as far as I could see, he was taking company money and taking me on a snarkhunt.

After the Corn God story ended, the kids were sent off to bed—they ran off hooting and hollering and as likely to sleep as to fly to the moon. The adults moved closer to the fireplace, and the pregnant blond said she wanted to hear Jed's song, because she had a bet about the words. There was a ripple of laughter and at least four voices immediately started in on a song that was vaguely familiar from my childhood—at least the tune was:

This here's a story about a man named Jed
a poor engineer barely kept his family fed
then one day he was shooting at some fool
when down to the ground came a government tool.
Drone, that is—federal scold, 'lectric bee.
Well soon Jed was bugged by surveillance in the air;
All his neighbors said, "Jed move away from there!"...

It wasn't quite the same story—I didn't remember what my family sang, but it wouldn't be anti-government like this. After the song ended, Rosie said she wanted to hear one of the Arabian Nights. I knew those well enough to know they were full of innuendo and crude humor, and there was no way I was gonna sit here with a bunch of smoked brains while they smirked about the dirty jokes. So I picked my way across the room and into the bedroom, shutting the door, shuffling my feet to find the edges of the mattresses, and locating my assigned bed under the far window. Despite the hubbub in the next room and my misgivings about the next day, I fell asleep fairly quickly.

* * *

I am back in my apartment in the East Village; the red brick walls protecting me, the clamor of street bikes and trailers' comforting syncopation. Tomato and garlic odors waft through my window screen from the pizza place downstairs. Four feet from the tall ceiling, my loft bed is warmed by the rising heat and I snuggle under the wool spread, looking down at the tidy living room—blue twill sofa and Bentwood rocker pulled up to the iron-and-mosaic coffee table neatly stacked with production data for my quarterly rooftop dish report. Another full and satisfying day as a white-collar grunt, pushing pixels and paper instead of shoveling and sweating. Tomorrow I will get Javier in LA via satellite and... oh, but the satellite glitched yesterday, didn't it? And Rob had shaken his head and said, "Well, I'd warned you. It's barely functional, what do you expect? Los Angeles is about to become a foreign country, or a dream..." And I woke; the sound of trucks became the soft snores of the sleepers beside me; the room reeked of chamber pot and mold. For a second I thought I was back in the slums. I started to shake, then pinched myself savagely. No—I wasn't going to fall apart! I was in Ohio. The apartment was waiting for me. In fact, I was promised a mid-town apartment with two bedrooms and a view of the East River if I secured two client towns. *Hold on to that thought. Hold on to it.*

As dawn highlighted the dirty burlap window screens, I got off the lumpy straw mattress as quietly as possible, and used the chamber pot. Not only was it nasty, but no one here cared about using it privately. I rubbed the sleep from my face. Even though my beard and mustache felt scratchy and weird, I was glad I'd let them grow before the trip—no telling when I'd have a chance to shave. And most men didn't, out here. I slipped my soft leather tiretread shoes on, shrugged into my jacket, shouldered my pack and tiptoed outside for some slightly fresher air, letting the splintery pine door ease shut behind me.

The rain had stopped overnight, but the front overhang dripped, making thin music in the puddles. A scrawny man whom I had met briefly stepped out of the RV on my right and peed against the side of it. In my family's commune, he would have been flogged for that. Any urine went onto the compost for fertilizer. But this place seemed too dispirited to care about soil development.

I was stiff and sore from the lousy bed and worried that I'd look too rumpled to pass for a slick New Yorker. Somehow I doubted there'd be any place to clean or iron my clothes. I'd be lucky to find some place to shower! I needed to talk to Geoff about that. How *did* you clean these old clothes, anyway? I stared past the courtyard toward the western fields and forest, where we were heading. The fences looked tipsy, neglected, and wilderness was erasing the square edges. Did I really dare try one more town before giving up? How far out could I go and still feel like I could get home safe? For the first time in a long while, I felt naked, weaponless and out of my depth. Did Cheyenne deliberately pick this guide who was as silent as a dead vid screen? Or were they all like this—those who were crazy enough to travel through the barbaric places alone?

Hearing the noises of the waking community, I went back inside. Two of the men and the pregnant woman were sitting in the living room with their morning joints. Loud swearing from the kitchen drew me quickly through the mess. Davis was beating his fist on and swearing at the old grinder—a manual model converted to pedal. Dandelion root coffee again. Geoff came through the back door carrying a dozen eggs. He started cracking them into a chipped beige ceramic bowl, and my gut turned over. In two days we'd had eggs four times. That was *more* than enough for me until we got back to the City. Especially after I'd seen the state of those chickens. I practiced smiling as the others wandered in and started breakfast—eggs, biscuits (no butter) and dandelion coffee. Yum.

Alerted by the cooking odors, the living room group came in, grabbed plates from the dish drainer and helped themselves. The twin boys sidled up to the basket of hot biscuits, grabbed two each and fled.

"Dammit, Lyle—come back here you thieving bastard," Davis yelled half-heartedly, almost on automatic. He was pouring "coffee" with slow trembling motions, straining to focus.

The rest of the group wandered in, the kids slipping past their elders and holding out plates, which Rosie slopped eggs onto. As they ate, some sitting and some leaning against the counter, the group argued about the day's tasks. I toyed with the scrambled eggs, which were frankly disgusting—too "eggy", if that was possible. But while they were busy squabbling about whose turn it was to sawdust the outhouse, I palmed a pair of the sticky baking powder biscuits that were already beginning to fossilize. If I didn't get hungry, I could always use them as grenades. And the coffee tasted like a tannery smelled. I would be looking for a *decent* restaurant in the next few hours.

"You ready to go?" Geoff went to the doorway, his pack slung over his shoulder. Predictably, no warning. I grimaced and returned to the living room to check for any stray belongings, though I knew I had them all in my pack. All the important things were secured in the e-bikes with strong combo locks, and the essentials—phone, emergency med pack, switchblade, company-issued mini pistol, trade drugs—were hidden on me. Geoff might trust these losers, but I didn't.

Sitting on the sagging couch, picking every crumb of the stolen biscuits from the curved upholstered arm, was one of the twins. He glanced up, then back to his scavenging. I remembered that kind of hunger. Impulsively, I whipped the two biscuits out of my pocket and handed them over. His eyes grew wide and he froze, looking at me. Then he grabbed the biscuits and bolted for the door in one motion.

I checked the bedroom then leaned into the kitchen and said goodbye to the ragtag family posed like a Norman-Rockwell-does-meth painting; they ignored me. I let the front door slam a little harder than necessary. *Good riddance*. A light drizzle had started again and I turned up my collar as I hurried across the yard. In the corner of my eye, a flash of azure near the corner of one trailer—a blue sleeve, quickly withdrawn. Bright color was as jarring on this farm as a violinist on a compost heap—yet somehow familiar. Geoff gave no notice, but I saw chickens veer out of their path to avoid that corner. So. Someone hidden. Inner alarms blared, and an odd image from the past flickered in memory—Artaud of Astoria, a squat, lumpy chieftan who'd terrorized parts of Long Island. His bashers wore sky blue as a blatant brag that they didn't need camoflage. I didn't turn my head, but strained my gaze and hearing as I headed to the barn. A *dink* of thin metal siding being squashed. How stupid would I be if I over-reacted? But it could be terminal if I under-reacted.

As I stepped inside the barn, I risked a quick glance back. *Yes!* Two men in blue were edging around the trailer. I had a few seconds. Could they have tracked me without Geoff's help? Doubtful. I casually walked past Geoff to my cycle, flipped open the saddlebag, and as I stuffed my pack in, I palmed a concussion grenade, frantically trying to remember the instructions. I couldn't risk looking at Geoff, or toward the door. Judging the distance as best I could, I pulled the pin and flipped the grenade toward the opening then dived into the straw. The *boom* shook the rafters and the air was suddenly thick, unbreathable. Choking, I scrambled up, leapt onto the e-cycle and switched it on. I brought it in a tight circle, to ram my way through if needed. Geoff and one Astorian were flattened by the thick rubber fragments, stunned. *Bastards.* I gripped the handles tight as I accelerated and hit a leg going out. The scream left me unmoved. There was one still guy in the yard—confused but standing. I swerved, held tight and charged him, spewing mud. He leaped aside, fell. A choppy, messy wallow through the yard, then out onto the road. Only then did I realize I was shaking.

Artaud! What the hell?? A petty slumlord, someone I'd worked briefly for, then handed to Metro, neat and sorted. The reward paid for my entry into the Apple. He should still be in work camps, his crew disbanded. But those *were* his bashers. I even thought I recognized one. But how could I? It had been more than ten years.

2

They wouldn't be far behind. I needed a hiding spot—sooner rather than later. They'd expect me to run to the limit. As Madison came into view, I veered back to the shed where we'd hid the bikes yesterday—I could watch for them, and once past, I could follow *behind* at a safe distance, the last place they would look. It had worked for me in the past.

The shed was filthy, reeking of mold, and deserted. I'd barely glanced in before, but it was piled with old computers, microwaves and other dead machines—a neo-Luddite contagion hospital. There was even an old PED-Xing sign—warning of pedophiles crossing—Melinda would love that. The un-glazed window looked out on the road, and I stepped back far enough to shield my face. That had been too damn close! The bastard must have set this up in the City—was Cheyenne in on it? Was anyone else? And *why*?? If I got back—when—I would find out. And enjoy being their nasty little surprise.

It was barely five minutes before Geoff's little RAMspeed rattled by, followed by two others—bigger but ancient. Yesterday's fears reemerged—I was stuck, four days from New York, at least two from the edge of civilization. Back home, it was Square Pants Square Dance day—*no, focus!* Geoff saw me as a stupid desk serf—and that was an advantage. They might not suspect until Geoff's bike battery started to run out. I could find the roads back to the rail-end, probably. The bike could go 40 miles without pedaling; maybe 60 if I could pedal enough to keep a tiny charge, and my legs didn't give out. But we hadn't charged since yesterday. The railroad—civilization—was almost three days—five charges—away. I vaguely recalled the charging stations—indistinguishable from other mold-ering farmhouses at a distance, but well defended and usually located by those huge concrete ramps that curled like mammoth apple peels down from the Pike. If I had to walk or pedal, it would be at least another day's travel. More like two or three. The bike charger could help a bit if I could wait until the sun returned—but I might starve waiting for that. My helmet—barely needed at our 15 mph average speed—had been left in the barn. It would have helped to keep off the rain. I sighed. *If I get back I'm gonna nominate myself for Employee of the Month. Before someone nominates me for Dumdroid of the Month.*

Fighting the mind-block that panic brings, I inventoried my bags. Geoff had called me paranoid for insisting on an even split of supplies, but now I realized the bastard had been trying to hobble me even more. Aside from the med kit, a small solar/hand-crank charger for the phone and a few packages of weak heroin for trade, I had five hand-sized survival bars, a water filter that was nearing the end of its useful life and the solar motor charger that took up half the bike compartment. I had a wallet full of cash, which probably was toilet paper out here, but the thick wad would be reported "spent" and duly stashed as a perk when—if—I got back. Two changes of clothes, all thin and lightweight like professional gear, and a waterproof poncho. And my pitiful weapons: knife, pistol—*that* had been a shock, wish my slum buddies could see this beauty!—one remaining grenade, some welded-nail caltrops. The bike came with a small box of maintenance tools, not that I could fix anything; that had been Geoff's job. I had an antique paper map that Melinda had given me, fragile and almost falling apart at the creases—Pennsylvania on one side, the Northeast region on the other. Most everything else we had planned to pick up in trade as we went. After all, we weren't falling off the end of the world, were we? *And I'd thought New Jersey was the outlands.* If only I'd taken the antique metal compass that my boss had offered as a joke—I'd been so positive the phone/satellite would be my all-knowing Guide.

I pulled out the phone—when my boss had handed it to me, he had quickly shown me apps for basic foreign language translation, a printable program with comm tower specs and materials, a special company GPS to track me at great expense but which depended on the glitchy satellite, a calculator—so important since I never mastered mental arithmetic—and a very small supply of my favorite jazz tunes, for when the silence became unbearable. But right now there was only one function I needed. The signal bars wobbled between one and two, but I frantically punched in my boss's phone number, trying to remember if there was a time difference. Thankfully, I worked in a company with its own internal phone system. On the other hand, if I hadn't worked for them, I wouldn't be lurking in this Hell for Misbehaved Machines right now. I could hear the phone dialing, then silence—I glanced again at the bars. There was no signal. The vastness stretching between here and New York felt like one of my childhood nightmares where—I shook my head and kicked my ankle against a jutting wood block; the pain jolted the panic away.

The fight-buzz was wearing off, and my muscles jellied. It had been ten long years since I'd lived in the madmax metro surrounding the City. Ten years since I became office fodder. *Got too comfortable, Martin, bo-yo—forgot barbarians don't queue for supplies.* I kicked myself. *Time to unpack all those bad memories, and remember the moves.* I didn't expect the company to give a day-old fart about me, but surely they would protect their investment? And how could Artaud afford to pay Geoff more than the company had? This stunk worse than East River sushi. I unfolded the paper map, mostly to reassure myself it was still there… my hands were shaking. Okay—my worst fears had come to pass. But it couldn't be worse than being 14 in a gang-controlled slum, could it? I'd survived on my own before—I could do it again.

Geoff had guided us from memory, but many of the roads on this pre-Adjustment map should still be there, and some towns, even. The major highways we'd been following headed diagonally northwest from Pittsburgh—but he would be expecting me there. I could follow behind them until the first charge station—then what? Would City money buy a charge? And smaller roads were as scarce on this map as empty City apartments. How many had become dead ends as the gravel was overrun by weeds? I refolded the map, tucked it away. What I really needed was an all-terrain bike, so I could cut across fields and let the sun guide me due southeast until I hit the railroad again. Oh—and a boat for the river. Yeah, right.

As I stared out, checking for townsfolk, I realized I'd been hearing a soft sound for several minutes—perhaps a rat scrambling, or… Carefully, I stepped away from the window and let my eyes adjust. At first, it was black as a lower basement salvage pit, but slowly the piles of debris began to stand out against the rough board walls and floor. That nightmare sense of animation that scrap heaps can conjure began to fade—these were only lumps of dead plastic, pipes and circuit boards that lay unclaimed by the stupid inhabitants of this no-power town. I breathed easier, scanning the room, craning my ears…only the furthest corner had any anthropomorphic piles remaining, and I stepped forward to see what they contained. And she stepped forward to meet me.

Oh, shit! I reached down instinctively before I realized I had left the gun by the e-bike. *Stupid, stupid, stupid.* I squared my shoulders and stared belligerently. She was a short, slim brunette with close-cropped hair framing a pale Celtic face, wearing farmer's overalls and a rollneck sweater begrimed and gray with dirt. Then the ancient barreled six-shot in her left hand seized my attention. She wasn't aiming it at me, not yet. She looked startled, not angry. Slowly she raised the pistol.

"Wait! I'm harmless—I'm just hiding here," I said quickly. "I can pay for help."

"Shhhhh," she cautioned, keeping the pistol trained on me. "Neither of us should be here. Why are you hiding?"

"I've been… a guide brought me from New York City, then this morning he tried to kill me."—*Gawd, you sound pathetic, Martin*—but this was my very quick plan B. Wounded lion, begging the mouse's help.

"You're from the City?" I could almost hear the capital letter. But neither her cautious expression nor the gun's direction changed; no easily-impressed farmer's daughter, this one. She glanced over at my bike and supplies, laid out on the seat. *Fatally stupid, Martin.* I'd known slum Amazons who were more than a match for any testosterhellion. But I didn't think she was one. Without moving my head, I searched for a weapon or diversion. Then she surprised me: she lowered the gun, and smiled. "Right. I saw you two in town, and I know Alex—a sneaky bastard if ever there was one."

Alex, eh? Well it would make sense that he had a few names. I grinned stupidly, continuing the hobbled tourist routine. "Yeah—I just found that out. And now what?" I looked stricken, not hard to fake. "If you could get me to the main road, or even a good back road, I think I could make it to the railroad—do you know where that is?" At least she wasn't making any move toward my supplies.

"Yeah, I know where the Pitts Burg is—we mostly avoid it, though you can get some good stuff at the Pencil Vanity Mall. You think you can get there alone?"

"The what?"

"You know—the Mall of Pennsylvania—that trading town outside the railroad wall. That's its nickname."

"Uh—we?"

She looked panicky. "My townsfolk—where I come from. A couple of us have been there, but there's nothing much we need. Our town is self-sufficient." A note of pride vibrated in her voice.

"Then what are you doing here? If you don't mind my asking," I added politely. No point pissing her off.

"These Luddites leave all their good scrap just lying around—why waste it?" She grinned, and I nodded eagerly.

"I could help you with that—I'm a technician back in the City, and I could show you which are the good parts." Okay—stretching it—I was a data-pusher, although I'd picked up things here and there.

She laughed quietly. "I'm a tech, too—you're probably surprised that there are any outside your big bubble, but we exist. Not everybody needs the Big Drip." She grinned at my look and added, "the IV, the artificial life support. That which you presume to call civilization." She gestured toward the window.

"I—" Too many thoughts were going through my head. There was something outside the Big Five that thought it was civilization? And that knew about—was *scornful* of—our City? There was a possibility of help?? But…technician? She looked like she had been rolling in the cabbage fields. I shook my head to clear it, and she mistook that for disagreement.

"I guess you were raised to believe you would be the birthplace of New America. But concrete and steel—"

"Excuse me, miz—I don't know your name—I just *really* need to get back to the road before these—uh, Alex—comes back for me. I am guessing th- he plans to dump me in the nearest ditch."

She glanced out the window and nodded. "Fine. I can lead you a back way down to the old Turnpike. And my name's Ciera."

"Martin. And thank you." Slowly I moved toward my bike, refusing to look at her. But I felt her follow me, not too close. So she wasn't that trusting.

"It's not a favor. You did talk about paying, right? And don't touch that pistol."

I slowly, gently reached for the small bags of H, held one up. "This is probably the best pain reliever you will find outside the City."

She shook her head. "Don't count on that. No, I was looking at the little solar charger—that could really be handy." She gestured me away, took my gun and examined it. "Cap pistol—useless," she said, and shoved it deep in my bag.

Cap pistol? Was this more of the setup? Shit. The charger wasn't something I could trade. Despite its glitchy connection, the phone was the only thread tying me to safety. My lifeline. The thought of being completely cut off squeezed like a tight band around my lungs. On the other hand, I at *least* needed to get safely away from her, and it would solve half my problems if she really could get me to the Pike.

"I tell you what," I said, "I'll give you half now and half when you get me to the road." I made a display of pulling the solar part from the charger plug, and handed her the plug. Her hand was freezing, and I wondered if she was more scared than she appeared. I shoved the other part in my bag, praying that I really did have the extra plug somewhere, in case I had to take off in a hurry.

As I finished packing, she shrugged into a hooded green camouflage jacket and said, "So—ride in front of me, and I'll give you directions as we go. And keep your hands on the handlebars—sorry, but you're a shining example of how foolish it is to trust strangers." She stepped toward one of the apparently scrap bikes and picked it up—hidden in plain sight.

I swallowed my snark—her dig was bull's-eyed. I had been a green-ass to trust that bastard Geoff. But I'd had no choice. In the last team meeting, when the new hire had suggested we just take a small battalion of soldiers, everyone else had hooted. The boss had said, "Never make a show of force unless you are prepared to use it. And one small battalion is not a force." Though right now I would trade my right testicle for a battalion of soldiers.

We wheeled our bikes onto the deserted road. Hers was an older version of my Yamahonda 450, one of the best re-assembled bikes on the market. My company had spared no expense. Hers looked more modern than these hinterlands could've provided. It even had the Duratread re-carved tires that reduced flats. So *some* place was trading with the Big Five. That was information worth pursuing. No, nix that—I was a negotiator, not a spy! A failed negotiator. And if I went back in such ignominious defeat, I would be lucky to keep my job, let alone be promoted. But maybe she knew of a town capable of a tower? Was it possible to hire another Scout at the railroad terminus? Incredibly, my city-bred pride warred with my survival instincts. I must be in shock. *First things first*, I reminded myself grimly.

In order to save what was left of the power, I pedaled the bike, and it sounded like Ciera was doing the same. We followed the deserted road along a scummy reed-clogged stream which reeked of manure, rotting vegetation and something nastier. Reminded me a lot of Long Island. A half dozen black-and-white cows gathered under a tipping oak tree, nibbling sparse grass. I was surprised to see a number of those diamond shaped metal signs still attached to poles, painted symbols almost unreadable. One said YIELD—Melinda told me that was a pirate or begger's station. It must have been a strange civilization. There were also some of the metal guard rails that apparently protected the cars from attacks coming over the fields. So these neo-Luddites hadn't *touched* their valuable salvage. There was no trash, as such—with few industries, I guess there just wasn't that much disposable. Yet the fragrance wasn't—couldn't be—natural. Probably runoff from the tannery. I glanced at Ciera in my sideview mirror—she was keeping far enough back that she'd have time to grab the gun that bulged under her overall bib before I could overcome her. I wondered about the safety catch on those old rotating-barrel pistols. I waited until we had ridden further into the farmlands before I held up my hand and slowed to a halt, letting her come up beside me.

"We need to get off this road—this is where he's searching for me." I tried to sound casual and was annoyed when my voice shook.

"Not much farther, then we'll turn off to the right. Look for the red—do you know what a fire hydrant looks like?"

I nodded, not trusting my voice. *Don't get angry!* After all, I was the one playing dumb tourist. *Don't complicate this until you're better hidden.* Part of me was still struggling to catch up with the sudden upheaval. Less than a half hour ago, I was on a business trip toward Chicago. And now I was like some poor dumb errand boy being chased across a field by a pack of cutthroats. I had a bike that was running out of juice and could barely go a trotting pace on these crap roads. A galloping horse—hell, even a good runner!—could outpace these puny e-bikes! How long before they doubled back? How did Artaud fit into this? My mind whirled as we bumped carefully down the pitted asphalt and I strained to look for any glimpse of that pinky-washed-out "old red". Or did they repaint their hydrants? With what? Red was expensive.

The husks of many crammed-in houses filled the field to our right—some kind of old suburban neighborhood. The shoddy building materials had almost melted back into the ground, but here and there a burnt, unsalvaged 4 x 4 stood like a pillar. Another long rectangular sign on a pole read, "Chow Mein Lane." Any side roads were invisible in waist-high weeds. A row of rusty cars that probably marked some sidewalk. A ton of steel—a half year's credit—rusting into uselessness. Someone needed to send a salvage team.

"Turn here!" she shouted, adding, "They haven't cut the grass."

Who? I thought but turned sharply into the road I could almost see, then all my attention was taken up by avoiding potholes, weed clumps and the occasional unidentified piles.

"Go to that shed, and then we'll stop a bit." I glanced in my sideview; she was pointing left, toward an almost intact metal shed not far away. I focused on getting there without blowing a tire. The rain chose that moment to intensify, and I shook my head to dash the water from my eyes. Rain trickled inside my collar like the icicle test Artaud once concocted. *Focus, Martin!*

The shed was more of a lean-to, with pockmarked corrugated aluminum walls and ceiling. One corner was dripping and bouncing slightly in the breeze. The packed dirt floor held nothing but a pile of stones. I gratefully rolled my bike under its shelter, while Ciera wheeled hers toward the other wall. She was skilled in keeping someone at safe arm's-length—maybe she *was* a trained salvager. I would need to deal deftly. It was tough to focus on her while worrying about Geoff and the Astorians. Even armed, I feared she wouldn't be much use if we ran into them. And with a cap pistol, neither would I.

"All right—we have a few minutes—so what are you doing in our country?"

Our country? Our *country*? Did she mean the countryside, or…? Weighing every word, I told her about the comm tower plan, emphasizing the trade and the totally voluntary nature of it. I painted myself as a naïve city type—left out all mention of clawing my way from the slums into middle management. "This morning G—Alex apparently ROB'd me—err, ratted on bargain. A couple bashers—hitmen you might call them—turned up as we were taking off. I lost them, but only just."

"So what was he going for? Money?"

"Not *my* money, but—" the fact was, Geoff got a quarter up front and three quarters on completion—so *someone* paid him mega to overrule the first contract, "—but it's expensive to get out here, I don't know why he waited so long." Why now? Why not a day out of Pittsburgh? Who would've known—or cared? *That* thought was a gut-kicker. I had no doting family, no steady partner—unencumbered out here equaled expendable. I'd counted on the company considering me important enough to defend. My cheeks were burning, and my fuse! Cheyenne had said Geoff was thoroughly trustworthy. The bitch.

"There *is* a rough kind of security around the Burg," she said, fumbling in her pocket and pulling out a strip of dried meat. The rain drummed over her words, but I think she added, "murder is punished, usually." And something indecipherable about trouble—she glanced at me as if to say maybe I fit that description.

Watching her enjoy her snack, I thought of my survival bars—I'd eaten two mouthfuls of the egg glop—but they had to last me back to the railroad. I shrugged.

"Okay—maybe Alex had better connections around here." *Not* those pot farmers—they couldn't organize an evening out.

"I've heard they do a thriving slave trade from any fools who wander away from the train." She looked at me with an appraising smile. "They sell back the rich and powerful fools. The others…" she shrugged, adding, "You only got this far 'cause of Alex—you *know* that, right? Walk into the wrong town and you'd never walk out. Could they get a good price for you, d'ya think?"

Was she cold-fusioning me? Or did she believe the same stories those pot farmers did? The Army still had authority out here—they must. Why else would they have sent a civvie like me on my way toward Chicago? The comm tower project was legit—I *knew* that. A flash of image from a school book, the old infantry going down in front of big guns... wave after wave of expendable peons... like me and my fellow desk serfs. Panic bubbled and overflowed like old Harry's infamous septic. Someone was going to pay big time. This was worse than those legendary swamps of New Jersey!

"Why should I trust you?" I blurted.

She laughed. "You can't afford not to. But also because I'm curious. Tell me what the City is really like, and I won't charge you as much. And your life is worth it, right?" Her mocking tone held a darker note.

Good—she *was* a curious farmer's daughter. But an armed one. Slavers?? I fought my writhing gut. There were no slaves on Long Island, though some of the jobs were as servile as they got. One was always free to walk out of the frying hopper into the grease. Why hadn't I done more research? *Don't panic, think!* Just like when a dropped concrete block had fractured bones in my foot. My mind was dropping into instinct mode, shutting down the higher functions. I pictured the mini pistol—six shots, close range only—dare I try to get it from my pack? But I needed her cooperation—she could lead me on a city shark roundabout, at this point. *You've been through worse*, I told myself, *remember the siege of Queens, remember that night under East 47th.*

"Sure I will, but not here," I said. "I want to get a couple hours away along a road they—he—isn't likely to take." I paused, considering. "If—" *what the fuck*—"if you get me onto the train, I'll leave all my supplies with you. Even the bike." I could get home without them, at that point.

Her eyebrows lifted, but she looked doubtful. "I hate getting *that* close."

Truth? Or had she never been there? Was I putting myself in the wrong hands? I tried to picture riding through this tangled countryside alone. I watched her; she seemed nervous, too—biting her lip, wiping her empty hand on her pants, holding the gun at her side but tensely.

"Let's take it in steps," she said. "I had another job today, remember? But I can get you into a shelter tonight—that's the med pack. I'll take you to an e-charger along the way. That's two of those drug packets. And I'll put you on a clear section of the old Pike Road tomorrow. At that point, we'll see if you want to chance it, or hire me for the rest. And whether I want to do it. That reminds me…" She looked around then walked over to the pile of rocks in the corner, studied it for a while, then knelt and started to rearrange it.

Was she mad? Adjustment shocked? Too young. Then what?? As I watched, she stacked a couple flat boulders and laid two others at an angle. A signal code? Like the trash code of Astoria—bits of toys and glass hidden in unmovable bins, since anything movable was stolen. Kids paid to do rounds checking on each message site. Primitive, but surprisingly effective. Half consciously, my hand was easing toward my pack.

"Don't even think about it, rube," she said, turning quickly, the gun already in her hand. I froze. She stood up. "Look—you need to decide if you trust me. I *don't* have to do this, and I *don't* take slaves. Do we have a trade, or are you going to clever-Dick your way into a shallow grave?"

Of course I didn't trust her. Or anyone. If I'd fully trusted Geoff, I'd be dead or a slave by now. In the last almost three decades, I hadn't trusted a blessed soul—and I didn't know anybody who *did.* Those must be the good who die young. The rest of us kept looking over our shoulders and even then…I put my hand over my eyes. This was the closest I'd come recently to walking on alligators—and she was asking me to trust her. An old feeling swept over me, like when I'd wriggled through the Queens DMZ and finally had to just follow the shark who snuck me into the City—a kind of resignation, deciding that even death wouldn't be as bad as languishing where I was. I dropped my hand and nodded.

"Okay then." She brushed off her pants and checked the charge on her bike. "I have probably ten more miles," she said. "Although it's mostly flat, so we'll do some peddling."

"I probably have seven, max." No sun, no charger—so I hoped she hadn't noticed it.

She looked away, as if calculating. "The next charger is fifteen miles from here—I hope you can pedal." She paused, then fished my pistol from my pack. "Put this in your coat—but if you touch it and there's no grizzly in front of us, I'll shoot. See if I don't."

It took us three hours to do those 15 miles—three grueling hours of drizzle, cracked asphalt, gravel, weeds hiding sharp metal—even with a small power assist, my back and butt were aching after two hours, and by the third, I'd fallen into almost a robotic state, thinking only of the time when I could stop, watching the battery needle dropping closer and closer to red. After a while, I didn't even look around to see if we were being followed. Most of the fields we passed were cultivated; none looked familiar. The rolling low hills, overrun by trees and shrubbery, were so different from the flat, diked Long Island sandscape or the concrete order of the City. I could be on another planet, like in an old mu-vid. I couldn't see any houses, and wondered dully who were working the fields. Along one open meadow, a series of long parallel mounds in a field had been left fallow.

"What are those big mounds over there?" I asked. "They're too even to be hills."

"Mass graves." Her tone suggested I shouldn't ask more, but I didn't want to. They didn't look new, so I guessed they'd been made during the

Adjustment—after the food and medicine ran out and people died off so fast there was sometimes no one left to bury them, a fact I'd heard in whispered stories, but that civilization had removed most traces of. Even Calvary Cemetery's vast acreage had been repurposed when they were desperate for defendable grain fields. Now all those headstones were stacked walls carving out farmers' plots. *Wheat from dead men's bones,* as the saying went.

Twice Ciera called to me to slow down, as she paused and examined tall wooden pole gates that were tattooed with odd symbols. At the third gate, she nodded and gestured that we were going in.

There was a crude metal bell the size of a skull hanging from the gate post. As she pulled a rope, the bell clanged like a burn barrel being hit by a rock. She opened the gate and let me wheel my bike through. My muscles were aching like I'd been hit by my own grenade; I moved slowly so I didn't stumble. She latched the gate behind us and followed me down a well-kept gravel road between fields of several kinds of grain-like plants. After what felt like a full mile, we came to a long one-story stucco house obscured by trees and vegetable gardens. An older man, stooped but still sturdy, stood with a hoe, frowning at us. I wondered that he would be so trusting of strangers, then I saw a curtain twitch in the house behind an open window—of course, he had backup. Ciera walked up to him and nodded.

"We would like lunch and to charge our bikes."

"Lunch is three grid each. Charging—" he glanced over at me, grinned. "—that'll cost ten grid. Or his rain jacket."

My muscles were still bouncing up and down on the lousy road; everything jangled. Sounded like they didn't use real money, but had some kind of shared currency. From Ciera's frown, I gathered he was gouging us. But I hoped she'd accept. As much as I hated to part with my raincoat, I had the waterproof poncho in my pack, and I was desperate to sit down and get some food in me.

After glancing at me, she nodded, and he gestured us toward a table with some benches on the grass. "Chargers in the side yard—go plug them in. Then sit there."

We wheeled our bikes around the side, toward what looked like the bastard child of an old gasoline pump, a solar heater, and a chicken coop.

We searched for something resembling hookups; even Ciera looked puzzled. Finally we found two and plugged in the bikes.

"I hope this doesn't blow their batteries," I muttered, but I really was too tired to care. With leaden feet, I followed her back to the benches. Sitting down, I realized I should have checked for dampness, but the water soaking through my pants was just one more bit of misery. I'd never make it back in less than a week, not if I had to pedal. Fourteen years was a long time for muscles without training. Geoff had let us power along paved roads—nothing like peddling over rough ground. I rested my head on my hands and tried to accept the possibility that I was going to die out here. It was like the time I'd fallen into the East River, plunging so deep I thought I'd never get back to the air. Ciera walked over and called something into the house, waiting in the doorway for an answer. On an impulse, I tried my phone, careful to keep it out of sight—if our grasping host saw it, he might decide that it was a better trade. The connection bars waffled as usual, but I quickly punched in, "Trouble. Help!" Commco had an office network hooked into the main cell network so we peons could get our orders. I almost sent it to my boss, at the last moment blipped it to Rivera in Accounting—not any kind of Player and hopefully chatty enough to let several people know. GPS should locate me. My head swam with conspiracy theories and I had no idea how much was fatigue.

After a few minutes, the man and a young woman came out with two trays. On each, there was a mug, a thick slice of bread with butter, a bowl of potatoes with more butter and a very small bowl of some kind of chili. We thanked them and I started with the bread because I figured that at least wouldn't kill me. Ciera started with the chili, so I asked her what kind of meat.

"Goat, I think."

I hated goat but I was going to choke it down anyway—I was ravenous. And there wasn't that much of it. The potatoes were good, the mug was full of a thin but decent ale, and it was obvious there were cows in abundance somewhere, because the butter was thick and delicious. Not at all like the half-soylent lard served in the company cafeteria.

"So, tell me about the City," Ciera said, putting down her spoon. "I hear they've managed to keep the power going almost like before the Chaos. I hear they stole all the transformers from other states, and whatever else they needed."

She sounded more curious than hostile, but I spoke guardedly. "It's not exactly like before, but we do still have lots of culture and convenience. Like theaters, bookstores, clothing stores—" *Keep it vague.*

"Who's making all the things? Like cloth, books—you know."

"Some factories survived the Adjustment. They're putting a few more steam-powered looms online every year in Jersey, Connecticut and Massachusetts—and a couple museum water-based mills have been revived in defendable areas. Books—well, we never had mass burnings—New York doesn't have many fireplaces—so there are a lot still around. Not so many new, I guess. The Island—Long Island—has a big Crafters Guild, and the Pennsylvania railroad corridor specializes in dairy and leather stuff. A lot of recycled goods come in from the South." That was about the extent of my knowledge, since none of that ever interested me.

"Aren't the people living around you resentful?"

"The towns around the City benefit from our trade and protection, so no, I don't think so. And we're working to expand the abundance, but it's not that easy, with our world trade cut off."

She looked down and wiped the chili bowl with her bread, but I could still see her smile. "*World* trade? You don't even have state trade anymore."

I was torn between bragging and wanting to watch what I said—it could be pure curiosity, but what if it were something else? What if she was a marauder looking to exploit the City's weaknesses? Well, not *her*—her town or gang. Were my parents' stories more than something to keep us behaving?

"That's not entirely true," I said slowly. "There is some trade up and down the coast, and certainly out to Massachusetts and Pennsylvania along the railroads. Wherever the Army can protect citizens. We get some things in from DC and the south through New Jersey. And the best technicians are working constantly to get the power grid back up."

She snorted and almost choked on her bread. "The grid? With people stealing not only the wire but the towers themselves? Isn't that why you're having to make a deal with some city to defend these towers? How big a grid can you manage if you need a soldier every 50 feet? The New York Army *can't* be that big."

Now it was my turn to look down and pretend to play with my food. This was the argument I had heard whispered all through Long Island, and on certain streets in the City itself. That America had broken down so completely that it couldn't be reconnected. What our great-grandparents had taken for granted—light at a touch, long distance flight, speaking with anyone anywhere—was lost to us forever. I honestly didn't worry about it; I'd never known those things and if they came back, it wouldn't be in my lifetime, so what was it to me? My primary concern was to scramble far enough out of the shark tank that I could confidently plan a year or more in advance.

"Look," I said patiently, "I'm not the City's representative." *But I was, wasn't I?* "I'm just a technician, out here to do my job—and at this point, I'm focused on getting back—" *and reporting the two-timing bastard* "and… getting new orders." I paused, smiled. "And I'm *really* grateful that you're helping me—that you've agreed to help for payment," I amended.

She smiled back; her eyes were green, I noticed, and she had a small scar on her right cheek near her ear. Attractive, in a grimy way. But not exactly friendly. I couldn't tell if there was pity or amusement in her expression.

"And it's the US Army, by the way."

"In your dreams. Five cities don't make America, even if they can talk to each other."

How did she know how many cities we had? *Shit*—was her town more than just the subsistence country farmers I'd seen so far? I remembered her bike. Maybe she wasn't telling the truth about hating Geoff. Maybe I'd fallen into his hands after all. Or worse.

"What kind of tech are you?" I asked, trying to keep my voice casual. But she still tensed.

"Mostly solar," she said, watching me. "I apprenticed to one of the best sol-techs around, and I can fix pretty much any board they bring me. Except the ones that got flared, of course."

"That would be useful. Solar is a really good local system. It's hard to find the type of board that didn't flare out, but we had one on our farm growing up."

"You grew up on a farm?" The doubt in her voice verged on disdain.

"Yeah. We grew beans, potatoes, apples and walnuts—and of course the usual vegetables." I could hear my tone get edgy—I never talked about my childhood. I didn't want to now. Even if it was a safer topic than City logistics.

She picked up on that, and changed the subject. "This afternoon we're gonna hit some really broke-down roads, but they won't be ones Alex is looking along. And I know a place for tonight where we can sleep safely. Someplace we have an agreement with."

I nodded and kept my face blank. To look distrusting could scare her off. She seemed to think she'd said too much; she frowned and tapped her spoon on the table. The host might have taken that as a signal—he came up and removed the plates. Standing, I shrugged out of my raincoat, and fished in the pockets to make sure I wasn't leaving anything. I turned so he couldn't see me transfer the weapons; I was grateful the food was already in my pack. There were just bits and scraps—a stub of a pencil, a button found on a road, a sticky hard candy that I'd spit out halfway to take advantage of a free beer. And at the very bottom, two tiny pasteboard rectangles—I glanced at them. Ticket stubs to Utoob Night, the last vid-concert I had seen, with Julee snug against me in the dark. Tears sprang to my eyes, and I crushed the tickets, digging my nails into my palm. *No, no, no, NO!* I was *not* going to fall apart! I hadn't cried since before I managed to wriggle into the City, and *dammit* I wasn't going to do it now! I slammed my ankle against the leg of the table and the jolt short-circuited the tears. It was just fatigue, that was all. Grimly, I stuffed the tickets and everything else in my backpack, handed my raincoat to the old guy, and limped toward the bikes. I unfolded and donned my poncho. A few minutes later Ciera joined me, and we unplugged our bikes. I was checking the bike packs, but she stopped me.

"He won't have stolen anything—thieves don't last long out here."

It was a wrench to trust her—muscles strained to paw through everything, to protect my stuff. She looked down at her console.

"Looks like mine charged full," she said. I checked mine and gave her a thumbs up. We rode back to the pathway, my muscles aching anew.

We pedaled as much as we could after that, to save battery—the roads were as bad as she had predicted: mostly flat, but we still weren't doing more than five miles an hour. The road morphed from gravel to broken asphalt to flat dirt and back several times. Tree branches, weeds, occasional rusted lumps of metal were strewn in our way and as we progressed, the shrubbery got deeper and wilder—farms giving way to brambles, sapling trees and the occasional moss-furred wreck of a building. The tangle of green was getting on my nerves—too many things could be hiding—I wanted orderliness, straight lines...smooth concrete buildings. We passed more eerie grave mounds, with a sense of others under the encroaching wilderness. It must have been hell out here during the Adjustment. Ciera led me down some winding paths, pausing occasionally to study a cross-roads, looking for I don't know what. Once or twice, I worried she had got-ten lost. But Geoff would never have picked these roads to search, so I could breathe a bit easier. It was just a matter of keeping my wits about me and watching this woman until I could be sure she wasn't planning on ROBing me. Maybe I could find out how she knew as much as she did—that information could be sold in the City. Once I got to the railroad, I would have plenty money left to buy my ticket back to the City. And I had City cred, too, once I got to the banking region. I wondered if they still had banks out here. Maybe I'd ask later.

As long as she got me there, I'd probably have to hand over my things to Ciera. It went against the shark code, but I'd feel like a ripe turd if I left her empty-handed. Things probably had very different value out here—who knows whether she was getting the best of the deal? So I'd go back in with nothing—but *someone* was going to pay up! I'd call in my debts among the management—all the times I kept silent about screw-ups, the time I'd "lost" some forms so our team didn't have to pay back bonuses. I'd even call on a few City friends—the fellow jazz freak who did "re-search" into private lives; the hobby-thief who thrilled to the risk of ampu-tation if caught. I'd find and expose this joker—let the company "dispose of" her—or him. Take the costs out of their louse-plagued hide.

As the road started to slope gently uphill, Ciera said we could use some battery, as we were getting closer to shelter. I adjusted the clutch into power assist. My legs couldn't manage much more. And if it came down to: *I have to* vs. *I can't*? I assumed she wouldn't be willing to wait as I rested for a day or two—but could I get her to hand me over to another guide? Did I have enough to trade with? How far out would the company come after me??

As the shrubbery encroached on the road, narrowing it almost to a pathway, without warning, four bikers appeared 15 feet away.

3

I slammed on my brakes, skidding, and Ciera stopped alongside me, pulling out her gun. Belatedly, I copied her. A second later, she lowered it, and used her other hand to wave.

"Lio!" she called. "It's Ciera!"

The riders, who had braked and whipped out weapons when they saw us, lowered their hands, and I breathed again. Stuffing my gun into my pocket, I followed Ciera toward them.

"They're neighbors from…where I live," she called back over her shoulder. She was being awfully cagey about where that was.

Getting off their bikes in the slanted sunlight were three men and a slim young Afro woman with cropped hair and an old "team cap" with some entwined initials on the front. She wore gray coveralls frayed into fringe at the cuffs. The three males—a dishwater blond about my size, a six foot black-haired possibly Native blood and a short, sandy-haired freckled teen—were dressed similar to me but more threadbare: jeans that had been patched and re-patched, random as a City notice board, faded checkered shirts and homemade leather jackets crudely painted in green/brown camouflage like Ciera's coat. Each had a cloth baseball cap and leather holster with a pistol. Ciera had greeted the sandy-haired one and they slapped hands when we met. He cocked his head, puzzled, and glanced at me quickly before speaking.

"You're far from Madison, yeah?"

Ciera gestured toward me. "Martin got crossed by Alex, that tracker dog from Pitts. Needs to get back to the train. He's from the City."

She put a slight emphasis on the last two nouns, and I wondered what it meant, aside from the obvious. Their response was mixed: the Nat-Indi looked disgusted, Lio enthused, and the other two faces were unreadable.

"Seems the long way round," Lio commented. "Is anything to do with Alex nosing around 'bout a stranger over Godbey's Inn? He had two big fat troubadours with him."

"You saw them?" I blurted. Their glares indicated I'd crossed a line, so I looked at Ciera mutely.

"Describe 'em, Lio."

He shrugged. "Alex you know. The other two had troubadour gear—sky blue jackets and black pants. One had bruises on his face. They *dressed* like musicians, but they were *shaped* like the security guards at the cattle swap. They said they needed to rescue a stranger—he glanced at me—"claimed chit from the New York Minister of Justice herself."

Ciera looked startled and turned to me.

"Impossible," I said, stunned. "They belong to—I don't know what you call it, but we call them slum tribes—and their leader is in prison. Last I'd heard, anyway." I paused, then spoke with hearty confidence I didn't feel. "There is just no way a high ministry official would hire those dumdroids for anything."

Lio nodded. "That's what *we* thought, but they flashed some cards, and Godbey believed them."

I shook my head vigorously, but my thoughts were fraying. "If—just on the remote chance—they were hired by the Minister, they would not regale in clown clothes. That was the uniform of that slum chieftain. I recognized them." But he'd just said that *singers* dressed like that out here; I remembered last night's jokes about the musicians. Was that just weird coincidence? Had I jumped to the wrong conclusion? Not totally—Geoff *had* been ready to turn me over to *somebody*. It just might be a different somebody.

"Well, if they're still searching for you, you're probably in a lot more danger than you figured," Ciera said, echoing my thoughts. Would she even want to keep going, if it got more dangerous? She stared at me. "If I didn't know Alex, I'd wonder… but he's a scrounge lizard," she concluded.

Lio murmured something to the dark-haired guy, then with feigned casualness, asked Ciera, "Think they're linked to—?" His raised eyebrows conveyed something cryptic.

She looked startled and glanced at me again. I had no idea what he was hinting at, so I shrugged and shook my head in puzzlement. She gnawed her lip then said, "I can't see Alex involved with…them. He's lone wolf."

"But for hire."

Annoyance bubbled up through my fatigue. Okay, I was a stranger, but I wasn't an enemy! Unless *they* had something they didn't want the City to know.

"Out of your line?" The dark-haired guy asked Ciera.

Now she looked affronted. "I've got good reason, Matty," she replied stiffly. The group had wheeled their bikes to the side, propped them on kick stands and removed some packages that turned out to be biscuits and some dried meat. The girl had a large leather water bottle that she passed around. I took a sip to be polite, but wanted to wait until I could use my filter. At first, it looked like they weren't going to offer me the food, but a dark look from Ciera shifted the package from Matty's hand to mine. Again, to be polite, I broke off a half biscuit and picked the smallest strip of the meat. I could pretend it was vat-extruded, if I closed my eyes. Except for the weird taste—salty and spicy; I couldn't even tell what meat.

They were standing around because the ground was still damp, and I was damned if I was going to give in to my shaky legs and sit, but I contrived to lean a bit on the saddle of my bike because it would be even more embarrassing to fall down. Occasional breeze shook drops on us, but none of them seemed to notice, engrossed in a coded conversation that I could barely follow.

"A line of gray was seen at freedom," Lio commented.

"What was the response?" Ciera asked.

"Nothing much, for now."

"Hadley's at the old red commune," the young girl spoke up for the first time.

"I know, Jilly," Ciera replied. "I sent word home. Might be a link up."

"Would he be happy 'bout that?" Jilly asked, then looked down after a sharp glance from Ciera.

"Miz Troy is in Springdale—day rents," Matty said, in what seemed to be a nonsequitor, but Ciera nodded. Lio was looking more and more unhappy, but it was obvious he admired Ciera and hesitated to say what was on his mind.

She grinned suddenly and turned to the third guy. "Jordy, would you change clothes with Martin? So we can slip past them?"

"Oh, set *me* up to get snuffed, huh?" Jordy replied, but he was also grinning.

She replied coquettishly, "But you get such a stunning set of clothes out of it—you'll look much nicer in your coffin."

Jordy lifted his hands, palms up. "It's okay with me." But the others frowned.

I wanted to protest—my outfit was worth three times his. But I had two modern sets in the bag, so I wouldn't look like a beggar once I got to the railroad. *If* I got there. Survival before appearance, dammit. And she would probably refuse to go on unless I was camouflaged. At least Jordy's clothes would be a brilliant disguise—no Citizen would be caught dead looking like a victim of the street drug HighnMighty. So we found a fairly dry clearing in the shrubs and swapped clothing. Jordy complained a bit about my damp shirt, and I was grateful that his was dry. I made sure that I emptied my pockets, and I ignored Jordy's low whistle at the sight of the phone. Back at the road, I found Ciera had been talking routes with Lio—they were discussing swapping the bikes for horses. It made sense in theory, but did I want to break my neck falling off a horse I couldn't ride? On the other hand, I had heard they could move quickly and they couldn't possibly need as much fuel as the bikes did. It might cut our trip by a full day. If I didn't break my neck. If she didn't dump me. Or was part of the trap. But I didn't see how she could have set up this meeting after she had met me, and she was clearly startled by the news about Geoff.

Ciera's friends took leave of us stiffly, with several warning glances at her.

"Oh—and be careful—big cat spotted five miles east," Lio called back as they headed away.

There was a definite tension in the air. She held her head up like a typical defiant kid—both proud and anxious. Obviously they didn't want her to go with me; obviously she was going anyway. Maybe she was saving face; I felt a little guilty about that thought. But only a little. She was a free adult. And if she succeeded, she would be getting my treasure trove.

We took their side road. The rough patched pants pulled and dragged awkwardly, making pedaling even harder. The leather jacket weighed a ton and smelled like cow. Once I thought the others were out of hearing, I called out, “That was a lucky meetup, huh?” letting my tone voice my doubt.

She didn’t try to deny it. “Wasn’t chance. These are our roads,” she said. “I was hoping to run into someone—get some news of the east. And it worked.” She again sounded defiant.

I didn’t reply, annoyed at their coded conversation. What else had she discussed? Was there a new team of thugs waiting to kidnap me? I had a mad urge to just scoot away and try this alone. My legs said, *yeah right.* On the other hand, it could have absolutely nothing to do with me—without phones, they probably had to share information like this all the time.

“Speaking of chance—when did you plan to tell me about the trouble times two?”

“Honestly, I thought you’d lead me to a main road and vanish. I didn’t want to get you involved.”

“That works as an excuse for the first two hours. What about the last three?”

“Look—trusting people doesn’t come easy. If you knew how I was raised—”

“I’m beginning to suspect.”

And I still suspect you. I felt guilty about it, but it was true. We rode in silence again for a while. The “road” was no more than a muddy double rut through the shadowy forest. The trees still dripped and an insane chorus of birds squeaked and chirped from hidden perches. One shriek that sounded like a braking train was particularly getting on my nerves. I tried to think, but all the energy was going to leg muscles. Once we got to an overnight place, I would rest a little and make plans.

“We’re not going to Godbey’s Inn, by any chance?” I asked suddenly. “Where is that, anyway?”

She laughed. “It’s a trucky town 10 miles north of here.”

“What’s a trucky town?”

“It’s all built of those metal shipping containers, you know? Like they used to drive around?”

“Yeah—I’d heard of them.” We’d actually seen one or two at a distance—the closest thing they had out here to skyscrapers. Stacks of metal rectangles, some with windows cut out, fading paint and cryptic lettering—a cross between a bus depot and the Lego Museum.

"And no, I'm not flare-brained," she added. "But they'd be gone, anyway."

And trying to find me in this wilderness was harder than picking one rat out of the New York thousands. Heck, *I* didn't even know where I was.

* * *

I had to ask for a break an hour later—my leg muscles were seizing. Ciera found a small dry area under thick trees; I heard a stream nearby. Getting off the bike carefully, I dropped to the ground, knowing there was a good chance I couldn't get back up.

"I'd move if I were you. That's poison ivy."

I sat up and tried to scoot away without putting my hands on the ground. "Thanks."

"Don't sound like that. I *could* have not told you at all."

She disappeared into the brush and came back a few minutes later with a dripping water bottle. I hesitated when she offered it to me—unfiltered water was alive with vicious, gut-sapping critters. But I was parched, embarrassed to sound fussy and too tired to fetch the filter. I drank; it tasted delicious.

"Does that bird have some disease?"

"*What* bird?" She looked around, then stared at me.

"The one that sounds like it's dying. Or it's a train stopping." I imitated the descending note. She shrugged.

"You said you were a farmer, and birds are strange to you?"

"I'm not a farmer. I grew up on a farm. I was cheap labor, until I escaped. And we didn't have many birds. They ate crops, so we netted or trapped them." From her glare, I could tell I'd crossed a line. "Why—what do you do about the birds?"

"Let them live," she growled. "unless they're needed for food, then kill them respectfully."

"A Greenie!" I blurted before I could stop myself. Damn—one of those eco-nuts. Most of them had died off during the Adjustment. So they said.

"Of course a Citiot would think that."

"A *what*?"

"City idiot. Citiot. Thinks steel and concrete will keep him alive." The scorn in her voice was acidic. But if she would guide me to the train, she could believe in the big-footed spaghetti monster, for all I cared.

She cocked her head and stared. "You say you can't trust people. How then do you live your whole life trusting complete strangers?"

"What? I don't follow."

"Your water, food, shelter, security—all of it is out of your hands. You trust—every day of your life—that they'll follow through. You couldn't keep yourself alive for a week on your own. And you *say* you don't trust. I don't get that."

An image flashed through my exhaustion—a tightrope walker I had seen once at an outdoor show—with ten people below him, holding a huge woven net, just in case. I shook my head, confused.

"I'm *really* too tired to argue," I said. "Can I nap for an hour?"

"Fraid not. I want to get to the farm by dinnertime. Try lying flat and completely resting your muscles for a few minutes. It really helps. And drink more water." She demonstrated and was quiet for a while. I lay back, grateful for any break. I must've drifted off because I woke to hear her say, "Okay, break over." She stood and brushed herself off.

I groaned, but got up and limped to my bike. If Geoff caught me now, could I defend myself? Even revenge was too much to think about. I fumbled in my med pack, found a strong pain pill and washed it down with some water. I also pulled out my map.

"Show me where we are."

"Oh, yeah—I saw you with that in the shed. Very nice. That should take care of the overnight by itself."

"Only after I get to the train!"

She smiled. "We're about here—" and pointed to a place about a 16th of an inch from where the river took a left/right jog. We were passing well south of a cluster of rumpled hills and small lakes, I was happy to see.

"Hard to believe it was an hour's drive," I murmured.

"What was?"

"Youngstown to Pittsburgh—about an hour and twenty minutes by car—Before."

"You're joking!" She stared at the map again. "That's—"

"Two full days on decent roads," I said, sighing. I wish Geoff hadn't told me that, rubbing salt in the wound.

"Cars could go ninety miles per hour." She sounded almost wistful.

"I think they were only allowed about sixty. A mile a minute."

We were both silent, contemplating that.

"Well, we're only doing about five an hour, so we better get going." She handed the map back and got on her bike.

The afternoon was a blur: forest, more fields, then weaving through a totally deserted, overgrown town—doors gone from mossy brick shops, all glass removed, dust blowing through gaping walls. The surreal sight of impossibly tall lampposts like sterile giant beanstalks. How did they change light bulbs Before? Then another scrubby forest. Ciera took the lead after a while; obviously I had no energy to take any kind of upper hand. It was galling, but it was a fact. The pain med had dulled the worst, but my muscles were still limp as a leaky bellows.

At one point, a low growl percolated through the shrubs, and Ciera told me to power up and move fast. We jolted over a barely-there trail; my teeth started to ache. Finally, she signaled to slow down again.

"What was that about?"

"Lio said there was a big cat—remember?"

"So? Cats aren't scary."

She stopped the bike and stared at me. I stopped, too—grateful for any rest.

"Are you kidding? Have you ever *seen* a tiger or lion??"

"No—what are they?"

Her bark of laughter was edged with fear. "I'll explain later. Let's keep going."

* * *

The sun was hovering over the far trees when we began following a line of thickly-planted shrubs that smelled like cat piss. The spiky leaves were a superb barricade. We reached a wooden gate framed with tall metal poles, maybe old plumbing pipes.

"This is it," Ciera said.

I pulled up near the gate, and dismounted shakily.

"Don't touch it!" she warned as she pulled up next to me and got off. "It's zapped." She pushed a small round button that was set near the latch, and only that. I looked up the pole—it was possible a small sol-panel was up on top. Did they have batteries? How deadly a zap, realistically, after days of rain? Maybe a salt battery? The path beyond was lined with the same tall hedges, and turned left a hundred feet in, so nothing could be seen. We waited in silence, several long minutes, and I felt the hairs on the back of my neck rising—some group could be surrounding us at this very minute. I fought down panic, glancing at her matter-of-fact expression. If this turned out to be just a hostel, she was being honest. Probably. I slowly took several deep breaths.

Finally, we heard a tinny jingle, and Ciera lifted the latch and stepped through. "Stay here and watch the bikes," she said, "I'll be back soon."

As she disappeared around the corner, I staggered over and examined her bike. She certainly was traveling light—there was one pack the size of a melon, with obvious security tabs so I couldn't look inside. No extra compartment on the bike that I could find. And I'd seen no bulges that would indicate she was carrying lots of stuff on her person. Either she had a place to stash what she needed close at hand, or—as she said—hadn't planned to be gone long. How did she think she could escort me to the railroad? My doubts grew. Could this be her homestead? For some reason, I thought not. I checked my phone again—one or two bars, briefly three—none. *Damn!*

A few minutes later, she came back along the path, accompanied by a tall blond and freckled man with big ears who looked strong enough to carry both bikes to the house. He studied me carefully but without hostility.

"I'll need to check you and your bike before I can let you in," he said. As I bristled, he added, "or I could wheel it in and store it in the barn overnight—you can take what you need from it first."

Neither option set well. Either I showed them my weaponry, or they would look it over themselves and possibly steal it. I almost grabbed the bike and just set off down the road myself—just get back to that railroad! My aching legs brought me back to reality again. Even if they were taking me hostage, I didn't have the strength to fight. Although my upbringing protested, I agreed to let him look through everything if I could keep it with me.

"That depends on how dangerous it is," he replied, smiling. "We don't get too many real strangers here, and tourism has been dead about fifty years. So declare your weapons, and we'll find a safe place to put them—

you have to have some, otherwise—" he shrugged as if to indicate how stupid it would be.

His casual demeanor decided me. I handed him the single remaining concussion grenade, the gun, switchblade and handful of caltrops. Ciera didn't comment. It was a pitiful amount of protection. And only this morning I had been thinking the Army was my backup. *You're so dead, Martin.* He quickly and efficiently searched the rest of my packs and patted me down—I was glad I hadn't tried to hide anything. Despite his saying they didn't get visitors, he seemed damn good at security. He paused when he felt the rectangle of the phone in my pocket, but moved on. Afterward, he walked ahead as we wheeled our bikes down the path. It turned left then right, revealing a large window, an arched doorway and plastered walls glowing pink in the last of the sun. As we emerged from the hedge, he indicated a side porch on the big cobb house where we parked the bikes.

"They're safe here," Ciera said. I didn't have much choice, but I double-checked the locks; I would hear the alarm if they broke into them. The light was fading fast; as we walked back to the front door, lanterns were lit inside, spilling a golden glow out onto the scarred wood of the porch. I paused and looked down—it almost looked like series of carved initials. Ciera chuckled. "They used old library tables for the porch," she said. "Lots of character."

The entrance was also recycled—arched oak double doors with carved scrollwork like City cathedrals, opening into a main room, oval with pale green plastered walls and the deep windowsills of cobb houses. Strawbale or mud buildings were rare on Long Island, because sandy soil made bad mud and straw was needed as mulch. But I recalled the town medic clinic was cobb-built. To the right, a fire crackled in a large ceramic stove that had a low recessed cushioned bench where two little boys and a girl, all in brown smocks, sat reading a book. They glanced up curiously as we walked in and went back to reading, heads together. There were doors ahead and to the left, and a faded red and green woven rug covered much of the wood floor, which looked to be more salvage cleverly fitted together. The eight chairs clustered around a large plank table were sturdy, if mismatched. There were even a couple of paintings on the wall. My spirits rose. Obviously, Ciera knew a much better quality of hostel than Geoff.

As I turned and surveyed the room, I was startled to see a tramp staring at me—and to realize it was a mirror! My hair was plastered to my head and my scraggly beard was dripping—I looked like a molting raven. The leather jacket hung like a rigor-mortised cow, hiding my narrow shoulders. My eyes were reddened, strained from fatigue and tension, the blue irises more startling. *I* certainly would not have allowed myself in.

The door ahead of us opened suddenly, and a stout young woman with brown braids in a crown around her head stood with a potato in one hand and an antique peeler in the other.

"Welcome, stranger," she said. "Hi, Ciera."

"Hi, Monica. Thanks for letting us stay over. This is Martin—from New York City."

Monica's surprise was gratifying, and the children looked up at us with new interest. But I was too tired to face a barrage of questions this evening. I wanted nothing more than to drop onto a blanket in a corner and let the night roll over me.

"You look like you're gonna fall down, Martin. Tell you what—dinner is not for an hour. Why don't you nap on the warmbench? Jody, Aston, Lyle—it's time to set the tables. Sometimes a cat nap really helps."

Surprised, I gratefully accepted. We hung our wet coats by the front door. Slipping my shoes off, I lay down with my back to the room, the pack nestled against my stomach. The bench was very warm, and the cushion soft. I had planned to lie there and listen to the conversation, but before I knew it, I was asleep.

4

When I woke to someone shaking my shoulder, I was too groggy to leap in panic. Slowly, as the babble of voices filtered in, I remembered where I was. A pinprick of tension bloomed in my chest, but I've always been a slow waker. Rubbing my face, I sat up and looked around.

The table was full—seven adults and Ciera, with an empty chair beside her and the table piled with meat, potatoes and several green vegetables. The aroma was tantalizing—my mouth watered like a starving dog's. With a start, I realized the odors probably weren't Synthy—they couldn't afford the chemicals. When was the last time I smelled *real* food that good? Ciera showed me to a small room with washstand where I made myself passable, then led me over and introduced me.

"Chip and Monica you met, and this is Gayle, Jon and Jason. On the other side of the table are Mina, her partner Su, Rory, and Lev."

They waved or nodded, half of them already started on dinner. Their skin tones ranged from ivory to mahogany, which surprised me after the very white towns Geoff had led me through. More like the City here. Thanking them, I sat down and looked at Ciera, uncertain of protocol. She handed me a green ceramic platter of shredded meat covered in a spicy red sauce with sautéed onions, and I had to force myself not to take a double helping. There were boiled potatoes and what looked like chard or spinach, as well as curly kale—not my favorite, but I was so hungry that I took full servings of everything. There was a bowl of gorgeous butter to put on everything, and I confess that I probably ate like a starving man. I looked up a couple times to see ironic smiles on the residents' faces, anyway. But at that moment, I honestly didn't care.

After some minutes of concentrated eating, the redheaded mocha-skinned man with a broad acne-scarred face—either Jon or Jason—asked casually, "So, did you come back out here to look for family? Surely you weren't looking for entertainment." He wiped his mouth on his dark green flannel cuff that had bits of straw clinging.

The rest of them chuckled, but looked at me curiously. Or maybe suspiciously? I smiled. I was feeling a lot more human after the food. If this was how they treated prisoners, I could live with that.

"Actually, I was sent out to see if there was a way to build and maintain a couple relay towers so that our connections with Chicago could, ah, improve." Nonchalantly, I glanced around the table—who looked interested? The redhead, and the guy who met us at the gate. Who looked suspicious or hostile? Monica looked a bit nervous, but the others didn't seem to care one way or the other.

"So they're thinking of expanding out to here, are they?" Monica asked with a frown.

I shook my head emphatically. "No, no, it was more like a trade deal—seeing if there was a town that would build or at least protect a comm tower, in exchange for some kind of goods or services. I don't think anybody from the City wants to move out." I smiled to take the sting out of that, and was surprised when they laughed.

"Nor do we want them to," Ciera said, grinning. "We like them where they are."

"And you're not interested in moving in?"

The laughter was twice as loud. I bit my lip—these bit-brains had no idea what they were missing! Then I glanced around, and reminded myself that they seem to be doing pretty well. At least on a very small scale. I kept my expression neutral.

"Well, to each his own," I said.

They passed the bowls around until we had cleared them—I felt full for the first time in three days, and a sudden craving to be full like this and heading for my own bed shook me so that I had to grip my sore knee under the table to stop the flood of emotions. The very normalcy of this place brought out how alien it was. Especially since my next steps seemed impossible. And the cat nap had not touched my deep bone weariness—how would I manage several days on my bike? I shut my eyes for a moment, seeing the City's speedy steam cabs—ruinously expensive—that could bring one safely all the way up or down Manhattan Island with so very little effort. I had only done it once, paid for by a very wealthy, lovely lady who I'd briefly imagined would like me enough to bring me into her luxury townhouse near the Park. Another blasted dream.

My thoughts were interrupted by the children coming in to remove the dishes; one of them brought some kind of cream pie and smaller plates. Even full, the sight of those mounds of whipped cream had me drooling again. Monica quickly divvied up the slices and the pie disappeared in a New York minute.

"Whose turn is it for the dishes?" The ebony-hued man, who'd been quiet through dinner, spoke up.

"As it happens, it's yours, Jason," Gayle said. She was smiling, her fingers coquettishly playing with her auburn dreds, but I immediately sensed it was meant to sting. From the quick frowns around the table, they'd also caught it.

Jason sat up, stuck a false smile on his face, and said, "Well then, I better get to them. Oh—by the way, I noticed the goat fence was broken by the apple trees—can't imagine how that got overlooked." He stared at Gayle, then pushed back his chair. After he left the table, there was a deep silence, with a few glances at Gayle, who shrugged and suggested that Monica and Jon get their guitars.

"We can show our visitor our folk songs." Again, the sense of a missile rather than an invitation, but I smiled back and told her I'd enjoy that. It would be good for a few laughs with friends once I got home. Four-chord songs were children's music.

But no one moved. Ciera turned to me and said, "If you don't mind, I think we would love to hear how the City manages to exist—how do they run it? How is it organized?"

I was wary but I owed something for that marvelous food. What could I describe that wouldn't be useful to spies? "Well… the City is divided into twelve boroughs, and there's a Council wonk in charge of each. They meet monthly—we call it Wonk Talk—and figure out what's needed. You can travel out of your borough to work, shop or visit, but it's hard to *move* out." I thought of the promised Midtown apartment—did I *really* believe that, just this morning? "There are lots of ongoing projects as the City—uh... improves, so we are used to things being a bit different from month to month."

"How do you barter?" Ciera was interviewing, with the others listening raptly.

"We still use money." I was surprised. "You know—dollars, quarters, dimes… They stopped the nickels and pennies—not needed." *And mostly melted down for wire.* I didn't mention that many payments were via PayPad; I doubted I could explain it well enough to them. Hand-scan pay had been fairly widespread before the Adjustment, but most of the delicate electronics apparently were fried in the flare. The government was on a big drive to repair the systems, apparently in factories north of Manhattan, and to make it the main pay method again. Really tricky with the power outages, though.

"I thought the dollar crashed."

"Well, I guess—but if the US says it's worth a dollar, it is." I scratched my beard, which still felt strange. "Even after the electronic trading crashed, people still had cash and I guess we all agreed to… value it." It was such a complex topic, how could I summarize? For example, there were still many under-table barters, but generally paper and metal money served for non-pad shops and those special extras you didn't want the City to find out about. The paper money was getting so worn out that handling it required special care. In fact, when they released a new batch of found money, I had friends who tried to collect the new bills and hang onto them. I could never afford to do that.

"Where do you get food?"

"From the factories and farms. Long Island, New Jersey, Pennsylvania—all of them bring food in, and get—" I stopped, remembering how poorly my family had been paid. *Paid in patriotism—what crap! Paid in promises.* Not to mention that fresh food was too expensive for most people. Factories made the vat meat and synth-flavored breads, greens and potatoes that most of us ate, not that I minded. "Uh—they get security, the ability to trade safely, a…a storehouse for their goods—"

"—which are your goods, now."

"Not necessarily. There are warehouses all along the river filled with stuff that the countryside owns. They know it's safe with us."

"Except for the five-finger tax." Monica cut in.

Too tired to argue with barbarian prejudices, I just shrugged.

"What do you like about living there?" Monica asked.

"Like? Everything!" *Especially compared to this wilderness.* "There are shows to see, and sports, and music playing all the time—"

"They must get tired."

"No—electronic music. Recorded music. It plays from speakers in many buildings. It's like a…soundtrack…" They wouldn't know the term. "It's like having a lot of musicians anytime you want. And video—little mu-vids—playing in some of the shops and parks. And restaurants have readymade food." *Even if it cost too much.* "And lots of people everywhere, so there's lots of things to do after work. The city has almost a hundred thousand residents!" I wondered if that number even registered with them.

Monica sniffed. "I heard in the Chaos—"

"The Adjustment," I murmured.

"Some 'adjustment'! I heard they told the people to evacuate, then wouldn't let them back in! Only the rich and the government got to stay."

I'd heard that, too, but wasn't going to admit it. My parents and grandparents had served in the Guard and were given their plots as pay for controlling the first panic. They flatly refused to talk about it. And I remembered Tuffy, one of the odder members of Artaud's tribe, who nevertheless had a sharp ability to pick out the truth from the slogans. He used to say, "We were combed out of that City like fleas off a dog. And then they groomed us to clean up their messes." But I didn't want to describe the Long Island slums, nor the obviously skewed privileges like energy and food.

Instead, I repeated the standard explanation. "Well, at first they didn't think they could keep the City going. With power down everywhere, those tall buildings *were* unlivable. It took *time* to get a local power system working again. And by then, many people had died." In refugee camps, of starvation or disease, Teg had told me.

The group fell silent, looking down at the table. Even though I hadn't lived through it, the Great Dying had haunted my childhood. Why should I be surprised if it had affected them? Despite the curtain of silence over the first 20 years after the event, despite the government's dogged attempts to erase any trace of the destruction, whatever happened had wiped out more than half of the population, and the survivors—who were dying of old age now—had passed their trauma down without a word. I hesitated, aching to ask how their grandparents had managed.

"I hear the towers still don't work." Jon spoke up suddenly.

"Enough of them do. Just—you have to know *when* the power will be on. It moves around the City. Like, Midtown is on from 11 to 2, and 7 to

10, so people on higher floors there have to get in and out only during those times." Was that telling Ciera too much? I didn't mention that most towers were abandoned above the 20th floor, slowly being taken down and reused. And I didn't want to explain all the Go-Time planning, the Shut Sundays, the calendar that each of us had to keep close, to navigate the City's many sections—that detail might be useful for spies. And the gravity-feed water barrels on roofs, the super-insulated ice boxes. It was a huge bonus working for a state corporation that gave themselves full power, *and* had a cafeteria. Not to mention hot showers. "We don't have to worry about crime or need to carry a gun around," I ended, "we can travel the whole City, and even most of the farmlands, safely."

"We feel safe here," Gayle said, in a defensive tone. I nodded; *don't piss them off.*

"I'd have thought there'd be more crime, with so many people," Jon added.

"Well, they deal pretty harshly with crime—" *hand cut off for theft, work farms, flogging for energy cheats, death for a lot of things*—"and also they make sure citizens have enough, so they don't need to resort to crime." That sounded naïve, even to me.

"We just shoot 'em. Or hang 'em," Jon said.

"Which saves on bullets," Gayle added. They all chuckled.

"Who decides who's wrong, though?" I asked. "Do you still have judges?"

Ciera shrugged. "Town elders, usually. If someone is caught in the act, no one needs to judge. We can't afford thieves, swindlers, violence or selfishness."

Almost sounded like a warning, like an old mu-vid—the horror under the pleasant façade. Or, to be honest, like many areas of Long Island. Most pertinent, I could disappear here without a trace. What value was I to them alive? Well, slave, as Ciera had said. I fought the urge to run, again. Tonight, if the damn phone cooperated, I would try texting Melinda—but no, she was Cheyenne's best friend. Then maybe Gillian, the partner of a top clothing exec who'd passed me her number the last lavish Fourth of July party—she might not remember me, but seemed the adventurous sort—her number spelled "HOTLUV", which is how I recalled it. I'd never told her I was too low down the ladder to own a phone. Maybe my plight would intrigue her... *Someone* needed to know where I was!

"Do they still have the famous massed transit?" Ciera asked.

I was pulled back to the present. "Um, there are trolleys, and since they banned all the cars that had survived—" *except for the very rich*—"it's a much nicer place to walk or bike, and really it's not a very big island. Since there's no reason to go out to the farmlands, the trolleys just loop around a few main streets." I didn't mention how strict the barricades were around the City, how much it cost to be smuggled in from Long Island or Jersey, how severe the penalty even for those trying to get *out* without permission. Spies or not, they would probably see it as a prison colony rather than a jewel that needed to be protected.

"What about the underground travel?" Jon asked.

"Because it cost so much to light and ventilate, they just abandoned the subways." Actually, much of that system was flooding, as the seas rose slowly but steadily. It was the same reason that Battery Park had been abandoned. I heard they'd planned to make giant dikes or floodgates, but that had only happened around the best Long Island farmland. Everyone downtown in Little Venice lived on the second floor and above. There were even rumors of troll colonies in the flooded subways, but I didn't believe it.

Monica and Jon finally went for their instruments. They returned to sit on the warmbench, and the rest of us moved our chairs closer to the fire. Gayle grabbed a basket full of fluff, and pulled the stuff apart on two square combs as she listened. A few others had handwork, too. I was feeling warm and full and thus almost falling asleep. They started off with a tune that I remembered from an Irish ceili I'd attended for my 20th birthday—the flame-haired girl who went with me had broken my heart shortly after; I don't think I'd listen to Irish music since. They were both skilled players, picking the melody and counter melody with smoothness and intensity that suggested much practice. But the music was fading in and out as I fought to keep my eyes open. I jolted awake to find myself almost toppling off the chair.

"Maybe we need a bit of a rest rather than music tonight," Ciera suggested softly.

"Of course—you have ridden a long way today," Monica replied. She led us through the kitchen, where Jason was still working with two older boys. She picked up a glass-sided candle lantern, lit it and pushed open a far door into a narrow hallway with two closed doors on each side and at the far end, steep stairs leading up. Monica pushed open the first door.

"Ciera, you sleep with the girls." She pushed open the door opposite and held her candle lantern high. "And Martin—I hope you'll understand that we will all sleep better knowing there isn't a stranger wandering at night." She looked at me with raised eyebrows. Half asleep already, I couldn't quite get it.

"I'll work it out with him, Monica," Ciera said. "Thanks for everything. See you in the morning."

Monica handed Ciera the lantern and left us alone in the hallway. Ciera showed me the tiny room—a thick blanketed mattress on a low pallet, a covered chamber pot in the corner, and narrow slit windows shuttered against the cold.

"It's a habit to, um, shut in any visitor they're not very sure of—I'll slide the bolt on this side and let you out in the morning. You've got your pack and what you'll need tonight. We'll be getting up at dawn, so I hope you sleep soundly."

I hadn't noticed, but the door had a thick wooden bar on the outside. So—*was* I a prisoner? Or was this just common sense? I slid it back and forth a couple times—the rasp was loud enough that I think I would hear it if anyone tried to get in. I shrugged.

"I guess I wouldn't trust a stranger in these circumstances," I commented, adding, "And thank you for this place. It's so much better then what Geoff, um, Alex provided."

She grinned. "Is Geoff another alias? Good to know. And yes, this *is* a nice place—though a lot more primitive than I could stand for long."

"Really? Then what—" I could see her tense; I waved my hand as if to say "forget it".

She shook her head and said slowly, "A totally manual farm is a huge amount of work. It helps to have a decent amount of power—to heat water, keep a few things cold, run a tiller…you know. All they have is the solar alarm."

I'd been thinking the same thing, but her comments surprised me. Then I remembered. "Yeah—you told me you were salvaging hardware from Madison. So you're using it, not just selling. I guess as a solar tech, you work where there's power."

I wanted to pursue it further, but fatigue was shutting my brain down fast. I told her goodnight and went into the room. She set the candle lantern just inside the door; it cast a strange light as I carried my pack towards the mattress. I heard her close and bar the door; I pulled out my phone and checked—*oh god*! There was a message! I fought with the flickering contact, and on the third try was able to read the text from Rivera—"Hang on! Coming!" A wave of relief washed over me, almost threatening to knock me over. The connection with the City, which had been flickering as badly as the phone bars, surged back strongly—I *would* make it.

I dropped my clothes on the floor by my pack and practically fell into the bed. I don't remember falling asleep.

5

I am running down a filthy alley littered with plastic farm crates full of rotting vegetables. I pause, but I know someone is chasing, so I run on. I dodge into a clothing store where Ciera, behind the counter, holds up bib overalls and says, "time to start paying back." Then I am in a concrete alcove, Geoff—or is it my boss?—is looming over me, taking my Citizen's pass and chuckling. I push him away, grab my pass and run—into a busy street, where a trolley full of clerks from Commco are laughing and tossing baby sharks onto the street where they thrash and die, gasping. I take a few steps forward—can I get on? But the Minister of Justice, dressed as the Red Queen from the Alice Saga, is on the steps, waving a wand that emits sparks or lightning. Then the rain starts, and in a minute is a gray curtain cutting me off from everything else. I feel the water rise to my ankles, then knees. Am I in lower Manhattan? I look around for a stairs or door to escape the flood. A moment later, I am choking as the water closes over my head.

No! I woke and sat bolt upright. I was alone in the tiny bedroom—the candle in the lantern was guttering as it drowned in hot beeswax; the honeyed perfume filled the room and wild shadows danced on the walls. A breeze, damp and chill, slipped in through the tiny slit windows, making me burrow back into my warm nest. The silence was eerie—I heard something hoot and a faint snoring from another room. The absence of usual city percussion again felt like a missing tooth. I shook my head to clear it. The nightmare was fading before I could catch details, leaving me with a sense of loss and danger. Then I remembered last night's text—someone knew I needed help. For the moment, resting behind the barred door, I felt safe.

* * *

Even though I had slept soundly after the nightmare, I was barely able to move the next day. My muscles hurt so specifically that I could have traced each one for an anatomy class. I was tempted, but skipped more pain meds—who knows how badly I might need them before I got out of this? As light filtered through the shutters, Ciera unlocked the door, looking apologetic. I tried not to hobble like a recyclee as she showed me to a small washroom with a basin of water and a towel; the water was warm but the soap was jelly-like and repellent. The company shower stalls' glorious hot water and bars of soap flashed in mind, and I vowed I would never take them for granted again. Then I slowly moved to the main room, where breakfast had been set on the table. Monica joined us, but the others apparently had eaten and gone. I watched Ciera press something into a blob of clay and pass it carefully to Monica. A debt token? It would come out of my bag eventually, but I focused on the thick oatmeal with some delicious honey, and a halfway decent cup of hot coffee. Roasted barley and something else I couldn't identify, but a pretty good imitation. I hoped it wasn't going to be $10 per cup like in the City.

"Since the last time you were here," Monica said, "I've gotten the weaving studio set up—do you want to see it?"

Obviously aimed at Ciera. I tensed. She hadn't yet told me if she was willing to go any further. Had they discussed this, and was I on my own? I looked over at her in time to catch her questioning glance.

"Well," she replied, still looking at me, "we have a long day ahead, but I'm sure we can spare the time."

I sagged in relief. Hurting this bad, I wouldn't be sharp enough to navigate, even with excellent directions. I nodded, more than willing to put off the pedaling. We carried our dishes to the kitchen, whose plastered walls were washed in pale yellow. It was a fairly large room, with plates and bowls standing vertically in racks on one wall, and cups hung from pegs underneath. I noticed the sink had a hand pump faucet of soldered plumbing pipes and a wooden ax handle, and the deep window sill was screened on the outside, glass-doored on the inside and held some wrapped packages. A pie safe and window fridge; that would be nice—in the City, we hung food over the sill in canvas bags when it was cold. Large wooden bins stood along one wall and in an alcove, a wine rack held two dozen bottles. That was impressive, even if it was homemade—with all the work that went into fermentation, a full bottle of wine was always priced over my budget.

Monica saw me looking and commented, "That's blackberry wine. They grow so abundantly out here we have to do something with them besides just making cobbler."

"Cobbler's good too," Ciera said with a grin.

We went down another hall, windowless but well lit from several round skylights—I glanced up; they seemed to be glass bottles full of water. The weaving studio was very well lit with a combination of high south windows and a wide glass northern window-wall set at an angle, probably to catch more sun. The panels were small and different sizes but none of them were cracked, and they seemed expertly set in. Beneath, on the clay-tiled floor, wooden trays of tiny seedlings were arrayed.

"Already starting the crops," Ciera commented, as she bent down to study them. The sun picked out highlights in her dark brown hair, and gilded long eyelashes. The overalls fitted her slim shape like they had been made just for her. She moved with such grace I had to imagine she wasn't feeling the effects of the ride like I was. It made me feel like an old man, though not quite too old to appreciate her.

"Yeah, it's tricky not to get dirt anywhere near the fiber, but we manage. Can't waste the light." Monica said. She walked over to a large wooden contraption that was mostly a couple of large square frames, joined with a large horizontal frame and what looked like foot pedals. A loom, I guessed. And a fancy one—a few of my aunts wove, but their looms were simply vertical frames strung with woolen threads. Not really relatives, but all the women in our commune were aunts, and the men uncles. Here, a curtain of threads hung down from a few of the frames, and another curtain ran horizontally across. I had never been that curious about where the fabric for my clothes came from, but looking at this very complicated thing, I wondered how long it would take to get enough fabric to make a tunic. Of course, they had machines to do that Before, and the steam mills north of the City did something similar now.

"Monica, it's gorgeous," Ciera said running her hand along the wood frame. "Who built it for you?" She sat down at the bench in front of the loom and moved a wood bar back and forth, then pushed the foot pedals—I could see it attached at the bottom and that caused strings to move, but I couldn't begin to understand the process. Hard to believe cloth was made out of string. And the string had to be made somehow, too.

"The Beaver Falls workshop. It was a big trade," Monica admitted, "we put half up in produce last year, and have guaranteed the other half for this year. They do such good work, it will totally change how we weave. And with Gail being such a good retter, as well as spinner, we'll have a lot more linsey woolsey coming out of here by next year." She picked up a piece of unbleached fabric; I could tell it wasn't wool, but didn't look like cotton. She offered it to me and I touched it gently. "Linen wears like iron, and wool makes it soft," she added. It felt smooth and lightweight.

"It might be really nice to have a tunic of something like this," I said. My aches and pains were preventing me from appreciating what was obviously a big deal to them. Ciera must have seen my expression.

"We probably should be—"

"But you haven't seen the sewing machine!"

Monica hurried over to a corner and lifted a cloth. Underneath was a small black machine that looked a bit like the kitchen faucet pump crossed with some hand barbells. I had seen pictures of a sewing machine somewhere, and vaguely remembered one of the aunts had one. Any sewing done around my house had been done by hand, usually by the children, and in the City there were tailors. Ciera came over and examined the machine, sat down and moved her feet back and forth on pedals on the ground, which made part of the machine move.

"Very impressive—you're turning into a regular tailors workshop."

"Yeah. So maybe your group might be interested—"

"I'll definitely mention it to them—we keep needing more fabric, that's for sure."

They moved back toward the door and I followed, limping slightly and stretching my muscles surreptitiously. Monica led us through a different hall, and out along the back of the house. The ground sloped gently away, and it was neatly partitioned—I recognized an herb garden, and it was quite a large one. As a boy I had enjoyed wandering through the herbalist's garden, sniffing the wonderful odors, with my hands obediently clasped behind my back. Even now, I could smell oregano, rosemary—I smiled and took a deep breath.

Monica bent down and picked several leaves. Handing them to me, she said, "these are St. John's wort and mint—if you rub them on your muscles, it should help the stiffness."

"Oh, good idea!" Ciera said. "And do you have any muscle cream, with comfrey or cayenne?"

"Both. Be happy to give you a jar."

A small cobb hut slightly detached from the main house suddenly erupted with children, who ran to a flat patch of field and started a game of kickball. The ball thudded against their wood clogs as if it was solid under the leather cover.

"We've added something to the schoolroom—come look," Monica said and walked swiftly to the hut.

Inside, three walls had deepset windows and one wall gleamed with something intricately patterned. I looked closer and realized someone had attached dozens of small foil food packets, the kind that were sometimes offered as antiques in the City. An almost-circular cartoon cat with a pink bow smiled out at the viewer, and the word *Hello, Kitty* was repeated in a banner over every cat. The overall effect was spritely and playful.

"Someone must have found a real middentrove of those," I commented. "I've only seen one or two before."

"Yeah—a peddler came by with bags of them and he really wanted some fabric. It took a little discussion, but we did agree that it would be a fun decoration for the schoolroom, and increases the light. Oh—and we got a new bike tractor from Middleton—a bit stiff to pedal, but Jon manages. Lets us use the horses for salvage hauling."

"Had you thought about a solar module? We've got one that's basically self-powered…"

As they chatted, we crossed a courtyard that the house encircled in horseshoe shape. Monica led us through a small pantry, where she took a small glass jar from a shelf and handed it to Ciera. Another short hallway and we were back in the living room.

Monica turned and hugged Ciera. "It was good to see you again. Make sure you come back with Ulni if she comes to get cloth."

Ciera grinned and nodded. "That's not usually part of my job, but I'll try. Thank you for being so generous on short notice."

"My pleasure." Monica glanced over as if considering whether to hug me. I stepped back and offered her my hand.

"I appreciate it, too," I said. "This is really a very impressive place."

"A bit more than you were expecting to find out here?" Monica asked teasingly.

I felt my face redden, but I smiled and raised my hands. "Not what I expected in many ways." I didn't want to say that I'd hoped for electricity and running water. But the food and bed had been more than fine.

* * *

Shortly after, we were on our bikes again, heading down the gravel road as the early morning sun shafted through tall, straight trees that made a natural fence on both sides, augmented by some woven vines up to shoulder height. The bright light and dark shadows in bands across the road made it hard to see, as my eyes had to adjust and readjust. I focused on the ground in front of me, forcing my legs to pedal, hoping the fence was thick enough to prevent attack. I bit back groans as my muscles were jolted all over again, though honestly the gravel was not nearly as bad as the various combinations we had traveled over yesterday. How would I survive two more days of this? If I hadn't had a sixth floor walk-up apartment, I would probably be done already.

Ciera was silent behind me and the road stretched straight without turnoffs, so the next hour gave me time to ponder my predicament. Was Geoff simply an opportunist? If not, who had masterminded this whackjob? Surely not the Department of Justice! Who did those bashers work for? *Were* they local thugs in troubadour costume? I couldn't believe local thugs would pay more than Geoff was getting for this trip. So there had to be a link to the City. I ran through the company dramas: Cheyenne's and others' blatant attempts at top management, my boss's continual flouting of the CEO's desire to build dishwork out into New Jersey, the constant tension between the silver spoons and the striving. And of course, the usual petty personality clashes. Would someone go through all this trouble simply to make my boss look bad? That they'd be willing to sacrifice me, I had no doubt. Cutthroat didn't *begin* to describe the modern office. You were either a shark or you were chum. I'd thought I was a shark…but of course there are always bigger sharks. But to sabotage the communication system?? What could be the advantage of losing the towers? As far as I could see, it would be a disaster if New York could no longer communicate with Chicago or DC. We were about to lose Los Angeles and Houston—for now—but we couldn't manage ground trade with them yet anyway. It had been mostly swapping information about things like weather. Warning of approaching storms was worth a lot of money, but we would have to make do with Chicago and DC's data, starting pretty soon.

We? It had nothing to do with me—I was just one of the peons scrabbling for crumbs the powerful threw out. I barely read the corner newsboards—the theater, celebrity crap and lottery boosting. The news I wanted came from friends and colleagues and the price of goods in the stores. The most valuable information was stashed in the halls of power, anyway—and journalists wrote what they were told. But didn't I hear something about rumbles from the so-called tribal chiefs in the outer slums? I'd shrugged it off as fearmongering. Ten years ago, just beyond the reach of the Army, there had been some especially nasty power struggles, and those who reached the top were sharks with a capital S. They threw their might against the borders of the City and got crushed. Could one of those have decided to sabotage this trip? Could Artaud still manipulate his minions, or another chief have taken over? In that case, the faster I got to the authorities, the safer for me and the better for this project. But would those two mangy dogs have the nerve to imitate officials if their backing didn't come from inside? What if someone in the City wanted this to fail? How safe would it be for me to cry foul? Or to wait out here for help?

"Turn left up ahead." Ciera's voice jolted me out of my thoughts. A broader shaft of sunlight suggested a road I couldn't yet see. I peddled a bit slower, and veered towards my right, to give me a better view before I turned into a blind alley. "What's wrong?" she called behind me.

"Nothing—I was just being careful."

"Good idea—but it's generally safe around here." She moved up on my left. Since the morning, she had been subtly more friendly. She'd handed back my weapons, and had even suggested I keep my gun and grenade handy in case of trouble today. She wouldn't have done that if she were handing me over to someone. And I was pretty certain now I wouldn't get to the railroad without her. Maybe she knew that, too.

The new road was also gravel, but less well maintained—weeds were growing tall enough that I had to constantly swerve around them. The fence of trees continued on the left, but on the right, behind a rusting barbed wire fence, a green sheep meadow undulated towards low distant hills. I could smell the glorious perfume of flowering trees—reminding me of the ones I used to stand under as a child and just breathe in. Several acres away, what looked like an orchard was being tended by a couple of stooping or reaching figures. A few more of those grave mounds dotted the fields, with the sheep nibbling their slopes. In the far distance, a white fish-tail shape jutted high over the fruit trees—maybe one of the crashed planes that had so altered the landscape just after the flare? Around New York, the only evidence of the massive Downfall were obviously-new cities built on the cleared ground. The ones that had flattened the Bronx had been recycled into new food factories and a prison. All the parts had been used, and they existed only as horror stories whispered by mischievous uncles who were shushed by aunts. Here, aside from the relic, the sun sparkled on the damp leaves and grass, and beaded the wire fences like a zircon necklace. The slight breeze found gaps in my crude leather coat, but it felt good.

"This road leads to the river," Ciera commented. "There's usually a bit of morning traffic, so that would be a good time to cross—they divide the cost of crossing among those who are waiting. It'll be slightly cheaper with a crowd, but still expensive."

I was weaving around a thick clump of yellow-flowered weeds and just grunted. Anything of value was expensive, it went without saying. The bike wobbled; I cursed as I pulled it up—my muscles were responding just a bit too slow, like an engine misfiring. I prayed that the distance to the river was shorter than yesterday's journey.

* * *

I was focused on avoiding hidden potholes, and so didn't notice the overpass until we were almost upon it. It looked like one of several places where Geoff and I had to divert our trip briefly from the main road because a bridge had collapsed onto a smaller road underneath—tons of concrete and steel rods twisted and now rusted so badly it looked like a bizarre bird nest. And in the center, a truck big enough to be a house, the cab crushed, the back van open and plundered. In a landscape of ruined, overgrown buildings, the huge pillars that had supported the arch still stood, covered with flaking painted symbols as high as two people could stand, two massive towers of useless concrete with weed-dotted ramps leading down from each in a wide curve like giant scythe blades. I knew of at least six massive working bridges in the City, so high that a 10-story tower could go underneath. They were mostly usable, with Army posts at each end to inspect crossing carts or bikes. The fees to use them were as steep as the ramps and rumor held that 50 years with only shovel-and-pick maintenance made the road surface very risky. Certainly the real estate under or near them was mostly abandoned and worthless. Looking at this mess, I had a new appreciation of the danger. No more visits to that funky jazz dive near 42nd St.

"It doesn't make any sense, does it, them building all that because they can't slow down and stop for another cart?" Ciera shook her head.

"Remember—a mile a minute," I said. "How long would it take to brake at that speed?"

She had probably never seen a mu-vid, so she had no feel for how fast people used to drive Before. Cars did incredible speeds—if the images could be believed. Of course, most of them crashed in the end, and my friends and I agreed it was droiddumb to risk life and expensive cars just to chase after each other. If they had raced along at twenty-five miles, no one would have been hurt. Somehow that didn't occur to the people who lived then. Standing in front of this heap looming half the size of some of the City's big towers, filling acres of land with concrete and asphalt, I tried to picture a society so rich it could afford to waste so much just for speed. I felt *really* small. *Just get me back*, I prayed, though I didn't know to Whom.

* * *

A half-hour later, we walked our bikes slowly to the top of a steep ridge and looked down. Ciera said this was the Beaver River—half the width of the Ohio that it emptied into a few miles south, but still too broad for a modern bridge. To my right, too far away to see the details, the ruined pillars of a Before bridge seemed to have a swaying hammock strung between; tiny figures were moving slowly over it, and I shuddered to watch them swing. Nearby, the remains of a town were obvious under the trees and wilderness, but on this side at least, there were no residents.

"The only way to get heavy bikes or carts across are the ferries," Ciera explained. "There's four on the Beaver, and who knows how many on the Ohio."

The ferry, which was coming toward us across a smooth flat patch of river, looked like a large raft with gigantic wheels in the middle of either side. Something was moving in the raft. Squinting, I realized it was oxen. One near each wheel, slowly walking—they must be powering the paddle wheels that drove the boat! I turned to Ciera, and saw that she was looking intently at nearby shrubbery, staring down at the small queue of travelers ahead of us—doing the kind of reconnoitering that I should have been instead of staring like a wide-eyed tourist.

"See anything?" I asked.

"I don't see two big fat guys dressed in blue," she replied. "But if they have any brains, they would have changed clothes also."

"If they *are* from Long Island, they probably won't care about disguises. That was the point of the sky blue," I explained. She looked at me quizzically. "The tribe is bragging that they don't need camouflage because they have power. They could afford to be identified in public."

"Well, that might be fine for the City, but they could quickly find themselves—" she stopped herself, as if giving too much away. I remembered last night's conversation. Well, good riddance if they got caught.

We rode down slowly towards the queue waiting on a narrow wooden dock—four scruffy mule carts assembled from doors and whatnot, with six scruffier farmer types leaning against them, watching the ferry and smoking some kind of weed—neither tobacco nor pot; the odor wafting back was almost like cat piss.

Ciera stopped at the edge of the cleared bank. "I'm not waiting out in the open," she murmured. "Keep the heroin handy—the ride costs between five and twelve grid each, but I'm hoping two bags will take care of it. We'll wait till it's about ready to leave, and get on last minute. And put on your cap."

I nodded, trying to picture how much further it would be beyond the river—and how soon before we would reach anything resembling civilization. I put Jordy's brimmed cotton beanie on my head, feeling like a total wank. But it did cover my hair and obscure my face.

The ferry slid alongside the jutting wooden pier, and the pilot moved away from the tiller, threw a large coil of rope, caught by two on the bank and dropped over a thick pole. The squeal and whine as the boat ground to a halt against huge rubber tires—bumping, bouncing, jolting—echoed off the trees and nearby hills. Several birds seemed to answer. Two pre-teen boys held poles in front of the oxen, slowing them, then turned them around. Three walking passengers and one mule leaped or stepped onto the dock. Ciera punched my shoulder. I jumped—and only my fatigue kept me from elbowing her in the gut. Her move would have started a deadly fight back home. Breaking personal boundaries was a challenge, pure and simple.

She seemed unaware of that. "Get ready—they usually load and go."

"No schedule? They don't wait for a certain hour?" I rubbed my shoulder.

"What for? If you want the ferry, *you* have to put up the flag and wait. A valuable boat is not going to sit tied up at a dock."

Indeed, I saw the boys lowering a bright pink square from a thin pole. The pilot was standing on the pier cradling a rifle as he scanned the river banks. I tensed myself to move quickly, then paused.

"What if he thinks we're thieves? Won't he shoot us?"

"I'll call out to him. Walk the bikes. It should be okay."

Should be. Great. She punched me again as the last cart wheeled itself onto the boat, and we strode quickly down the last slope, as she waved and called out, "Howard! Wait up!"

"How did you know his name?" I was fighting down instinctive rage at being punched twice.

"I don't—I can pretend I thought I recognized him."

The pilot had the gun in readiness but not aimed as we clattered onto the rough wood pier.

"Thanks for waiting," Ciera gasped, as if she was out of breath. I played along, and it wasn't difficult to look utterly beat. She gestured toward me and I pulled out the bags. As I was about to hand them over, commotion in the forest caused us to look around. The two bashers were coming out of thick shrubbery on their big e-bikes about 100 feet from us.

"Bandits!" Ciera shrieked. "Quick! Hurry!"

She practically threw her bike onto the deck, and I carry-dragged mine after her, fighting the bouncing and pitching. The pilot flipped the rope off of the pole, jumped on board, and the boys whipped the oxen, yelling, "Yee haw!" Everyone braced, and for a moment it seemed like one of the carts would slide and unbalance the raft—dropping the bikes, Ciera and I lent our shoulders to holding it in place. I glanced back in panic as I heard gravel spew—the thugs were racing down and onto the pier. The ferryman aimed and shot, but the bucking ferry sent the bullet wild. One of the thugs couldn't stop his bike and plunged into the river with a tremendous splash. A moment later, he bobbed up, spluttering and flailing. The other scrambled to help him back onto the dock, and Geoff raced out of hiding to help. I sagged against the cart, my heart racing, cursing Geoff but keeping it low.

"Well, they know where we are," Ciera muttered, before I could.

"And my disguise obviously didn't work." I was afraid to ask *now what*? Afraid there wasn't any good answer. "How soon can they get across?" I asked instead.

"Probably not for a couple hours—the next ferry is at least fifteen miles downstream, and this one doesn't come back again until new traffic gathers about lunch time. And they *won't* be allowed on it." She looked at me angrily, and my gut clenched—if she set me down on the other side, could I find my way home? It clearly wasn't just a question of knowing the route—this was as tricky as crossing tribe territory.

The ferryman secured his rifle in a vertical slot and turned to us. "Were they after you?" he asked, crossing his arms and glaring.

Ciera paused, as if considering denying it, then shrugged. "I don't know—I noticed they were following us, but I figured we were just random targets and that they wouldn't dare a crowd." I kept my face blank—they *weren't* following, they were lying in wait. Who told them??

He glanced down at my bike, and said "I hear there's a bounty—a bike of that make and year was stolen out of Army Depot in the Pitts. They're paying 50 grid for finding it."

She took a deep breath. I tensed—is this where she would finally let me fend for myself?

"Can't be this bike," she said. "*This* one belongs to Yuri of Middletown—on special loan so we can scope out the troubles."

The ferryman's head snapped up—he stared at her dubiously, but cautiously, for a moment. Then he nodded.

"In that case," he said, "ride's free—if you can pass some info back to me, seeing how I keep this passage open."

"That sounds reasonable. Agreed," she replied, and they slapped hands. With another nod, he walked over to collect fees from the cart drivers, who were blocking their wheels with wooden triangles.

The drivers had left the area near us open, avoiding us like contagion. As she came back, I stepped closer and murmured, "Why did you lie for me? I mean—I'm really grateful, but I don't understand."

She looked down, frowning. Maybe she wasn't sure, either. She stared over at the carts. "Well—firstly, I said I would get you across, and I don't break a promise. Secondly… I don't kick a crippled dog—I mean, I don't leave someone—anyone—just when they're needing help. That's not the kind of person I am." She looked up at me, as if daring me to dispute it.

"I… It's really unusual, where I come from. It's not—"

"I don't doubt that. The City breeds sharks, is what we're told."

So much truer than she had any idea. Too damn true. Weirdly, I felt even more vulnerable—if I followed my rules, I would be the same kind of bastard as that foul threesome at the docks. But I didn't know these other rules—oh yeah, some of the storytellers liked to tell long sagas where the hero acted, well, *heroically*, and never cheated or power-grabbed, no matter how much trouble it got him or her into. We all enjoyed them, even while agreeing that kind of action was basically insane. The mu-vids never had those kind of stories; the heroes in those knew how to take care of Number One. Was she telling the truth? She wasn't with Geoff, anyway—and it was harder and harder to believe she was conning me. Did she *really* act without a personal hook? Surely she would still expect payment down the road. If she expected heroism from me, she'd have a long wait. I knew my limits.

"Who's Yuri?"

"One of the big town presidents. That will take a few appeasement gifts later, also. But if we get the information—"

"What information? *What* troubles?"

She looked directly at me. It was obvious she was deeply suspicious. I shifted uncomfortably, knowing I hadn't given her all the details, but I'd outlined the major ones, hadn't I?

"This isn't the right time, but when we get to the other side, we need to talk."

So we braced ourselves and our bikes against the rocking of the ferry as it made a mostly straight line towards the other bank. I watched the gray water swirling, trying to carry us downriver, the ferryman wrestling with the tiller and the oxen straining in their stalls as they walked along their treadmills, some sort of wooden boards connected by wires or chain links—it was a remarkable design. And if the City hadn't been surrounded by brigands, it might be an excellent way to move across the Hudson or East rivers. New York ferries were smaller, faster, armor-plated warehouses, and big loads went over the bridges, with armed guards. Was crime so much less frequent out here, or were we armored because we could afford to be? There was that "we" again—I never thought of myself as a "we" in the City, why was I doing it out here? Maybe because this incomprehensible rural setup was so definitely "them".

The other bank got closer and larger: a flat open plain with few trees. A couple patched mega-ad tents nestled in flat areas, their huge antique images faded to pastel. Clusters of wood and brick buildings crowded the wooden dock—in fact, two wooden docks about 100 feet away from each other—and I could see a handful of people queuing on the upstream dock. I couldn't see where the road led after that. If we weren't closer to Pittsburgh than the map showed, I'd need a longer break. I doubted I was sharp enough to take the train back to the City. After all, there were lots of ways to be swindled all along the line. I'd be tempted to stay overnight in the terminus hotel before riding—if not for this gut-deep urge to get home ASAP. That reminded me—I eased my phone barely out of my pocket and checked for coverage. No bars. How could they track me like this? Sighing, I tucked it back in.

When the boat docked, we followed the cart drivers off, rumbling over the scarred wooden planks, pedaling past a painted sign, "Welcome to Horseferry", then up a mud road marked "Honey Sign Lane" toward some wood and plaster buildings dominated by a large two-story clapboard house with a hanging painted sign: "Destry's Inn". It had porches running across the front on both floors. The western wall had been stripped of its white paint by weather and the porches sagged slightly; some of the ornate scroll trim over the windows—all of which had glass—looked handcarved. There were traces of dark red paint in the grooves. Possibly a couple hundred years old.

"Honey Sign Lane?"

"There used to be a sign advertising honey there years ago." Ciera shrugged.

Hanging around the porch, a couple of shirtless teenaged boys in brown sacking pants—one tall, scrawny blond and the other shorter, hefty and dark-haired—were watching us. Wheeling her bike up to them, Ciera asked, “How much?” The blond held up two fingers and she handed something to him, and gestured for me to leave my bike. I glanced at my locks, made sure they were secure, then handed it to the dark-haired boy. Despite their attempts to seem disinterested, I could see the gleam in their eyes. I hoped she knew what she was doing.

Ciera led me into the dark front room. When my eyes adjusted, I could see it was a restaurant with a long bar against the back wall and a small side room that was brighter because of three windows lined with viney plants. There were no lights or light wells to alleviate the gloom, and it seemed like the five clients and the tall thin woman behind the bar were used to it. Ciera threaded her way past the diners towards the other room. We took a table as far from the others as possible, very close, if my nose was correct, to the bathrooms. The woman followed us, and Ciera ordered two meals—just like yesterday’s lunch, there were no choices—and stamped a sheet of paper the woman was holding. Our waitress nodded silently and walked swiftly back towards the bar.

Ciera turned to me. “Okay, now we talk. This has gotten too serious, and I need to know.”

“I’m telling the truth—I knew nothing about those two until I saw them in the barnyard! I used one of my concussion grenades to get away, and I certainly didn’t stay long enough to ask them what they were there for!”

“But what about the rest of it? If they’re not from Justice, who hired them? The Army?”

“I’ve been asking myself that this whole trip—why would the Army do it? And I don’t think they’re bright enough to be authority—they really are just dumb bullies.” I realized that, despite being very thirsty, I also had to use the facilities. I turned to see where the bathroom doors were. “Excuse me a minute—I’ve got to, um, wash up.”

She grinned wryly. “Not in there, you won’t. But pee if you need to.”

I hurried to the back corner and entered the restroom—a pit toilet with a wooden seat and a pile of leaves in the corner... perhaps for toilet paper? Luckily I only had to pee and it didn’t take long, because I was holding my breath. Various occupants had carved initials on the wall, and possibly “decorated” it with other substances. So much like Astoria rude decor. Wiping my hands on my pants, I went back to the table.

There were already two plates on the table, with potatoes, a large chunk of dark bread, something orange and maybe a small bit of ground meat. Two glasses contained some clear brown liquid that I hoped was beer. Ciera had already begun. I sat and started on the potatoes; they were surprisingly good. It didn't take long to clear my plate. And the beer was palatable.

"If you weren't sent out here to spy for the Army, then were you taking messages about—" she looked around and lowered her voice, "—you know, the situation—to somebody else?"

"What are you *talking* about?"

She leaned forward and murmured, "The revolt, Martin—I don't believe you don't know anything about it. It's too coincidental that you show up just when it's about to get started." I stared at her. She snorted in frustration, and continued, "Fine. Don't tell me, and I'll just drop you off right in the middle of it. Maybe that's where you want to be."

"Ciera, I *really* don't know what you're talking about. I really *did* just come out here looking to see about the comm towers!"

She narrowed her eyes and studied me. After a moment she sat back shaking her head. "You're a good actor, or you're really in trouble. For now, I'll pretend you don't know. What we hear is, some locals plan to take over the railroad—real soon. Word has gotten around, and everyone is worried. We know the Army will fight back, but we don't know where the blame will fall. Will they believe it's only a single group, or will they blame all of us? Will they use it as an excuse to take over more territory? Can they even expand out this far? That's what we need to know."

She didn't look like she was lying. There'd be no reason to, and besides I'd know weasel words if I heard them. *Would I? What about Geoff?* Confidence suddenly drained like a dam bursting—what the hell did I know about this world, or who was telling the truth? There was going to be a war?? And it was happening right between me and my real life. I pictured the train ride out: the Wall undulating closer and farther from the tracks as lucky towns were chosen for inclusion; the wheat and medical poppy fields' ragged young green within the Wall's protection. The towns well-organized on the usual pattern, people unarmed, dressed in up-to-date fashions—I'd even noticed a few solar-panel streetlights. I hadn't noticed any soldiers—the corridor *had* to be defended, but hardly enough stationed there for a war. There had been flocks of children laughing, running to school and once I had glimpsed a garden concert out of the train window. And someone wanted to grab that for themselves, with all the bloody carnage that entailed?? Slum battles flashed through my mind. Abruptly, I stood and rushed back to the foul pit toilet closet.

"Give me a minute!" I hollered through the door. The stench brought tears to my eyes. No—who was I kidding? Tears flowed and I hunched over, trying not to touch any of the stinking wood. Sobs shook me. I stuffed my cap against my face to smother all sound. *No, no, no, no.* I bent double, teeth clenched against the bubble of pain and fear pressing up from the deep, locked spot in my chest. *No, no, no, no* was all I could think. *No* to everything—to the whole stinking, fucked-up journey so far. To the people who used me like a chess piece. To the intrigues and lies and unwritten rules. And I knew it was more than the past week. Everything. All of it. All my life scrambling, never making escape velocity. Maybe there *was* no escape. No chance at all. I wanted to scream it, to gasp it, to vomit it out. I leaned over the open hole and disgorged lunch. I heaved and purged until I felt empty as an old grain bag, a hollow bag of skin.

6

I still trembled a bit, but the worst was over.

"Are you all right?"

I took several deep, choking breaths, then forced out a hearty "yes!" It sounded like a strangled goat. Two more breaths, tried again—"out in a minute!"

I leaned against the reeking wood, no longer worried about the slime, or germs. Trifles. I was gonna die. Maybe not this week. Maybe I'd even get back to the City. But the slip-slidy structure of my world was suddenly stark and clear. I would die, no escape. This elementary fact had never been in my face like this, and yet it felt core—that all my skills and learning were attempts to cover over it. I could scramble all I wanted—get as high up as a CEO—eventually the waves would close over me and I'd be history—not even that. Who would even notice my absence? What the hell was life *for*?

After an unknown time, I became aware of Ciera knocking gently.

"Martin—are you okay?" There was real concern in her voice. I was touched. Slowly, I opened the door and walked out, remembering too late to brush off the tear stains. Ciera glanced once, then looked away. We walked back to the table, which had been cleared. Ciera sat, and patted the table in front of my chair. Woodenly, I sat and leaned forward on my elbows.

"So what I told you really was a surprise?"

I nodded, not trusting my voice.

"Then I guess you can't tell me how strong the Army is."

I shook my head. I was looking down; I didn't really want to see her expression.

"It was nice where I grew up," Ciera said, apparently changing the subject, "We had enough to eat, and the adults took care of us. Most of us stay in the village all our lives, unless we marry away, but there's a ceremony when we're fifteen. They take us out, show us the mass graves, and—depending on how iffy things are—maybe a deserted town, or a struggling one. We don't actually have to go too far outside for that. And most of us are shocked to learn the truth, that things haven't really settled down since the Chaos. That life outside our village is in fact pretty brutal."

"I know life is brutal—I grew *up* knowing that."

"But not, maybe, how unstable it is?"

I was still numb; her words were coming through a filter like spongy gray foam. I tried to think. It was true that the harsh world in and around the City was very structured; I knew the rules, even if they were mostly *do unto others before they do unto you.* And this new crisis was probably just a bigger version of that. But she was talking about something different.

"I think my village can be gentle because we live in balance," she said. "At least, as much balance as possible, given that the Chaos isn't over yet."

"What do you mean, not over?"

Ciera waved her hand toward the windows. "It's only been fifty years since the solar flare—it takes a while for civilization to collapse or recover from something that big. The Grandparents say there's been about ten years of plateau, but that it can't last. When we've salvaged everything we can reach, and that wears out, we'll need to be ready to live without all that stuff. Same with you in the City, only worse—it sounds like you're not even preparing for downshift."

"But that's what the comm towers were for!"

She shook her head. "No, that's trying to keep things as they are. That's not the same thing as preparing to lose them. If you stepped back for even a moment, you'd see that a big city can't be sustained. It's too dependent on the outside, which it can't control. This new revolution shows that you can't keep sucking off resources without pushback."

She was probably right. I didn't know, and it felt too big to grapple with. I needed to think about what to do next. Or did it even matter?

She was drumming her fingers on the table, staring off into space. The host lady came to the doorway and paused. When Ciera noticed her, she nodded, stood and said, "Well—we'd better focus on getting some horses. It won't be long before someone else recognizes your bike."

We retrieved our rides from the boys, who had been sitting astride them and polishing the mirrors, preening. The road east was well-maintained gravel, so full with traffic that I had to work not to hit any of the walkers, two-wheeled carts, bicycles, double bicycles, even some pedaled cabs with riders clutching stuffed bags. I glanced around halfheartedly for my pursuers, though Ciera had said they wouldn't be able to catch us soon. Then I just tried to keep up with her, peddling and allowing myself a bit of power boost.

A sense of absurdity welled up, and I saw myself flailing and pratfalling like in those crazy sitcoms where everyone seemed to have the sense of a concussed duckling. *Martin Barrister, Seinfeld* of the '60s. Crazier than the bungee-snake dance on Elvis Eve.Well, I still had all my pieces and it had finally stopped raining. Gratitude for small things—that was the ticket.

The sun had come out when we were crossing, but I didn't dare use the solar panel—that would be like yelling "Here I am!" Our conversation replayed over and over, but she was still speaking a foreign language. What point was balance, with everybody and his brother poised to grab whatever you had? What point was anything, if death was the only end? I thought of my apartment, but the furniture and the posters on the walls seemed like a dream. My legs still ached, my back was on fire, and my head was stuffed with sponge. I wondered why she continued to help me—surely she was outside of her region, and moving closer to the danger. Was *she* the spy she suspected me of being?

The towns were closer here, and more populated. They'd been re-built on the ruins of a huge old city—the regular geometric broke-down walls were everywhere, though at times overrun by sapling trees and wildflowers. It looked like people decided to clear a space here and there and rehab some buildings into a random town. Though there were no obvious power stations, once or twice I thought I saw lights on—not candle flicker, but steady glare—in a house or shop. Buildings were in good repair and clothes seemed less haphazard. The streets were also straighter and crossed each other at right angles.

We stopped two "towns" over, in front of a block-square concrete building now sectioned into a handful of smaller shops shoehorned into the massive stone walls. One sign said "Troy's Stables" and two more advertised a blacksmith and a farrier. A wood and stucco second story had been added, roofed with corrugated steel tied down with steel cables. Inside there were stalls made of old multi-colored doors, housing at least a dozen horses, with the accompanying smell. There were a few life-size wooden painted horses, secured by metal poles up through their middle—various harnesses and horse blankets were draped over and around them. On the left, a cluster of manual bikes, e-bikes and small pedal carts stood near a doorway. Hand-painted on the wall behind them: "Excursions—day or hour" and in smaller print "Guide Extra". A tall middle-aged woman with brilliant red hair appeared in the doorway, paused, then walked toward us, stately as a queen. She smiled warmly as she approached, but I sensed steel underneath.

"Greetings, Miz Troy," Ciera began. "I am Ciera from the Engel band, who know Rojas of Boardman, who know Smiths of Poland, who know Lins of State Line."

The woman nodded. "I, Troy of Hilltown, who have traded with the Smiths of Poland, and with Yuri of Middletown, and belong to Stablers of West Penn, greet you. Do you come for new bikes?"

Ciera shook her head. "We would have horses, if we could."

Troy's eyes lit up. "And trade the bikes?"

I stepped closer to Ciera, and frowned at her. She avoided my glance, but shook her head. "No, if it please you, we would pay to store the bikes here, and take two horses as close to the Mall as you have stabling."

"The Mall is not safe now," Troy replied, and bit her lip. "I have heard—" she paused and looked over at me. Somehow she knew I was a stranger—so much for my disguise. "I have heard that horses are being… 'corralled' in that area." She looked meaningfully at Ciera, who nodded and sighed.

"Then how close do you recommend?"

"No farther than Ambridge—and mind you, swing wide of the river until you're well past the old train yard in Freedom. Rumor says that's where they are—" again, she bit her lip. "And there is a voluntary quarantine in Newconomy—only medteams going in or out. Best way is to take back lanes to Old Ridge Road, and take that south until it ends in Ambridge. The stable there will take my horses. And the old 65 will get you down to the Mall, but you'd better not be riding anything they want."

As Ciera and Troy negotiated price, I wandered around. A preteen boy and girl were mucking out stalls, two gray-haired, scrawny men leaning near them, chatting in gruff murmurs and glancing at us. I wondered if my bike was going to cause trouble here. I hope Ciera told her to hide it. Hearing a rhythmic metallic clang, loud then soft, I finally recognized the blacksmith—that would account for the nasty burning smell. A damp breeze swept into the huge doorway and I shivered, trying to picture what might be up ahead;

where "help" might locate me and what it might be. A thought froze my blood—what if *Geoff* had convinced the company *he* would save me? I needed to text Rivera—"no Geoff!" Fighting the new despair, I fought to recall any rescue possibilities I might have forgotten…and came up blank. The truth was, I had come out here expecting something like the Long Island communes—more primitive yet orderly, places treading water, just waiting for a little boost from the City. I had not in my wildest dreams thought that it would be a different country. Ciera's first question to me, why was I in her country, came back with bitter irony. *Why* had I volunteered? It'd taken me years to carve out a safe space—and success had made me sloppy. This gamble had looked like a good one—served me right for trying to snarf a fast bennie. And yet, in the City, I was surrounded by people who were actually hefty from overeating, who wore sparkling jewelry and owned little machines that gave them enormous advantages. It was hard not to be hungry in the City; hungry for everything.

But back to now. Was there way to sneak in further along the train line, avoiding this revolt, maybe even head cross-country through Pennsylvania and entering via an armored ferry? *Yeah, right, Martin—keep dreaming.* Without a safe place to regain strength, I was vat pink. And who would take City credit? I *had* done research before the trip—of course I didn't just "trust"—but it was a blank past the railroad terminus, except for gov-speak about how de-pop the country was, ripe for resettlement as soon as "resources" allowed expansion, etc. Even then I realized they didn't know Bo Diddly; it was now blitheringly obvious that if they did have info, the comm towers would have been already resolved. I had been sent out as a test probe. Ten years on desk had dulled my shit detectors; office shenanigans where the risk was loss of status or a smaller desk had gradually morphed to seem "dangerous". How *could* I have forgotten that deep terror of lurking death? And here it was again, and me almost an old man. That was the problem with adventures—they were only fun when you were watching them in a dark theater with some salted corn strips and someone to put your arm around. Shaking my head, I began to clear my bike pack, stuffing everything I could into my knapsack or pockets. I double-checked the fiberglass compartment. Every last scrap would be needed to get me on that train.

Ciera was gesturing while the woman played with a small frame of vertical beads, pushing them back and forth. Perhaps that was the trade ritual? Eventually, she put it away, and they walked toward the stalls. I followed, dreading this next part. The woman indicated two stalls at the end; a milk white horse and a dappled brown watched us with quiet, dark eyes. She slapped hands with Ciera and walked away. Ciera turned to me.

"Do you really not know how to ride a horse?"

I shook my head. "When I was a boy, I rode a mule or two, but they were pretty worn out."

She was busy putting on the leather riding gear—the straps around the nose, the saddle, which needed a blanket underneath apparently. I felt stupid standing idle. She finally handed me a pair of canvas bags strung between a thick leather strap. "Here—try to get all your stuff into these bags and balance the weight. What doesn't fit can go into mine. You'll fall off wearing the knapsack." After she had done the white horse, she briskly worked on the brown.

I'll probably fall off even without the knapsack. Once again I pulled out my stuff and rearranged it—both too much and too little. When I finished, Ciera took them and attached them behind the saddle. She led the brown horse towards a bench, and indicated I should step on the bench and get on the horse. Lucky I was too tired to be scared. I did as she said, bracing a little as the horse sidled.

"Put your feet into the stirrups—those metal holders—and press your heels down. That should keep your feet in. You can also hang on to that knob on the saddle—those two things should keep you in the seat even if you can't steer." I shrugged wryly at the dubious look on her face. "Hold the reins—these ropes—loosely in your hand. Troy says this horse will follow mine, so you won't have to steer. We'll go slow, and with luck no one will have any idea who you are." She hurried back and mounted her horse, then rode it toward the doorway. My horse picked up its head and followed—the mild jolting was actually more gentle than the bike, and I grabbed the knob tightly, strained my heels down and clung with my aching legs as we walked the horses towards the road. I didn't dare risk a glance back at my bike, but I felt like another string connecting me to home had just been severed.

I tried to imitate Ciera's posture as we rode along streets that were fairly thick with traffic. I had a wild memory of an old cowboy mu-vid I had seen, with men on horses thundering after a herd of cows. They were using both hands to spin ropes and throw them around the wildly veering cattle. They must have been stitched to the saddles.

Two blocks lined with shops drew clusters of all ages who mostly ignored us. I breathed easier. Men and women wore patched jeans like mine, though several women had long skirts in bright, flashy plaids and stripes. As the day warmed, sweaters and capes were being carried. A couple nine-year-olds were hauling buckets of water from the central pump to a pottery shop, the water sloshing on their bare feet. Down one street, gangs with crowbars and sledgehammers were crawling on the ruins of a brick building, clinging to steel pillars, shouting warnings to each other as parts of walls crashed down. Other workers darted in, grabbed the pieces and hauled them towards a row of carts, each holding a separate material: bricks, metal, wires, and random junk. A scream followed one crash; I couldn't see where the injured was, but I winced—I'd felt falling stone. I pictured these scavengers trying to take down the 50- or 80-floor towers of the City. It was breathtaking: the huge black netting strung across the street under the top floors; the acetylene torches flaring, too bright to watch; the half-assed wooden elevators on the outside that carried raw materials down. Taking a tower apart floor by floor before it collapsed in the street killing hundreds—*that* was scavenging! These amateurs probably hadn't even studied engineering.

A flash of pale blue at the corner of my eye sent panic coursing through me. *Stop daydreaming!* It was only the coat of a young woman hurrying across the street. I concentrated on maintaining my balance, and was congratulating myself on doing pretty well, when a bicyclist raced out of a side street causing my horse to sidle, and I clung by arm muscles alone as one foot slipped out. A moment later, I managed to get it back in. After that I paid better attention.

* * *

We eventually left the town behind, following a road sloping upward toward another forest. The edges of this one had been clear-cut some time ago, and new saplings were about a foot tall. I could hear the thwack of axes farther away, and to my right a narrow dirt path led upward. The sun was making up for its recent absence by glaring down. Movement caught my eye and I looked to my right—in the half-wall of a ruined building, a head pulled back into the shadows.

"That building—" I called out, "what do you think it was?" Instinctively, I knew it would be foolish to say I'd noticed the person. I eased my gun out of my pocket, more to warn the stranger than from any hope of hitting anything.

Ciera turned and looked; reaching for her gun. She glanced at me and I drew my finger across my throat, hoping she knew that gesture. She nodded and nudged her horse into a faster pace. We followed the road over low hills then curved south. No one followed us. About mid-afternoon, as I heard the trickle of a running stream, Ciera called back, "we can stop here a while."

"That's fine—but where's the brake?"

She halted her horse, and I was grateful that mine walked up to it and stopped. Gracefully, she bounded out of the saddle, grabbed her reins and mine, and tied them to a thin tree.

"Press down on the saddle with your hands, lifting yourself off a bit, then swing one leg over, standing on the other leg, then just kind of jump backward."

I still ended up on my butt on the ground. But I was off and in one piece; a small blessing. New muscles were hurting; hadn't I run out of those? I muttered excuses, stumbled behind a tree and relieved myself. Various vines and brambles woven in a vicious serrated net pulled and scratched at my legs and caught in the jean's patches. Back at the horses, I found Ciera had filled a pottery water jug and I drank gratefully, no longer worried about anything too small to see. Micro bugs be damned. We sat in dappled shade under a tree in early leaf. She shared part of a bread roll and some cheese, and I gave her one of my survival bars. We hadn't spoken about trading for a while, and I had lost count of what I owed her. My fatigue had progressed to a kind of lightheaded fizzy energy that I knew was too thin to be useful. But I tried to seem alert, and asked her to describe the rest of the journey.

"Like Miz Troy said, it's getting dangerous. But there should be someone in Ambridge I can contact."

"*Should* be?"

She sighed and fiddled with the bread. It dawned on me that she was way out of her depth—too far from home. Had she even crossed the river before? Her friends had been disapproving—maybe I should've asked more of them. She had sounded very formal with the stabler.

"That person in the building—did you see him? Is there danger from bandits around here?"

She shook her head no, and didn't seem perturbed. "I've been told this area is well patrolled, and anyone who's hiding in the ruins is a squatter rather than a bandit."

In my experience, the two went together—how else did squatters get their supplies? But I had a bigger question.

"I need to ask again—why are you doing this for me?"

She glanced up. There was more worry in her expression now; I realized she must be at least six years younger than me—not a kid, but…

"I wanted… I want to help the village prepare for this—problem," she murmured, looking down. "Even though we live a couple days' ride from the war zone, most of us have relatives closer than that—anyway we can't rely on distance alone."

That seemed a pre-rehearsed argument; it wasn't me she was trying to convince. Would she get in trouble for this? My gut clenched; would she *survive* this?

I responded carefully. "I was thinking during the ride—I don't believe they'd have sent me out if the Army was ready to expand. Commco—my company—is tight with the government. It has to be, it's the communications monopoly. And it doesn't make sense that they'd send a… a peon… out into the wilderness if they had better options." I grimaced, but peon I was. "They *must* be short of military *and* wary of this area. I was a test balloon—I mean, a—a throwaway test." And my text back must have told them what they needed to know. The reply had been a feint. There would be no rescue. The food felt like dust in my mouth.

Ciera nodded slowly, then reached toward a blobby mushroom, brushed it off and nibbled it. She grinned at my alarm. "So maybe they won't be pushing out the walls?"

"I doubt it. I'd have seen *some* signs of massive construction—in some places, the walls are less than a mile on either side of the tracks. You can't hide a major buildout of the walls." I hoped that was accurate. Sometimes it was hard to tell what was official Wall, and what were the old highway walls that apparently had protected drivers from the flanking houses. What if they were building a second, outer wall? But even that would require lots of material and equipment—and Army bodies. "It all seemed pretty tranquil along the route," I told her, "not like anyone was adjusting to big changes."

"I'd like to be more certain," she said. Looking away, she added softly, "I—five years ago my husband was killed in a skirmish, when two tribes clashed in an area we were scavenging. We knew nothing about it, wandered into it—not all of us got away."

The pain in her voice pierced the fizzy fog I was in. Husband! And dead. And seemed like she blamed herself.

"Sacrificing yourself won't help your town," I said, remembering the bloody fights I'd survived, mostly by luck. "What do you think you can find out? And how would you get it back to them?"

"I don't know. But I said I'd get you to the train."

"Maybe that's not possible." I was beginning to lose the fizz, morphing into something like the morning after rum punch. "We—we *could* find it's already happening—and we can't just stroll across a battlefield." I was grateful the fatigue was keeping the worst of the fear at bay. *No way back.* And if the revolt succeeded at all—but I couldn't believe the City was that vulnerable. It would crush the fools and anyone close by, then back to normal. Whatever that was. Since lunch, "normal" seemed a joke, a thin curtain like the one that mu-vid girl pulled back revealing the wizard to be just an old salesman.

She shook her head. "We can get as far as Ambridge. Then see what's happening. We'll have to punt from there."

It seemed to me we were punting already. But I didn't say that.

Looking away, she continued, "I've been thinking, too. Even if you don't know details, you could—because you're City—you know—find *out*." She looked at me hopefully.

Turn spy?? Risk my neck to maybe get a few details that *might* help? I hoped my face didn't show my shock. What kind of old stories had *she* been hearing?

"How?" I asked, "if you're right about the rebels, they'll have passwords, body language—all *sorts* of ways to tell a stranger from a brother." I thought of all the weird struts I'd learned as I made my way from the far reaches of the Island toward my City goal. *They should have made a mu-vid of them.* "And the Army requires uniforms."

"But there are always vendors—and what I hear, the Army buys what it needs along the way," she insisted. "You could go up selling something…"

I tried not to be harsh. "What do I have? What could you get me to offer them?" *That they wouldn't take if they wanted,* I didn't say.

She looked down, reddening, the disappointment and worry so clear that I looked away. I thought of Sati, who I loved as a seven-year-old—she'd had dreams far beyond the commune, dreams constantly dashed by Life. I wondered if she'd survived. And in what shape.

"I hereby release you from your promise to get me to the train," I said, aiming for mock solemnity, but missing the mock. "Seriously—what I think I should do is rest somewhere—maybe you can help arrange that—then finish the trip in a couple days. When I'm fresh." I tried to ignore the roiling in my gut. I hadn't felt so homesick since the second day I'd run away from home.

Cocking her head dubiously, she replied, "Maybe. It's obvious you're exhausted, and I'm getting pretty tired… But we need to get the horses stabled, at least. She charges by the day."

Some things never change. We searched around for a stump or rock to use as my step up. Once on the horse again, I vowed this would be my last time. Give me a machine any day!

* * *

The afternoon passed quietly as we wound down the hill, literally along the edge of a ridge that alternated slope and cliff straight down into tangled gulches, with concrete posts but no fencing left along the drop-off. Who would be stupid enough to ride that close? Brick and clapboard ruins jutted from the dense growth, mostly houses standing alone; I wondered how they had managed so far from anyone else. No one lived out here now, from what I could see, as I searched the ruins for any movement. Traffic was rare; we passed two mule carts led by boys barely 14 who didn't give us a second glance. The sun slid in and out of dark gray pillowy clouds, threatening but not raining. I felt my life was in suspension—something unknown was being weighed in a balance I didn't understand, and it could tip either way.

7

Ambridge was another reclaimed town. We passed blocks of rectangular brambled ruins—like drawings of ancient civilizations that my teachers had—before we arrived at anything functional. There was a haunted feeling about it—ruins in the City were much more like salvage operations, every McScrap recycled; these looked totally abandoned. After the edges of town came the smellier businesses—tannery, composter, asphalt-melter and finally, the stables. I gratefully used a mounting post to get off a bit less awkwardly. I removed the saddle bag and transferred stuff to my knapsack. Time to trade off this useless equipment and stop lugging it. The stuff I needed—some speedo to push my exhausted body a bit farther, a few more pain pills and a traveler's guide to this looking-glass landscape—I had no hope of getting.

Ciera led the way downtown, which was also downhill. Red brick buildings from a century or more ago were interspersed with the poured concrete-and-glass boxes from the turn of this century—their huge panes were gone of course, and on the first floor the vast openings were filled with old doors, huge restaurant signs of cracked plastic, variegated wood planking or corrugated tin, held in place by thin wood and wire scaffolding with vertical posts pounded in front—some sidewalks had been broken up to make low walls barricading alleys between buildings, and in one place had been piled and mortared into a small leaning hut. Looked like a lot of the asphalt road had also been torn up, not difficult once the weeds had broken it into chunks. New city from the bones of the old. The second floors of the concrete buildings seemed to be open to the air—maybe gardens? I saw bits of greenery along the edges. Nice sleeping porches in summer…I remembered the rooftops of the Long Island farm—deadly on a summer's day but a blessing at night, sleeping safe from wild dogs, letting breeze cool the sweaty 80 degree nights. Some even rigged wet cocoons, but I'd never bothered.

"Got a grid, lady?" A voice from an alley made me jump. A hunched old man with a long beard the color of tobacco stains on cobweb, wrapped in a wrinkled, filthy gray coat shuffled out with his hand held forward. He looked a lot like the beggars on the Island, the ones who were methodically kept out of the City, but Ciera stared at him like she had never seen a begger. Before he could do something dangerous, I fished in my pocket and found an emergency bar, and snapped it in half, then pulled out one piece and handed it to him.

"It's really healthy food; lots of energy," I said as he tried it dubiously. I gestured for Ciera to walk quickly away—he didn't look very strong, but who knew?

"Down on his luck, they used to call that," I said as we turned a corner.

Ciera kept glancing back. "I'm surprised they allow it," she said.

I was dying to ask her—*who* wouldn't allow beggars? The town didn't look like it had walls or guards, so how could they keep them out? But I remembered she was as much a stranger here as me, so I kept quiet. As we crossed an east-west street, I glimpsed the river down the hill and across town, gray through a clearing in the trees. Wide and slow, it was dotted with sailing vessels, dinghies and canvas-hooded barges… looked like a steady business up and down the Ohio. One speedier boat must have had an actual motor.

"Do they have pirates too?" I murmured. Where did all this activity come from? Was the Army aware that the people out here were so industrious? True, there was a lot of rubble and wilderness and the towns looked like kids' forts, but here they seemed to be thriving. Of course, the communications tower project assumed some ability—but so far that had seemed laughable. I looked around. Nothing like a power source was visible. Ciera had mentioned solar—but unscathed panels and parts weren't easy to come by. They couldn't find enough just on the scrap heaps, could they? My friend who worked the rooftop solar farms had told me of the acreage of black panels that constantly needed tending. If *they* had such acreage, it was well hidden. And solar was a tiny percentage of the City's power. What was I missing here? Then my own predicament flashed back, landing on these musings like an iron girder. I shook my head. I must be delirious, wondering about the barbarians when Rome was about to be plundered. *Focus on getting home*! At least *there* I understood the rules, like a rat well-trained in my maze.

"What I don't understand," she said, breaking into my thoughts, "is how you could even live in these concrete boxes for more than a week without going crazy."

Looking past the inept retrofitting, I saw the usual stone and steel buildings, the strength and protection they provided—no leaking or rotting if properly maintained. I saw order and discipline and yes, the genius of mankind taming the wilderness.

"I don't understand how you could live in those mud huts that are constantly falling apart," I replied.

"Monica's place was not a mud hut, and it's durable for the next 40 years at least. There's no life here," she retorted, "doesn't it shrivel your soul to never see any living thing?"

"There's people—don't they count?"

"Only as predators," she replied dryly. "But I suppose in your place you have greenery stuffed in the cracks?"

She must have spare energy, to want to keep debating. I wish I did. "We have vertical gardens, rooftop gardens, hydroponic gardens—there's lots of greenery. And the City has one of the biggest urban parks in the world." Much of it was a farm now, but that was beside the point.

"If you actually lived with Nature, you wouldn't *need* a park. Why wish for greenery and shut yourself away from it? And it can never feel alive, not really. There's no natural curves, it's all angles that never appear in Nature—I would go crazy after two days."

I refrained from saying that I was going crazy with all the greenery—no sense pissing her off.

We walked steadily downhill, and I hoped Ciera knew where she was going. After several blocks, the streets gradually came to life: some bony mules tugging carts, two-wheeled raw wood barrows mounded with crates and sacks, men and women peering into a haphazard cluster of shops: shoe repair, a basket shop, a salvaged goods store. I didn't see anything of the flashy decorative items we citizens prized, like plastic boxes assembled from gift cards, or the lovely plastic pictures they used to put on their tables under plates. These salvaged goods were useful, like belt buckles, plates and mugs and hardware. A guy in orange overalls picked up useful street trash and two street sweepers chased what was left using twig brooms. People glanced our way and went back to work. There were no more beggars, so perhaps this town *had* zones and we'd just passed through their slum. I didn't get any hint of invading army, so possibly we'd arrived in time. In time for what, I didn't know.

Something that had been pricking the edge of my attention swam into awareness: all along the brick and concrete, circles and squares of lighter wall showed a massive salvage operation had removed practically all the metal. Lamps, signs and brackets had probably been reborn as the steel shutters and storage barrels I'd noticed outside various shops. Even the corner street signs were missing. The only words visible were the ancient painted-brick shop names and advertising—that old cocaine Cola, a green and white crowned fish lady improbably advertising coffee, and some sports team called the Flyers, maybe an airplane team—still on the walls in pinks, greens, blues and blacks—the reds of course bleached out. No matter what Ciera thought, it was comforting after all that unidentified greenery to have stone buildings on either side, even if they were only two or three stories tall.

The clatter of a machine startled me—a high-pitched whine from a motor overlaid with the clanky rattle of something heavy rolling down an ancient conveyor belt. Another sound conspicuously missing during this trip. So there *was* some kind of power. There was an erratic screech from a worn-out flange as something hit it wrong. I remembered my mother playing a Spike Jones "Symphony" that sounded similar. As we passed a clothing store where random patches were obviously high fashion, a pair of grimy guys stood arguing by the door. My hyper-fatigue made them vaguely teapot and candlestick shaped.

"I saw them take Toma's mule out from under him! And if he wasn't quicker than a starved dog, he'd have been scooped up, too!"

"And where was you, to see all this?"

"Hiding behind a cart! You don't think I'd be out waiting for them? It's *started* I tell ya!"

The stick-thin redhead scratched his nose. "Jasper said it wasn't till next week. And *he's* got a dad in it."

Suddenly they noticed we'd paused to listen, turned and glared at us. Ciera put on a blazingly sweet smile and walked over.

"I ask pardon for overhearing—but I'm heading south, and I've heard there is...trouble."

"You don't want to go south, Missy," the potbellied one said. "No one's doing *that* right now—in fact, if you head over to 65—" he gestured—"you'll see a steady traffic come north."

"The Army's gonna come down like a big boot and don't care who's underneath," Skinny added. They both glanced at me—was I doing something wrong? How could everyone tell I wasn't local?

"Oh well, if it's already started..." Ciera said, "is there a place for refugees? I'm... looking for my brother's family."

"Up in the Old Village, in the Feasting Hall—that's what Lorie at the Merc says," Potbellied replied.

Thanking them, she hurried us away.

Around the corner, she paused. "I can find you a place to rest while I look," she offered.

My legs screamed *yes*, but I couldn't risk her disappearing; she was the one familiar part in this craziness and I was too tired to start with a stranger. That was what my mind said—my gut was screaming something much more basic. I shook my head.

"Thanks—but maybe I can help somehow." Sounded flimsy. "Would there be a safe place for this bag?" I shifted it off my aching shoulders.

She bit her lip, thinking. "I'd hate to risk losing the stuff. Besides—we look like refugees this way."

I sighed, re-shouldered the lumpy canvas satchel and followed.

"I'm guessing that if my—colleagues—are anywhere in town, they would be where the refugees are collecting, because that would be the best place to get information," she said as we threaded our way north. "Besides, the Old Village is a commune, and we do some trading with them. If it's not too incredibly crowded, it might be a good place to rest."

How far is it? I was dying to ask, but there was still a very small reserve of pride left. I forced my almost dead legs to plod along next to her, reminding myself that this was very small stuff compared to the gang initiations and the territorial wars that seemed to happen monthly when I was in my teens. *But you were in your teens,* my legs responded—*a whole lot more agile, and lots of cheap energy*. If this was a taste of getting old, I wouldn't mind giving it a pass.

"So your town sent folks already to—scout?" I asked, as much to distract myself as anything. I searched for any sign of Army or other outposts of civilization. But this town looked like all the other ones outside the railroad walls—acting as if the City didn't exist. A vast non-civilization civilization. My conception of the world kept expanding and contracting, like the one time I had done a hallucinogenic.

She glanced over at me before replying. "There are members who trade here from time to time, though like I said, we're mostly self-sufficient. I've been here once, but others come regularly. It made sense that they would come over to see if things…have changed." I noticed she was very cautious, talking abstractly and glancing at passersby.

Some of the streets were crowded compared to the other towns, but some streets looked like they were only kept clean and open to connect the various small hubs of activity. I tried to estimate how much effort it took to keep a square block maintained. I'd never really thought about the energy required to keep New York going—although I *had* heard it whispered that the Company had its own team of "specialists" who "acquired" the various bits needed, no questions asked. I was startled to notice that there were no power poles, no wires, no transformers—how had I missed that? Maybe it was true that the City had scraped the nearby states in the first few years after the flare crashed the grid. The lack of visible grid and lightposts was one of the things subtly knocking me off balance—they even had overhead wires in some of the train towns we'd passed through. They *were* civilization, in a way. On Long Island, the setup that provided a few pumping stations or central refrigeration units was so precious that would-be thieves were given the death penalty on the spot. And the Reserve kept line-of-sight monitoring 24/7—what had seemed canny suddenly seemed more like desperation. *Were* we scrabbling to avoid the inevitable?

* * *

Unfortunately for my aching legs, it was at least twenty-five blocks to the colony or whatever it was. And the rain decided to return as a thin drizzle. As we reached a wider street, we met a steady flow of travelers going our direction. The refugees looked tired—all were on foot and carried lumpy patched cloth sacks, even the little children. Women of all ages and heights but all worker-thin led children in long hand-linked chains like undulating snakes. It looked a bit like the May Day dances or the Hokey Pokey Festival. A few old men tottered under huge bundles. Some looked scared but most showed that same dazed exhaustion that I felt—well beyond fear into resignation. Tall or broad-shouldered men were glaringly absent—hiding or conscripted? No carts, horses, mules, bikes—so Troy was correct. I was glad we didn't get here on e-bikes. I revised my opinion of Ciera upward yet again. In her own way, she was as canny as I had been in my youth. Was now, in the right setting. Which this *wasn't*. If I got back, this should forever remind me not to overestimate my abilities. *If* I got back… I suddenly saw myself in Homer's Snaffle-Jazz Café, regaling attentive friends who paid for my drinks and meals to hear all this strangeness, … I'd never really told them much about my slum years, because so much had been illegal—but this, *this* would be free credit and knows where it would lead? That buoyed me for another few blocks.

As the crowd plodded by, some stopped at a crossroads, pushing toward a stone fountain that brimmed with clear water. I wondered how safe it was, but they clearly didn't care.

"Will they feed all these people?" I asked, shaking my head. At least they looked too tired to riot. For now.

"Sure. They'll be calling supplies in from over the river, I'll bet," she replied.

"Why—do they know them?"

She glanced over at me. "No—what has that got to do with it?"

"From what I can see, most of these people aren't going to be able to work off a snack, let alone do enough to earn three meals a day." I looked around. "Hell, most of these are children too young to do anything at all."

"So—in the City, you let people starve if they can't work?"

I saw horror on her face. "Hey—don't blame me! I don't make the rules. But yeah—it's not like we have a lot of free food lying around." Long-buried images of scarecrow figures slumped in doorways surfaced—I pushed them back down. That was part of what you learned growing up, that there wasn't enough, and that not everybody survived. Surely it couldn't be *that* much better out here in the country? Now she looked as if she didn't believe it.

"So you just feed them all, and hope for the best?" I asked, thinking of that beggar.

"I suppose at some point, if the food got really scarce…" I could see she didn't want to continue that thought. "My grandparents told me a little about the Great Famine—when there just wasn't enough for everybody. And ever since that time, we've worked really hard to make sure it didn't happen again."

And she accused the City of wishful thinking! Well, I certainly didn't want to force feed her bad news. I changed the subject.

"Do you think they're all safe from the battle here?"

"I hope we're far enough north for now—if the fighting has started, it's a day away. It might be confined to the Mall."

I didn't want to mention the Army tanks. Those monsters could go straight across a city's ruins, smashing whatever was left. If they brought those out, the only thing to do was run. That was the worst part of fighting—it dissolved into chaos so damn fast. I'd only seen tanks once, parked at a Guard gathering to celebrate some anniversary—the huge gray steel monsters with treadmill feet had given me nightmares for weeks. I didn't even try to describe them to her. And besides, I was saving my breath for walking, and trying to breathe through my mouth because the stench of unwashed bodies—and unchanged infants—was nauseating.

* * *

We finally got to a brick-walled complex that took up several blocks in each direction. I couldn't see over the walls, and the crowd was jammed up at the gate.

"I know another way in," Ciera murmured and led me past the glut, down three streets and into an alley. At the far end was a plain steel door with no visible handle. Ciera knocked, a complex series of raps and pauses, and in a moment the door opened a crack. A gray haired man with a warty nose looked around at us suspiciously.

"Brother, I am of the Engel band on the Lake, and we come to help. And to meet up with Hadley and Megan if they are still here. I am Ciera, and this is Martin." I waggled my fingers at him, feeling stupid.

He stared a minute, then opened the door wider. "Come in before they find this door," he muttered, "it's a madhouse out there."

"I know, we passed them," Ciera said. "Thanks and I hope you could use more hands right now."

"All we can get." He led us through a hall past a series of storage rooms—racks of slapdash wooden crates, rectangular metal tins, huge glass carboys of liquids. The containers were both familiar and unfamiliar—most looked pre-Adjustment, which meant this place had done some really good salvage. Guard families had spent a lot of credit locating and buying aluminum containers, mouse-proof and extremely lightweight, but they also collected glass jars with metal screw tops. This place had less metal, more wood and glass. Ciera was right about them bringing in supplies: a group of teens were passing us, to and fro like ants, bringing bags, boxes and bundles into various rooms. I saw quart jars of pickled cabbage and dilly beans, braided strings of onions and garlic. Moist-earth potato fugg wafted from one room. Past the stores was a huge kitchen—steamy, hot and crowded. The din made it hard to hear, but I think Ciera said they could feed two-hundred at a time. Impressive.

Most of the people were wearing the same red short-sleeved, pointy-collared shirt and black pants—unusual, and in very good repair. Those in the kitchen had matching red aprons. Something made me think of Guard uniforms, of the supposed-equality that a uniform conveyed—spoiled of course by the insignia of rank. If they had the ability to make this many identical clothes, they must have access to a decent size fabric mill—another astonishing thing. They were also mostly smiling, despite the impending attack or siege. It almost seemed like your average work day. I wondered if they were a religion, or just organized to work together. I couldn't see everything in the time it took to walk through, but I got the impression of efficiency, and a *lot* of manual labor.

I was turned around by the time we reached the Feasting Hall, and I paused a minute in the doorway to take it in. As big as a concert hall, two floors high, lined on south and west walls with small-paned glass windows that created an arch of light on the floor not quite reaching the corners. But overhead, two large tubular light wells drew sunlight into the rest of the room. Chairs lined the closest blank wall, and tables along half the other wall held the remains of a buffet. The scuffed oak floor was full of refugees on blankets, mattresses, or just sitting on bare wood. Just beyond the tables, a few wood and cloth screens made several tiny cubicles where members were interviewing refugees. Men and women dressed in red/black were moving among the ones on the floor, bending and talking, handing out supplies. Someone had rigged up a very clever solution to the odor of crowds—a long horizontal pole with large but thin wooden fans hung from the ceiling on the opposite side from the main double doors. Ropes attached to a crossbeam at one end allowed people to tug and create a decent breeze—and they were encouraging bored children to take their turn at the "game". I smiled and shook my head. How, in this confusion, would we meet up with Ciera's friends? I glanced around and saw Ciera a few yards away, gesturing at a frowning couple who shook their heads at each of her statements. Looked like they had found us.

Ciera noticed me and waved me forward. I nodded warily at them as I came up. She introduced them as Hadley and Megan, then plunged back into their argument. Hadley was a pale, dark haired man a little older than me, slightly taller than Ciera, dressed in gray coveralls like her, with an unbleached longsleeve shirt with sweat-stained armpits. He already looked harassed and was not taking this well. His sleek good looks would better fit a sly grin, but he scowled at Ciera, hands on hips like a big brother. Which, it turned out, he was.

8

But what are you doing *here*?" he spluttered. "You were collecting in Madison!"

Ciera's expression waffled between chagrined and defiant. "I was, yes, but Martin here got in trouble with a bounty hound—Alex—d'ya remember him? Well, I said I'd get him to the Pike—"

"Pretty far from the Pike," Megan observed. She was a well-muscled brunette with braids wrapped crown-like over a broad, beak-nose face. Definitely more brawn than beauty. She was dressed in the red shirt of the colony, with tan trousers.

"Yes, well, we were chased by two singer-slavers, so it seemed wise to lose them over the river. And then I figured I'd bring him to the 65, and could hook up with you two." She smiled brightly, but they weren't buying it.

"And now what?" Megan asked, putting her finger on the problem.

Ciera spread her hands. "That depends on how bad it's gotten."

A crowd of refugees jostled us as they pushed toward a food table being loaded anew with pitchers, cups and bowls of biscuits. Sensing that the traffic would pick up, Hadley waved us closer to the windows. He glanced around over the heads of the proto-line forming, noticed someone, told Ciera "Wait here!" then threaded the crowd towards a tall black man in the group uniform. They held a heads-together conversation while Ciera and Megan glared at each other, then he came back.

"We're supposed to be helping set up new composting toilets," Hadley said. "You can help us in a minute."

"I think we need some rest first," Ciera said, glancing at me. "We've been pushing it hard for two days."

The other two studied me, not hostile but not friendly. I might be on my own again sooner that I wished. Yet that fear didn't penetrate the fatigue and I simply nodded. Sleep first, then I would deal with whatever came next.

"All right, you can rest in our room for now," Hadley said with a sigh. "But don't think this discussion is over."

Megan led us around and through the crowd, to a door that led into a long hallway. There was a guard politely but firmly turning away those who wished to see what was on the other side, but he recognized Megan and let us through. Some doors were open along the hall, and I could see small bedrooms with bunk beds, four to a medium room and two in each closet-size room. Megan led us to one of the smaller rooms, and indicated the bunks.

"I'll come back and get you in two hours," she said. "I hope that's enough time."

"It will definitely help, thanks Megan," Ciera responded as she dropped her bag in a corner. The walls were smooth plaster, with light yellow wash. A pair of tan leather packs leaned under a narrow window near several closed wooden crates about the size of a stack of books, and a couple undyed heavy linen jackets draped over the only chair in the room, an ancient mahogany straightback. The bunks of square-planed logs took half the space, with slats holding lumpy mattresses covered with coarse linen sheets and a single brown blanket each.

"Take the bottom bunk, Martin, and let's rest while we can."

"Thanks." I was almost too exhausted to talk, but the tiny pilot light of survival still flickered. *Know thy enemies*—or at least thy unfriendlies. "Who is Megan to you?"

Ciera was already climbing into the top bunk. I sat down gratefully on a straw-filled mattress and eased off my shoes. "She's Hadley's wife, my sister by marriage. She came from this colony." Her shoes sailed off the top bunk, landing with a thud.

"So, do you always send couples out together?"

She was silent a minute before answering. "Unless there are children, yes. Most of us would rather face the danger together than worry when the other is out alone or with others."

Damn! I'd forgotten about her dead husband. Obviously, I was too tired to make decent conversation. Muttering an apology, I lay down and was asleep instantly.

I woke to the sound of Ciera and Megan arguing—more acidic than the discussion with Hadley. Groggy, I lay there pretending to be asleep until awake enough not to put my foot in my mouth. Apparently they were discussing what Ciera should do next. Megan's tone suggested she had little patience with Ciera and the resentment in Ciera's voice was very clear. A shaky relationship to begin with, and this wasn't going to help it.

"...the rebels plan to take the fight closer to New York," Megan was saying. "The Mall is only fifteen miles from here but their tunnel is at least two days farther east, where the Army would not suspect."

"So, you're saying they're going to blow up the railroad tracks?"

I was suddenly sharply awake. Blow up the rail lines?? Destroy the only chance I had to get back to New York?? And then a fleeting image of me already on the train, unsuspectingly riding toward that explosion. I tried not to move but my body must have betrayed my attention and they stopped talking. I opened my eyes, and got up shakily. It would take several more rest periods for my muscles to get back to normal.

"Did you hear that, Martin?" Ciera asked. She was standing, arms akimbo like she was squaring off for a fight.

"About blowing up the railroad? Yeah, I heard. Is it possible?" I shuffled into my shoes, bending to pull the unfamiliar front flaps up. How did people manage in these antique monstrosities? I apologized at the loud rumbling from my stomach. Now that I had rested, my body was demanding food.

"We don't know," Megan answered. "But my point is, the fight is going to be several days from here, and so we are pretty safe for now, unless the Army gets the idea to just bomb the hell out of everywhere for pure spite."

"They won't do that," I replied. "They only have a couple of planes, fewer bombs, and they definitely need to keep this area as a resource—bombing it would damage infrastructure they will want later—not that they are ready to move out right away." I gave her the quick version of my task out there. She nodded and acknowledged that Ciera had described some of it earlier. "So I doubt they want to drop bombs everywhere." I concluded. It was still pretty muddled in my mind, though. Was Geoff's betrayal some personal vendetta by someone I'd ganked? It wouldn't be impossible for someone to make fake ID cards for those bashers. And a good vendetta was worth an awful lot of effort. Or *was* it somehow connected with this rebellion?

Before we joined a work team, we were given red aprons to wear. I noticed they had a tiny embroidered image of a man's face—he wore glasses and had white beard. I asked the gaunt brunette who handed the apron to me, "Is this your group's founder?"

She laughed. "Heck no. We have no idea who he is, but his initials are KFC. We found these outfits—hundreds, no thousands, of the same ones in all sizes—enough to last us for years—in a big warehouse. They were individually surrounded in that see-through plastic fabric, in perfect condition. So we decided that was a good way to avoid envy about dress."

It made sense, even if they looked weirdly uncivilized, and I felt strange with the long plain panel of cloth impeding my movements. But no odder than the patched jeans and leather coat. I must look a total wank; this would be worth an insta-pic to save and laugh at some day.

We joined the buffet line and got a bowl of cabbage soup and bread roll served by a tall, wiry commune member (*communist? communista? communarian?* My groggy brain had gone off the rails.) He grinned and winked at Ciera, and she grinned back before leading me to some chairs in a corner occupied by a young woman who pulled her six-year-old boy up and gestured us over when she saw the full soup bowls. Ciera nodded thanks and sat down.

"What was that all about?" I asked, trying not to spill my meal before I could get it inside me.

"What all?"

"The wink and the smile… or is that some code that I'm not supposed to know?" Soon as I said it, I realized how dumb and jealous it sounded. "I'm just trying to figure out how things work around here," The soup was much better tasting than it looked.

"Just being friendly, I guess." She dipped her bread into the soup and scarfed it down, then held the bowl to her lips and just drank out of it. Intolerable manners where I came from, but I copied her. The first couple years on my own, I'd found it impossible to blend in, because my elders had literally beat rules into me and the upwelling of panic when I broke those rules was stronger than my need to fit in. The City's rules were less obvious, and the punishment not so immediate, but it was still hard to shift modes; my muscles tensed as I noisily slurped up the last bit of cabbage. I had to resist apologizing.

"Okay, sis—time to get to work." Hadley had come up, and he cuffed Ciera on the shoulder. She laughed and swung the empty bowl into his stomach, not hard enough to hurt, but I jumped. Another weirdness—physical violence was serious where I came from, never joking. They noticed my expression.

"What? What's wrong?" Ciera asked.

I shook my head. "Nothing. It's just different around here."

They both looked at me oddly, then Hadley led us through the kitchen to drop off our dishes and explained that we were assigned to hand out clothing to the refugees, for now.

"More than happy to," I said, "but I need to use the facilities first." I had no idea whether I was talking about a pit toilet or a flushing one. Or perhaps just a tree.

"Staff bathroom is down that hall," Hadley said. "Then we'll meet you in the Great Room."

I nodded and headed toward the bathroom, which turned out to be a composting toilet, much better smelling than the one in the restaurant. I was wondering how to discuss plans for my next step without seeming ungrateful. Obviously, I did owe some labor for the food and probable shelter, but without a contract they could easily keep me here, working me so I couldn't rest up—and I was getting crazier, more frantic, every minute I was away from the City. On the other hand, I surely did *not* want to be at the site of that explosion! I needed to find out more, and I didn't know how.

* * *

Coming back into the Great Room, I saw Ciera and Hadley standing near a portable screen of wood-framed wool cloth, obviously arguing again. I noticed that another door from the back area opened on the far side of their screen, so I retraced my steps quickly. Sidling out of the doorway, I eased behind a triple-jacketed old woman sitting on a blanket with a scrawny two-year-old in her lap. I stood next to the screen and leaned in, trying to appear casual.

"He's already given us a 2065 Yamahonda 450 hybrid with variable power-assist and its own charger!" Ciera's voice was terse with an anger I hadn't heard from her.

"So? There's nothing saying he wasn't sent out here with lots of goods specifically to find out what we're doing. Bikes like that might only be a week's salary back there." Hadley's voice had the resonance of someone who knows he's right and is trying hard to be patient; I remembered that tone from my own older brother. But he was wrong about the bike. I couldn't have earned one of those in two years.

There was a moment of silence, and I wondered if he had convinced her. Why was it always so difficult to prove a negative? I clenched my jaw to keep myself quiet.

"He doesn't—he didn't seem clever enough for that," she answered finally. *Thank you very much, Ciera.* "And beside, he's had several chances to use force—and he has weapons, and hasn't tried anything. How would he know that I had any info to share? It's not like I'm the town cryer."

"No—and that's beside the point! You've stepped over so many lines to do this, Ciera! What the hell was in your mind? How many markers have you left for us to pay? How do you think our family will be judged?"

"What does it *matter* how our family is judged? Besides, Malcolm and the others have always resented us because we had most of the land around the lake, and even though we gave up more than three quarters of it, they're still always grousing that we kept the best for ourselves."

"You don't know what you're talking about, sister! Don't you remember the time the Prudys were sent out? You don't know how bad it could get!"

"There's no rule against traveling—"

"There doesn't *need* to be—everybody *knows* that you don't go off on your own wild goose chases, risking not only expensive town equipment, but also an able-bodied citizen," Hadley's voice took the tone of the lecture, and probably one he had given her before. "The town has invested in you, Ciera—and you owe them something for that."

"So what was I supposed to do—leave him in Madison, or point my finger in the direction of the Turnpike? He would have starved by now."

I wish I could have heard a bit more concern in her voice, but it was mostly the anger of a younger sibling. On the other hand, if something like that had been tried in my family commune, there would've been no discussion—Hadley would be able to beat her and lock her in some room until elders passed judgment on the transgression. For all his anger, it didn't sound like he was going to do that.

"So—do you think he's important enough that someone in the city would pay for him?" Hadley asked. I tensed.

"Hadley, that's not what we do! I am *not* a slaver and I am not going become one."

I un-tensed fractionally. It was still possible her older brother could overrule her, though there was a bit more steel in her than I'd imagined.

He sighed. "No, I guess not. So—what good is he? No, no…don't get fussed. Your heart was in the right place, and…I might've done the same thing myself." That last admission was obviously wrung out of him. "But what can we do? There's no way we can get closer to the railroad at this point." He sighed again, and one of them bumped against the screen. I froze. Could they see me from here? It didn't seem likely that my shadow would go through the thick wool, but I stepped back just in case. "I think you need to go home now, sis," Hadley continued. "We will do what we can to get him someplace that's safe for a Citiot."

"No…I...think it could be really dangerous if I set off now. Even though you are theoretically right," she hastily added. "In a day or two, it could be better."

"Or it could be worse—a lot worse."

"Then we would all have to leave—and it would be safer as a group." Even I could tell these were spurious arguments—she really didn't want to miss out on the excitement. At that moment she seemed so much younger—and I cursed myself for getting her involved with this. Not that I'd known. But if I could have revealed myself, at that moment I would be joining my voice to her brother's. How could I get on the train, and leave her in the middle of a potential war zone? With a huge knot in my stomach that had nothing to do with the cabbage soup, I retreated back into the kitchen and out the correct door, hoping they wouldn't think I had been gone too long.

* * *

The job of handing out clothing was easy because the group was very organized: the impromptu plank tables were full of clothing piled by size and then by type—people would come up, explain what they needed, and be handed whatever was available in their size. Nobody fussed, and I began to understand how the residents of Madison got some of their stranger outfits. New clothes in the City were generally similar in color and shape, and I had never really thought about it. The newsboards claimed it was fashion, but a friend who worked at a clothing outlet assured me the few machines still working were very limited—"what you see is all you can get." Here they certainly had variety, but the clothes had been patched and washed almost to tatters. A young blonde woman stood between me and Ciera, so we couldn't chat, which gave me time to figure out what I needed to ask of her.

Obviously, if Hadley thought I was a spy, there would be no help from him, despite his promise to his sister. My pack still held enough trade goods to at least get me food for a week, if she could tell me where to pick some up. And if I could get a couple days of real rest here—even if it was on my own in town—I could head eastward, leaving her here in this relative safety. I half regretted giving up my e-bike, even with the rebel threat. I tried to picture the map. Didn't Megan say we were only 15 miles from the railroad? Couldn't I walk? I didn't need to get on the train, only to contact civilization again. A shudder of relief went through me just picturing that. Once within the walls, I could flash my citizens pass and use my credit—and the cash in my bag—to buy my way back by whatever other vehicle was available. The rules I knew, that were bred in, would be back in force. And maybe I could get some extra credit by turning over whatever information I gathered about this rebellion—once I was safely home. And *then* I could make trouble for whoever had not come out to rescue me.

Rescue! I suddenly realized my GPS was constantly, if incompetently, broadcasting my location. If rescuers *were* coming, even if they were friendly, I was leading some kind of authority—maybe Geoff!—to this group who were confident they were out of harm's way.

9

I touched the phone inside my pocket. It had been on mute for most of the trip, but turning it on and off still triggered a little jingle. I barely knew enough to use the basic functions. How could I shut it down without making noise? Glancing over at Ciera, I remembered I had never mentioned the phone to her, nor had she seen it. But surely she must assume I had *some* communication device. And it wasn't like the GPS was working all that reliably. Still, as soon as I could find a moment alone, I would shut it down. Better that I be out of contact until I could get away than get them embroiled in whatever this crazy situation was. A flicker of the despair I had felt since lunch jolted me. I was stepping back and forth between two worlds; not the rural and the City, but the worth-living and the hopeless. How much of what I thought was solid was really bubble-thin? Was all this plotting and scrambling really worth the effort?

I shook my head to clear it. My immediate problem was that phone noises were just too strange out here—it wasn't like I could step near some beeping machine and hope it would obscure the jingle. Maybe if I found one of those clanky machines we'd passed earlier...but this building was swarming with people. Even the outhouses had constant queues—and this group, weary and passive as they seemed, still might tear apart anyone caught with "spy equipment". It began to feel like I was walking around with a live grenade in my pocket.

Everywhere I went, the community was as busy as a dug-up anthill, but plenty of laughing and chatting people, despite the crisis. As I was assigned various small tasks, I listened in. I overheard a young man explain to a refugee that the commune had been here since before the Adjustment, and had been well set up to make a smooth switchover. A religious community many generations ago, it had turned into a kind of museum, preserving low tech machines and processes, and then a community of Greenies took it over and built it into a working organization again. From another conversation, I heard about its factions and splits, and that there was a branch community at the Mall of Pennsylvania, and messages were being carried from Mall members who still had relatives in this town. Some of the interviews I overheard were sounding them out about moving to other towns and communities and even looking for potential marriage candidates.

There would have to be a very fine balance of population in order not to outgrow the food supply but still have a good enough supply of workers, and I wondered how they managed that. The City mandated birth control injections for all women of birthing age, unless permission was granted to have children, as a new generation of workers were needed. That was another of the essential New Jersey factory products that was judged too important to let fail during the worst of the Adjustment—or possibly they had started it again soon after the worst had gone by—I was a bit fuzzy, since my history and economics lessons had been tucked in between the many jobs on the family farm.

It was two long hours, working at various odd jobs, before I got my chance at the phone. Some canisters of milk had come in and were needed in the "summer kitchen" where they were making yogurt. I volunteered quickly and lifted the odd wooden carrying yoke onto my shoulders, hoping I didn't drop the heavy metal cans in my fatigue. I staggered a bit as I trudged down a flagstone path—the kitchen was two houses away and around the corner, and an increased rain was keeping most folks inside. Glancing around, I picked a moment when I was out of sight of the main building and hopefully out of earshot if I muffled the phone with my coat. I set the cannisters down and took the phone out. At least opening the lid was silent. As I reached for the Exit icon, I saw a text message waiting! Eagerly, I poked at the icon and was flat-out confused by the message: B CRFL G. PLT 2 RSKU U LIE! HI UP DNGR. U R PWN. What the hell?? I couldn't turn it off until I could decipher that—damn! Couldn't risk it now—I closed the phone, picked up the cans and hurried to the kitchen.

The odor of warm fermenting milk hit me as I stepped over the threshold. The "summer kitchen" was a large room with a wall of windows both glassed and screened. The high ceiling had a pair of rotary fans—off now—maybe powered by solar? On long granite-topped wooden tables in the center, a dozen workers filled pans with milk, then placed them on what looked like brick ovens that lined a short wall. Others were pedaling some butter churns—if they had solar, they didn't have batteries. Along three walls, upper shelves held a large mismatched assortment of cooking equipment; they were good salvagers. This group was also chatting away merrily: two ginger-haired young women who might be twins, a black man with gray streaks in his short hair who pedaled a churn with gusto, four teen boys who were washing crocks and pans in large sinks near the door—all stopped suddenly as I walked through. I eased the milk containers' yoke off my shoulders—*don't spill them now*!—and smiled brightly. They were waiting for something. After a long moment of silence, I realized they wanted my "credentials."

"Um…I am Martin, a visitor with, um, Hadley and Megan…" *Did I give last names?* "Of the…er…Engel band. They asked me to bring these."

The group relaxed; some smiled.

"Thank you Martin," a plump gray-haired lady said, summoning two of the teens who came over and easily lifted the heavy canisters to the table. "I'm Sudan of the commune. Are you…coming up from the Mall?"

How much should I tell them? The garbled text message nagged me—I wanted to get away and read it! But again, something was expected.

"No…I…I traveled with Hadley's sister Ciera from Ohio. We arrived this afternoon." I noticed two or three frowns—what did I say wrong? Did they still say Ohio? What did I know of territories?? "And—and they are expecting me back in the Hall to help," I finished quickly, half bowing as I backed out.

I hurried to leave down the road, glanced back—Sudan was watching. *They aren't all trusting*, I thought, half striding, half stumbling around the corner. I couldn't risk the phone right now. Unless…

I asked about the nearest bathroom again as soon as I got back inside and someone gestured down the hall. It was another neat composting toilet—a bucket of sawdust by the seat and only the musty odor of compost below. I sat in the dark and opened the phone, then punched up the message—it was complete nonsense—or was it? My father had mentioned a strange texting code that people used to have when phones were available to everyone. But our relationship was prickly, so he'd given no details, although I remembered that his friends used to chuckle about some of the word combinations. Quickly, I checked the caller ID and got another shock—it was Cheyenne! I looked again—I could see "lie," but the rest was gobbledygook—what was she doing?? Someone knocked gently. I shoved the phone into my pocket. I needed more time!

But each time I vanished to open the phone was one more risk of getting caught. Throughout the afternoon's chill drizzle, as I helped them carry the poles and patched sheets being used to create auxiliary outhouses, my thoughts were whirling, my nerves tense to the point of snapping. I was vaguely aware that they were sparing me the muddy job of shoveling—but it certainly looked like they had plenty of strong younger volunteers, so I refused to feel guilty. Each time I went back for another load of supplies, I watched for any moment to step into hiding and re-read a portion of the code. I had nothing to jot it down with, and couldn't memorize nonsense phrases in my exhausted state. I was so frustrated I could scream, but forced myself to act as cheerful and eager as the rest of those around me.

The work of setting up this refugee camp was amazingly smooth. Because I was looking for every opportunity to slip away, I noted that no one else was doing so. And that was even without a monitor! While we didn't use whips or staves on Long Island, there was always somebody taking notes. And you didn't want to be in that notebook. After I'd dropped a load of old sheets on a pile, I turned to the hunched, tiny old man who was measuring each one with a long ribbon tape measure.

"They're doing a lot of hard work," I commented. "there must be some stiff punishments, huh?"

He looked at me, frowning. "Don't know what you mean."

"The punishments—for not doing that." I gestured toward the busy workers. "Why are they working so hard?"

He stared at me as if I'd grown another eyeball. "Because they want to?"

"Just that? But—*why* do they want to?"

He dropped his tape measure."Because they live here? Because—they're part of this group? What kind of a strange question is that?"

Once again I was faced with a different set of parameters—I couldn't even ask the question right. Nobody worked that hard for no reason! That should be obvious. But either he wasn't willing to tell me, or the punishment was so subtle it was invisible. I shrugged, smiled and turned back to work.

* * *

Late in the afternoon, an argument broke out about whether or not to use a certain pile of lumber that a blonde guy insisted was for some important new building. While they hotly discussed it in carefully polite terms, I took a few steps back around the building and flipped over the phone again. Carefully I reread the message, trying to add the vowels back. The first part, I think, said "be careful of G"—Geoff. So maybe she'd been fooled, too? The full word "lie" stuck out. And the PLT—polite? Pilot? No—*stupid Martin*—plot. So it was "plot to rescue you"! A lie. Damn! As I feared. "Hi up—danger"? So—not an office plot. The little bubble of hope that this was just some nasty vendetta popped and I could feel my stomach sucked into its empty space. Obviously, if it was something bigger than the company, she didn't dare tell me what it was. That sentence alone might've been a big risk, if anyone was monitoring calls.

It was quiet suddenly, so I pocketed the phone and stepped around the corner again, looking politely puzzled. I hefted some of the lumber they pointed to, and hurried back towards the digging. What was the last part? Could I text back? But for the next hour or more, there were no opportunities to slip away. Finally, as the dinner break neared, in desperation I faked a twisted knee and grimacing, asked to be able to return to the room or at least to the Hall to rest. Grudgingly, Hadley nodded and I hobbled off. Still in their line of sight, I did not dare step aside, but once in the front entrance, I nodded cheerfully to the short, squat woman peeling potatoes and keeping an eye on the door, and headed back towards the store rooms. "They need some ruberbrmm," I mumbled in passing. The kitchen was still in turmoil, so no one spared more than a half glance, even towards a stranger without a red shirt. The bathroom was occupied but the first storeroom, lacking a door, lined with wood shelves full of honey and jam, was empty. I stepped to the far corner by the purple, blue, red, orange and gold in wax-sealed glass jars, praying no one would have reason to come in for a moment.

The last part of the text was something about *urrr*... Then I said the letters softly under my breath—"you are"! And the last word? Whatever, it wasn't good news. Dare I text back? Three bars. My heart was slamming my chest, but I speed dialed and texted "Thanks. Help."—no time for more. I still didn't dare shut the phone off, so I pocketed it and walked along the storeroom hall and when I reached the back door guardian, I told him I had gotten lost and could he direct me to the Feasting Hall? Cheerfully, he gave me some right-left-right directions and I made it back to the crowds in the big room, carefully hobbling in case anyone was watching.

What now? If Cheyenne was telling the truth, I should avoid any official rescue. If she was lying, I could be trying to evade the very people who could help me. Memories of the first winter on my own in the favelas of Long Island swam into my mind: trusting no one, often shorting myself of the exact help I needed. As a 14-year-old, I didn't have experience enough of people to decipher friend from foe. I hoped that I had learned something over the last decade plus, but now I had less strength to respond if I guessed wrong. I considered my officemate: Cheyenne never made any attempt to hide her plays for power. A tall, sleek, dark haired Native-Asian beauty, she used every bit of her svelte allure to attract the kind of patronage, male and female, that would move her up the corporate pyramid. And yet I remember Melanie once, when I was caustically describing one of Cheyenne's attempted seductions, angrily telling me about the woman's special trust fund for poor kids who wanted to study engineering—something that, Melanie said, did not come cheap. I had discounted that as some kind of self-polishing resume checkpoint. But Cheyenne did not *need* to text this to me. Even if I was—a pawn! That's what she had written!—even so, she could have let me go under. And I certainly didn't have any power that would boost her upwards. Was it—could it be—just being nice? I couldn't fit that into my picture of her. Maybe there was someone else that she was trying to defeat, and my returning would spoil that other person's plan. That must be it.

And when it came down to it, I didn't give a damn *what* this was about. The higher-ups always had their mini wars; the rich were addicted to money and fell over themselves getting more, and the only thing I wanted was to stay out of the way. Why should I care, as long as I got back to my apartment? Even if they ganked me and I got demoted or fired, I could deal with it. No—fired meant I lost the apartment. But I'd get another one. And then I pictured the railroad exploding, the satellites winking out… the roots of the city withering. Maybe I'd been out here too long—the thought of supply lines cut, a city full of hungry, scrambling people felt more real and more dangerous than it ever had. Maybe Ciera was right about this being a temporary stability. Maybe the railroad touched a lot closer to my apartment than I wanted to admit. And what could I do about *that*?

10

Late afternoon wore on; I had my knee wrapped by a medic to bolster my excuse and I was put back on clothing detail, this time joined by a skinny, squint-eyed guy who looked about sixty, incongruously named Pippin, with the mix of features we called *Meltpot Max*—his ancestors had come from many groups. Head and shoulders above me—and I was at least as tall as the others in the room—he could survey the room easily, and appeared used to this monitor role. I hadn't seen Ciera since the outhouse job, and knew I couldn't go looking—my pride forbade it anyway.

The refugee influx at the main door was slowing a bit—maybe folks didn't travel at night and just bedded down along the way; maybe this was all that was coming. An old woman like a dried plum came up and asked for a shirt—hers was patched in six places and worn through in two more. I rummaged in the pile and found a soft, dark green long sleeve shirt, missing two buttons. Her eyes lit up and she took it eagerly.

"Feels good to help out, don't it?" Pippin commented as he handed a pair of black pants to a boy of ten.

I looked away, afraid my face would narc me out. Honestly it felt weird. My training—only giving out what was earned—warred with my survival instinct—never giving *anything* away—and both were slowing my gestures as I handed over usable stuff to strangers. But I needed to fit in.

"Yeah—it does," I replied, may be a bit too heartily. "Do you—does the group give out charity regularly? Or is this a special situation?"

"Charity? I dunno what you mean."

The weird "other world" sensation hit again and I tensed. It wouldn't take much to get in trouble here. "Um, just—you know—sharing with strangers."

"What goes around, comes around," Pippin answered cryptically.

I'd only heard that in reference to retribution, but I nodded wisely. He wasn't fooled—he chuckled as he found a shirt for a small girl. "Your tribe don't share the wealth?"

"We don't have much wealth to share," I said honestly. Things always seemed damn tight when I was growing up.

"Where you from?"

Shit. I knew it was going to come up but, distracted by the text message, I still hadn't thought of a good story.

Pippin looked at me slyly. "Rumor says you're a wall townie, dumped by a guide and white-knighted by Ciera," he commented, smiling. Not hostile, at least. Well, if they knew that much and hadn't thrown me out, I might be safe here.

"True. I'd come out trying to find some old business contacts and the guide my company hired suddenly, uh, turned on me."

Pippin rubbed his chin, nodding; his afternoon stubble was dark and noticeable—one of the few here who shaved, and it was obviously a losing battle.

"Must be a bit different for you," he said.

"Oh yeah. I can't even begin to tell you."

"Been to the City once. I can kinda guess."

I stared at him. "You've been *inside*??"

He grinned; it was clear he knew what that involved, so he'd either managed to get in or he'd gotten close enough to know how hard it was.

"Strange place, that—" he said, breaking off now and then to smile and locate clothes, "the concrete never ends, Nature's banished and everyone's a clone. Looks the same," he amended.

"The same? No, that's—" I paused, looking down at the rag pile in front of me. Different perspective. "I guess...our new clothes are somewhat similar…"

"*Somewhat*? You couldn't stamp out cookies as alike as you Citiots—sorry. Not just clothes. You walk the same, same haircuts—and shaved naked!—and all the same blank look on your faces. At first I thought you were zombies." He chuckled.

His comment about no beards sounded almost envious. "Zombies?" Then I recalled an old mu-vid about dead people eating brains. *Gross!*

"No offense. But you *looked* like your city—all orderly and smoothed out so nothing original showed. Didn't stay long, lemme tell you."

I nodded, carefully keeping my face a blank. Had he been spying? Like they said back at that first commune, tourism had been dead 50 years, so it wasn't *that*.

I suddenly realized he was one of the Survivors—old enough to remember all of it. And he was smiling! Most Survivors I knew were as brittle as ice and about as friendly. Whatever had happened right after the power failed, none of them got through it whole—and none would look back for any amount of money or pleading. But here he was, smiling. I glanced at his arms and noticed the inky scrolls of tattoos just showing at the wrist; a sure sign of an elder. Maybe he'd—

"How did you manage?" I blurted, before I could change my mind. "You're—old enough. How?"

"How did I survive?" he asked quietly. His smile dimmed, but he didn't retreat into what I called the Cave of Cold Rage, like my relatives and their friends. "You really wanna know?"

"Yes!" Did that sound freaky? "I—no one would say *anything* when I was growing up and I could see how it hurt them. Shouldn't we know? In case—"

"Yup. Best idea. Citiots—sorry—wanna pretend it didn't happen. Out here, we make sure kids know—when they're old enough."

I tried to picture growing up with the real story, without this thing being The Terror—so bad *no one* would talk about it. One of my first big, scary puzzles in life—all the official records were upbeat govspeak, nothing more. All the details suppressed or forgotten. And if you asked someone who'd been there—it was like you'd zapped them with a live wire. And *I'd* even stuffed that memory down below my waking brain. Normalizing.

He paused. "Hard to give a short version." He rubbed his chin.

"How—how did you cope—right after it happened? Did people go mad?"

"Not where I was living. You gotta understand, some folks seen this coming and downshifted so they wouldn't crash. Already had some solar, wind, hydro—and backup supplies. When suddenly we couldn't get news, things just seemed quieter. We dug in; set up like it wasn't coming back on. Which it didn't."

"But after months—no one could last that long!"

He chuckled. "We're all here today. Big problem was refugees, straining resources. I was ten, you realize, but I heard later that teams were set up to protect what we had and help where we could. Triage, I guess. The oldest trucks didn't have computer parts, so we used 'em to haul the newer ones into a sorta corral, made it easier to defend. And eventually a great source of metal and parts. Called it the Great Wall—lotta black humor back in those days. Everyone worked till they dropped. Even with this—situation—it's a lot easier now."

What was humorous about a Great Wall? "Who was in charge?"

"No one, as such. We had teams, but around here there'd already been lots of talk, so even the deniers quickly got with it and we hauled ass to make it livable—not like the ones who just waited, and waited, for the Feds to rescue them." He was silent again and I suspected there was a lot even he didn't talk about. "And it really helped that we already knew how to cut power use to a fraction. There wasn't the long hit and miss that the City had. So I've heard."

So after all, I really couldn't know how it had been for my grandparents and parents—because it had been different out here.

"So, how do you get your stuff? Like clothes and tools."

"If you can believe it, there's still plenty from all the huge stores and warehouses. The Great Dying took a lotta folks, and we try to make that cheap junk last as long as we can. We've turned a couple of those places into our own warehouses, and each member town gets an annual allotment."

"You haven't run out?"

"Of some things, yeah. We do without or we barter with your edge towns—they still want a lot of the crazy junk like disposable shavers, and we get—some good basics. A lotta people know the home crafts now, so we're getting by."

Pippin straightened up suddenly, glancing over the heads of the crowd. "Shit," he muttered, "tattoo." He spun and grabbed the arm of a 10-year-old girl who was scurrying by. "Go tell Jared—tattoo in the room."

"Tattoo? How'd he get past Will…or Marna?"

"Too late for that. Go tell him." He turned back to me. "Hold the fort, will ya?"

Then he was pushing through the crowd more energetically than I had seen community members do. He came up to a scrawny young man, perhaps sixteen, and now that he'd mentioned it, I saw some kind of blue tattoo on his cheek. I guessed its meaning—the Long Island tribes each had their own way of branding outcasts, those who didn't fit but hadn't sinned enough to kill. Artaud's gang snipped a piece of the ear, Big Lulu's uptown band took the first and fourth fingers of the right hand, and Mickey's clan cut three short scars on the cheek, deep enough it wouldn't vanish. And of course, the City cut off the hands of thieves. I don't know why I was surprised, but I was; somehow I had gotten the impression everybody got along out here. Pippin had taken hold of the youth by his shoulders, and though the tattooed one struggled, Pippin's height allowed him to hold on until two more members came up—a broad-shoulder blond man and a hefty, well-muscled woman in her 30s. The three of them steered the teen back toward the entrance. I didn't see Pippin again for a half-hour or more, and it got busy for a while and then suddenly there he was by my elbow. I jumped, and he apologized.

Embarrassed at being caught unawares, I asked, "What happened to the outcast?"

He shrugged. "Got another mark, and we sent him on his way. And warned the guards."

So there *were* guards. They did a very good job of hiding their weapons. Torn between curiosity and sounding naïve, I continued, "There's always some, I guess, but everything I'd heard made it sound like you all got along." I looked down and fingered a denim shirt that had been reversed, the buttons re-sewn on the inside, the double-bound seams barely hinting that it was inside out.

He was quiet a moment, then said, "Wish we did. But like you say, there's always some. That's human nature. We try our best to give kids what they need, but sometimes what they need is pure rebellion and not even the most dangerous adventures seem to cure that. And there are others who have to take rather than being given—they're greedy or they're impatient…And there are some legacy families, I guess—long history of drugs and alcohol, just can't shake it, and eventually they cross the line." He sighed, and for a few moments we were busy helping a couple mothers find new sizes for growing children, while donating clothes that they'd outgrown. I wondered how all the washing got done, because most of these clothes looked pretty clean.

"So you tattoo them and send them away? How do they survive on their own?" It was a dumb question and I knew that even as I asked it.

Pippin's expression was a mix of grief and annoyance; he bit his lip. "We're not sure if they do. But of course there are lots of different towns and groups 'round here—some tolerate rebels better, some places're less organized so the outcasts can live on the outskirts. Mostly they don't come back, 'cause we've warned them. But some—" he hesitated, "some are angry and have to prove they were right. If they come back, we mark them again, and—" he was silent. After a moment, I knew I wasn't going to get any more details. But it was probably something like the "three strikes and you're out of it" rule in the slums. And most people considered that generous. Some people just didn't learn.

I was beginning to feel exhausted again, realizing I was half asleep on my feet. Bringing some donated clothes through the kitchen to the clothes stores, I caught a whiff of something coffee-like and hesitated. How bad a faux pas to ask for a cup? Even a mouthful. I hadn't brought any speedos with me, not knowing the trip would be so brutal.

"Could I—do you mind if I had a cup of—that?" I asked a young man barely shaving age.

He grinned, "Of course not—that's what it's for. And you look dead on your feet—if you don't mind my saying."

Yup—just about how I felt. Luckily mirrors were rare out here. I accepted a ceramic mug and sipped as fast as the steaming brew allowed. A girl of ten hurried through the kitchen with two chickens, one under each arm, both cackling loudly.

"Jinna—outside! No live animals in here!" A woman called to her, but she had already reversed directions, heading out the door.

"I'm looking for Rom—where is he?" she called back. The broad-shouldered blond I'd seen at the tattoo incident, definitely in danger of conscription if the rebels saw him, pulled away from washing dishes.

"Coming, Jinna!" He grabbed a couple knives and followed her out. As much to get out of the way as anything, I went after him.

Jinna had put both chickens into narrow metal funnels that held them upside down. Damn—butchering! I skittered back inside, but even that glance was enough to bring back nasty memories—the severed necks, hot blood flowing, the grossest part—that I was always forced to do—pulling out the guts and organs, hot and squishy between my fingers. My brother

Mick had delighted in it, but I felt sick for days after. Luckily meat was a rare ingredient and the birds ended up in soup, barely recognizable. The girl hadn't seemed upset—was she one like my brother, or was this yet another "different world" scenario? I left the mug on the sink, thanked the boy, and hurried to bring back the new pile of clothes.

"What took ya?" Pippin asked.

"I—stopped for a bit of coffee. Sorry." I put the clothing—medium-size shirts and pants—onto the middle table.

"Primetime. You look like you needed it. Did it help?"

"Uh—yeah." I was still grappling with butchering images. Seemed my whole life I was doing ugly jobs, hungry for the *why*. "Pippin—um—do you remember what it was like—before?"

He laughed, showing yellowed but solid teeth. "That gets asked a lot. Well maybe not so much anymore—young people don't know enough to wonder." He sighed. "Almost as hard to describe as 'just after'—maybe harder. You've got *some* pre-Chaos trinkets, I remember—" he glanced over, obviously curious.

"Yeah—we have mu-vids in theaters and recorded music and some diesel-powered machines. And electricity, of course. And the big state companies have computers." I left out the antibiotics and other medicines, in case they didn't know about that.

"So you've got a *start* at knowing."

"But—like: flying *anywhere*? Or knowing anything in an instant? Or seeing people's faces long distance?"

He looked startled. "You can't do Internet video? I thought you talked with the West Coast."

I grinned wryly, thinking about the failing satellite. "It's mostly text, and the voice connections are weak and scratchy. The computer system cut back to green screen recently, to save power." Which was why those colorful phone icons looked so cool, but I didn't say that. "But—you could go to a store and just buy *anything*?"

"Yeah—stuff from anywhere. What I most miss is bananas. I *really* loved bananas. And cinnamon. Couldn't describe the taste…"

"I—I have some idea, since we have syn-flavors still."

"Sinning flavors??"

"Synthetic. They say it was one of the New Jersey industries declared essential—and for the first couple decades, people were just eating bread with different flavors on them, but that was enough to keep them going. A whole meal in a loaf of bread or potato—steak, tomato, lettuce, carrots, butter—and of course, dessert. Chocolate flavor was actually given out as prizes, I heard."

"That is *so* weird." He shook his head. "But I guess it makes some sense. Bread and circuses.' You all got used to the fake stuff?"

I thought of the chickens out back, now just blood and feathers everywhere. I shuddered. "Yeah—why fuss with all the bugs and crap when it tastes just as good out of the vat?"

"I remember folks being hooked on what we called junk food—it was just fat, salt and sugar, with some food coloring, and *flavorings* of course. Eventually they didn't like the real stuff. They really suffered out here—withdrawal was painful, I was told. Though I remember some chocolate-coated cupcakes that were really good." His expression grew wistful.

Fearing I was crossing the line, I asked, "Is Pippin your real name?" I couldn't believe someone could name a boy child after an apple.

He laughed loudly then, turning heads. "Nope, my *real* name is Fingal—mother was from the islands, a Celt. But the way they misspoke Fingal pissed me off, and at one point Pippin stuck." He was grinning, to my relief. Back in the city, no one but the authorities asked for your real name. Mine was Josephus, but I'd been Martin for 14 years, and it felt like my real name now. As much as I hated my childhood, I hadn't wanted to embarrass my parents in case I had gotten caught or involved in something that turned into a nasty public spectacle, like being executed. Better that Josephus Martin Gearhart Barrister died and now existed only as a memory somewhere on Long Island, and attached to a number in my official documents.

As we worked, he told me stories of his boyhood, about the machines that did household work, and most of the office work too. Even more elaborate than in my office. About how most children's toys were machines, and about how most of them broke quickly and were shipped overseas to be taken apart. " 'Cause there were some nasty chemicals in there, and we didn't want our people getting sick," he said, then corrected himself. "Didn't want to *pay* our people, so we gave it to the slaves over in China or Indonesia. I still wonder if they didn't end up with a bargain, after all—we don't even have those piles of dead machines to recycle now. Some of those metals would've been really handy."

"But they just had so much stuff that it lost its value," he continued. "Can you imagine, some of them were actually building houses out of piles of tires and glass bottles! They wasted hundreds and thousands of tires and bottles to build *walls*! Like no one else could find any other use for them." He shook his head.

It seemed bizarre to me, too—building out of mud and straw was one thing, but nowadays a good glass bottle was worth it least a meal or two.

He talked about blocks of street lights that burned all night, cities that were lit up and could be seen from outer space—of satellites that sent back pictures from space. I'd seen one or two of those at school, and the senior management floor had two large posters. I still couldn't wrap my head around the fact that I'd been looking at the whole planet. It seemed too tiny, too much to grasp that those lights were whole cities. Pippin talked about television, something I'd heard about but that also was hard to imagine: having a choice of hundreds of mu-vids and even getting news as it was happening on the other side of the world. To be honest, I didn't understand why they needed that—what could we do about the other side of the world?

Pippin must seen the frown on my face because he added, "Does seem like a lot, I know, but we thought we had free energy back then, and somehow or another, people lost track of where it was coming from. Even though I lived through it, I still don't understand how people got so far from the facts. I was a child, though."

"I'm not sure why we needed to know about the rest of the world," I said. "Didn't we have more than enough to deal with here?"

He chuckled, but his eyes were grim. "Oh yeah—definitely more than enough. But back then people did things because they could—no one asked whether it was *necessary*. It's like that old joke about climbing a mountain because it's there."

"People climbed mountains just because they were there? There was nothing at the top?"

"Right. And we're talking about real mountains, with snow on them, not these hills we've got around here, for all they're *called* mountains. Snow year round, though not so much anymore."

This was definitely getting out of my sphere of knowledge. I changed the subject. "Did cars really go a mile a minute? Were they always crashing, like in the mu-vids?"

He grinned. "Sometimes even faster. And they did crash, but not nearly as often as in the movies—a lotta what was in those movies is pure fantasy, right? Do they mention that? They spent millions of dollars building fake cities, burning up fake houses and cars. Heard they had cars that would fall apart if you banged your hand on 'em, specially made for crashing. And I know they had fake people to fling around in those disaster scenes, 'cause my uncle had one—he'd gotten it from a movie set where they were filming in Latrobe. They used to film all over, had to get guards to keep people off the set, and they hired ordinary people to walk around on the fake streets so that it looked real."

I shook my head—I always thought the people that went through the Adjustment got crazy because of the chaos, but maybe they were crazy beforehand. "Why did they spend so much money making fake mu-vids? Wasn't there enough to vid in the real world?"

"We'll never know that," he replied. "So much info about back then is just plain gone. When the computers crashed, all the info on 'em just vanished. There are bunches of old books and magazines, but they talk about things like it was normal and were mostly trying to get folks to buy things."

I fingered a large pink blouse, which brought up another question. "Were people really as large as this?" I asked, holding up the blouse, which was big enough for two people at least.

"Oh, that needs to go back to the tailors—we'll make a couple new things out of it." He took the blouse from me and set it aside. "I do remember seeing some really fat people. They talked about it on the news a bunch. Some of the pictures almost seemed fake. They'd say it was an epidemic, making a lot of people sick—had to do with all that junk food. Around my family, we ate pretty healthy and got a lot of outside yard work. There were some pot bellies and big butts, I didn't know anybody who was 300 pounds or more…Oh, there was one guy at the hardware store…"

"300 pounds??" People only got weighed these days at the Guess Your Weight booth at the Fun Fair, but I knew I was about 165, and most guys I knew were about the same. I tried to picture carrying around 300 pounds. I could certainly understand why they'd want to eat that much, but I didn't understand how they got away with it. Pretty much anyone showing extra flab was penalized for hoarding, except in the Park Avenue strata.

"How...how do you think it will turn out?" I asked. "All of this, I mean? You've seen a lot—is it gonna work?" My questions were incoherent, but Pippin seemed to get the idea.

"I'm afraid it depends on where and who—this isn't one country anymore. Different parts are gonna fail or survive—they're doing that now," he began, rubbing his hand across his stubble and looking out unseeing across the crowd. "I've thought about it a bit. Manual labor only gives you so much—and we'd all gotten used to a lot more. Question will be whether we can get used to less, and whether what-all we've set up is sturdy, or still too dependent on far-flung details."

"What you mean—far-flung?"

Pippin lifted a shirt of shiny forest green silk. "Everything we make takes some kind of raw material," he explained. "And for years—hundreds of years, I think—we got those raw materials from all around the world. Got used to having them. Some of our simplest items had two or three things from the other side of the globe! Now, we do a good job of recycling, but the fact is we can't get that stuff anymore. So when it's gone, it's gone. 'Course, that was the problem before the Chaos, only they didn't want to see that," he added with a dark chuckle. Then he scowled. "And worse than that—they built things that need sophisticated care so the poisons don't get out and destroy us."

"Nuclear plants—I know about those."

He turned and stared at me curiously. "Whaddya know?" I got the impression he hoped I knew a lot. Which unfortunately I didn't.

"I know my family had a preparedness drill in case the Indian Point plant—melted? That's the way they talked about it—melted."

Pippin nodded. "That's what I remember—somehow it can melt and that's a really dangerous thing. There are instructions in a lotta places about needing to keep the power stations running, or at least shut them down in a really special way, otherwise radioactivity, whatever that is, gets out and kills people without anyone seeing or smelling anything."

"Yeah—it gets into your bones or lungs or something. But I know the City has kept the Indian Point plant going safely, and—from what I heard anyway—they had made special plans to keep the plants in the surrounding states going or shutting down safely. Of course, it's been 10 years since I heard anything definite—but when I was... sent out... last week, the information I got made it sound like there were no dangerous areas around here." But would they have told me the truth? I was beginning to doubt it.

"I know there's a bend in the river southwest of here that people pretty much cleared out of early on. I hear the only people living there are desperados—it's wild country, and I've not heard of any army out there maintaining anything."

"I thought that nothing could live if the plant melted."

"When I was little, folks used to talk about places called Chernobull and Fushima and how people still lived there, they were just kind of crippled. And it's a plain fact that we don't have any idea what-all has been left for us in the soil and the air and the water. They left us a crippled world," he finished.

"Who did?"

"The Boomers—the ones who made the world go boom," he replied, spitting the words like a curse. "I didn't have kids," he added, "after all I'd seen, I didn't have the heart to watch kids of mine struggle, knowing it could very easily get worse—much worse." He was looking around the room, and I could tell he was staring at the children who played so heedlessly in the big room.

Survival had commandeered so much attention all my life, I never thought about 50 years from now, 100 years…to see the "tribe" as consisting of... everybody. That felt overwhelming—impossible. How could anyone care—really care—about that many people? I took a deep, shuddery breath. In an instant, that awareness snapped back like elastic and I was again confronted with my need to get back to the City. Once I was safe, maybe I could do more.

11

As it got closer to evening, the issue of where we were going to sleep became more urgent. That closet that Hadley and Megan were sharing was too small for four, and all of the staff rooms were full. I couldn't stomach the Hall with its great unwashed masses. As much as I didn't want to lose track of Ciera, I began to think about finding a room in the town. I watched as group members lit and hung oil lamps from angled brackets around the room. Maybe if I left her half of my stuff, she would trust me to come back. Or at least figure we were even, what with the bike and all. I was still scared about being on my own, but Cheyenne's message and the fact we were within walking distance of the terminus made me feel both urgent and a little more confident. And Hadley might find a way to keep me here as serf.

After waffling while helping prepare food, I broached this to her (all but the last part) as we were standing in line for dinner, which was a buffet of large pots of food cooked easily in mass quantities and served on plates, thus: potatoes, cabbage, beans and hunks of bread without butter. Definitely not gourmet, but filling.

When I'd asked, Ciera looked at me dubiously. "What's wrong with sleeping here?" she asked.

"If 'here' is the big hall, it's smelly, noisy and crowded. If 'here' is Hadley's room, it's too small. Surely *one* of the things I have to trade would get us—or me—a quiet room where I'm not *so obviously* a stranger."

I watched her face as she parsed this. If I were still being tracked, I was a danger to her and others. Had she mentioned to the others that Geoff was still looking for me? Somehow I thought not. She frowned, and in that moment looked really adorable. *Don't even think about it, Martin.* Her big brother was only the *first* obstacle.

"I guess hiding you makes sense," she sighed.

"I'll leave half my stuff, so you trust me. I just need basics."

She stared at me disconcertingly. "I do trust you, even if the others don't."

Damn. I didn't want her trust—did I? Well, yes as a practical item, but I didn't want her to think I was a nice guy—I was a shark and I knew it.

"I—I appreciate that," I said slowly, "and I don't intend to cheat you or run off… I just need sleep and a quiet place to think."

"I'll ask Hadley after dinner."

I could guarantee Hadley wouldn't let her stay with me—and I was annoyed at my own disappointment. *Focus on getting home!*

We took our plates to a group near the windows, where Hadley, Megan, and a white-haired couple sat under a golden puddle of flickering lantern light. The old woman had some Middle Eastern blood, from her features, and the man had lively brown eyes behind the first pair of glasses I had seen in a while and a ruler-straight nose that my parents called Roman. They were well-dressed, the woman wearing a rich green wool shawl, the man's beard clipped and neatly groomed. Given the crowd, only the elders had chairs, and I eased my sore muscles down, watching my meal carefully so that it would not get to the floor first. Fatigue was again turning my muscles to rubber, only rubber was never this painful. My mind was buzzing with the cryptic message, the hope that Cheyenne got my reply, wondering where Geoff was, and a recurring mental image of a train being blown up. It all seemed as unreal as a mu-vid about aliens or monsters. Surely this wasn't *my* world! My attention was caught by Ciera's outraged, "no way!" so I listened in, thinking they were discussing the uprising. But the older couple were trying to tell a story about some previous uprising, while Hadley interrupted with comments and Ciera shook her head in astonishment. I gathered it was about the town she was from, and I craned my neck to hear over the general hubbub.

"Well, dear, they *did* invade the mall—I was there," the woman said.

"It was during the Great Dying, before the mall, before the wall was built—when the Pitts had a lot of supplies," the old man added, "and your father led the charge. Oh, no—must have been your grandfather… I'm losing track."

Hadley interrupted, "I'm sure they were going after something essential—mother used to comment about how one small missing piece—"

"But Mrs. Alito—they weren't brigands!" Ciera cried out. "We've always believed in peace."

The woman shook her head. "Peace is easy when you have what you need," she stated flatly. "It is a lot harder when you are going without or if your town might fall apart. Just look at the City—look at how much they come out and steal because they are afraid they cannot do without it."

Ciera half glanced at me, but turned back as the old man continued, "We were after water filters, medicine and wheels—and I'm pretty sure we raided the local library and took away a pile of books. I was just a kid soldier, of course, but I remember four of our guards were killed, and I think we got two of theirs. And it will be like that again," he insisted, "We've been lucky there was so much to salvage we didn't need to battle, but we're running out and there will be fights. This fight is about that too, I'm sure of it."

"Were you there as part of the—team, Mrs. Alito?" I asked, curious.

She laughed, a delightful trill that made her seem 10 years younger. "No my dear, I was one of the treasures," she said with a twinkle in her eye. Her husband grinned.

Ciera's jaw dropped. "Don't tell me we were doing barbarian raids on women!" she almost howled.

"It was a bit more complicated," Mr. Alito explained. "I'd been there a couple times before, and we had met—in fact, she had rescued me from a couple of jerks who wanted the pack of meat I had brought into trade."

"Yes, I was darn good with a gun at fifteen," Mrs. Alito said, grinning. "So when they came back to grab what they couldn't trade for, I was afraid he wouldn't be coming back again—so I made him take me with him. Of course we returned to my family later." She patted his knee, and I could almost see the daredevil couple they had been. It was their version of my slum "adventure"—more fun as a story to be told later.

"But our town was *founded* on harmony and balance!" Ciera's voice was tight with frustration. "Didn't the Treaty of Midland set out rules so that we could trade rather than raid?"

Hadley looked uncomfortable; the old couple looked at Ciera with tenderness, but Megan snorted and spoke for the first time.

"That was years after the Great Dying. And what happens when we run into those who don't believe in harmony and balance? Do you think we can just convert them, instantly?"

Ciera scowled at her. "You come from this commune," she replied. "You have basically the same guidelines we do."

Megan waved her hand. "Of course, but what about the tattoos? What about those who refuse to go along with guidelines?"

"Ciera, our parents taught us well, but I think they didn't want us to know—" her brother started, but the old man interrupted him.

"Not everybody needs to deal with the ugly underbelly," he said with a warning edge to his voice. "It's a huge accomplishment that for the most part, our people witness only harmony; they live in harmony every day. I'm proud of that."

I realized I was letting my dinner get cold and started to eat, tucking their comments away to think about later. How much real history was in their stories? I was on "input overload" now, and couldn't focus until I got my feet on safer soil. It was impossible to know what bits I could forget and what might be essential later on. Later—when I was back in civilization.

Civilization. There had been so many times when I had chafed at the routine I now recalled longingly—waking, coffee and toast, dressing for work, company trolley… doing most of it with my mind on something else, no danger that I might not make it to the office. The sheer repetition made it fade like breathing into the background. And here I was as I had been in the slums: praying for a bit of routine, some confidence that I would be doing the same thing tomorrow. I'd gotten it, thrown it away, and now I swore I wouldn't do that a second time.

Although Ciera seemed unwilling to let it go, Hadley changed the subject abruptly, asking the couple how the commune at the Mall was doing—or had been before they'd had to evacuate.

"Well, by and large we were getting along, although a lot of the group seem to be getting antsy for some of the gadgets, weren't they, Chrissie?"

She nodded. "We were too near all the fancy stuff—and they used to say *Before* that it was contagious, that need for stuff. Almost as bad as the need for liquor. It looks pretty, and then you just want it."

Should I mention the stores that I passed on my daily trip to work, full of polished and mended trifles with the glow of Pre-Flare to draw the eye? I didn't know if this couple had heard my real story. The shops I could take or leave, but I knew what she meant—I'd seen people clustered around the windows with yearning in their eyes. The others were nodding as if this was wisdom, but I blurted, "But surely the answer isn't just to hide yourself away?"

Mrs. Alito inclined her head thoughtfully. "I don't call it hiding. It's removing temptation, surely, and it's also refusing to let desire lead you around by the nose. Need is different than desire, and if you fill your needs, and leave the rest of it, life feels pretty full. But when you let other people tell you all the things you don't have, suddenly your life feels empty."

I shifted my sore legs, trying to avoid cramp. "What if your life *is* empty?"

She didn't answer, instead saying, "When I was little, I used to watch all kinds of outrageous sales gimmicks on television. They let anybody say anything back then. I didn't know any better—I thought those things would make my life a twenty-four-seven party. The first time I got one of those games they advertised and opened the box and found out it wasn't full of sparkly sound effects and music and people laughing hysterically—it was just cardboard and plastic and about as dull as a cardboard box could get—I was devastated. I would like to say I never believed them again, but they were really sneaky ads. The songs were stupid but hard to get out of your head and we used to sing them when we played outside, though they didn't mean anything. And my mama could sing all the ads that they had when she was a girl—those things would just get inside your head. I tried to tell the younger folks that, but I guess you have to be disappointed over and over before you realize it's nonsense."

Another Survivor. I was still trying to grasp that there must have been enough people out here who managed through the chaos to survive, reproduce, and make these towns. And that their Survivors seemed less, well—broken—than ours.

We were interrupted by the brawny blond man Rom coming over and telling us a group was going to start some charades. He gestured towards a larger group gathering near the small cubicles, and apparently dividing into two groups. Megan stood and gathered up our plates and bowls. The older couple said they were content to watch from a distance; Hadley turned to Ciera and asked, "How about it?" She glanced at me and I said I was both too exhausted and too unfamiliar—I hadn't played since childhood. I didn't say it wasn't my favorite game even then.

"I'll come over but just watch or maybe you need a scorekeeper," I offered. So we said goodbye to the Alitos and joined a group of about 20, most wearing the group outfit but some from the refugees. I was astonished to see smiles on most their faces—as if they weren't right in the middle of a crisis. The old saying, *acting like it's a beautiful day when it's pissing down acid rain* came to mind.

Ciera and Hadley joined one group; Megan had disappeared into the kitchens to help wash up. Someone said the theme was "how-to books". The groups went into their huddles, to create the names that the other group would guess at. I sat on the ground next to a slim ebony woman of about 30; she had a pleasant face, and short crimpy hair, but it seemed like there was something glazed about her eyes. She was not exactly focusing on anyone, and I wondered how well she could see. Cheerfully, she commented, "It's good the youngsters still have energy after all that hard work." That made me feel a little guilty, but I ignored it and asked her if she was from the Mall. She nodded.

"Was there a lot of—trouble?" I asked. In front of us, the groups separated, laughing, and exchanged two wax tablets that I presumed had the first charade.

"It wasn't bad yet," she answered. "Some of us decided to get away early. Much rather walk than run."

"That sounds sensible," I replied. "Were they really taking all the vehicles?" I glanced at her again—how much would she have known if she was blind? I tried not to stare—but I'd never seen a blind person, only heard about them. One of my uncles talked about a blind brother who worked in one of the factories, able to do handwork by feel.

She inclined her head toward me, close enough that I almost drew back, but I braced myself. She spoke lower, so as not to interrupt the game—Hadley was standing in a pool of light, gesturing, putting up fingers, tugging his nose—and the others were calling out possible answers. One scruffy young refugee called out, "muddling!" And that set everybody laughing hysterically.

"It's *all* muddling," another one replied, while Hadley shook his head impatiently.

My companion murmured, "I was given to believe that they were borrowing, though many of us wondered how they would manage to give them back, especially after a battle."

"So there'll be a battle?" I was still really having a hard time believing that anyone would be stupid enough to go up against the Army. Didn't they have any idea?

"Well I can't see the Army giving in without a fight," she said chuckling. I wondered what she saw that was so funny.

"Aren't you afraid—" here I was trespassing—you never asked strangers their feelings. But she just shrugged.

"I guess. But I just take each day as it comes—seems like it's even more foolish to act like things aren't gonna change. How much warning do you think they had before the Chaos hit?"

I'd wondered about that sometimes—whether the lights all just went out *like that*, or if they'd had some kind of warning, some chance... to do what? It was all too far in the past, and besides, like Pippen said, we would never know what they had been thinking, because everything they'd been stashing on the computers had flared and died. Oh, I had heard rumors that some of the machines had survived, and certainly the City had managed to repair or stash enough computers that a small network was available to the government companies. But they were as likely to tell the rest of us as a gold coin was likely to pop up in a slab of pink.

The other team was struggling to guess now, and from the grins on Ciera and Hadley's face, they thought they'd come up with a fairly impossible item. The volume grew until somebody shushed them—pointing out some refugees were trying to sleep. Then they put a lid on the noise, but the gesturing and gleeful body language continued.

"I—probably not much," I told my companion—should I be saying my name? "But I don't see why we shouldn't wish for some stability—"

"Oh, *wish*—of course! That's natural. But not the best survival tactic."

"No." I agreed. But what I struggled to ask was—how could she stay calm and even cheerful, given that situation? It seemed like my whole life I've been glancing over my shoulder. Could it be because they were farther away from the center, that they felt less scrutinized? More free? Because I couldn't believe they were in any less danger—quite the opposite.

"The Idiot's Guide to Leadership?? There's no such book!" a black woman exclaimed.

"There is! There is! We dug it out of some clone house and it's in the library in our town," Ciera insisted with a grin.

There was muttering from the other team, but Hadley confirmed the title, adding "There's a whole series of them—Idiot's Guide to Arithmetic, Idiot's Guide to Farming, Idiot's Guide to the Dog Grooming—I thought it was a joke, but most of the information in them is correct."

"Why the hell would they want idiots being leaders anyway?" Rom asked, shaking his head. "Probably what got them in trouble."

The woman beside me was laughing along with the others. I had seen books like that, and even stranger ones, as some of the gangs sold salvaged books along with their main trade. I especially remembered the one—"Five Minutes to Total Organization"—that Tuffy had brought to the bonfire one night. He read us segments that had everybody laughing—but I was laughing so as not to be different; we had just gotten back from another brawl and I was still shaking. I couldn't understand how they could just forget about it.

My thoughts were interrupted as the group took a break. Ciera flopped down on my other side, brushing my shoulder as she sat entirely too close. I tensed, then forced myself to relax. The group was crowding together, sitting wherever they could squeeze in. Megan and a young man brought trays of mugs, and began to hand them around. When one reached me, I almost sipped, but luckily I noticed they were passing them until the farthest member had one—I passed and kept passing until the blind woman beside me was holding a mug. Then I sipped; it was cold beer and very delicious.

Ciera was flushed with excitement, sweaty and oh so desirable. I tried not to concentrate on her shoulder inches from mine. She grinned at me, then sobered—either remembering my plight, or noticing I wasn't as enthused. I smiled back, but couldn't relax. Their behavior grated against everything I'd been taught about polite society. They were so... *familiar* with each other! Ciera, resting on a young man's shoulder briefly, Hadley giving Megan a pat on the ass as she brought the mugs—even close family didn't do that in public! And the interrupting and talking over each other—a deadly insult in the office, and a beating for a child. Aunt Gloria had been shunned for a year before *she* learned manners.

Sitting next to Ciera, my elbows tucked in at my sides, I caught their glances—they thought I disapproved. And in a way I did, though I also wanted to throw off the cold military manners of my clan, and the no-go personal space of the slums. But I had no key inside, no switch to flip that would relax me enough to laugh, tell stories, and touch strangers carelessly. The endless dictated rules of society didn't work in this semi-barbarian town, and I didn't speak "barbarian". But I wanted to—oh how I wanted to! I was even tempted to get drunk on the delicious beer, but I'd probably give too much away, and then their generous tolerance would change to something more ugly.

* * *

In the end, they seemed curiously accommodating and found me a spot alone in one of the goat sheds, with a fairly clean blanket on top of a bale of straw. I told myself that it was a lot more comfortable than the same blanket on the floor of the great Hall, and at least I had a bit of privacy. The shed, a 10 x 20 wooden room with hayloft and two barred windows, had been mostly raked out—I assumed they used the manure this spring on their fields. Lucky for me. The ripe odor of goat was even comforting, bringing back early summers working—and rarely, playing—with my cousins. It was well after dark when they brought me over, after all of us helped settle the refugees and set up for breakfast.

Understandably, they didn't want to risk any kind of flame, so after the guide showed me the room and left, I had to feel my way to the straw bale and drape the blanket as best I could. Stretching myself gingerly back, I tried to untangle the events of the day; it seemed a lifetime ago that we'd crossed the ferry on electric motorbikes. And two lifetimes before that when I believed I was on a simple business trip. That was so clearly stupid now that I couldn't fathom how I ever imagined it was legitimate. Where the hell was my brain? I shifted and the straw creaked and squeaked. I suddenly remembered rodents would nibble on sleepers' toes; I'd sleep with my shoes on.

I remembered a conversation in the kitchen earlier when I was helping to shell peas. The motion had brought back weary childhood evenings; my hands fumbled as an echo of their old pain spread through my fingers. The sheer force it took to feed ourselves! As soon as I was old enough to understand, I had cheered for the synth food creators who made nutrients in vats. Let the machines do the work. To drive children into nightmares just to eat was an insane life.

Ciera had been chatting with Bev, a short, broad cheeked, latte-hued woman with gray hair, but something of my thoughts must have shown on my face.

"Not used to handwork?" Bev asked.

"*Too* used to it!" I snapped. "Grew up shelling peas till my fingers were raw."

They looked shocked. "Why push so hard? Where's the balance?" Ciera asked.

"*What* balance?" I asked bitterly. "Too much work for every morsel."

"Didn't you send most of it to the City?"

Bev glanced at me, then Ciera. I didn't know if she had been told where I came from, and preferred it not be public. Let her think I was one of the refugees.

"So?" I countered, trying to signal her to be discreet.

"So—the problem is the City is sucking up resources. You wouldn't have to work that hard just to feed yourself."

"It's improved some since then." Something in me hated to defend that cutthroat place, but I had to. "We—they—have rooftop and hydroponics and vertical gardens... and lots of progress in vat-grown."

"Yuck." Bev made a face. "Chemicals instead of real food."

"It *is* real—it provides all, er, their nutrients. It's just machine made."

Ciera sighed. "They *tell* you that, but everyone knows—they knew before the Chaos—that there are things in real, organic plants that we *don't* know how to add to fake food. And we need those things."

"They've made progress since then. And besides, not having to farm gives us—them—time for better things. Like theater and painting and music."

"Those things should come from abundance and balance. We're creative when we've done our work. You have fake abundance and imbalance with some people having too much—and the proof is that some of you have to overwork. You can't have magic abundance."

"It's not magic—it's science." I jerked at a pea pod stem and ripped it open; the peas scattered and bounced. Muttering apologies, I retrieved them. Why was I arguing with these people? Who *cared* what they thought?

"Science is a lot of what got you—the City—in trouble," Ciera persisted. "If they hadn't relied on the grid—"

"But no one could have known the flare would be that bad—"

"Oh, they could—" Ciera said, overlaid by Bev's sharp, "If it *was* a flare!" I stared at them both. Bev shrugged and added, "Don't you think it's suspicious that no one from other countries have contacted us?"

I continued to stare. As far as I knew, we *had* been contacted—that sort of stuff was handled at the top. "Umm…no—a flare would've caught them, too."

"Only one side of the world would have been hit. And there are sailing ships. Museums have plenty. By now they'd be here—if they wanted to be." Bev got up to grab another sack of peas.

Ciera whispered quickly, "Some think the Russians or Chinese did it—hacked the US grid, then convinced the others to leave us down and out."

When Bev got back, Ciera switch topics to what the plans were for moving some refugees into longer-term living areas. I kept my mouth shut and my head down.

* * *

Reviewing it all as I lay on the straw, it still didn't make sense to me. We had more in the City than they had out here! And yet they believed they were richer. And that Chino-Russian conspiracy theory! I shook my head. What had been just common fact in the City began to look like one of several realities to choose from—but surely one of them was correct and the others false?? This small tribal band seemed to be getting along all right on their point of view, but maybe it only worked within the small area that they controlled. I reran that thought and realized it could just as well apply to a citizen's point of view. A sudden feeling of falling shook me, as if an unseen earthquake had dropped the floor 20 feet. Gripping the sides of the straw bale, I told myself I was just overtired, and what I needed most was some really good sleep. But first, I really needed to check my lifeline—I pulled out the phone, holding it between my body and the straw bale to muffle any noises. I flipped it open and looked at the screen, which was so bright I could barely see it. Had there been a reply? There were no alerts, but the connection bars seemed fairly stable at three, so I keyed in Cheyenne's office number and laboriously texted my question—*what help can you give me?* At the very least, I thought, she could alert some agency with a story of my emergency without revealing that she was aware of any larger plot. If she was warning me, maybe that meant she wasn't particularly hostile toward my position… I suddenly noticed the battery was very low. I sat up, fumbled in my pack for the charger, attached the plug and started the hand crank. I was too exhausted to fully charge the phone, but to let it die was suicidal. The crank was awkward and my muscles were exhausted, but it worked off some of my anxiety. As I cranked, I stared at that tiny illuminated screen, full of colorful icons that seemed surreal after almost a week in the hinterlands.

"You lied to me. Bastard."

I jumped and looked toward the door—Ciera was standing there; at least, I could see her feet in a small pool of light, and I certainly recognized her furious voice.

12

She flipped back the lantern shutters and the glare illuminated the shed. As I watched the emotions play across her face, I fought to control my own. I glanced down at the phone. It was a little too late now to correct my oversight, but what harm had been done?

She was struggling hard to keep her voice even, which dropped it to a low growl. "It's been two fucking days and you never said a *word* about talking to the City. You lied, Martin. Why? No—" she interrupted herself, waving her hand as she walked toward me. "Doesn't matter why. I guess—" she swallowed hard. "I guess Hadley was right."

"No, wait." This was so frustrating—it wasn't like I'd actually played her! "The phone hasn't worked most of the time. That's why we need the comm towers!"

"Then why did you bring it?" The scorn on her face made it ugly. "Just a pretty toy?"

"I was using it to impress the people in the towns we met—show them there was communication so they'd want to help us." It sounded smarmy, even to me.

"So you were just scamming them? And so scamming me wasn't that big a deal." Her tone was flat; she'd written me off.

About to protest again, I thought about all the times I checked for messages, the times I texted. She was right—I had lied, by omission. I hadn't done it to hurt her; I hadn't thought about it! I spread my hands, noticed the phone, and put it back in my pocket.

"Okay—you're right. But it wasn't... it was just looking for a Plan B. Nothing that would've hurt you—but seeing if there was someone else who could help me get back. Just in case. In the City, you have to have a lot of options."

"In the country, you don't play people like options—you treat them like friends...or enemies." She swallowed again, looked away, then glared back at me. "There's no room out here for people who lie to get what they want." She winced slightly; I wondered if she was remembering her story to the ferryman. "I was so stupid, telling Hadley you weren't spying on us—"

"But I'm *not*! All the stuff I told you was the truth—I really *was* doing the comm towers, I really got ganked by Geoff, and I really didn't know how to get back to the train." And I really didn't know how to regain her trust. Probably the first time I had ever been trusted, and I'd fucked it up. I suddenly felt tired in a way that had nothing to do with this trip. "Is there—is there anything I can say to convince you?"

She looked away. "I can't think of anything," she replied, jovially. It didn't even sound like her voice.

It was like getting face-smacked by a rake, something I had done once as a child, which was more than enough. It was too treacherous here; I couldn't keep my footing, couldn't figure out what the rules were. Even ordinary English was a different language out here. A rising panic made me twitchy to escape.

"Since...since you don't believe me, all I can do is leave you as much stuff as I can spare, as payment—because I do appreciate it—and just take enough to rest a few days and then find my way as best I can."

She bit her lip, turning away. "They'll be even more suspicious if you leave," she said. "They'll know you're a spy."

"I am *not* a spy! I'm just an idiot from the City who was sent out with not enough info! You *know* I haven't talked on the phone since you met me—wait, look—I can show you everything I sent and received and you can see there's nothing in there—" I pulled the phone out and hastily pulled up the outgoing message menu. Despite herself, Ciera moved closer, frowning as she stared at the screen. I figured she had probably never seen one of these phones—at least not a working one, but she surprised me again.

"There are only a few left around here," she commented, "only the president of a big town or head of security would have one. I've only seen one twice."

"You mean, you all have been using our signals for free out here??" And maybe overhearing our messages? That would explain her knowledge, then.

She sneered. "Why not? It was the City that robbed us of most of our equipment. Why shouldn't we get a little back?"

I couldn't argue with that—it was precisely that kind of thinking that the City applauded. I opened my last text to Cheyenne, grateful that I had gone full alphabet rather than that silly code.

"You see?"

"That just proves you're asking for backup."

"Okay—look at this one." I opened the one before that, which said *thanks*… Okay, the one before that, the one that finally said *send help*. And I showed her the two responding messages, Rivera's brief one and Cheyenne's, and again got a shock—she could read that easily. "Shit—I should have asked you sooner. I had no idea what this one meant. And I only got it this afternoon. And by the way, we don't own phones either. This one is company property."

"Which is why you couldn't read it? Code is a lot easier and faster to send." She couldn't keep the smugness from her voice, but I was relieved to hear less hostility. Cheyenne's message certainly showed I wasn't spying. Didn't it? I let the silence linger, and finally she shrugged. "Okay, maybe. But they haven't known you as long as I have—they wanted to send someone else out to check on you, but I—" she didn't finish, and I stumbled over my own reply.

" I… I told you I'm not used to people trusting me, or my trusting anyone. Trust makes things so much more complicated."

"No, you're wrong—it makes things simpler." Was there doubt in her voice?

It was that different reality again. I couldn't introduce her to mine without a trip into the City, which was not going to happen. Fatigue was dumbing me down; I needed to get out of here; find some place where I wouldn't be attacked in my sleep. But leaving Ciera was almost as big a wrench as shutting down the phone—"Let me find a safer place to sleep. I'll leave my stuff with you tonight, except the phone and my weapons. I owe you the rest. And if you want, I'll come back tomorrow to prove I'm legit." *But would I?* Was it safe? I couldn't decide that until sleep restored some brainpower. But I needed to see *her* at least. "If we could we arrange to meet first somewhere... about...about how I could get some supplies, I—I'd be grateful." I cursed the emotion in my voice, and didn't dare say anymore.

She was silent for a long moment. "Alright—I should be able to slip away. Let's say noon at that fountain we passed. Wait if I'm late. And I think there are rooms about two blocks north and four west. If it's still there, it's called the Hill-town Arms. Take the drug packs—one should get you lodging and food. I'll bring you to the gate."

It wasn't the main gate she led me to, however. We passed the summer kitchen and wound along several dark paths in an area I hadn't been. I could hear the river close by. We reached a thick wooden door set in a brick wall that seemed unguarded. She silently lifted the bar and opened the door enough for me to squeeze out. I glanced at her, caught her confused expression and hurried out without a word—before she could see how confused *I* was.

* * *

As I walked along unfamiliar empty streets, old slum habits came back like bad relatives. I walked as close to the buildings as possible, glancing every which way and making my footfall soft and irregular. I was especially careful not to trip on things I couldn't see—the Old Man's Shuffle came back though I hadn't used it in 10 years. Light from a half moon had precious little to reflect off of, but gradually my eyes adjusted and I could walk a bit faster. I followed her directions past brick buildings that seemed lifeless except for faint telltale cooking odors. Windows were shuttered or skin-covered; I could see nothing beyond them. Apparently light was in short supply or very well hidden. Praying that the inn was still functional, I crossed one block and turned right at the next.

The dark closed around me, as if it was trying to penetrate. Here alone, without even my pack, with the most pitiful defenses, too tired to think straight, I flashed on one of my worst memories: that pitchdark night I left home, wandering, a half day from the farm but in another world, the fact of my utter ignorance of how to survive racing through my muscles and causing me to shake like I had flu. I had gathered the few things I could safely steal, but just like tonight, the sum total of what I carried was so pitifully inadequate that I might have just as well tried to leap off a cliff and fly.

And yet I had survived—somehow, one minute at a time, I had made it through the nightmare of gang initiation, fights for food and territory, the friends made and lost either to death or drugs… every day certain that I wouldn't make it any further, I had nonetheless made it. I wish it gave me hope in the moment, but I was too aware that each second was still a crap-shoot.

I tried not to waste time cursing myself, but it hit me hard that I'd lost shelter, support and yes—Ciera. And for a stupid oversight! That was another thing that I had hoped was totally behind me—the feeling of juggling frantically, knowing you have too much in your hands and can't afford to drop any of it, and knowing in your gut that you were going to—you had to!—because you were just not a good enough juggler. I had a flash of memory—one of the weird Wu twins, juggling knives and some stolen melons for the amusement of the gang, who of course were cheering for the knives. And eventually, one came down and sliced into his ear, almost severing it. The look on his face—the utter surprise that he could possibly have made a mistake—that was kind of what I was feeling right now. I hadn't seen this particular catastrophe coming. But wasn't that the definition of catastrophe?

An uneasy feeling—a prickling between my shoulder blades—arose as I pushed my aching legs to hurry along the narrow street. Like the others, this lane was deserted. Yet I felt *watched.* Was that just old memories coming back? No one could see through the windows, so it would have to be another walker. Dredging up old techniques, I found a doorway deep enough and turned as if striding through an open door—flattened myself, turned… and waited. In a minute, footsteps crept closer. Gun in hand, heart in mouth, I leapt out, aimed—and stopped.

Geoff!

He reared back, startled, then relaxed into a grin. Despite the gun pointed at him, he almost sneered.

"When was the last time you killed someone?" He asked, easing his left hand toward a hip pocket. In answer, I shot his wrist and despite a total lack of practice, I winged him. He jumped, clutched his wrist with the other hand (thus disarming him, as intended) and called me a few choice names.

"Next shot in the chest," I said calmly as I could. I probably couldn't cold-kill him; I'd never been able to do that. Besides, I wanted info. "So the GPS *has* been tracking me?"

"What GPS?" he snarled. "Citiot boy—there *is* no GPS—never was! God, that's been dead for decades! I'm a *tracker*—the City couldn't find you without me. Why they *want* you is more than I can figure out—but it's none of my business."

Stunned, I half-lowered the pistol, then pointed it again. "No GPS? So how do they know where *you* are?"

"Ham-op. The old basics. I checked in at the church and even nearby the pot farm. If you knew where they were, you could call home," he taunted.

"I *have* called home, bastard," I replied, thinking *ham*? Not meat. Wasn't it some kind of antique wireless code with dots and dashes? Or was that Mores? My aunt had shown me a dot-dash alphabet once. It had seemed totally ludicrous. "You've seen my phone. How does it work, if not by satellite?"

"It's ham op, too—just a basic send/receiver, translates text to Morse code. The pictures are fluff. Have you ever talked on it?"

He must be lying. The rich, who had cell phones, and the companies, who had many networks, all talked about satellites. How were we talking to Los Angeles, if not satellite? *Don't get distracted!* Those mysteries were for later, after I got home.

"So—who's paying you? And for what? I have a few more shots and I can put them to good use." My rage was bubbling and despite having never used a gun, at this moment I was willing to plant a couple more non-lethal hits to get him to talk.

"How much for the answer?" He was grinning again.

"How much for your life, asshat?" I wanted to smash his face. *Calm down—don't let him rile you.*

Suddenly remembering the bashers, I stepped against the wall and glanced in the other direction. Empty, so maybe Geoff hadn't brought them.

"I'm counting to some number, and when I reach it, your shoulder's Swiss cheese," I said, "unless you give me a name—*now!*"

Uncertainty erased his grin. He put his wrist to his lips, then lowered it. "They want you trussed up in a safe place—it was supposed to be at the pot farm, but you screwed that up. And I don't know names, fool. No one gives names."

"Then contact details—tell me what you *know*!" I stepped closer and aimed at his shoulder. "Three, two…"

"AF748—does that help?" His grin returned, but his eyes held cold rage. I realized a second too late he was kicking out—he caught me in the left knee and I howled, but didn't drop the gun. He spun and raced off and I didn't dare risk a wild shot bouncing off the brick.

"Catch you later, dude." His voice echoed as he sprinted around the corner, and with my knee in agony, I couldn't follow.

I cursed under my breath until the white hot pain had eased. Of course Geoff wouldn't know his clients—especially not if they were powerful. The fact that he'd met with Cheyenne was now in her favor—she wouldn't have been so open about planning a hit. But what good was I, locked up? And who to?

I limped toward the possible inn, keeping close to the walls, supporting myself on wrought iron railings, barrels or the walls themselves, trying to figure out how to cover my tracks. If Geoff was as good as he seemed, even this close to the railroad I might never get back without help. I wonder how they viewed gunfights around here? But Geoff hadn't flashed a gun—did he even have one? Come to think of it, I hadn't seen one though I assumed he would have been armed. He probably still thought I was a stupid desk jockey. I needed to find out about this GPS problem! Once I got to the hotel, maybe I could text Cheyenne again—though she wouldn't get it until she got to work tomorrow. Dare I ask Ciera and Hadley what they knew about how the phones worked? Probably not until I'd made amends in some way. I needed time to think and a chance to rest!

But things were about to get more complicated. I heard another set of footsteps, flattened myself and swiveled my gun as a small silhouette eased out of an alley.

"Martin!" Ciera moved closer, and I lowered my gun with shaking hands.

"Damn you, girl—what are you *doing* here?"

13

I leaned against a slimy brick wall that stank of horse piss. Fatigue and aftershocks threatened to knock me to my knees. And one knee was throbbing.

She moved close enough to murmur, "Don't *you* start now. I wanted to make sure you got there—safe. That was Alex, wasn't it? I heard you fighting. Are you—all right?" She had a small bag over her shoulder, and I recognized my knapsack.

"Just a kick in the knee—not bad." I grunted. I had to get off my feet and somehow ice this before it swelled. "My shot clipped his wrist, so maybe he'll back off now."

"I doubt it. But let's get you to the Hill-town."

That was rich—her thinking she was taking care of me! But she had been, hadn't she? Right now that hurt more than my knee. Gently shaking off her arm, I hobbled beside her for the remaining two blocks, and was relieved to see a painted sign on a double door indicating night visitors should knock three times. The knocks brought a burly Scandinavian-type geezer in a coffee brown overall who didn't look armed but asked us to keep our hands visible as we walked in.

The lobby was larger than the pair of candle lanterns on the front desk could illuminate—huge shadows swallowed the far corners. What I could see was similar to the very few hotels I had been in: the chest-height registration desk, a pair of wide upholstered chairs and tiny tables nearby, some framed photos of anonymous landscapes behind the desk. Ciera murmured her litany of connections, and he recited something similar; I was too tired and sore to catch it. I slowly reached in and held out one of the heroin packets—"Can we get some lodging for this? And food in the morning?"

He took and examined the bag, and Ciera assured him it was real. I was glad for her sake that it was. I knew she couldn't go back tonight, and that she had done some serious damage to her valuable connections by following me. I had so many mixed emotions about that I couldn't sort them out. And I was probably too sore to take this golden opportunity, if she was offering it, to get to know her better. Best to focus on survival for both of us—though I had many friends who had the opposite response during great danger: *fuck it*, literally. Party like it's 1099. Or something.

He stared at us as if wanting to ask more, but he simply said, "Room Four, down the hall." He handed Ciera a flat metal key with a round plastic tag—a "4" was embossed in gold. No keypad locks out here? I looked around for some kind of light to take with us, as the hall beyond was as black as a subway tunnel. Ciera walked over to the registration desk, picked up a clear glass jar no more than 3 inches tall, and used a small rolled piece of paper to transfer flame from lantern to a candle in the jar. She carried that towards the hall; I followed. Last night I had been locked in like a prisoner, the night before that shared a dirty mattress on the floor with Geoff—I could only hope my future was looking up.

The room itself had almost no resemblance to the hotel rooms I had seen—I had a sudden, uncomfortable memory of a very hazy evening spent with an ebony-skinned beauty who was the sister of a friend who rapidly became unfriendly afterwards. The room didn't have a bedframe, just a mattress on a pallet slightly raised off the floor near a metal grate from which warm air was gently flowing. Some kind of central furnace, then. The mattress looked thick, though, and it had sheets, and there were two thick blankets folded at the bottom. As I got closer, I noticed a small sconce just over the mattress, apparently for the candle jar.

"Could be worse," I murmured, setting my pack near the mattress. The room seemed enormous without furniture—I knew it normally would have a table and chairs and a dresser, and once upon a time there would even be a private video screen. And of course the tiny candle barely illuminated the area where we were standing. I gently took the candle from Ciera. "If you don't mind?" I said, then made a cursory check of the room. Nothing but drifts of dust, the chamber pot and some mouse droppings. Satisfied that there was no one lurking, I came back and put the jar on the sconce. It cast a feeble glow that didn't reach much beyond our bed. *Our* bed—I wonder if she had thought of that. She might not be any more used to these towns than I was. At least the mattress seemed large enough to give us each some room.

I winced as I sat down, and fumbled in the knapsack for the medicines. I had two pain meds left, but I definitely needed one now. I hesitated, then bit one in half and tried to swallow without water—who knew how much more I might need it later on? Ciera sat at the other end of the mattress, leaned toward me and handed me a water bottle.

"Do those pain medicines help quickly?" she asked.

I took the glazed pottery jug, removed the cork and drank as little as possible. There must be a place to fill it up here, and I had my filter, but did I want to be wandering around in the dark?

"They're pretty good—these have some poppy juice as well as willow bark extract," I replied. I rested the cool ceramic against my knee. The urge to get some ice was almost like a craving; symbolic of all the other things I couldn't reach out and get, I suppose. I knew without asking that it was hopeless.

"I wish I could get you some acupuncture—that would help immediately."

"Is that the stuff with the...needles?" I shuddered involuntarily. "I was never really good with...sharp things."

"If they're sharp enough, you can't even feel them—but it is a little hard to sharpen needles these days," she admitted. "Once, though, we found a stash of the old disposables, as thin as a hair—I swear!—and they barely touched the skin and Marta was in heaven for a while… Marta's our acupuncturist in...town."

"Where do you live? Why can't you tell me? It's not like I'd know where it is, anyway."

She toyed with a button on her shirt as she answered."Evansville, we call it. It's really a very nice town, on a big lake, and hidden from the main roads so that unless you know it's there, you don't find it. Sometimes groups come to fish, having heard of the lake, but we have…various ways…to make sure they don't get there."

"So they're never seen again?"

"No! Not at all!" She looked startled. "We're not killers—we just have the place rigged so that it gets a lot more difficult to travel, the closer you get to the lake. Brambles, carefully placed wasps nests, extra deep mud puddles. And some—headache-maker devices that I think were military.

Eventually they give up. About 500 townsfolk live on and around the lake, so there's lots of us to protect the town. And we don't go in and out much."

I remembered what she said to her brother about her family giving up their lakefront property—I wonder if she had come from a wealthy family—but I'd heard most wealth had vanished after the Adjustment. Certainly out here, they wouldn't be able to get their money from banks. Could they?

"We've worked really hard to set it up so that we have enough power—solar and hydro—and we make sure that all the important skills are passed forward. Nobody owns a lot, but we all have enough." She was looking down, but I sensed that she didn't completely believe that.

"Enough of *everything*?" I asked, and she looked up defensively. "Hey, no place is perfect—I grew up in a place so friendly that I ran away at fourteen."

She grinned and shrugged. "It's not anything like food or clothing…" She hesitated. "There's just so many unspoken rules, and sometimes it feels like there's no way to do or be anything other than what they want you to be." She looked down again. "I know we have it really good in our town, but that's why I became a salvager and a solar tech—I wanted to go out and see—" she waved her arm—"everything."

I sighed. I remembered that feeling, and remembered exactly the time when it vanished: Mackey had led the charge against the Jamaica Joes, but they were a lot stronger than we had any idea. I was about three steps behind when one of the Joes smashed a baseball bat flat in Mackey's face. Luckily my instincts kicked in as the blood splashed on me and I was out of there before I really had a chance to comprehend what I'd seen. I couldn't go far, or I'd have been beaten by my own gang, but I stayed on the outskirts of the battle, and focused on staying out of range. But the sight of Mackey's smashed-in face had apparently registered, because I had nightmares for months afterwards.

"*Everywhere* includes a lot of stuff you don't want to see, believe me." She made a face and I knew she was equating me with Hadley. "No, really," I continued, "I totally understand that one town might be too small, especially if you don't really get to choose who you are. But honestly, there's some nights when I would trade a lot of my independence to get back some of my innocence." Then I remembered her dead husband. She'd seen that, and still wanted to see the world.

Feeling suddenly generous, I double-checked the phone battery was at least half full and gestured to Ciera.

"Want to hear some really good jazz?"

She looked around and then at me, quizzically. I smiled, inched the volume up slightly, and selected the first track on my saved music—Night in Tunesia—the trumpet began its soulful moan under the jumpy snare of drums. Ciera stared at the cell phone for a couple minutes, then halfway through the song, she looked up and asked "Is that someone you know?"

I was startled. "No, of course not—he's been dead for ages. The whole band has." I shut down the song because I couldn't stand to talk over it. "It's one of my favorite pieces though."

She spoke carefully, as if aware she could hurt my feelings. "It's not someone you remember playing, then?"

I wasn't sure what she was getting at. I shook my head, then selected the second song, prefacing it with, "This woman is still alive, and I wish I could get to hear her. But her concert's too expensive." The music swirled around us, and I was filled with longing for the streets full of antique neon lights and the dark cafés with synth-tobacco aroma wafting from pierced tin canisters.

Ciera listened politely, but I could tell she wasn't impressed. Perhaps she was more of a folk music fan. I let the song finish, then shut down the phone, to save the battery. I had hoped… I didn't know what I'd hoped for, but I felt disappointed somehow.

"Music doesn't sound the same when there isn't somebody playing it," she said finally. "I know they used to have recorded music all the time, but it seems like such a weird and lonely way to listen to it. There's something special about seeing a performer enjoying... I don't know how to say it. I just know that it doesn't feel like music unless you're with a bunch of people, playing and listening."

"Well, yes—of course it's wonderful to hear the live music, but we can't always do that. This allows us to listen whenever we want to."

"But like I said—it seems…I don't know—like you're stealing something. Like you don't have to give the players your attention because you've sucked their music into your little box… and then shutting them up in an instant because you are tired of them. It sounds weird when I say it. I don't know how to explain." With that she fell silent, and once again I felt the huge gap between us.

And the vast distance to civilization—not necessarily miles, but the distance between sitting here in the dark with a candle, knowing there was no power anywhere around, versus the scheduled dark hours that could be filled up so creatively in the City. I thought of what Geoff had said about no GPS—could that possibly be true?? Could there be *no* threads connecting me to the City? But *some* information was getting back and forth—two people knew I was out here. Was that enough? I glanced up at the candle in the jar—the flames seemed to be guttering in the melted wax, on the verge of going out. I glanced over at Ciera, who was watching me.

"What will you tell your brother?"

She winced. "He already knows some. After you... left, I went back to tell him it was okay—but I just couldn't flat out lie." She was running her finger along the edge of the mattress, refusing to look at me.

"He must've gone IED."

"He wasn't happy," she glanced up and smiled sourly and I pictured the fight that had happened. "I showed him that you left the knapsack, and I told him I knew where I could find you. And that you'd come back." She looked down again and I knew that wasn't all, but I didn't want to press her. After a moment or two, she continued, "Pippin spoke up for you—he told Hadley you weren't a spy. That carried some weight. And I've left a bond."

I shifted a little closer toward her on the mattress. I wish I felt like I deserved her faith and Pippin's, but it made it worse. With what I might have to do to get back home, how could I handle debt to other people?

"What kind of bond?"

She waved her hand. "Oh—just some things I own at home. After a... while, I told him I'd go after you to make sure you came back. I said we'd be back tomorrow a little after dawn. He had no right to stop me, and he knew that." She got quiet again.

So very different from my family! "But that probably won't be the end of it, right?"

The candle guttered and went out. The dark was so sudden and pressing that I gasped. Without thinking, I reached out and my hand met hers; I squeezed gently.

"Well, I guess we're here overnight now," I said, in a feeble attempt to joke, "I'd never be able to find my way to the lobby by feel." But I was thinking *now what?* Aside from sex, how does one pass the time in such a primitive setting?

"Tell me what a typical day is like for you, all the little details, because what's ordinary for you is probably strange for me." Her voice startled me; I released her hand and leaned back against the wall.

"Well, I usually get up around 4:30 AM; probably a leftover from the farm, and also the slums where truly 'if you snooze you lose'—often your life. I don't have to be at work until 7:30, and I don't have an elevator in the building, but the power does go off in my building at 5:15—living in the lower-class areas means you don't get the primo hours—so I have to wash and make breakfast quickly—synthcafé in hot water boiled on the electric ring, with some precooked Baco waffles, usually. I get a second breakfast at work, but I'm a hungry boy. If it's Monday, I head out for the early markets, to see if there are any good bargains. Like I said, the company provides our meals, but they don't worry much about variety or taste, so food is still a treat. It's never certain what the grocers will put out, though there's generally some of everything: grains, fruits, meat, veggies. But the packaging industry is basically gone, so we have to bring our boxes and bags down and fill them up from the bulk containers. And of course, no one can afford a fridge, not to mention the power that is out for several hours each day, so most of us don't buy perishable food before we are going to eat it. Some people have insulated ice boxes. The vat food keeps well, but most of the bulk food tastes pretty similar. Actually we don't get real fruits and vegetables, we get 'fruit strips' and 'veggie strips' which probably have a lot of filler, though they are handy for a sandwich. And the vat meat is like the vat tofu—we buy chunks of it that we can slice and grill or fry or cut into chunks for soup." I was grateful I couldn't see her expression in the dark. I bet my menu sounded pretty disgusting to her.

"Tuesdays and Thursdays if the weather's good, I go to a park, to watch the dogs that the rich bastards' servants come down to walk. I would love to have a pet, but that is so out of my price range it's not even funny. On the neighbor's farm they had a sheep dog, and he was pretty friendly unless you touched one of the sheep. I was really broken up when a rustler's arrow got him. Now I get my fix from watching the dogs frolic in the park, and some of the servants know me well enough that I can even throw a stick sometimes. And I know that sitting at the desk too much is bad for muscles so I do a bit of jogging around the park." *Not nearly enough*, I mused wryly.

"I guess that's part of the weird side effects of so many jobs not being real," she commented.

"What you mean, not real?"

"Well like just sitting at a desk all day—are you actually making anything?"

"I'm making…information," I replied, though I knew exactly what she meant. When I first got the job, I had been thrilled that I didn't actually have to work, not like shoveling or cleaning or delivering messages.

"I'm sorry for interrupting—what about the other days?"

"Wednesday morning is usually laundry—there's almost always a line at the laundromat, and once you get a washer you have to stand by it to make sure your clothes don't disappear. These are the old washers and dryers, without those electronic gizmos, just basic warm wash, rinse and spin. The laundromat's in a different section of town, so it's operational from about 5 AM to 11 AM, and then again from 8 PM to midnight. Wednesday mornings seem to be less traffic, which is why I picked it—it's hard enough to stand there for about two hours when the clothes only take about an hour total to wash and dry. It's usually mellow rock, but at least they have music there. Someday I'd love to be able to hand it over to the counter clerk and pick it up the next day. That costs at least twice as much."

"Um—what's a mellow rock?"

I swallowed a laugh. "It's a type of music—I don't know how to describe why it's different from jazz except it's got a different rhythm and the melodies…I don't know how to describe music."

"That's okay, I probably wouldn't understand anyway. Sorry to interrupt again."

"Friday is the day the newspapers are posted on the corner boards, and there's always a line to read them. I don't mind waiting in line, because I've met some interesting people and the people in front almost always shout out the biggest news so we don't have to wait, and we can be discussing it while we wait our turn for the details. Of course, I do get some news at the office, since Commco taps into the news net."

"I'm not sure I understand—I've heard about newspapers, but why would they need them anymore?"

I shrugged, though she couldn't see that in the dark. "I'm not sure if need is the right word," I replied. "Newspapers were really big in the old days, and the authorities are doing everything they can to bring things back to normal. The news isn't much—stuff about famous singers or actors, production stats from various industries, notices about new goods that will be available. But the speaker over the news board plays instrumental soft jazz and the quality is so good I'd stand there just to listen to the music."

"Sounds like it's really important, this artificial music." I could hear the doubt in her voice.

"The music and the vid—video—screens sure make it easier to wait in the lines, which we do a lot. And we can't afford our own players, most of us. Not all stores and restaurants have vid screens, but many do, and there are public screens also, usually at the trolley stops or other places where we have to wait. Some of the stuff they play is weird, like old public service announcements or music vids with people doing bizarre things—but since 90% of the vids are pre-Adjustment, we don't expect to understand them all. They show short features, because otherwise people would block the area, standing for an hour or two to watch a full mu-vid. If you want to do that, you have to go to a theater, and that costs a bunch."

"Do you all still have phones and things?" Ciera asked. "You said the cell phone wasn't yours."

"It isn't. We've gone back to public phones for local use, located in the corner convenience stores, where you call another convenience store and they send a messenger to go fetch your private party." Should I try to explain to her that we called the corner stores *just sold the last one* stores? She probably wouldn't get it. "It's mostly not worth the price, and long distance means you have to go down to the phone bank at the phone company, and pay a fortune. But I don't know anyone who has someone to talk to long distance, so it's mostly a moot point. There's a messenger service in each borough—they will run or bike your message around the city. I—I used to do some of that before I got my office job. And of course the rich have their own arrangements, as they always do."

"So you think you all can just keep doing that, pulling things out of the countryside around you and pretending like the city is just like it used to be?" Ciera burst out.

Once again I had the feeling she was seeing things way different from what I was describing.

I shrugged uncomfortably. "Probably not. I never really thought about it much. My friend Rada works for the national salvage board, and though he can't tell me anything about where they are salvaging because that's a national security issue, he says that the salvage operations are taking longer than they used to, which probably means that they are having to go farther away to get the usual stuff for reusing and recycling."

"What do you—your city—go out for?"

"I think most of the portable stuff in the City was used up in the first decade or so...so probably pretty much of everything. Metal from cars and junked houses; glass jars from landfills and old stores; cardboard, paper and wood from all kinds of abandoned places and intact furniture when they can get it. All our little trinkets and luxuries are salvaged, cleaned up, and sold as 'new again.' I know there are foundries in Pennsylvania along the train line that recycle and reprocess the salvaged metal. One thing that you Greenies were right about—plastic wasn't worth the effort. Oh, there's some stuff that still good after fifty years, but most of it has just totally broken down and can't even be recycled. Some towns have started using it as gravel on the roads, though it turns into powder eventually. Some use it in sandbags, though mostly it's not heavy enough."

As if feeling guilty, she changed subjects. "What do you do for fun?"

"My hobbies mostly are jazz, baseball, and mu-vids—when I can afford them. I had a friend who was really interested in history, but it's not a popular subject 'cause everyone is focused on moving forward. And I collect the little bits of art I can afford. Drawings other than machine schematics are really cool."

"Do you draw?"

"No—there were no spare papers or pencils growing up. We used charcoal twigs and wooden boards in school, and even those weren't supposed to be wasted. Once, the teacher praised my sketch of the classroom flag. But mostly, they would erase my doodles and insist I get back to lessons."

"Have you ever gone hiking?"

"No—unless wandering around the city is considered hiking. Once a colleague took me to the rock climbing walls in Midtown—that was a freaky experience, but fun. They'd hooked up pulleys and safety ropes on a couple of the empty buildings, and the walls had plenty of toe holds, and there was enough danger to make it exciting. A spendy hobby, so not one I picked up. Oh yeah, there are thrifty climbers who just do it themselves on the ruined buildings, but your body could lie there for weeks if you got it wrong. Mostly, I like to get together with friends and socialize."

She was quiet a moment, and I knew she was thinking about how stiff and formal I seemed this evening. How could I explain to her how different manners were, without insulting her? But she had another question in mind.

"What did you mean about everyone focused on moving forward?"

"Like, the City is constantly running Progress Drives, where we are asked either to volunteer time or to put up with some 'minor inconvenience' like going without meat for a month or power for a couple days, so they can make some new arrangement that will supposedly benefit all of us. I don't know that I've seen much benefit, but on the other hand I haven't noticed the City slipping backwards at all, which is reassuring."

I thought about the daily routine—the mind-numbing but safe round of interactions. "I don't have high hopes, having grown up working like a serf," I said, "I just want to be able to live a bit more easily, have enough both to support myself and a little left over for fun." *And hopefully find a woman who likes me well enough to hang around for a while.* But I didn't add that, under the circumstances.

"Those who do not learn from history are bound to repeat it," Ciera muttered, then louder, "What you actually do in your company?"

"My job is to keep track of the maintenance details for the various receiver dishes that are on roofs around the City, and to alert my boss if it looks like there's any major problem. Someone else has to do the actual maintenance, someone I've never met, but his name is Guy, and he's always sending me notes complaining about how bad these dishes are and how we're gonna lose them soon—and I don't think we've lost more than four in the ten years I've been there."

"Do you get paid, like money? Like they used to get paid by the hour?"

"I'd heard people used to get paid hourly, and I suppose some still do—maybe the cleaners and the maintenance people for the City—but we sign a contract to work as much as they need us, in return for room and board, and an allowance for extras. So my apartment isn't really mine, it's part of the workers' complex for the company. And the food I buy is from my extras money. We have set times for breakfast, lunch and dinner, and go down as a group for whatever they are serving that day. None of the meals are all that special, but they usually feed us enough, and at least we know we'll get fed. Most of us work six days a week—you have to apply if there's a specific day you want to have off, though there's six official holidays per year. If you're sick, you go into the company hospital, and if you're lucky you come back out."

"It sounds like they own you!"

"There are worse things, believe me. The jobs that don't own you don't take care of you either and if you're not sure where you're gonna live tomorrow or what you're going to eat, it's real hard to focus on work. Like I said, before I got in at Commco, I worked as a messenger for a couple of city offices, and none of them paid enough for me to actually have an apartment or eat three square a day. I shared a room with four other guys in a room big enough for two, but we worked in shifts, so only two of us needed to sleep at any one time. I also had to pay for my own clubs and knives, because carrying packages could be a really dangerous job, let me tell you. And it was strenuous, so I always felt like I was hungry."

I fell silent, caught up in memories of that first amazing year when I got the job at Commco, but not sure I wanted to share that with her. The day I was hired, I went on a binge—I took Darcy, the guy I actually shared the room with, and two other friends down to one of the best jazz places in the mid-class district (the richer districts were off-limits) and we ate, drank, and I was very merry. And the day I moved into that one room apartment, I had a lump in my throat and a grin on my face all day. I just leaned against the walls and stared around—furniture, curtains, a nice loft bed above the living area, even a gas ring … The bathroom had a toilet and tub, though the only sink was in the kitchen corner. But I wasn't sharing it with anybody, for the first time in my life—and I was only 19. I considered myself a huge success—I made it a priority to keep that apartment, no matter what I had to swallow at work.

For a while I had dreams of making it even bigger, telling myself this was just a plateau and once I got my bearings, I'd leap even higher. But as I got to know the system better, I realized it was even more cutthroat than the slums. You moved higher up the ladder at the cost of your—I guess I would call it individuality—everything that made you a different person. You could go up, but you'd never get to the rich levels, and you were almost a machine, with no thoughts of your own—or at least none I could see. They managed every moment of your life once you became a senior manager. And if those managers had original ideas and were utterly unable to act on them, that must have been a kind of hell. Better that I had a small bit of money and a decent chunk of independence. And yet I jumped at the trip to Ohio precisely because I thought it would be an easy way to get a few more perks without becoming a senior manager drone.

I shook my head and apologized for talking so long about myself. I was clinging to memory, out here where my life seemed like a rapidly fading dream.

"I want to hear more about you," I said. "I had no idea that people had—survived—outside of the walls. How do you manage to get all the things that you need?"

"That's what I wonder about you," she chuckled. "Out here, it's simple—you know the people who are making the things you need, or you make them yourself. And food and water are nearby; you don't have to wonder if they're gonna be there for you. I would be so scared, living in that concrete desert…"

"How can you call it a desert?? There's theater and restaurants, music in lots of cafés *every* night, and every now and then a parade. There are museums—the Museum of Progress is opened twice a week, and there are lots of other little—"

"Those are the extras. They're not what you need to stay alive. You act like survival is guaranteed in the City, but so many things could break down…" She was silent, as if she realized she had been criticizing me again. "You asked how we do it—we keep things simple, so theater is a bunch of us dressing up and acting. And we don't have museums, but there's so many things lying around from Before that I guess we don't really need one. We do have a library—and there's lots of information there. But the Grandparents decided that it would be better to have less and be sure of having it, than to insist on luxuries and bankrupt ourselves paying for it."

I struggled to find a way to say it politely, but in the end I just blurted, "But without those things, I'm not sure I would want to *stay* alive. You call them luxuries, but I lived without them for years, for 18 miserable years, and I can't imagine living without them anymore."

"What about friendship, the beauty of nature...love?"

"I don't have to give them up in the City—there are some parks, so we do have nature—and it's not like love vanishes because we have theater."

"I remember reading," she said slowly, "that people got so busy rushing after these luxuries and paying for them that they ended up with no time for friendship or love—or nature. They tried to cram those into five minute segments and of course that's impossible."

"Love is most nearly itself when here and now cease to matter," I murmured.

"What?" She leaned closer to hear me.

"It's… It's just a bit of poem that I heard once. *Love is most nearly itself when—*"

"*—here and now cease to matter*. I know that—it's from T.S. Eliot, from the East Coker section of The Four Quartets."

My cheeks burned in the dark as I admitted I had no idea what she was talking about. The only lines of poetry I knew were from mu-vids or from friends quoting. Nobody bothered to name authors or titles.

"Do you know more of it?" I asked.

"It's a very long poem. I can give you the stanza," she replied, reciting:

Home is where one starts from. As we grow older
the world becomes stranger, the pattern more complicated
of dead and living. Not the intense moment
isolated, with no before and after,
but a lifetime burning in every moment
and not the lifetime of one one man only
but of old stones that cannot be deciphered.
There is a time for the evening under starlight,
a time for the evening under lamplight
(the evening with the photograph album).
Love is most nearly itself
when here and now cease to matter.
Old men ought to be explorers
here and there does not matter
we must be still and still moving
into another intensity
for a further union, a deeper communion
through the dark cold and the empty desolation,
the wave cry, the wind cry, the vast waters
of the petrel and the porpoise. In the end is my beginning.

I was silent when she finished, afraid my voice would shake too much if I said anything. Her voice had been quiet yet vibrant, and the words themselves...! Who could have written such incredible words? It was like they caught fire inside my head, without me having to understand quite what they meant.

"But my favorite part of his poem is actually from the section called Little Gidding," Ciera said. "I think it may be my favorite of all poems:

We shall not cease from exploration
and the end of all our exploring
will be to arrive where we started
and know the place for the first time.
Through the unknown, remembered gate
when the last of earth left to discover
is that which was the beginning;
at the source of the longest river
the voice of the hidden waterfall
and the children in the apple-tree
not known, because not looked for
but heard, half-heard, in the stillness
between two waves of the sea.
Quick now, here, now, always—
a condition of complete simplicity
(costing not less than everything)
and all shall be well and
all manner of thing shall be well
when the tongues of flame are in-folded
into the crowned knot of fire
and the fire and the rose are one.

I was completely stunned. A few of those lines were familiar, but the effect of the whole was like a bomb. I wanted to hear it again and again, but I knew it had already permeated some deep part of me. She shifted on the mattress and leaned against me gently, resting her head on my shoulder. I could smell the odd perfume of human hair. The weight of her body against mine was like an electric shock even through my clothes. I didn't know if I was doing absolutely the wrong thing, couldn't even muster enough brain power to sort through the possible consequences. My body was telling me I wasn't quite as tired as I thought, and before I had a chance to change my mind, I took her gently in my arms and we stretched out on the bed.

14

The next morning I didn't really want to wake up, wanted to lie there half asleep, entangled with her and the blankets. But the sun was slanting dimly through the skin or parchment window panes, and my bladder was screaming at me. So I slipped off the bed as quietly as possible and went over and used the chamber pot.

Light did not improve the appearance of the room—blue gold wallpaper was faded and peeling in several places, with darker squares where something had hung. The carpet had been ripped up, leaving pitted wood flooring and treacherous tack strips near the walls; fake beadboard was leaning drunkenly above them. Every light fixture had been removed, along with the wires, the holes patched over with sagging burlap. A real armpit of a place, and I was glad we had arrived in darkness. I had missed it the night before, but in a tiny closet alcove there was a tray table with a steel soup pot and a towel; the pot was full of water and there was even a very small bar of soap. I had no idea what the protocol for sharing a towel was, so I dipped the soap in the pot and rubbed it on the parts I most wanted to get clean, then awkwardly splashed a bit of water to try to rinse.

"Why don't you use the towel?"

I didn't turn around. "I wasn't sure—I wanted to leave some for you."

"You could dip a corner in and use it as a washcloth, then dry off. And I don't mind sharing a towel with you. Under the circumstances." There was a smile in her voice.

After I'd done the minimal wash-up, very aware she was probably watching, I turned around. She was standing, and she came over and gently took the towel from me, smiling, but maybe with a little doubt in her eyes? I had enough doubt for the both of us, though I smiled as brightly as I knew how. Where did this go from here? What would her brother say—or maybe do—when he found out? Some of my friends were highly territorial about their sisters. Did she use birth control? I knew I didn't have the nerve to ask her that. Leaving her to her ablutions, I retrieved my clothes and before I dressed, I found that muscle salve that Monica had given us and rubbed it on my calves and shoulders. It had a minty fragrance and I could feel the muscles getting warm.

"I did promise Hadley that we would get back just after dawn," she said, stepping into her clothes with all the grace and glide of a belly dancer. I watched, hypnotized. She was wearing the same coveralls and camouflage jacket as when I first met her, but they looked different somehow.

"Then let's get breakfast and head out," I replied, when I could find my voice.

The hall was just as bleak—wallpaper confetti and dust-smothered cobwebs, though it did look like someone swept from time to time.

"I hadn't realized how nasty this place was," Ciera commented. "I only knew it was here."

"I guess people do what they can—and maybe there just aren't that many travelers."

The lobby was huge; the far side that had been in darkness last night was set up for dining—a long table with ten chairs, at which four were eating. We walked across clean but pitted ceramic tile past a bricked-up fireplace. The red/gold wallpaper had darker squares from missing pictures, replaced here and there by bright amateurish oil paintings. The large windows had been bricked in down to a four-foot square filled with a wooden grill that looked quite sturdy. I wondered how tricky security was around here. I patted the gun in my pocket as I crossed the room warily, though they could hardly get away with violence in a public place. Could they?

Just before the table, on our right, there was a small buffet and a new attendant stood by—a well-muscled young woman with crimped black hair and broad cheekbones smiled at us and began to prepare two plates. Combined hotel management and security? Handy. Breakfast was two biscuits, a smidge of butter and a dollop of purple jam, a slice of grayish ham and a cup of mint tea. It could be worse. We brought our food to the table, and sat a couple chairs away from the foursome, who actually seemed like two couples. One pair—a hunched white guy with a fight-crooked nose and graying skimpy beard murmuring with a tall, coffee-toned younger man sporting dyed blue hair—barely acknowledged us. Slightly more friendly was a young woman who looked so similar to Ciera that I was startled—

she could have been an older sister, but her face was harder, more closed; maybe how Ciera might have looked if she'd gotten her wish to "see everything." She had been chatting with a blond man whose left cheek was scarred, a red welt running up to his tiny freckled nose; he was wearing a loud red and yellow checked jacket.

The woman acknowledged us with a question. "Any news of the world?"

I was taken aback, but Ciera replied quickly, "Refugees coming up the 65, apparently trouble at the Mall. And I'm Ciera."

The woman leaned back stiffly and I sensed a different ritual here. I put my hand on Ciera's to stop her repeating the usual litany. She glanced at me with a frown, then nodded as it became apparent the woman would not give her name. Instead, Ciera said, "And from your travels?"

That seemed to be more to the woman's liking. She replied that it was all quiet up north but there had been frackquakes by Youngstown. At that, the other pair turned to listen and the older man asked, "Was there damage to the roads? Can a cart get through?"

The young woman shrugged and said 376 looked okay for the most part. Then she pointedly asked him, "Any news of the world?"

He scowled, less willing to answer, but eventually said that areas to the east had some new permitting rules. "A new boss, apparently. Tolls are costing more."

"Pricing themselves out of trade," his companion added.

"Oh? Where does one check in now?" the blond man asked.

"Franklin Park, if you want north or east," the old guy replied. They began to discuss routes and rules with the wariness of poker players, watching each other closely and trading information as if bartering goods. I gathered that there were loose coalitions of towns, and travelers needed to know what areas were covered by what agreements and which towns were the gateways, as showing up suddenly in a town without a permit could be a very dangerous thing. It sounded almost as treacherous as Long Island, and I was fascinated, but my plate was empty and I knew we couldn't put off our return much longer. I nodded to the group, and we brought our plates back to the attendant, thanked her and left.

Unlike the hotel, the streets looked a little livelier in daylight. Though the roads were empty, the sidewalks had some bright painted, soil-filled barrels holding sprightly green seedlings. Some of the brick rowhouses had been painted or at least scrubbed down, and here and there a door had been decorated—an intricate Celtic knotwork, a bold and splashy poppy. Definitely seemed to be life in this part of town. Then I remembered where we were heading, my gut clenched and I forgot my interest in local architecture. Ciera seemed tense as well, though she pointed out a budding tree, and a tangle of beads in a window, trying to act as if we were out strolling.

"What—what should I say when we get back?" I had no desire to make things worse. I wasn't even certain why I was going back, except to be sure she wouldn't get in trouble.

She glanced at me nervously, then sighed. "I don't know—unless you can think of something that would really prove to Hadley you weren't…from the Army."

"I could show him those texts just like I showed you." That reminded me—I'd texted Cheyenne last night. I pulled the phone out and checked. Nothing. Maybe she couldn't get through. Maybe she didn't want to. I stuffed the phone back in my pocket. I glanced over, watching sunlight glint on Ciera's hair, still tousled from last night. As if sensing my attention, she ran her fingers through her silky dark-chocolate locks and looked over at me. I desperately wanted to know what she thought about last night—was it just a fun evening? Was she Making Plans? But I wasn't going to ask, especially since I hadn't had time to think through my own response. And what of my plans to get home, now? Aside from the logistics, could I just walk away?

And then the walls of the community were in front of me. The knot grew in my stomach as I pictured her brother and the other members. What did I know about their taboos? But he had let her leave yesterday, or rather, had had no right to stop her. So perhaps this was just a matter of reassuring him that I was honest, that my interest in her was just what it seemed.

She tapped on the scarred metal door where we'd first entered, and the same guy let us in, smiling. A good start. He waved us toward the kitchens and we found our way through the same kind of bustling crowd—an aproned old woman holding a steaming pot, four young men arguing over trays of corn muffins. People nodded and kept working. Maybe only a few even knew we'd left. Pippin charged down the hall toward us and stopped suddenly.

"You're back—good. There's a meeting in 'bout fifteen minutes, after breakfast is done." He smiled at both of us, but I sensed some tension.

Maybe we weren't home free. Was the meeting about us? I wracked my brains for something I could offer to repay their hospitality and ease their suspicion. My pitiful supplies were already hocked to Ciera, and I knew less about this revolt than they did.

We entered the Hall before catching sight of Hadley. He was chatting with a tall black woman while constantly scanning the crowd, and when he caught sight of us he hurried over. His expression was set in a smile that did not reach his eyes, and he nodded curtly as he got closer. Ciera stood beside me, in front as if to protect me. Or claim me?

"I'm glad you're back," Hadley said, glaring at me, then smoothing his expression, biting his lip and nodding again. "There's a meeting to discuss the rebellion after breakfast. Ciera, as a member of my party you are invited. Martin—"

"I know I'm not invited," I broke in. "I understand, and I just want to say that I am *not* a spy and had no idea I'd run into your sister in Madison—"

He waved his hand impatiently. "We don't have time. But if you don't mind assisting us, we would like to ask you some questions." His formality was pointed.

I looked around the room—there seemed to be fewer refugees; half of the pale oak floor was now visible and I wondered if people were already finding new homes. Perhaps relatives came to claim them? But then I saw a new line coming in at the main door, looking weary, confused and relieved. "I'll tell you whatever I can, but I haven't had a lot of info about the military since…since I left home fourteen years ago. You don't see them much in the City."

Hadley nodded and walked away; he'd barely looked at his sister. I glanced over and saw a hurt look, quickly erased.

"Come on, Martin—let's get a second breakfast," she said, and headed for the buffet.

Several people who I recognized from yesterday came over and chatted—I couldn't remember their names, but they seemed friendly enough. They asked Ciera about her community, and she praised the solar and hydropower and communal kitchen and workshop.

"Each of them is big enough to let a dozen people work on small projects. Good classroom size, too," she explained. "Just the basic tools, but group solar ovens, for example, make the best use of the heat. We have five large fresnel lenses. We also have a hot bath and sauna—large enough for twenty-five or so. Really nice in the winter."

A wiry black man no higher than my shoulder asked, "Why do you keep hidden? Is it some kind of El Dorado?"

The others frowned; one woman elbowed him. Ciera looked dismayed, wary, but she answered, "No—we just made a decision a couple generations back that we wanted self-sufficiency, that we would do better when we could count on each other for what we needed and our mutual survival depended on each other." I could tell she was reciting some kind of community dogma, and after last night's conversation, that she might not believe it. Another woman quickly changed the topic to the recent warm spell that had caused the early cole crops to flourish.

The hot oatmeal with honey was delicious and I cleaned my bowl quickly; I had passed on the scrambled eggs, though they looked good. I was racking my brains for helpful information and mostly coming up blank. Or worse than blank—reviewing what I knew about the military opened up closet doors that I had sealed long ago: getting beaten at five for fussing during a National Guard parade; my mother embarrassed and tight-lipped as we left the grounds of the triathlon where I'd only come in 8th. So many days and nights of pure frustration as I chafed to be something more than a tool. No—I didn't want to go back there again. And after 14 years, what information would still be accurate?

As we were finishing up, Hadley rejoined us and told Ciera the meeting would be held in the summer kitchen. She quivered with suppressed frustration—clearly, she didn't think he was treating her fairly. And it was true—he was neither being honest about his opinion nor letting her have a chance to explain herself.

"Hadley, if you have a minute," I said, pulling out the phone, "I'm happy to show you this, like I showed Ciera last night, so you can see that my texts were purely about getting myself home after my job fell apart." I held it out to him and held his gaze firmly. Slowly, he took the phone, and—not asking for directions—flipped it open and punched some keys. I watched as he read the texts.

"What are these pictures for?" he asked finally. He tilted the phone and gestured towards the icons.

"They're apps for things that I was supposed to need on this trip—like translating to another language, and displaying specs for the communication towers, and the agreement form they were supposed to sign." I took the phone back and tapped the translation icon; when my boss had shown it to me, it expanded to show a couple boxes where I could type in a phrase and it would translate in the next box. Now, despite tapping several times, nothing happened. I frowned and tapped the spec sheet app—again nothing. A chill went down my spine. I had two thoughts simultaneously: *Hadley's gonna think I'm lying; was Geoff right about the apps being fluff?* But they worked when my boss showed them to me. I glanced up at Hadley, and shook my head, I knew I looked confused, but did I look honest? I took a deep breath, let it out, and tried the agreement form—that, at least expanded into a document showing the contract. I let Hadley read it as I pulled together my chaotic thoughts. Could my boss have handed me another phone? Did something mess up the software in the last few days? Or had I been set up, never meant to arrange a single tower?

He handed the phone back and said, "We're going to talk a bit and then someone will call you in, and maybe you'll have some information that's helpful."

"I hope so," I replied. They left and I looked around, saw a corner where I might be undisturbed a while, and zigzagged through the crowd. Two long days and there still hadn't been much time to pull my thoughts together. Not to mention new pieces of the puzzle kept falling into my lap. I recalled a fragile 500-piece jigsaw that had occupied a side table in the commune dining hall, and how I'd spent hours struggling to put together the damn blue sky, which was all the older kids would let me work on. Without color or texture, the only thing to work with was shape—tiny changes in contour. This felt more like someone had jumbled two puzzles together and I first had to separate them. But the shape of things was always important.

I watched as children danced around seated refugees, blithely unconcerned as long as they were full and rested. That's how I used to be a long time ago—last week—knowing there was a larger world outside of my own, but content to live in ignorance. No chance of putting *that* genie back in the bottle. What did it mean that all of these people lived outside the City, not needing what we called civilization? Was it a sign that America could become bigger than five cities? If so, why were citizens never told about these folks? A foot away, a young blond woman changed a 2-year-old, deftly removing shirt and pants from the wriggling girl, pleading with her to sit still. There were plenty of workers out here who could contribute to progress. Was New York just reluctant to extend its benefits out this far? Or, as Ciera and her group hinted, was New York plundering as far as it could reach, not caring who they stole from? And was this rebellion the pushback? I thought about Pippen and the Alitos, and Monica and her household, and of course Ciera. Once I was back, I would never see them again. And the roll of days would keep unwinding, carrying me with it—to where?

Seeing a pair of pre-teen boys wrestling near the cubicles, I flashed back to my slum years—being a scrawny young teen in a hardened group of men and women wasn't much different from my family fascist commune, but with less shame attached. Amazed that they gave me credit for whatever I could do, I'd scrambled to learn everything. Willie's Warmongers was the first to take me in; despite the name, they were more focused on salvaging, refurbishing and selling weapons on the black market than in actually using them, though of course one always had to defend territory. As a malnourished 14-year-old, I mostly fetched and carried—rusted axe heads, armfuls of hardwood for handles or staves, metal pipes, scraps of steel to be cut into the nasty hurling stars from some Asian shogun's imagination. The one thing missing was anything that fired a bullet. When I finally had the courage to ask why, one of them—Tuffy, I think—pulled me aside and told me the story of Magda's Missing Mob. Everything got turned into a saga out there, since there were few books and hardly any readers. But the story was chilling enough for a mu-vid: one of the slumlords had decided that she would sneak around government gun taboos, and set her gang to refurbishing a stash she had located somewhere in the wilds of the Island. Apparently they had just sold their first batch on the market when the Army descended—"not for arrests and trials, no"—they came in with guns that sprayed bullets like rain, murdering the entire gang and *all* hangers-on, whether they were involved or not, grabbing all the guns and parts, and—for the first time in a decade—driving a tank straight into the area and flattening the entire territory. The kind of warning that even the dumbest gang leader could hardly ignore.

"They couldn't have done better if they had hoisted the dead bodies into one of their planes and dropped them down splat in our laps," Tuffy finished. "Everybody got the message." And, I found out, the area had been left vacant and had become a kind of neutral territory where gangs sometimes met to negotiate tricky deals.

I suddenly noticed Pippin standing in a doorway, craning to look around. I stood up, and when he saw me he waved me over. This was it—what did I have that could help them? Was I willing to give them info, not knowing how it would be used? Did I have the right to ask them if they were part of the rebellion?

"I'm glad to see you back, son," Pippen said, patting me on the shoulder. I tensed, knowing he meant it as a friendly gesture. I returned his smile nervously; so—he was actually glad to see me? I followed him along the path to the summer kitchen, glancing over at the new privies I had helped set up. This place worked really well, and seemed so much happier than my family's commune. Could something like this be imported to the Island? They definitely knew a few things we didn't.

Inside, the kitchen was crammed with several dozen people seated or standing wherever they fit, the young cross-legged on tables and oven tops. There was a watchful silence as I entered, and for an instant I tensed to flee. I looked at Hadley for my cue, but he deferred to an older woman whose broad face was a reddish brick brown, flat-cheeked and hawk-nosed with straight black hair tied at the nape of her neck. She smiled at me with no trace of hostility but I found it impossible to relax.

"Greetings, Martin, I am Erma," she said. "We appreciate your helping us in this situation. I am not sure what you know about this rebellion—" I shook my head and raised my palms to indicate I knew nothing, "—but we are hoping you might have some information about how the Army might respond, considering that we are not part of it."

That answered one of my questions. "Like I told Hadley, I know almost nothing about the Army because we don't see them in the City. I didn't see any signs of work on the Wall or extra troops along the corridor as I came out—"

"Can you describe the ride to us?"

I closed my eyes and reviewed the two-day trip. "We started out across the river, since rail doesn't go into the City itself. The first part of the trip was through some pretty large towns—mini-cities I guess. Even though the buildings were much shorter than City towers, there wasn't a lot of green. The Wall there is really wide—not a corridor so much as a whole segment of Jersey. That's where they have a lot of factories, and it's well guarded, plus I think most of the citizens would report any troublemaker instantly, so the Army doesn't need to just hang around. After about half a day, we were out in the countryside, and you can start to see the Wall on either side of the train. But a lot of the farmland is inside, at least for the first day. I noticed on the second day—after we'd stopped at a hotel in someplace called Easton—that the Wall got much closer, and in some places, it was only a couple hundred yards away from the track. And then it would bulge out as they let a town come inside their protection—there were at least a dozen towns that we passed on the second day."

"We heard it was just a bunch of the walled towns that decided to merge," a gray-haired black man commented—was he the one churning butter yesterday?

"Do you remember a town called Harrisburg?" Erma asked.

I shook my head. "They weren't calling out the towns where they stopped—and they only stopped twice each day. I got the impression they stopped where the passengers wanted to get off, and those people knew which town."

"You mean they just stopped anywhere?" Hadley was astonished.

"No—from what I could see, my guide and I were the only citizens who weren't with the Army or government." *Was Geoff a citizen?* I'd always assumed so; maybe not. "It actually takes a lot to get permission to go out. Strictly business—and only senior managers or Army brass have business that far out." I didn't tell them how that had un-nerved me, until pride or overconfidence kicked in. Then I spent the time daydreaming how I would describe all these up-ranked types to my friends over drinks.

"Those Army personnel on the train—did you notice anything about them?"

I could tell they were hoping I would have some miraculous bit of information. "I wish I could say that I noticed something different, but I'd never been out on this train so I have no idea if there were more or less Army than usual. Some of them were chatting quietly—"

"Did they look relaxed or tense?" Erma asked.

"I guess—most people look tense in the City," I replied, and Pippin snorted. "They didn't look especially tense. One thing I know—most of the time, the military is just reserves. Unless it's changed in the last 10 years, the Army and the National Guard have most of their people working on farms or repairing machinery or doing useful work—very few of them are just sitting around with their guns waiting for problems. So unless they've known about this rebellion for weeks, it'll take them a while to bring troops out." *Especially if the rebels blow up the tracks,* I thought. And that was probably the goal.

"So that means any troops they bring out would be missing from important daily chores and farm work—it would be costly." Erma said, nodding.

"I would think so," I replied. "And—again, unless there was a huge recent military buildup—they have only a few planes and fewer tanks. Most of the troops travel on e-bikes, horses or on foot. The trains seem to be mostly for bringing goods—the one I was on had one passenger car and seven box or tank cars. I don't know much, but it doesn't make sense to me that they'd lay waste to the countryside, not if they could catch the rebels." I left it unsaid, but they must know that they couldn't hide rebels without consequences.

There was a low murmuring as members couldn't restrain their comments. Then several members began shouting out questions. *Shit, there'll be trouble now.* But Erma simply listened and then waved her hand for quiet and pointed to one of the boys I'd seen in the kitchen the day before.

"Mick—what's your question?"

"Do they have bombs?"

I shifted uncomfortably—I didn't want to be an expert on this. I noticed one or two older members were murmuring their own opinions, "...can't get the steel to make casings...would have to find a military depot... probably stockpiled enough to last forever..." Erma let the low conversations go on while she waited for my answer. Why didn't she stop them? Where were the group manners? This wasn't order, and it wasn't chaos—it was something in between. Belatedly, I focused on answering.

"I've never heard of them bombing anywhere around here in the past ten years. Have you?"

They glanced at each other, especially at the elders. Most shook their heads. A pock-faced girl of about 16 said, "I heard there was a big explosion around Youngstown—"

"No, that was a gas tank exploding," someone called out.

Eventually they agreed they hadn't heard of bombings. And they would know more than I did, especially if the City didn't advertise their battles. There was a subtle relaxation around the room.

One of the older women I'd seen in the kitchen called out, "What if Ambridge built their own wall?"

That was greeted with laughter and playful objections. "Someone would have to be porter!" "Where would we get all the bricks?" Who's got time after their chores?"

Someone else hollered out that the rebel talk had only mentioned a strong protest—nothing about taking over a railroad! "Where are they getting all the soldiers?" he finished. That started another round of multiple conversations. Erma let them go on for a while then waved them to silence.

"What should we watch for?" she asked me. "What might be the signs that a large army troop is coming?"

I was at a loss—how did I describe tanks and planes? Had they ever seen mu-vids? If they had phones…

"Uh... I guess the first sign would be a really loud machine noise in the distance if planes were coming," I started. "Like a giant buzzing but steady—has anyone heard a plane?"

Pippin raised his hand and nodded. "Kind of like an angry hive of bees amplified by a giant tin washtub."

I nodded, remembering hives from childhood. "Good description. Tanks will sound just as loud and there would be a lot of destruction and collapse noises because generally they just go over rather than around." I thought about the large highways that Geoff had led me on—they'd collapsed in too many places for tanks to be able to use them. And after seeing the broken overpass, I doubt they would risk valuable tanks on elevated roads. "They're slow but basically unstoppable. If you hear or see them—you'd better run. Planes can be shot down, but only with really large guns."

"Best we have are rifles for deer or critters," Pippen commented. "I remember seeing pictures of those guns—so big they had to be mounted on trucks."

"Guns might be a sore point," I said, remembering Tuffy's saga. "They definitely want to be in control of all weapons that fire bullets."

"But that would leave us defenseless!" someone cried.

"I think that's the point," someone else chuckled.

I nodded. "From what I heard, they definitely don't want to risk being shot at. Not to say you give up weapons, but just know that if they think you have a lot of them they might come out to take them away. Shooting should be a last resort, and you'd better be prepared to back it up. Booby-traps might work better."

Conversation grew loud for a while, and Erma waited. I thought about my family's commune meetings—the rigid silence, the specified order in which people were called. I looked around. Half of these these people wouldn't even have been called upon, being too young or too unimportant. And yet this confusion seem to work—and people were involved, deeply. I tried to imagine growing up in a place like this. That brought up a stab of pain, so I dropped it.

Raising my voice, I suggested, "It would be a good idea to have some people looking out for movement from the east. If you haven't already done that." *Don't insult them.*

But nobody seemed insulted. Erma nodded and said that besides interviewing refugees, they had a number of lookouts and had posted some really good runners. "The big question," she said, "is what will we do if they are coming?"

Hadley jumped in. "But Martin doesn't need to hear—"

She cut him off. "I don't think that's a problem," she replied, deliberately looking around for any objections. People shrugged, some shook their heads. No one seemed that worried. I avoided looking at Hadley, avoided smiling or showing my relief and... gratitude. Here was a whole room full of people trusting me! I shifted away from that thought fast, as emotion bubbled up. *Think!* What else could I help them with? It was hard to think in a room full of excited conversation. The only time I'd experienced that was at the jazz clubs, and we were never discussing anything important.

"The only thing I can think of," I said, raising my voice slightly. The room quieted. "Is that the Army will probably not want the hassle of chasing down widely-scattered people and goods. They would probably just hit some big, symbolic or supply-laden building or area." As I said that, I realized we were living in just such an area. Not good news. "So it might be a good idea to cache bunches of important stuff in separate places, whatever you can spare to hide away right now. And –" *Was this a crazy idea?* "try to set up some big-looking building on the east edge of the town that they might be attracted to. You might even pretend to defend it and then run."

Pippin and the Alitos laughed, but the others looked puzzled. It was probably only a mu-vid type idea. But I was pretty sure the Army would make a big gesture and then stop. That was their mentality, as I knew to my regret.

They debated this for a while, with people calling out pros and cons, and some of them suggesting buildings that might work.

"What about leaving them a big stash of something that looked important—something they would have to retrieve and pull back, and then we could booby-trap the place before they returned?" the young blond chicken butcher suggested—Rom, his name was.

"Such as?" an old lady asked.

"Well.... We've got that huge pile of sol-panels that are fried. They look good, but we can't get a bit of juice out of them."

"That might work," I said eagerly. "I know for a fact that they're always looking for new panels. And I'm guessing they won't bring a solar technician with them on a foray."

I thought about some of the other ploys the gangs had used. Artaud had his group disguise their refurbished e-bikes in pairs as old wood carts, setting a special-made box on top. I remembered how brutal it was pushing them across town toward the buyer—a job reserved for the newer members like me. Disguise was crucial because the authorities didn't like to spend a lot of time looking around in the slum areas. Mickey and his distillery gang hid their stills among the smokestacks of coal-burning forges that also allowed them to build more stills and tools. Big Lulu's methane production was damned hard to hide, but she counted on the Army's sense of self-preservation—the vats were raised overhead, and anyone attempting to destroy them would either be blown up or smothered in a mass of humanure. But the prime guideline along the edges of the City was definitely to avoid trouble whenever possible. In retrospect, I realized the Army must have known all of that was happening and for their own reasons allowed the black-market commerce almost under their noses. There were other gangs that dealt in the more traditional goods: pornography, prostitution (all sexes) and drugs. I had never even tried to get in those, partly my squeaky clean upbringing, partly stories about how brutal they were. And there was one strange white supremacist group tucked in on some of the tidal islands inside of Long Beach barrier—islands that often disappeared in a surge, but rumor said the whole community was up on steel stilts and acting like it was Fortress Earth—one of those odd mu-vids that had been popular in the slums. Because even the slumsters, poor as they were, wanted the entertainment that had survived the Adjustment. Each gang had its big screen—sometimes as big as 22" x 48"—safely protected in a powered headquarter building, and the trade in mu-vids was as intense as the food trade. Usually that same headquarter building had its own rooftop garden, and the one thing that had helped me get into a gang was my knowledge of planting, puny as it was.

I realized someone was asking a question; I jerked back to the present. "I'm sorry...?"

"I said, is it likely that these rebels will even be able to blow up the rails?"

I chewed my lip and shook my head. "Can't answer that. Too much depends on whether the Army has any hint of it happening." The wildly unexpected sometimes succeeded—but only once. In four years, I'd gone through four gangs: Willie's Warmongers, Big Lulu's, Mickey's and finally Artaud's. Each time, I'd found some stunt to fake my death, and convince the new gang I wasn't a deserter; each time it had to be weird and sudden. *Let people see what they want to believe.*

I glanced over and noticed Ciera smiling at me; a flush swept from my knees to my hair. She had a habit of tilting her head slightly that caught my breath. I grinned back and then tried to refocus on the conversation.

The members were arguing about how far the trouble would move up the 65—would there be actual battles here, or just fallout like loss of supplies and more renegades?

"I've heard it's best to prepare for trouble and hope for luck," I said. "Maybe decide what things are too important to lose, and hide them now?"

Many nodded at this, and the group seemed to spontaneously break into smaller clusters, talking intensely. Erma came up to me and shook my hand; I had to steel myself not to jump. I really would have to get used to all this touching.

"Thanks for your input," she said. "We'll work on the details. Since we've got so many tied up here, do you think you'd be able to lend a hand outside?"

"Yes, of course," I said, "and if I think of anything else, I'll let you know."

She thanked me again and I left the summer kitchen, walking slowly toward the big house. As I turned the corner, Ciera caught up with me, slipping her hand in mine and swinging it a bit.

"That helped," she said, "though I don't think they were ever as suspicious as Hadley, and he's just mad because –" she was quiet, looking away.

"Because...?"

She blew a loud raspberry. "Oh, he's just set on marrying me off to this carpenter back in town. Nice guy, very steady—Lord, how steady!—but not someone I could live in a tiny house with." She looked embarrassed, and I struggled not to smile. Of course, the *big brother knows best* trick. I relaxed a bit; I could manage *that* kind of trouble.

We went back to helping get new refugees settled. After yesterday, I was more familiar with the set up; I fell into an easy routine of handing out clothes and for an hour or two was even manager. I caught myself smiling; despite the rebel threat, I had an irrational feeling of safety here. On one level, not the social one, I'd always had an ability to adapt; it was rusty, but I could feel it coming back to me. *Just look around for how others are acting, and do the same.* Even in this outlands, that strategy worked. Ciera was helping with the meals, and occasionally we would nod and smile across the room.

About lunchtime, I got a break and went over to get my bowl of whatever was cooking. Turned out to be a kind of cabbage and potato stew flavored with dill that was pretty good. Ciera joined me in a group by the windows. Rom and the blonde woman who'd helped with the tattoo—Astrid, she said—and a couple others I didn't know were sitting on the floor in a patch of thin sunlight, chatting about a surprise find—yards of oilcloth in good shape, uncovered in a collapsed building. "It would make wonderful awnings," Astrid said.

Rom shook his head. "Nah—that stuff falls apart in sun. Unless it's specially designed. Better for raincoats."

"Or situpons," a freckled teen boy interjected.

"What are situpons?" I asked.

"Waterproof cushions," Rom replied. "Usually with a shoulder strap for carrying. Really handy if you're out in the field, or even traveling through a town. At least in spring, when things are always damp." The group chuckled.

"Don't they have them in the City?" the boy asked me.

I glanced warily at Ciera—how did I describe the City's habits and—yes, luxuries—at least compared to out here?

"We, um, don't need them, I replied. "Most of the time we don't sit down outside anyway."

"Why not?"

"We don't have time, mostly—City jobs usually last ten hours a day, and then you have to stand on line to get what you need, and that takes another hour or so each day. We sit inside—in theaters, and cafés—and there are benches in the park, I guess..." I trailed off; thinking of the City was too painful. I suddenly recognized my "jump mode"—that transition time when I'd refused to count on any one place, funneling my attention instead on keeping my feet and jumping from new situation to new situation. *Out of the frying pan, trying to avoid the fire.*

"Why does the City treat us like the enemy?" the teen boy asked. There were wry grins from the older folk, but he wanted an answer.

I shrugged. "I think they're just so big they don't see you at all. They are brutal; they know what they want and they intend to get it. If you're in the way..." I shrugged again.

"Then why did you stay there?" he asked. The woman next to him slapped him lightly in the back of the head. But the rest of them were listening.

I could feel my face getting red. I looked down. "I guess—there weren't any other options that I knew about. Where I grew up, they worked heart and soul for the City and... they barely got crumbs. At least inside, I was getting something." *And I didn't have to murder or rumble*, though I didn't say that. They all had guns out here; how often did they use them? The towns seemed so peaceful—had I traveled through at a peaceful moment, or did they know some magic the City didn't?

Pippin came over to us, carrying a thin board to which a piece of paper had been clipped. He handed it to me, and I handed my empty bowl to Ciera, puzzled. He pulled a pencil out of a hidden tunic pocket and asked, "Could you maybe sketch out what a tank looks like? And maybe if you've ever seen one of those big guns? I've tried, and I guess I don't remember enough."

I stared at the pencil and the blank piece of paper. They would have cost a half week's salary. I had one stub that I had managed to liberate from the office—it had been a risk, since stationary theft was a chopping offense: a couple of fingers or even a hand, depending. I sketched on the end sheets of books that I had bought or found. Eagerly but carefully, I tried to capture what I remembered—the tank's shape, squat and thick like the rectangular lid to a casserole, with the long gun as pot handle. The strange wheels wrapped in a link bracelet of steel—like the treadmill of that ferry. I did a little side sketch of the hatch on top open, with a soldier peering out.

"Hey—that's really good!" Ciera said, peering over my shoulder. The others murmured approval.

Pippin leaned forward like a tilting sunflower, watching the picture emerge upside down. "Yeah—I think you've got it. That's what I remember. What about those mounted guns?"

I paused—I hadn't left room. Glancing up at him, I unclipped the paper and turned it over. I tried to remember the large bombardment guns that had been parked near the tanks during the Guard picnics, an irresistible draw to all the kids, untouchable and proudly guarded by the junior cadets with their spiffy uniforms and bits of tinsel on their shoulders. The truck wasn't hard—it was basically a pickup truck, and the gun was similar to tanks, only with a swivel mount and a visible trigger system. I was surprised I remembered as much as I did; I guess at the time it had been important to me.

"Primetime! You did a damn fine job," Pippin said, taking back the board and pencil. He hurried away.

"You said you didn't draw," Ciera said.

"I don't, really. You can't draw without materials, or training." The group was breaking up after lunch, standing and stretching a bit. Rom tapped Ciera on the shoulder, and asked her to look over some panels they had outside. I waved and went back to my clothing table.

The refugees kept coming, and I wondered how bad things were getting at the Mall. Given the uncertainty, perhaps it would be better to stay here for a couple of days and scope things out. They didn't seem like they would kick me out, and I could feel a little strength and energy coming back. I just needed to get my bearings again. Maybe... maybe I could even learn enough to bring some improvements back. Or something. The wedge of despair was still twisting inside, telling me how helpless I was. But they had something here, and if it wasn't a pipe dream, maybe it was worth learning. As long as I could keep my jazz, and theaters, and sports, and pink....

* * *

The afternoon wore on, as I helped in various tasks—carrying supplies from a couple of horse carts waiting at a side gate into the pantries, bringing more blankets and mattresses down from a second story room piled full, even washing several sinks of dirty dishes. I still wasn't good at chatting; they still held me at a slight distance as if unsure, but it wasn't unfriendly—just a bit awkward. As dinner was being set up, I saw Hadley, Megan and Ciera cross the room, having an intense discussion. I had a sudden pang—what if *they* decided to leave? After all, they didn't live here, and at home they would be farther from danger. I hurried over, fighting to breathe normally.

"...have at least five cases of inverters north of town," Ciera was saying.

Hadley shook his head impatiently. "It's too dangerous to get them now, and it would slow us down."

"But the Army could come and sweep them up! Those inverters would last us for years! We could probably get them for five barrels of salt fish. At least Rom thinks so."

"Yeah, but Rom's not in charge of that trade," Megan said, with apparent relish. I wondered how she could be willing to leave, given her family was here. And she definitely was strong-minded; I could work with that.

"Hello," I said, as casually as possible. "Any more news of the rebels?"

Hadley glared at me, but Ciera answered, "No sight of them yet, and the refugees are saying there's been no battles. Most of them are just being cautious." She turned to Hadley. "And the fact that they are moving up here suggests they don't see trouble coming this far."

He snorted. "As if they know? If we had one decent spy report—" he glanced at me, then quickly away. "Maybe it would be worth the risk. But we're only fifteen miles away."

"A full day on foot!" Ciera obviously didn't want to leave. Hope, fear, desire and confusion tumbled inside—I had a crazy flash of watching my clothes in a dryer. That was my gut now.

"Nevertheless." Hadley said in a classic big brother voice. "Nevertheless."

Like a burst pipeline, crowd noise spewed from the far corner through the room. We turned in confusion. It was a babble—fear, anger, questions—but finally I caught "*rebels!*" in the din.

Hadley grabbed a boy snaking his way through the mob. "What happened?"

"Rebel *train*! Came in from the North—stopped here. They're coming to get us!" he gasped. Hadley let him go.

"They're coming to get supplies," I said grimly.

15

It took me a moment to grasp the other point: rebels had a train? How??

"I thought all the trains stopped in Pittsburgh," I murmured, barely aware I was speaking out loud.

"Well, they keep the tracks in repair around here, and use hand carts up and down the river, because it's so much easier than a horse and cart," Ciera replied. "But I'd never heard of real trains."

More proof that this place was more sophisticated than I thought. But that would have to wait. I grabbed Hadley's arm—no time for politeness—"Quick—how much stuff can you waterproof? How much is sealed?"

"Why??"

"Throw it down the privies."

Ciera gasped and Hadley stepped back, horrified.

"I'm serious," I persisted. "It's an old slum trick—be sure it's water-tight, then throw it or lower it down shit holes. They won't look there. It's that or lose your best tools and starve."

They exchanged glances, but I saw I'd convinced them. Megan strode over to one clutch of members and Hadley ran toward another. Ciera and I tried to stay on our feet as the refugees panicked and fled the Hall—maybe right into rebel guns.

What could I hide, and where? The essential map, meds, phone and weapons were on my body. The solar charger—I shook my head. This was always the dangerous decision—resist or give in? Hide or try to act as small and powerless as possible and hope they don't want to waste ammo? Who were these rebels? I needed to *see* what was happening.

"Ciera—tell them I'm gonna check it out—find out what they're do-ing." I turned and elbowed my way through—greater good and all that—and out to the street. The sun was already sinking toward the river, and the last of the light flared golden on the tops of the buildings. I braced against the wall until I could see the direction the crowds were going. By now, they'd figured out where trouble was and were running away. So I snaked a path in the other direction, keeping my eyes open, waiting to see where the prey became the predator.

It happened three blocks away. I saw more gray shirts and jackets, more clumps of men with rifles on their shoulders. The rebels seemed to be stopping people randomly, just grabbing a few here and there. I needed a better vantage. Glancing around, I noticed a red brick house on the corner, with a wide front porch complete with grapevine trellis. It took a moment to pull myself up, buoyed on a surge of fear and anger. Crawling up to a window, I started to check for locks—then remembered the "glass" was parchment-thin hide. I slit it with my knife and crawled in. I moved through the gloom of a bed-sitting room to the other window, carefully cut a slit and peered through.

It was a street of mixed shops and homes. The rebel gray uniform was visible along two blocks. Something about it pulled my memory, but it was just a detail. There were a few soldiers battering doors and looting, but they seem to be picking carefully and moving fast, so they didn't have much time. Good. They *were* robbing residents and refugees, but for the most part were not hurting them for fun. So this likely was an organized salvage group, looking for specific supplies, and not a "slash and burn" mob. I watched for a few more minutes, trying to see if there was a pattern—how far would they go and in what direction? I saw some breaking off left and right, but the main group kept together and it looked like the splits came back promptly. Another good sign, if only the group weren't so close to the commune. I wonder if they knew about the place. They must—didn't that town guy say his friend's father was a member of the uprising? I needed to hurry back and warn the colony not to hide too much—the rebels needed to find *some* food or they'd tear the place up looking.

I groped toward a back room, slit and looked out a window, caught a glimpse of a back porch, fumbled my way toward the correct window, praying no one was home or that they were too scared to move. I shimmied down the porch pillar and crept toward the street. There was a side street not far away where I saw no uniforms and few residents. It's one of the hardest things to do, to walk calmly, or at least to imitate the general movement, when one is trying to escape. The overwhelming urge to run like hell seems to come up from the ankles and work like a riptide on the legs. I also knew better than to whip my head back and forth looking for soldiers, but since I was theoretically a resident, I could at least hurry, doing my best to look helpless.

Back at the commune, I saw the group was working fast and efficiently to "dispose of" most of the tools, lowering them down in baskets. At least most of the privies were very new. But some were also wrapping small items in layers of cloth and dipping them in hot wax—these must be very precious, and heatproof, items. I found Megan and passed on the word about the demeanor of the rebels, and about not hiding too much—not that they were in any danger of that, with maybe ten minutes left before soldiers arrived. In one corner, I saw young men digging furiously, and others holding wooden crates that I assume were full of potatoes and root vegetables—if they could cover that neatly with something, they might get away with it. I hope they had posted a lookout.

The fear-rush was wearing off—it didn't last as long as when I was young—and all the soreness and fatigue came slamming back. Deciding this was a bona fide emergency; I pulled out another pain med and swallowed it without water. I forced my legs to carry me around the chaos, looking for Ciera. She was helping a group that was filling hollow walls with canned food—hidden panels must have seemed a great idea during the ups and downs of the Adjustment.

"I just hope they don't know about them," I murmured. "They might get mad."

"What do you mean?" asked a brunette with a bowl haircut, one blue eye askew; the other impaled me with a lance-like glare.

"It's possible the rebels—being homeboys—not only know this place is the central shelter, but that it has hiding places. That sort of information gets around."

"Only members know about *these*," she snapped, then turned back to work.

I refrained from pointing out that I now knew about them, and in past attacks, likely others also had found out. I touched Ciera's arm and led her aside.

"Look—this will be very dangerous in a few minutes. If we head back to the inn—"

"Run away?? Are you serious?" She pulled her arm away angrily and I felt an old shame sweep me. Before I learned the "save your ass" code of the slum, I'd grown up with all sorts of brave patriotic nonsense. But most of the Guard families lived in orderly, safe towns—I'd had no chance to discover what courage was—and wasn't—until I'd escaped. No one in the City pretended to be brave.

"It's just strategic retreat."

She glared. "Didn't realize you were a coward."

"Who just went out to spy, huh? Was that cowardly?"

She frowned. "Then I don't understand…"

"There's *times* to go face-to-face and *times* to disappear and let them get on with it."

"We can't *all* disappear."

I paused, looking around. "You *could*—a mass desertion actually could cause less damage—you can't defend it, in any case." Not without a couple dozen guns and a killer instinct.

She glared at me again. We were in different worlds. I bit my lip.

"So what are you going to do?" I asked.

"Stay here with my brother and the others. Face them *bravely.*" Her emphasis on the last word bit hard. Was it courage or stupidity if it got you killed? I agonized—even an organized scout party can get nasty. Was she safe with the crowd?

"I think I can be more use to you all if I'm out of the lineup," I said finally. As a stranger, I would almost certainly do something to call attention to myself—and rebels would *not* believe the comm tower story.

She looked puzzled a moment, then scathing. "Go, then—run and *strategize*, if you want to."

I ground my teeth, biting back the useless explanation—I'd just have to prove it. Somehow. I fumbled through my pockets then handed her my gun. "This is easier to hide than that cowboy gun of yours," I muttered, "you shouldn't be shooting from a distance anyway—not if you want to live." I also gave her the med pack and the paper map, touched the phone but couldn't hand it over. She stared at me, her eyes huge.

I turned and pushed my way through the crowd without looking back. I snatched up a mismatched outfit from the clothing tables as I walked by—at least I knew it was about my size. Thank you, efficient commune.

I heard someone yelling orders in the distance as I stepped out of the main gate. Obviously soldiers knew about the side gates. I pushed the sick worry away as I tried to think of a plan. If I brought back info about the train, that would help, wouldn't it? It would be damned hard to get close without getting swept up by them. But how else to get information? First, I would scope out what was happening. Adopting a stoop and a shuffle, I headed back toward the main street.

A half block away, I took a moment to change clothes, in case my description had been circulated, tying the loose brown wool pants with a hemp rope grabbed in passing. I turned off the phone, tucked it into the thick gathers of my underpants—awkward, but definitely safer if anyone checked me for valuables. The heavy leather jacket, cap and jeans got stashed behind a tall bin on the side of a house that looked ransacked: door handle smashed off, a few small boxes scattered on the porch like afterthoughts. I flicked open and carried my knife inside my cuff with two fingers, like I'd been taught; instantly near to hand. Then I headed for the shouting.

Mercantile Street was several blocks of red brick storefronts only lightly glazed with old graffiti, the old window secured with colorful wood shutters, with painted cloth banners over the doors, indicating name and hours. Many said, "sunup to sundown"—solar lights must be rare here. At least the early drizzle had flattened the dust and stopped before it created much mud. Soldiers were going through every shop, calling back and forth as they worked their way slowly down the street, owners standing by the doors in various poses of resignation. One crate full of squawking chickens was losing feathers as a man carried it on his head—his grimace showed it wasn't all that was raining down on him. A gangly soldier coming out with an armful of bulky canvas bags even patted the woman by the door on her shoulder. *Spoils of war.* Maybe there was some deal about repaying or sharing spoils. No battles that I could see; just surrender. Some of my tension evaporated.

Standing in the shadow of a doorway, I thought quickly. Hunching over probably wouldn't be enough; I needed to adopt the "dead arm/limp" that I'd learned years ago—effective against forced labor, as long as the aggressors weren't bloodthirsty. At worst, I'd be put on light duty. And the "dead arm" tucked into my belt allowed me to hold my knife loosely out of sight. I wanted to get close enough to learn about this group and their railroad plans. Why would they blow up the railroad if they had their own trains? That bit of information must be wrong. I eased out of the doorway and moved slowly toward them, head averted, trying to look like I had an errand.

As I limped out to where the uniforms could see me, I realized I was shaking. All the old fears of authority crawled up my spine and wrestled with my resolve. *Don't tempt the Man. They can throw you in a hole so deep you'll never get out.* How many times, since earliest memory, had that been uttered, usually during a beating or the subsequent isolation? Nobody questioned the ones in charge—they had all the power and you had none. It didn't matter if you were right. I struggled with a five-year-old's terror as I walked forward. I knew I was a coward; it didn't take me long in the slums to find out that I had gut-wrenching fear every time there was a fight. In the City, I'd turn away when my friends talked trumpo—I knew firsthand that you don't know you're a coward until you have to be brave. I'd never embarrassed myself—when it came down to it, I'd put my mind somewhere else or goaded myself into just jumping in, but I never got over the terror. I never really found what I'd call courage. Sometimes I'd wanted to ask Teg if he, underneath his calm exterior, had any of the same feelings—but guys don't talk like that.

"You! Come over here!"

I steeled myself, enraged at my timidity. Looking up like a good citizen, I continued my exaggerated limp, careful to keep my left arm pinned in my rope belt, knife tip poised on my ring finger; tricky not to twitch it even a little—did I remember how?

"Yes?" I answered. Did I call him Sir? Or what? The little mannerisms were going to be trickier than the cripple routine.

"Carry this—oh. Shit." The rebel had a red stripe on one shoulder, so not a grunt. He was a dandy, obviously not used to work, with a neat caramel-toned mustache and sweeping sideburns and a tiny goatee. After a moment, he gave me a bag that I could carry in one hand. I made an eagerly pathetic attempt to keep up with him as he strode down the street, past soldiers dragging canvas sacks on handcarts. The slight clatter of glass suggested jams and preserved foods were inside—the glass jars were at least as valuable as the food. In spring, food stores would be tight—if the residents starved, would there be a backlash toward the rebels? The mood of the residents was getting darker—I saw more frowns, more suppressed anger, as they stood aside for the salvagers. There was a definite feel that a limit was being reached. As if he sensed the tension, my soldier hollered to the others around him. "Back to the Beast, boys! We've a train to catch!"

"Hey, Colonel, ah got a Dutch uhvun!"

The young soldier holding up the cast iron pot had a strong southern accent. Weren't these *local* rebels? What was going on?? Suddenly the gray uniforms triggered a memory—some famous rebel army wore gray, didn't they? In the country's only civil war? But that could be a coincidence—gray wasn't unusual; dyes were expensive. And after all, if you're going to get the uniform stained and dirty, why waste money on color? But I remembered jokes around the office about the DC branch being made up of Confederates, and about DC getting too ambitious, told as humor, but all too plainly not. As I walked, I listened more closely—about half the voices sounded southern. I glanced at the rebel mob as they strolled down the street—some looked steel-fit and deadly, but most were young men. A few boys seemed 14 or younger, probably those who were "big for their age", those who too often drifted into violence because it was expected of them. They seemed confident and eager, so I guessed they knew very little about the Army they were facing. Even though I heard you could make gunpowder from pig shit, I doubted they'd seen big explosions, let alone planes with bombs. And although there were far fewer of those, it only needed one to take out a crew like this. Most would shit themselves and run, if they survived. When I'd seen the five-plane Air Force take off from The Guardian airport, the noise alone was terrifying. We weren't treated to bombs that day, as they flew toward some disturbance in Connecticut, but I'd seen mu-vids of war and could easily imagine the devastation.

The street ended by the river, where a large steel-girder bridge still mostly crossed the wide blue waterway. "Mostly" meant that one narrow path had been preserved over the length of the span—possibly a walkway or maintenance path, but now a handful of pedestrians waited at the tollbooth at this end. Gray-suited guards lounged by the booth. I didn't see money pass hands, but clearly some record was made—the passerby stamped something onto a long roll of paper or cloth—hard to see at this distance. I supposed the tally was settled periodically. Pretty good system, as long as you knew where your customer lived. But this evening, the soldiers were inspecting and claiming anything useful.

Just beneath the bridge, where a trestle spanned the underside, the train—engine and four cars—sat in a wreath of steam. The steep embankment obscured the lower part; the concrete stairs leading down was crowded with soldiers. I tried not to stare too openly, but as I followed the colonel along the top of the embankment, my glances showed a black monster with a huge smokestack and a bin behind the driver's cab that was piled with coal. I vaguely recalled that Pennsylvania was coal mining country—they'd found enough for the few miles they were traveling south. But then what? Attached to the engine were two eight-windowed passenger cars, a fenced flatcar and a boxcar that the soldiers were busily stuffing with their stolen goods: beer kegs, grain sacks, hastily folded sheets and blankets, axes and shovels and the squawking crate of chickens were handed down. The cars were in worse shape than ones I had seen in a Brooklyn museum.

"Put it down over there." The colonel gestured toward a pile of canvas sacks near the top of the stairs. I nodded meekly and limped over, then my eye was caught by a canvas-roofed table and chair set-up in a clump of young trees. On the table was a metal box with several knobs and dials, and a short-haired young blonde was fiddling with the knobs and listening with her head almost against the box. An older man—supervisor without a doubt—was standing over her. They didn't notice me. I slowed and let my path drift closer. Was this one of those ham ops? She was frowning, straining to hear something, which she turned and repeated to her boss.

"Tell them will be leaving in—" he looked at the activity around the train "—in an hour. Probably at terminus by 0400 hours."

I winced—anybody who told time in four digits had no mercy and no sense of humor. I limped toward the intended pile and carefully lowered my bag, then turned casually to study the ham-op. Did it use the satellite? Or was there some other way to catch the sound waves? I was totally fuzzy on all things mechanical, partly because it was still status in the city to be a desk jockey rather than any kind of hands-on fixer. I had a passing acquaintance with moonshine stills and bicycle gears, but nothing high tech. There were others in the office who were hobbyists, following the mechanics and engineers around, pretending to be supervising, while actually learning from the "grunts". Raul was one of them, and he would enthuse about how satellites worked whenever he thought he wouldn't get jeered. From him I got the vague idea of ripples in the air, that somehow are caught and then sent out again. But as to why machines were needed or how they did the work, I was completely untutored.

Not all of the bustle was around the train—there was a group gathered around the mess tent (I always wondered about that term—my family referred to meals as "mess" though they were never messy.) The smell of boiled cabbage was strong, but also grilled meat that made my mouth water. How many bags of flour, eggs, chickens, etc., would it take to feed this lot? I pictured Abe, my brother named for a president and destined for the Guard from birth (so the story went—but maybe they'd waited to see who was most adept—it clearly wasn't me). Abe had started in cadets at six, then gradually spent more time in training, till we only saw him on holidays. He was the golden haired boy, literally and figuratively. He even had special "conferences" with my parents and other elders, giving reports we mere mortal kids couldn't hear. I'd listened through the old central heating duct every now and then, but it was just boring details of plane and tank strength, forays and such—if I wanted to know that, I'd have joined. But now I wished I had listened a little more closely, so that I would have even of vague idea of what was going on here. I wondered if Abe would be called out for this. And the other Guard. My folks were too old, but how many others that I knew would be conscripted?

My colonel was conferring with two others with striped shoulders, so I eased toward the mess. I wanted to get back quickly and figured the "back-door" lay beyond the diners. This apparently was a quick grab-and-run; some were already taking down the pole and awning areas, storing the rolled-up tents in canvas bags. Where did they come from? I strolled along the sidewalk, acting purposeful, and listening hard.

"Gawd, I hate these salvage victuals! Nothin' like the hogback we'll get at home."

"If we get back. Still a battle 'r two to get through."

"I hear it's a feint."

"A faint what?"

"A *feint*! A fake out. We're only to draw fire."

"Oh—and that's *better* than a battle??"

Another argument was about *where* they were:

"We're right outside New York."

"Nah—I figure we're still a coupla days away."

"Any place is better than the hole we came from."

"Don't let the captain hea' you say that. He could find wuse holes."

A hawk-nosed man with gray hair came over to the diners and shouted at them until they had hustled their plates to the portable sinks and started moving the mules from their corral to the flat car. I took the occasion to sidle in the other direction, limping slightly faster. What I'd heard made me more confused. If this was a feint, complete with train, what did the main company look like?? Was New York in more trouble than it could handle? I dodged behind some tall shrubbery, wild and misshapen, and thought hard. They were leaving—that was good for the community as long as no one had been hurt. But this sounded big—big enough to spill back from wherever the conflict flared. This was a small army but it *was* an army—and it wasn't ours!

"Gotcha!" Arms flashed around my chest from behind and a strong grip pinioned me. Without thinking, I stepped hard on a boot arch, causing Geoff to swear softly but vehemently. I tried to break his grip with an elbow, but he was strong and good at twisting a joint where it would hurt the most. My knife was uselessly pinned.

"Let me go, bastard—do you want to get us *both* conscripted?"

"Let's just march back to town, city boy. You've got to be in the right place to be rescued—and it needs to happen soon."

"Huh?"

"Captain! Spies here!"

Instantly all eyes were on us. Geoff froze but didn't slacken his grip. Since my arms were pinned, I kept up the cripple act, letting my mouth drop into outraged innocence, standing still in his grasp.

Four of the regulars surrounded us, two with pistols aimed. A burly short man with salt-and-pepper hair and gold braid on his jacket hurried over to us, followed by the colonel who had used me as baggage boy.

"Who ah you?" he asked. His thick accent was worse than a foreign vid.

Geoff spoke quickly. "This here's a spy for the Army, suh—I sawh him down in Pitts, tawking with one of the Army wall guards, last week." His twang was quite authentic, and I wondered how many accents he had mastered as part of his job.

I worked to sound slow and confused. "Sir? I was in Horseferry last week. I never been to Pitts."

The colonel who'd commandeered me commented, "He's so crippled, I can't see him getting from Pitts to here on his own—his arm and leg are crap."

"Yes sir, it happened after I hit my head. I was fourteen. Lame ever since."

"Let go o' him," the captain ordered, and studied me as Geoff stepped back. I prayed that he had no knowledge of how muscles wither from lack of use. I seethed with rage at Geoff, but also at myself—how could I have been so careless?? Breathing thanks that I'd left my modern gear with Ciera, I prayed the captain would avoid my crotch if he patted me down. The phone would be a deadly giveaway; keeping it in place had definitely helped the limp.

Geoff spoke up. "A bit o' pressure—if yuh know whut I mean—would get him to talk. You'd see I'm right."

It was a dangerous game he was playing. All I could tell under torture was his other name, our route from the City, and rumors that *must* be common knowledge in order to have reached commune ears.

"I hain't got time for this. Crippled, yuh say?" That to the colonel.

"Yes, sir."

"Then get him on boawd and we'll take him tuh Pitts. And tawk along t' way." He frowned at me, more annoyed than worried, it seemed. I knew I didn't look—or smell—impressive. Not at all like a citizen, thankfully.

"And take t'other one too, till we see what's going on w' him."

"Sir? I'm just a—a friendly," Geoff protested.

"Shut up. We'll find owt what yew ah."

As the colonel led me away, I suppressed a smile at Geoff fuming between his escorts. His set jaw told me he hadn't planned for this, but that didn't help me. He probably had more contacts at the Mall than I did. I almost laughed at the black irony—I was getting closer and closer to civilization—and at this rate would never get there alive.

16

"Given that we probably won't get out of this alive, would you mind telling me what the hell is going on?"

We'd been stuffed in the box car with the supplies. I was wedged and jostling against two lumpy canvas sacks that whiffed of horse and were crammed with hard lumps—jars, maybe. Definitely not feathers or straw or anything comfortable. I'd done a good enough job faking the dead arm that they had only a rope tying my good leg and arm to a metal pipe handle in the wall of the box car. Geoff was trussed much more thoroughly, lying across two boxes, his head close enough that I could murmur and the young guard sitting in the far corner couldn't hear over the rumbling wheels.

"I should've cut my losses," Geoff grumbled. He was talking mostly to himself, scowling and struggling with the ropes. "I figured it was some kind of nasty 'venge. But when we got those forged IDs from someone who wasn't scared of the Ministry—that's when I should have dropped and run." His wrist was bandaged where I had winged him, and I could tell it still hurt.

The train was rocking and clicking, and the growl from the engine was much louder than in City trolley cars. They weren't going fast—either cautious about rail conditions or not able to get the boiler hot enough—I guessed no more than 10 miles an hour. Still, that would get us to the Mall in about an hour. I had that much time to find out what I'd gotten myself into. And how to get out. I wasn't lying—I knew my chances of getting out of this alive were slim. I was trying not to think about that.

"Do you think it really was the Ministry? Why would a government agency want to sabotage the comm tower project?" I asked.

"I don't think it had anything to do with that. I think you were bait," he sneered. "Not sure for what—but when they told me what towns to aim for, I knew they weren't serious about the towers. Either that, or they were bodaciously ignorant."

It was a fake? I thought about Madison, the Neo-Luddite burg. "Did you try to tell them the towns were wrong?"

"That gorgeous dark-haired bitch who hired me just didn't want to be told—she'd been given the names of the towns, and that was that." He paused, stared at me, then apparently made up his mind. "Look—let's help each other out. Get out of this mess, and put our heads together later. Looks like we both were ganked. But we can flip the sleeve ace—what d'ya say, huh?"

"Sounds like a good idea." Not that I trusted him as far as I could throw him—and I'm sure he didn't trust me. But he definitely owed me help getting out of this. "How did you get the IDs?"

"Use your other arm, why don't 'ya? We can overpower him." He obviously didn't want to reveal his tricks.

I shook my head. "And then jump off a moving train? Too dangerous. What about the IDs?"

After tugging futilely at the ropes again, he said," I radioed back to say you had gone." He scowled at me like this was my fault. "…and they said to stop at—a certain town—where they would produce a signed authorization to do whatever was needed to get you back. To whoever was waiting."

Too many questions roiled around. "A place that could print government authorizations?"

"Or close enough it would pass."

"So there *were* more sophisticated towns nearby?"

"Yeah. That's why I knew the mission wasn't legit. That and when we stopped at the church overnight and I radioed back, they told me someone would be trying to kidnap you and I was to let it happen, then find out who it was."

It still sounded like sabotaging the comm project—but I couldn't figure out who would benefit! Surely the inter-departmental wars hadn't gotten that savage. The City needed that contact with Chicago! I racked my brains—would some other group be put in charge if my company failed? Since I'd never paid attention to politics or the pissing wars of the rich—basically the same thing—I had no idea.

"So you didn't know who those bashers were? You were working with them!"

Geoff rolled his eyes. "Like I cared? They contacted me at the farm; said they were only going to hold you for ransom, and offered me—well, some seriously useful trades. And since I'd been told to cooperate, I went along with it."

Was this truth or his cover story, his way of getting me to help him? It was hard to believe he'd spend so much time tracking me down unless somebody was dishing out mega cred. Nobody on my level. And he said he wasn't rescuing me. Could I believe him that somebody *was* intending to rescue me, once they had flushed out some kind of enemy? But he didn't *say* that, did he? He was only instructed to find out who it was. I was disposable, unless I had information they needed. And at this point I didn't. Nothing to bring back to them. I thought about how close we'd be to civilization when we arrived, if—the big If!—we could get away from this group, whatever it was. And then I thought of Ciera.

"So was that a hamop whatever on the table back there?" My mind clicked from impossible choices onto something irrelevant.

He frowned, as if trying to figure out what the hell I just said, then nodded. "Ham radio. Mostly short distance, but repeaters can be set up, and some folks know… about other rigs, so there's no telling how far their messages are reaching. You should be careful about learning too much—could be really dangerous."

"Oh—and I suppose not dangerous for you?" I tried to sound scornful, but in fact I was curious.

He shrugged. "I know how to trade that info, make it worth the danger."

I suddenly noticed the train was slowing, and within a couple minutes had stopped. Geoff tried to sit up, but he had no leverage. My mouth got so dry I could barely swallow. This could be where they searched and interrogated us. I couldn't reach the phone, but I gently eased the knife past my fingers, down behind the canvas sack. It was useless against an army. We lay there for what seemed like ages; there was nothing to measure the time. Even my racing heart was unreliable. Finally the door to the car opened, and a pair of brawny soldiers came in, quickly untied my bonds and hoisted me to my feet. I had been cramped for long enough that it was no problem at all to fake lameness. In fact, I was lucky I didn't fall down. But when one of them grabbed my "bad" arm, I let out a howl and then apologized—but he stepped aside before he could feel how strong that arm was.

"I won't give no trouble, sir," I said haltingly, as obsequious as I dared to be, "no trouble at all." I didn't even glance back at Geoff—if it worked that we could cooperate on escape, so be it. Otherwise, he was on his own. I could hear them helping him to his feet; I hoped they had him tightly. I knew he'd leg it away without a second thought for me.

A handful of soldiers waited to load more goods into the car—so they'd gone on another salvage raid. It was inky black beyond the garish yellow fans of light from the passenger car windows. I could hear the gurgle of running water under the hiss of steam, and dimly made out that it was coming from near the engine, as I was led in the opposite direction. They brought me up ornate metal steps into the first passenger car, much more spacious than the storage car, though there must have been a dozen officers busy inside. The reek of unwashed bodies and cheap cigars was almost eye-watering, and the air was blue with smoke. The radio setup was crammed in a nearby corner, with the blonde soldier hunched over, straining to listen in the relative quiet of the stopped train. Around her, the muttered conversation occasionally got loud and she glanced up in annoyance but obviously did not have enough rank to complain.

I tried to catch bits of conversation as the soldiers pushed me through to the back corner, toward a pair of restaurant-type wooden booths covered with papers and a large map. Without turning my face toward the map at all, I strained to decipher anything. The problem with middle America was there were very few landmarks—I'm sure I'd recognize the East Coast, and the Great Lakes area was distinctive, but the farmlands and hills around Ohio and Pennsylvania were just a great green lump. I guessed that the red lines that snaked through were railroad tracks, and the circles could be cities, could be forts. I suddenly realized what I might be bait for: if New York suspected anything out here, a project to extend communication towers would certainly draw out any who were already attempting to colonize! I tried to memorize the dots so I could add them to my map later. But I knew I wasn't any kind of decent spy. In the gangs, I was simply one of the grunts, unskilled in knowing what information was valuable or how to get it without being discovered. Of course, they didn't intend me to be a spy—just bait. I turned back to my immediate crisis, finding some plausible story and concentrating on consistent "disabilities." I forced my expression into that blank panic of an innocent who had no idea what was going on, acutely aware of the phone tucked into my underpants—if they found *that*, I'd be hung on the scaffolding that was filling the engine tank with water. I was relieved to see the colonel who had forced me carry the bag was present.

The captain was sitting at the back table. He looked up from the pile of papers with a frown of annoyance.

"Ah don't really have time fo' this," he complained. "So if you were spyin', ah'll be happy to make shoa you regret it."

One of the other officers spoke up. "I recognize Sydney—" he indicated Geoff. "He's, er, been useful. You know—info, and all that?"

"So—one of ah spies?"

"Um…not…necessarily…"

The captain scowled. "Ah hate mercenaries. Profiting off'en the struggle, eh?"

"No sah!" Geoff stood as straight as possible while being held; using his soft Southern voice, he protested, "I was working f' you—I just needed monah to get *others* to tawk—yuh know how it is."

"I do indeed." The captain didn't look convinced, and I breathed easier. Then he turned his glare on me. "What's yo' story?"

I spoke slowly, both to make myself seem less sharp and to give myself time to make the story believable. "Like I said sir, I'm a... I'm just a local—I was in Horseferry, came in to see family, and then that Colonel there," I pointed with my good arm, "made me—I mean asked me—to carry a bag over to your train, sir, and I did, sir…and that's all. I don't have any idea what-all is happening."

The colonel nodded. "It's true that he was on Main Street, not near the train—I needed help, and he was close by."

The captain's frown deepened; he leaned back against the bench. "Well, it goes against all mah principles t' kill an innocent man. But I can't let ya'll just walk away and blab 'round."

I could feel the ice of terror building in my gut and spreading up my chest, threatening to paralyze me just when I needed to be able to think.

"So ah'm just gonna keep you in that car fo' now," he continued. "Ah'm thinking the surprise part o' this will be done inna day or two. After that, yuh can't do much harm. Might be tough, yuh getting back from th' Mall—"

"But I'll figure out something! Thank you, Captain sir, you're an honorable man." I was babbling with a tinge of hysteria, but that strengthened my disguise.

"And Sydney here can keep ya'll company—like ah said, ah don't want anyone spoiling our su'prise. So you two just sit tight. If you try t' escape, though, we'll shoot yuh. Understood?"

"Yes sir," I said vehemently. I could feel the relief washing over me and causing my legs to wobble, and I willed myself not to pee in front of the soldiers. Behind me, Geoff also mumbled his assent, and the soldiers led us back to the boxcar. They were even nice enough to let us stop and relieve ourselves by a tree. In the dark, I could smell cook fires and saw partly-shuttered lanterns bobbing and weaving. Apparently the soldiers were camping overnight here—wherever that was. I wonder if they would feed us, but that was probably asking too much. *You're alive, be grateful.* And I was, but I was getting hungry, too.

In the boxcar, which was now crammed to the ceiling, we were tied up in a sitting position, wedged between two crates of chickens. In the dark, I could not see them well but certainly could smell them. When the car guard left us alone, I asked Geoff what he knew about this uprising.

"They said you were helping them—but only for the money? Or are you one of the rebels?" But even as I said it, I knew he was a mercenary, first and only.

He looked over at me with disdain, trying to decide whether it was worth his while to talk, so I reminded him that we were going to help each other get out of this.

He shrugged and said, "All I know is there's been building up from the south. Towns and forts following a new rail line—they used an old spur to bypass the Pitts and it's got as far as south of the Ohio." So I was right about the red dots.

"You think Washington is trying to expand?"

"I don't know who else it could be. I know it's been tricky moving around in some areas that the New York Army used to have authority in. Seems like as New York backed off, DC pushed forward."

"New York backed off?" That was news to me.

But it *would* be, because I never paid attention to any of it. I was so sure the City was stable, it never crossed my mind to worry. The sliver of despair that had struck—was it only yesterday at lunch?—again wormed into my gut. What point in making plans to get away? Such a stupid life, maybe it should end stupidly. For an instant, I thought Ciera's voice murmured nearby. I winced. How could I protect her or the others? Their town might be right in the path of this expansion, and how do you move an entire town? Or hide it?

You trust strangers every day of your life, she'd said. Suddenly I could see the nightmare that would unfold if someone cut off City supplies for even a few days. No citizen could afford to hoard food, even if we could keep it fresh. Maybe this was why my parents hadn't yearned for the City. Should I stay out here? If I even got out of *this* situation, obviously. I tried to picture myself living among the Greenies, back to manual labor and the lamplit evenings full of...charades? A wave of resistance flooded me—give up the music, the restaurants, the lighting, water and heat that made up a decent life? I couldn't! I fought the downward spiral of thoughts, and told myself fiercely to *focus*—get myself out of this and worry about the rest later.

The train wasn't moving, so they *were* camping overnight. The guard came in with water and piece of bread. Since they wouldn't untie us, he had to feed it to us slowly. I tried not to choke as water went down too quickly, and I thanked him even though it had barely quenched my thirst. Despite my upright position, the blind tunnel of the near future, and my ravenous hunger, I fell asleep.

* * *

I woke to rocking as the train picked up speed. It was still night, so I had no idea how long I had slept. I glanced over—Geoff was wide awake, looking around at the supplies with a calculating expression. My muscles were aching and I wondered if I even had the ability to run if we got a chance. The young guard at the end of the narrow aisle was half asleep, his head nodding beside his lantern then jerking upward. Watching him carefully, I yearned after the knife, but it had vanished under the new booty. *Dammit*. Would the general let us go eventually? Despite everything, I just couldn't believe they were going to attack the City, even this far out. It was suicide! Or was it? How strong was Washington DC? They were our *allies*, despite the jokes around the office. What had changed?

After another vague while, the train stopped. I caught my breath and tensed—end of the road? Hopefully not mine. Thankfully, it wasn't a long wait—four soldiers climbed into the baggage car. They hustled us out as others unpacked the supplies we were sitting on. A short young man with a uniform half again too large for him directed the soldiers to drag us forward. We tripped over at least three or four separate trackways and, though I couldn't see very far, I could sense a few railcars nearby. He had them tie us to an old metal scaffolding about 10 feet from the train, in pitch darkness. Just beyond the rails, some scrapwood shacks and tattered canvas tents that might have been the rebel camp were illuminated by the glow of three or four campfires. In the distance, I thought I could see the Terminus, the massive retrofit "wall" that protected the citizens of the United States against the barbarians outside, or so we'd been told. The two-story high parapet was dotted with down-pointing lights, to illuminate the area below. Normal security, or were they expecting trouble? Spreading away from the Wall, small pinpricks of light picked out a shadowy trading area that seemed active even at night—the Mall of Pennsylvania. I stared around, remembering what I had first seen in daylight as I exited the railroad three days ago.

The first shock had been that it wasn't a wall so much as a line of walled-off blocks: on the inside, I had seen what I thought were buildings nestled right against the Wall, but when I turned to look outside, I saw they had simply bricked up the windows and doors of the rowhouses and then piled and mortared rubble in the streets and alleys between. Not pretty, but effective. And the next surprise was the Mall was actually a sprawl: at least 25 blocks square, dotted with the same brick row houses and warehouses, but these had windows draped with every item imaginable, and every flat field or lot was crammed with tents, awnings and temporary stalls.

Geoff had hurried me through it, after we'd picked up the bikes inside. I remembered the weird, barely intelligible chants that rose like a wave of noise from a horde standing beside the gates as we came through: "*tin pots, tiiiiin pots, shiny tin pots... Get yer wood bowls here—best in the West!... Elastic, really strong eeeelaaaaastic... lead solder, get yer lead solder here...*" Of a dozen who got off the train, we had been among seven leaving through the double-height, double-door Wall portal. The others scattered toward booths. We'd powered up the bikes and Geoff led me on a hair-raising path around burlap stalls, scrapwood booths, wood carts, oversize wheelbarrows and a throng of people who were *not* looking where they were going! Thank God for my messenger service years. In a lot of ways, this part of Pitts resembled Long Island slums, but still with an alien feel. We whizzed through a couple of blocks of intact rowhouses displaying clothing and fabric, then another several blocks of iron workers and scrap metal dealers—it must have been a huge job to haul in all the hanging and piled goods and to pack up the temporary table-booths each night, back into the houses or into covered carts that probably doubled as living quarters. These cart "homes" ranged from neat wooden caravans to ramshackle corrugated tin boxes barely large enough for two people to stretch out. Many brick buildings had ironwork grills on door and window and there were low growls and barking from unseen dogs. No entertainers visible. Those inspecting merchandise were stern-faced and I saw many hefty men and women whose stance screamed "bodyguard". There had been a few food booths and beer vendors, with no shortage of customers. It looked like a complete madhouse. I was relieved when Geoff located the ramp onto the elevated roadway and we were heading out of the Mall.

The clash of wood against metal brought me back. I stared at the preparations going on stealthily around me. Men with torches and lanterns raced back and forth, casting strange shadows and turning the cars into grotesque monstrosities. I was hearing more than seeing, but it was obvious they were moving fast, clearing the track in front of the train. Why had the City picked this spot to end the railway—why not keep going? It was disturbing to think I was at their last defensible outpost. In any case, I knew there was no gateway or passage for a train. Would the rebels be mad enough to try to break through with the engine? But that seemed exactly what they were planning, because I could hear the cars behind the engine being decoupled. The clink and tap of the hitch being removed, the sudden lurch of the engine forward just enough to be sure the cars wouldn't follow, and then the sound of rapid shoveling and steam building. They were gonna ram the wall! What did they hope to gain?? Then I remembered the soldier who said this was a feint—so perhaps they wouldn't carry it through? But why would one put such a valuable engine at risk if it wasn't going to do anything except distract the Army's attention? I suddenly realized in all the busy confusion, no one was keeping an eye on us. Wishing for my knife, I dug my fingers into the knots, tugging quietly but frantically. Slowly I untied myself from the scaffolding.

"Don't leave me here, Martin—I can help you get back to someplace safe," Geoff whispered urgently. I paused, considering. There was no way I was gonna trust that bastard again. Since the captain wasn't bloodthirsty, I assume they had tied us in a fairly safe area, but maybe they wouldn't *come* back. As rapidly and quietly as I could, I loosened a knot on one of Geoff's arms.

"Now get yourself out of that," I whispered. The moment he was free, he would abandon me or worse, try to kidnap me again.

"Bastard—I won't forget this," he hissed.

"You're welcome," I replied, and hurried away.

Even though I had my night vision, the bits of light were so erratic they almost made things worse. I threaded my way carefully across steel tracks and wood ties, around tipsy steel sheds, a few wheeled carts, some of which reeked of tar and worse. And I could swear I smell methane—so someone here had a fuel depot? I hadn't smelled that since the City. I banged up against a 50 gallon metal drum chained to a scrawny tree, and hurried away, my pulse pounding in my ears. I wanted to get close enough to see their next move from a safe viewpoint. About three blocks away, on the edge of the railyard, I noticed an outside steel stair zigzagging up a four-story brick building. Just like in the City, the bottom segment was folded upwards, but desperation gave me extra strength and I caught the bottom rung on my second try, hauled myself onto it, and continued up the rickety metal steps until I had reached the roof. From there, I had a glimpse of the Wall, or rather, the fans of light draped along the top like a golden banner, illuminating the brick barrier laid across the old rail lines. Dawn was starting to break beyond it in the east, as if the glory of the City was spreading toward us. The crowded angles of the outdoor market emerged from the shadows. In the stillness before the main traders woke, I could hear the engine clearly, and it crossed my mind that maybe those who were supposedly asleep were in fact waiting silently to see what might happen next. I heard the engine coughed into gear, at first slow but, by the time it got to where I could see it, going faster than my e-cycle could have gone at top speed—heading straight for the Wall with no sign of braking. I strained but I couldn't see anyone in the cabin—could they be sending this crewless? Or was this some kind of suicide mission? In less than a minute, the engine reached the Wall and hit it full on—smashing the bricks and toppling the upper portion onto the engine, which wedged into the gap. I shook my head. What had that gained them? The next moment a huge explosion blasted rubble, stone and metal everywhere.

17

I flattened myself, covering my head though I was blocks away. A large chunk of something whizzed by and dented the steel air vent in the middle of the roof. I squirmed nearer to the low ledge wall, propelled by instinct. Were they *totally* Trumpoid? After the echoes of the blast died down, I peered over and saw the squadron slamming wood planks across the rubble, climbing over the twisted wreckage of the engine and Wall, piling inside as fast as they could. Some feint! This had to be a declaration of war—but by who? Regardless, my hopes of getting safely to the City had collapsed with the Wall—even if I got inside, they would conscript every able man and woman as soon as they'd heard about it.

I leaned back against the ledge, taking deep breaths. The damp stone jutted against my right hip, and dampness seeped in through the wool pants. My ears were still wonky from the explosion, like hearing the world through a tin bathtub. I was Acme'd—the ground was gone and I was hanging in midair. In a heartbeat, my world upended: we weren't islands of civilization in a depopulated wilderness! I saw fortified, frightened cities, hoarding scraps of the past, playing Rocky but being Bullwinkle. And in the valleys and along the ridges, a different civilization was growing—with maybe a better chance to succeed. All of it so fragile that war could take it down, city and country alike.

I couldn't go back now, not to my old life. Could I? But where else? And ultimately—what for? My friends and I grabbed perks, playing the lotto of life for leftovers. Now even our dreams of comfortable serfdom might be desperate delusion—we'd be crushed as the silver spoons who already had as much as they needed warred with other silver spoons to get more.

Should I contact the office? Even at dawn there'd be a handful of workers. Surely they'd hear soon. But if this was top-level stuff, maybe the first they'd know about it would be a squad coming in to enforce a conscription order. I shuddered. This was worse than the deadly dance between Long Island gangs, cutting loose and praying I'd land safely in the next one. The phone rubbed against my hip. I fished it out of my pants and turned it on, figuring the noise, even if noticed, would be the least of someone's problems. As I waited, I thought *isn't it better to be free out here, with the admittedly slim hope of landing somewhere safer in the future?* Then the ever-present wedge of despair pierced me. I was getting old, still struggling too hard—what was I aiming for?

I remembered something Teg had said one night when we had chatted alone with a couple stolen beers, sour but potent. He didn't often shift from his attitude of amused cynicism, but that night he confided that what he most wanted was a spot somewhere in the City or the Island where he could make a difference. He'd prefaced it with the words, "this shows I haven't outgrown my childhood fantasies," and it sounded like a guilty secret. I remember asking what he meant by making a difference.

He was quiet for a long while, then shrugged. "I'd just like to know that my time on this earth had been noticed by someone, in a good way; that I wasn't just a bubble rising to the surface of the cesspit and popping, vanishing as if I'd never been there."

Infected by his sincerity, I'd babbled something about him already making a difference in my life, about how much it had helped me to learn some of history and to have an idea of the cycles of civilizations. I didn't dare tell him that his friendship, all by itself, had made a huge difference—*that* was giga taboo. But even so, I thought I saw his eyes tear up, and he looked away, then nodded. Nothing more was said about it.

Leaning against the cold concrete ledge, seeing my City threatened by someone mad enough to risk the gains so laboriously re-created, Teg's wish stirred deep in my heart. A saying of my great-uncle Lars—"you're not really dead until you are completely forgotten"—came to mind. At this rate, I'd be dead the moment my heart stopped. Maybe a week later. I'd rejected my family's military devotion to the City, and I still thought their zeal was misplaced, but it must be a comfort to believe your life was making a contribution.

All this actually went by in a couple of breaths, as dawn grew brighter. I checked the phone and was thrilled to see full connection—but the battery was almost dead. I hesitated. What would I tell anyone? This close to the Wall, could they just reach out and grab me? The City had a nasty—and insistent—way of asking questions. After an agonizing moment, I turned the phone off, stuffed it into my pants pocket, and peered over the ledge. Most of the brick or concrete buildings were one or two stories; at least half were empty shells. One took up an entire block, roof-less but solid—a walled farm or corral? I looked beyond them. The Terminus Wall met the elevated highway at an odd angle about eight blocks away, forming a branch wall, since the highway was bricked up beneath, just like the Els cris-crossing Long Island. It hid the river that must be on the far side. On a distant hill, probably across the river, I noticed a half dozen broken skyscrapers like jagged teeth—was Pittsburgh that big a city? Or rather—*had* it been? Because those towers looked totally abandoned. The rising sun hit the pillars and no glass winked back. Pittsburgh was just a name to me, like DC or Chicago—I'd never really thought about its size or fate. Honestly, my world had been no bigger than the City and surrounds—it was dawning on me that this country was fucking *huge*.

The clash of metal brought my attention back to the streets below: I saw a small battle just outside the gap in the Wall and people on foot below me, a few pulling tiny carts, heading westward like a line of spiders trickling out of a building that was just starting to burn. I had seen *that* once before—it was unsettling how they knew and responded to danger. Looked like there was a similar instinct in humans. I wondered how those inside the Wall were managing, with no option to fade into the countryside. Where could *they* go to hide?

I weighed my narrowing choices. It was dangerous to go inside or call right now. Maybe I could call or text Cheyenne later, after things had "ripened" a bit, and feign innocence, see how things stood. And in any case, I wanted to make sure Ciera and her crew would be okay before I went back. I thought of this morning—yesterday morning now—how waking up beside her had filled me with a glow that was more than just good sex. Ciera had wanted to find out how this battle would affect them. Okay. Ambridge was supposedly only 15 miles north, so I could grab a bicycle or if the worst happened, I could walk back with the info. Now I wanted a better weapon, and to avoid that battle. I scanned the area, made a mental map, decided on a block to aim for, and climbed down the staircase, dropping to the street and managing to stay on my feet.

The Mall was now as busy as a knocked-over anthill, full of people intent on gathering enough to flee or protecting what was left. Some were muttering to each other, but most were grimly silent. Everyone leaving was on foot, and I wondered if the rebels *had* taken all the vehicles, like Troy had said. No one even glanced my way as I threaded through them, looking around for a decent club or miraculously abandoned gun. Street signs had been recycled, not that I knew what streets to look for. I did find a bit of 2 x 4 leaning against a wall and deftly scooped it up as I hurried by, but kept looking as I moved into what seemed to be the metalworkers area. There was a lot more iron on the windows and doors, and some ornate light fixtures on the brick buildings.

Many of the brick walls bore the unmistakable signs of fire—if that charring had happened all at once, the blaze must have been enormous. The acrid tang of scorching permeated the street. How long did the odor of a big fire last? I decided it must be the metalworkers' forges. The area looked like it had been lived in for years. There were more glassed windows than in Ambridge, and those wouldn't have survived a fire. I noticed patterned fabric curtains, and a few windows had trifles dangling—like a painted wooden rooster, or giant hand with one finger pointing up. By one set of concrete steps, there was a new iron hitching post with the top shaped like a horse's head.

Finally, a block away, I saw a metal-caged cart being plundered: a small crowd formed and reformed as people leaned in past a dislodged grill, grabbed something and hurried away. They passed me carrying swords, knives and hooks. I wriggled between two scrawny leather-clad boys no more than 12, spotted a large butcher's knife and lunged for it before one of them could snatch it. Then I raced away without looking back. One task accomplished.

Reluctantly, I turned my steps back toward the unhitched cars and the rebel camp. For a few blocks, I was going with the flow of refugees as they followed the walled highway 65, forming a second wave of refugees that would hit Ambridge tomorrow. Then the buildings ended and the rail yard began. It stretched for eight or ten blocks vaguely parallel to the highway, and behind it was a steep hilly wilderness of shrubs and gnarled trees. Now that the sun was up over the Wall, shafting through the narrow streets from behind me, I could see abandoned rail cars dotting the tracks, mostly converted into housing or shops, now deserted. They gave me a bit of cover as

I crept closer. The overnight campfires had been dowsed. How many soldiers would be left to guard? Glancing around the end of a flaking, royal blue steel boxcar, I saw a young soldier walking my way, waving back at his fellows. I held my breath, listening as he strolled jauntily toward me, maybe looking for a private place to pee. As he rounded the car, I grabbed him with one arm around his chest, pinning his arms, and held the knife to his throat.

"Don't fight me!" I hissed. "I just want information. If you tell me what I need to know, I'll let you go, okay?"

He stopped wriggling. "What d' you wanna know? I'm not gunna give away secrets," he added, with a touch of defiance, ruined by his next line. "I dun' know enny, act'lly."

"Tell me where you're from."

"Me? Car'lina, origin'lly. But I've been livin' in Lil Virginia, at Fort Cumberlan'."

I pondered that. It confirmed the southern origins, and maybe where the railroad came through.

"I know you're just a private, but do you know where you travelled through to get here? I'm not with the other army," I added. "I'm just a citizen back near the Ohio, trying to decide how much trouble I'm in." I let the knife touch his throat as an added incentive, though I doubted I could use it on a kid of about 14.

He was silent a moment, then said, "I only know we marched through a cuppla forests, bivouacked at Connellsville, marched no'th for a while, past what usta be a big airpo't—there's a couple of huge planes sittin' there! Bigger 'n houses! Then we got to th' river—th' Ohiya, I guess—and crossed a real rickety railroad bridge, had to go single file, and then met up with the railroad train in a big yard and rode south agin. I don't know the towns."

Not very helpful, but what could I expect? I tried to memorize his response, in case it was useful to Ciera's group.

"Were you ordered to take over the towns you passed through?" I asked.

"No, we weren't that many—" he stopped, as if unwilling to give numbers. "It didn't 'zactly make sense t' me, traveling that far, the long way 'round, but they don't tell me nuthing."

"That makes two of us, brother. Alright," I said. "Lay face down and count ten, and then get back to your group." I could tell he'd already had his pee. He scrambled down to the ground and I left at a run. I dodged around a few flatbed cars, and skidded around a tanker, then headed back into the maze of shops and tents.

I paused in a doorway to think. That hadn't given me enough, but my gut was telling me I didn't have the courage to steal a uniform to pass myself off. One night trussed up was enough. Obviously there was no picking up gossip from these oh-so-silent residents. But there *had* to be more clues here—they picked this place to start a war. I didn't want to go back empty-handed!

I stepped out of the doorway. It was amazing how quiet the town was. Grim-faced, people were dismantling what they could of their homes, filling wooden crates and rough-wove bags; grabbing jars, clothing, hand tools, with no hesitation. I wondered if they'd had to do this before. Even the dogs had been muzzled, or were trained to be silent. A hunched, scrawny black man about twice my age pulled hammers and pliers from a display board in front of his square canvas hut, untwisting wire quickly and plucking the tools into a dirty canvas bag, hefting it now and then to test the weight. A pre-teen girl two sheds down was trying to stuff a couple chickens into a wickerwork cage—they weren't cooperating, but even they weren't squawking. The silence was unnerving. I paused to breathe deeply; it felt like I couldn't get enough air. Once, a huge hurricane swept through Long Island, wind and flood grabbing at everything we owned. Only seven, I'd thought the world was ending. Now, watching that engine blow up the wall—what if madmen were in charge? All of *my* plans had been based on the people in charge being sane and having enough self-preservation to keep the cities stable.

I walked randomly, letting the crowd steer me, alert for any hint of an explanation. What did I own to barter for info? Nothing, since I'd left it all with Ciera, expecting to be back within the hour. I wonder what she thought of me now? *Almost* nothing, I amended. The phone in my pocket must be worth a small fortune out here. I paused inside another doorway, a concrete alcove that stank of piss. I tucked the butcher knife in the rope belt at my back and massaged cramp from my hands. Fatigue was making me stupid. One part of me was screaming that civilization was a few blocks away—and another part remembering how well the City enforced its rules.

I'd been happy to go along with its stupid regulations because it gave me the 3R's: refuge, rations, recreation. Now I wanted to know what they didn't want to tell me. Maybe I needed to treat it more like a slum boss, one of the biggest.

And maybe that's all it was. The sudden thought turned me cold. *Were* the cities just large tribes, as arbitrary and arrogant as Artaud or big Lulu? I shook my head. *Focus*! All I needed now was some background information on this battle, and a status update indicating where the danger was. Surely, among all of these fleeing people, there was someone who had some information. Or maybe I should ask the ones who weren't fleeing.

The sun was lifting above the buildings now, causing steam to rise from damp brick and cobbled streets. Looking more carefully, I saw maybe a third of the citizens were packing to remain in place, barricading their building or carts, some of them stashing goods down open trap doors. I wondered how extensive the cellars were around here. Big enough to hide in? Apparently not, or why would so many flee?

I racked my brains, trying to remember any stray bits I'd learned about this hinterland. We were told these outer citizens were trying to earn their way closer to the City by being useful—salvaging from nearby wilderness, slaving in the workshops that made things like leather or cheese that was brought in by train. As I'd told Ciera's group, each train had many freight cars but only one passenger car. It took an extraordinary event for a regular citizen to travel either direction. Melinda told me they sometimes organized field trips for the small town officials, who would bring back enthusiasm and push their citizens harder. And I vaguely remembered such clumps of poorly-dressed, awestruck folks, blocking traffic as they stared upward at our towers. *Our*—I was doing it again—I was *not* part of "we the City", especially not now! I'd never felt part of it, despite the constant boosterism that filled the news, the windows of the shops and the speeches of our bosses. *Progress, progress, progress*—I'd always known it was too good to be true, only I'd had no idea how big the lies were.

The sound of crackling, metallic voices coming from a gray brick rowhouse slowed me. It sounded like the ham-op the rebels had. Cautiously, I sidled up to the middle house of the triplex and peered into a streaky glass window, past pale blue curtains. A knot of men and women were huddled around a table on which rested a small box with dials; they were listening intently. It was too garbled for me to catch the words and I gnawed my lip in frustration. Could I risk asking for help? My concentration flickered like the sounds, broken by thirst and a gnawing hunger. I massaged my gut.

"Have a problem, friend?" The speaker behind me suggested that I certainly did now. His voice was deep and throaty.

Without moving, I replied, "I just wanted to see where not to run—where the danger was centered. If they know. I have other info about the rebels."

"*Do* you now? Better come inside."

Smooth as a pickpocket, he snatched the butchers knife from where I'd tucked it. Stepping away and to my side, he knocked on the door with a long staff he was carrying. The end of the polished wood was tipped with brass, easily able to kill. A teen girl opened the door. Slowly I crossed the threshold, making sure my hands were visible, praying I had enough info to trade.

It was a large-ish multipurpose room, with the kitchen area—sink, woodstove, shelf/cupboard unit—at the back through a large arched doorway, a worn black couch and Bentwood rocker off to the right, and an ornate dark wood table in the center. As a middle rowhouse, it only had windows back and front, but a small light tube came down mid-ceiling to prevent it from being a cave. To the left was a closed door under stairs that led upward. The walls' floral paper was faded to a ghostly lavender; fancy ceiling trim was flaking azure over white. Definitely an attempt at elegance; I was reminded of the graceful lines of my old apartment. They used to build really well.

Five people ranging in age from teen to senior, none of them looking overfed, gathered around the table: a gray-haired old guy, a short middle-aged woman with caramel-toned skin and black hair tucked up in a blue patterned scarf, two tall swarthy men who looked like brothers sharing some Mediterranean background, and the slip of an Asian girl with coal black eyes and ebony hair to her shoulders who had opened the door. From behind my forced smile, I studied them for danger signals. For a few minutes, no one said anything, though they stared at me. Every ear was focused on the squawking box. "*...the wall, and ...squad inside...*" And then a metallic shriek and a different voice: "*Bring troops back out, head south ... –oats near the West End Bridge and regroup in Mount Oli–. Check in again 30 minutes. Is that clear?*" The first voice responded, "*Clear.*" And then the radio fell silent.

The group straightened up and turned to me and my captor. Glancing over my shoulder, I was startled to see it was a short young man of about 17, thin as a twig. Obviously his voice was the biggest thing about him. "I found him outside," he told the others in the deep baritone.

"My name's Martin," I said quickly, "the rebels had been holding me on their train until we got here, and then I escaped. I'm just trying to find out enough to avoid walking into trouble again."

One brother grinned ironically, as if I already had. The woman, who wore a modern tunic several years old and a tan wool skirt that hung around her ankles, looked me over carefully and asked, "Why did they hold you captive?"

"Some other guy accused me—thought I was a spy—I convinced them I wasn't. But then they didn't want me out to spoil the surprise."

"Why not kill you?" the baritone asked.

I shrugged. "Sounds like their leader is an honorable man, says he doesn't kill innocent unarmed people."

"That's a relief," one of the brothers commented, "though it sounds like they're leaving pretty quick." He was wearing an antique navy suit jacket a bit too short in the sleeves, an old button-front white shirt and baggy blue trousers with an angled button front flap. His nose was as straight and sharp as a chicken beak, and his curly hair was charcoal black. His brother wore the more common leather jacket and patched jeans garb.

"I overheard one officer saying that this is just a distraction, a feint—that the main whatever is somewhere else," I said.

The brothers exchanged glances and one commented softly, "Then it's true, what Russ said." The other shrugged and shook his head, obviously not convinced.

"I'm from back by the Beaver River, in Horseferry," I said, keeping part of my story. "I just wanted to know how far the danger zone is. They came down through Ambridge along the rails, though no one had any clue that they were north of us. Do you think they have a lot of equipment? How could they just blow up an engine like that?"

The woman said, "We wondered about that, too. In any case, it's obvious we need to get away from here."

"Is it, Zara?" The eldest man, who'd been quiet up to now, stood with his arms crossed, one finger stroking the thin gray mustache over his lip. His red linen shirt was faded from washing and his brown trousers had a knee patch, but he had a gold ring on his pinky. "If they are leaving as fast as they came, either the Army will be following them quickly, or it will be patching the hole. It won't have time to spare for us."

"I agree," said the baritone with that aggressive importance that only young men imagine themselves to have. "We might have to suspend trading for a little while, but surely the big battle is up along the line near Harrisburg, and they'll just patch this hole, maybe put an extra guard or two along the wall. But they don't have much more." The others nodded.

I sagged in relief. It made sense that the people living in the gap between two worlds would be aware of military strength. Slum lords searched out each other's weaknesses, and those unfortunates who were subject to the lords' whims searched even more acutely, while their own underdog plans were overlooked. Arrogance would likely be the same on whatever level this played out.

"I don't know if you trade up to Ambridge or with any of the groups beyond, but I know they rely on this area for supplies—I want to help. What can I tell them—what do you suggest they do until this blows over? *Will* it blow over?"

The older man sucked his teeth thoughtfully—the others looked like they were about to speak but waited; so he had the authority. While he was thinking, one of the brothers went back to the kitchen dresser and pulled out a tray of flatbread, then reached into a small wooden box for a ceramic pitcher, bring them back to the table. I heard my stomach growl and clenched my arms over my gut to silence it. Half smiling, the woman gestured with her mug and asked if I would like a drink and a bit of bread, and I nodded enthusiastically. Thank goodness for this outsider hospitality ritual! She went back to the cabinet and brought over a ceramic cup, gray with elegant blue dripped glazing. The other mugs were equally well made, obviously pre-Adjustment. In fact, the whole room reflected moderate wealth, albeit salvaged. The man with the pitcher filled each of our mugs with what turned out to be a delicious pale ale. The flatbread was crispy and I devoured it in four bites, slightly embarrassed, but what can you do?

"The big question is," the old man started, "how much territory can the Southerners hang onto?" There were nods as he continued, "It's one thing to override a territory—any half-assed wave can flood a beach—it's another thing to stay put. This has the feel of an opening in negotiations, not an invasion." He talked as if he were retired military, and I wondered how many outside the Wall had been trained like my parents and relatives.

"The problem is—if you're wrong about that," I noticed the others slightly leaning away from the brother who spoke—"we stand to lose even more than just our homes."

"Leave then, Asrah," the old man replied impatiently. "We will do what we can to protect your place and position."

Asrah jolted as if he'd been slapped. He scowled and shook his head.

"I'm wondering if it's worth trying the tunnels," the old guy muttered, half to himself. "If they know about them, we'd be screwed. If not, it's worth finding out what's going on inside."

I held my breath. Was he talking about tunnels *under the Wall*? I thought of all of my clothes and gear still up in Ambridge, stuff that would've helped me fade right into the inner town. Getting in without alerting the border guards might be worth it. Now I regretted having told them I was from Horseferry—but I couldn't confess to being a citizen. Not until I knew their position.

"What could we learn there that we can't learn here, Justin?" the other brother asked. Zara carefully placed a cover on the radio, carried it to the couch area and tucked it into a hole in the wall, then replaced a panel, seamlessly.

"For one thing," the old guy replied, "we could find out if they took anything—or anybody—back with them. Was it simply a scare tactic, or did they have a mission?"

The group was silent, each deep in their own thoughts, and I could hear the continued exodus outside, the shuffling of many feet on concrete, the occasional clang or crash. I clamped down on my excitement. These folks had information—would they let me walk away with some of it? Now that I knew there were tunnels, could I find them on my own? Between hunger and fatigue, my mind kept blanking like a computer screen flickering on and off. Stick with them, I decided—if they'd let me. So I needed to convince them.

"While I was captive, I heard one of the soldiers saying he was from Carolina, wherever that is. And he said they stayed at a fort in Connellsville in someplace called Little Virginia."

Justin looked at me with interest. "Little Virginia was once West Virginia—it's just south of us. Carolina's much further south—that means they're pulling people from quite a distance. This might be bigger than we thought." He tugged at his mustache, then turned to the young girl. "Mare, will you go to Aida's forge and see if Elontee has come back with information? " He turned to me. "You said they came down from the north? And nobody knew?"

I nodded. "There were rumors that somebody was commandeering horses and carts from around Ambridge all the way down to the Mall—but I wasn't paying much attention. And there were a lot of people coming North from here, either kicked out or leaving ahead of the problem. We all thought it was local rebels, though—and I didn't hear *anything* about a train. Until it arrived. And then they grabbed me to help carry their booty."

The girl scurried out the door as I was speaking, and the atmosphere changed subtly. Zara pulled a pair of flattish pistols from a drawer in the table, tucked one in her skirt pocket, and handed the other to the old man. Two brothers patted their jackets, as if reassuring themselves. This group was prepared for *something*.

While she was searching in a drawer, coming up with some ammunition, Zara commented, "There *is* a local group of idiots who think they can step on Army toes without being crushed. They had been clearing folks out of the area the Southerners now occupy. I think they just found out that they're in over their heads."

Something like a snort of laughter came from Asrah. "A pox on them for stirring up a hornet's nest. I hope they get to take the blame."

"But the Army won't know the difference between them and us—that's the problem!" his brother exclaimed.

"Zir, the Army won't have the time or manpower to worry about it," Justin said impatiently. "They've just found out there's somebody who can blow up their wall, who has trains, and who apparently struck in at least two places. Who do you think they're gonna be focused on?"

Zir nodded reluctantly. "But they might grab some of us to see what we know," he mumbled stubbornly.

"We'll just have to keep on our toes," Zara said. "Though I'm sure it's something the General will be taking advantage of." She smiled in approval and the old man smiled also. The brothers didn't look impressed. "I guess that means our book club is canceled today," she added with a bigger grin.

"Good. I thought Brothers Karamazov was really boring," Justin commented. "Just because it was the only thing we could get six copies of is no reason to waste time on it. But I hope Mick's veggie cart gets through."

"Maybe I could go down to Hamlin and catch it," Zara mused. "There's only going to be early coles and old potatoes anyway."

"Don't grumble because it's not vat—we'll need everything just in case they cut supply lines." Justin responded.

Book clubs and vat food—it sounded more like the City. Hope surged. Maybe they wouldn't take it too hard if I revealed… but wait on that for a while.

Zir went to the window and glanced out. "So what now?" He asked. "I hate waiting."

"War is mostly waiting," Justin replied. "And one way or another, this is war. New York is not going to tolerate this level of challenge. Miller told me they'd baited a trap further out in Ohio—I wonder if they caught anything that far out?"

I tried to keep my face neutral—could they be talking about me?? Or maybe I wasn't the only one sent out. If they were looking to see how far the Southerners had intruded, maybe they sent a couple of us poor suckers to various areas. It was getting way too complex. I needed to focus on safety and information, in that order. But a rebellious part of my mind kept distracting me with images of my apartment, with my hard-won trinkets like the half-melted Duke Ellington record, two brittle watercolors, the cobalt blue bottle that the seller swore was Revolutionary War surplus and an old leather baseball glove with *Spaulding* burned into the palm—all of them useless and yet…And what if I never saw Finnigan or Ramsaur again? Or Melinda? The thought of *never* going back was short-circuiting my thinking.

The two brothers had their heads together, murmuring. Now Zir turned to Justin and said, "We're going to check on today's delivery. It probably got held up, but if not, I'd hate to miss it. And maybe there's word from Natrona." He glanced at me, obviously not wanting to say more in front of me. Justin nodded, and the brothers left.

"So what are you going to do now?" Zara asked and I realized she was speaking to me.

I grimaced and answered honestly, “I have no idea. I’m really torn—part of me wants to just go home, and part wants to find out something worthwhile.” I didn’t mention which home I was thinking of.

“Well, you can stay here a while, and we might be getting some information you can bring back—where was it again?”

“Horseferry”, I said slowly, sensing that she was suspicious.

The 17-year-old protested, “you don’t even know his family!”

That was it! I’d forgotten about the litany of connections that was always exchanged. I frowned and quickly said “Engel band, I’m… husband of Ciera Engel.” Frantically, I tried to think of all of the other names she had dropped, but my mind was blank.

“Morris, could you go and get those vegetables before someone else decides to hoard them?” Zara asked, not taking her eyes off me. The 17-year-old mumbled some protest, but left quickly. We eyed each other for a few moments in silence.

“Where are you really from?” she asked quietly. There was no threat in her voice, but there was a gun in her belt.

“From the City,” I admitted, “in fact, I might have been that bait you talked about a moment ago.”

Justin harrumphed behind me, and Zara nodded. “I knew you looked too pale—you’re an insider, no question.”

So *that* was how they could all tell—I hadn’t thought about my skin tones, how sitting at a desk all day would definitely look different from working outside.

I raised my hands palm up. “I had been sent out, I *thought*, to arrange for some new communication towers. But on the third day out, my guide tried to kidnap me, and I’ve been trying to figure out what’s been going on ever since. The Engels helped me, but I’m not part of their clan.”

“You know you can get in big trouble claiming a tribe out here,” Justin mentioned dryly. He pulled out a chair and sat at the table, resting his elbows and staring up at me.

“No, I didn’t—that’s one of the many, many things that I don’t know about out here,” I said with a grimace. “It’s been a real education.”

Zara chuckled. “I’ll bet it has. And you’re still alive, so you’re doing pretty well.”

“More lucky than anything else,” I said. I thought hard—if they had tunnels, and had been inside, maybe I could safely scout, see how hot it would be for me. "If you'd like me to help, I'd go with you inside– I probably could find out more, because I have city credit and a citizens pass." I would have to use them carefully to avoid conscription. Having an escape route would help.

As I suspected, they didn't jump at my offer. Zara looked at me thoughtfully, and Justin sat back in the chair, stroking his mustache, looking at the window but, I suspected, seeing much further away.

I had never done well with others' silence; after a moment, I continued, "I've been out here only a couple of days, and I'm already realizing that what they tell us inside is half of the truth, at best. Before I spent my days as a paper pusher, I fought my way through the slums of Long Island, and managed to survive in several slumlord gangs. But that wasn't as difficult as this is."

Justin glanced away from the window. "So you know about loyalty to tribe?"

"Noooo....," I dropped my gaze. "In fact, the gangs were a great example of looking out for yourself. Yeah, we had to obey the slum boss, but each of us knew that the others would grab any advantage, and though in a fight we would watch each other's backs, there wasn't anything like trust, not that I remember. And then I got the City, where it definitely was shark eat shark, and look out for Number One."

He didn't reply, and once again I felt forced to fill the silence. "I've been impressed by out here—confused, but impressed."

At that, Justin snorted, kind of a laugh. "My ex-wife was from the City," he said, glancing at me. "I used to live north of Allentown, where there's a little overlap. We met on—I guess you would call it a raid." He grinned. "I guess it wasn't City proper, more like north of the City; used to be Bronx."

"That's all the factories and...prisons," I said, slowing as I realized what I might be saying.

Another snort. "Yeah—she didn't much like the factories—said there wasn't much difference between them and the prisons. She really liked it out here for a while." His voice grew softer and he looked down. "But she never got the hang of trust, either."

"Who was this group you were with back in Horseferry?" Zara interrupted.

"After the guide turned on me, and I got away, I met a member of the Engel band, and followed her to Ambridge. She said her town was self-sufficient, but on rare occasions came down to the Mall." I left off the detail about the red uniforms, until I knew I wasn't putting them in danger.

"Oh—refuseniks," she said.

"What??"

Zara shrugged, and waved her hand like brushing a fly away. "There's a bunch of survivors who have turned their back on everything the cities offer. Or so they say. We call them that because they are refusing to integrate. There's a lot about the City that's bad, but I still think they might be our only hope."

I tried to wrap my mind around yet another point of view—more like what I'd imagined the outside to be, but now hard to fit into the puzzle.

"Zara, just because they've tried to re-localize doesn't mean they're anti-civilization," Justin said.

She pulled the mugs from the table and walked them to the sink. "They think they can go it alone—wait 'til they get to the bottom of the salvage piles."

"They're farther out than us. Makes sense to have the basics nearby. Remember that blizzard two years back? No one could've gotten farther than a couple miles from home."

"Except for that crazy guy on the dogsled," she chuckled. "I about fell over to see a couple big dogs dragging a toboggan—piled as high as it could go, too...Do you think you can find out what's going on for us in there?" Zara asked me, abruptly.

"I—I left my city clothes, and money back with the Engels, but I can prove I'm a citizen, and I can tell what's different by looking. Our towns are pretty standard, you know," I replied. "I want to know what's going on too, and if you help me get in, I'll share whatever I find with you."

"And then stay inside?" Zara sounded doubtful.

That, of course, was the $64 billion question—where was I safest? Where did I belong? I shook my head. "I…I don't think I'll stay. Firstly, they won't be happy with me for messing up the job, and second, if it wasn't a legitimate job—if I was just bait—they won't want to see me walk back into the City." I was sorting it out as I spoke, and realized it was the simple truth. Unless I wanted to play the stupid innocent victim, and forever keep mum about my real adventures, I needed to find an answer that was more workable. That, and conscription could even nail oldsters like me.

And it came down to who had acted to help me, and who had treated me like a disposable. Loyalty had to be earned. I fumbled in my pocket, and pulled out the phone. "I'm not that familiar with what-all it can do, but as a sign of trust, I'll share this phone with you, if it helps." I held it out to them.

18

Justin sat up straight and Zara came over, staring suspiciously. She glanced at Justin, then slowly took the phone and examined it. "I've seen these city phones," she said. "It's like a portable radio."

"No, it's a satellite cellphone," I said, then remembered what Geoff had said—was it really just another form of ham-op? "It's really low battery, though."

Justin took the phone from Zara and opened it as if he'd handled one before. Examining it closely without turning it on, he said, "it's a fancy one, but it's a short-wave radio. I might be able to find a charger for it. Do you still believe in satellites?" He asked as if he was talking about elves. I felt my cheeks get hot. I shrugged.

"I...I used to," I replied. "Now I don't know what to believe." If we didn't have satellites, how were we talking to Los Angeles? But did I know for a fact we *were* talking to Los Angeles?? But why would they want to *fake* that? This was really looking like that mu-vid where the pigtailed girl pulled back a curtain and the big wizard was an oily snake salesman. "I just used to do my job, and as long as they fed me three meals, and gave me a place to live…" I realized how puny that sounded. I shrugged, feeling my face get hotter.

Justin looked at me with a slight smile on his face. "You know, most of us are just trying to survive now that everything's falling apart," he said softly. "We just try to find the things that work, and keep doing them—and hope they don't stop working. Maybe not a noble philosophy, but a workable one."

Zara gave a sound between a snort and a raspberry. She ran quickly upstairs and came down with a bundle—I was surprised to see modern tunics and pants. After a moment, I realized I shouldn't be; if they were going to go inside, they certainly couldn't go dressed as they were. I looked down at my own clothes and grimaced. I hoped she had something in my size.

"When in Rome..." she said, sorting the pile on the table. "It can be tricky, living on the border. We've got one foot in each world. Neither fish nor fowl, as my grandmother used to say."

I wondered what Rome had to do with it, but I'd heard the other saying from an old man who lived on the road near school. He was a defrocked priest and trader in scrap glass, describing himself as neither fish nor fowl on the few times that I had found—or filched—some glass to sell him. I accepted a gray tunic and black pants in good repair and probably no more than three years old. The collars had changed slightly in recent years, but out here in the far-flungs probably nobody would notice.

"One thing," I said with a bit of embarrassment, "it, um, unfortunately it's been three days since I've had more than a tiny chance to wash up. And I'm afraid I wouldn't pass inside, as rank as I am right now."

"You're right that they're pickier inside," Zara agreed. "And you're in luck—we actually have a shower." Her pride was evident, and with good reason—showers were a luxury item in the City—our company had a superb locker room. Hot showers were available once a week, and I took full advantage. But I was used to scrubbing up in the sink. "I guess you could call the water lukewarm, but it's definitely not cold," she said, as if not wanting to disparage her bit of luxury.

Justin directed me to a walled-off section of the back porch, overlooking a small garden with a chicken coop crammed in one corner, and a wickerwork fence with a few broken limbs at the back. The alcove was just big enough to shed my clothes onto a straightback chair and step under a wide metal shower head. He instructed me to pull the lever under the shower head just long enough to get wet, then turn it off, soap up, and rinse off. Given that the day was brisk, I knew I wouldn't be standing in there long. But even a cold shower would feel good, grimy as I was.

He handed me a pile of new clothes, and I was grateful to see that underwear was included. In Ciera's world, I must be in debt up to my eyeballs now. I turned to put the new clothes carefully on the seat of the chair.

"Before you put the shirt on, put this under." He was holding a sleeveless tunic made of small squares of leather sewn together so they would bend. A shirt of armor! I flashed on the cobbled-together slum armor—bits of leather, tin, wood... anything that would deflect a blow—but that was worn on the outside, and some of it decorated to make it look more macho. Especially the helmets. I accepted it with enthusiastic thanks; it was at least as valuable as my phone.

"It's my specialty," he said proudly. "By day I'm just a cobbler, but after hours…" He grinned and patted the armor. "Everybody in the City wants my stuff."

More like everyone in the slums, but I didn't want to tell him that. On the other hand, how did I know if citizens were wearing armor under their tunics? It hadn't occurred to me before.

He handed me a towel, I thanked him again, and he left me alone to get on with it.

She had been right about the temperature of the water—it wasn't shocking, but there was no temptation to linger. I figured it must be from an overhead tank, and if they were using passive solar, the recent gray weather wouldn't have been helpful. I sluiced off the grime and felt energized by the cold. Toweling hurriedly, I noticed the various bruises and scrapes—I hadn't been this purpled in a decade. But I was still alive, and near to civilization, and maybe nearer to finding out what I had gotten dumped into.

As I came back inside the house, Justin walked over from the stove, took the wet towel and asked, "It's your call, but do you want to shave, too?" He gestured for me to leave my old clothes in the corner on a box.

I blinked—how stupid was it to have forgotten that? "Of course—" I started, then hesitated.

He nodded at my expression, and said, "Yeah, it's tough on the edge—I keep my beard neatly trimmed, and there are several inside who have semi-variations: mustache or goatee, or something. If you shave now, when you come back out you'll stand out over here."

And even more so up in Ambridge. I fingered the coarse but full black beard on my chin. How weird to have something as simple as facial hair be such a problem! In the City, I'd operated on autopilot, no worry at all that I would stand out.

"Ah...I think I'll leave it for now," I said.

"Probably a good call—it's such a pain to keep it shaved."

As we were chatting, Mare arrived breathlessly. She paused in the doorway, opened her mouth to speak, but at a signal from Zara, followed the woman to the sink corner where they spoke in whispers. Justin glanced at me and I nodded. Of course they wouldn't trust a total stranger; I was glad they were letting me join them inside. I wandered out to the sitting area, pretending to study a picture on the wall, waiting until the conversation ended. It occurred to me they might have plans to silence me after I helped them, but I couldn't see this couple as coldhearted murderers. Could book club members also plot deliberate assassination? What were my officemates doing now? Why did those two ideas come out together? Was Cheyenne young enough to be snagged for conscription? Such random thoughts tumbled in and around my almost physical awareness that time was passing and I was no further toward my goal. *Should* I strike out on my own?

Just then, Zara patted the girl on the shoulder and sent her away again. "It looks like Jontee is scrambling—knowing the Army has ID'd some of them, he's pulling out troops and heading west," she told Justin.

"West?? Out toward Ohio?" Whoever Jontee was, he wouldn't be good news for Ciera's group.

She glanced at me. "There'll be folks watching out for him and his gang. Seems to me you'd be better off bringing back as much of the story as you can."

Obviously, she could see right through me and/or read my thoughts—I'd had some aunts who were like that. Aunt Gracie, in particular, always seem to know my plan before I did.

"Yes, well…then we'd better go before the news dries up. I know citizens—the first buzz doesn't last long."

"Alright, but you need to remember to follow our lead. We don't want to compromise any..."

"Friends. Yes, I know. I'll follow you." I hoped that my urge to be home didn't totally overwhelm me once we were inside the Wall.

We wore old-fashioned baggy canvas coats over the modern clothes, which made me wonder how many people out here actually knew about the tunnels. Was this a small group, and were they connected with the rebels? Zara hadn't sounded impressed by them, so perhaps not. But there could be different rebel bands.

We left their house and Justin led us south, toward the bricked-in highway. The exodus had slowed, but the tide was definitely against us. They nodded and waved to various people as we strolled along, and Zara even slowed to check out an item someone was bundling away—I wasn't sure if it was an act or if they really didn't feel any urgency. But my impatience was growing like carbonation in a bottle, and it wouldn't be too long before it popped. Many buildings were still ruins, ivy growing up the wall and trash—once an old junk car—stuffed into the doorways.

"That's Asrah's and Zir's place," Justin commented as we passed a huge, block-long brick warehouse. There were no doors or windows on this side, and I wondered what they stored, but no point screwing this fragile link with useless questions.

We moved through what looked like the food market, though most shops were closed. Still, a medley of pleasing odors threaded through the overall tang of dirt, animals and un-identified burned objects. A green ribbon or strip of red was hung on several doorknobs, and when she saw me looking, Zara commented, "Green means they're open but you have to knock." Normal? Or another sign of caution? I shook my head and psyched myself up to enter the real town in a few minutes.

We were at least ten blocks away from the gap caused by the engine, on a street that reeked of sawdust, varnish and fresh wood. One shop—square blocks of concrete, spattered with old graffiti—had one boarded window and one open window with a plank counter. Blonde wood bowls, plates and spoons were laid out like treasures. Another three-sided corrugated hut displayed painted shelves and small chests. I had a wild urge to bring back a wooden bracelet as a trinket for Melinda, then shook myself—totally LOLkatz! Panic did that to my mind sometimes. A crowd still lingered here, men and women in sleek leggings and green cotton tunics, some embroidered with the popular meandering braid pattern—the first hint of civilization. They were gathered in clumps, arms crossed, watchful, speaking in quiet voices. One group clustered around a man speaking rapidly and gesturing broadly, his voice not audible. We had passed someone who had a guard's alertness. He'd nodded, but now I doubted I'd have been let through on my own.

Justin led us to a newish two-story gray clapboard house with shuttered windows and a windowless steel front door that looked totally out of place. The steps to the porch were rickety, needing repair, and there was a young man with broad shoulders sitting on a straightback chair by the door, whittling something and whistling tunelessly. His face was lumpy and pitted as if he'd survived some kind of pox. He glanced at us as we walked up, nodded at Justin, then stood and opened the door for us. As I stepped inside, I wondered where his weapon was. Or was it more a question of "go in and never come back out"? I didn't dare look around.

We were in a small living room that felt abandoned even though it was furnished: lumpy brown sofa, twin end tables and an oil lamp, even a dusty braided rug. It felt like a stage set, so I wasn't surprised when Justin and Zara shrugged out of their coats—I hurried to follow—and Justin picked up the lamp, then led us down a hall into the kitchen. This had more sense of being used; a dirty mug sat in the sink. Zara opened a small box from the counter. Striking a strip of metal onto a gray stone, she got a spark to flare in some curled sawdust as neatly as a master tinderer. She lit the oil lamp and Justin led the way down some back stairs. My throat was dry as we descended the creaky wooden steps, and I told myself it was the dust, but in fact I was getting more anxious the closer we got to the inside. They hadn't given me a gun and Morris had taken my butcher knife with him, but at least they'd given me a slim carving knife that was definitely sharp enough to de-bone someone. I gripped it tightly.

The basement was damp concrete with a tinge of mold overlaid with an oily smell. A sliver of light seeped from narrow horizontal windows set high in one wall. Justin led us across into the dark; eventually the lamp revealed a steel door with a combination lock—the old-fashioned kind that turned like a door handle only with numbers around the edge. He spent a bit of time turning it backwards and forwards, and finally it popped open. Before he opened the door, he murmured, "We've got about three hours before someone comes by and locks this—so let's not dawdle." He touched Zara on the shoulder, and she smiled reassuringly. I suddenly wondered—were they a couple? She was at least ten years younger, but that might mean nothing out here.

The tunnel was rough concrete, arched and low—I had to stoop a little, and once or twice I stumbled on the uneven surface. A slight breeze was coming from somewhere ahead of us. The oil lamp flickered and my companions' shadows leapt wildly back and forth—it might have been easier to walk with my eyes closed. My palms were sweating and it took a strong effort to keep from turning around, running back. I stifled a wild chuckle. Here I was on the edge of what I'd been yearning for these last three days—and I was scared. Today felt like one of those fun house rides where the room slowly turns and the walls become the ceiling and the ceiling becomes the floor. No matter how this turned out, my world would never look the same.

The tunnel ran for about five blocks, mostly straight with occasional bends and twists. I saw a large chunk of metal pipe jutting from one wall; they'd had to dig around existing plumbing. I tried not to think about the weight above me, but I never been happy underground. If this went on much longer, I was afraid I'd embarrass myself. Just when it felt like my breath was solidifying in my throat, we saw a concrete staircase leading up. Justin stopped, put out the light; I heard the clink as he set it on one of the steps, then he whispered to us to move slowly and quietly. I touched the side of the wall, almost touched Zara's back, and fumbled for the step with my foot. I focused on not stumbling, refusing to think about what was ahead. After what seemed like a million stairs, I felt Zara pause and heard the soft creak of the door. Justin's silhouette was thrown against the concrete as he eased the door open. I swallowed a couple times and warned myself to not embarrass all the gangs I'd belonged to by acting like a coward. Then he gestured and we swiftly took the last couple stairs, and I entered what looked like a library.

I had to blink and let my eyes adjust. I had only been in a library twice, yet recognized it instantly: a small room, divided by low bookshelves running parallel to the long, book-filled walls. That distinctive moldy paper smell blew up my nostrils and I had to grab my nose to keep from sneezing. We seemed to be alone, and this room had high windows so I couldn't see the town. Even with no lights on, after the gloom of the tunnel it seemed exceptionally bright. Justin tiptoed quickly to the door on the opposite wall, paused a moment to listen, then opened it a crack and peered around. He gestured us toward him.

"It's closed today. I want to get over to the café, I'm guessing that's where folks will gather and besides Bromley is on our side. Put that knife away—oh. Good."

I'd slipped the knife up into my right cuff, balancing on my ring finger as before. Justin nodded his approval, and added, "Do we have a plan?"

Zara nodded and I gestured with my left, palm up—it was all the same to me. We followed him through the larger front room, out the door and down two steps into the street. It was a short block of neat red brick rowhouses, three concrete steps to each door, bent iron railings. Each house had a small lamp at the front door, each window ornately arched, with glass panes and demure curtains screening the residence from inquisitive eyes. The sidewalk was well swept. It was a street that might have won awards in the Annual Street Association competitions. I shivered, uneasy—something was off. But I had no chance to consider further, as Justin was lead us quickly up the sidewalk past a trio of citizens—huddled, whispering, taking no notice of us—and around the corner to the left.

We were at the edge of the Mercantile section; if the town was standard, I knew there would be a breakfast/lunch café down the block and to the left. There would be another ahead three blocks and to the right. It was obvious that a lot of this town had been here Before, but as I passed the sewing alterations, the cobbler, and the jewelry repair in proper order, it was also clear that the town had been retrofitted to the standard and thus very similar to the others. Just like the City wasn't *totally* standard, but had been retrofitted as effectively as possible, shops and businesses trading places decades ago. The best examples of Newtowns were on the civilized part of the Island, the rebuilt areas of the great Downfall, the ring of towns in New Jersey and Connecticut and along the train lines and the Niagara Corridor.

It was all normal, nothing out of place. The corner news boards, the cameras—probably half of which were broken—and the color-coded recycling bins along the street. Even a few speakers playing mellow rock, the melodies drifting past us. But my stay outside had tilted something—this felt too easy, too *pat*, and instead of relaxing, I had to force myself not to dart glances into every shop and alcove. I guessed we were heading back toward the rail line; behind us, beyond the southern part of the Wall, I could see those towers—fifty stories or more—across the river. There were some ten-story buildings on this side, many blocks away—could they they have powered elevators this far out? The jarring differences between modern construction and Before was really evident in this place, as if they were halfway finished the transformation. We passed a very ornate stone church with real stained-glass windows and that pointy, useless steeple that made churches look so odd compared to normal buildings. The streets were relatively empty, and I knew most people would be at work, except for those on disability pass, or family leave (rare enough) or elective holiday (even rarer.) This was the time of day where retailers restocked their shelves, and tradesmen delivered new goods. There were two biogas trucks chugging up the street, along with a few horse drawn carts and even a couple of tri-wheely pedallers.

Justin turned left at the corner and we threaded our way past two clumps of citizens outside shops, trying to appear as if they had just bumped into each other. But I could tell from the tension that they were AWOL from something, trying to get information just like we were. I hoped the guards wouldn't be around here soon to scatter them back to their jobs. I took two hurried steps, caught up with Justin, and murmured my concern, adding that I could get the coffees at the shop so we could sit and listen. He glanced at me, then over at one group and nodded sharply. I didn't hear any emergency vehicles or fighting, so we were probably far enough away from the main trouble. The train station had been located in the industrial section, and this was retail. The trouble could be spreading, though.

The café was much more crowded than normal—there was no way that this many employees would be given their break at the same time. I wondered what kind of excuses they had given to get away—or perhaps the usual routine had broken down so much that nobody cared! In that case, it would be random chance whether guards would be policing around here or the other shops.

The café was the usual perky red and white decor, glossy painted walls and counters, furniture bolted to the floor. Apparently the curved bucket seats molded of re-pulped and varnished waste cardboard had originally been new extruded plastic, if my friend Raul was to be believed. The pictures on the wall were the usual scenes of American progress—those golden fields of grain and shining skyscrapers taller than anything we currently could manage. This one also had a couple pictures of glossy red race cars—the kind you'd see in City museums. Maybe there had been a race track around here in the old days. All the tables were filled with citizens sipping from white ceramic mugs and nibbling the fancy cookies and crustless sandwiches that were a specialty of this chain. But their expressions were tense, and they leaned close, murmuring to each other as they glanced around at the rest of the room. No one was acknowledging the emergency openly, but it was clear everyone knew something had happened.

I motioned to Justin and Zara to stand at the back counter near the occupied stools, as if waiting for a seat. My heart was slamming in my chest as I eased forward into the food line, rubbing my fingertips against my thumb, wondering whether leaving my impression on the Pay Pad would ring alarm bells. Surely they would be too busy to pick up one stray citizen today. Maybe the emergency had overloaded the circuits—it happened from time to time, when the usual routine was disregarded and too many citizens used the same auto-process simultaneously. And in fact, when I got to the counter, I could see that people weren't using the Pay Pad, but instead reciting their number. I breathed a sigh of relief—exposure post-poned. I ordered three coffees and three large deli sandwiches from the lovely Afro-Asian girl behind the counter—the hell with my budget—recited my number, and stepped to one side to wait. Zara came up behind me and murmured that she'd help carry. In my anxiety about the payment, I hadn't been paying attention, but now I tried to eavesdrop. It was a strain because most people were keeping their voice in privacy mode, where only those leaning toward them would overhear.

"…just fell like a giant had toppled it…"

"only the 17th AC was in town..."

"Yeah, and it blew out the vatfreeze, half the Silver Line and Gozone!"

I murmured to Zara that some of the trains, the local food storage and a popular nightclub had been damaged.

A man appeared at the door, looked around wildly and eased over to a table midway to the counter. It seemed like everyone knew this was new info, and strained to hear. I could see the message being passed from lean-ing body to leaning body, like a ripple in a pond. Finally it got to the cou-ple standing next to us.

"They zinged the Hote and hooked the DefMin's bottom two!"

I gasped and Zara looked at me blankly. Very quietly, I translated, "They've kidnapped the two youngest children of the Minister of Defence from the town hotel." So Justin was right about the soldiers having a goal besides destruction. That would *have* to provoke a full scale war. The knot of panic in my gut tightened.

We got our order and juggled the plates toward Justin, who had claimed a small table in the corner. Despite the excitement, I was ravenous and devoured my meal. The vat-pink slices had that wonderful sweet spicy taste, and the cheese slice was a pepperjack. No lettuce leaves, but possibly they didn't get out this far. The bread was soft, the sauce was creamy and I was briefly in heaven.

"What else do we need to know?" I asked, talking around a big mouthful; I had to repeat myself after I'd swallowed.

"How many Army are assigned here?"

"One troop, the 17th Armed Calvary," I answered. "Overheard that just now. They'd be on e-bikes, not horses," I added.

"Okay—and it would be good to find out if the disrupters are on." Justin was also enjoying his sandwich.

"Disrupters?" I glanced from Justin to Zara. They seemed surprised I didn't know.

"They jam the signals—the radio signals—at the low end all the time," Zara explained. "But sometimes, in emergencies, they block the upper signals and nothing can get through. Except whatever wavelength *they're* using," she finished bitterly.

"Quince would know," Justin said, glancing around. The place was still buzzing, but it seemed like folks were beginning to leave, with apparently casualness. The info was going to be spread far and wide. "Let's see if we can get to him. But first I need to stop at the cert shop."

We bussed our plates and headed further down the street. The retail shops—personal care supplies, herbal medicines, stationary, a musical instrument shop with two inlaid guitars featured in the small glass window—were newly built and yet so familiar I could almost believe I was walking through my home town again. It was a creepy feeling, suddenly, and I had to force myself not to glance around for relatives and old friends. People could live their entire lives never seeing any more variety than was allowed on the twenty-square block retail center, the social events blocks and the fun-fair that operated on the edge of the regulation flat green park/sports field. Even marrying away didn't change the look of town you walked through. Authorities said this had been discovered to be what most people liked—to be able to count on exactly the same shops, the same experience over and over—and after the Adjustment they quickly structured things to be "back to normal." Only it didn't feel quite so normal, now.

Just past the furniture district, two buildings down a narrow lane, Justin paused at the door of a bedding shop. Glancing around, seeing no one, he opened the door and we followed him in. It was a cramped room with four low aisles to our right, the shelves stacked with neatly folded sheets and blankets. On our left, towels were stacked on wall shelves. There was a small aisle to the back counter, where a wizened man with a broad nose and bushy eyebrows was hunched over a little printing machine.

"Morning, Mackey," Justin said. "Is that card ready yet?"

"Have it for you right here, buddy. Got the ring?"

Justin slid a gold band across the counter. Mackey put it on his index finger and admired it. Then he turned and opened a small drawer with a tiny key. He pulled out a bioplastic card that looked like ID. I tried to keep a blank face—this had to be a forger! I was dying to look at the card but it quickly passed from Mackey to Justin, who slid it into his pocket. Zara was shifting from foot to foot, and she quickly turned and led us back out.

Four blocks later, we stopped at a clothing store and Zara led the way in. The man behind the glass counter—a pear-shaped redhead with a large moustache but cleanshaven cheeks—waved cautiously. I could tell he wasn't pleased to see us. There was a tall gray-haired woman browsing clothes on the far wall. Justin and Zara paused to check out the rack of identical green tunics, and I copied them, then moved away toward the wall of black pants. There were some black leather belts of a five-braid design that looked pretty cool, and I was tempted to buy one. On impulse, I found one my size and brought it to the counter. Quince—if it were he—was startled.

I placed my hand on the Pay Pad but it sat there, dead. My gesture startled Quince even more. Justin came over, glared at me quickly, and murmured, "How are the siggies today?" I stared down at the pad. They operated on wireless, so the fact that they were down...in confirmation, Quince gestured wordlessly at the pad. I repeated my action, to show Justin that nothing was happening.

"Bugger," he muttered. "Thanks. Adios." He tugged me away from the counter; I left the belt—probably no chance of coming back for it. But when would I be wearing nightclub togs again anyway?

"Anyone up for scanning the scene?" Justin murmured as we stepped out.

Zara looked panicky and shook her head. I struggled to pull my thoughts together, working against a panic that felt a lot like what I'd felt in Madison. "I... I think we could get to the hotel near the station. Even with the... problem... there would be some visitors, and we wouldn't look as obvious." But I was acutely aware that neither of them had passes. Unless Justin had just purchased one? Mine was back in Ambridge, though my number served. "The hotel will be about eight blocks north, then two to the right. About three blocks from the rail line, if I remember."

Justin smiled. "That was my guess, but I'm glad you know." He glanced around. "We should walk about a half block apart."

"Right—citizens aren't usually out this time of day," I agreed. "Only approved transport and a few other workers." We'd travelled a block north, and there was no one in sight. I glanced around, saw a news reader board and carefully unpinned the sheet of news. I handed it to Zara. "You'll be bringing this to another board to post." She nodded and started walking with short, hesitant steps; I saw her start to glance around then arrest the motion.

"Justin, if you walk with slower steps, but use the phone as if you are making notes on what you see in the shops, you won't get questioned." He smiled again, pulled out the cell phone and kept it in sight as he paced up the street.

That only left me. Unfortunately, I didn't have a gimmick, so I opted for brash self-confidence. Most of the time folks left you alone if you acted like you belonged there. As I walked behind them, I worked on my story: I was from the City, sent out to review dish procedures with the local tech, but due to high occupancy, ended up having to take a visitor room more than 10 blocks from the workplace. I tried to guess where the communication offices would be—that was a wildcard in most cities. The large corporations managed to override what should be their assigned place and ended up near amenities such as parks, cafés—wherever the hell they wanted to be. But that gave me an excuse for being slightly lost.

I had the insane feeling that I was living two lives at once—like a very strange mu-vid I had once seen, where the main character got split in two and was moving in parallel worlds. That vid was incredibly odd when I saw it, but now I *knew* how it felt. There was a part inside responding to these normal streets like an Army brat coming back to visit family. But another part was jumping up and down and screaming, "This is too weird! This is—" and I would shy away before the thought could go any further. I felt the knife on my fingertip, I brushed my other hand against the smooth cotton tunic, and reminded myself of the many battles I had walked toward as a teen, not knowing how any of it would turn out, but knowing I had to do it. I was a little older, a lot creakier, but it was the same thing. And maybe it would always be the same thing. That lay like a lump in my gut—

that there was no safe, quiet place, anywhere. I thrust that thought aside and stared ahead, watching Zara's figure dwindle about three blocks away. She seemed to be speeding up, whether from nerves or not being aware that we were losing her. I sped up, figuring I could pass Justin if necessary.

Just then, somebody—taller than Zara, possibly a man—came up to her from a side street, and they spoke a moment. I saw Justin pick up his pace, and I trotted faster, letting the knife slip into my hand. By the time we had covered the next block, the man had gone and Zara had resumed walking. I slowed a little and re-hid the knife, anxious but not willing to blow cover to find out. It was a tense six blocks, though.

* * *

By the time I saw the hotel's broad stone façade and four story faux-towers—a combination of leftover structure and some obvious renovation—I had almost forgotten the man in the jumble of thoughts and fears. I *needed* to get back to Ciera and her group; I *needed* to bring more information than this. There was little or nothing I or they could do if there was war. On the other hand, what did I know of what they had? I caught up with Zara and Justin at the corner of the hotel, by the ornate signpost, "Hotel Rockefeller"—yet another chain industry.

"...going to do a flyover ASAP!" Zara was saying. She glanced at me.

I understood her worry but I had to know. "Zara, I'm not the enemy—"

"Shush! That discussion later," Justin interrupted. "Tell us, Zara."

She swallowed, straining not to turn her head to look around. "They're falling in with New York; says the free trade deal will go through if they swing this. They have enough soldiers—" at that, she did glance around.

I didn't see anyone who looked even vaguely military. The sidewalk in front of the hotel had several clumps of chatting citizens, and—there! The cluster of men in gray tunics and pants on the concrete front steps, leaning against the stone ballustrade and chatting. There was something in their stance... Belatedly, I took the news sheet from Zara, folded it and refolded it until it was small enough to fit in my pocket. It felt a little like a time bomb.

"Okay—so Teg's gonna play nice. What does he want from us?"

My head snapped around. Teg?? No—couldn't be. It just couldn't be.

19

My mouth was so dry I could barely speak. "That person—that Teg you mentioned—how old? I had a friend, years ago…"

They studied my face; I knew I was shaking, and I took a deep breath and tried again. "A man—ten years older than me—he was blond and we were in a gang together." I must've sounded like a total signfeld. But my thoughts were scattering like scared pigeons. *Don't tell them he died.*

Zara again seem to know what I wasn't saying. Her smile was tender as she said, "This Teg is blond, but no more than twenty."

"Couldn't be my friend, then." I turned suddenly, unable to keep my face blank. There was nothing to knock my ankle against, so I let the knife tip poke my palm enough to wash pain through my body and chase out shameful emotion. A crazy hope, just crazy. I shook my head and turned back to them. Justin was studying the hotel sign diplomatically, and Zara nodded and patted me on the arm. It didn't feel as weird as it usually did.

"Anyway," she said, "his troops will be guarding this area, and rebuilding the wall."

"Then they might be needing extra... supplies," Justin said.

"Yes, Lars mentioned that," she replied. "I just hope he knows what he's doing."

"If he doesn't, nobody does," Justin replied grimly. "No large troop presence. Do we need anything else here?"

Though it felt like stepping out on an invisible bridge, I needed to find out who the inside players were.

"I think...I think I might get a bit more information from my office—it's worth a try anyway." I saw the look on their faces, the suspicion that they couldn't avoid, and I raised my free palm outward. "I just need to plug the phone in for a boostcharge at the hotel, and I can text somebody, and

Zara can watch. Justin—it might be too suspicious if all three of us go in, but a couple is no more obvious than a single. Sometimes less so."

Zara looked even more frightened; she glanced over at the hotel, and I knew she was seeing those men in gray. Tentatively, I reached out and patted her on the arm—how could that motion be soothing? But she relaxed a bit and smiled at me. Justin nodded abruptly, handed me the phone and said, "I'll walk around the block until you come back out."

"If you make it a two block circuit, I should be back out after one go around. The zapper chargers at the hotel are really efficient, they tell me." As long as I got enough to call, I didn't care.

With a glance at Zara, he walked away, strolling toward the pizza place that was always located a half block from the hotel. I took a deep breath and headed towards the main entrance, and Zara trotted a bit to keep up.

"If they ask, we are a couple on a wedding trip, coming to see your sister married," I murmured as we climbed the steps of polished concrete. In the City, some of the steps were fancy materials like granite and marble, but anything new was re-fab concrete, at best with marble chips. I didn't glance over at the men in gray, and nothing in my peripheral vision suggested they had noticed us. There was a young woman and a three-year-old girl by the mahogany and glass double doors; wearing embroidered pale blue tunics; of the wealthy class. I gave her a half bow as I passed, as good citizens were supposed to. Zara caught my motion and repeated it, and we passed into the lobby.

This place had as much relationship to the Hill-town Arms as a Tiffany lamp to a candle stub: the indigo-on-gray floral stenciled walls were framed in mahogany that gleamed russet. The rug was a thick unbleached canvas woven with thin gray stripes; it was meticulously swept. The counter at the far side of the room was brushed steel and glass, with fancy strip mirrors, and the reservationist behind it wore a white tunic with silver buttons. Luckily, we didn't have to go that far—if I remembered from my brief rendezvous with a well-off married woman, the chargers were generally in the phone alcove just inside the entrance. I veered to the right and sighed in relief that no one else was using the alcove. Stepping into the three-sided booth with its narrow shelf and built-in plugs, I glanced back and gestured Zara to join me, though it was a bit of a squeeze. I could feel her trembling as she tried to lean casually against the doorway.

"Hurry up," she breathed.

Awkwardly, I slipped the thin knife into my pants pocket, praying it wouldn't slice a hole in the cloth. I grabbed a zapper plug and connected the phone. One of the little icons started blinking and I guessed it was charging. It seemed impossible that it was less than a week ago I was learning how to use the damn thing. I opened it and awkwardly thumbed a text: *What's up? Something's wrong out here*, and let Zara see it before I sent it to Cheyenne.

"If she's not at her desk, or doesn't reply, I'll—" I didn't have to finish, because already a reply came through: *Still alive? Gd. They say DC gt U.* I groaned softly at the code, but puzzled out: "Good. They say DC got you." I texted back quickly, *Got away. Can't get back yet. Who in DC?* I looked over Zara's head, but so far no one was paying us any attention.

All of it. Rumbles on. 2k reward 4 capture DC capt or above. All of DC?? My hands were sweaty; Zara's anxiety was catching. "Rumble means a fight, in slum talk," I murmured to her. Odd Cheyenne knowing that.

Conscription? I texted back, as I tried to think of any other info Cheyenne might be able to give me.

16 to 22 now, she texted back. *RU OK?*

I sounded out the letters. *OK 4 now*, I replied. *Gotta go.* I closed the phone and quickly unplugged it, slipping it in my pocket and picking up the knife at the same time. I wasn't sure but possibly the desk clerk was eyeing us. Audaciously, I draped my arm across Zara's shoulders, leaned protectively over her and steered her gently out the door.

"I apologize for the rudeness," I said, "but I didn't want the clerk taking any photos."

"What rudeness?" Zara asked. "Oh, yes—you all don't like to touch each other. That took getting used to." She smiled at me as we navigated the stairs. The men in gray were gone, and there was no sight of Justin on the sidewalk. "Should we wait here?" she asked.

"I don't think so, but just so we don't miss him, you go one way, I'll go the other—down two blocks and around. We'll meet up with him at some point."

We separated at the foot of the stairs, and I headed around the hotel sign and down the block, looking for Justin's gray hair inside any of the stores I passed, just in case. There were one or two walkers; a few more came out of stores as I passed. It was getting to be lunch time, and the workers—those who didn't belong to a huge corporation with its own cafeteria—would be getting out to eat. I hurried a little, because I didn't want to be obviously searching for someone in front of a lot of people. It was a relief to know that conscription was starting with the younger crowd—so I might be safe if I went back. Might even be a hero, I mused. I turned at the corner, and halfway down the block, I saw what had held Justin up. Or rather, who.

The red armbands of the Survellence Activists were obvious on the couple talking with Justin. I could see Zara had hesitated at the corner beyond and I moved fast to forestall her. This was going to be tricky. With barely a moment to get my thoughts in order, I hailed Justin as I came closer.

"Hey! Did you get lost coming back to the hotel?"

By now I had covered the distance and came up to the group, wishing I knew what name Justin had given them. The pale, crewcut, clean-cheeked man barely came up to my shoulder but the brunette beside him topped me; both had that smug righteousness that SA was known for. There was no safe way to just ignore Snitch Anonymous, but I put on my jovial, boss-handling smile and said, "Has he been asking for directions? He has a tendency to get lost on his way to the bathroom, I'm afraid." I laughed at my own joke; they didn't laugh with me. *Shit.* This might be tougher than I thought.

"Passes, please," the woman said. She allowed a half smile to break through. Obviously she thought she was going to nail a reward today.

"Citizen," I said politely but with an edge of annoyance, imitating those senior managers who delighted in stepping on toes, "I'm afraid both of us left our passes in our rooms when we were asked to evacuate a little while ago. *Surely* you are aware of the current state of emergency?" My tone suggested I thought she was entirely too stupid. Justin, I was very glad to see, had put on a look of good-natured dim-wittedness, looking back and forth between us.

"A good citizen would never leave—" the man interrupted, but I cut him off.

"A good *citizen* follows directions, instantly and without question, sir!" I stared him down and he finally looked away. "My number is 553 dash 234 dash 78. Buddy?"

"554 dash 450 dash 45," Justin said quickly.

"Hey! I hadn't realized we were born so close together!" I exclaimed, grabbing his elbow and pushing him toward Zara. She had turned her back and was studying a shrub. I turned to the couple. "Good day, citizens," I said firmly and followed Justin.

It was agonizing not to look back, and I was so glad Zara had guessed enough to walk in front of us around the corner toward the hotel. We walked without speaking to the end of the block, and at the corner I finally risked turning around—the street was empty. I let my breath out, not realizing I'd been holding it. My mouth was as dry as a morning after, and I almost staggered as we came up to Zara.

"Quick! To the right and around the corner—then hurry to the library. They may have put word out."

We retraced our steps in silence, several paces apart, and I strained for sight of the building. The streets seemed oddly empty for lunchtime—apparently folks had gotten the word and gone back to work or home to chew on it for a while, and to wait for further developments. Or could there be a *shelter in place* order? It took less than ten minutes to get back to the library. I had a moment of panic—how would we get back in if it was closed? But Zara worked the pin pad and the lock clicked open. We hustled inside and I could feel the relief flood over me in waves.

I leaned against the nearest bookshelf. "That was too damn close." I smiled to take the edge off.

"Thanks for saving my butt," Justin said. He had his arm around Zara and was hugging her tightly; her eyes were closed and her cheek was wet. So they were a couple.

"It was me who put you in danger," I replied, trying to sound casual. I was *not* going to tell them how dangerous that could have been. I wondered briefly if anyone really had the number Justin had recited and whether the poor slob would have an excuse. If it were me, I would flat out declare that the snitch had remembered it wrong. The problem was—I had unthinkingly given my real number, because the taboo against giving a phony one was too deeply rooted. So if they did report back, and it did work its way up to—well, whoever does all of that spying stuff—someone would put that together with my phone call… Suddenly it wasn't looking too safe again for me.

"Let's get back," Justin said, "I want to be there if they show up needing supplies." He pulled a small box of matches for the oil lamp—too precious to use unless there was no other choice?

The trip wasn't nearly as long on the way back; a peculiar fact I'd noticed often before. We shrugged into our coats in the living room, and Justin opened the front door slowly. The same guy was sitting on the chair, and Justin paused to give him something, possibly a payment token? The crowds had thinned. There were a few shopping; tension was still in the air as if everyone had an ear cocked. Their random movements felt odd after being inside—here were men and women of all ages, who would be indoors working just on the other side of the Wall.

"I want to stop at Aida's and see what's come in," Justin muttered as we hurried along. We were walking north again, along the bricked-in buildings and rubble infill that constituted this part of the Wall. I glanced at some of the ex-houses, trying to imagine them with glass panes and doors, in a different age, when this town—this city—had twice or three times as many people, and there were no partitions. I tried to picture gasoline-powered cars and trucks filling the streets, and people dressed in velvets and silks and even plastic clothes, snacking on portable food and throwing away garbage into big bins that they said used to dot the sidewalks. And no horses allowed inside the city. It all just seemed too weird.

Once again, as the fight-buzz wore off, the fatigue flooded back—my legs wobbled like loose springs and my brain was fizzing like I was half drunk. I'd gotten almost no sleep last night and very little the night before—not that I was complaining about *that*. I'd just left the town that I'd been trying to get back to for three days, and it felt like it had been a near miss. The safety of civilization had evaporated into the reality that I was well and truly AWOL. Having to dig out my number again grated on a part of myself I had buried 10 years ago. Maybe the trade-off hadn't been worth it.

The sun sped in and out of fast-moving gray clouds, casting and erasing shadows on the brick and concrete buildings. This area didn't look evacuated, yet I suspected there were far fewer goods on the streets than usual. I could smell methane again, and I wondered if that was a common power source here, and where they created it. Big Lulu's humanure methane plant had been set up in a huge abandoned building, and though the stench was unbelievable, the resulting liquid brought piles of money. It wasn't the safest fuel, however, and I'd breathed easier in many ways once I'd left that gang.

We were still following the Wall and left the woodware area, entering a hybrid block: elegant metal and wood shelves; small oak tabletops with ornate wrought iron legs; large iron cooking pots with shaped wooden handles. Then Justin turned left and we entered the metalworking section, and that acrid stench that I remembered from Troy's stables came wafting down the street. Justin had said Aida was a blacksmith. He pointed out her shop at the end of a block of old warehouses with no windows but huge doors. As we got closer, a group of fit-looking young people—three men, two women—walked out of her open doorway; their pace and bearing immediately marked them as soldiers. They were bulked up under their denim tunics—maybe Justin's armor? They didn't glance at us as they walked by silently—there was a sense of mission that I'd encountered so often in childhood. This wasn't a casual patrol. I took a deep breath to steady my nerves. I'd lost all sense of what might happen next; adrift in an unfamiliar pattern, trying to pull the pieces into something approaching sense. Once I got back to their house, I would negotiate some kind of transport back to Ambridge. My sense of urgency was growing; what if she thought I'd run away??

We turned into the doorway; in the center of the room, in front of a large metal furnace whose chimney jutted up through the roof, a woman in a sleeveless gray tunic and leather apron was slamming a huge hammer on a red hot iron bar; her bare shoulders dripped with sweat, and her forearms bulged. Chestnut brown hair was cropped above her ears, a business-like haircut where a forelock could be dangerous. Her leather apron was pockmarked with stains and scorches. She was no taller than Zara, but I guessed she weighed almost double with muscle—she turned, plunged the iron bar into a pail of water, sending a cloud of steam like an explosion into the air behind her.

"What ho, Aida?" Justin called out as he led us in. His voice was cheery, as if we hadn't just escaped a Snitch. She looked up and grinned in response—I was shocked that neither seemed—well, they weren't acting like there was a war on. Then she caught sight of me. And her expression became watchful. That was more like it.

"May I introduce Martin, who nipped in with us just now, and gathered a few pretty posies for us?"

I glanced between Justin and the blacksmith—the code wasn't impossible to parse, but I wasn't sure why it was needed. Then I noticed in the shadows a couple of young men busily assembling metal plumbing pipes; one was welding them to something round.

"Portable forge from old pipes, brake drums and lawnmowers," Justin murmured, following my glance. "One of her more popular items. But just local help." So perhaps not everyone knew the whole situation.

"They are pulling 16 to 22," Zara commented. Aida had stopped hammering; the iron bar was cooling from red to dull scarlet.

"And Flyboy's going to do his magic soon," Justin added.

"*Is* he now?" Aida gestured toward the back of the shop, where a couple of chairs and a table were pushed into a corner under a tiny, grimy window. A bit louder, she said, "Your job is almost done—but come look at this."

As we gathered around the table, I muttered, "In case it's of interest, there's a $2,000 reward for the capture of a southern soldier rank of captain or above." I leaned back in the straight chair, and felt it creak beneath me.

Aida's eyebrows shot up, and Justin punched the air with his fist. "That would be worth getting," he said.

"Might be more danger than it's worth," Zara replied, worry thick in her voice.

"Might be too late," Aida said. "Elontee watched the grays vamoose—pontoon boats across. No more'n 50 or 60 all told, she said. They skirted the Haunt and kept on south—got whatever they wanted and scarpered."

"They got some official's kids," Zara told her. "Do we know if New York has taken hostages?"

"Might be why they want the captain," Justin commented.

Aida pushed aside a pair of tongs and pulled a couple of sheets of paper from under them. She scanned a page then looked up. "We can keep eyes at the key points, but nothin' we can do if they come back. Where the hell did they hail from, anyway?"

Justin glanced at me. "Martin says they came down from north of Ambridge. Crossed over the Ohio on an existing railroad bridge and then came south."

"I'd heard rumors since about HorseFerry," I added, "but everyone was saying they were locals."

"So we need eyes up there, too," Aida said, frowning.

"I can't speak for the people I was with, but—"

Zara shook her head. "They're refuseniks," she said, "they don't care about this stuff."

"I don't know if that's true," I replied slowly, "but even if so, this might have changed their minds." In truth, I had no idea what they planned to do about it, since I'd left as soon as the crisis had erupted. But any sane person would be looking to protect themselves even if it meant new alliances.

She shook her head again. "I can't abide those people. It's like they want to dress up in bearskins and live off dandelions."

"I don't understand a lot right now," I said, rubbing my face with my hand, "but the ones I met out there don't fit that description at all."

"Zara's a jeweler, did I mention?" Justin said, a hint of apology in his voice. "Ornaments aren't quite as popular where you don't have civilization." *So that's where the gold ring came from.*

"But I do a snazzy set of vac tube pins, as well," she snapped back at him. He patted her arm, but she slid it away.

"Well, this changes a crapload," Aida commented. "We need eyes everywhere now. Our back trails might not be safe for—"

Justin interrupted her with a sound like a cough; he and Zara sat up stiffly and the blacksmith picked up the hint. So there was still something they didn't want me to know. I shrugged; lack of trust was more familar anyway.

"I plan to head back to Ambridge as soon as I can," I said. "I could bring up a proposal or something, if you wish."

"Could be, could be..." Justin nodded, stroking his mustache. "We'll think it over."

We were interrupted by a couple of burly, filthy men who walked a small mule cart into the forge and hollered at Aida, "Where do you want this?"

"Same corner as always," she hollered back, rolling her eyes. "It's the coke delivery," she explained. At my puzzled look, she continued, "The stuff I burn in my forge. Comes from coal."

"I wondered if coal was available around here," I replied. "Because the engine they were driving wasn't a solar powered train."

"*Solar* train?" Aida asked, half distracted by watching the delivery men shovel piles of gray rock into a corner stall. From her sour expression, she did not suffer fools gladly.

"Inside, they power some of their trains with solar, though I think they have coal as backup," Zara said.

"I didn't know that," I murmured. The train I came out in ran on steam, but from the solar panels on top of the long locomotive, I had assumed it was purely sun-powered steam. But of course, that wouldn't work in the rain, and batteries would take up too much space. And biogas would be too explosive. I shook my head—Ciera was right: I had taken my surroundings for granted, just assuming they were there as if by magic. Even during the hardtimes slum years I didn't pay much attention to how things got there. I was focused more on people and on power; the making of things was not nearly as important as the stealing of them.

"There were a lot of people leaving today," I said, "but a lot of them *weren't*—is there a reason why?"

The three of them exchanged glances; Justin shrugged. "Some people are more skittish, maybe. We've had—difficulties—before, usually one group fighting another, and people have different ways of dealing with that."

"A bunch of families sent their slower members north, in case things got difficult and they needed—flexibility," Zara added.

"We hear the General's group snuck up the asses of the local rebs while some were waffling 'bout going in. Pitched battle for about an hour. Then the rebels decided to fade," Aida said.

"Sensible," Justin commented. He turned to me. "Why did you want to know?"

"I just wondered because on Long Island, if someone abandoned territory, it wouldn't take but a heartbeat for another group to just swoop in and clear the place." I searched their faces, pretty sure they were not saying everything, just trying to find out a bit more about local politics. Not that I pictured staying forever, but it might help Ciera's group.

Zara made a sweeping gesture. "Most of the folks around here know the golden rule," she said.

"You mean 'those who have the gold makes the rules?'"

They laughed until they realized I was serious.

"No, the old rule—'Do unto others as you would have them do unto you,'" Justin explained, still fighting a smile. "It's a lot easier to live at peace with your neighbors," he added. "It used to be pretty wild here, but people have seen the advantage to being a bit more fair-handed."

"And those who don't, get educated quickly," Aida quipped, then stopped at a look from Justin. "As best we can, we'll watch people's stuff 'til they come back," she said.

So they weren't going to tell me exactly how things were run—I suppose I'd be wary under the same conditions. I thought about the plundered knife cart and wondered if the rule only applied to those who scored points with their neighbors. I just flat didn't believe that people were nice without reason. And there was that trust issue again—*I* sure wouldn't leave and trust my neighbor to look after my stuff. My apartment was locked tight. That reminded me—the Ambridge community said they had a place down here.

"Have you heard of a group where everyone wears red button-up shirts and black trousers?" I asked. "The group in Ambridge said they had a sister colony here."

They shook their head, but Aida commented, "Unless they're the ones over on Buttercup Way that use the weird church." She grinned. "Place must be a bugger to keep up—everything curved and the roof like a mushroom. I think they wear black gear."

It might be worth finding out," I said, "because that would give the group in Ambridge a reason to cooperate with you."

"Thanks," she replied. "We'll check it. Reminds me –" she turned to Justin, "looks like the Council's meeting today. Rebels will be paying up—or else."

He harrumphed and Zara said, "Serves them right if they lost their places here, but I bet they won't do that."

"Nope, "Aida replied, "we still need their shops. But there'll be fines, and *this* time some cash better filter down." She scowled and I ached to ask more. This was the first place that didn't sound like it had a slum boss.

"Aida, can you get someone over to the General, and let him know I'll be available if he needs... supplies?" Justin asked.

Did he mean his armor? Or was he in charge of something more lethal? How prepared were they for battle? Living this close to a different civilization, they must be more wary than Ciera's group. In the slums, no one dared fight the Army, so if someone was unfortunate enough to draw official attention, the usual plan was to scatter, let the Army make their symbolic slap-down, and then come back and pick up the pieces. But this was so far from the City, despite being technically part of it, there might be a different strategy. And knowing that strategy would help Ciera and Ambridge.

Speaking of supplies… "As they came down, the southern Army stopped a couple places and grabbed a lot of goods from the residents," I said. "Maybe they didn't take it all when they left—there might be stuff worth salvaging in the boxcar."

"Thanks, good heads-up," Aida said, "But for now the train's off-limits 'case they brought up some nasty Southern bug."

Damn—I hadn't thought of that. Did that put me under quarantine? I glanced around, but no one seemed to be considering it. And it was probably too late, given how long I'd been hanging around Justin and Zara. Contagion was taken very seriously in the City—though they couldn't identify germs like Before, anyone who got sick with fever had their family and colleagues put on watch, and sometimes quarantined. The Flu Sagas were many and tragic, so nobody argued with the Health Department when they came around.

"Let me know if there's anything else you need, Aida," Justin said, getting up from his chair. "I think we can be grateful that this wasn't worse, but I'm sure it's not the end of the story."

"Damn cert," Aida said as she accompanied us to the door, "We'll need reserves on red level 'til the Army moves again."

* * *

When we got back to the house, Zara invited me to stay for a meal. Justin had gone into another room, and hadn't come back.

"It's close to dinner, and I know *I'm* hungry," she joked, a little shakily.

I accepted, although I was desperate to get back—what if Ciera had left with her group? Would anybody tell me where Evansville was?? That thought nagged like a sore tooth. I had a goodly amount of information, though I suspected Justin could tell me more. But I'd run out of things to trade. In fact, I was probably in hock. Zara pointed to the plates and utensils in the cupboard and I brought some to the table. "Set it for four," she instructed.

"Do you mind if I ask—this general's group—are they the rebels? But you said they were joining with the City…" The number of separate groups involved in this fracas made me feel déjà vu with the Long Island slums.

"Teg runs a number of important industries out here," Zara explained, "he's got a decent-sized methane plant out by the old landfill, and somewhere or another they dug up a huge trove of giant tires that they trade to the City for their planes. And a bunch of other stuff."

"That's right—you said they were doing a flyover. Did you mean the City?"

Zara was slicing up some pink; the smooth rounded shape glistened slightly. "You don't mind Spam again, do you?"

I'd heard it called that years ago. "We just call it pink. And I love it, especially barbecued pink."

She chuckled. "That's good too, this one's the Middle Eastern version, with synth-spice that goes good with lentil stew. And no, I didn't mean the City. Teg's group have their own planes that run on methane. I think more than anything else, those have helped him get ahead." She paused, as if wondering if she should have told me that.

"I just want to be clear that my loyalty is not with the City. I don't owe it anything." I brought the meat to the table and following her pointing, retrieved the pitcher of ale from an ice box. "But... doesn't the Army—object?" I couldn't imagine the authorities not grabbing any kind of working plane.

Dishes rattled in the sink as she scrubbed. I was startled at the sound of running water and I turned—there wasn't much pressure, but they had running water in the kitchen, too! Was it a piped system? Or just a tank on the roof? She put mugs in a wired dish rack then turned to face me. "I'm not sure how he manages, but they've never been able to find them, and he doesn't rub their noses in it. And today it sounds like they're just as happy that he can do something to find out about the Southerners."

"I…I hope he doesn't trust them too much, because in my experience their promises aren't worth a computer service agreement." I paused; she probably wouldn't get that.

But she laughed uproariously—so some of the City's jokes filtered this far out. "I think he knows that pretty well. It's not something I've ever wanted to do, but a good trader has to keep the upper hand. So I guess he holds out just a big enough carrot that they don't shut him down."

Sounded like a pretty smart trader. I thought about my friend Teg—he'd been savvy. Not that it had helped him. The problem with random violence is it hit the useless and the brilliant without differentiating.

Zara walked over to the couch, opened the panel that hid the radio, but pulled out a small hand-sized device. "I thought it would be nice to have a little music with the meal." She carried the device to the kitchen cupboard, and set it on a stand, then fiddled with it and a moment later, classical music—some violins and woodwinds—played softly.

"You have recorded music!" I was astounded. "You have to be filthy rich in the City to have a player like that."

She smiled slyly. "That's one of the advantages of being a supplier—you can skim a few things off the top." She adjusted the volume. "We've made enough money selling these and other things to the City that we could afford to keep one or two for ourselves. Do you like Brahms?"

"Actually, I prefer jazz—I even have one or two songs on my phone, because I didn't think I could go a couple weeks without music."

I was about to describe my favorite jazz nightclub when we heard voices from the other room—Justin and somebody else. Must be another entrance. In a moment, the door to the bedroom—or what I thought was a bedroom—opened and a blond haired young man wearing a shirt of Justin's leather armor under a pale gray camo zip jacket and carrying a leather helmet followed Justin into the room.

I stared—if that young man wasn't Teg, he was his younger brother. Or son??

20

He glanced over, registered my stunned expression, and looked more closely. Justin also noticed and asked, "Seen a ghost?"

"Something like that," I stammered. The crisis faded; I was in a bubble of memory. "Are you—Teg?"

He glanced sharply at Justin, frowning. Justin's smile flickered and died. I cursed myself for forgetting protocol.

"I only ask," I explained quickly, "because I had a friend—a good friend—back in Long Island who had that name and who—I swear—looked just like you. He—he died in a gang fight. Or so they *told* me." Again emotion welled up and I swallowed hard so I wouldn't look LOLkatz in front of these people.

Zara had brought a basket of bread to the table; she froze there watching us. Justin looked warily at the young man; he must think I was dreamsurfing, since my friend was dead. But Teg stared at me thoughtfully, and a slow smile spread across his face.

"And what might your name be?"

"Martin. But they called me Marty back then." Like that mattered now. Images welled up unbidden, of nights around scrapwood fires, wrapped in whatever blankets or rags we could find, drinking homebrewed beer and bragging about raids—hard to believe it was my life.

The young man nodded and set his helmet on a side table. He shrugged out of his jacket but left the armor on. "And you're out here from Long Island?" He pulled out a chair and sat. Zara brought over a bowl of mashed turnips and took the chair opposite him. I waited until Justin sat, then took in the last chair, with the young Teg on my right. There was something about him that put me in mind of a brindle cat that had lorded over our family barn—silent, hyper-alert and deadly to vermin. He was like that but much larger—I suddenly thought of the big cat Ciera had worried about. Maybe that's what a lion or tiger was like.

"It's a bit of a long story," I said, as food was passed around. His intense attention was unnerving; he seemed as likely to shoot me as listen, but he was hanging on every word. "The short version is I was sent out from the City and I've discovered I was just a lure to get the southerners out of hiding, only their plan to kidnap me failed. Several people have helped me in the past couple days—and they were strangers under no obligation. That wouldn't happen in the City or on the Island. So I'm—curious—about the situation out here."

"He saved my butt inside the Wall just a while ago," Justin broke in. "A couple of bastards with red armbands stopped me and he talked his way out of it as smooth as anything." He chuckled as he folded some bread around the slice of pink and munched on it. "Did you talk your way out of the kidnapping, too?" he added jokingly.

"Well, I—actually, I did," I admitted with a smile. "I was always pretty good with this limp and dead arm gimmick that made me look helpless. Takes a bit of practice to not move your arm at all, but it saved my life a couple times."

Teg nodded. "Always best to avoid fighting if possible," he said around a mouthful of turnips. He was eating hearty, and I wondered when he'd last ate. And why he was here, but of course I didn't ask. Something to do with supplies, Justin had said, and definitely none of my business.

"So the southerners tried to kidnap you?" he asked.

"I don't know *who* tried to kidnap me," I replied. I explained about Geoff and how he turned from my guide into my stalker. Perhaps a good story would make Teg forget Justin's indiscretion. "In the end, the southern Army grabbed both me and Geoff. The captain wouldn't kill an unarmed innocent, as he said, and left us tied up near the train. I got away, and I don't know what happened to Geoff," I finished.

"Did you see what they had in those rail cars?"

"They stole a lot from the locals as they came down," I explained. "Mostly food. I didn't see many weapons in the car, but the soldiers carried rifles or pistols. They had a ham-op radio box in the passenger car."

He nodded, then changed the subject abruptly, asking Zara, "How's the gold and silver trinket business going? I might have someone to buy a bauble for soon."

"It's definitely improving, thank you. For a while there, business was pretty slow—that happens after the holidays. But I used the time making more tube pins." She looked chagrined and paused; Justin frowned, but Teg continued smoothly.

"Well I'm sure the word has gotten around that nobody makes Celtic knotwork like you do," he said, reaching for a piece of bread. "And Justin? Enough leather for your shoes?"

So they were going to stick to safe topics. I hadn't expected to be taken into their deep bosom secrets, but I was itching to find out just a little more about where the danger was. I thought about the flyover that Zara mentioned—what it would be like to soar above the ground like a hawk, seeing more than you could from a City tower on the East River, moving across the landscape like a cloud. Several old aunts and uncles had tried to describe the sensation to us kids, but the best I could picture was the dangerous view from the top of the barn roof, where we could see a mile or two away. As I'd discovered, City towers with views were strictly off limits to peons.

They were chatting about appliances now—Zara was bragging about having a new methane-powered washer that saved the outrageous cost of using Tony's Tubs somewhere in the Mall. Justin talked about a bicycle-parts windmill he had found somewhere—he was deliberately vague, glancing at me—and how easily it could be reproduced. Teg talked about the early crops north of the city, how the recent rains had slowed growth. Zara volunteered the news that there was a new yeast dealer in town.

"He's getting apples from up in the valley, and the yeast I've gotten has been excellent," she commented. "Made great sourdough."

"I'll tuck that away," Teg said. "Open to all trades?"

"Seems like he's interested most in glassware and good linen, but that's only from what I've had to offer," Zara replied. "No list posted, so maybe he's open to haggling."

"We found some bright-colored yarn—the wool was moth-eaten but some of the acrylic stuff was still good," Teg said.

"I think it depends how it was stored," Justin cut in.

"Aye, there's truth in that. Our raiders found truckloads, so get the word out that it's available, will you?"

"Sure," Zara said. She began to clean up the dishes, and I rose to help. My muscles were itchy with inaction, and I wanted to ask her about transport back. I was already in debt, but maybe there was a way to leave some token or agreement to pay for a vehicle or animal. *Vehicle*—I'd never be able to ride a horse alone. Troy had a stable here; maybe she'd want me to bring some cycle north to safety. I was desperate enough to even leave the phone as bond if necessary. I refused to think about the fact that I didn't actually know the roads to Ambridge, having ridden down on the rails.

Following Zara to the kitchen area, dropping my voice under the noise of the rattling dishes, I asked, "Have you heard of Troy's stables in the area? I'm thinking of getting a ride from there."

Zara looked at me dubiously. "Yes, I know them, but I think the transport there was either borrowed or vanished mysteriously before they could put their hands on it." She hesitated to name the rebels, but at least she'd said *they*, not we.

I sagged against the counter. "Would you know a way to get back to Ambridge? About fifteen miles north of here up the 65."

She thought for a while, washing the dishes and handing them to me to dry. Over at the table, Justin and Teg were in deep, quiet conversation. I put a cobalt blue ceramic plate up on the rack. None of the dishware matched, but it was uniformly gorgeous and would probably fetch a year's salary if sold in the City. Artaud would have given his right arm, or at least his right henchman, for this stash of dinnerware. Was the salvage so much better out here, or was it true that most of the City salvage ended up in the luxury towers? Maybe life wasn't *tough all over,* as the authorities kept telling us. With my safe retreat cut off, maybe it was time to find out if there was an even safer place. But then I thought of the jazz, and the mu-vid theaters with their incredible images of the past and—if Pippin was truthful—of things that had never been. The moments I was swept away into those other worlds were some of the best in my life. Even when friends and colleagues let me down, the music and the images didn't disappoint. But Zara had music and syth-food, so maybe there was more out here.

"I might know where a bicycle could be borrowed," she said eventually. "But—there would have to be some kind of trade." She looked at me with a doubtful expression.

I nodded, frowning. Clearly I was more than broke as far as credit went. But wait! "If I zipped in and out of the tunnels, I could pull enough credit to buy something to trade—if you have any idea what would be good." *And were willing to let me use the tunnels again*, I amended silently.

"Maybe," she replied in a tone that said *no*. "Maybe we'd be going back in a day or two."

A day or two would be too late. I fumed, wondering if I could walk the 15 miles without collapsing. Wondering if I could steal a bike—and deal with the consequences later. Zara went to the ice box and pulled out a small square vanilla cake with white icing. She handed it to me and I brought it to the table. Justin and Teg looked up and the young man hummed in appreciation.

"Looks great, Zara."

"Actually, Justin made it—he's got such a sweet tooth that he keeps us well stocked in cakes."

She laid out some smaller plates and forks and cut the cake into four generous pieces. We helped ourselves and she brought back a pitcher and four glasses. Actual glassware glasses. I picked one up and stared at it, feeling a bit like a country hick. But glass was even less common than the lovely ceramic dishes. Plain water glasses were really rare and I'd never actually used one. The water in it shimmered and I thought I could understand why they had been so popular Before.

Glancing at me, Teg seemed to pick up his conversation with Justin where we had interrupted it.

"I have enough personnel," he said, "but you being such an expert, it would be really helpful if you could advise us on-site, just so we don't waste all the effort."

Vague but definitely not trivial talk. I wondered if they would prefer me to leave, and I was about to suggest it, when Justin answered, after a flicker in my direction.

"Are you sure you wouldn't be slowed down by an old man?"

Teg shook his head. "One, you're not that old, and two, we'll be pacing ourselves. And you don't have to—go the distance. Just help us out at... base camp, if you would."

Zara was looking back and forth between them; from her expression, she didn't know what was being proposed either. Worry was tight across her face; she'd already almost lost him once today. Justin looked at her, possibly thinking the same thing, but after a moment or two, he nodded slowly.

"It's an important job," he said. "Definitely worth doing right. I'll come."

"I promise I'll bring him back whole," Teg told Zara. She blushed and looked down. Ashamed of worrying?

"If it's important…" she replied.

"Definitely. Crucial." Teg looked over at me, cocked his head thoughtfully, and asked, "Would you like to come with us, Marty? We could use an extra pair of hands."

I paused with my fork halfway to my mouth. Was he legit? It was damn sudden to trust me, but on the other hand, Justin and Zara had decided pretty quickly, too. And for all I knew, they were as big in this organization as this guy. But I needed to get back to Ambridge! Every hour I stayed away increase the chances that Ciera's group would move on, or run into the retreating rebels who might now be acting in panic. Still, he seemed to be the source of inside information—worth waiting in order to bring back something really helpful to her? Maybe he could even extend his protection… A guy with his own plane could be useful.

Teg smiled, and added, "We're bringing stuff through a mixed zone, and if Justin told the story right—and he usually does—your skill would be handy in case we run into citizens who don't need to know." His voice took on a wheedling tone that was all for show. "It's too late to start to Ambridge alone," he said. "We'll be done by dawn, and you can leave then."

Justin and Zara were watching me intently, and with a sinking heart, I realized this was the best way to settle my debt with them. And a night's thieving, or whatever they were doing, should leave me a clean slate, and if I could manage it, maybe a ride north.

"I—I still don't know enough about your customs, but I suspect I owe you big time for all you've done," I said to Justin. He waggled his head with indifferent agreement. "I'm really worried about the group I left behind," I continued, and Zara broke in.

"Aida is sending a runner to open negotiations," she said. "They won't mind carrying a message saying you'll be a bit delayed."

That didn't leave me much excuse. I nodded—did one shake hands? It didn't seem so. Teg stood, rubbed his hands together and smiled briefly; it was a shark's smile.

"Great!" He said, grabbing his helmet. "Let's get going." It was a couple hours before I realized I hadn't told him about Ambridge.

21

We left by a back door, across the yard and through the woven-twig gate into an alley so narrow that the overgrown shrubs tore at my jacket and hands. The sun had gone below the tall hills, but it was still twilight, bright enough to see where we were going. Teg walked like a hunter, long silent strides and a twisting torso as he checked alcoves and crosspaths. I didn't see a weapon but I was sure he could produce one instantly. Justin followed a step behind him, with me a step behind that. In the next block, Teg paused, turned to us and said, "Wait here." He loped up the back steps of an empty-looking rowhouse and came back a few minutes later with his jacket a bit more bulgy, and led without comment down the alley.

We crossed several streets of brick rowhouses of the kind I was becoming familiar with—narrow, stark, unadorned. But many of them were in good repair, and I could see flickering lights behind curtains of all types—cotton prints, wool blankets, old magazine or book pages. He led us to a corner occupied by a very odd brick building, painted strawberry-yogurt pink, with pointy-arched windows that were boarded up, and a tower topped by a stone onion-shape. This had to be an old church. But Justin told me it used to be a very popular pub. We climbed chipped stone steps to a door nailed shut with three large cross-boards. Teg pulled it open easily—I recognized a common slum disguise.

Inside, there were oil lamps on various small tables, and a group of men and women lounged along an enormous bar, sitting on wooden stools and chatting, while the man behind the bar served drinks from somewhere—the shelves were empty, and the room otherwise looked dusty and unused. They all rose as Teg walked in.

"Tootle pip," he called out, walking up to the bar. The others moved aside to make space; they watched him with expectant smiles. Maybe this job wouldn't be so difficult; they apparently didn't think so. On the other hand, they were young and fit. There were four men and two women starting from my height and going upward—all clearly well muscled under their gray camouflage jumpsuits. The two women, one ebony and the other slightly lighter, had hair cropped above the ears like the men. The darker woman was striking, a face out of the old modelling magazines; the other was plain, but only in comparison. One man, a pale redhead, was almost a giant—I'd barely come up to his shoulders and he'd make two of me. He stood beside a white blond man with pale blue eyes and a piece of an ear missing. The other two were dark-skinned, gaunt, and seemed a mix of ethnic types, not quite as *Meltpot Max* as Pippin, but impossible to cubbyhole. They waited alertly as Teg pulled things out of his jacket and placed them on the bar: a roll of velvet cloth, a small paper map, and an old pair of Army binoculars. The roll of cloth clinked and I suspected lock picks.

"Haji, Desan, Jerome, Rory, Chala, Shawna,—this is Martin. He comes from Long Island."

They murmured at that, looking impressed. Had they heard about our gangs? What would they expect of me?

"Everyone revved up and ready?" he asked, not pausing for a reply. "And you've studied your parts?"

Desan and raised his hand. "When we get to the tower," he said, "which of us—"

Teg waved him to silence and turned to me and Justin. "Would you mind taking that lamp and going to fetch the two knapsacks that are in the basement? That door just there."

Justin obeyed without hesitation, and I followed him down the stairs, knowing we were sent away purely to miss the information. On the one hand, it made a lot of sense that only those who needed to know were given the dangerous facts, but I was getting a bad feeling about this "general"—young and cocky—who knows what kind of plan he had concocted?

We got to the bottom of the creaking stairs, and Justin moved hesitantly past tar-splashed wooden posts as thick as old trees. I moved close and murmured, "Justin—do you trust him? Or is that something you can answer?"

He hesitated, glancing back up the stairs, and said in a half whisper, "He knows what he's doing. I've seen him pull off some amazing things. He doesn't give much away, but I trust his promise to get me back." He moved forward and located the pair of knapsacks leaning against a huge old iron furnace. He picked one up and handed it to me.

As I slid it over my shoulder and started back toward the stairs, I considered his response. Teg had not promised to get *me* back—not specifically. But it sounded like Zara and Aida also admired him. I didn't trust people without a bit of history, but his uncanny resemblance to my old friend nagged like a sore tooth. I'd be keeping my eyes open, and myself braced to run, if it came to that.

Justin patted my shoulder and I paused. He gestured silently at the stairs, then gestured palm down for me to wait a little bit. Made sense—I didn't want to be embarrassed being sent off on another stupid errand.

"How long have you known him?" I whispered.

He shrugged. "About five years, since I moved to the area. I told you I lived outside the City—well, for a while I actually lived *inside*—went back with my ex-wife to the Bronx. But I couldn't stick it out in there. I felt like a puppet, with all the rules and everything the same—just like inside today."

I had to agree; today even the half-finished outskirts inside felt artificial, like those movie sets Pippin described. "So you both came out again?"

"I came out; she stayed inside," he said bitterly, then shrugged again. "They are really different worlds. He glanced up and I nodded. "So I lived in a northern town for a while—that's where I met Teg. I helped him set up some radio outposts—I'm good at that—and he told me about the opportunities down here. So I wandered down and met Zara...and I stayed."

"Justin?" Teg called from upstairs. We hurried up and put the knapsacks on a table. They were fairly heavy and thudded as we set them down.

"Careful," Teg cautioned us, "there's a couple of grenades in there."

Now he tells us? I tried to keep my face blank. The rest of the team seemed to have been filled in on us and were polite but silent. Teg let us out into the night, and I resigned myself to not knowing what came next. Not much different from the slum gangs.

A few blocks away, at the steel door of a block-long warehouse, we were met by Asrah and Zir, who recognized me with shock, glancing from me to Justin and back.

"It's okay," Teg murmured. "He's our inside guy."

Their expression changed to cautious welcome—which of us were they worried about?—and they gestured us into an enormous room crammed with aisles of shelving. I'd only seen something this vast once, when Big Lulu's group had raided a large old store-turned-gangtown far out on the Island. This was huge, although it was hard to judge even by the light of chimneyed oil lamps that the group picked up by the door. Certainly the glass jars and metal pipes just in front of me would have been enough to keep a gang in beer and bacon for years. Justin had acquired a small wagon that he pulled behind him, as we trekked up and down. Tiny pin lights glowed at the end of each aisle, something to navigate by, but not enough to show the goods. Even that was impressive, and suggested solar power on the roof. When someone lifted an oil lamp, I saw stacks of glass jugs that Mickey's distillery team would have drooled over. Next came wood boxes marked with odd labels: JJ Mid Gain 12AX7, KT88 Golden Gate, 12AX& Tungsol Reissue. Teg pointed—Zir picked out a box here and there, opened them and removed small glass vials, placing them into a larger box his brother held. I noticed the files were plugged with some kind of metal with wires sticking out. Didn't seem like computer parts—maybe for cars?

Next, we stopped at shelves loaded with guns—not pistols, but larger, more complicated pieces needing to be cradled in one's arm, with strange metal boxes sticking out at the sides and straight rifle butts as well as handles. Nothing I'd seen before, but undoubtedly a death sentence within the City. And you'd probably be grateful for death by the time they gave it to you. My mouth went dry just looking at them; I watched as Justin and the others pulled gun after gun off the shelves and loaded them into the wagon. I recalled Tuffy once claiming that gunbattle mu-vids were deliberately destroyed by the authorities, in order that we never know what had been. "*They* still have them," he'd assured me, "but even the black market has a hellish time finding any. They want to be sure when they come out blazing, that the shock alone will kill you." He said even the car chase mu-vids had been snipped to erase the gun battles. I had seriously doubted that such mu-vids or weapons existed—the Guard didn't have them—but here was proof the guns were real. If rebels had these, the City was in deep shit.

"Do you have ammo?" Teg asked. Asrah nodded, trotted down the aisle, and came back with an armful of metal boxes like the ones attached to the guns. They loaded those into the wagon and we continued down the rows. The darkness around us, as the oil lamps flickered and bobbed in Desan's and Shawna's hands, was thick and alive like some fiend waiting to pounce. What had I gotten myself into? My old gangs seemed more like boy-cliques now; I prayed I wasn't going to see what real warfare looked like. We stopped again, and Zir pulled a metal box off the shelf, handing it to me.

"Be real careful with this."

I realized it was a radio box, like the one I'd seen at Zara's but bigger. Knobs and dials poked my arm as I held it, and it was surprisingly heavy. What was inside? I had a weird flash of myself sitting at a café table, trying to describe all this to my jazz friends—another world, another life, and maybe one I'd never see again.

"You'll need a couple of these," Asrah said. "Got them last week and they are checked out." He handed two red hand-sized plastic rectangles—black on one side with a tiny bulb on the end—to Justin, who whistled softly. I recognized them suddenly—solar powered flashlights, absolute gold on the Island. Artaud had wielded his almost like a scepter. Justin flicked the light on and off for each of them—an almost blinding light, in fact a very useful weapon in the dark—then left them off. He handed one to Teg, who stuffed it in his jacket pocket. I wondered how long each light would last.

We continued walking the endless aisles, detouring along rows with the brothers stopping here and there to pick up something and tuck it in a box or the wagon. Finally we reached a door on the other side that led to a tiny office. Zir put his lamp down on a wooden, paper-topped desk, and picked up a leather-bound book about the size of one of my family's Bibles. He opened it and held it toward Teg.

"As agreed," he murmured. Teg glanced down at the page, taking a moment to read it, then took a white stick from the table, and wrote something on the page. Justin did the same. *So they extend credit out here*, I thought inanely. That was one that the inside gangs hadn't solved—it was cash or trade on the spot, no deferrals or credit. No trust. I wonder if these folk swapped hostages to be sure.

The rest of the group began to load the goods into large knapsacks, even the guns—so they weren't for immediate use. I breathed easier. They crammed a few extra things in our two knapsacks. Justin took the radio from my hands and wrapped it in a thick blanket before stowing it into a blue backpack that was braced with a metal frame. He carefully placed the glass tubes into cloth bags and placed them on top of the radio. Then he shrugged that backpack onto his shoulders with a grunt.

Once everything was stowed, we followed the brothers out of the office through a door where we eased out quietly, leaving the oil lamps behind. Night had fallen, the street seemed deserted, and a damp breeze blew down between the grubby buildings. A slightly less than half moon appeared and reappeared between slowly shifting clouds. It took me a few minutes to get my night vision back, and meanwhile Justin guided me with a hand on my elbow. Teg was in front and the burly bulk of Rory loomed in the rear as the group followed narrow streets, their footfall almost indistinguishable from the bits of tumbling debris. We turned onto a cobblestone alley—large humped stones like in the City's lower Bowery, their hills and valleys tripping me up more than the buckled asphalt of the larger streets. My pack was full of the guns and my back was stiff as much with fear as effort—could they go off if I joggled them too much? But I was the disposable pack mule.

At crosstreets, a high faint light glowed in long shafts—so we must be near the Wall, perhaps following it south again. Pitted concrete walls, yellowed in the light, were pierced by corrugated truck-sized steel doors, chained shut and covered with old hieroglyphic symbols from Before. My eyesight began to adjust, and I could see irregular forms, gray except where stray light picked out faint color—barrels, a ladder chained to a wall, a hitching post. Once or twice I thought I saw figures up ahead, but they melted into the darkness by the time we arrived—avoiding trouble? We passed the building that I'd climbed this morning, then down a tiny two-person-wide alley to a corner where my eye was caught by an ornate Victorian house—there were lamps behind the curtains, their light revealing elegant carved porch pillars and arched window frames. Oddly, the house was across from a windowless two-story warehouse, and a block down, the same kind of warehouse faced an ivy-covered church—what kind of planning had this city done, Before?

We passed into a non-residential section—blocks of solid walls, high windows, narrow steel doors—storage or factories. Another couple blocks and it opened onto flat lots full of eccentric Mall booths, their occupants asleep...or watchful? We passed a large red and yellow sign leaning against a pole, the double arches of an old eatery, now defunct. I was surprised it hadn't been grabbed—those massive plastic signs, much more weatherproof than typical plastic, were popular shed roofs back East. *That's* where I'd seen the KFC face before! The odd association jolted me. *Focus!* The darkness felt deeper, more threatening, as buildings were left behind. I saw a bright light ahead—Teg had turned on the flashlight. Was he confident no one could see it? I recognized the elevated highway in front of us, and held my breath—what now? At the Wall, the group paused as Teg bent over a lock on a gray metal door while Desan aimed the flashlight. There was a rattle like he was using the lock picks. The door opened noiselessly and we walked down a half-block tunnel to an area walled on the right. Teg turned off the flashlight. I sensed we were Inside.

Here, lamps dotted the streets at wide intervals—a very faint light that nevertheless carried a long way in the blackness. Where there were lights, there might be cameras; I hoped they knew that. I noticed Teg was leading us through the darker segments, moving slowly and erratically, perhaps enough to fool motion detectors—would they have *them* this far out? They were costly but the City was full of such security devices, and all citizens knew that "shortcuts had long consequences." We continued south for a couple blocks, under another elevated road, then I sensed a large structure to our left. Tall verticals broke the beams of distant lights, and I imagined I could make out the open framework of something vast—at least two blocks long and eight stories high. "Old stadium," Justin murmured. "I'll tell you about it someday." Then we were near the river—I could hear it—turning left and following a one-story wall bristling with razor wire on the top. It was a long walk with no buildings or alleys to shield us. The group had gone completely silent and I cringed whenever my footsteps were the only ones audible. I focused on the creeping gang-step that allowed one to pass silently through enemy territory. I no longer felt like a citizen of this place—ten years of adaptation had melted away in a few days. After two or three blocks, buildings began again on the left—not the old brick row houses but "modern" steel and polished granite with lots of windows, mostly intact. It was the kind of office area that the City touted as "proof" that life had never regressed to the window-breaking, car-burning anarchy of the Adjustment. Such large windows were almost impossible to make now and those offices were generally occupied by government or corporate executives. This far out, I wondered if they would risk being so close to the edge of the Outside. I'd noticed some steep hills to the north—my bet was executives would have claimed the view from safety rather than this river-front property.

Teg signaled us to stop in front of a four-floor office building whose sleek steel and granite face was unmarred by erratic painted messages or the scorch marks of the inner-city. The windows and glass door of the first floor were black on the inside—curtains or panels. He scratched at the glass and a moment later the door was opened and we slipped inside. A light was turned on, and I blinked, adjusting. We were in a large room with office desks in typical rows, on which sat a dozen or more soldiers in gray camouflage jumpsuits bulked up by Justin's armor. A tall black woman with cropped hair, broad cheeks and a hawk nose greeted Teg solemnly with a slow fist bump.

"All is ready," she told him. "The crossing is prepared, and guards change in ten minutes."

Teg nodded and flashed one of his brief smiles. He gestured me forward. "This is Marty, who will help us with the guards." Under her curious stare, I felt myself go cold. What did he mean?? I thought I was along *just in case*. Teg told me to hand my knapsack to her, so I shrugged out of it carefully and stretched my shoulders in relief. She made no move to unpack them, and I wondered if they were payment rather than tools for the evening—I sincerely hoped so. Gang scrums had been bad enough with bats and knives—I never wanted to see a battle fought with those things. They seemed totally capable of "raining bullets like hail," as Tuffy had described. What could they do to a human body? And leather armor would be useless, I suspected. She and Teg moved to the other side of the room, talking quietly.

A young man with a gaunt pockmarked face, cropped black hair and bright blue eyes had brought out a tray of mugs and what looked like cookies; our group dug in with relish. The mugs held cider, slightly alcoholic and very tasty. The cookies were chocolate flavored, and I savored them, wondering how they managed to get such a rare chemical. Justin was chatting quietly with a sandy-haired fellow in the corner, and Rory was conferring with a redheaded man almost as large as himself, comparing pistols that had appeared from nowhere. My muscles couldn't endure this level of tension much longer; I tried to stretch them, telling myself that at least for the moment we were out of danger. But what did Teg mean?

As if sensing my stare, he turned from his conversation with the woman and came over. "In a few minutes," he said, "we'll be approaching a bridge to the south side. It has been bombed, like the other bridges, but we have a workaround." He flashed one of his smiles, more like a dog baring his teeth. I tried to keep a blank face and meet his eyes. "Even though nothing can get across the bridges, they always have it guarded. I propose that you approach them and explain that you have been kidnapped and have escaped—use most of your real story, so it will be believable. While you have their attention, we will slip past, and then I'll come back and spring you." He stared at me and I knew in that moment that it was agree or die. He had a slum lord's cold certainty and a lot more intelligence. *Don't let him see you resist!* Don't give away the inner doubts even for a second. He knew I was too far into this to have any hope of backing out. *The bastard!* My mind spun as I nodded slowly, agreeing while racing through the slim options I had. If worse came to worst, I would in fact be mostly telling the truth—I would be with guards who would want to know how I got there, but I was a citizen and entitled to protection under the law. A small part of my mind was yelling that was a theory which most citizens took great care to avoid testing. How would he "spring me"? Why would he need to? I was disposable—a very handy tool he had picked up at Justin's.

I swallowed hard and asked, "How long do I have to keep their attention?" Let him think I was gullible. "I mean—I want to know how long to string the story out so there's no… danger."

He looked past me, calculating and I risked a quick glance around the room. Justin was watching us but his eyes flicked away as I looked over—yes, he knew this had been set up, damn him. And I had walked into it—once again, my shit-detectors had failed. So much for loyalty to tribe. But I wasn't their tribe, so they probably didn't even feel guilty. I thought I saw some guilt or shame on Justin's face before he turned away. I wondered if Zara would even send that message as she promised. *Tricked again, Martin.* That should teach me to trust people.

"If you can keep them talking for 15 minutes, we should be done by then," Teg said, and I dragged my gaze back. Taking a slow deep breath, I nodded. I was sure I wasn't keeping the bitterness out of my face, but what did he care? The woman extinguished the lights. With my gut full of bile, I followed them out the door, glad I couldn't see Justin. Well, I would have plenty of information to give the guards in return for my safety—but Teg must know that! Confused, I looked over at him, faintly outlined by a light high overhead; he flashed another smile. *What the hell??* As we filed down the street, Justin touched my elbow again to guide me until my night vision came back.

"We'll pick you up again, promise," he murmured. I stepped away and he dropped back. Would he have said that if I was disposable? Was he just making sure I didn't cut and run? My mouth was bone dry and I longed for a simple glass of water. Well, I could ask the guards for that, I thought with a bleak chuckle. It would fill some time.

Too quickly, I saw a deeper darkness rising up above me—the thick steel of the bridge even blacker than the night. There were fewer lights here, and I noticed several that were out. Had that been prearranged? Who was this woman who apparently lived inside but was loyal to Teg? At least some of her crew, maybe all, had followed us out. My mind persisted in dwelling on trivial details in an attempt to avoid thinking about the next few minutes. Teg was moving slower now, the entire group creeping carefully through the shadows under the buildings. A pool of light at the base of a massive concrete pillar identified the guards' shack. My legs had their usual impulse to flee, and I steeled myself, remembering Rory's pistol. The safest thing was to go through with it at least for now, and see.

Teg paused just outside the circle of light. He turned and I knew even before Justin tapped me on the shoulder that it was—my time. I walked forward, feeling like a sacrificial goat. Teg leaned forward and murmured, "You said you were good at bullshitting—just play the helpless victim again and it will be all good." He and the others stepped back into the shadows. I ran my fingers through my hair, panicked for a moment at the thought of my beard, and then just ran toward the shack.

A guard was outside in an instant, leveling a pistol at me, so I called out, "Help me! Please God help me! I'm a citizen—Martin Forrester—I was kidnapped." I paused, leaned down with my hands on my knees, gulping breath, refusing to look at the guard, refusing to consider what happened if he didn't believe me.

"Hey, Jodi—check out a Martin Forrester, will ya?" The guard yelled back into the shack. Turning to me, he asked, "what's your number?"

"Uh—553 dash 234 dash 78," I said, trying to sound dazed and confused, trying to squelch the rage. That would have to wait.

He called that number back into the shed as I slowly straightened up, hands in view, setting my expression into hopeful confusion. It looked like he was buying it. He still held the gun on me, but his panicked tension was gone.

After a couple minutes, a woman's voice inside the shack called out, "He's legit! Kidnapped by rebels."

"Oh ho!—you'll have a lot to tell us," the man said. "Come inside and I'll pat you down and then we can talk."

I stepped in; the shack was a single room big enough for a pair of desks, a back counter with a sink, a single electric hot pad, and a bunch of snacks. Some built-in cabinets above were marked *Emergency, Communications, Night Shift ONLY.* A back door was unmarked—toilet or escape route? The woman turned out to be a short muscular brunette with a bowl haircut, latte-hued skin and big brown eyes. She sat near a device that looked a bit like an old stapler, that would click on its own occasionally. She kept an eye on it and also watched me with something between fear and awe. The man told her to keep the gun on me as he patted me down. I had forgotten to get the phone back from Justin, so it wasn't there to be found. I felt mixed regret and relief at that.

"Everett, what should I tell headquarters?" Jodi asked.

The man gestured for me to sit on one of the straight-backed chairs. "Nothing yet," he replied. "Let's get the whole story then we can call it in." She turned to the device and tapped it a couple of times in an irregular rhythm.

"First, could I have a glass of water? I'm dying of thirst." At least my hand, trembling as I took the glass from Everett, helped the illusion. What next? Should I spin a story, watching the clock, or just blurt the truth? I remembered Justin saying he'd tell me about the stadium—surely he wasn't that coldly calculating? Did he believe he'd see me after this? But could Teg be lying to *him*? I'd suspect that man of anything, after seeing how calmly he'd forced my cooperation.

The room took on the clear edge and slowed reality that I'd experienced twice in the middle of battle, as if my mind was pausing at every instant. The guards watched me, Everett with a smug smile and Jodi with a rookie's wonder. I glanced at the clock—five minutes to eight.

22

"Well," I began, "you probably have my record—I was sent out by Commco, to get a couple comm towers set up in the wilderness. I did my best, but the first town was an utter failure, and the next morning, as we were getting ready to ride out, two bashers crept up on us and...grabbed me. They overpowered my guide, I think, but they hit me on the head, so that part is fuzzy..." I described a trip similar to my real one, but in the company of kidnappers. I told the guards that all my goods including my phone had been stolen, and that I thought some kind of ransom note had been sent. I left out any reference to Ciera or her acquaintances. I could do that much for her. *Yeah, big heroism, Martin.*

Jodi turned back to the large sheaf of papers on her desk. She scanned one of them and shook her head. "Negative. No ransom request was received."

"Um, maybe that report is outdated?" I said, keeping an edge of barely contained hysteria in my voice.

"Maybe," she said doubtfully. "There might be a new one coming in with the next shift."

Yes! Shift change was supposed to be any time—and now I was looking for it, I could see both guards had their eyes on the clock, and part of their attention on the door; they would be tired and more than happy to make me the next guy's problem. I spun the story out slowly, hoping that some of the gaps could be a poor victim's fatigue and confusion. Twice I thought about Ciera and my voice clogged in my throat, but they took it as delayed shock. It was harder to concoct something about the handover to the rebels, but I kind of glossed it and kept going, and thankfully could tell the story of the train trip fairly straight. As I got to the part where they were interrogating me, a noise outside caught our attention. I heard muffled voices of surprise and then a louder voice yelling, "What the fuck is that??"

Both guards grabbed their pistols and ran to the door. I gasped, then called out, "Don't let them get me again!" I half rose in my chair, wondering if I could flee past them. And go where?? The guards called out to a *Raul* and a *Varunka*—so the next shift had found something. Or someone. Looking around, I noticed what looked like a cell phone on one of the desks. I braced myself as my two guards raced outside. Grabbing the phone, I jumped to the door and looked out—there was a weird globe of bright orange bouncing or wafting down the street a half block away, chased by the pack of guards. And suddenly, Teg was at my elbow, tapping me, muttering, "Hurry—up!" He turned and ran and I followed on shaky legs.

Apparently he'd meant *up* literally—he was climbing a metal ladder on the side of the bridge piling. The ladder was in shadow but if the guards checked, it would take only a moment to find us. I followed hard on his heels, my legs trembling; a jolt of pure panic helped push me up the final dozen rungs to a lower steel scaffold. Teg pulled me into the shadows and froze; I sank to my knees and tried not to shake.

Three stories below us, the guards had caught up to the huge globe, surrounding it.

"Weather balloon," Teg murmured." Hopefully they'll think it's armed." He chuckled. There was no light up here, so I couldn't see his expression, and luckily he couldn't see mine. He'd actually come back. He'd actually come *back*! This was gonna take a bunch of re-thinking and now was not the time. He stood and gripped my arm as I clamored up on shaky legs. Slowly, we moved along what felt like a very narrow metal mesh flooring; I tried not to think about the three-story drop. He moved aside and guided my hand forward to another ladder. "It's another couple flights, I'm afraid," he murmured, letting me go first.

I prayed the adrenaline wouldn't wear off till we got to the top. The rungs were round metal pipes, not easy to stand on and somewhat slippery. I gripped the rungs above me tight enough to strangle them, and slowly pulled myself upward. Around me, I could sense the metal scaffolding, and I kept my head close to the ladder—one hard knock would have sent me backwards into Teg. *Just. One. More. Step.* I repeated that over and over, and we finally reached another landing.

"Could I—could we rest a moment?" I asked, ashamed to have to beg for a break.

"Yeah. You wait here, and I'll send someone back for you," Teg replied, then I heard him clamoring quickly up another ladder. Eight years younger than me, according to Zara, but at least twice as strong and fit. I sat there, breathing hard, trying not to think about being at least five floors up on an openwork bridge. I heard shouts below—they must have discovered I was gone. Would they think to look up? I leaned back against the cold steel. Now I was on the City's radar again—would they assume I'd been re-kidnapped? *Had* I been re-kidnapped? Damned if I could make head or tails of this.

I heard someone climbing down, and a young man called my name softly. I answered, scrambling to my feet, ducking to avoid metal struts. How would I make it up there, let alone whatever came next?

He came close, touched my arm and traced it to my hand, then pressed a bottle of water into it. "Teg said you might need some help—would you like a speedo?"

"Yes! That would help a lot," I replied with a sigh of relief. He placed the pill into my palm, and I washed it down gratefully. It would take a bit of time to kick in, but even knowing I had it would give me a bit of strength. He guided me to the next ladder and I began to climb, focusing everything on the movement upward.

The climb was agony, but somehow I made it, emerging from a mesh hatch beside a wide flat road that looked solid. Hadn't Teg said this had been bombed? The air was much cooler up here and I shivered; I could feel the speedo kicking in as I stared around, trying to figure out where I was. I had never been on such a bridge before. The half moon gave enough light to see the outline of Pitts far below, sheltered by the erratic Wall, its security lights a glowing gold halo. Beside it the width of the gray river shimmered like silk. It was so much higher than I had ever been, I felt some—what was it climbers got? *vertigo*—so I turned away from the magnificent view. Two narrow shafts of light swung slowly back and forth across the asphalt in front of us—team members using the flashlights. Others seemed to be struggling to carry a very long strip of metal scaffolding toward the middle of the bridge. The young man accompanying me pointed forward and I plodded over, watching my feet, not quite trusting the solidity of the asphalt. It was far beyond surreal now—this could easily be one of my nightmares.

It was a long bridge with two huge steel arches, pale yellow streaked with rust and dirt, one soaring like a giant's grape arbor far above us, the other far off toward the other city. A giant's rope curved low on both sides, with smaller ropes tied vertically to hold up the roadway—of course the "ropes" were thick steel cables, but my exhaustion skewed it, making them seem normal and me ant-sized.

As we got towards the middle, I could see a gap in the road—at least 25 foot, much too big to jump across. Obviously where they had bombed. I glanced at the cables—several had been severed, and it looked like the tension rested on a very thin remaining strand. I swallowed hard.

Justin was leaning against one of the barricades, hunched slightly forward, breathing loudly. He wasn't wearing the large knapsack. At least I wasn't the only one out of shape. I walked over, anger and relief and a strange kind of triumph surging around in my gut. Did I curse him out or demand an explanation? They had come back for me, after all. But they'd lied to get me here—and what else were they lying about? He glanced up as I got closer, and waved me over.

"Quite a climb, huh?" He spoke in short gasps, still drawing breath deeply. "On the other side is The Haunt. You heard about it?"

"No—it's really haunted?"

He shrugged. "I've never been. But the story is that the city bosses bombed these bridges right after the Adjustment, to protect themselves from rioters, but it backfired. They were trapped and became cannibals—with only a few left at the end, battling each other for food. Legend says the ghosts of those who were eaten still wander, looking for revenge." He chuckled but looked more scared than amused. "Others say it's the ghosts of the cannibals—or they're zombies now—still roaming around looking for food."

"Oh, super—and we're walking right into the *middle* of it?"

I glanced over where the soldiers were working almost at the edge, calling out instructions quietly, struggling to get the large metal scaffold piece upright. Teg waved us over.

My vertigo came back as we got closer; I stayed as far away from that jagged edge as possible, wondering what they were doing. In a minute, my question was answered—most of them stepped back, while a couple bent over the metal piece. I heard the low humming whine of machinery—they had rigged up some kind of pulley and winch, attached by thin cables to the stanchion of the bridge. We watched, by the light of a flashlight trained on it, as the metal piece slowly angled downward like a drawbridge, attached to a similar length with short braces, looking almost like a narrow railroad track. There was no sound but that machine as everyone watched tensely. Then, with a thump, the makeshift road touched down on the other side. The group unfroze, punched and patted each other, laughing. Then they paused again, watching as the woman team leader came up and shouldered some kind of weapon—a crossbow. I had seen drawings but since they were ballistics, gangs avoided them. Thrown weapons yes; anything spring-loaded, no. Someone aimed the strong flashlight across the makeshift bridge, barely catching the far end. She aimed and shot—something flew across and thunked into a solid upright at the other end. She dropped the bow, took hold of some kind of rope, pulling it backwards and tying it to an upright beside her.

"All right—now let's get going," Teg called out softly.

They were going to cross on that?? Okay, it was metal, but it was as narrow as a felled tree—and we must be at least 14 or 15 stories up! The speedo was causing my heart to race, and my mouth was as dry as ashes. The group members had scattered, and some came back pushing three wheelbarrows full of bags and boxes. Where had *they* come from?

"It's best if you look a little ahead, not down at your feet," Justin wheezed beside me. "Walk slowly and put your weight in your ankles, if that makes any sense. Pretend you're walking on a curb."

I must have stared at him like he was crazy, because he gave a brief chuckle. "It's hard to see, but Elontee just created a small rope handrail that we can steady ourselves on. It'll be all right." He patted my arm.

Perhaps it was good that this felt like a nightmare; the sense of unreality numbed my panic and I followed the others up to the makeshift bridge, which was wider than I had feared—several metal beams together, it was at least as wide as the alleyways we had come through. But below it was nothing, and that nothing sucked at my feet, making it hard to take one step after the other. I tried to follow Justin's instructions, resting my hand lightly on the rope just for comfort, looking at the feet of the guy in front of me, trying to pretend I was walking through an alley, forcing my brain away from any thoughts of rivers or heights or falling toward... *Just. Keep. Walking.* Suddenly, I don't know how, I was at the other end and stepping off onto asphalt again. I stumbled forward, half running, trying to get solid ground around me again, letting the delayed tremors shake my body. I swallowed repeatedly to keep from throwing up.

It didn't take long for the rest of the group to cross, even the wheelbarrows. Then we were walking down the other side, toward the part of the city that held the huge dead towers. As we approached the end of the bridge, I noticed the soldiers were now holding those deadly guns. What the hell was over here? Surely they didn't believe in ghosts or zombies. I kept to the middle, with Justin and the three who were wheeling the barrows, letting the others create a protective ring. Justin reached into a jacket pocket and handed me a pistol—a flattish angular piece that felt smooth and powerful. I breathed a little easier holding it. Until I thought of those guns.

We came down onto river frontage lined with modern buildings, tons of untouched salvage. Where the lights hit it, I could see much of the glass was shattered, still lying in shards, a glassblower's treasure chest. I heard the growls of a feral dog pack and gripped my pistol tighter. Elontee and another soldier who were carrying crossbows moved to the front. We crossed the esplanade and walked up the street in front of us, with the wheelbarrows in the middle. An inch or more of soil or dust, blown in over decades, muffled our steps. The growls got closer. As the first dog came around the corner, a crossbow arrow speared it and as it thrashed, the pack fled. Silent and effective. Elontee paused to retrieve the arrow. The group continued down a street of old four- and five-story Victorian relics, reminding me of New York below 14th St. It was a familiar, crazy juxtaposition of styles and centuries, weirdly illuminated in the swaying flashlight beams. I tried to focus on looking for danger. I intended to throw myself flat if *anything* popped up—stay out of the way of those guns.

After about five antique blocks, we entered an area of sleek glass towers rising on both sides higher than I could count the floors. Here, too, much of the glass was blown out, lying in drifts, the metal frame windows gaping like open mouths. I thought about New York's emergency deconstruction, and the areas where no one walked unless they wanted to be pinned under tons of concrete. It was inky dark in this sky-less corridor and several soldiers paused, put something on their heads and in a moment had flashlights, small but bright, adding to our visibility. As their gaze swept back and forth, I caught glimpses of office chairs, café tables and wire seats, even backpacks and those printed cloth shopping bags lying both inside and outside the shattered glass front of shops. Cars were still parked at the curb, windows open, caked with streaky dirt, tires flat. Whatever had scared people away had kept people out for 50 years. I didn't believe in ghosts, or monsters, except human ones. But *something* had convinced enough people to stay away. So what were *we* doing here??

I had a sudden panic that we were going after the southern rebels, as we trudged block after block. But that would be foolish, with so few, and wouldn't the plane do a better job?

Without warning, a group of howling men jumped us from a large alcove.

"Down!" Teg hollered, but I was already hitting the street, pulling Justin down beside me. The blast from the guns, like chattering teeth at hearing's pain threshold, and the shriek of shattering glass froze my limbs—all I could do was pray. It was over in a few seconds, and the silence rang in my ears. I gulped a breath.

"All clear!" one of the women called out.

Slowly, I rose to my knees and patted myself to be sure I wasn't bleeding. I seemed intact, and I glanced over to see Justin rising shakily, but with a smile. I looked the other way, and unfortunately at that moment the guards with the headlamps chose to examine what was left of the bodies. Ripped apart as if a pack of dogs had descended, there were red heaps of flesh, arms and legs ending in bloody stumps. I clamped my teeth together and looked away. Talk about butchering!

One of the soldiers who'd been handling a wheelbarrow clutched his shoulder and Elontee hurried over, a roll of bandages in her hand. Another soldier was sucking his hand, but otherwise the group looked alive. I heard a babble from...where the bodies were. I listened without turning.

"You can't enter Hell, this is our Hell!" the voice said. "Our Hell, our punishment—you don't belong here!"

"What the hell is he talking about?" Shawna asked.

"Pun intended?" Teg responded. "They think the Apocalypse has happened, and they have been sent to the underworld. From what I gathered last time I was here. Come on—let's keep going. Take his weapons and let him go."

My legs were like jelly as we continued down the street, the voice of the crazy fading behind us. The soldiers in front were now inspecting each alcove as we passed, their headlamps raking the shadows, their guns poised.

"These AK guns are dangerous here," Justin murmured.

"No shit, Sherlock," I replied.

"What? No, I mean the bullets ricochet—bounce off the buildings. It could be as dangerous for us as for them," he explained.

"Then why did they bring them?"

"Well, maybe they didn't know how many we'd run into. Or maybe they're good against zombies," he added.

Thanks, I needed that image, I thought.

Finally, Teg gestured for the group to stop. He pointed towards large double doors of black "smoked glass", blazoned in gold letters *UPMC*. We climbed shallow stone steps, the barrows being dragged backwards, and entered the building.

A two-story lobby of polished granite and marble, elegant except for the thick dust that lay on floor and reception desk, graying the purple upholstered chairs and the sleek blond wood tables, billowing up as we walked toward a bank of elevators. I put my hand over my nose to avoid sneezing. Surely he didn't know how to make them work??

But instead he led the group toward a blank metal door at the far side of the hall—the emergency exit. And of course there would be stairs all the way up, no matter how insane it was to think someone could walk 50, even 75, flights to get in or out of the building. It had been one of the requirements before the Adjustment, one of the many games that had been played with residents, promising a non-existing safety from fire or extended power outage. This one had the usual pushbar with red warning sign that an alarm would go off if used. With a wide grin, Desan walked over and pushed the door open, and we paused. But the alarm had died decades ago, and the stairwell was simply a black concrete pit, airless and as dusty as the lobby.

"Okay, team—grab what you need and get moving," Teg said. About half the group started rummaging in the wheelbarrows, removing their knapsacks and pulling out objects. Rory had Justin's blue knapsack on one shoulder, carrying it as lightly as a jacket. He unshipped it and Justin pulled out the bags of tubes, then the radio. He rested that in a wheelbarrow and began explaining in a low voice. Desan came over with a handful of wires and a screwdriver, and Justin attached the wires to the radio, continuing to instruct them. More gear came out and Jerome joined the group discussion.

My curiosity overflowed and I stepped closer to Shawna, who was leaning against the wall.

"What are they doing? Unless you'll have to kill me if you tell me," I added half jokingly. But only half—remembering Teg.

She chuckled. "I guess you could say we're building one of your City comm towers," she answered. "This is the tallest building around. Gonna get an antenna up on the top, with enough wire to bring the control room down to a manageable floor. It will be a remote station, anyway. If it works, well..." She smiled and fell silent.

Ironic—I was finally part of a comm tower project. "We don't have to climb all the way up, do we?" At this point they'd probably have to shoot me, cause I wasn't gonna make it.

"Nah—just half the group. We're going back now. Come back for them later."

I couldn't imagine Justin walking to the top of the tower either, and was relieved to see him pat Rory on the arm and come back towards us. The climbing group shouldered their knapsacks, shook hands with Teg and entered the stairwell. Rory carried the radio and Desan held the streamers of wire. That left me, Justin, Shawna, Teg and four of Elontee's soldiers.

"Before we leave, I want to sweep some of the building for resupply," Teg said. "This was one of their biggest medical centers. Shawna and Nick, up one floor—check for examining offices, check the drawers for any medical gear. The meds would be too old, but the tools will be fine. Montel, Jon and Grady, you check two floors up. That's probably all we have time for now."

The soldiers removed their knapsacks and left them in the wheelbarrows, then headed into the stairwell, each pair with a headlamp. The three of us were left with Teg's flashlight. He went over to a knapsack, and removed a metal thermos.

"Water—have a bit but don't drink too much," he said passing it to Justin. Justin drank and passed to me, and I sipped gratefully, washing the dust down my throat. Teg passed the flashlight to Justin and drank some water, then replaced the thermos. We made our way to the lobby. Teg thumped one of the chairs, thought the better of it, and sat down in the dust. He snapped off the flashlight.

"This will give us a moment's rest," he said.

I sank into another chair, and Justin eased himself down beside me. "I definitely need to exercise more," he commented. As the last hours' events caught up with me, rage began to bubble up again. It was pitch dark inside, but I could sense Teg was moving, and I tensed—should I move farther away? Should I demand answers? Some inner survival circuit tripped and my comment died in my throat.

"Tower team to base, over," Teg said. I startled—was he talking to me or Justin? He repeated it, and I suddenly realized I could hear his voice coming from my pocket! He also paused, moved slightly—lowering his hand?—and asked, "Marty? What is that?" The underlying harmonics of his voice sent ice up my spine.

I fumbled in my pocket, remembering the little phone just as I pulled it out. I held it toward him, saying, "As I ran out of the guard shack, I grabbed this off the desk—one of their phones?"

"Shit—those bastards were intercepting us," Teg growled. I felt him move and again tensed, raising my arm to block any blow. But he was speaking into his phone. "Base—17 switch, out." I could hear the crackle and whine like the ham radio, the pitch rising and falling, and then he spoke again. "Tower team to base, do you copy? Over."

I heard a crackle and then a metallic voice say, "We copy—what was the problem? Over."

"Bastard guards had our frequency—stay off that one. Switch as per the list. Over."

"Copy that. Otherwise all right? Over."

"Going fine. See you soon. Over and out." His clothing rustled as he stuffed both phones in his pocket.

There was silence for a moment and I touched the pistol in my pocket—a crazy thought, since I couldn't see to shoot him. But I wasn't gonna go quietly, if he decided to cut me out of the team. Then I heard him sigh, and he said, "I suppose that was a lucky grab on your part."

"Yeah, you might never have known they were on to you," Justin said. His voice sounded shaky, and I wondered if he thought I was in trouble.

"I just grabbed it because I'd left my phone with Justin," I explained. I hadn't felt this combination of resentment and fear since I'd been hauled up in front of Big Lulu for losing a stash of screws and washers.

"Oh, right—and I left it back at the house," Justin said apologetically.

"I don't need it now, and sounds like it could have been bugged anyway," I replied. I felt a hollow, like an empty tooth, but told myself I had lived for 28 years without a phone—I couldn't be lost without one now.

Just then we heard voices and footsteps in the hallway. Teg flipped on the light and walked over, illuminating Shawna and the other soldier who were piling stuff into a wheelbarrow.

"There was a good stash of needles and bandages and some stuff I don't recognize but took anyway," she told Teg. A moment later, the other three came down, each with a full armload which they dumped into the wheelbarrows.

"All right, we're outta here," Teg said. The soldiers grabbed the wheelbarrows and followed us out of the building.

"It's tempting to grab some more of this stuff while we're here," Justin commented as we crossed the large courtyard and got to the first block of shops. I was more worried that we had only two guards, though the three who were wheeling barrows had guns strapped to their backs. Were there other feral gangs lurking? I couldn't stop straining to look into shadows, though without a light I could see very little. And the pistol was in my hand, for whatever good it would do.

"We'll be picking up more stuff, I promise," Teg replied. He pulled out his paper map, consulted it and turned down a different street. How long would this adventure continue? The speedo was helping me keep up, but I was hungry and thirsty and those few moments weren't enough of a break.

A couple of blocks away, the flashlights revealed a huge old-fashioned building of massive stone blocks crudely carved as if by hand, though the size of the building would have made that impossible. Each block was as big as an apple crate, mortared with a neat ridge of cement, and despite the unwieldy size, the builders had created a castle-like structure with turrets and arches, strangely graceful. There was even a stone bridge from one of the buildings to the other above the road. What I would have given to see this in the daylight! All I could glimpse were the details revealed by the several flashlights sweeping up and back.

"It's the courthouse," Teg explained, "I need something from here. You boys stay here with the wheelbarrows—Shawna, Justin, Marty, come with me."

He led us up wide stone steps under a huge archway. The massive wooden door had a steel grate blocking it, but Teg pulled something from his pocket, fiddled with the lock, and in a few moments, pulled the grate away. It shrieked on rusty hinges, and the sound echoed down the street. I turned back, afraid that our presence had just been announced to the whole city. But Teg waved impatiently and we stepped into the building.

Despite the 19th century exterior, the building had been modernized into a plain-vanilla office set-up, with lots of white walls, gray desks, generic paintings and beige carpeting, all now thick with dust. Tracks in the carpet said we weren't the only ones who'd gotten in. I gripped my pistol. Teg seemed to know where he was going, leading us down one hall after another, everyone following blindly. He stopped in front of a wooden door with a frosted glass window painted with *Archives*. He ushered us inside, then swapped his flashlight for Shawna's headlamp. As we waited by the doorway, he paced up and down the aisles of wooden cabinets with very shallow drawers. He stopped and pulled out a couple drawers, and I could see these were maps—piles of paper maps. How had he known these were here? And what was he looking for? I knew better than to ask, but curiosity was itching inside me.

Eventually, a hiss of satisfaction said he'd found what he'd come for. He pulled several large sheets of paper carefully from the drawer, rolled them up, and moved on to the next drawer. He found others and eventually brought a thick roll back to the door.

"Marty, if you don't mind, would you hold these very carefully?" It wasn't exactly a question, and I didn't get the sense I could refuse, but it least it was polite. We followed him back outside where the other soldiers were sipping water and nibbling what looked like nutrition bars. One of them was holding a gun at the ready, but they seem to have far less tension than I would have.

Teg led us through the abandoned streets, working our way around fallen or tossed metal barrels, some of which still held crumpled bags and tin cans. There were downed limbs off the trees, which had grown massive, arching overhead and breaking the sidewalks with their roots. The wheelbarrows were definitely having a hard time. Teg waved us into an alcove, after Shawna had checked it, turned to the soldiers and asked, "can we stuff this all into the knapsacks?"

"And leave the wheelbarrows here?" Shawna asked incredulously, then bit her lip. The others tensed as Teg frowned. I held my breath, but all he said was, "We can come back for them. I know a place to leave them."

The soldiers scrambled to fit everything inside their bags, Shawna moving the fastest.

"Now that they're empty, they should go faster—and in two blocks, we can safely leave them."

None of the streets looked familiar, and I wondered how we would get back to the bridge. And I was dreading that crossing, even though I know I had done it once. I glanced at Justin—he must be exhausted too. A spasm of fear passed through me as I pictured him or I going off that narrow metal strip, falling, falling... I shook myself—no point making it worse.

We passed the same shop a second, or was it a third time? I tapped Justin's shoulder and asked, "Are we going around in circles? I've seen that shop."

"It was a chain—they had them on almost every block. That reminds me—" he hurried to catch up with Teg. "Would you mind if I nipped in there and get us a bean grinder?"

Teg laughed. "Are you sure you can carry it back?"

"It'd be worth trying."

Teg handed his flashlight to Justin, who stepped in gingerly through the broken glass door. We could see his flashlight sweeping the counter, then he set it down as he fiddled with something. I saw him tuck the flashlight under his arm and pick up a small machine. He moved slowly across the room, weaving around the tables and chairs. Finally he made it to the sidewalk, and Teg took the flashlight from him. I looked at the machine, and wondered why he would want one if coffee beans didn't exist anymore.

We were crossing a set of five streets that met at angles, and Teg had his flashlight trained on an odd greenhouse of some sort: arches of glass or maybe hard plastic, some of which had shattered. But it looked too small for more than a couple tables of plants. As we got closer, Justin muttered, "Oh shit—he wants us to go under the river." I was trying to figure out what he meant when we arrived at the greenhouse and I saw the old escalators coming up out of the ground—it was a subway! Fancier entrance than the New York ones, which were boarded up in any case, but definitely the old moving stairs that would take travelers into the lower platforms where the subway trains ran. I was stunned—I thought that was only a New York thing. And then I realized what Justin meant—we were gonna take that tunnel back under the river!

23

There was some barely-heard muttering from the soldiers, but no one questioned as Teg ordered us down the stairs, taking the barrows with us.

"They're on high alert at the other end of the bridge," Teg said, "It'll take days for them to relax again. And you know how carefully they watch the river."

I almost challenged him—I wouldn't even go down the *City's* subways! Did he have any idea if the tunnel even went across? But I couldn't walk that bridge on my own, if I even could find it, so I'd be stuck here with feral crazies—assuming Teg let me object and live. I trudged down the stairs, feeling my way down strange jagged steel steps, using the cracked plastic handrail to avoid falling.

It was darker than a blanket over my head down here, the lights from the flashlights as meager as candles. My heart lurched—what if our lights gave out halfway across? Had he thought this through?? He told the soldiers to set the wheelbarrows against the wall, and led the way through the metal gate onto the platform. I'd never been under New York, but the elevated platforms were very similar to this: white-tiled walls, bare concrete floor, a few empty frames where posters used to hang. A sign hung along the edge of the track said "Gateway Station". We climbed off the platform onto steel tracks with wooden ties like the railroad.

"Careful, now—just walk on the gravel, not the ties. They're slippery," Teg said. "Our patches are holding, but only just."

Not merely slippery—there was a couple inches of water, lapping over the ties. After a couple stumbles, Teg organized pairs, each with one light, which made it somewhat better. But it was dank and cold, the walls dripped and maybe it was getting harder to breathe. How did air get in and out of these tunnels? How long would the tunnel be? I tried to picture the width of the river, and how many steps it had been across the bridge—anything to keep from picturing the tons of dirt over my head and the river above that. I swore when I got across that I would leave immediately, find my own way back to Ambridge. How did I know this guy was even sane??

As I stumbled along next to Justin, once or twice grabbing his elbow to keep him from falling, I tried to picture this as an operating subway, with trains rocketing through here—it probably took less than 10 minutes to get under the river, at the speeds that I had heard the subway cars could go. Riders would barely notice this black hole. Despite Teg's comment about patches, my mind kept returning to an image of a rockfall—something totally blocking our way, something that would drive us all the way back and then we would have to cross the bridge on legs that could barely cross the street. *Think of something else!* I thought about Ciera and the commune—would they have gotten word by now? Why hadn't I asked Zara if I could have gone with whoever they sent? My debt had stopped me, then. Now lack of sleep made me so stupid I was a danger to myself. I thought of my apartment, but that brought no comfort, because there was no way I would be able to sleep there again until I satisfied the authorities that I was a good citizen. And how the hell would I do that? This was all too big for me. Something was going down that was gonna shake the City and I didn't want to be there when it did, did I? But where else? *Don't worry about it until you get through the night*. One emergency at a time.

"Almost there!" Teg's voice startled me. His light, which was noticeably dimmer, was angled toward an opening on our right—it was a subway platform! Had we gone all the way through? I took a deep breath as Justin patted me on the shoulder.

"We did it—we did it. Zara's never gonna believe this," he chortled, still clutching his grinder. I smiled and focused on not crushing the maps nor tripping in the last few feet, and then we scrambled up onto the chest-high platform, Shawna giving Justin a leg up. Teg led us up the frozen escalators. I noticed even the soldiers were moving really fast, as if they couldn't wait to get out. This was not the usual escape route, then.

It was still dark outside, though after the tunnel, it looked more like deep twilight. I took a deep lungful of fresh air. It must be somewhere around 3 or 4 AM. There were a couple of lights in the distance, so we were still inside the Wall. The speedo was wearing off and when it did I would drop where I was and sleep for hours. I looked around—a couple blocks away was that huge metal skeleton that Justin called the stadium. So we weren't far from the gate we came in on. What a night!

"Let's get this stuff into the warehouse," Teg said, turning left toward the stadium. Open air around me gave me a bit more strength—it was astonishing how wonderful fresh air could feel. How far up the skyscraper was the other group by now? Could they really get an antenna on the top, and how far could a signal go at that point?

All flashlights but one had been switched off, and that one was a dull yellow, probably in its last hour. This area was mostly flat empty space, with a few hulks of metal or cracked plastic strewn around. Directly in front of us was the walled-off Highway 65, but we veered left again and walked parallel to it, navigating through the broken concrete from a smashed ramp. We were slightly north of the stadium, in an area of older buildings that had apparently been cannibalized for parts. Teg stopped at a burnt brick shell about head-high with doors and windows missing, the floor treacherous with splintered beams and rubble. He led us toward a fallen door leaning between an inner wall and floor. Two of the soldiers hurried forward and lifted the door—which was hinged on top and concealed a staircase going down. One soldier secured the door with wire, and the rest of us followed Teg down creaky, wobbly stairs. At the bottom, someone lit an oil lamp and I looked around at a small but well-stocked storeroom—shelves similar to Asrah and Zir's, with parts of machines, boxes labeled "medical", "wireless", "brewing"... a real hodgepodge. The soldiers unpacked their knapsacks, and Teg inspected each item then directed them where to store it. Once again I felt unneeded and very tired. Is this where I asked to leave? I hesitated. If Justin could hang in there, so could I. And when I was done, I should be debt-free. There were no chairs, so I leaned against the wall, still gently holding the roll of maps, and tried to make sense of what I was seeing.

It reminded me of the gangs—they had specialties, but also scrounged anything and everything, trading what they didn't need. They stashed in small hideouts, since no one put all of their precious salvage in one place. This was very cleverly hidden in wreckage, rather than secured in the same sense as the brothers' place was. But who knows what was secure out here?

I leaned over to Justin, who was watching hungrily. "How did you get those wheelbarrows up to the bridge?"

"They were up there before—that and our little bridge—they'd been brought up one by one, in prep for tonight. This was a one shot deal—security along the river is really high, and even if they don't realize we went over, the little diversion Teg arranged will have them on even higher alert for a good long while. They are always looking for boats, so that was never an option."

I wondered how they got past the guards when I wasn't around to help them. Had that been a test? I remembered a couple scams in Mickey's gang, impersonating repair crews in order to get at a restricted place. If I were a guard and someone told me that scaffolding was necessary to keep the bridge from falling on my head, I'd have let them through, and the hell with regulations. That weather balloon was good—it had looked so alien, but I'd seen one once, now that I thought of it—there was a weather station near us on the Island, with a lot of gizmos to try to predict patterns. I wondered again about the satellites—was it all a huge lie? *Were* we in contact with Chicago or LA? How would I ever know for sure? The silver spoons didn't allow peons to question—the only way we would find out was if a satellite crashed in front of us or they admitted to lying, which wasn't going to happen.

"All right, crew—next we get the fuel." Teg was at the foot of the stairs, waiting with the oil lamp. He showed no fatigue or impatience, nor any sign that he expected resistance, even after a very long night. And the crew followed without a murmur, Justin and I lagging behind.

"How long is this going to take?" I whispered to him.

He looked uneasy. "I'm not sure, but honestly—it's best to just do it." Which confirmed my instincts. Teg wasn't somebody you got on the wrong side of.

Once again we were walking with the walled highway on our right, through an area technically inside but obviously abandoned. Two blocks over, I recognized the doorway we had gone through, and Justin looked over at it longingly as we passed. In front of us, the Wall angled and ran down past the stadium to the river. Here it was another mash-up of buildings and rubble-filled streets. Teg led us to a much-graffitied gray brick building, opened one of the boarded windows—it swung easily on hinges, another camouflaged entrance—and the group scrambled through it. I was grateful for some old boxes and barrels "casually" strewn beneath the window to give us a step up. On the other side was a bare living room, thick with dust, and a short hall that ended in a front door. Shawna hung to the rear of the group, and carefully brushed the dust with a large clump of wool from her pack, erasing our footsteps. The front door opened easily, and I was startled to see that the outside was a faux-brick surface, as if the door had been filled in. This group was bonza with camouflage! We went down the concrete steps and continued across rubble-strewn fields.

There were no lights here, and flashlights had been turned off, so we moved slowly and I tried to stay alert; I'd be soul-shitted if I fell, after keeping my feet so far. The half moon was already riding low in the sky, hovering before us over what looked like a blasted landscape. A city without noise was so strange I shook my head a couple times to be sure it wasn't my ears. Was this what the Dead Cities sounded like? The silence was broken only by the rattle of dry leaves or garbage, and our soft shuffling as we headed toward the only two-story building around.

It was concrete block construction with a row of large vents along the top and bottom—ribbons of light were leaking from the lumpy vent covers. I'd been smelling methane, and it must be coming from the building. What were we getting fuel for? Surely we weren't going to bring it back across the water?? These fuel depots were more dangerous than fossilized grenades without pins. And if we were stealing…! It was suicide trying to fast-finger fuel from a tank.

Inside, a vast room was lit by actual light bulbs. Of course they couldn't risk the danger of any kind of flame—still, a huge expense. But whoever ran this could afford it—this digester set-up was even more elaborate than Big Lulu had, and she was the Shitfuel Queen. Not that you ever said *that* to her face. She'd assembled steel barrels for the various steps of processing. These rows of tanks were made from auto bodies; the curves of hood and backs not even much hammered out, but pieced together into odd multicolored egg-shaped tanks that must have held gallons of sewage. This must be where all the night soil carts ended up. Yards of that ropy-looking flexible metal tubing led from the digesters to narrow tanks that probably filtered the sulfur out. I could hear the gentle bubbling in the final waterbath filter, and at the end of the process, pipes led into several really huge tanks. I wondered how many pressure-release valves they had installed, if any. If this plant blew up, it could take out four blocks! Maybe it already had once, I thought, remembering the streets outside. Three workers were checking the set-up even in the middle of the night—at least they knew not to leave it alone.

Teg walked over to the workers and spoke quietly, then gestured two of the soldiers over. A worker led the pair to an alcove by the holding tanks, and they came back wheeling two large steel gas canisters on hand trucks. So they had a compression set-up, too! Even more amazing. The soldiers gently maneuvered the hand trucks outside and our pace slowed to a crawl as two soldiers shined flashlights on the ground to be sure the hand trucks wouldn't be bumping and joggling—on these cracked and damaged pavements, that was like surgery on a roller coaster. I felt like some wannabe's bodyguard, not needed but being dragged along, and I could see Justin was exhausted also. This boy general had more stamina than the Playboy Energizer Bunny!

After another three blocks, Teg stopped at a one-story cinder block building, completely nondescript on the outside, with two steel-covered windows and a small steel door. A slightly unpleasant smell drifted out. Teg had the methane-toting soldiers wait outside, and the rest of us followed him in—as we stepped inside, the odor of frying fat overwhelmed me and I gagged. The place was lit by traditional oil—or should I say fat?—lamps and in the center of the vast room were three huge bubbling vats—this was a rendering facility! Another thing I had become familiar with in the slums but had tried to forget: the need for machinery oil meant that every bit of animal fat available, no matter how stinking—and some hinted, two-legged—was rendered by cooking and filtering until it was pure enough to work as grease. It was a nasty business and the leftover putrid waste had to be well hidden. Any neighbor who caught you dumping generally buried you in it, permanently.

We didn't stay long—a broad-shouldered, potbellied guy brought out a canister of grease about the size of a bread box, then we headed out again, making our painfully slow way across the abandoned streets. Fuel and grease indicated some machine. Of course, the plane—how big was it? Surely he didn't want us flying with him?? That would be my Dixie-Masonic line tonight. As much as I had always wanted to know what it felt like, this was *not* the time or place. I would have gone up with any of my uncles in a heartbeat, but this daredevil? I'd sooner jump up and down on Big Lulu's tanks.

Another block and we stopped at another warehouse, but this one had a wall of small frosted windows and there was an irresistible smell of bread and roasted meat; my mouth was watering. But who would be cooking at such an odd hour? When we went in, I discovered it was completely for the General—a restaurant with no outside advertising had rousted its workers in the middle of the night to make a meal for us. He could probably arrange a burial just as quickly. There were four tables set, and two waiters by an old-fashioned hot buffet of heated covered metal dishes.

"We still have a bit more than an hour, so get some protein in you," Teg said, standing aside to let us eat. I was surprised he chose to go last, but soon I was totally caught up in filling my face with fresh biscuits, ham—I didn't even balk at the eggs. They had tea rather than coffee, but it wasn't bad, with fresh milk and honey. As I ate, I looked around—it was just a warehouse, but with at least 20 tables in one half, and the hot buffet, shelves of dishes and stuff. The other half of the room had a low raised platform in front of a red-curtained wall. A theater? An auditorium? Why hidden? Why in one of the seediest areas in the city? On the other hand, it might be hard for the City's foes to meet in large groups anywhere in sight... or maybe weddings were illegal here? My sleep-starved mind was throwing up all kinds of absurd ideas. But the Long Island slums also had some very odd customs, so who knows? The food was refueling me, and right now that's what mattered.

We each had seconds, and time to enjoy it; I was grateful for the break. If this-all was about the plane, we'd have to wait until dawn. The more I thought about it, the more I realized there was no way to hide the noise of an airplane motor. The southerners would certainly know they were being spied on! Did that matter? Did he figure they'd suspect the City? As I went back for a small bit of thirds, I stopped at his table; he was eating alone. That should have told me something, but I was tired.

"Teg—are we waiting for dawn to launch the plane?" I asked. "How will you keep the noise down? I've heard planes and they're ear-splitting."

He looked up at me, surprised, though he wiped the annoyance off quickly. He gestured for me to sit opposite. I'd made a mistake, but it was too late.

"So you've heard planes before?" he asked, as usual turning my questioning him into his questioning me. "Army planes? What kind?"

"I believe they were Spitfires, the old World War Two planes with gunners and spy cameras. The electronic-driven planes were flared-out, though I've heard rumors they've modified a few."

"Have they now? That's interesting..." He forked eggs and toast into his mouth and chewed deliberately, looking off into the distance. When he refocused on me, I thought I could see a dangerous glint. *Nice going, Martin.* "Are there many?"

I was aware the info could friendly-fire my family, so I was glad to sincerely say I didn't know much. "I saw five in the one squad that usually patrolled up around northern New York and Connecticut. They protect the Niagara Corridor."

"That's where you get your water, right?"

"No—that's our power plant—up by Niagara Dam. It got top priority after the flare and still has. The water comes from reservoirs in the Catskills, but they might be linked somehow. Anyway, it's a highly-secure area; only Guard and Army families allowed to live and farm along there."

"So—no huge squadrons of bomb-dropping airplanes?"

I wasn't fooled by his joking tone. "My uncles said all you need for superiority in the air is five more planes than the other guy has. And as far as we know, no one else has planes." I watched him carefully; his smile widened but he said nothing. Surprisingly, he did finally answer my question. "Yes, as you so astutely noticed, we are gathering materials for a short flight."

"Surely you don't have plane big enough for all of us?"

"Are you hankering to go up in the air?" He seemed amused. "Sadly, it is a one person plane—more than enough for our needs."

I hoped he couldn't see the relief on my face. He gestured me back toward the buffet and I hurried to get my last few bites. What would the City do if they knew someone else had planes? Would that kind of information be worth money? That was a stupid question—of course it would. The *question* was: could I manage to negotiate that money my way? But as I brought my food back to the table where Justin was sopping up the last of his egg with a corner of toast, I thought about those who would be betrayed. The City wouldn't care where it dropped its bombs. And if it decided on the scorched earth response like with Magda's mob, it would be game-over for this area.

There seemed to be a faint glow on the eastern horizon as we left the restaurant and headed due west. We were still at a snail's crawl, and the tension grew as we blindly followed Teg. To soldiers, any pace slower than a quick stride instinctively meant some life-threatening situation. It was another long five blocks but finally we stopped by a two-story concrete-block garage that still had its huge rolled-metal door. Teg tapped lightly on the metal and instantly it began to slide up with a rattling growl. When it reached head height, we ducked underneath into the darkness and stood just inside the door. It rattled and clanked back down, and as it hit the concrete, someone snapped a flashlight on, and by that light one of the soldiers lit a couple oil lamps from a shelf by the door.

The room we were in was somewhat smaller than our "restaurant" and completely filled by an old towtruck, and behind that the plane. I caught a glimpse of a blue-gray single-seater, its silver propeller tipped in yellow and the two-decker wings painted with some kind of circular icon. Even though it was in good repair, the plane was ancient.

"I didn't know he had a working tow truck, too," Justin murmured. "Only ever seen one other."

Frankly, the plane looked like it was put together with canvas and fence poles. I was doubly glad I wouldn't have to go up in it. I knew old planes were rare as honest politicians, because during the Adjustment people had gone crazy and destroyed whatever planes hadn't crashed from the sky. The biggest planes had been impossible to move to safety and religious zealots had set airports and factories alight in their frenzy to blame Progress for the problem. The Guard had too much else to do to defend anything but military property. That's what my uncles said, anyway—the younger ones, not the Survivors. *They* never said anything about Just After.

The soldiers were busy pumping gas into the plane, and a couple greased wheel axles and checked a tiny motor underneath a lifted-up hood. It was maybe twice the size of an e-cycle motor—hardly more efficient than flapping your arms. Teg had gotten into the cockpit and was examining something by the glow of his flashlight. Justin, Shawna and I stood off to one side, waiting.

Eventually, the preparation was completed and someone stepped to the metal door and began to haul on a rope, and the rolled metal clanked and groaned upward. There was a definite gray brightness to the sky now, and I prayed that our adventure would be done as soon as Teg was aloft. I wish I felt confident he wouldn't find me if I took off.

One of the soldiers hopped into the tow truck and started the motor. After a few minutes' warm up, the truck pulled slowly forward, the tow rope tightened and the plane trundled behind the truck, moving slowly across a parking lot toward the highway. Certainly it couldn't take off from this two-block flattened space? I vaguely recalled planes needing a very long flat strip to take off. We walked behind as the truck carefully towed the tiny plane down the street toward the shallow ramp to the highway. This road had all its metal fencing, poles and overhead signage stolen for scrap, leaving a naked curve of concrete arching up. I watched, stunned, as the truck started up the ramp, angling around to ensure the plane missed the brick retaining wall, barely fitting. Suddenly I realized—the highway! A long flat surface! I couldn't help grinning as I followed. They paused at the bottom to let the truck and plane finish the trip, then jogged up.

"Clever, huh?" Shawna asked with a grin as we trudged behind them.

I could see this elevated section of 65 was in good repair—they probably made sure of it. The motor sounded like a wild thunderstorm in the dawn silence; Zara could probably hear it at home. Since the noise of this adventure couldn't be hidden, maybe residents knew better than to be curious.

Teg switched his helmet for a smooth leather pilot's cap, like my uncle Zach kept on his mantelpiece, with green-glass goggles. He climbed the left wing, walked it, then dropped into the cockpit, which was open except for a small windscreen. The truck turned around and parked behind the plane.

"Better him than me," Shawna commented as we watched.

"How did he learn to fly?"

She shrugged. "I have no idea—just one of the many weird things he's learned to do."

Someone heaved on the propeller, getting it spinning. The plane started up with a choking and sputtering, but finally the motor caught and roared. Teg drove it down the highway, picking up speed, and just when I thought he would *have* to turn at the far bend, the plane lifted off from the ground and sailed upward. I caught my breath; I felt like a seven-year-old again, watching the Guards' planes leave The Guardian airport. It was such a miracle that a huge piece of metal could soar through the air! We watched him turn to the left and head south, over the downtown island and beyond. Soon the plane was a small speck in the air, with a buzz no louder than a bee.

"He'll probably be gone half hour or so," Shawna said, waving me and Justin down the ramp. "We might as well wait someplace comfortable." Most of the others stayed there, leaning against the wall and chatting. She led the way back to the garage, to a small door a little farther down from the huge truck entrance.

Inside was an old office with three chipped and scarred wooden desks, Army green wall cabinets, one of those antique water bottle stations with a glass bottle half-full, a lot of papers strewn on a long counter to our right, and several broken-down straightback chairs. At the far desk, an old guy was hunched over small piece of machinery. He was scrawny, with a thatch of white hair, tattoos curling down his bare arms from under a short-sleeve gray tshirt and more wrinkles than a well-used bed. He glanced up when we walked in, and waved us over excitedly.

"Shawna! Come hear my latest find!" He started pushing buttons on the machine and there was a brief hum and burbling.

"Syd collects messages," she murmured to us. "I'm not sure where he digs them up."

Messages? But nothing could surprise me after this night. So I thought. He waited until we got close and pushed a button and a woman's voice came out of the machine, saying "*Your call is important to us, and we really appreciate your patience. All our client service specialists are currently busy* –" the message cut off sharply.

"The rest of it was glitched," Syd said. "But the first part's really clear, don't you think?"

We murmured agreement. I glanced at Justin for explanation; he just shook his head and raised his eyebrows. Syd reached for another small machine on the desk, pulled it closer, swapped wires from the first machine and pushed a button. A man's voice said, "*Please listen carefully, as our menu options have changed. To check your bank balance, press 1. To arrange a payment, press 2. To speak to a representative regarding overdue payments, press 3. To find out location and hours, press 4. For all other calls, press 8.*"

Syd grinned up at us. "Even though there wasn't a glitch, somehow I missed whatever the message was between four and eight. But it's impressive, huh?"

I understood the part about checking a bank balance, but not at the press of a button. I glanced at Shawna who was suppressing a grin. "Yeah, Syd, I've never heard messages that good." She led me over to the counter where there were blue ceramic cups stacked three high. "He's totally nuts about these things—voices from his childhood, apparently." She handed each of us a cup then went over to the water station and poured herself a drink. I set the roll of maps carefully on the counter.

"What does Teg use the plane for when he's not spying on rebels?" I asked. After all this, I felt entitled to some answers. Maybe Teg could check out a safety zone for Ciera's group.

"I've heard he's trading pretty far out," Justin said and Shawna nodded.

"He's found several towns way North of here—by the lakes," she said. "They have a good setup with barging along the water, and he found a decent landing strip. The trades are worth all the methane it takes to fuel Monty—that's what we call it. I just wish it could carry more."

"Has he talked them into sharing their salt yet?" Justin asked turning to me, he explained, "they've got an old mine up there, and we just can't get enough, even with all the grocery warehouses."

"Long Island has a desalinization plant," I said. "Well, mostly a lot of labor-intensive drying out of seawater." Once again, I realized I hadn't thought of being without something that basic.

"I think he's found... a few things they want." She was being cagey, but I was distracted, thinking that a plane could make the trip to Chicago—couldn't it? How long would Los Angeles take? It used to be common, even daily. I was pretty sure the Army kept their planes for local security—but theirs were so much bigger. How far would you go if you couldn't count on getting more fuel?

"The towns were really stuck last winter—I guess the lakes freeze and Teg actually landed on the lake and brought them some food. He says he needs to keep them alive to trade with us," she chuckled.

"I'd heard they needed guns, too," Justin said. He put his grinder on the counter, grabbed a desk chair, pulled it over, and sat. I grabbed another and eased into it. How was I going to walk or pedal to Ambridge this morning?

"Yeah—for wolves and for some other group further north. Hard to part with them but—" Shawna shrugged, leaning against the counter. "He has a plan. It's bigger than I can picture."

"Yeah, me too," Justin replied. They were both silent a minute, and I remembered Zara had called him "General Teg"—so maybe he had aspirations of leading his *own* country? At least he bothered to keep his people alive, unlike the City.

"Has he done any more on the salvage town?" Justin asked.

"I'm not sure. It's hard to get folks to head out to the middle of nowhere, knowing they'd have to rely on his plane to bring in basics. Even his most loyal followers are hesitating."

"I get that. He swears there's some incredible salvage out there, if we could just find it." Justin said. "If I were 20 years younger…"

"I think he'll get a crew together. He's amazing at convincing folks," Shawna said. "He got the Ross Park militants to fold."

Justin noted enthusiastically. "Yeah—I never thought they would calm down. The farming's been much easier up there recently."

"He's convinced them it's better being inside than outside," Shawna said.

That sounded too much like the City and the slum gangs for me. Once you have an *us*, you have a *them*, and even if the war is pushed further away, I was learning it only makes it worse eventually. Peace was needed for growth, for stability. And maybe that required making your own "safety zone".

"If he wasn't bringing those sacks of wheat down here from whatever town he's getting them, we would've been in trouble this winter," Justin commented. "And the razor blades were really, really handy. Not just in trades, but for Zara's work."

"Yeah," Shawna agreed, "he's finding some amazing things. Having that extra market for all the radio tubes has come in handy, too."

That must have been what they pulled out of those boxes and brought to the tower with the radio. I had no idea why a radio needed glass tubes—one day I'd ask Justin to explain the radio to me.

Shawna and Justin chatted about various people whose names meant nothing, and I found myself half dozing on the chair. I longed to put my head down on the desk, but tried to stay awake and listen, in case I heard anything useful. But that was the problem—what was useful?? In this confusing onslaught of information, I couldn't tell what bits would be helpful to me or to Ciera. I'm sure it would be good for her to know there was someone who could fly a plane, and maybe do some spying out in her area. But would the group accept the necessity for it? How well had they managed with the rebel salvage team? I had a brief moment of panic thinking of all that could have gone wrong—I forced that image out of my mind and tried to review what I knew.

There was a group close to the Mall who did at least black-market trade with the City. This group also had their own private network, trading items that I had only seen as antiquities. And most importantly, this group had radios, guns, and access to a plane. They might be very small, but they weren't helpless. And they had a culture of sharing that was absent in the City or the Island. They weren't allied with the rebels, either local or South, nor did they seem to be allied with the City. A bit like Ciera's group, they wanted to create their own society, but these also wanted some of the luxuries that New York could provide.

Shawna looked up suddenly, and I realized I had been hearing a humming that was gradually getting louder.

"He's coming back. Let's go."

We headed back to the landing strip; my legs felt like bungee jump cords as I stumbled after them. The last several days had been passed in a stupor; I was losing even the memory of feeling rested. I fell back into my *Just One More Step* mantra.

The soldiers had parked the truck halfway down the ramp and they waited at the top, close to the wall. The buzz was getting louder, and I saw the plane coming in from the west, aiming straight for the flat length of highway. It got larger and lower, and I held my breath. I was glad it wasn't *me* aiming at concrete! How did Teg know when to aim away from the road, and how did one judge that distance? I glanced over, and saw the others were tense as well. The buzzing became a loud roar as the plane descended, touched the concrete and bounced, hit again, joggled a bit and roared straight up the highway, right at us. I braced myself to run. But with a squeal, the plane slowed, losing speed until it stopped five feet away. The soldiers raced to do something with the wheels, ducking under the propeller which was slowly coming to a halt.

Teg climbed out of the cockpit and balanced along the wing, then hopped lightly down.

"The rebels are about twenty miles away, and they're still heading south," he reported. "I don't see any sign that they're planning to come back anytime soon."

"That's a relief," Justin said. "Now we can get back to routine surveillance, and doing something about these idiot locals."

"The City's gonna want some of those locals, Justin," Teg said. "We might be able to save most of them, but the leaders are gonna end up inside."

Justin nodded with a frown. "I know," he sighed. "They played with fire, they get burned. But their families –"

"I already have a plan, Justin," Teg said. He headed down the ramp as the soldiers worked to hook the plane back to the truck. Shawna, Justin and I followed him. Apparently the plan was not going to be revealed.

The four of us made our way back to the gray building/portal, but instead of using that, we turned left and headed toward the bricked-in I-65. At the corner where the two walls met, Shawna bent down and pulled a round cast iron grating up from the street, sliding it, rasping, until the hole was clear. The sewers?? Teg was underground more than a wharf rat! He gestured for us to go first, and Shawna led the way down the iron rung ladder, then Justin, then me, feeling my way, listening so that I wouldn't step on Justin's head, willing my wobbly legs not to slip, grasping the roll of maps in my left hand. I tried to keep my right hand on the side of the ladder so that Teg didn't accidentally step on my fingers. I was so close to being finished that I was getting superstitious—my family always said that disaster hovered at the end of a job. But we got down without incident, and Teg turned on his flashlight again. The battery was definitely dying; the light was reddish gold and didn't carry very far. I was glad to see the sewer was fairly empty—certainly no one used flushing toilets anymore, but in the City some scrags dumped inconvenient garbage down convenient manholes. This held only mildly moldy rainwater trickling along the center of the tunnel. We followed him down a narrow side route, and I again had to resort to my mantra *Just. One. More. Step*. Luckily it was a very short trip, probably just under the Wall, and there was another ladder leading upward that I climbed awkwardly but gratefully.

We came up in a very narrow alley between a building and the Wall, well shielded and deserted. Even after dawn, the light was poor here. Teg brushed himself off and smiled at us; I thought of wolves and sheep.

"Good job, thank you," he said, shaking hands with Shawna and Justin. He paused a minute in front of me, then put out his hand. I shook it, my whole body stiffening. "Marty, would you mind doing one last favor for me?"

He was looking directly in my eyes and again I sensed I couldn't refuse. "There are a couple objects I've found that I'm really hoping you can identify—as someone who's been inside and also on the Island. Would you come with me for just another, say, half hour?" He was searching my face for signs of disloyalty. *Or?* It suddenly occurred to me that he might not want to take the chance that I could bring all this information back inside. I didn't look over, but I sensed that Justin had gone still with shock. Not a good sign. But it was very clear that saying *No* right now was not an option.

"Of course, if it doesn't take too long. I need to be getting back to Ambridge very soon. They're waiting for me." Had I made that believable enough?

"No problem. And I might be able to find you transportation, too," he said, taking the maps from me, waving goodbye to the others and gesturing for me to follow him up the alley. I didn't dare look back, as I walked closely behind. He *had* come back for me, and he *hadn't* attacked me for having that phone. Automatically, I patted my pocket, but instead of the phone I felt the pistol. A jolt of relief and panic swept me—I wasn't completely helpless. Let's see if he was telling the truth now.

Three houses up, he led me up the back porch into a kitchen that looked well used, though I didn't hear anybody. He reached into his jacket and I tensed, easing my hand toward my pocket. But he pulled out a blue plastic token the size of a quarter and placed it on the kitchen table, then led me to a door which led into the basement. Was this another storehouse? At the bottom of the rickety wood steps there was a large candle, which Teg lit and held high as he moved through the clutter of stacked boxes, chairs with busted seats, even an old couch angled upright against the wall. It was an unusually long basement, and I suddenly realized it was yet another tunnel—this area must be honeycombed! How many residents were aware of these?

"Sorry, it's a few blocks away—but won't be long now," Teg called back to me. The light didn't carry back well and I had to feel my way around the obstacles as I followed. It *could* be legit—it would make sense he wouldn't want me to see where his treasures were stashed. And at the moment he had both hands occupied. But it could be an ambush. The room narrowed into a hall or tunnel, a little less cluttered but not empty. I wondered how much trade was stored down here, or was this simply junk they didn't know what to do with? I tensed each time I went past an object I couldn't see around. My breathing was shallow and it felt like the last of the speedo was coursing through my veins. Legit, or *literally* a dead end?

I slid the tiny pistol into my hand, feeling that wild energy that comes from the nearness of death. Teg eased his way past several wooden crates that blocked the hall. What if I was wrong?? This side trip seemed too convenient, but why would he want to kill me now? He'd had plenty of opportunities. He hadn't really needed me since the bridge. Why show me all that stuff then kill me? What did I know about what he was thinking? And did it matter? Better that I get him before he nailed me.

As I raised the gun, Teg ducked between two crates. *Damn!* I followed, keeping the gun out of sight until I could get another chance. He slowed to hold an overhanging basket out of the way, then continued snaking his way down the meandering path. I took a deep breath, aimed again—and almost hissed as he turned left suddenly. Where were we *going*? Was he setting me up for ambush? Torture? How could I explain his death to Justin? But that was less important than me surviving.

Two more quick turns as I raised and lowered the gun twice; my hand was trembling slightly by now. I thought of the feral crazies, what was left of them after being mowed down. The way bullets tore into flesh was sickening. I didn't want to see it. But I wanted to live. Once again, as Teg started down a slightly wider aisle toward a staircase, I lifted the gun, my finger slowly squeezing. The plane flashed in my mind—a power baron he might be, but there were hundreds counting on him to protect the little they had. Kill him, condemn them to death. And, now that I was right up against it, I couldn't shoot a man in the back. Just couldn't. *Shit.* I shoved the gun in my pocket, and followed him up the flight of stairs, straining every muscle to be ready for an assault, hoping I remembered my hand-to-hand training. He opened the door at the top and walked inside. He said something softly, and added, "someone to see you," and stood back to let me enter.

Confused, tense in every muscle, I walked through the door. Lying on a wide couch, blanketed up to his waist, a blond man with a scarred face rested on one elbow and stared. I stared back. Despite the wounds, I recognized my old friend.

24

"Marty." His voice was like gravel in stream. "Tegson sent word—but I thought for sure he had been mistaken."

"How often am I mistaken, father?" the junior Teg cut in, grinning broadly. "I recognized him from your stories."

He'd told stories about me? There was a lump—no, a boulder—in my throat that was stopping me from saying anything. I took a few steps forward then stopped again. My heart stuttered and I swayed as I thought about the moment in the tunnel—how close I had come.

"Marty? You were never tongue-tied—far from it." Teg said with a smile, skewed as the right side of his face barely moved.

"I—I haven't been this surprised in a long time," I said. I looked around for some place to sit—I didn't think my legs would hold out for another second. Tegson grabbed a straight-backed chair from under a table and whipped it around behind me. I dropped into it and stared again at my friend. "I'm sorry—it's been such a wild couple of days…"

"Wilder than the raid on McMullen's distillery?" he asked with a chuckle.

"Oh my God—I hadn't thought of that in years. When Pig dropped the lamp underneath the keg and we thought 15 gallons of pure moonshine was going to explode!" A wild exuberance boiled up and I started laughing, realizing that it sounded half hysterical. I shoved my fist in my mouth to stop, and shook my head.

"All these years I thought you were dead," I said finally. "Couldn't you have gotten word to me somehow?"

"How? *You've* jumped gangs. You know you can't go back or let them know—"

Of course. He'd pulled the same stunt that I did, disappearing into the wilds and hooking up with another slum boss. It still felt like a knife, though—

all those years him walking around—"walking around maybe on the next street!" That burst out.

He shook his head "No—I moved a lot farther away. I realized the slums were the worst kind of trap, and despite what they told us, the City was a dead-end. I ran to the edges, out beyond the Protectorate. Do you remember the time we captured that skinny, half-dead kid with the beak nose that I said had to be a Roman descendent?"

I nodded. "Artaud wanted to torture him even though he swore he wasn't from another gang… but *somehow* he got away." I cocked my head at Teg and he grinned.

"That's right. He told me where he'd come from, a place in Pennsylvania that was just hangin' on, but which had some bodacious resources. I could see it was a better place to grow some wings than with Artaud's clan. And I had a six year old." He gestured toward the door Tegson had left by. "Once I found out about him, I knew I didn't want to stick around. And you?"

"I made it into the City—can you believe it? A million to one chance." My elation was dimmed by his last comment. Maybe he thought I was a fool.

"I knew you had it in you. And how did it work out?"

I hesitated. Up to a week ago, I would have told him it was sensational. Now?

As if he could sense my confusion, he nodded. "Dreams change," he said, looking down, then looked up with a grimace. "And now the idiots in charge are trying to make sure the whole bloody thing blows apart again."

"Do you know what's going on??" I leaned forward. "I feel like I walked into one of those tall tales we used to tell around the fire—the one where the girl followed the rabbit down a hole and everything was backwards. I thought I was going out to help set up some comm towers, but it turned out I was bait. But I don't know for who—do you? Who's coming up from the south?? I left some—very nice people—in a town northwest of here, trying to help the refugees who've been fleeing from whatever's going on. And I think they're easy targets—and I'm trying to find out enough to tell them which way to run so that they're out of the way." That jumble probably made no sense to him.

Teg's son came back into the room carrying two large mugs. He handed one to me and I gulped it, and almost choked. It was a rich dark ale, stronger than I'd had in quite a while. I switched to sipping.

"Teg-son-of-Teg over here has been keeping up with the admittedly rapid-changing situation." My friend's pride was evident, and his son grinned.

"I don't need or want to know the details that might—compromise anything—I just want to know where my friends in Ambridge—actually they live somewhere middle of Ohio—do they still call it Ohio?—where they can go so they're not right in the middle of all this. What I found out from a soldier was, they were coming up past a big airport, through the middle of Ohio and then doubling back down."

The young man frowned and took a step closer. "Did you get exact locations?"

I shook my head, and closed my eyes to remember. "He said they had started from Fort Cumberland, and took a winding railroad line past something like Con-ville, or Conly-ville, past a place that still had the old passenger planes, and crossed over the Ohio where there was a island in the river. I know they came down from the north to Ambridge right along the river. And nobody there had any clue they were coming. That's all I know," I concluded.

"That's basically what Justin told me you'd said. Nothing more about where they came from?"

One detail flashed in my mind. "When we were getting horses, the stable master said to avoid the town of Freedom—she didn't quite say it, but the sense I got was the rebels were hiding there. Oh, and Geoff, my guide, said something about a town near Madison that could print out City authorizations. I don't know its name."

The young Teg grinned. "That gives a little more detail. Thanks." He turned on his heel and left the room quickly.

"Things are going to get difficult real fast," Teg said, then paused. "I can trust you, can't I?"

"Of course! I wish you had trusted me back then—did I just say that?" I shook my head. "Nobody trusted anybody back then."

"No—it wasn't something we did. But I—as much as I trusted anyone, I did trust you."

"Then why didn't you tell me?"

He gestured with the mug. "I didn't have time—the whole thing came together in a matter of hours and I had to go for it."

I looked at him, seeing again the tall, brawny daredevil. The way he was lying there now—he probably couldn't get up. As if sensing my thoughts, he said "It's a real tough dance, isn't it? Jumping from one shark pod to the next, fighting your way in and then fighting your way out again. And no way to know when you might get slammed. You want to know what happened, don't you?" He didn't wait for me to answer. "It was about five years ago. I was—no, I guess I'm going to have to give a little background."

He shifted on the couch a bit and suddenly I worried—would I have to help him? Were the two of us alone here? But he settled back against the cushions and continued.

"This has been building for a while—between New York and DC, I mean. I know at one point, they really thought they could get at least the original thirteen colonies patched together again. But there were so many resource gaps—by then I was watching from the outside, and I could see the New York sniffer dogs coming farther out, not turning their noses up at third-hand goods—the clues were there if you knew where to look."

"Then it was just pretending? Telling us that America was still—a country?"

"Remember I told you about Rome? There are always those who believe, even down to the end. And there are always those who never did believe, but are ready to take advantage of the believers. And there are a few—usually just a few—who see the writing on the wall and know they have to adjust to a different reality. In New York, there were those who didn't want to share the coal, grain, wool—the things that were easier to get up here. They started muttered that DC wasn't contributing its share. When Philadelphia fell apart—do you know about that?"

I shook my head, once again feeling like the stupid student he was lecturing near the bonfire.

"It used to be common ground, and then—I'm not sure exactly, but a tug of war started, and the people who lived there got sick of it, and started to sabotage the rail line, to hijack the goods as they came through—and within a couple years the place became a DMZ. That's 'demilitarized zone' in oldspeak."

"I know—remember my folks are Guards?"

"That's right, I forgot. Anyway, once that easy connection eroded, there was a lot more distrust, and maybe easier for those who sensed a gap in power. Tegson was 17 then, and going on countless raids to find out what-all was going on. It scared the shit outta me, of course—you don't know fear until you have a child. But he was telling us that New York was building up extra military, and twice he got down as far as Hagerstown and found out that DC was also spreading a bit. Of course, the swamps of the Capitol were getting much worse, so they had to go inland in any case. Dumbest idea ever, building a national capitol on a swamp." He chuckled, and I could see the old Teg under the scars and the weathering.

"I don't think even the authorities, those who thought they were prepared for this, knew how half-assed it was going to be," he continued. "Once a system breaks down, it's a crapshoot. Everything was interlocked so amazingly—you wouldn't believe it Marty—and you pull out a pin here and a cog there, and before you know it, things are running on three wheels and parts are flying everywhere." Teg grinned—on some level, he was enjoying how well his theories fit.

"Who is 'us'?"

"Like I said, I moved out to Pennsylvania, and saw how much there was to build on. There were a lot of folks scrambling, but I knew enough about history to sense what kind of group could survive, so we pulled together a fortified town and established some trade routes. We were up on a river that had its own dam, so it wasn't hard to come up with some hydropower, some grain mills—the usual stuff. Even have a huge underground—Anyway, then I started thinking about what the City was gonna need, and how much they'd be willing to pay—and one thing that is always gold is information. We have a scout team second to none, if I may say so, and I saw this mess building up, so I had Tegson contact the City with some info, and offering to be an auxiliary force if necessary. Not that we told them how big we'd gotten!" He chuckled. "Just some small-town loyalists, ready to help..."

He shifted again, and I wondered if he was in pain. "But back to the accident. We'd been doing a percentage business, finding new salvage sites for the City bosses. They've got a great team, but there's only so many of them, and it's really fuckin' amazing how much junk there is just lying around out there. I swear people must have been sitting, absolutely *sitting*, on top of crap—they couldn't possibly have used... but there was a lot more of them, back then. I keep forgetting. Do you know there once was over 8 million living in New York City?"

"How much is that compared 100,000?"

He laughed. "You never were good at numbers. That's 80 times more. Eighty cities the size of now."

I tried to wrap my mind around that number, and failed utterly. "Where the hell did they put them all??"

"They filled up those big towers—and there used to be some really big ones, before we were born, towers they took down after the fires, in order to get at the metal and other stuff. They said there used to be ones 100 floors tall."

"Naw. That's just one of those urban myths."

"I don't think so." He reached awkwardly to put his mug on the floor and I jumped up and took it from him, setting it on a table nearby. "Thanks. I think a lot of those tall tales were true, frankly. It was an awesome civilization. Too bad it ate itself up. Anyway—where was I? God, my mind wanders so bad these days… Okay—just like most accidents, it happened in a fraction of the second, when I wasn't paying as much attention and got overconfident. We had found what seemed like a real treasure trove of heavy machinery, where a river must have buried a town in a mudslide—this was middle Pennsylvania. A wall we were tunneling under collapsed, pinning my legs, and crushing them, but I didn't know that then. The group was really quick to get me out, but it first it looked so bad we all thought I was gonna die. Fortunately, we had an excellent medic, someone who knew the herbs and also had studied as much information as she could glean from the old medical texts. She put me back together as best she could, and I was in a cast and half delirious for months—but even though I recovered, all those breaks meant my legs just don't really support me anymore. I can walk with a walker—one of those wheeled metal-pipe gizmos that old people used to use, back when they used to keep them alive artificially—but I can't take part in the forays anymore. Luckily, Tegson was more than ready to take over."

"He certainly has a lot of skill and self-confidence." I hesitated—should I mention how I'd been used? Would Teg be proud of his son's ruthlessness? I wasn't sure I wanted to know.

"You look really uncomfortable in that chair, Marty—come sit on this couch—there's plenty of room." Teg slowly shifted his legs off the couch, leaving me space. I was going to protest, but I was half falling off the chair from sheer fatigue, helped by the beer. The couch was tall-backed and I was able to rest my head on the cushion; it felt wonderful and I let my muscles relax, hearing Teg's voice coming from farther and farther away.

* * *

When I woke, I was stretched out on the couch and alone in the room. I jerked to my feet, startled. How long had I been asleep?? The sun looked bright behind the thin blue curtains. I rubbed my eyes and looked around.

Aside from the couch, there was a well-upholstered armchair, a dark wood dining table with pillared legs and four matching chairs, two bookshelves packed with more books than I'd ever seen except in a library, a soft blue area rug and a desk at the window—a pleasant, comfortable room. Was this his home? Didn't he live much further north? I heard voices, so I walked through the door into a small kitchen, more like a hallway with stove, tiny icebox and sink along one wall, narrow enough that I had to ease around Tegson to where Teg was sitting on a metal pole chair with wheels, chatting while his son cooked. The smell of bacon and fried potatoes was irresistible. The room widened at the end to accomodate a small round table ringed with four chairs, and ended with what looked like a door to the back porch.

"Have a nice sleep?" Teg asked with a chuckle.

I looked around for a clock. "How long was I out?"

"A couple hours."

"No! I've got to get back to Ambridge! I've been gone so long already!"

"You needed that sleep—you couldn't have traveled anywhere in the shape you were in," Teg replied. "And now you need some food."

Of course he was right, but that didn't ease my impatience. It had been more than a day since I'd left. Had Zara actually sent the message? Did they know where I was? I joined them at the table, wincing a bit at how awkward my friend was—even with loose pants, his legs were obviously twisted and barely holding him up as he clung to the metal bars of the walker. But he seemed skilled in seating himself, and his cheerful demeanor didn't change. Tegson was more gentle and warm—almost an entirely different person—with his father. I again breathed thanks for my cowardice with firearms.

"I think I was telling you a bit about the accident and the aftermath, when you zonked out," Teg said, in between mouthfuls. "We were a pretty large group by then, and I was happy to see that there was at least a half dozen really capable members who split up duties when I wasn't able and of course Tegson here took on the surveillance and defense planning."

"Was that why you needed to get the maps?" I asked.

Tegson stiffened and glanced at his father. I could see he didn't trust me and I didn't really blame him.

"You don't have to answer that," I said.

"Thanks. I think I won't for now." He smiled briefly to take the sting off, and Teg quickly jumped in.

"We're always looking for old records. There's both too much and too little. And it's all jumbled together. There were libraries but many of them didn't survive the fires. People were so careless before they realized there was no fire department—or water—to rescue them. They say New York looked like a birthday cake with lit candles—that's why we don't have the biggest towers anymore. But I heard that there were fanatics who defended the main library and some of the museums—literally living there, hoarding water and killing to make sure that not a bit of flame came near their precious treasures." He paused to enjoy more of the breakfast. I was trying to eat mine slowly, my gut still half asleep. They even had synth-coffee, and I savored it. "The other thing about libraries was—apparently just before the flare, they were actually throwing out books, switching over to the electronic media that everyone was sure would be the wave of the future. And of course that all disappeared in an instant. So we've had to scramble and find smaller libraries that couldn't afford to switch, and to look for information wherever we could. We've found shelves of books glued together as decoration in restaurants, for instance. Bugger to get the glue undone."

"Would any of that information be useful anymore? Things have changed so much."

"There's a lot that's still *very* useful—and we want to save it for whoever survives."

I pushed the last corner of bread around my plate, sopping up any leftover juices and fat—trying to pull my thoughts together.

"I see you believe living out here is better," I began.

"*Much* better," Teg interrupted.

"Okay, much better. And I can see there are small groups a bit like our slum gangs, but they seem to be more generous. But like I told—the others—I don't know if I could stay out here if there were no music, or theater or—so many fun things in the City."

"Bread and circuses," Teg said with a scowl. "Aren't those things especially good *because* your job is just paper pushing?"

"I…I hadn't thought about it that way. But yes, it's true that my job doesn't make a lot of sense and I wouldn't do if I weren't paid really well. But—"

"I'm not saying culture is bad. And I'm not saying we don't have any out here. But I'm saying some kinds of culture, especially some of the stuff they saved from before the flare, is a kind of junk food—subtly addicting, and reinforcing the need to follow all their orders in order to get these little special rewards. They used to do experiments with rats, where they would push down on a lever to get a reward, and the City has set up something like that. You work as a semi-slave, and they feed you treats of various kinds."

It was obvious I was not going to get Teg to meet me halfway on this, so I dropped it. The immediate problem was helping Ciera's group anyway. Teg picked up on something in my expression.

"So what are you gonna do, Marty?"

"God, Teg, I wish I knew. I can't go back to the City now—even with what I just said and even though I got a really nice apartment. Well, it's not mine, belongs to Commco."

He sat up straighter. "You work at Commco? What area?"

I just do the dish reports—I keep track of the ones that need repair, what roofs, etc.—it's pushing info around. Which sure beats digging potatoes." I grinned briefly. "But I've been out here long enough to see that the City will die if they can't keep the supply lines open. And I know for sure I'm not top of the list if they start rationing." I remembered some really brutal nights, when there wasn't enough in the gang's supply to feed everybody. "At least they drew lots in Long Island," I finished.

Teg nodded; he knew exactly what I was thinking of. "Yeah, the City never draws lots. Their priority list was set decades ago, and if there's any jockeying, it's so far up it we'll never see it. Anybody who's not living within sight of the Park hasn't got a chance."

I thought about Melinda, Rivera and Cheyenne—what the hell were they gonna do? What the hell could I do for them? My helpless panic must have shown on my face, because Teg waved his hand as if to dispel my thoughts. "Maybe you can warn them," he said, "but they probably won't believe you. Would you have believed it, a week ago?"

I shook my head. "No—it's like... I don't know if you ever saw that muvid about the girl and her dog and that scary wizard –"

"Oz. He was the Wizard of Oz. It was my daughter's favorite movie," he said quietly. Tegson jumped up suddenly to get the coffee pot.

"You have a daughter?" Before I'd finished, I knew the answer.

"Had. One of the usual spring flu's came through, took out at least a third of the town."

"I'm...sorry."

He nodded and said gruffly, "You still haven't answered—what are you gonna do?"

Tegson refilled our cups, put down the coffee pot and left the room.

"I know I'm going back to Ambridge, at least for now," I replied. "I want to give them enough info that they're not directly in the path of this mess."

"That'll be hard, if you don't know where they live."

"Well, the Ambridge colony is out in the open, and they don't have any protection. But what the hell kind of protection can you *have* against an army??"

"You mean, other than another army?" He smiled. "There are bunches of caves in Pennsylvania, did you know that? Some of them are big enough to hold an entire town."

"No shit? But you can't live underground all the time."

"You don't have to. You just have to have it as the sanctuary, and be sure that your above-ground town looks deserted if need be. Precious goods stored behind false shelves. Then you can bugger off to the basement, as it were, and hang out until the bastards leave. They used to have caves in Italy, that could literally hold the whole city and had 16 or 17 levels."

Something about the way he said it made me think he knew some of this firsthand. And that would be just like him, figuring out somewhere to hide that no one would think to look. Was Tegson using the maps to look for more hide-outs?

"Another handy spot is—have you ever seen a real mall? Not this mess—that should be called a bazaar, technically. But covered –"

"Yes," I interrupted, "there are a couple in the City, where there's five or six stores in one building so you don't have to shop in the rain."

"Well picture that but about as big as this mall out here—or at least eight or 10 blocks square."

"Covered??"

"Yup. Back when they had so much stuff they were sitting on it, they could also afford to put gigantic roofs over basically a town. And what's left is basically a town—divided up into little houses, with lighting built in if you can get sufficient biogas or solar and batteries, with kitchens and huge bathrooms. And best of all, completely fortified against the outside area, because they didn't have many windows to the outside."

I tried to picture it, and again I failed.

"Now, some of them got trashed pretty badly," Teg continued, "and the ones around the City got recycled damned efficiently, but in a coupla places the Great Dying happened so fast that the mall was basically as it was left—abandoned and empty, but intact."

"Why empty?"

He shrugged. "I'm not sure, but I think they were failing even back then, and they planned to knock 'em down and start again with something else. Hard to believe how much they knocked down and trashed—the landfills are just packed with really good stuff. We've got workers dawn to dusk, pulling out perfectly good crap."

"The...the City tells us landfills are really dangerous."

"Probably because they don't want you grabbin' your own stuff," Teg chuckled. "Sure, there's some toxic stuff there—but we found a bunch of bunny suits and—"

"You dress up as bunnies??"

He laughed so hard he couldn't speak for a moment. "Right. I guess that hasn't come down to newspeak. Those were the suits workers used when they were making the really high tech stuff, or working in hospitals—full-body covering, gloves, booties and a mask could protect you from a lot. We liberated some from a toxic waste dump and make sure the workers are protected, and then the stuff is disinfected before we trade it away."

"But the hardest part is always the food," he continued. "If you've got fields or flocks, it's tough to avoid losing them. Sabotage sometimes works." He stared at some inward image, and seemed almost to have forgotten I was there.

"The best defense is a good offense, sometimes," he said finally. "Keep them fighting far away from you, or at least long enough that you can move to someplace else."

He pulled himself back to the present and looked at me quizzically. "If you're determined to help them get through this—whatever it becomes—I'd advise you to have them link up with these locals here—form a surveillance team and use whatever they have to keep track of what these DC Southerners are doing. I think it will be quite a while before New York decides to come West, and they will be saving their firepower for DC. But that's not to say there won't be a bunch of refugees if the City gets in trouble. But I doubt they would get out past mid-Pennsylvania, purely for logistical reasons. We're watching that situation, and have made plans –" he hesitated, then continued "to accommodate as many as we can, but only if they're willing to go along with our way of doing things."

"So—are you going to fight them? The southerners?" I asked. "Or the City, for that matter."

"No way. We have a lot of skilled guerillas, trackers and runners," Teg said, "but that's not the same as an army."

"Justin said something about 'any wave can overrun a beach but it takes a lot more to hang on to it.' Hey, is that why Long Island ended up such a mess when the City can come all the way out to Pittsburgh?"

Teg nodded. "Exactly. So we haven't tried to push back. Let the City think it owns this whole area. Let it think it can swat us down at any moment—it won't bother to do that as long as it doesn't see us as a danger. But it's big, and clumsy—and we're not."

"What about the Southerners?"

"I don't know. Tegson says they are hungrier, but also following standard army-think. They haven't really thought in terms of guerrilla war, despite this little foray. That gives us a chance maybe to be the bridge, or flow between—and live not as peons, but as our own people."

"*We the people*...Didn't the country's—decree or something—didn't it start like that?"

Teg sighed. "I would have thought your folks would have taught that document above all."

I reddened. "They did, but I didn't really listen—I didn't believe anything my parents said, not after I saw what they did."

"It was the Constitution, and for years it was the guiding light. Then, unfortunately, it became the convenient excuse." Teg's expression darkened and again he was looking off at something I couldn't see. "Remember I told you always to beware of companies whose names claimed some kind of goodness? Instead of just 'Murphy, Doctor', you had 'Health First' or 'Safe Drugs'– the more they claim it, the more suspicious you should be. And for too many years before it all fell apart, *We the People* actually meant 'we the rich people'. And when things did fall apart, the rich were the ones who had the ability to grab the lifeboats. Luckily, they were too stupid to do a good enough job and some of the rest of us survived. And now, things seem to be shifting a bit, and who knows? Maybe *We the People* will come back for real."

I wished I had his confidence. The people I had met in my life would not easily coalesce into "we"—not unless there was a fairly good size "they" to fight against.

Tegson came back in the room. "I'm heading out now, to get—the goods," he told his father. "I can get Marty started on his trip." He held up a red plastic token with something written in black.

Teg and I exchanged glances—he seemed as loath as I to cut short this visit. We needed weeks to catch up! Teg looked away.

"Probably a good idea," he sighed. "Marty, that chip will get you a loan of an e-bike over at Lonnie's—Tegson can show you where."

"And here's a small map to show you the route," Tegson said, coming over to the table and spreading the paper. We bent over it, and Tegson ran his finger along a road that paralleled the river. "I can't spare the map, but it's a fairly straight route—the only time you need to get off 65 due to a rockfall is just about here—" he pointed "—and get on again here and take 65 into Ambridge. Turn right at a ruined bridge across the river where the buildings start. Five blocks then turn left. And then it looks like straight up this road to the colony."

I startled, knowing I hadn't told him exactly where the colony was. But Teg had told me how good they were with surveillance. I wonder if they knew where Ciera's town was.

"Thank you," I said, "although that doesn't seem enough."

"Thank you for helping last night," Tegson replied lightly. "And it will help us if you help the others survive this conflict."

"Well, it might be that those folks will be happy that a shark wandered into their territory," I said. "Too many of them seem to believe they can avoid fighting."

Teg sighed. "Don't take this wrong, Marty—but you were never a shark. You never stepped on others; if you stole a bit of extra to eat—that's just common sense. Sharks *enjoyed* the kill."

I shifted uncomfortably. I never did enjoy it.

"And besides," he continued, "you were too generous to be a shark."

"Now, that's not true! I learned really early how dumb it is to be generous."

Teg shook his head and told his son, "Marty would always be the one who would split his meal with a newcomer."

"Well, I knew what it was like to be hungry," I muttered.

"And you also tried to teach others what you'd been taught," he said.

"Well—I never thought of that as generous."

"The others weren't doing it."

"Marty was very generous last night, helping us with the task he didn't fully understand," Tegson chipped in.

"I didn't get the impression that I would be allowed to say no," I said carefully. "Once I was in the middle of it, I didn't have much choice."

Tegson chuckled, and his father looked at him curiously. "Well, it was kind of an initiation," the son responded. "I heard they had them in Long Island."

"Yes, but usually we knew that's what we were going to do. I was—surprised," I said. I wondered if there'd ever be an occasion to tell him just exactly how close to death he'd come because of his actions.

Teg struggled out of his seat and stuck out his hand. "I'm... damn glad we ran into each other again," he said with a catch in his voice.

I shook his hand slowly, looking at him, then away. "I hope this won't be the only time we talk," I replied.

"Not at all! You're always welcome, and it sure seems like this brouhaha will mean you're in contact with the group here. We can keep in touch through Tegson."

I nodded, not trusting my voice. With one more glance, I turned away and followed Tegson through the door.

25

Tegson led me back through the debris-strewn basements, the timber-propped tunnels. Why was his father's location a secret? We wandered this way and that, coming up again after several blocks.

"Lonnie's is three blocks that way, then take a right. This token is all you'll need," he explained, handing it to me. "And I'm in contact with Justin, so any time you want to get in touch, ask him." Nodding, his expression already focused on something else, he turned and left.

I couldn't begin to untangle all my feelings as I watched him stride up the street. I'd have the same combo of confusion, delight and anxiety if I'd found a winning lottery ticket in my box of laundry soap. In a daze, I turned around and realized that I knew where I was, and could find my way back to Justin and Zara's. It was an overcast day; gray skies but no threatening clouds; chilly but not freezing. As in Ambridge, the street signs and poles had all been recycled, but some names had been carved or painted on the corner buildings. I walked down Rope past Western. There were dozens of people walking or pausing at shops, as if it were a normal day, instead of the possible beginning of a war. Is this what Inside was like? Were people always this blind, or did survival mode filter out long-term problems? I caught a couple curious glances, and I looked down. I was still wearing Justin's armor underneath my jacket, and maybe I still looked like an insider. I shifted to a confident stride, staring down the road as if on an errand. When I caught sight of the house, I quickened my steps, praying they'd be home.

In fact, Zara and Justin were chatting with the trading post brothers and the skinny kid who had first challenged me. When I tapped on the door, the kid opened it and stepped back with a shocked look. I glanced over his head and waved at Zara. She jumped up, called my name and hurried to the door. The boy—Morris, I remembered—stepped aside suspiciously, but Zara hugged me then held me at arm's length.

"We weren't sure you—weren't sure if you'd gotten in trouble," she said. Justin waved at me from the table. I knew the brothers were aware of the sortie, but I wasn't sure about the boy.

"Just a brief detour to visit someone I used to know," I said, looking at her intently, hoping she would guess. But she just looked puzzled and led me to the table.

"Well, sit and have some ale and flatbread," she said.

"We'll finish up our business in just a minute," Justin added, then turned to the brothers. "It's okay to keep talking."

Asrah seemed dubious but picked up his thread. "We should be able to get at least three dozen tubes from the glassblower by next week. If Zara will have the other parts finished?"

"Definitely," she said. "Even if I have to miss the book club again." She grinned and looked at me as if drinking me in. I returned her grin with warm contentment. Now there might be three separate groups who would be happy to see me if I showed up. It was a novel sensation.

"Are the pins going to be bi-polar?" Zir asked. She turned back to the conversation, discussing details in a jargon I didn't understand, so when Justin stood to clear up the dishes, I hurried to help. Bringing the plates over to the sink, I asked him quietly, "Do you know if Zara sent word to Ambridge for me? And was there word back?"

"We were going to see Aida in just a little bit—she'd be the one who'd know," he replied. "Did you...was Teg...all right?"

I paused. Obviously he didn't want to detail his worries, just as I didn't want to tell him more than he should know. I still considered Tegson a lion with a cat's fickleness, though perhaps my special immunity had increased.

"Yes, everything's fine. And my next big task is to get back to that group. He gave me a token that should get me an e-bike over at Lonnie's, if you know where that is."

"It's down the street from the forge—we can stop to see Aida and then get you on your way. Do you know the roads?"

"I—I looked at a map and I think I know the way. Highway 65 is in pretty good shape and I think Geoff and I actually passed Ambridge the first time, but didn't stop." My impatience was growing, like a physical itch. "Oh—but I need to give you back your armor." I started to take off my jacket, but Justin patted my arm.

"Leave it for now, just in case. We haven't got enough lookouts to be sure you won't run into trouble. And I can fix you some food and water."

I thanked him, choking up slightly. Such a different world out here! I assured him I would get the armor back, "...and maybe I can help the negotiations with Ambridge, if needed."

"You think you'll be out here for a while then?" He stroked his mustache, acting casual—but I think he really wanted to know.

"Yes—for a while. I've never liked to hang around inside a burning house."

He chuckled at that. Zara and the brothers stood and she escorted them to the door, where Morris had been apparently standing guard. Zara said something to the boy which sent him out the door, and she turned and hurried back to me.

"Martin! I was afraid we'd never see you again. Justin told me about last night, though I don't think he told me the half of it." She glanced over at him. "And then apparently you disappeared with General Teg."

I agonized about telling her—surely if Tegson wanted them to know about his father, he'd have mentioned it? And they would have known to tell me me when I asked earlier. So for some reason, my friend was a secret.

Zara saw me waffling, and hurried to add, "Your business with him is your business. I'm just glad—" I could see her struggling not to say anything negative about Tegson.

"Everything's fine, and he thinks it's a great idea for me to get the group up there to become part of at least your surveillance system—I honestly don't know enough about them to know what they have. But as...Teg...suggested, right now joint surveillance would be crucial. No one seems to know enough about what's happening south of us. Did Justin tell you about the flight?"

"Yes, and I wish I could've seen it." Her eyes glowed like a child's. "I used to watch birds and ache to fly."

"I'm not sure I'd want to go up that high—believe me, the bridge was high enough!" I replied, smiling. Relief at having gotten through the wild night flowed over me again.

Justin had been busy in a back room and came in with a lumpy knapsack. He gave it to me, saying, "You should get up there in a couple hours, max, but just in case, there's a bit of food to tide you over. I put your phone in the small pocket here." He pointed it out.

My phone. My lifeline or my albatross? The image of the Ancient Mariner with a strange bird hanging around his neck flashed in my mind, and I could hear my uncle Roy telling the story in his gravelly voice. I shook my head. Obviously still not enough sleep.

"Would you mind if I washed up before we left?" I asked. "I don't want to go back to the group looking like I slid down the garbage pile."

He chuckled. "You don't look so bad for a guy who's been up all night, but of course—you know where the shower is and I think Zara has even cleaned your old clothes." He rummaged in the knapsack, and pulled out a pair of pants.

"Actually," she said, "I just found a better pair—I'm not sure I could've done much with those brown pants." She looked apologetic and I reassured her they weren't mine.

"I just picked them up off the donation table, to give me a disguise." Would I even remember where I had stashed my old clothes up in Ambridge? Did I care? It didn't take me long to wash up, and it felt good to be able to put on clean clothes, and brush my hair, which was getting shaggy. Within a half hour, I was ready to go.

The atmosphere in the street was still casual, as if everyone had forgotten yesterday. Zara saw me looking around and said, "It doesn't take long for word to get around—probably everyone knows the Southerners have left and the Army isn't currently planning punishment. As for the rest? We've learned to live from day to day."

A bit of the old slum attitude, I mused. When Life was a wringer washer, expect wrinkles. No long-term plans. But that wasn't true either, since most trades and living arrangements required long-term planning. So what was "living day to day?" A kind of attitude, I supposed—a detachment from what you wanted to have happen, a refusal to put faith in your own plans. Focusing on enjoying that day for what it had, not on some nebulous future. Probably why I didn't fit well with the gangs—I'd always been focused on the City, using them as my stepping stones. Most of the others had seemed content to be where they were, though Teg had also been an exception. A dangerous gush of emotion welled, and I bit my lip. I would sort it all out the moment I got some calm and stability. Another long-term plan.

Aida's was crowded, but not with customers. The back table was full, with three or four standing behind the chairs, looking over and sliding their comments into a spirited discussion. Aida came out of her small office, sheets of paper in one hand, a pitcher in the other. We were halfway across the room before she noticed us.

"Justin!" she exclaimed, "you got news for us?" She set down the pitcher and papers. The others turned in their chairs or looked up; most of them grinned, but I noticed two participants frowning—a seated redhead whose curls were tight as a poodle's though her nose looked more like a pug's, and a short man behind her who resembled the Middle Eastern brothers. So even this group had its naysayers?

"First steps went well," Justin replied. A young blonde got up from her chair and allowed him to sit. Zara and I stood behind him, and I was reminded of the slumsters' Council talks where designated speakers were backed by their supporters at a wooden telephone cable spool.

"It will probably be tonight before we will know if the second part worked," he continued. "There are definite crazies over there, I can tell you that. One of them babbled about being in Hell and how we weren't supposed to be in *his* Hell—" Justin shook his head, and the others leaned closer, intent. "And they were armed, so I wouldn't like to go back there a second time. Maybe during the day, but then they could see us better too."

"How did you get over?" A nondescript young man asked, but the woman next to him elbowed him and he fell silent. Justin chose to ignore the question.

Aida asked, "So it's a cert they're still heading away?" Everyone seemed to know who she was referring to.

"Yes—they were heading due south with all speed, and likely trying to get their hostages as far away as possible."

I thought about those children, and wondered how the Army was planning to get them back. I supposed that silver spoons would be returning to their defensible homes and staying put. Closing the barn door after the horse was gone.

I leaned over and whispered to Zara, "I need to go—can we see if any word came back?" Much as I would like to know the group's plans, I didn't want to be distracted for another hour, and they looked ready to talk much longer than that. She gestured to Aida, and they stepped over near the office and exchanged murmurs.

Zara came back and said, "The messenger was sent, and has returned saying the community would consider the proposal and send word down in a day or two."

"But did anybody tell—"

She patted my arm. "The messenger relayed your message about coming back as soon as you could. They said they'd pass the word on."

Not nearly reassuring enough. I had to get going, now! Even though it was a wrench to leave my new friends. After a moment's waffling, I hugged Zara, and patted Justin on the shoulder, he glanced up, realized that I was going, and stood.

"Safe trip, and let us know how it turns out there," he murmured, extending his hand. I shook it firmly and thanked him for everything.

"I promise I'll get the armor back," I said.

"I know you will."

I turned and left before the eye rains started—all of this trust was unnerving. Zara accompanied me to the door and pointed up the street to a bicycle wheel hanging from a post in front of another brick building. I thanked her again and hurried off.

* * *

Lonnie's had more cycles and tri-wheels than I'd seen in one place. And parts were stacked and hung all around the walls: I recognized wheels and handle bars and the ingenious metal flex-chain that connected the gears. But a lot of the pieces were weird—it would take a master puzzle-maker to connect them into anything useful. I glimpsed a back room with lathes, more gadgets and a long table. Two pre-teen boys were dragging an e-bike up a ramp from a basement—he must have hidden them during the crisis.

Lonnie was a large man with a barrel front; he must be doing well to be able to put on what they used to call a beer belly. Bald on top with a ragged fringe of black hair, large ears, and a wide mouth, he stood with arms on his hips and his head tilted, waiting for me to speak.

I handed him the token and said I'd heard I could borrow an e-bike. He glanced at it, then startled like a spooked horse and examined me dubiously.

"Yeah, this will get you any model you want, but you better not have stolen this—just sayin'."

I smiled, enjoying the secondhand power. "No, it was given to me. I'm heading to Ambridge—and he would appreciate my getting to where I'm going quickly and in one piece."

Lonnie turned and perused the lined-up bikes, then pointed to one with a gray leather saddle, a hefty motor and a flat mesh square over the back wheels for carrying supplies. Not quite as powerful as my original e-cycle, but it looked good.

"You need to get this back within the week," Lonnie said.

"Isn't there somewhere in Ambridge I can drop it off?" Having to bring the bike back seemed to make the trip pointless. Unless she came back with me...

He paused, looking down at the token, as if it were a message. "Weeeell.... I suppose you could... problem is, we don't have trade with them up there." He looked really uncomfortable. I thought about Tegson; I didn't want to get the guy in trouble.

"Okay, no problem—I'll get it back to you within the week. It's likely there will be messages coming from there in any case." I thanked him and after a brief lesson, I hopped on the cycle, powered it up and slowly drove away.

It felt really strange, after all the walking, to be biking up a street toward the highway. I ignored curious glances and maneuvered around the mangled asphalt, bounced along cobblestone alleys past brick rowhouses in all stages of repair, ever closer to the elevated road, trying to picture where the entrance ramp was. There were just enough one-story warehouses and salvage shops in this southwest corner of the Mall to block my sight of it. I paralleled the highway until I saw the curved road—I had to detour half a block to find the beginning, but then I was up on the elevated section, and the way looked clear. I opened the throttle a bit and started toward my uncertain future. Would she have had time to think about—us—and would she have... reassessed her opinion of me?

Most of the guard rail fence was gone, of course. I couldn't see over the edge to the closest buildings, but the ruins of the old Pitts spread out on both sides for a couple miles. I glanced to my left, where the river was a wide band in the distance, and the foreground a scattering of large concrete box warehouses—was *that* the building where the plane was hidden? The area was even more trashed in daylight. To my right, blocks of small brick row houses—Zara and Justin's somewhere among them—jammed like fat books on a shelf, gradually giving way to fenced-in garden plots and then whole blocks cleared and planted. The railroad tracks ran parallel to the highway, and I thought about the crazy ride in the baggage car as I rejoiced at the wind blowing my jacket and ruffling my hair. At this speed, I would be in the colony in an hour and a half! The wide expanse of road was so empty that I was startled when another e-cycle puttered up a ramp and headed toward me. I tensed and slowed a bit, reaching for my pistol. But the rider, in brown leather with a leather helmet and goggle glasses, blew past me at a high speed, not even acknowledging me.

My mood dropped as the elevated road quickly descended into an ordinary concrete four-lane, paralleling both the railroad, which had somehow shifted to its left, and the river beyond that. Now I felt vulnerable—although there weren't a lot of streets that connected, and there often were walls or cliffs on my right, attack would be much easier. I powered up the bike and focused on moving as fast as possible. What happened to the highway? Had I really gone this way with Geoff? It looked so different after all I'd been through that I couldn't be sure.

Fortunately, the concrete was well patched, as Tegson had said, though there was much more traffic on the river—small boats, even several rafts—than on this highway. The absence of road traffic could be the battle or the theft of vehicles. I passed maybe a handful of walkers. There were many ruined towns. Buildings were picked clean and their bones were all the unliftable bits, sticking up through the brambles. Large tree stumps everywhere suggested cold winters. Saplings poked up randomly. I thought about all the places Tegson's troops hung out, buildings disguised as total wrecks, so I didn't quite believe *all* this devastation. On the other hand, it would make a lot of sense to be gathered in defensible towns and this looked too open.

I mentally revised my travel time, and focused on speed and peripheral vision. Often I was traveling through young forest, though trees had been cut clear on both sides to prevent ambush. I really wished I had a helmet to go with the leather armor, and I half-consciously began to vary my pace, swerving a bit back and forth to become a more difficult target. The sky was leaden and there were no shadows, luckily—no place to hide and aim. I glimpsed narrow streets of ruined brick bungalows overgrown with vines. There were more huge warehouses, those giant stone boxes that before the Adjustment held only one store in a town-sized building. Without windows, it was hard to see if there was anything inside now. Once I passed a large house that looked occupied and had a wooden sign dangling from the porch: "$5 A Night." Either an inn or a brothel.

Because the road was so straight, it was easy to see the predicted rockfall ahead, and I slowed, searching for the street I was to take off. This would be such a perfect place for an ambush! I braked enough to handle the bike with one hand and took the pistol from my pocket. If only I knew where I was going! The detour seemed permanent, and the side road was well maintained, passing an old gas station, a couple brick houses, the foundation shells of four woodframe buildings burnt to the ground, and a gray stone church. I counted two streets then turned left, and paralleled 65—so far so good.

Then something thudded into my back, glancing off. Without looking, I floored the bike and raced down the block, around the corner, then veered sharply into a driveway and behind a gutted house. Ditching the bike, I raced to the remaining upright wall and looked back. Three men on foot, two of them with bows, were trotting down the street, searching. They were too far away but I couldn't risk them getting closer. Resting my arm on the brick, I aimed at the first archer and caught him mid torso; he clutched his gut and fell over. The other two spun, looking wildly for me. I took out the second archer with a shot to his shoulder, then as the last bandit danced and jiggered toward an old street post, reaching into his jacket, I shot again, but it went wide. He pulled out a large pistol, and got off two shots toward my brick wall, to force me down and let him get closer. I darted toward the other side of the house, clambering over fallen brick, swearing softly as my foot slipped off some rotted wood. I wasn't going to let him catch me there. As he got closer to my hiding spot, I crept around the wall's far side, waited until he had passed around, then raced over. I jumped him from behind, slamming him to the ground, pinning his pistol underneath. If the others weren't hobbled, I didn't have much time.

"I either tie you or shoot you—you decide," I grunted, struggling as he tried to get up. He was small but wiry, stinking like a pigsty and swearing as well as any slumster. I held the pistol against his temple and he froze.

"Tie me," he said, "but if my mates get you, you're dead."

I ignored that, kneeling on his crossed arms, putting my pistol away and trying to find something to tie him. It wasn't like I carried that stuff all the time. I forced him to his feet by twisting one arm almost to breaking point, then pushed him toward the ruined house. Holding both pistols, I jumped away and told him to take off his jacket and hand it to me. Glaring, he did so, and I noticed an old scar slewed across the right side of his face from temple to chin—an old hand at this, and more dangerous. I made him lean over a low wall and I tied him up with his jacket then forced him to sit facing the wall. Then I raced back to the bike and headed out. I glanced over—the two others were still on the street though both were moving. Shaking, I steered the bike back toward 65, then down the highway out of town.

Closer to Ambridge, the highway closely paralleled the railroad, and I began to see refugees heading south in small groups. I warned several of them about the bandits, and told them to be extra careful. I recognized the crippled bridge, where the train had parked, and I took a right and headed into town.

As I motored up the road that had been thronged with refugees—was it just three days ago?—my heart was revving with the engine. Would they even let me in? But surely, if everyone was allowed.... Where would I stash this bike? My mind was catching on trivialities, not willing to think about whether she was even still there. I passed shops where the soldiers had looted—shoppers were going in and out like nothing had happened. Finally, I pulled up to the main colony gate. They were ushering a group out—going back home? Another long walk, but unless they lived right next to the explosion, an intact home was waiting for them. And here? I didn't see any obvious destruction, but inside might be a different story.

I wheeled my bike up to the gate, where the porter, the hefty blond woman who had helped apprehend the tattooed one, eyed me curiously. I could see a second person hovering just beyond the doorway—the cast shadow might have included a gun.

"I'm Martin, I'm...with Ciera and Hadley and Megan—I left to find out what was going on. Could you—could I come in and find them again?"

She thought for a moment. "Are you the Martin who got kidnapped by the rebels?"

"Yes," I replied eagerly, "so they heard about that? I was taken down to the Mall, and I have information that could help you."

"Go on in," she said. "You can park your bike over there—" she gestured toward the alcove "—until you find a place to store it. I'm Astrid."

"Thanks, Astrid. Please be careful of it—it's not mine, and it's on loan for a week only." I would find a better place soon—but now I had to find *her*! I hurried inside, pausing at the threshold to look around. The Hall was still fairly packed, refugees resting on the floor and getting food and clothing from the various tables. Nothing seemed to be changed and I wondered if they had repelled the raiders after all. I reminded myself was only a bit more than 48 hours. The overcast day didn't bring much light into the room, and I strained to find any familiar face. It was Pippin's height that caught my eye, and I eased through the crowd and went over to where he was dishing out stew.

"Martin! Good to see you, dude," he called out, handing a soup bowl over and coming around the table. I was grinning like a stoned idiot, and his smile was broad. "We heard you got tangled up with the rebels somehow."

"I got too close, trying to see what they were doing, but at least they didn't hang me for spying," I replied as he put his hands on my shoulders and held me at arm's-length.

"Yup. Seems like all parts still there."

"Is—are Ciera and Hadley still around? Have they gone back—" I couldn't finish.

"Out back, helping with the sheets. Since it's dry, this is a laundry day. Hadley might actually be chatting with Erma," he said. He patted my shoulder. "I know you're anxious to talk to her, so go out there, lad." He pointed me down the hall with directions to get to the back door and the wash house.

Dammit—my heart was pounding as badly as on that bridge! That was crazy, after all I'd been through. But when I saw her slim figure against a white sheet as she helped pin it to a long clothes line, I caught my breath. I hadn't had time to think about how I felt, but now it was damned obvious. She'd gotten in under my defenses and I really need to know how she felt about me. Still, I hesitated, watching her gracefully bend and pick up another sheet, shake it smooth and lightly toss it half over the line.

Another woman noticed me and called out, "Hey!" Ciera turned and froze. It took all of my strength to walk forward and close the gap.

All of the various clever phrases I had considered as I was riding up vanished and I ended up just calling out, "Hi." She was surprised—maybe worried? Then she strode up to me and smiled.

"When did you get back?"

"Just now. I saw Pippin, and he told me where you were." I felt dumb as a muted vid—I wanted to hug her; it would be stupid to shake her hand, even more stupid just standing here. Impulsively I reached over and fingered a strand of her hair. "It's good that—I'm glad you're okay," I said.

"I'm glad *you're* okay," she replied. "They said the rebels kidnapped you."

I glanced around—all of the launderers had stopped and were staring. "Is there—could we go somewhere and I could tell you about it? I do have info that could help the group—and your town, maybe."

She looked over at a willowy dark-haired woman who gestured her off. Ciera grabbed my hand and walked me back towards the building. I squeezed her fingers and fought a lump in my throat. Images of the bridge, and the crazies in the Haunt, and yes, that last wild moment before I had re-discovered my friend, flashed through my mind. Now that I was back, I was pulsing with the fear that I had been swallowing the past two days.

She steered me through the kitchen where we grabbed two mugs of coffee and headed for a corner of the Great Hall. She nodded and smiled to the others, and once again I felt the warmth. We settled on the floor under a window, where the thin overcast day at least gave us a bit of light.

"What happened?" she asked. "Some said you were kidnapped, some said..." She frowned. Some? Hadley, maybe?

"I was doing okay, spying on the train and the soldiers—who come from the South, by the way—and then that jackass Geoff crept up and grabbed me and wanted to take me hostage, and that alerted the soldiers and they arrested both of us."

"Now, don't talk like that," she chided.

"What? Why?"

"You're insulting jackasses," she said and giggled, with an edge of something else. Maybe she'd really worried. Guilt mixed with joy that she really *did* worry. I took her hand again and held it as I continued.

"I was able to convince them that I was a stupid incompetent—just like I convinced you—" I couldn't resist throwing that in, "and the southern captain wouldn't kill an innocent, so he took us with the baggage down to the Mall. They actually rammed the engine into the Wall then blew it up!"

Her cheeks were bright pink. "I never thought you were...that incompetent," she said looking away. She was a worse liar than I was.

"Doesn't matter now," I said, "what's important is that this wasn't just local rebels—the battle is between DC and New York and it's gonna involve everybody! There's a group near the Mall with really good information—" I hesitated—should I tell her about the plane? No, she would tell her brother everything. "They found out the Southerners have already gone back, and so for now probably no more battles, but this isn't gonna end here. Your town will have to do something to make sure they aren't the battleground when the war breaks out again."

I searched her face, looking for signs that she didn't believe me. All I saw was a worried confusion.

"There's lots more to tell," I said, "but I want to know how you managed with the troops. Did they end up taking much? Was anyone hurt?"

"They came through and demanded food and medical supplies, and Erma gave them quite a lot, and then gave them an ear bashing about leaving refugees helpless if they took anymore," Ciera replied. "Our local boys obviously felt guilty, but, yeah, there were some different accents and *they* didn't much care, as long as they got what they wanted." She bit her lip and looked down. "They started breaking open cupboards, while the local boys hung back, and gradually disappeared. And all of a sudden it was just about five of the out-of-towners, searching in one room, and...they found themselves staring into about two dozen guns." She looked really uncomfortable, and I worried that someone had gotten killed. "Erma quietly told them that they could take what they had but if they came back, they'd better bring the full Army and a lot more guns than they were carrying. I don't know if she meant that, but those guys saw how it was, and backed out quickly. I don't know what they did afterwards."

"So no one got hurt?"

She shook her head. "Not here. But we sure have been spending a lot of time washing crap off of our supplies," she said and giggled again. She looked as swoggled as I felt. "I didn't think—didn't know this group would be willing to kill five soldiers who weren't shooting at them." She looked crushed. I wondered how often she'd had to use the gun she carried. Maybe she thought it was just for lions?

"Maybe they wouldn't have," I said. "Maybe they would have disarmed and jailed them, like the southern captain did with me and Geoff." She wanted her town to be peaceful and self-sufficient—and the odds of *that* in the coming months would be slim to nil. She'd have to learn.

"When I got down to the Mall, I found people who were trading with the City but also had their own system—they have radios like the Army, and have been able to find out what both sides have been doing. One of the southern soldiers told me—"

We were interrupted by Hadley and Erma walking up; her brother frowning and glancing back and forth, Erma smiling in welcome.

"Martin, we heard you had returned," she said before Hadley could speak. "We got word from the Mall group but we hope you will be able to explain further."

"I'd be happy to do that," I said, jumping up. "There's a lot more going on than it first seemed, and I think—it could get bad."

She acknowledged that with a calm nod. "We are gathering the members now," she said. "Could you join us?" She looked at the cup in my hand, and asked, "Have you eaten?"

"I'm fine for now, in fact—" I pulled my knapsack off my shoulder, and rummaged in it. "Friends gave me some food for the trip, and I don't need it now, so perhaps you can use it."

"Thanks," she replied, "we can drop it in the kitchen as we go."

Ciera scrambled to her feet, and said, "I'd like to be there, too—Martin was saying this would affect our town, and I want to find out how, if you don't mind?" She was deliberately refusing to look at her brother.

"Of course you may. This is not a closed meeting—we are simply restricted by space. But you have also known him longest—" Erma's smile showed that she knew exactly how the situation was, "—so you can certainly be part of the discussions."

26

We followed them across the room, and Hadley took a moment to whisper something in Ciera's ear that made her frown. Possibly he was still advocating for that carpenter, I thought, and suppressed a grin—not the right time. I tried to focus on a coherent story to convince them how much danger they were in, and that Justin's group were worth linking up with.

I almost laughed again when I found that we would be meeting in a barn. True, it was a very large, open space, and the cows had been turned out. But it seemed so clichéd, so *moo-vid*, to be punny. The bales of hay were crowded with members who craned to watch as Erma led the way to a wooden podium set at one end in a natural light shaft. Like most wooden barns, it was not as tight as a house; spears of light angled down and lazy dust motes swirled, but it was too dark to see most faces. There had been a low murmur through the room, but that stopped abruptly as we four walked forward. Erma gestured for Hadley and Ciera to sit in the semi-circle that I presumed made up the Council. I saw Pippin and several others that I recognized; Pippin smiled and nodded.

Erma stepped up to the podium, and in a loud clear voice, she announced, "Some of you will have heard that we received a messenger from a group living near the Mall, telling us that there may be a bigger war breaking out between the major cities, and asking for our cooperation in keeping this area secure."

From the gasps and murmurs around the room, I could tell there were some who hadn't heard, or at least not to that level of detail. Erma raised her hands and the group fell silent.

"They gave us some information, notably that the soldiers who came through here a couple days ago were from the south, as part of a larger attack on the city of New York, presumably by the city of Washington, DC.

Their information was that hostages had been taken and carried south, and they assumed that negotiations would start between the two cities, which for the time being would keep other battles from happening. While I don't know this to be absolute fact, it would of course be a good thing if we had some breathing space. Martin here—" she gestured towards me—"has some additional information that I think will be very important as we try to decide what to do. Martin?"

She left the podium to me, and I reluctantly walked up. Scanning the crowd of at least 50, my mind momentarily blanked. How much of what I knew was secret? No one had said anything, but I knew instinctively that Justin wouldn't want all their activities shared with strangers—not yet. So this had to be convincing, give them enough defensive weapons, but not strip the Mall group naked. A tall order.

"The last couple of days have been so crowded that I couldn't possibly tell you all of it, without at least four bathroom breaks," I started. The crowd chuckled, and some of the tension eased. "But the group that sent the message is both honest and talented. I was impressed by their surveillance skills and their preps for...staying independent, even if the two cities start to battle it out. That will take a lot of luck *and* skill, but I think they could offer you—and your group down in the Mall—important help and what they want is news from this area." Did this sound like a sales job? I wanted it sincere—did I even know how to do that?

"What I learned from the southern soldiers was that they came up past the old airport, then crossed some railroad bridge a bit west of here and followed the river down through Freedom, I think, which is where they picked up the train. That means there's probably more of them on the south side of the river, and maybe you didn't know about that?" I looked around and saw a mix of puzzlement, worry and some nods of confirmation on the nearest faces. How much surveillance did this group do? Since the train got through, it wasn't enough.

"I didn't see the message you got, but I believe their group wants to trade information at least—and possibly also goods. But it sounds like the priority is to find out whether there still are soldiers on the other side of the river, and how many." I glanced at Erma and she nodded.

"Are they going to fight the soldiers?" Rom asked. He was straining forward as if itching for action.

"I don't think so—they told me they had good surveillance and communication but would definitely prefer to stay out of the way while the cities battled, and just try to protect what they have."

The crowd murmured its approval for this approach, then quieted as Erma gestured. Turning to me, she asked, "Whose side are they on?"

"To the best of my knowledge, they're not aligned with either side. In fact they seem to be trying to arrange things so that neither city can expand out and claim this area," I replied.

The group broke into excited discussion, and it took Erma a little while to quiet them. I used the time to think through various facts, trying to decide which were safe to reveal. Maybe not the tunnels, but probably more about the hostages. Definitely more about the radios, though not the tower project, or those big guns, and definitely not Tegson until he wanted to make himself known.

"They have asked us to set up surveillance teams and to relay that information to them so that they can have more advanced notice of any soldiers," Erma said, "and that seems to be a sensible task, and a good trade if they give us similar information."

I nodded. "They were able to find out that the hostages were children of the New York defense minister," I said, but had to stop as the exclamations and comments grew loud. It *was* a bastard act, I thought. Of course, this group probably wouldn't understand how those children were used to being pawns—as scions of what amounted to the nobility, they were traded and groomed and bound into stilted childhoods. Such children were often used among the rich to form alliances. Heading south as valued hostages with another group might not be much different.

Erma finally succeeded in quieting the group again, and I continued. "From what I could tell, the rumors about an attack happening further down the rail line were also correct—it was a double attack, one to steal the hostages, and the other to keep the Army from coming out and catching the soldiers. Justin—my contact—thinks that the local ringleaders will have to surrender or be handed over, but possibly the punishment wouldn't extend much further." As an experienced citizen, I was much more pessimistic. The city would grab any goods they could squeeze out.

"Their group has patrols that allowed them advance warning to the east, north and south," I said, "and which allowed them to send refugees toward safety—and they are quite grateful, by the way—but they were surprised and upset by the train from the west. So that's where you'd come in—finding ways to check the borders and relay info," I concluded.

"Thank you, they did make their gratitude clear, and promised repayment of debt for our care of the refugees," Erma said.

She asked for questions and Pippin immediately raised his hand. "Did they think that the Army would be coming out here? The New York Army, I meant."

"They thought the Army would be focused on repelling the Southerners, and wouldn't have additional troops to send to this area. Unless the southern troops were massing here. But they did mention there might be refugees from the City, if supplies get cut off there." Again I pictured my colleagues, my jazz buddies—was there any way I could warn them without endangering my new friends?

I noticed a ripple of whispering, similar to that in the café when Justin, Zara and I were spying—something being passed from the back to the front. When it reached Rom, he raised his hand and asked, "Gordy wants to know if we are going to get our vehicles and animals back?"

"I don't know anything about that," I admitted. "I know the other group is going to contact the their local rebels and negotiate to perhaps save the rebels' families, and maybe you could ask for both vehicles and the stolen supplies back." Unless the Southerners had taken the supplies from the train to fuel the long march south.

I saw Hadley whisper to Ciera. She leaned away and elbowed him. Whatever he was trying to convince her of, she wasn't buying it. I thought briefly about our situation—could she stay here with me if he went back? Would I be forced back to their hidden town? I knew I needed freedom right now—I needed to see Teg again, and to stay in touch with Justin and Zara. Surely, she'd understand that?

Erma thanked me and I sat on the only empty straw bale, about four seats away from Ciera. Erma waited for quiet, and then continued. "As some of you know, once the rebels had come and gone, the Council sent a scout party to see where they had come from. It has only been a little over a day, but I am happy to report that one of them has come back already—Ari, can you tell us what you found?"

Ari came out from behind a pillar, a short, light-skinned African-Asian man with short cropped hair. He came up to the podium with a nod towards Erma.

"A couple of us followed the railway up, t' see where that train came from. Louder?" He adjusted his voice. "When we got t' Freedom, it was clear that there'd been a buncha activity, including fixin' up some of those old trains. The place wasn't 'zactly empty, so we couldn't explore like we wanted, but we kept following track that was neatened up recently. We got t' the ol' bridge at Rochester, where the Beaver comes in and we could see someone'd started to do repairs on th' trestle that crosses the Beaver River. There's no other railroad crossin' the Ohio between there and Freedom, so we think that's where they came over. It's not ready for a train yet, but it's close. Bob and the others kep' going, but sent me back just t' let you know." He nodded slightly, turned, and walked back to the shadows where he had been standing.

"Thank you, Ari," Erma said. "I think that validates what Martin's group had said, and I think it confirms our need to address the situation. I propose that we request some explanation and details from those locals who were known to be part of this—we are their neighbors, and we need to know where their loyalties lie."

The group chattered noisily for a while, and then Rom stood and waved them to silence. "Erma, I respect your opinion, but I also fear to give away our position too soon," he said. "Those neighbors have already shown by their actions that they favor the South. If we go and ask them, why would they tell us the truth? I suggest that we increase our surveillance of the railroad depot at Freedom, and that we get a patrol across the river, and see what might be there."

I nodded; Rom was thinking strategically, while Erma was still thinking like a neighbor. There was more noise and excitement, then Pippin stood and turned to the group.

"That suggestion has merit," he said, "but it's also dangerous. We don't have the means to communicate with our groups if we send them out that far. And not to downplay the importance of this crisis, but it's also Spring and we need everybody in the fields for planting."

A little nervously, I jumped up. "That's one thing that the other group could help you with," I said. "I know they have radio equipment that's portable and would allow your groups to stay in contact. Devices like this—" I pulled my phone from my pocket and handed it to Erma.

There was a lot of excited chatter; Erma examined the phone, with Rom and Astrid looking over her shoulder. Erma looked at me questioningly—did she suspect I was a spy? But surely Hadley had told her? I hoped I hadn't just blown it. And I hoped Justin would be willing to trade—if not handhelds, then the small boxes. Pippin was right: sending spies out without contact was dangerous.

Finally she held up her hand and the group quieted.

"This would help a lot," she said, "and perhaps they could be part or all of the repayment they promised." She handed me the phone and glanced around at the Council members, then continued, "If the group allows, I would like the Council to meet and make some preliminary plans. Then we will bring it to group vote. Do I have your agreement?"

A chorus of yeas and nays broke out, but the yeas were louder. "Then I declare this meeting over for now. We'll reconvene as soon as we have something for you."

In the glut of bodies leaving the barn, I pushed over to Ciera and faced Hadley's scowl.

"You're not getting rid of me easily," I told him, "So I'd make peace with that, if I were you."

Ciera grinned at me then at her brother, pulling her shoulders back and raising her head. "Right," she said, "get used to him." With another brilliant smile, she pulled me away, toward an empty stack of hay. "I still want to hear the rest of your story."

So I told her of the train ride, the exploding engine, the meeting with Justin and crew. I gave her a sketchy description of our trip inside the wall, leaving out info that might give away the tunnels.

"But when I got inside, it felt too weird," I said, "like it was fake or something. Something about your freeflowing towns got under my skin."

"Of course," she replied, shifting so she could snuggle against my shoulder. "I told you the cities are too artificial. And speaking of under your skin—what are you wearing??" She tapped my chest and the armor thunked.

"That's another thing the group could trade with you—really good leather armor."

"I hope we won't be needing that. What did you do next?"

I put my arm around her and breathed in her scent. "We came back out and I—met some more of the group, and they—will you keep a secret?"

She frowned. "If it doesn't hurt my town."

"It won't. It's just until I get an okay from these new folks. There just wasn't time."

She nodded, and I continued, "They asked me to go with them to help put up a comm tower."

She pulled away and looked at me in surprise. I grinned. "Yeah," I said, "it's ironic, isn't it? Theirs was just a big antenna, but yeah, it felt odd." I pulled her back into my arms. "We went into a part of Pitts that's been deserted, cut off for decades. Full of crazies, but also lots of salvage." I couldn't help thinking that some of the stuff I saw would be worth going back in for. Was the rest of Pitts so rich in salvage that they could afford to leave that to the crazies? What else was going on there? "Anyway, we ended up walking under the river to get back out."

"What??" She tried to pull away again, but I held tight and kissed the top of her head; *my* excitement would be obvious if she leaned in wrong. "You can't walk under a river!"

"One of the benefits of civilization," I told her. "Tunnels for the trains, and this one was still good. It was a bit—unnerving—but we got out okay."

She was quiet a minute, then said wistfully, "I'd like to see something like that someday." I had a sudden strong urge to introduce her to Teg—have her meet the man who'd taught me more than anyone. And see what he thought... I stifled a laugh, as I realized it was like wanting to take her home to parents. Seeking approval.

"Maybe you can go with me when I go back—"

"You're going back??" This time she did pull away. "When??" Her expression shifted from anger to hurt to confusion.

"I'm not leaving permanently, but I borrowed the bike, and they said I had to get it back in a week. It was my only ride. And someone has to meet with Justin's group—and maybe I can get them to trade the phones and... other things." I thought of those big guns. That would change the odds totally. But I didn't know if I wanted them out here.

She sulked and leaned back on my shoulder. "You need to stop disappearing."

"It wasn't my fault. Blame Geoff."

"Where do you think he is now?"

I hoped he'd gone with the rebels, but couldn't count on it. "I think with all this, he's decided he's got better things to do than kidnap me. Probl'y realizes the contract is dead, under the circumstances."

She sighed. "It's been a weird week."

"You got *that* right." I was really afraid to ask, but I need to know what was coming next. But she was ahead of me, as usual.

"All right—what do we do? About us, I mean. I don't know what your city relationships are like."

"Can't help you there—I'm not sure myself," I said with a wince. "I came from a clan that married kids off to form alliances, then through slum gangs where there were no steady relationships 'cause people died too fast, and then into the City where status was so strict that I kept running into class issues every time I thought I was hooking up." That about summed up my love life, and it was pretty pathetic. "What about your group?"

"There is some…marrying off, but mostly to provide a good living for the couple," she said slowly, "and some restrictions because so many of us are cousins, one way or the other. But we used to have dances and gatherings so teens could get to know each other, and if we liked each other, and there weren't restrictions, we usually got to marry."

I couldn't help it; I tensed at the mention of marriage so quickly. She may have picked that up, because she hurried on.

"They usually gave us a long time to decide—up to a year or so without pressure. So we have time to get to know each other before my group would be asking me. But the town has discovered committed relationships are better for community than sleeping around. But this crazy new situation will probably interrupt routine."

"I'm…glad, since I want to stay in contact with the group at the Mall. They helped me as much as your group has and I still feel like I owe them. Maybe we both can go down to the Mall."

She turned to face me, smiling, her eyes huge. "I'd like that! I'd have to figure out a way to fix it with Hadley, but our group is going to need some kind of representation."

"He's acting just like a big brother, and I'm betting he'd say no. Do you have to follow his word, or is there someone else you can ask?"

She looked down. "I've never thought about it much," she confessed. "My family has been reasonable, and after my parents died, my older brother and sister took over advising me. There's the Council I suppose, but well-brought-up people know the rules, that's all."

"So you have an older sister too? What would she say?" I tried to picture an entire extended family protecting Ciera—what I gotten myself into?

"I think Risa would understand more, but she's also traditional," Ciera said slowly, picking at the cuff of her jacket. "The thing about my town is that we *do* depend on every member, and therefore… we can't just selfishly do what we want." Obviously her inner battle was intensifying.

"Well," I replied, thinking fast, "you would be doing your town a great service if you helped them survive whatever this is gonna turn into. And since you already like to be outside the town more than others, it seems like you would be the natural go-between, or at least investigator."

"That makes sense, but how do we convince Hadley?" She looked up with a wry grin.

Almost as if he was called, Hadley appeared at the door, looked around, and walked toward us. "Ciera! It's time to get back!"

She jumped up but stayed by the hay bale. I got up more slowly, taking a deep breath. If I couldn't convince Hadley to leave her here, I would have to go with her—I didn't want to split up again so quickly. I just couldn't. So I would *have* to convince Hadley.

"Ciera, I need to talk to you," he said, getting closer.

She took my hand. "You can talk to me here. And I'm not going back, Hadley. I need to stay here for now."

He glared at us, obviously struggling to keep his temper. After a moment of silence, he said, "I hope you know what you're doing, Ciera. Even if you are—interested—in someone outside of town, we have protocols for that. You can't simply walk away from your job."

"I'm not walking away—I'm…switching jobs for now," she replied. "Someone has to know what's going on so we can tell the town. You go back and tell them what's happened so far, and I'll collect more information so that if something happens suddenly, I can get word back."

He wasn't buying it. He glanced at me with an expression that said he thought I'd put her up to this, which annoyed me because all I did was put words around what she already wanted to do.

"Ciera, I hate to say this—but if you don't go back now, you've broken faith with the town. And you know the consequences."

She looked stricken and squeezed my hand unconsciously. Was he threatening to kick her out? She stared at her feet, biting her lip, then after a moment looked back up and I recognized that defiance. She was still gonna stay. My heart lifted and relief flowed through me.

"There are protocols if I've broken faith," she replied steadily, "I have the right to say what I thought I was doing. And this is an emergency, Hadley, even if you don't recognize that—"

"I recognize it," he broke in. "I know there's danger here, and I thought especially at a time like this, you'd be thinking of your town—"

"I *am* thinking of the town! Like I said—I plan to stay and get more information, or even go with Martin to the Mall and find out what this other group can offer our town."

He glanced at me, eyes widening in panic. The big brother part was winning.

"Ciera—the Mall still is too dangerous, even if there's no battle at the moment—"

"Actually, I would be able to keep her quite safe there, because like I said, that group has amazing skills both at surveillance and at hiding what they want hidden. And I still have citizenship, and a pile of credit just the other side of the Wall that I can tap into if needed."

"I don't need you to keep me safe," she said, tossing her head and half glaring, half smiling at me.

"All right, then, we both would be safe with my friends at the Mall," I amended. I squeezed her hand to let her know we needed to stay allied against Hadley. Or at least against his objections.

I could feel his tension, as if wanting to bodily pick her up and carry her off. I know I'd feel like that. But she was grown—heck, a widow!—and I planned to keep her safe no matter what she said.

"Be it on your head," he said finally. "Megan and I are leaving now. I plan to be back next week, if the town approves. I want you to be here—" he paused as she glared at him. "—I'd like you to promise me, if you would, that you'll be here, or at least let Erma know where you are." For a moment, he looked stricken. "I don't want you just disappearing."

"We won't disappear," I said quickly. "I want to stay in contact, because this is gonna need all of us."

He looked at his sister and she relented. "I promise I'll be here, or Erma will know exactly where I am," she assured him.

He nodded, looked at her, then hugged her tightly. Then he turned and left without a word.

I glanced over and saw tears run down Ciera's face. We'd both made a commitment now. I was AWOL and maybe so was she. I gave her a few moments to compose herself, then asked, "Do you want to see him off?"

She shook her head. "He'll be back in a week," she replied, not confidently.

"Then maybe we can go and ask—someone—if we can get their room, before someone else does." I hugged her tightly. "I want to have some private space tonight." She lifted her head and kissed me and it got intense for a few moments; I knew it would be painful walking around for a while, and tonight was *too* far off. May be a "nap"?

Finally she broke free and said, "Okay—let's find out our next job, and see if we can get ourselves into any group going down to the Mall."

The colony was as stirred up as when the train had arrived—frowns, whispered conversations and scurrying around, with refugees milling anxiously in the center of the room. Many of those looked like they were packing—I guessed if a major war broke out, they'd want to be home. Which might give the colony more freedom to maneuver. As we crossed the Hall, the Alitos came over to us.

"Martin, we wanted to ask you—" Mrs. Alito said.

"—if it was safe to go back, in your opinion," her husband finished. They looked at me like two ancient birds, bright-eyed but small and fragile.

I frowned. Who knew where was safe? "Do you have family there?" I asked.

"Our daughter's family—they stayed to watch the farm outside the Mall. "

"Well…I honestly can't say anywhere is *that* safe," I said.

"Which means here isn't much safer than there," Mrs. Alito said.

I agreed and repeated what Tegson had reported about the troops. "So unless your family was involved in the fight—"

"No—we didn't see any point in pulling a tiger's tale," Mr. Alito said.

"Then I'd go back. This could be a long crisis."

"That's what we thought. Thank you." Mrs. Alito hugged Ciera and gave me a kiss on the cheek. "I hope you two stay safe. If you're down our way—"

"We might be!" Ciera said.

"Then look us up—corner of Hall and Shelby northwest of the Mall."

I watch them ease through the crowd, heading for the big double doors. I tried to imagine what it would be like getting old and not being able to dodge trouble like I could now. Compared to Tegson, I was already old. Unfortunately, the odds against my getting that much older were not great.

I looked around futilely for Pippin. The Council members were still missing, so the meeting must be going on. I thought about what Pippin had said about planting, then remembered Teg's warning about moving out of an army's way when you had crops in the field. Should I mention that before they started planting? Maybe they should find safer locations, or maybe plant earlier crops? I vaguely remember discussions as a child about weather patterns and finding the fastest-growing crop with best chance of surviving.

Ciera had the bright idea to check with the porter at the gate to see how rooms were assigned. The man told us staff rooms were the responsibility of the residence manager, who probably was still in the meeting. So we shelved that and asked who assigned jobs.

"Because we're staying even though Hadley and Megan are leaving," Ciera told him.

I had a moment of fear that we wouldn't be welcome without "our" official party, then remembered I was still an important source of information, and relaxed. The man told us we could just help out at the food table or anywhere else that looked busy until the Council came out of session. So we headed back across the room, slowly dodging the women and children who were trying to cram the little they had into patched cloth duffel bags and backpacks. Some of them had the wildly bright-colored nylon duffels; a fabric that supposedly was plastic but had lasted longer than the smooth plastics. And those colors had never been reproduced; they almost hurt my eyes. They were status symbols in the City so it was amazing to see them here. On the other hand, what did I know of the class of these refugees? When war broke out, everybody ran, not just the poor. And, huddled on the floor, they all looked poor.

It looked like lunchtime so we joined the servers, Ciera passing out bread rolls, and me putting a scoop of butter on each plate. As we worked, I asked her how it was that trades were arranged here.

"Are you worried about your stuff?" she asked with an impish grin.

I smiled. “No, I’d mostly forgotten about them—except for the pain meds and phone, they didn’t do me much good out here. I was wondering how you and I will pay for food and shelter, and how I’ll pay back Justin’s group if we stay with them down there.” I thought about last night with Tegson—I wanted to avoid *that* kind of payment in the future!

“Well…it can be pretty complex,” she began. “Firstly, our town has a trade agreement with this colony, and also with this town.”

“Two separate agreements?”

“Yes—the town itself has a Council and this community is represented, but also has its own rules.”

That made sense. “So it’s like you each have a tally sheet and just chalk up debts? Like you did at Troy’s stable?” That scene passed before my eyes and I added, “and what were those little beads she was playing with?”

“That was an abacus, a counting board,” she explained. “They’re very handy. We have someone in town who makes them. And yes, kind of like that arrangement—which reminds me, I owe my town for that also.” She winced and I thought about how many trades she had entered into, to help me. I had a lot of repayment ahead.

“So do I remember you put a mark on the sheet at the restaurant, and that somehow gets back to your town to pay?” She winced again and I felt guilty reminding her. We needed to sit down and make some notes. “We still owe the ferry man information,” I exclaimed. “Is there a way to send someone down to tell him what we know?”

“Good point—I’m guessing the Council will send runners to the towns they trade with, but we can ask specifically that he get some info. I could write a note.”

“But back to trading,” I said, “I know I, or we, owe a couple people along our route, and will probably owe more soon, so how do we know what to trade, and how much it’s worth?”

“You have to agree between you,” a middle-aged lady with curly gray hair and shaped like a potato sack, commented from my other side. “Pardon me for eavesdropping, but trading is important, and it’s good to learn it right. What we do is bring out the goods or describe the service, and then ask, ‘and for this, might I have’ and then you tell them what you need.”

Ciera leaned around me and told her, “That’s true, but there are also guidelines already set—some things have been given equivalents.”

"Yes, that's a start, but it still depends on whether the other person thinks the trade is worth it," the woman replied. She was dishing out bowls of cabbage soup, and had a queue, giving me a moment to ponder. It sounded similar to the slums, except that slumlords factored in power/status and tried to cheat the other person. I assumed they weren't trying to cheat out here, so that also meant really trusting the other person to be honest and not greedy. That was the part I didn't understand how to do.

"So, since you trade a lot with some places, I guess you're careful to make good trades so that they'll trade again?"

Ciera nodded. "It all balances eventually," she said. "Sometimes we'll be in debt to another group for months or years until we find something that balances the account. But those are pretty big trades," she added.

I thought about Monica's description of how they got the loom—part of their crops this year, and what happened if there was a disruption? That was another group that needed to know what was going on. I got a knot in my stomach, as the number of innocent targets multiplied.

"What's the frown for?" Ciera asked. "Do you think we're stupid for trusting someone for so long?"

"No, I was thinking more about Monica's group, and the other towns—if Justin's group can't figure out a way to keep the fighting out of this area..." I didn't have to finish.

"There must be a way to keep the peace around here," she said, staring straight ahead. The person in front of her waited politely for a roll and I finally nudged her. Startled, she dropped a roll on the woman's plate and apologized.

"It may be too soon to know that," I said, "but the group down in the Mall is keeping an eye on the armies—at least we should get some warning. If a good surveillance can be set up here." I realized I was repeating myself, but what could I do? I remembered Justin's comment about *most of war is waiting*—now I felt that keenly. Waiting for the Council to get out, hoping they made some sensible decisions, waiting to get back to the Mall and find something *useful* that I could do about all this. And of course waiting to know where in hell I would finally end up—the thought of this stretching on for months or even years chilled me.

"I wonder if this was how the Adjustment felt?" I murmured.

"What?" Ciera was distracted filling the plates of about six children from toddler to 10-year-old; the youngest one wanted two rolls and she had to explain that they got one and could come back if they needed another.

"I was just wondering if our grandparents had to go through this much *waiting* during the Adjustment, when they didn't know what had happened or what to do about it," I explained.

Suddenly I noticed Pippin come through the double doors—why wasn't he in Council? Or had they broken up? I tapped Ciera's shoulder and pointed him out, then waved. He waved back and came over, making slow progress across the floor full of refugees balancing plates on their laps.

"Were you in Council?" I asked. "Have they made decisions?"

He grabbed a plate and started down the line. "Been in town, checking with shopkeepers. They're gonna meet tomorrow. I said I'd be there." He collected his roll and pat of butter then accepted a bowl of cabbage soup from the middle-aged woman. "Thanks, Patty."

"He's one of our best diplomats," Patty told me. She hollered over her shoulder, "Soup kettle's getting empty!" and turned back to me. "He helped with the treaty of Midland, way back when," she said, with an enthusiasm bordering on hero-worship. "I don't know why the old fart won't get married," she added. I smiled, wondering if she considered herself a candidate.

"Is that the one where they agreed to trade not feud?" I asked.

"Yup—that's the one. Most of the towns have kept to that, and we've all done pretty well." She scowled. "This war might blow it all to hell."

"It might," I admitted. "But one of the guys I talked to said if we could keep them fighting somewhere else, we'd have the best chance at surviving."

"Makes sense. But what if the other towns have the same idea?" I hadn't thought of that. I had no idea what—or who—the wilds of Southern Jersey or West Virginia held, or whether they could try the same snakey idea. But I was willing to bet Tegson could out-snake them, whoever they were.

I noticed refugees looking over toward an area blocked by a screen. A murmuring started among them and the staff.

"I think Council's gotten out," Ciera said.

27

She was right. Erma came around the screen, followed by Rom, Astrid and a couple others. They headed for the food tables and we handed out their meals. As Erma passed me, she murmured, "Could I have a word with you?"

"Of course! Now—or do you want to eat first?"

"Now is fine—get your meal and come over to our circle."

I looked over and saw that Ciera had heard and Patty already had a bowl of soup waiting, so I rounded the table and followed Erma. I noticed everyone was watching the Council curiously, but no one came over to where they were eating as a group, sitting on the floor. I settled myself next to Erma, curious and a little nervous.

"I wanted to ask you a bit more about this group," she started off. "I realize you were only there a day, but what is your sense about how allied they are to the City?"

I had a delaying sip of soup. "Several of them stated that they definitely want to be independent, but they don't mind trading with it. They seem to like our—the City's—luxuries more than you do, I think. But I only was *here* for a day, so I know as much about you as I do about them."

"True. But you seem to be adapting well." She flashed a rare smile, showing charm that probably helped her into leadership.

"It's not so easy," I admitted, "the City is really different."

"So I have heard from Pippin," she said. At his name, he shifted around and leaned toward us. "We were just saying you thought the City was very different from here."

In answer, he laughed uproariously, startling several people. "That it was, that it was. By the way, Erma, town meeting is tomorrow at ten. I said I'd be there. Will we have a plan by then?"

"We'd better have," she replied. "If these armies are moving quickly, then we should, also. I'll call another meeting after lunch."

"We're not gonna get a lot of other work done today," he said.

She sighed. "True, but what's the point of getting work done if it's all going to be undone? Better we find out what we need to know."

"Pippin," I said. "You mentioned planting—maybe it would be better to wait until you have some idea where the armies are and might go?"

"Plants have a certain time they need to be in the ground," he replied.

"Yes, but there's a little leeway, depending on weather and specific seed strain, isn't there? I grew up on a farm," I added.

"You? Grow up on a farm?" He chuckled.

"They do have some on Long Island, you know," I said, smiling but stung. Apparently everyone saw me as a tower turd.

"Well, we also have a scion and seed swap about now—with the other towns roundabout here. It's an important place to get new varieties," he said.

"Anyway," Erma cut in, softly but firmly, "we're trying to assess whether they would push the trivialities we don't want, rather than respecting our choices. That's one of the things that splits us and our fellows near the mall."

I thought about Zara's contemptuous opinion. "I had heard something about that... difference," I said. "And I know there are some who think it's foolish to go without. But others definitely believe everyone has the right to choose. They tolerated me, a citizen," I added, "I'm different in the other direction."

"As long as they don't insist we change," she said.

"It sounded like their aim was a stable culture outside big cities—both of them—and they seemed really focused on the practical goals of trade and information."

"And yet, Norma wasn't wrong about trade causing the downfall of civilization, in a way," Pippen said. "It was the long supply lines that people depended on that screwed everything when they vanished. We have to be careful not to rely on goods from too far away."

Erma frowned. "That's true, but there's a real difference between goods from around the world and goods from three or four hours away."

Pippin shook his head. "Not as much as you think. It's capabilities versus distance—they had supersonic jets and huge ships that could go fetch around the world. We have a horse-drawn carts and if we're lucky a few motor vehicles that can go perhaps a couple hours without recharging or refueling. Almost the same equation."

It was obvious that they had discussed this many times before, because neither seemed surprised at what the other was saying. And Ciera's townsfolk were even more adamant against outside goods. Could a town really create enough to be self-sufficient? Teg seemed to have studied this, and I couldn't wait to ask him. Maybe this time I wouldn't fall asleep before he'd fully answered.

Erma was saying, "...if the group agrees, we will send a delegation to the Mall to negotiate, and meanwhile we will contact our town partners, to let them know and to get their cooperation."

"There is a ferryman out of Horse Ferry who was helpful getting us—Ciera and I—out of danger. We promised to send word back since he keeps that passage open."

"We can do that," she said. "We had planned to contact the ferries and alert them."

"That's gonna take a lot of legwork," Pippen complained. "Some of our best runners are also our best crafters. And we lost some of our transportation, too," he reminded her.

"We'll do the best we can. Rom is working out the logistics for the trips. Though it would be wonderful to have a few more phones," she said, half to herself.

A few *more*? Then I remembered Ciera saying that the large towns had some, using our satellites—but if the satellites didn't exist?? I needed to find out how the radios and phones worked. I remembered the one I had grabbed.

"Erma? One thing I found out is that sometimes one phone can listen in on another—I hadn't realized that." I hesitated, but she nodded complacently.

"We know that those phones have only one frequency, but there are radios that can change frequencies. Did your group have those?"

My group? Meaning Justin, I supposed. "The group at the Mall had several different kinds, and some of them could change something. I'm sorry, I don't know that much about radios *or* phones. I was given mine just before I came out here." I remembered that moment, but it felt like a different person had received it. Just eight days ago.

"Well, let's hope they have enough to share," she said, scrambling to her feet.

I stood also and asked if Ciera and I could join the delegation.

"You, certainly—since you know these others." She paused, considering.

"Ciera is needed to represent her town, and also—" There was no way I could say I really needed her near me, but Erma seem to understand.

"I suppose one more will not be that big a problem."

"And we are both willing to pay for whatever we cost—though I still am not totally sure how you do that around here," I said.

She smiled and said, "I'm sure you will, and you have already helped us a great deal. They said you suggested contacting us. Thank you for that."

"If my phone would be helpful to you now...and Ciera has the solar charger for it." I held it out to her and she took it with a smile and a nod. Oddly, I didn't feel quite as naked without it. At least while I was in the colony grounds.

The second meeting was a repeat of the first—the crowds on the hay bales, the Council in the front ring. The light was a bit brighter this time, as the sun had broken free of the thin clouds.

Erma gestured for quiet then started. "The Council proposes several items that we will ask your consent on individually. First, we will send information to our trading partners and ask that they stay alert and give us information. That will require four or five runners. Second, we will send a delegation of five down to the Mall to negotiate with that group. They will travel with four colony members who are returning to that area, and who will give us shelter. Unless the group disagrees, the delegation will include Rom, Astrid, Siegfried, Ciera of the Engel band, and Martin as our go-between. Third, we will begin preparation for a surveillance group to go across the river, though that may take a few days to pull together. We realize that pulls a possible dozen workers from our group, but in this situation, we believe it is important. I'm sure there will be town members who also wish to help us—Pippin will speak at their meeting tomorrow—but I think it is important that we ourselves get the information we need. This has the potential to be extremely disruptive."

That was an understatement. I kept my face blank.

Erma let the discussion go on for several minutes, then waved them to silence. "Before we vote on this, are there any pertinent questions?"

A man stood in the far back. "Is this deal with the Mall group going to detail what's traded?"

"Good question, Chas. The only thing we would ratify without consent would concern the communication devices, and the return of our vehicles and animals in partial payment for our assistance to refugees. One thing we do not know is whether this group represents the refugees or could make arrangements to represent them. Ongoing trading agreements would be brought back to the group to be voted on."

A woman stood up from the middle. "Has the Council considered the fact that extending trade routes almost always costs in terms of time and effort and legwork? It is said our civilization collapsed because the supply lines were just too long." She sat down.

Erma's expression showed that she recognized this was an opinion rather than a question. This must be Norma. She simply said, "We have considered that, thank you." She was a shrewd leader, refusing to be drawn back into discussions that had already taken place.

She waited a moment, then said, "Let us now vote on the three plans." The voting was noisy but I recognize the same kind of organic order as that first meeting in the summer kitchen. Erma was not manipulating the vote, but was also not allowing others to manipulate. It was a different model and sometime I'd like to find out more.

I was relieved and the Council was pleased that the group approved all three plans. As the meeting broke up into clumps of discussion, with others leaving to get back to work, Erma came over to Ciera and I, and said, "Martin, I realize you must be very tired, but we want to leave just as soon as we can. It's 2pm now. If you took a short nap, would you be willing to head back around five? That should get you there by dusk."

I had to bite my lip to avoid grinning that my "nap request" had been granted so easily. But I knew I also needed some rest. I glanced at Ciera. "Yes, that would be fine—I don't want to hold anything up—" again I had to stifle a laugh; I was getting giddy from lack of sleep. "And I think Hadley and Megan's room is empty right now. Unless you are very efficient."

She smiled. "Probably not that efficient. So if you would like to rest, we will get the other preparations ready and wake you in a couple hours."

"I came in on a borrowed e-bike, which is at the front door, hopefully—it's possible Ciera could ride behind me on that."

"That would certainly help. Now I need to find a few other vehicles."

I hugged Ciera and whispered, "So you get your wish. Now let's—um—rest until they come get us."

She kissed me swiftly and we left the barn hand in hand.

* * *

Our time together was too short, but I did manage to also get a little sleep before the discreet knock on the door. I called out that we would be there quickly, and we dressed and headed for the great Hall. Ciera carried my knapsack, and I had the one Justin prepared for me, though it was empty. The group was waiting near the big front doors. Rom and Astrid had oversized backpacks and also each carried a heavy cloth sack. Siegfried, who was a slim, dapper man with a salt-and-pepper beard, wore well-made brown tunic and pants, and carried a knapsack like mine. The four refugees—a young woman with a three-year-old, a nearly bald old man and his wife, who had a thick gray braid to her waist—were introduced as Molly, little Hermie, Arvin and Julia.

"We located three bikes and a decent horse and cart," Rom said, "so Ciera gets her own ride."

"Hooray for that," she responded. "I never trust another driver." She grinned like a child going to the Fun Festival. I hoped I'd have time to show her a bit of what I'd seen.

"My knapsack's empty," I said. "What can I carry for you?"

Astrid gestured toward a nearby table. There was a book-sized wooden box of elegantly carved wooden door locks, two cloth-wrapped cheese wheels as big as my head, three hard sausages as long as my forearm and four fresnel lenses that I recognized as old car headlight glass.

"Some to use, some for trade. That should be enough," she said. "And Erma wanted you to have this back." She handed me the phone and solar charger—I took them gratefully; I suddenly wondered if I could contact Justin on this, and how. Definitely would have to ask him.

I packed quickly and followed them through the doors. The sky had clouded over, with a threat of rain. My borrowed e-bike was sitting under cover with the other transport, guarded by a sturdy 11-year-old boy who thrust his chest out and stood at attention when we arrived. Rom thanked him seriously and handed him a token. Their bikes had wide cloth belts to attach the knapsacks, with what looked like old seatbelt latches as buckles. I was surprised there weren't more people to see us off, but Astrid explained that everyone would be tied up filling in for the various travelers. She pointed across the green to where a half a dozen people were coming together and then moving apart—I had thought it was some sort of dance practice, but she explained they were twisting ropes from smaller spun flax cord.

"It takes a large group to do the twisting, especially as the ropes get thicker," she explained.

There *were* people out on the town sidewalks, despite a light off-and-on drizzle, watching our progress south—so word had gotten around somehow. Despite a strong horse maintaining a decent trot, we were still at half speed compared with my morning arrival. I felt like a small parade, with the long-box open cart flanked by four e-bikes. Our packs were used as padding for the colony members crouched and holding waxed canvas over their heads. I could see some shops doing repairs—salvagers had damaged windows and doors. The shopkeepers waved as we passed, and Hermie waved back enthusiastically. "We going home? We going home?" he asked frequently, until his mother shushed him with a biscuit.

"Rom," I called out, "there's a place we have to get off 65, and it's got bandits—we're gonna have to be fast, and we're gonna have to be prepared. We should divide our attention in all four directions as soon as we see the rockfall, and go as silent as we can." The drizzle was more like a mist, but I wished I'd retrieved that cloth cap of Jordy's.

"Right. Hear that group?" he shouted. I had given Ciera the bandit's gun, and I patted the pistol in my pocket. I wished there was enough armor to go around; I fervently hoped that had just been a gang of three. Rom took us along a back street to Highway 65, but I recognized the half-broken, foot-traffic bridge as we passed. The same trickle of merchants were queuing by the tollbooth.

"Has anyone tried to fix that so they could drive over it?" I asked, thinking it needed an additional guard.

"Not so easy to build out across that gap," he called back. I thought of Tegson's group and said nothing.

We made good time heading south, as Arvin skillfully steered the cart around clumps of walkers. Ciera's frown suggested she felt a bit guilty to be passing them, but they waved cheerfully enough.

"Better that we make their path safer," I called to her, but it was hard to converse over my shoulder and our conversation lagged. I noticed Rom and Astrid on the other side of the cart were pedaling, and Ciera was using half power, but I mentally justified my full power—this was my second trip today, and I'd need to be alert along the detour. And frankly, I was out of shape.

We were never totally alone on the highway, as the groups I had started to see on my first trip continued to flow south. I worried about that rockfall area—how many had fallen victim to those bastards? When we got to the detour, I could see the walkers had made a footpath up and over the rockfall—which explained why they'd crossed in safety. I pulled out my gun and held it up, gesturing to the others. We fell silent and Arvin nudged the horse to pick up the pace a bit. Molly pushed Hermie out of sight.

There was no sign of the threesome except the bloodstains on the street; the real rain was still holding off. I did a quick reconnoiter at the house, but Scarface was gone too. I worried we'd be attacked purely to get back at me, so I told Rom I'd pedal ahead, to draw them out if they were lurking. I stayed a block or more up front as we proceeded along the side street, darting glances, my muscles stiff with tension. *I should have given Ciera the armor*, I thought, *I'd feel better.*

The treeless rubbled block seemed endless; too many half-walls to hide behind and the gray sky dragged my spirits lower. As I reached the far corner, I heard a single shot and someone gasped—I wheeled the bike and raced back. They had paused mid-street; everyone looking around and Rom clutching his arm.

"Don't stop! Go! Go!" I yelled, racing the bike around the group and into a likely alley. It was deserted; I u-turned and sped out, fight-speed flowing in my veins. The others had hurried ahead, Arvin whipping the horse into a lurching gait. I thought I saw a hand emerge from over a crumbling wall, and I fired in that direction. How many bullets did I have? This was *not* my kind of fight!

"Turn right at the corner!" I hollered, and we raced the three streets back to the highway. Another group of four ragged toughs was poised on the last building, set to leap with bats. I sent two shots into them and Astrid shot also. They missed and the toughs scrambled up, over and away.

"Let's get another several blocks away and we can check your shoulder," I called to Rom as I came up alongside. His sleeve was red, and I could see the burn marks where a bullet passed, but it wasn't pumping blood.

"Flesh wound, let's keep going," he said. We kept up speed until I waved them to stop. Astrid leapt off her bike and flagged Rom down. She tied his arm with a cloth hanky or scarf. Hermie peeked over the cart brim, his eyes wide.

"It's okay now," I told him, hoping it was true.

* * *

The rest of the trip was uneventful and took a little over an hour, getting us to the off ramp just about dusk. Arvin directed us up an unfamiliar street, a typical mix of brownstones, small garden plots and shops. We even passed a corner pub before we got to a very odd building, red brick like the others but with walls curved into an oblong. The roof was conical, spreading down like a gray sand heap. Not quite like Aida's mushroom description, but definitely more roof than wall; it seemed like it should have been thatch. Beside this, a two-story smaller building was just as curved but a little more proportional. Every door and window was arched, and the overall effect was elegant if odd.

"Welcome to Colony House," Julia said. "If you go down Buttercup Way to the back of the building, there's a shed to park the bikes." She gestured down the narrow alley. "We'll take the horse and cart to the barn a couple blocks from here."

Hermie scrambled out of the cart, squealing, "Home! Home!" He disappeared through a narrow wooden door with scroll-like iron hinges, held open by a middle-aged woman who was grinning broadly.

"Welcome back!" she called out. Julia and Molly, carrying sacks, followed the boy inside, while Arvin drove the cart up the street. We drove the bikes down the alley and spotted the shed just beyond the two-story building—it was a normal square wooden shed, put up more recently. I worried about the rented bike—would it be safe here? Dusk was deepening and I didn't want to risk walking back from Lonnie's tonight, but I couldn't imagine trying to pay for a lost bike. A broad shouldered young woman came out from a back door holding an oil lamp, skipped over, handed the lamp to Rom and hugged Astrid tightly. Definitely sisters.

"So glad you could get here, sorry it had to be this way," she said, releasing Astrid. She showed us where to park the bikes inside, then stepped back around us to the doorway, and dragged the double door shut. I hurried to help and we dropped a heavy wooden bar across. I glanced at the windows—they had thick wood bars skillfully notched into the frame; I breathed a little easier. The oil lamp cast only a dim glow, so we had to pick our way around garden tools and small carts toward the back door. She led us along a single-wide pathway to the next building.

I found we had come in the back—the front of the main building was flat across, and a large double door flanked by two single doors formed one wall of the great Hall. There were pillars and arched ceiling supports around the edges of the room, forming smaller alcoves where it seemed various activities were permanently housed—looked like a medic's station, and another one had a loom, and in another a table piled with hides gave off the tang of leather. The ceiling did not vault as high as it should, and I realized a false ceiling had been installed to make a loft.

"Dinner's not for a couple hours," Astrid's sister, Inge, told us. "We'll get you settled in your rooms first." She led us through a narrow hallway to the smaller building, which consisted of two identical floors: a hallway with four rooms on each side—obviously a dormitory. We went upstairs and Inge gave Siefried the first room. I was surprised when she ushered Rom and Astrid into a single room, but I was pleased that Ciera and I had our own, though it was so tiny there was only space for a wooden bed slightly wider than single, a wash-stand with a white bowl and pitcher, a projecting candlestand over the bed and a row of pegs to hang clothes. But it was ours, and it was private, and I intended to make good use of it that night. I went to the basin and splashed water on my face; it felt wonderful. There was a narrow arched window near the wash-stand, and as I dried my face I looked out on the small garden plot across the alley. I saw a few small leafed plants, but mostly the dirt had yet to be plowed; there were long rows of straw mulching to keep weeds down. A waist-high wicker fence surrounded the plot and beyond it, some scraggly, shrubby trees suggested they'd done some coppicing to provide the wicker branches. As I stared, the rain began—a few dark spots, then a pattering, and soon the fence and plants were dripping. Someone was saved a job of watering.

Ciera bounced on the bed slightly. "Better mattresses than Ambridge," she said, "but the ones at home are stuffed with wool and they are soooo comfortable." She looked up at me enticingly. "Do you think we have enough time?"

Just as I stepped toward her, a knock on the door and Rom's voice calling, "Come on down and meet the group," interrupted us; Ciera sighed.

"Definitely later," I said, opening the door and following Rom and Astrid down the hall.

Two long tables had been set up in the middle of the big Hall; I was surprised that the whole group seem to number less than 60. Apparently this was a very small breakaway group; I wondered how recent. Several of them were wearing long black aprons, but other than that there was no uniform. Although the tables were set with plates, mugs and utensils, I saw no sign of food, and this seemed to be some kind of visiting time. Members were chatting in couples or wandering from cluster to cluster; about a dozen were hunched around a pair of quilting frames set up at the far end under the relatively strong light of what looked like a gas lamp with mirror reflectors. Men and women sewed and chatted; laughter floated down the room toward us. The group that came with us were in a circle of chairs where folks had various handwork: knitting, carving, some mending, and one young woman was doing something lace-like, barely looking at her hands as they busily looped thread.

I noticed about ten off to one side, peeling potatoes into buckets, chatting and casting unfriendly glances toward us. Seemed like some of the ill feelings of the split remained. If it was like my family, the feud would never end. There were about a dozen children of all ages dancing around but generally quiet. Rom and Astrid went over to the handcrafting circle; Inge brought Ciera and I over to an older man, almost as tall as Pippin, with a flat wool cap on his head probably covering a bald spot. He had very dark eyes that sparkled alertly, a long face that ended in a prominent jaw; I immediately recognized the group leader from his stance. That stance differed so much from Erma's that I could easily imagine the two wouldn't be able to work together. Inge introduced him as Jordan, and he shook our hands.

"Welcome to Colony House," he intoned. "We are grateful for your help in housing our more vulnerable members." He obviously didn't know that we weren't members the colony, and I couldn't help thinking that Erma wouldn't have made that mistake. But we politely acknowledged his greeting, and thanked him for housing us. With a nod, he moved on to the quilting group, and we wandered over to where Rom and Astrid were chatting with a black couple; the woman had a six-month-old in her arms.

"…going to take time away from jobs," the slim black man was saying.

"But it might prevent another disaster like the cattle raid of '64, if you remember that," Astrid replied.

"Only vaguely," the man replied. "But I know what you mean—a stitch in time saves nine, something like that."

"Exactly. And here's Martin and Ciera. Martin knows the group we're meeting, and he warned us about the problem, and Ciera is from a town a couple days away from us." Rom introduced the couple as Jared and Jalisa, who were the colony's tanner and seamstress.

"And the new parents of little Jakarta," Astrid added with a smile. I had seen that kind of baby hunger on other faces, and I hoped Rom was in favor of a family, for her sake. I wondered what kind of permission they had to get to have children out here. And I wondered about Ciera, but I figured she knew what she was doing, and seemed to value her independence and freedom. I was relieved to see she wasn't as gaga over the baby. I thought about Teg finding out about his six-year-old—how would that have felt? Scary, among other things.

Rom and Jared were discussing leather goods, and I sensed a deal being firmed up—I wondered if this was a secondary goal—Inge had sounded like she didn't see her sister much, so maybe there wasn't a lot of contact. Another thing to find out.

I noticed several couples about Ciera's age sitting near an alcove where lengths of cloth hung on racks. A broad-faced, sandy-haired man was tuning up a guitar. I nudged Ciera over that way.

"Do *Walls of Limerick,*" a young woman asked him. He nodded and began picking out the lively tune, which reminded me of one of my favorite jazz pieces. When I mentioned that to him, he frowned and shook his head.

"I'm not sure I know what jazz is," he said.

My worst fears confirmed. How could I live out here without jazz?

"It's like what you're playing, except that the beat is a bit more lively, and…different." I pulled out my phone, fumbled with the app then played the first of my saved tunes. Some stared as if it were magic, some grinned, but I could tell the guitarist was listening, not staring; his expression was awed and after a moment or two, he broke into a smile. When the song ended, he nodded his head and began fingering the strings, coming up with a credible version.

"I like it," he said. "Definitely a nice rhythm." He played a little more, repeating the first song, but with a livelier tempo that could be called jazzy. I grinned and nodded—maybe it wasn't hopeless out here. Someone else asked for another tune, and we pulled up chairs and listened, and some of the tension of the day began to melt away.

Some time later, a loud voice broke into all our conversations. "Will the serving crew please report to the kitchen?" a girl of about ten called from a doorway.

A half dozen people broke away from conversations, and the rest of the group meandered toward the table, still chatting. We waited to see what places were open, then took our seats. The leader said a brief grace—something else the group in Ambridge didn't do, but which was familiar from childhood. Then large bowls were passed down the table. I reminded myself that Ambridge had been dealing with refugees; maybe this was how they normally ate. I caught fragments of conversation: "...Larry got himself into this—and they are going hard on the rebels... heard a plane overhead last night, I'm sure of it!...keeping the wool clip from coming down..."

It had only been last night that Tegson had flown his little biplane—it didn't sound like the speaker knew it was a local, and I was glad I hadn't mentioned it. Did this group have any part in the rebellion? It didn't sound like Aida knew them. Should they be part of this negotiation? How many groups *were* there in this area? How many did Ambridge trade with? Did they have to negotiate crossing a territory, as the slum gangs did? I vaguely recalled the strangers' conversations at the hotel breakfast. How many would need to be involved to really ensure safety? I sighed, thinking about all I had to learn if I was going to stay out here. Was I? Could this have just been a minor scramble, something the cities would work out and forget? But that was wishful thinking—I couldn't unlearn what I knew now. Wherever I ended up, it would be different—because I was different.

Dinner was a very passable stew with a lot of potatoes and onion, but some lamb and good spices—so this group must trade with a chemical supply...or a greenhouse. I vaguely remembered many of these spices could be grown, though not in big quantities. I turned as Ciera laughed—she was joking with the blond guitarist, and I felt a pang of jealousy. Would I get used to the casual friendliness here? She'd never put up with my questioning whether this was normal behavior for her. I'd have to say something tonight, so that she understood what was normal for me.

The dinner concluded with another prayer, and a reading from some kind of inspirational book—something about loving one's neighbors, which I thought was a little inappropriate, given the situation—but maybe that was the point. I remember my parents speaking with scorn of those who insisted on love and compassion in situations where "the enemy was at the door." The family brand of Christianity was much more militant, "praise the Lord and pass the ammunition", etc. I was getting sleepy after filling my belly, and I wasn't paying attention, wasn't even thinking ahead to my night with Ciera—for a moment I was content to just sit in the warm, letting tomorrow take care of itself.

Finally the lecture concluded, and the group pitched in to remove the tables and chairs, clearing the floor. The guitarist was joined by some kind of flute and a violin, tuning up in the corner.

"They are having a dance in our honor," Astrid whispered to me as we lugged chairs to the alcoves. And indeed, the snippets of music coming in between tuning up sounded very energetic. I sighed. There wasn't a lot of dancing in the City, at least where I hung out. Dancing required a lot of self-confidence, which left me out. As the group members began to line up on the floor, and someone called out "Drowsy Maggie". Ciera looked at me and I shook my head.

"That's not one I've heard of, so let me watch and maybe I'll recognize it," I told her. She nodded and paired up with Jared, who at least wouldn't be cheating on his wife so publicly; Jalisa was nursing the baby off to the side, her wide grin showed she didn't mind. I would have to learn to dance, or get used to Ciera's other partners.

The dance was a typical back and forth, turn your partner, dance down the aisle, etc. They were all similar—just enough difference that you couldn't just jump in. So add that to the list: trade rules, code of honor, riding a horse, natural foods—I would have to start again relearning everything I thought I knew. With a good solid meal in me, it didn't seem as daunting as at other moments, but this would be the fourth time, by my reckoning—my childhood, the slums, the City, and now this—each time learning from scratch.

The dancers laughed and twirled, and those on the sidelines clapped and some sang along with the music, *The Wind that Shakes the Barley*. When that tune came to an end, the partners re-formed, with some swapping out from the sidelines. Ciera looked like she wanted to keep going, but glanced at me and came over. She paused to grab two mugs from a drinks table, and sat down beside me.

"Don't you dance in the City?"

I shook my head, then sipped the excellent cold ale, which had strong hoppy overtones. "We mostly listen, because the music is played in restaurants or theaters where there's really no place to dance. My family commune used to have some dances though. So that looks slightly familiar but it's been more than a decade."

"We'll have to get you dancing again!" She punched my shoulder, and I winced; I obviously would have to get used to that, too.

After the second dance ended, a new tune began—*Rakish Paddy*, someone called it—and Ciera urged me to my feet.

"This one is an easy one—I know you can pick it up," she said, tugging me towards the dance floor.

It was a melody I vaguely remembered, so I let myself get pulled into the line, and did my best to follow the motions of the others. Luckily these dances were very repetitive, so if I fumbled the first time, by the second repetition I could manage. It was strenuous, though and I wondered how they had the energy after a full day's work. I twirled my various partners, including Astrid and Jalisa, and I was congratulating myself as the dance ended and returned to our seats.

"Well, it'll take a bit of work, but we'll make you into a dancer, I'm sure," Ciera said as she plunked down into a chair, slightly breathless and grinning.

I noticed by the fourth dance that most of the older people were sitting out. The musicians ended after eight dances and two middle-aged women came to the center of the floor.

"This here's story of a time long ago, East of the Sun, West of the Moon…" one of them started, and there was a smattering of applause. Storytelling was good—it didn't require anything of me, and I could sit with my arm around the back of Ciera's chair, almost touching her, a typical teen ploy. I didn't dare drape my arm across her shoulder for fear that I'd embarrass myself by getting hard. Save that for later.

The story was about a young man off on a completely improbable adventure, running into magic animals and old hags, always showing courage and inventiveness—I had heard so many around bonfires and, like the dances, they fit a pattern though the details changed. The two women did a zestful job, with lots of gestures and changing voices. I recalled Magda of Mickey's tribe, who could make her voice sound like an old man's, a little girl's, and many believable barnyard noises. An unusual gift, much appreciated.

Eventually the evening ended and group members said good night as we headed toward the stairs. Ciera had acquired a thick beeswax candle in a brass holder, and as we got to our door, I could hear Siegfried snoring in his room. Rom had told me he was the main negotiator, so he'd rightly put sleep above dancing.

As I closed the door behind us, Ciera put the candle on its stand and came back and hugged me. I wanted just to make love and forget about everything else, but today's questions wouldn't let me.

I kissed her gently on the tip of her ear, and said "We haven't talked at all about what we'll do about, um, living arrangements. I know this rebellion is going to require a lot of attention for a while. But it sounds like you have procedures you have to follow—what is involved in 'hooking up with' a stranger?"

She pulled away slightly and looked at me with a mix of tenderness and worry. "Usually, it's not totally a stranger—it's somebody from another town who we got to know through somebody else, so the first thing that happens is the town gets references, I guess—somebody vouching that the stranger is reliable and things." She looks slightly embarrassed and I brushed my lips against her forehead and cheek.

"Hmmm...references could be a problem," I murmured.

"I don't think they are absolutely essential," she assured me, hugging me tightly. The next few sentences were spoken into my chest but I think I heard "then he has to agree to be blindfolded going in and out, because the town is hidden, you remember..."

"Blindfolded? You mean no one except people born there can see the path going in? And Megan puts up with that?"

She turned her head so I could hear better. "Well, she doesn't like it, but she does accept it. It only lasts until the town decides you're a full member."

"I think this new situation might make that a moot point," I said, helping her ease out of her jacket. Maybe this whole discussion should wait 'til the morning.

"I don't think the town would agree to come out into the open," she said. She tugged at my jacket, then my shirt.

"They may not have any choice, if the rebel army comes back through that area—this isn't just a couple of tourists wandering through—you'll either have to bring in help to defend yourself, or you may find yourselves running away."

She pulled away and glared at me. "We're not gonna run away, and we're not afraid of rebel soldiers!"

Damn. I knew I should left this to the morning. Was the whole town as pigheaded as Ciera? Would they truly think they could stand up to an army bristling with weapons?

"I didn't say you were afraid, but you saw how the other soldiers came in—you said yourself the Southerners didn't care that they would be leaving women and children without food. What if there had been a lot more than five of them?"

She pulled away and sat down on the bed—in the flicker of the candle, her frown took on fanatical overtones. What had I gotten myself into? I stood there feeling stupid, and a little annoyed. Courage was all well and good, but there were times when you knew the other guy was stronger. At least it seemed like Aida's group understood that and were not going head-on against the armies.

My real worry was that I didn't know how to discuss things with Ciera without getting her angry. How did one figured that out?

"Look, it's not something we have to decide tonight. I was just asking about *us*—about whether we'll even *stay* there, and when. Given the situation, I mean."

She looked at me in horror. "Not go back to town?? But—I grew up there!"

Well, that gave me part of my answer. I chose my next words carefully. "I'm not saying *never*—I'm just saying that for now, I—we—might be more useful out here, because there's going to be a lot of surveillance and trying to figure out what the cities are doing—at least everyone thinks that I can be useful advising them." I looked at her helplessly. If she insisted on going, would I follow, blindfolded and not knowing how to get back out?? A slight shudder passed through me. "You said you wanted to see everything—I think this is your chance."

She nodded and smiled. "I know—and I do. I hadn't realized I'd get homesick—" she paused and swallowed, looking away. "But I'd like to be helpful here, and I want to see this place, especially all the places you had those adventures." She smiled up and raised her hands toward me. "But let's deal with that tomorrow."

I came to her gratefully, blocking out everything except her skin in her eyes and her smile. It was more than enough for now.

28

The next morning at breakfast, I asked directions to Lonnie's, to get that out of the way. A young man offered to guide me since he was going in that direction. Reluctantly, I agreed—I planned to step in at Aida's afterwards and I didn't want to reveal their group location until I knew it was okay. As I sopped up the last of the eggs with my bread, I told Ciera I'd come back for her and show her what I knew of the town; she wasn't happy but said she'd wait. Astrid and her sister were already working near the big loom; I asked who we were to contact about the negotiations. She looked confused.

"Well, they told us we could leave a message with a man at a warehouse, and then they would contact us. I was hoping you knew something more direct."

"I do—and I'd be happy to set it up, if you don't mind my going alone. I didn't think to ask them about what details were okay to tell you."

"That totally makes sense," Astrid replied. "Tell them we are available whenever."

The young man, Paolo, was walking, so I pedaled slowly beside him, as he described the area, naming neighbors and mentioning their crafts. Many of them had shops at the Mall, he explained, but could be contacted at home if the colony wanted something. Yesterday's rain had given over to a weak sunshine, clouds drifting like strands of wool across a robin's-egg sky. A few hidden birds were singing, and a slight breeze brought odors of garbage, coal smoke, and the mustiness of damp cellars. Spring growth would have a struggle here, despite the patches of garden we passed. We also passed three carts collecting house wastes, and Paolo explained they were brought to composting heaps and a methane plant just outside the town, though he called it a city. And because it was so big, he explained—I hid my smile—it attracted a large number of unsavory types.

"We've only got the bandits under control in the past couple of years," he explained, "and now this—it feels like it's just one thing after another."

I was amused that someone in his late teens would sound so world-weary, but I kept a blank face.

"How did you control the bandits?"

"A combination of intimidation and redirection," he said loftily. "We have night patrols, and during the day the shopkeepers keep watch. Each street has to contribute at least one to the night patrols. When we hear about bandits, we would search them out and break up their groups. We punish anyone who traded with them—severely. And then we'd try to talk the gang into going honest. The younger ones often switched sides when they found they could get what they wanted without the risk."

His attitude of superiority was pure LOLkatz. He was probably younger than most of the people he was talking about.

"How did you know whether you could trust them, given that they'd been bandits?" *Once a fastfinger, always a fastfinger.*

He waved his hand. "We don't trust them immediately, of course. They get put with some mentor and have to prove that they're being honest for a good long time. Some of them don't make it and run away, but most of us stayed."

He bit his lip and glanced over at me. *So it was like that, was it?* I kept my expression neutral, and nodded seriously. "That sounds like a very good system," I said, pretending I hadn't heard his slip.

We were into an area I vaguely recognized, more industrial and warehouses. At the end the block, we turned left and I saw the bicycle wheel hanging from Lonnie's shop.

"I see the place now, thanks a lot," I told him. "And I can find my way back."

He looked like he wanted to hang around, and I remembered the urgent curiosity of a low ranker, but I wasn't going to satisfy it. Reluctantly, he waved and kept going down the street. I peddled the bike to Lonnie's; I'd stay inside for a bit just to make sure he didn't follow.

"That was quick—just overnight," Lonnie said when he saw me.

"Actually, I got here last night, but it was too dark and I didn't know when you closed," I told him.

"Then why were you so eager to drop it off at Ambridge? Just curious," he added, like he had just remembered Tegson's token.

"I went to a group there, to negotiate, and they liked the proposal so much they came back immediately. We're hoping to link up surveillance along the river." I figured that was vague enough.

"Hot damn! That's exactly what we need!" He was quickly but efficiently checking the bike for any signs of problems. I kicked myself that I hadn't done that before, but it seemed the bike was okay. "I don't like it that the damn cities think they can brawl out here."

"If all New York can manage is one narrow corridor, I can't see them rolling out much further." And now I knew, having been bait, that they didn't have any better options this far out. But I wasn't sure how Lonnie figured into the group, so I left it at that.

"And anybody idiot enough to blow up a train engine has got to be too stupid to win a war," he said.

He might not be aware of the hostages, so I just thanked him and went to the doorway. I peered out, searching the street and any shadowed areas to see if Paolo was lurking, but it seemed clear. So I hurried down toward Aida's, my heart racing. No matter how this played out, it was exciting to know they'd be glad to see me.

Aida was busy at the forge, pounding some twisted length of iron. The steam and the stink were so intense I wondered how she could stand it. It was almost as bad as the slums. I hailed her as I entered and she stopped, glanced down at the iron bar, then left it on the anvil and came over.

"Hot dangity, that was fast—what happed?"

"They liked it so much that they're already in town, hankering after a deal," I told her with a grin.

She punched the air triumphantly. "Ya told Justin yet?"

"No, if I didn't find them here, I planned to go to the house. The Ambridge group is already sending out some surveillance teams, but they can't go far without radio equipment. I mentioned you-all have some, and I hope that wasn't wrong."

She led me back to the table and offered to make tea or coffee; I said I just eaten. She hollered to a young girl who was in the corner sorting scrap metal. "Jilly—go on down to Justin, tell 'em Martin's back. Scurry!" She turned to me. "Should be at work, three blocks thataway."

"That's where he makes the armor?" We sat at the table.

She chuckled. "S*hoes*, Martin—the *shoes*. The rest we don't talk about." But she grinned to take away the sting.

"Right—sorry. I *do* need to know what is—private—and what is okay to mention."

"And we never got to telling you that." She sighed, leaned back. "It's been a wildwhoop these last days. Our group is more rumor than fact, okay? The fewer people that know particulars the better."

"I've tried to say as little as possible. I told them about the hostages so they'd understand the stakes, and confirmed what you'd said, but I never mentioned the tunnels or—" I stopped. I didn't even know what *she* knew! Maybe only Teg could tell me what ultimately was secret. I needed to talk to him urgently.

Aida grinned as if she could guess what I was thinking. "Yeah, it's a bitch, ain't it?" She sighed. "And add in that we only just met *you*, so how do we know *you're* on the up? 'Cept that the General has you thumbed up, sorta."

"Only sort of?" But I knew Tegson didn't trust me as much as his father did. "Fair enough. I'm hoping that as I help negotiate this, you'll trust me better." I shook my head, remembering the meeting in Madison, where I glibly asked that old man to trust me… was I still the same Martin?

"For the record, I know you went to the Haunt, so you know 'bout the bridge, the guns and you saw the plane," she told me.

I nodded. "And I've learned a bit about your group's wanting to be independent from the City, while still trading—and I totally agree. I was amazed when I came out here to find so many people living and working, almost like they didn't need the City."

She laughed. "D'you think it was bare-ass wildness?"

"Kind of—except I was being sent out to contact *towns* so there had to be somebody. But I thought you'd all be connected to the City somehow."

"Can you tell about your trip?" She looked really interested so I gave her a brief version of my original assignment, the weird turn it took and how I hooked up with Ciera and eventually the colony at Ambridge.

"So the City wanted towers out to Chi-town? They *are* trying to spread?"

"What I *thought* I knew was that we were already connected not just to Chicago but to Los Angeles and Houston," I explained. She whistled, shaking her head. "Now I'm not at all sure—everyone out here says the satellites are dead, and without them, there's no way we could be talking to the West Coast or the Gulf. But I don't know why they would be pretending, or where we're getting the information if it's not from there." I shook my head, the original puzzle popping up after being shoved aside the past couple days.

"Los Angeles—didn't that get knocked down by earthquakes all the time?"

"I have no idea. Unfortunately my schooling was stuffed between long days in the field. I got my best history and geography from—" Just in time, I caught myself from talking about Teg Sr. "—from some of the guys in the slums, but I have no idea how much was true and how much was tall tales."

"Same as us—we have some books, and stories from the grandfolk, but they're getting old, minds wandering—hard to know what was what." A look of yearning and anxiety passed over her face. "If even *half* those tales were real, it must have been assing marvelous! I know the General—" she caught herself, hesitated, and continued, "wants to see what we can bring back, like some of the miracles that were ordinary. He once took me to an assing *huge* factory full of iron and steel-making machines. Used to run by themselves. I looked up at those kettles—so big I was like an ant!—That's when I knew how much we'd lost."

"Hey, Martin!" We turned to see Justin hurrying in, waving. He slapped me on the back when he got to the table, pulled out a chair and sat down. He was grinning and red-faced, as if he had been running. A warm satisfaction rolled over me, and I grinned back. "When did you get in?"

I told him about the trip down, and the bandits at the detour, suggesting they send someone to deal with them or some refugees might not get back safely. I described the group that had come with me, and their willingess to meet whenever he could arrange it. "We were just going over what I can and can't say—I wanted to give them enough info so they understood how dangerous it was, but there was a lot I didn't tell them."

"Thanks, and I'm sorry I didn't do the legwork on that," he responded. "The tunnels?" I shook my head, and he let out a long breath. "Thank the Goddess. We figure the City would be all over us if they found out."

"I'm sure they would. You saw how tight-assed they were about just being out and around without ID."

He nodded, frowning at the memory. "So—is your group wanting to trade?"

I bit back a smile, thinking how they were both calling the other group "mine". Nice to be in demand. "Yes, but the way they do it is whole-group votes on anything big, so right now they're only authorized to talk about surveillance—and getting some portable ham op radios." I watched him, hoping I hadn't put him on the spot.

But he nodded. "We figured there's going to be a lot more demand, so we've really pushed the production, and also have upped our offering price to salvagers. I think we'll have at least a few we can trade them."

"That's good, 'cause as soon as they have them, they're gonna send out some patrols south of the river to see what's out there."

"Bonza!" Aida said. "Our patrol's combing south of the river looking for anybody left back."

"And the tower worked," Justin informed me. "Elontee and the group came back last night, and the first signals look really good."

"You're gonna have to explain to me how all that works," I said, "but it'll have to be later. I need to get back to the colony and tell them when you want to meet. And then I've got to show... someone... the town." I grinned, feeling my face redden.

Justin grinned, and punched me on the shoulder. "Fast worker," he chuckled.

I admitted this was the woman I had originally met, the one Zara sent the message to. "I was really glad that she was still at the colony. She's coming to represent her town in the negotiations." Or was that wishful thinking?

"The General might want to be there. Could we set it tomorrow 9 AM?" Aida asked.

"They said they were open to whenever, so I'll let them know." Privately, I was worried that they had hoped to do this faster, but it made sense that we needed everybody important to attend. We could always leave soon after, if negotiations were quick, and meanwhile they could plan with their branch group. "And would you mind mentioning to the General that I wanted to speak to him? He'll know what it's about. Oh—and there were a lot of people asking about their animals and vehicles, that the rebels took. Do you have any idea of their whereabouts?"

Aida seemed impressed and nervous that I would ask directly to speak to Tegson; he probably didn't come when called. "Been chasing down the ringleaders," she said, "*persuading* 'em it would be *healthy* to get that kind of thing back."

"Some of the bikes and horses went further east, I'm afraid," Justin said, "but we're doing what we can. We will definitely know more by tomorrow morning."

"They're not holding you responsible or anything, just asking for help getting them back," I assured him. "I got the impression that some of their transport had been hidden, but the problem with locals is they all know what people have. There's going to be a town discussion in Ambridge today, and some of that will probably get hashed out. But if they're stuck without transport, where could they go if they *could* afford more?"

"Well, 'f they've got trade, there's a couple places might have passable beasts. I've shoe'd a few."

More resources out here than I'd imagined. Things seemed more abundant than in the City. Was that because there wasn't an upper echelon to skim off the cream? Or was it merely fewer people with the same amount of salvage?

"So what next?" I asked, then glanced at them and added, "Just tell me what it's okay to know—I want to help, not screw things up."

Justin chuckled. "You already know plenty, and I'm not that worried," he said. "Now that we have the antenna, we can send folks out where there used to be a poor signal, and make sure there's no one lurking. The militia is doubling their training, and the town is calling in a support tax, either goods or time, so that we can handle this emergency without things falling apart. And of course, we're working to round up the rebel leaders, and I guess the General is in negotiation with the City to turn them over."

"So the militia—that's the General's group we met?—they patrol or are they just kept in reserve?"

No, Elontee's soldiers are a special group," he explained, "they're trained to do a lot more than just defend. The militia is mostly defense, but we have to be careful."

"Face off against the City, and they'll come out and crush us," Aida broke in.

I nodded slowly, remembering what Teg had said about appearing small and helpless. "So—I'm guessing it's a bit like the slums, where most of the defense is making sure you're not in a position to get hurt? Like removing your treasures before somebody gets them, and setting up booby traps that can look like accidents?"

"That's right," Justin said, "so it takes a bit of special training for these youngsters—I'm showing my age, aren't I?—to know not to attack openly, but to know enough sabotage they can respond, since we can't predict what's going to happen." He winced as if remembering the chaos of the past few days.

"Having a deal with your group to send oldsters and kids North if there's another scrum would really help," Aida added. "And securing the road."

I wondered where the Ambridge group would send *their* people if problems erupted that far out. *Just let it not get that big,* I prayed, remembering my father's constant quip about there being no atheists in foxholes. The war probably wouldn't affect Long Island, but how many would be conscripted?

The sun slanting into the window reminded me—Ciera was waiting! I didn't want her racing off on her own. So I thanked them and followed my morning route back to the colony. She was pacing impatiently, though she tried to hide that by pretending to hand something to a little girl. But I'd stopped to watch her from the door, enjoying her lithe figure, so I could tell she was gonna bolt out of the building, which she did immediately, tugging me along the cobbles. I directed her down Buttercup, to avoid Justin's group until they were ready.

"The Mall is this way," I said, "and let me show you where the train exploded." I led her towards the Wall, following the tracks once they angled into our street, pointing out the post where I'd been tied and the building where I hid and watched the explosion. I cautioned her to hang back a block, in case there were soldiers. Others were also hanging around, casting glances toward what was left of the engine. I was amazed the gap had been almost filled, leaving half the engine buried in it. I saw no guards, but they'd be on the other side. Keeping citizens in. My view of the City kept flip-flopping.

"Wow," she breathed. "Was it—did they do it on purpose?"

"I *think* so, because there was no one in the cab when it hit. And the rebels had big planks to put over the hot rubble."

I led her south along the Wall. She was taking in everything, eyes wide, and I smiled, remembering my own astonishment at these bricked-up windows, doors and rubble-filled alleys.

"And—the City is just on the other side?" Was there fear or yearning in her voice?

"Not New York City," I said "but what's left of Pittsburgh, only there's apparently a lot more over the river. It was a lot bigger than I had any idea."

She nodded, her attention flitting from thing to thing. Some of the other passersby looked at us curiously, and suddenly I worried. I leaned close to her and murmured that, since I didn't know the area well, it might be good to not look like strangers. She tensed, becoming aware of those around us, and shifted her pace and attitude to a more casual one.

"It seems like it goes on forever," she murmured, "like it would be easy to get lost."

"Yeah—I still don't know a lot of the streets, and I don't want to have to ask directions." I was startled just then to recognize the house where the tunnel started—it seemed like the same pock-faced young man was sitting on the chair. I didn't acknowledge him and immediately pointed out something on the other side of the street. A shop full of glass jars and tubes—and in the back, a flare and sizzle as a glassblower replied his trade. Was this where Zara got the tubes they talked about? Ciera examined the jars eagerly, saying there was someone in her town who would be thrilled to have some. Then she frowned, and I could see her waffling—self-sufficiency warring with temptation. I could see what the Alitos were talking about now. Yet they *did* salvage...so what was the difference, in their eyes?

Our steps took us to the woodworking blocks. The streets were fairly crowded; the buyers were as intent as when I'd first seen them—haggling with stall owners, passing some kind of token. Some of them had notebooks with recorded purchases, but it seemed few were immediately taking possession—was this some kind of wholesale market? The sellers seemed to know we weren't the usual buyer, and few of them gave us much attention. Ciera hovered between eagerness and scorn, touching a piece, then shying away like it burned. I wondered if she'd ever seen so many things for sale. There was more variety out here, although in sheer numbers the City had more stuff. Along with handmade items, there were carts and booths full of salvaged wooden things, some unidentifiable. Others I recognized the item but didn't understand the purpose. For example, there was a little house that was hollow, but instead of a door, there was a two-inch-wide hole—some kind of ritual object?

"Oooh, a birdhouse!" Ciera exclaimed, touching the faded flowers painted on the sides. She looked over at another—the head of a cat, with its mouth open in an O. "That's just sick!"

"If it's a birdhouse, yeah—I agree." Privately, I thought it was just the kind of humor my family would enjoy.

Some of the other things were painted flat boards apparently showing someone's butt as they bent over, and a lot of wooden chickens, though the polka dots and stripes made me wonder if they'd really known what a chicken looked like. There was an entire row of soldiers with hinged jaws that I suddenly recognized as fancy nutcrackers—a lot of work to go through for a simple tool, but my family'd love the uniform. Ciera hurried across the street, her eye on something, and when I caught up, she was holding a set of blocks with numbers—alongside them were longer blocks with days and months in faded letters.

"That's a perpetual calendar, deary," explained the stall keeper—a bone-thin man with slightly Asian features. His gray jacket was patched with so many colored squares it seemed oddly polka-dotted. The lack of other buyers at his stall made him more attentive to us.

"It's an interesting idea," Ciera said, examining the blocks in her hand. The man turned and whipped out a wooden frame holding four shelves of tiny drawers numbered 1 to 24—couldn't be a calendar, maybe a filing system?

"This one is special," he said with greasy charm. "An *add event* calendar—you put little treats inside the boxes, see? He opened one drawer after the other, though they were empty. "The rich used to put diamonds and gold in each box," he confided.

It would be believable for the Park Avenue set, I thought, but would they be likely to have boxes of simple wood? I recognized a sales pitch when I saw it.

"What about this, then?" he asked, pulling another item from under his table. It was a chicken, plastic rather than wood, and I wondered why he had hidden it. Were there rules about what each vendor could sell? He quickly turned a knob on the side, and set it down. I was startled to see the dang thing walking jerkily across the table, and we laughed out loud when a tiny egg fell out of its butt.

"This one's a real rarity—but I could get you a dozen for 50 marks," he said watching us eagerly.

Marks? They had a different credit scheme out here—I glanced at Ciera who looked just as startled. I declined politely and we hurried away.

We crossed a block and she caught sight of some cloth rippling from a building and dragged me in that direction. I hadn't been in the clothing and fabric area before. One outdoor table had multicolored folds of yardage that even caught *my* eye, as indifferent as I was to such things—reds, pinks, gold and blues glowed like gems.

"This is silk!" she exclaimed, fingering a sky-blue piece with a woven floral pattern of slightly darker blue. "Do you think it's Pree?"

"Pree?"

"Before the Chaos," she said impatiently. "They say some silk lasts hundreds of years."

The shopkeeper—a tall willowy blonde—was haggling with a stooped, older man over a stack of unbleached yardage. Was it safe to ask that question? Would it mark us as strangers and would she care? Reluctantly, I tugged Ciera away; we could come back after I found out more from Justin or Teg.

"Do you think there's a section for solar parts??" she asked, striding down the block, looking around so constantly she almost stumbled. I caught her elbow and steadied her. The sun gleamed on her hair and her puppy-excitement gave her a sparkle that I could watch for hours. She was much more interesting than anything for sale.

"Probably. The Mall goes on for blocks and blocks. I'm guessing there's shops for almost everything." We were getting closer to the metalworking, and I was torn between steering her away, and the risk of getting lost. I directed her up a street, thinking perhaps I recognized the route we took out of the warehouse. There were fewer shops and more rowhouses, and fewer walkers, so we could chat more freely. Ciera seemed as interested in the buildings as the stores.

"Everything is brick! I wonder where they got so many?"

"Don't they make them out of dirt? I think they had to because they didn't have trees," I replied.

"They certainly don't have trees now," she responded looking around. "This is even worse than Ambridge—just streets and streets of buildings—where do they grow their food?"

"I think they have farms just outside of town," I said, remembering Zara's concern with deliveries, "and somebody brings in carts every day and maybe you can order from them."

She frowned. "I wouldn't want to have to rely on somebody else for my food."

"But surely you can't make all of it yourself?" We'd paused on a corner. I noticed a roof-less box cart with baskets of muffins and bread being inched down the street by a boy of fifteen.

Ciera had noticed it too; she watched as the delivery boy grabbed some bread, ran up a stoop and knocked on the door. The person inside took the bread and the boy trudged back to his cart and kept pushing. There was a similar cart block away, but it had an overhead rack from which dangled some kind of dried plants; the girl doing deliveries was moving more swiftly than the bread boy.

"We don't grow all of it," Ciera replied. "But I know where the rest of it's made—I can walk down to the place, and I know the person and..." She took a sudden deep breath, and I wondered if this was all too much for her. I certainly couldn't help sort it out; I'd been on input overload for at least four days now. At least some of my despair was easing, due to finding Teg, and maybe because there were people who were happy to see me.

"They were talking in Ambridge about where to get bricks to fortify the town—there are certainly more than enough here," she said, switching back to a safe topic.

I pictured some of the ruins we had passed. "True—there still seems to be more salvage than anybody would need for generations."

"Yeah, but you only need to be missing one or two things to have it all fall apart."

"Like food?"

"Or water. Or one crucial part for a solar pump—I just don't know how they did it, back then," she sighed. "How did they keep all their machines going, with parts coming from everywhere? And getting them from strangers!"

"You can't actually grow past town size without getting your goods from strangers," I opined. We just physically don't have the time to personally approve everything we own, do we?"

We had reached a mixed block where the goods were mostly pottery and kitchenware. She paused, looking at a strange ceramic container shaped something like a giant bee. "I guess that's one reason our town decided not to grow very big."

"I don't understand how you can justify salvaging like from Madison, but then say you won't trade with other people because that's not self-sufficient."

She looked over at me, startled, as if the question hadn't occurred to her. She chewed her lip, looking down. "I…I guess getting it by ourselves feels like still relying on ourselves, and trading. We *do* trade—it's just that we don't count on others for our basic supplies. Grandfather Engel used to say that counting on strangers is like building your house on someone's cart—because if there's ever a problem, they'll take off and leave you hanging."

At last, a sentiment I understood! "True, but something like this—the rebels, I mean—shows that one town alone would be really vulnerable, but a lot of towns might be able to do something. One of the slum sayings was, 'if you don't organize, they will organize right over you.' Meaning just because you don't believe in self-defense, doesn't mean the other guy won't attack you." I thought about her dismay at the thought of her town raiding for its supplies. "I have to agree with Mrs. Alito—it's easy to be peaceful if no one's attacking you."

"But when there's more than enough for everyone," she complained. "trading can get us what we need, especially, as *she* said, if we know the difference between needing something and wanting it." She looked sideways at a very glittery trinket box with almost half its glass rhinestones still intact. Was I wrong to have brought her here, showing her all these geegaws that her town wouldn't allow?

"Maybe in some cases basic needs are enough, but like I said before, I lived seventeen hard years with just the basics and I never want to do that again. It's the little extras, the creative things that make beauty, that bring fun into my life."

"And I don't think you have to go without them," she argued, facing me. "You just have to find the right balance—not going after the extras in a way that cancels out the basics—I can't express it well." Her frustration was obvious.

I think Teg would mostly agree with her, and he probably could say it better, too. I really wanted to hear them discuss this—philosophy was never my strong point.

A sudden commotion made me turn, then push Ciera behind me. Two men twice my size had started shoving at a nearby stall. One pushed the other into a utensils cart, jolting it and knocking off a rack of spoons, which clattered to the cobblestones. The victim, red-faced and swearing, caught his balance on the corner, knocking forks everywhere, then plowed headfirst into his foe, sending them both into the side of a wicker stall, which crashed sideways. Someone screamed and a tall lanky young man raced up with a thick oak staff and knocked each man hard on the head, ending it.

"Damn brawlers," he muttered. He held up some kind of badge, which reassured the crowd, and he sent a small girl running off—for backup, I supposed.

Ciera pushed out around me and glared. "You don't have to protect me!" She said, "I can handle myself."

"Sorry, it's just—instinct, I guess," I muttered.

Three men and a muscled woman I recognized from Teg's group came running up. They hauled the unconscious—or dead?—men out with little fuss and carried them away. I wondered what the penalty for brawling was, if getting arrested was that savage. The stallkeepers began to clean up, helped by a few customers, while the rest of the street settled down again. Ciera had walked off, pausing to stare at some trinket. I came up to her but she wouldn't look at me.

"Look—I'm sorry—I didn't know how bad it would be. Was it so wrong I didn't want you hurt??"

She glared up, then away. "I don't need another big brother."

You'd think she'd be grateful. "I'm *not* your big brother. Look—I'm… just paying you back for helping me a couple days ago. Okay?"

That seemed to go down better. She grudgingly let me escort her along the street.

"I'd suggest finding something to eat, but I don't know how to pay for it," I said, taking a light tone. "I haven't seen any pay pads out here."

"What are pay pads?" Despite her sulk, she sounded interested.

"Inside—on the other side of the wall—they're machines that know how much you have in the bank and let you buy things with your fingerprints—or vein prints—I'm not sure."

She stopped and stared at me like I'd gone whiterabbit.

"Vein prints?? And what's a bank?"

So apparently they didn't have any. "It's where you store your money. Only not really—it's just credit on a list. I guess like your town debt lists, but all in one place."

She frowned, half distracted by a blue and yellow teapot. "And you tell this bank how much you owe?"

"It keeps track for me. And I can spend the credit anywhere—it's not just an agreement between me and a shop, for instance. Makes buying a lot easier."

"How does the shop know you can be trusted?"

"The *bank* can be trusted. That's what makes it easy. The shops have their prices listed on each thing and you just buy it if you want it. If you want to know what you've spent, you make an appointment to go into the bank and look at your records, though the pay pads can show your balance."

We came to a corner and I hesitated. Some of these areas were probably dangerous. *And* I didn't know the rules. I pointed in a direction I thought would get us back to the colony. Ciera was still struggling with the bank concept.

"Why would a bank go through all that trouble for you?"

Huh? I thought through her question and realized her error. "No—the bank gets *paid* to do it. It gets a little bit of money for every transaction—it makes money by handling money."

Again, she looked at me like I'd grown another eyeball. "Sounds weird," she said finally.

Would it be like this for too many things? Was I fooling myself that we could translate our lives to each other? I remembered Justin's first wife.

* * *

When we got back, we found Rom in a heated discussion just outside the shed.

"...didn't have permission to borrow them, and they're damn lucky we don't prosecute them for theft!" he told a pale, almost albino, middle-aged man who came up to his shoulder. I noticed three more bikes in the shed—was the colony finding some of the stolen goods on their own? Rom noticed us hurrying up and he broke off the discussion, and waved. "Did you two have a good time?"

"There's an amazing amount of stuff there!" Ciera exclaimed, then paused, calmed herself, and added, "Of course there is no way to know if it's good quality."

"We know which dealers can be trusted," the pale man said. "If there's something you're interested in."

"Thanks Lars, nothing in particular—I was just noticing..." she subsided, her face reddening.

"Have you found us some of the stolen bikes?" I asked Rom.

"We can check three off the list we made," he said, grinning wryly. "Only 34 to go."

"Justin is running down a few more for us," I assured him, "he says they'll know more tomorrow when we meet them."

"Is that Justin the shoemaker?" Lars asked. Something in his expression made me think he knew about Justin's other work, or maybe just suspected?

"That's the one. When I first got here, just after the explosion, he and his…partner, helped me—very generous and as honest as anyone I've met out here." I heard the belligerence in my voice, but couldn't stop it. If only there was a way to know the players! The slum gangs had been well established, and the newcomers were sat down and instructed as to who was who—it was that kind of lesson that helped me know where I wanted to jump next. Maybe if I got Rom alone…

"He makes good shoes," Lars said, almost grudgingly, "and buys some of our leather." He still sounded like he didn't like Justin. I hoped any of this started to make sense soon.

Rom said, "They've asked us to help with the afternoon chores, so I put you two on tenting—that's stretching new yardage that's been fulled. It takes several hands to get it hung correctly across the porch."

"What will you be doing Rom?" Ciera asked, impertinently.

But he just grinned. "I saved the fun job for myself—I'm going to help them grease the axles on the tiller."

"Oooh, better you than me," she joked. "Where do we go?"

Lars directed us to a side courtyard that I hadn't seen—a narrow, gravel-paved alleyway containing a long, single-story wooden building with a large overhanging porch. Three women, including Inge, were arguing about the best way to get a large heap of spring green wool cloth hung. We came over and reintroduced ourselves, and Inge asked me to fetch a ladder from inside the building. I stepped into the gloom and searched for anything with rungs. I saw large metal barrels, an array of shovels and rakes hanging neatly on one wall, loops of hoses awkwardly piled in a corner—I wondered how they made those, without plastic—and finally, resting against what looked like an old cast-iron stove, a six-foot wooden stepladder with large brass hinges at the top. I brought it outside, to where the women had lifted the damp fabric out of the tub and were holding it above the gravel, extending the yardage the length of the building.

"Set the ladder up at this end," Inge commanded. "And Dora, you climb up with your corner and get it on the clamps."

I noticed large nails sticking out at regular intervals across the overhead beam, with metal spring clamps hanging from them, the kind we sometimes used at work to hold thick documents together. The cloth reeked of stale piss, and I suddenly remembered a bunch of aunts sitting around table chanting and pounding cloth soaked in urine—as a child I was both repelled and fascinated. Dora climbed and carefully attached her corner with the first clamp, then carefully stretched the edge of the cloth and clamped it again, and one more time, then climbed down, moved the ladder a bit, and continued to clamp and stretch. Inge directed the others to hold the fabric evenly, and she herself anchored the lower left corner on another clamp on a post. Gradually, the length of fabric was straightened and slightly tugged into shape. I hurried to move the ladder for Dora, since I felt useless otherwise.

"Tell me again why you have to, um, piss on the cloth?"

Inge laughed. "It's the easiest way to get the natural grease out of the wool," she explained. "Old piss turns into ammonia, which dissolves the grease. And pounding closes up the gaps in the weave and tightens the fabric. Before this, our women had a waulking session, singing and pounding the cloth."

"I think I remember that when I was young—seemed like only women were allowed, not that I think men would've fought them for it."

She laughed again. "Aye, that's an old tradition and even with all our modern equality, it seems more fun when we women do this together. After it dries, stretched like this, it will hang straight when the seamstress cuts it into an outfit," she continued. I mentally added yet another step to the complicated process of getting the clothes I wore.

I had been hearing young voices chanting in unison, a little too far away to hear what they said, and I finally asked Inge what it was.

"That's lessons for the six to eight-year-olds," she explained. "The schoolroom is down the alley, and they probably have the window open on such a nice day. You don't have anything extra you can teach them, do you? We're always looking for new things to share with them—they get restless."

I shook my head and muttered something about my own lessons being pretty sparse, as we headed back to get another chore assigned. We ended up in the kitchen, peeling turnips for dinner, always an easy task to assign to the unskilled. Astrid had joined her sister in the kitchen, and they were chatting happily as turnip peels flew into their buckets. The place was much smaller than the Ambridge kitchen, but had a stone tile floor and the kind of professional steel and enamel appliances that indicated commercial kitchens. Most of the appliances no longer worked, of course, but the brushed steel shelves full of equipment were sleek and gleaming, the huge stoves looked like they'd been retrofitted for wood and there was a hum from a large two-door refrigerator that surprised me. They used oil lamps, so I couldn't understand how they would have working cold storage. Inge saw me staring at it and commented, "The group decided that keeping food cold was worth a small generator. We don't have as much solar around here, but the methane is available. Spendy, but it powers the fridge and a water pump."

"Do you have a well here? I thought cities had water systems."

"They used to, but it took a huge amount of energy to run. Early on, this city just dug wells and when we arrived we bought pumps. There's always the river, but few of us liked the taste of filtered and bleached water. So far the water table hasn't fallen too low, though townsfolk tell us there was a point where the pumps weren't working. I'd hate to think of having to cart water thirty blocks."

"They're talking about irrigation canals over at Town Hall," a dishwater blonde in a bright pink blouse commented. "And I'm sure they're gonna tax us for it," she added with a frown.

"Well, better they do *that* than form our own bucket brigade," Inge replied.

"Two summers ago, in that bad drought, we had to dig a well almost 100 feet deep," Ciera said. "Not only was it dangerous, but hand pumps don't really draw up that far, so we had to go back to the old bucket on a winch, and that gets really tiring." The others murmured agreement, and I flashed on the image of the City with dry taps—there were rivers on each side, of course but that water had always seems so filthy I wouldn't even bathe in it and you can't drink seawater—well, I had tried some after the desalination plant got through with it, and it was still nasty.

Four of us got a crate of turnips peeled and quartered and into large kettles quite quickly. Next, Inge led us into the main Hall and asked if we could help bring the spring linens down from the loft.

"Many hands make light work," she said. I saw a steady line of members trudging up and down the narrow wooden stairs at the back of the Hall—it was tricky because only one person fit, and so it looked like three went up, and then three came down, and brought their armfuls of blankets and sheets towards the dormitory.

"You're doing this fairly early, aren't you?" Astrid asked her sister. "We don't usually switch winter and summer fabrics until end of April."

"Well, we have more cotton and linen than we have wool, thanks to good salvage, and we want to make the wool last. And maybe it's a bit warmer in the city then in Ambridge—but we agreed it was time."

Two men were maneuvering a braid of carpet down the stairs, and we all held our breath—there was a thin banister, but I couldn't see it holding if somebody pitched sideways. There was a group sigh as the rug successfully reached the floor, and the men trotted off toward the dormitory. Ciera and I got in line to head upwards. I was curious about the loft—one of the worst parts about self-sufficiency, I thought, was the incredible amount of goods one needed to keep handy. My apartment was tiny because I could go to a shop and get what I need, and buy new clothes when the old ones wore out, and the company provided my main meals. Everything a group took on for themselves required tools, materials and obviously an organization that knew when and how to swap the seasonal stuff out. Even the slum gangs had their specialists.

It was a vast, dusty attic, with rows of dried plants, braids of garlic and onions hanging from the upper beams; the tang of apples suggested a fruit store. Aisles of chests and shelves ran the length of the single room, off into the gloom. Five members were busy uncrating and unwrapping the sheets and blankets, handing them to the carriers, who were mostly younger. I told myself I would do this till my legs gave out, and then find another assignment. We each took an armload of cotton sheets, smelling of wormwood, lavender and fleabane but surprisingly not musty. It was a little awkward carrying a full armload down such steep stairs, and I let my elbow graze the wall to help my balance. We followed the teen boy ahead of us into the dormitory, depositing our sheets in a ground-floor room where two harassed-looking women were directing smaller children to take individual sheets and blankets to certain rooms. Quite an organizational task.

As we got back to the main Hall, I saw a boy of about nine looking around anxiously. He caught sight of me and trotted over.

"Aida says to tell you we are not meeting at the forge, we are meeting at the old school—Page and Fulton Street." He jiggled from foot to foot, waiting for something—a tip, I suspected. I looked around for one of the members who could tell me where this place was. Jared had just come in with two hides slung over his shoulder, tilting him almost sideways. I ushered the boy over to the leatherworking alcove, arriving just as Jared flipped the hides onto the table.

"We've gotten word of the meeting location, but I don't want to let this one go until I'm sure we know where it is," I told him. I had the boy repeat the address and Jared nodded. He fished in his pocket and found a copper token that looks suspiciously like a penny and gave it to the boy who scampered away.

"Yes, we know of the old school—that's not a problem."

"How will we be sure we get there on time?" I asked. So far I've noticed people were fairly casual about time, and I hadn't seen clocks or even sundials. My parents had kept three mechanical clocks meticulously wound, guarding the time as if it had been sacred.

"You haven't seen our clock?—You gotta come see this!" Jared led to me to the front of the hall, where the big doors opened out onto wide stone steps, letting in a soft, fresh breeze. Just inside, over the double door, was a simple hanging wall clock with no case, so all the wooden gears and ratchets were clearly displayed, and the pendulum—a large brass circle, slightly tarnished—swung back and forth sedately, as the ratchets clicked and paused, clicked and paused. It was a little difficult to see the face in the gloom of the entrance, but a mirror had been cleverly angled to reflect light from two round windows on either side of the clock. At least on a sunny day, it wouldn't be hard to check time.

"Impressive," I said, and meant it. "How are you sure it's the right time, though? Is there a town clock?" In the business section of the City, there were clocks every ten blocks, actually displaying the time in digits, and none of them were off more than a minute from each other; I vaguely knew there was a clockmaster company that made sure of it.

"Yes, at the Town Hall there is a main clock, though I don't know how they set that one. I know that Before, they had one main clock somewhere in the world and *everything* was set to it—I can't imagine how. But we also have two really good sundials on cleared spots in the hills—so we have a fairly accurate way to check the time. And we even have someone in town who can make and fix clocks, which isn't easy. So we won't be late tomorrow, if that's what you're afraid of—" he grinned at me, "but for all I know, we don't have the same time as Ambridge, for example. In general, most meetings aren't set exactly—or they're set near noon, dawn or dusk, which everyone can tell. And I guess for war, they have those radio things so they can attack at the same time," he added, frowning.

We went back into the main Hall, where they were setting up the dinner tables in the center, putting chairs around, maintaining a steady chatter. I helped with chairs, and kept an eye out for Ciera. Eventually she came back into the room and I waved her over.

"What do you think about representing your town in this meeting tomorrow?" I asked her.

She looked up with a touch of defiance. "Why—is there a problem?"

"No—we just hadn't talked about it. Unless you've discussed it with Siegfried. I've got no one to represent, so I figure I'm just audience." Her touchiness made me uneasy. It really wasn't my business whether she had authorization or not, but would they hold me responsible for her actions? I hated unspoken rules.

"I'll just get the information, and bring it back home," she replied. "Then they can decide what to do. We would generally have a meeting for something this big anyway," she added.

It was a bit easier to join in with the pre-meal socializing, but I mostly stayed near the musicians, listening and nodding my approval. I let the dinner conversation wash over me, thinking ahead to another pleasant night with Ciera, and a second night where I'd get enough sleep. The meeting tomorrow would go as it went—I had told the truth that I felt like audience rather than participant. And then what? That was the big question hanging over me—where did *my* life go after this?

That evening in the room, we were quickly in each other's arms again, but I sensed the tension in her, and as we stood near the bed, not yet undressed, I asked her, "Is there something wrong?"

"No, she said quickly, but then paused and corrected herself, "Well, kind of—I'm worried that all of this is going to really mess up my home town."

"There's not much you could do to stop it, and is it really your job?" I murmured, as I brushed my lips across her hair. She smelled so good that I wished I could take the smell of her everywhere with me.

She sighed "I guess not, but it still—even though the Grandfathers say we can't keep our plateau forever, it's still not easy to think we've got the changes ahead."

"Major understatement," I observed with a chuckle. "I've been struggling with that ever since Madison! My life is so changed I don't recognize it anymore—and if I'm not going back—which I'm not," I hurried to assure her, "then I don't know where I belong." There. It was out in the open.

"You belong with me, silly" she said, and kissed me gently on the cheek. I captured her lips with my own, and the conversation was forgotten as we were caught up in each other.

29

After finding the old school, we were escorted into a room where the chairs had been rearranged into a double circle, and the desks pushed back to line the walls. One wall was paned glass windows, washed so well the sun streamed like gold and lit up the pale wood desks, the worn beige and brown checkerboard tile floor, and along three sides, the old plastic white walls that teachers used to write on, though the ink that would stick then wipe off was long gone. One half of a white wall had been removed and a slate board put up, a large, impressive slab of smooth gray stone with a metal tray underneath full of chalk. A young woman stood alongside with a lump of chalk, poised to write whatever was needed. There was also a scribe in the corner, a sandy-haired boy of 15 hunched behind a small student desk, with inkwell and paper. The mall group clustered near a table of refreshments, and Zara waved as we came in. Tegson hadn't showed—too busy, or too important? I brought the two groups together and introduced them.

"This is Justin, Zara, Aida, Elontee, Asrah, Zir—and I'm afraid I don't know these three," I said, "but this is Rom, Astrid, Siegfried, Ciera... and Jared from this local colony." I noticed Zara smiled broadly at Ciera, who looked slightly confused. I hoped my face wasn't getting red—I hadn't told Zara that much, but she seemed to guess a lot more. They introduced the rest of their group as Melany, Horace and Petal—all local merchants who shared a desire to "stamp on this kerfuffle", according to Aida. We took our seats in the circle, and I suddenly wondered if "the General" preferred to keep his face and identity secret—that's what I would have done. Elontee or Justin would report back.

Elontee began by asking Rom's group what their requirements of exchange were. "Because we have had to begin our relationship on such a serious footing," she said, "we realize we don't have the usual time to develop trust."

"We had talked also about that," Siegfried replied, "We have a dire situation and need to work together, yet we know little of each other. Martin has vouched for your group—"

"As he has for yours," Elontee replied.

Whoa! I don't want to be in the middle! My expression must have revealed my panic, because Elontee continued, "and that's a good start, but if we are to get off on the right footing, perhaps it would be good to swap a member or two, both to better educate ourselves and to reassure each other we are going to honor our commitments."

So they did take hostages, I thought, looking at Rom's face. None of the Ambridge faces showed much emotion, and I wondered if these were the usual negotiating team. Good poker players, except Ciera, and she was struggling to act calm, but her tapping foot gave away her excitement.

"Certainly, that would be permissible," Siegfried said, "and perhaps we could arrange a short apprenticeship at the same time, so that we would not lose useful working members? For example, we have weavers who have space for an apprentice, and our orchardist is doing the last pruning and could be instructive."

There was silence for a moment, then Justin said, "Well, I could certainly use a couple of hands in my cobbler shop, if someone wants to learn a thing or two about shoes."

Elontee nodded. "Then we will send two of our members with you and you can send us two. As to the communication devices—" she looked over at Zara, "I believe we have two box sets and two handhelds that we can provide. We understand that you hope this will be in payment for taking care of refugees?"

Siegfried replied, "If those refugees were of your community, we would deem it honorable to help offset the meals and clothing and shelter. We did not make any formal count, however, nor do we know how many are your community members."

Aida answered that. "We have several communities in town," she said. "Asrah's mayor, and I am deputy. We're running a count, to see who sent folk your way and to get some payback. But two of radios for sure, since you had a mob show up and you were open-handed. If the refugee count is bigger than guessed, we'll credit you more. You know these are tough to get?"

"And we have located ten carts, eight horses, and four bikes that we believe belong to your community or your town," Asrah added, looking embarrassed at Aida's casual tone. "After this meeting, perhaps someone will come with us and see if you can identify them. The rebel train cars have been put in quarantine, but in two weeks we will release to you whatever goods they left behind. We believe much is still there and they were looking to analyze the goods we commonly have, or maybe their plans changed."

"That seems odd, but we respect your information sources," Siegfried replied. "We have a partial list of vehicles, though some of the outer towns might not be on it. We were so concerned about starting this surveillance that we decided to come down here before they held the town meeting, which was yesterday."

"Yes—the surveillance," Elontee said. "Although our first reports suggest the southerners have not left anyone in the area, we don't want to rely on that, and will be maintaining patrols on the south side of the river at least for the next month. The more of the river boundary that can be guarded, the better."

I thought about the long drive to Ambridge, how much of that river seemed totally unwatched. How would two small groups be able to keep a tight border? They needed at least four more planes like Tegson's! And that would be too many because it would put the City wise and send them out to smash a dangerous precedent.

"Is it true that you have heard the two cities are negotiating rather than fighting right now?" Siegfried asked.

"Our sources inside said that DC is denying these were their armies, and both are speaking about 'regrettable rogue militias' and insisting they still want peace," Elontee said. "Unfortunately, we don't believe that will end all military responses. After all, if they've denied their armies once, they can certainly deny whatever they do next." The murmurings on both side of the circle were agitated. *But at least they aren't blockading the City, or dropping bombs*, I thought and that gives these groups a chance to put something in place. I wondered what Tegson was doing now.

"We are a small community," Siegfried began, "but we are reaching out to our trading partners, and certainly to the town we live in, and will be asking for volunteers to help patrol our areas. Most of the bridges across the river near us have been broken—" I glanced at Elontee, and she looked down, suppressing a smile. When she looked up, her face was unreadable. "—but we will increase our surveillance on both sides. We discovered that the group meeting the train crossed a recently repaired railroad bridge near a town called Rochester, where the Beaver River meets the Ohio, and that the local rebels seem to be resurrecting the old train yard at Freedom. We do not have a militia strong enough to intervene there, but any town rebels, at least, will be confronted and their properties forfeit if they do not cease and desist. That is my understanding."

Siegfried glanced at Rom and Astrid, then asked, "Will you be confronting these southerners, and how? We are concerned that open warfare would catch us at a severe disadvantage right now."

Asrah shook his head. "We don't have an army, nor can I see us raising one. But we understand from Martin that even the New York Army is mostly reservists who are usually busy raising food for the City and doing other essential tasks. What we hope to do is watch and have as much warning as possible—certainly more than we had this time—so that we can minimize damage, and perhaps deal with small groups that come to pillage."

Rom's group nodded and glanced at me; I squirmed uncomfortably. They were making me sound like the expert here, and that just wasn't true. But that's what happens when nobody has good info, I thought. Hopefully these patrols would quickly make them the experts and I could fade back. I wanted to focus on Ciera and me, in any case.

The discussion went back and forth about the best way to patrol, and what Rom's group would provide in payment for the other two radios, at least until refugee count was finished. As much as I wanted to listen, I found my attention wandering, thinking about what was happening in the City, whether Cheyenne and my officemates knew more than we did out here or maybe a lot less. Would it be safe, would it be worth it to try to find out more from her? And where was I to go next? I had done my job to bring these groups together, and going on patrol in a strange place didn't seem like a good idea. If I was to stay outside, where would I live? There were too many variables! Before I made any decision, I wanted to see Teg again. After this, I would ask Justin to get me contact with Tegson, and hopefully get permission to bring Ciera to meet Teg.

Elontee called a refreshments break, and I got up and stretched sore legs, then headed for the table. Someone had made or bought chocolate cookies, and they were delicious, well saturated with chocolate flavoring. I urged Ciera to try one, and enjoyed the surprise on her face when she tasted it. I refrained from telling her it was synthetic.

Zara sidled over and murmured, "Justin and I would like to have you two for lunch after this, if you can?"

I thanked her and introduced the two women more fully. "Zara was the one who sent my message to you when I was stuck here," I explained to Ciera, adding, "and Ciera was the one who helped me get to a safe place after my guide dumped me."

Ciera smiled politely but seemed wound up, and Zara's knowing expression worried me. I thought about the older woman's contempt for "refuseniks"—could she restrain herself at lunch, or was I risking a battle? Ciera was like a cork in fizzed wine right now. But Zara seemed welcoming, and I needed a break. I accepted and asked whether "your other guest" would be joining us. Zara looked confused for a moment then realized I was talking about Tegson.

"I'm not sure," she replied. "Honestly, there's no way to track that one." She smiled nervously.

"I mentioned to Aida I'd like to get in touch with him, but I haven't heard, so if he doesn't show up at lunch, maybe Justin can—"

Justin heard his name and turned away from his conversation. "Justin can what?" he asked with a smile, adding in a softer voice, "it's going well, don't you think?"

"Martin wants to get in touch with...the General."

Justin glanced at Ciera and said, "Of course—I'm sure that's possible. But I made lasagna for lunch so we can enjoy that first."

The negotiations resumed, with Elontee suggesting a formal agreement about future refugees. Siegfried agreed, with the caveat that his group had to vote on any details. Justin agreed to send a trainer to help Ambridge get the best use of the ham ops, and formal contacts were designated. Asrah handed Siegfried a list of possible trade items for future discussion. The group broke up shortly before lunch, and everyone agreed it had been very productive.

As we walked down the wide concrete steps of the building into the warmth of the spring afternoon, I tapped Rom on the arm and told him

Ciera and I were going to have lunch with Justin. He nodded and said "We'll probably have a small group meeting after chores today—if you could get back by mid-afternoon, we can discuss whether more needs to be done before we go back."

I agreed, and we waved and followed Justin and Zara in the opposite direction.

"Well Martin, what did you think?" Zara asked as we strolled. I suddenly remembered our trip inside, how stilted and fearful. How could I have ignored that level of surveillance? Another black mark against the City.

"It seems helpful to have this connection between towns," I replied, "but it's not like I'm any kind of expert. I'm a Citiot, remember?" I was only half joking; what did I know?

"Well, as you said, there's a lot of similarities between the slums and us out here," Justin replied, "maybe there's only one good way to deal with bullies like the City."

"Maybe it doesn't make sense to deal with them at all," Ciera cut in and I winced. Zara frowned, but she refrained from commenting. *Thank you, Zara.* I had briefly considered warning Ciera, but I was afraid it would backfire.

Justin replied carefully. "I think that the bigger an area gets, the more it has to trade with those that don't always share their beliefs," he said, "and it's harder to live with just the basics in a crowded town. From what I read, it was the very fact of more people in an area that caused specialization and a lot of extra—ah, here we are."

He ushered us in the front door and I quickly made some inane comment about the decor and was relieved that Ciera allowed the topic to shift. Zara moved to put on her music player, but I tapped her on the arm and shook my head. She frowned but put it back on the sideboard. Ciera was examining the bright paintings on the walls. We busied ourselves for a few minutes getting the meal onto the table, and soon we were digging into a rich lasagna that had been baking in a haybox all morning. Justin explained the principle of it as he set the casserole dish out—"if you have it insulated well enough, the hot food retains enough heat to keep it cooking safely."

"I think there was something like that when I was growing up, but at the time I wasn't paying attention. I'm afraid that our group was fairly rigid and it was the young women who learned how to use those things."

Ciera and Zara both snorted, and I was glad for one topic they could agree on. "That just gives the women a really good weapon in case there are disagreements over compensation," Zara joked. We laughed and for a few minutes chatting ceased as we enjoyed the meal.

After a while, Justin leaned back, smiling as we praised his cooking, then asking Ciera, "So did you enjoy your tour? We have some pretty good things to trade here."

I could see her struggling, so I jumped in. "I was wondering what barter system is used. One man mentioned marks, and I noticed many buyers weren't taking the goods—is this some kind of bulk trading system and how do they pay?"

"Yes, most of the buyers are either dealing for a town or come from the inside. 'Marks' just refers to a unit of credit, I suppose—and even though they quote you a price, it's all negotiable around here."

"But do the marks represent something fixed, like on the inside we have dollars and cents still? And we have banks that handle the transactions—I was trying to explain that to Ciera yesterday."

"We have guilds that regulate what can be sold and the basic price," Zara explained. "It seems more efficient to have those that understand the materials set the rules, and they handle the records of marks. That allows them to keep watch over merchants who might be gouging buyers or seriously undercutting their fellow guild members. New buyers or those who come from the inside have to deposit a certain amount in guaranteed trade at the guild house before they can use the Mall—the guilds provide a letter of credit they can show to the sellers, who mark off the cost of whatever has been purchased."

"Hence the 'marks'?" I asked.

Zara shrugged. "Maybe," she said. "The buyers will get their goods at the guild houses, and it's there they can negotiate for bodyguards to bring them back to wherever. We've done a good job of eliminating bandits, but there are always a few that want to get their goods cheap—only it's not so cheap if they get caught." She and Justin chuckled, and I thought of Paolo.

"I had heard that some of the bandits were given the chance to reform."

Justin nodded, and filled up everyone's glass—Zara had brought out lovely clear glasses for the meal, obviously looking to impress Ciera. "Yes, if we get a sense that the young one could possibly change, we offer them an apprenticeship and a chance to prove their honesty." He didn't mention what happened to the others, and I didn't ask. No sense spoiling a delicious meal.

Zara got up and returned with a square pan that she said was carrot cake. "Didn't have time to frosted, but I think it still rich enough," she said setting it on the table and serving it. I ate with relish, wondering fleetingly how good a cook Ciera was—or would I be expected to do that? I certainly had no experience with it.

"Will you be going back today?" Zara asked.

"Well, I really do want to speak to—our friend," I said. "I don't want to go back before I do that." But did I want to go back at all? I felt like a piece of drifting garbage, tumbling down the street without any goal.

"I'll get word to him after lunch," Justin said. "Can he contact you at the colony?"

"Ciera and I were going to take a last quick tour, and be back there by midafternoon," I replied.

"It's hard to be this close to—where Martin comes from—and not to be able to see that," Ciera said wistfully.

"You don't want to go in there!" both Zara and Justin cried, and I nodded agreement. I saw Ciera's expression harden, and I knew the advice had backfired, as usual. I had better get her out of the area before she decided to do something impulsive and foolish. Maybe seeing my friend could impress on her the dangers of overconfidence.

"I thank you for bringing out your special dishes," Ciera said. "In my town, that is a way to honor a guest, and I presume it is the same here?"

Zara agreed, and I felt embarrassed to have thought she was showing off. At the farm, we'd used the word "honored guests", but it seemed we were mostly impressing them.

After a few more thanks and *hoping to meet again*'s, Ciera and I left the brownstone and walked toward the mall.

"I want to see if we can find the solar section," she said, walking swiftly.

"Thinking of doing a little trading?" I joked, striding beside her.

She glanced at me with a flash of annoyance, and I warned myself to hold my tongue until I knew what a safe joke was. "I don't see any harm in finding out what they have for sale," she said, a bit huffily.

"Hasn't your town sent reps over here before? How do they decide which towns to trade with? Just curious," I added quickly.

"Well, I'm more on the salvage side, but I know some towns have been trading partners for a long time. There *is* a way for new groups to start trading with us; I think the town Council makes the decision."

"Who are on the Council?"

"Mostly the Grandparents," she replied, "but they're training their replacements, since most of them are getting pretty old."

We were hurrying through the pottery section, heading south toward an area I had not been, except perhaps on that night foray. "Do you have guilds like Justin described?"

"Not that formal, because we know everybody. But there are definitely master craftsman, those who know the most about a certain skill, and they have a lot of influence. They're the ones who decide who can apprentice, for example."

"You don't get to choose what you do, then?" I thought about the tests that my parents' commune put us kids through, to figure out our skills. Never wanted to go through *that* again.

"We get to say what we are interested in, but we always discuss it with the Grandparents and the Masters because they can see our skills better than we can, sometimes." Was there a little doubt in her voice?

We had come out from the brownstones into a space that was predominantly temporary stalls—windowed horse carts and old metal travel trailers parked in a scatter on old asphalt lots. The goods here seemed to be a mix of plumbing fixtures, garden tools and machine parts. Ciera slowed to check the tables for whatever she was looking for. The sun had warmed up the area, and I shrugged out of my jacket, holding it loosely over my arm. I could smell methane again, and I thought about that warehouse we had visited to get gas for the plane—I hoped there was nothing like that close by, because at best they were accidents waiting to happen. Was it my imagination, or were the buyers and sellers out here a little more scruffy, a little less...savory?

"We had to go through exams, not to test what we've learned, but what we might be good at," I told her. Maybe hearing some of my difficulties might make her less defensive. "Things like how to count the sides on a many-sided box without touching it. Or recognizing what thing in a group of things was the different one."

"I think they used to call those intelligence tests," she commented. "We saw something about that in a book at the library."

I felt my cheeks burn. Testing my intelligence? *Well thanks very much, Dad.* "In any case, it just made me feel pretty crappy. Not that I failed or anything," I hastened to add, "but just fact that I was asked all those questions, like they didn't believe me about anything."

The carts were crammed together, making the pathways a squeeze for horse-drawn vehicles. I wondered how these temporary booths were moved, or *if* they were. Perhaps this wasn't as temporary as it looked. Many carts had side windows that folded down to make counters, and there were poles sticking out from the roofs from which dangled enough gadgets that any passing breeze started up a chaotic orchestra. There was much too much to look at, and I wasn't that interested, so I focused on making sure we weren't in danger. There were lots of places where someone could jump out at us. The crowds were less polite as well, pushing and shoving past us. I pinned the pistol in my coat pocket between my elbow and hip. Lucky I wasn't carrying a knapsack, because it would have been fast-fingered.

"You said your group was sexist," she said, "does that mean you are?"

"Huh? No—I had enough years outside my commune to know that women are just as good as men at most things."

"Only most things?"

Uh-oh. "I don't assume someone can't do something," I said, trying to keep a defensive tone out of my voice. "I try to treat people as... themselves. But I don't know how to cook—that's not my fault. There was always one cook in the slum gangs, and in the City we mostly have precooked food. And you can't cook much on the electric plates in my apartment anyway. What kind of things are you looking for?" I said, trying to shift the conversation.

"Anything about solar panels," she responded, "and you'd be surprised what you can cook on small heater."

She could be so *stubborn*! I had a sister who was this bad—constantly having to correct whatever I said. How soon before *that* got old? I ignored her comment and pointed out some new-looking strainers that were large enough to fit across a sink.

"Would your town allow that kind of gadget?" I wanted to know how primitive the place I might be settling in was. Though if they had solar…

"You make us sound like we are barbarians!" She turned and glared at me and I stepped back in shock. Where had *that* come from?? I looked at her blankly, trying to think of something neutral to say. But she didn't give me the chance. "You probably think we're a bunch of barefoot... hillbillies!" she spat out, "Well, we have everything that we need, and we don't have to come out and raid—" she waffled a bit on that, then rallied with another wave of rage. "We are just as good as you Citiots!"

Stunned, I just stared at her. Her face was red, and after a second she turned her back on me and bent over some gadgets on a table. I was afraid to glance around and see who had witnessed that—what the hell was going on?? I reviewed what I'd said, looking for what set her off, but I didn't see anything, and I felt my own anger rising. I had swallowed a lot, but maybe she needed to know she couldn't push me like this! Rather than apologizing, I walked over two carts and examined a tray of what looked like can openers—as if anyone would dare open a metal tin 50 years old! I was fuming, caught flat out, and now I wondered if I should even go back with them. Maybe it wasn't gonna work, if this is what happened after a single day together. I remembered our ups and downs on the trip to Ambridge, realizing a bit too late that she'd always shown this defensive streak and smug POV. Even though she'd been out of her turf by the time we crossed that river. She didn't know how the rest of the world lived, any more than I did.

"It's not like you can say your way's better, if you don't even know—" I turned and glanced around quickly—she'd gone!

30

Panic hammered in my chest, as I took several fast steps past where I'd seen her last, glancing up smaller passageways, cursing myself for turning away in such a dangerous place. But it had only been a moment, she couldn't have gone that far! Unless she had run, but certainly I would've heard that? With all the others shuffling around, she *couldn't* have run that fast. So where the hell *was* she?? I dashed, circling around the area, widening my search as I caught no sight of her.

What the hell would I do if she really was gone? I cursed under my breath, every foul word I could dredge up. This was too much! I wouldn't let her out of my sight again until I got her started on the trip to Ambridge. Or at the very least, turn her over officially to someone. I could *not* handle this, on top of everything else! Where the hell *was* she?? Could she have been dumb enough to duck *into* one of these carts? And why?? I stopped flat, suddenly panicked with the thought that someone could have grabbed her to get back at me somehow. Could Geoff actually be around here? But surely he's given up on this kidnapping! Did they have slavers here?

"Ciera!" I called out, then a little louder, "Ciera!!"

"I think this is who you are looking for."

I spun on my heel. Tegson was standing there with a faint grin, and beside him, Ciera, biting her lip with that same half defiant, half apologetic frown she'd shown Hadley when we'd first arrived at Ambridge. I sucked in a deep breath, realizing I hadn't been breathing. I glanced from one to the other—had *he* grabbed her? But no—though I wouldn't put it past him to have lured her astray, to remind me who had the power.

As if confirming my fears, he said, "I got word from *two* people that you *really* wanted to see me. And I had word you were wandering the market, so I came out and ran into this very pleasant young woman." His tone of voice was almost taunting. I realized they were about the same age, so I was happy to see annoyance flash across her face.

"Thank you...f..for getting in touch so quickly," I stammered. I'd be damned if I would let her hear me thanking him for rescuing her. "I had hoped you would put me in touch with… my friend," I ended, glancing at Ciera.

"Certainly—we can go see him now, if you wish."

He made no attempt to leave her behind as he led us through the tangle of carts and trailers, over to yet another decrepit building—he must have these safe passages cached all through the area.

"I'd like you to meet good friend of mine," I murmured to Ciera. "He's—hidden away. Even Justin and Zara don't know about him." My emotions were roiling—this might be the worst time to go, but I had no choice. I just prayed she would be reasonable during the visit—and maybe Teg would have a better idea of what was going on with her! She seemed more subdued now, but watched Tegson with a disturbing interest. The last thing I wanted was her to be involved with his group—he'd put her in harm's way without a second thought.

As usual, the house's back stairs led into a basement that had been knocked out, forming part of the tunnel system. I glanced over—Ciera was wide-eyed and tense, but it didn't seem like she would back out. We wandered through a maze of corridors, but finally I noticed the wooden stairs we had first used—that moment I'd almost shot him slammed back into my mind and I gasped. He looked back, but I smiled and said it was nothing. A moment later we were blinking in the light of the living room, and Teg was greeting us from his seat in the comfortable armchair, a blanket around his legs as before.

"It's good to see you again so soon," he said with a warm smile. "And this must be Ciera."

She looked startled and I replied, "Your son has an amazing surveillance team—there's little he doesn't know. Ciera, this is my old friend Teg—we survived one of the slum gangs together, but I never thought to see him again. It was a shock to find him living here."

Tegson had disappeared into the kitchen, and I heard him clanking about. I could sure use a mug of that strong ale!

"This isn't my permanent home, Marty, you know," Teg said. "I described a little bit of the town I come from."

That answered one of my questions. "So you're just here to keep… an eye on things?" Once again, I was caught not knowing what was okay to say. Before

I put Ciera irrevocably in the middle of this, I needed to find out what the hell it was about!

Tegson came in with a tray of mugs and some iced muffins. It was amusing to see the change in personality when he was with his father, but I wasn't dumbdroid enough to trust it. Ciera hadn't said much, glancing from one to another, but she came to the table and took a mug and a muffin at Tegson's invitation. She obviously found him attractive—I needed to let her know how dangerous he was, but not in a way that dropped her deeper in this. Tegson brought a mug and a plate to his father, and I caught Ciera's startled look as she realized Teg couldn't get his own. Clearly, I couldn't ask Teg any of the important questions with her listening. I cursed my impulsivity and the bad timing.

"Help yourself, Marty," Tegson said. "I'll be back in about 45 minutes—that should be long enough, right?"

"Yes—thank you very much." I picked up a mug and tried not to guzzle. The dark ale was delicious again.

"Have a nice visit." He left via the tunnel door.

"Have a seat—" Teg gestured toward the couch and we sat. Our unfinished argument hung like a live sparking wire between us. "What did you think of our city?" he asked her.

"There...there's a lot of it," she started, then sipped deeply from the mug. "We—our town—doesn't do a lot of—extras—but it looked like the shops were very busy." She was struggling between politeness and defiance. My second thoughts about bringing her were far too late. Well, maybe Teg would get to see my problem, and we could discuss it later.

"The meeting between Ambridge and Justin's—or Aida's—group went well," I said, filling in. "I think there will be some better surveillance along the river now."

"That will of course be a good thing," my friend replied, and his tone told me to drop it. *So now what?* I thought furiously. Maybe history?

"Teg—you once told me there was a maximum size a city or country could get to, and that we always went over that and crashed. What size is it?"

"It's not one specific size—it depends on resources, but there *is* a max for each civilization. And yes, we've always gone over."

"How do you know?" Ciera asked, a note of defiance rising in her voice.

"History," Teg said simply. "Even though history is always written by the winners, once the winners lose, there's always a next civilization—eventually—who cheerfully document what they got wrong."

"We had Roman history in high school," Ciera said, frowning in concentration. "They conquered the whole Mediterranean and even up to Britain, but that was too far, so they fell, right?"

"It was both the distance and the fact that they had overused the areas they'd had for a long time," Teg replied. "Marty—could you get that book up there—the green cover, about half an inch thick? Thanks."

I jumped up and found it on the shelf. The book was fragile, page edges browning, tears patched with thin glued paper strips, the spine mended with long strips of fabric. I brought it to him, but he waved me back to the couch.

"It's by a man called Tainter. Open to page 49," he said. Ciera found the page quickly. I felt as dumb as a post, but at least our tension had eased. "The bottom section is about Rome, and mentions the major decline in pollens that they found in an archaeological dig in 1983, which pointed to overproduction and consequent exhaustion of the soils. But note how he also mentions the success of the Empire created this situation ironically by preventing the usual local food shortages because of their large networks, intensifying agriculture for profit by shipping long distances—the balance was destroyed and when the fall happened, it was huge. And that's the United States in a nutshell."

Ciera was paging through the book, eagerness and uncertainty warring on her face.

"Another author called it 'overshoot,'" he continued, "and every species from bacteria to humans fall prey. We can't help ourselves."

"So, if we're doomed to crash, why bother?" I blurted. The book was so crammed with numbers and charts that I couldn't fathom how someone had the time to read it, let alone gather all that information and write it.

"You're confusing history with personal," Teg replied, "Unless you think there's no point in living just because you're going to die, you take the journey and appreciate what you can." His voice changed and I could tell he was quoting: " 'The greatest obstacle to living is expectancy, which hangs on tomorrow and loses today. The whole of the future lies in uncertainty—live immediately.' That's Seneca, a Roman who lived around the Year One AD", he said. "It is tricky, but the secret is to appreciate the world around you, but not to get too attached."

"Like Elliot said in *Ash Wednesday*, 'teach us to care and not to care,'" Ciera murmured.

"—'teach us to sit still,'" Teg finished and Ciera bit her lip at her unintended faux pas. But he smiled at her. "T.S. Elliot is one of my favorites. But also the Chinese poets—do you know Doo Foo?" She shook her head.

He glanced at me and I made a wry face. "You know I don't know squat." I could see he was enjoying showing off. I was still trying to grapple with the year one. I suppose there had to be one... I just couldn't picture it.

"Well—you can learn. Doo Foo—spelt *t u f u*—lived in the eighth century in China, and his observations about the world are still fresh today. 'These times have brought us hardships, sorrow; in or out of court, there are few free days.' Apparently we haven't changed that much in twelve hundred years." I couldn't tell if he was pleased or sad about that.

"So—if there's a maximum size," I persisted, "how do we know when we're near the danger point?"

"Ironically it looks like a Golden Age," Teg replied. "There's huge abundance and everyone gets used to luxury."

"That's why my town doesn't want to get attached to luxuries!" Ciera twisted on the couch to face me. I nodded, hoping she wouldn't explode again.

"There's a balance, but it's pretty hard to get right—and it's dynamic—it keeps changing based on resources," Teg said. "The best is to live within the renewable resource frame. But humans haven't done that for centuries."

"*We're* doing it," Ciera insisted.

"No—not even out here," Teg said. "Recycling is good, but we still have far too many people for what the land, sea and air can provide."

"Even with the Great Dying?" I was astonished.

"Even with that," Teg said solemnly. "That's why we rely on salvage. Do you really think we'd be able to make absolutely everything from absolutely scratch?"

I shrugged helplessly and even Ciera was silent. Then she said, "The Grandparents say they'll be another crash after all the salvage is used, and we'll have to get used to less."

Teg nodded. "And it will support fewer of us, I believe—and yet we need a certain critical mass to make a civilization." He sighed, looking sadder than I'd ever seen. "We're trying to revive a number of the old industries to be better able to use the scrap—to use every last bit—which will give us time to think of something better."

"Us?" I couldn't see this group making airplanes.

"Our grandchildren, or even further ahead, with luck," he replied.

"But, though that is a noble reason, are you *sure* that you're not falling into the same trap?" Ciera asked."Thinking that machines are more efficient, therefore we should spend our precious time and energy making them so they can put us out of work? The Grandparents have warned us against thinking that efficiency is the primary virtue," she added, staring at him earnestly.

He nodded and sipped his beer. "Oh, granted—the planners before us were totally fixated on efficiency, and had left out resilience. But for the nonrenewables, we are stuck—we either learn to live without them completely, or we focus on the the most efficient way to use what's left—and I think a combination of both is the better choice. Do you have any idea how primitive life will be without your solar panels helping to run your pumps, your methane factories and batteries allowing your e-bike—heck all the metal that is needed to *make* an e-bike! Or even a manual bike, for that matter. By the way, Marty, did you know that those fashionable tunics that everyone wears in the cities used to be hospital uniforms? They called them scrubs. The City located hundreds of thousands in warehouses and voilà—you had a fashion trend."

"So we're not getting newly-woven outfits?"

"Not most of you—that's why they don't stay together very long—they're really old fabrics. The rich are getting new cloth, but you probably figured that."

"Oh, yes. The rich get whatever they want. On our trip—Ciera's and mine—we stayed over at a commune that had no power except for their alarm system," I said, happy to be part of the conversation. "They seem to be doing quite well, though most of their stuff was from salvage. Are you saying we can't even make things like glass or metal? We saw glassblowers today."

Teg waved his hand impatiently. "You forget that they need raw materials—it's not just *making* steel, it's finding the iron ore, the limestone, and the coal, not to mention the small bits of chromium or magnesium. Even when Pennsylvania had steel factories mostly run on human power, they still brought those ingredients from at least four widely-flung states. We'll probably get to that stage, but we might not stay there. And if the idiots in charge continue with their blind worship of the old days, we're not even going to get that far before it all falls apart." He frowned, as if he'd said too much.

"I'd like to know what machines you think are worth revising," Ciera said, "but first I need to use the outhouse." She lifted her mug. "It's all this good beer," she added with a smile.

Teg directed her out through the kitchen to the back. The moment I heard the second door slam, I turned to my friend urgently. "I need your advice! I think

I like...I love her—maybe. But I'm not used to this world, and her town actually hides itself and I'm afraid I'll be stuck—and we just had a fight and I have no idea why—"

Teg was grinning broadly; I wouldn't have put up with that from anyone but him. "Well, when it comes down to it, the town I live in is partly hidden as well," he said. "And anyone who can quote Eliot is okay in my opinion. This is a hard time to start something, I know—but I met my second wife in the middle of something similar—we had foolishly alerted the City to our project and they came out to crush us or at least teach us who was boss. We managed to get away, and we had eight good years, before she passed." Teg's smile dimmed for a moment, then he smiled at me again. "I'd say go for it, Marty—we don't get that many chances to really love. Grab the ones you get."

I heard the back door open again, and had time only to murmur, "But where should we live? How do I make a living out here?"

Ciera came back through the kitchen before he had time to reply, and he took up another topic as if we had been discussing it.

"...when Mickey's gang tried to expand territory, they found too much of their booze disappearing before it got to the buyer," he said, as if in midsentence. "It's another kind of leaky supply line."

I nodded as if I knew what he was talking about, and Ciera resumed her place on the couch.

"As to your question," Teg said to her, "although I think the City is crazy for trying to restore the *whole* grid, a more effective local power supply—maybe a grid that encompasses just this city or region—would be an enormous boost and allow many other improvements. If we could get an old coal plant going, even at much reduced rate, and enough infrastructure to have reliable power to homes and factories nearby, then we could shift our labor to creating some of the basic goods that we only have as salvage now—like cloth and glass and metal—and we would have the ability to freeze food."

"That's the trap the Grandparents warn us about," Ciera said, shaking her head. "The problem with that is you then have to use a certain amount of energy just to keep them going, because you count on them. It's not like you've got 10 weavers who are independent—you have one factory that if it shuts down, loses about 10 weavers worth of work. They used to have something called 'too big to fail', and a factory like that quickly become something we couldn't afford to lose."

She was getting excited, but I didn't see the anger that she'd unleashed on me. *Wish I knew why.* I sat back and listened to them argue, understanding perhaps three quarters of it, and not having much of an opinion, though maybe if I stayed out here I would.

I was impressed with Teg's ability to discuss these topics without going into details of what he or his son were doing. I suspected they had a lot of big plans, and I wondered if they would consult others before putting them into effect. Perhaps Ciera was right—noble causes could quickly blind you to your actions. In my experience, only dictators got to act absolutely. As much as I admired my friend, would I want him as my dictator? I glanced down at my beer—it was strong stuff and making me think some very odd thoughts.

Teg and Ciera had switched to quoting poetry at each other, an area where I was totally lost, so I just sat and enjoyed the lines quoted, some of which made sense, and some which would take a lot of work to decipher. Teg argued that most of the modern poets just previous to the Adjustment were garbage, where Ciera quoted several that she thought were worth keeping, and expressed her belief there were many more, "if we could just get at the computers where there poetry was stored."

"Yes, the burned library," Teg said. "Not literally like Alexandria, but certainly a library that vanished in a catastrophe. Marty, remember how you couldn't quite grasp how many people used to live in the City? Well, try to imagine having 120,000 libraries full of books, and the top hundred libraries together held about 550 million books—that was one estimate of what the US contained. And the worldwide Internet when it went down was about 10 times larger, to the best of our knowledge. One trillion pages. Though they said most of the stuff on it was crap."

Suddenly Tegson was in the room. I was startled that so much time had gone by, and relieved that no arguments had erupted. A sudden thought struck me as I turned to thank Teg. "Will you be staying nearby for a while? Since I don't know where to get hold of you otherwise, and these visits are too short..."

"Yes, for the foreseeable future," he replied, "and I will be sure to leave some kind of contact if we go back. And maybe sometime you can actually visit for a couple of days so we could get in some really good discussions."

It was less difficult to leave, knowing it was possible to see him again. Tegson took us back through a different tunnel, and we stepped out of a house very close to Justin and Zara's.

"I think you know your way back from here," he said, at the back door of the portal house. "And I need to go—this is a busy time." He was off before I had much chance to thank him, and I had a stray panic—what if something were to happen to *him*? Was there anyone else who knew where Teg was? No one was immortal, and surely they had thought of that?

"What...what do you think of my friend?" I asked, leading her back toward the colony. After being inside, the day was so bright I was squinting. I tried to guess what time it was—had we missed the meeting?

"I liked him," she said. "He really has an amazing memory—almost like a Grandparent but not quite as old. Is he crippled?"

"He can walk using a kind of cart," I replied. I took a breath. "And his son—I need to warn you that his son is—"

"—the General. I figured that out," she cut in. "And it sounds like you can only get to your friend through him? And why can't Justin and Zara know?"

"I haven't yet gotten a chance to ask that. But until we know, could you not say anything? And his son's name is Tegson, but the others know him only as Teg. There's still a lot I don't understand, and I think we need to be careful." I was torn between giving her some examples and knowing how easily advice backfired with her. Maybe if I told her she *should* make a friend of Tegson? It felt like a Fun House mirror.

She was quiet most of the way back, and I didn't dare bring up the argument—maybe it *was* just being overwhelmed by everything. And now we were walking back into another big decision—do we go back to Ambridge? Where did I belong?

The meeting had started before we arrived, so we took a couple chairs at the back and I tried to catch up. It sounded like Jared was making a case for this colony to be involved, but there were a number of members shaking their heads—including several of those who I had seen looking so unfriendly.

"If we get distracted by external obligations, we might neglect our own, or end up seriously overworked," Jordan said with his pompous intonation.

"It's not honorable to leave other people to protect us," Jared replied, "not to mention the high probability that they will ask us to pay in some other way. We are town members, and they mentioned at the meeting they'll be asking for repayment from anyone who sent refugees. My guess is they'll demand a bit extra for these patrols. If we are going to be sending people or goods, it would be better we do so up front, where we are part of the team and aware of what is going on." He sat down to a murmur of approval, many people nodding at the sense of his argument.

A dumpy middle-aged woman stood up. "I agree with Jared—we don't know how bad this is going to get, and it could get *very* bad," she said. "It could be a lot worse than bandits, and in the end, it will be essential that we have allies, unless we want to end up wandering like the Israelites, looking for some new home." She sat down with a thump.

My attention drifted. Ciera squirmed beside me, and I realize she wasn't paying much attention either. We would be going back today, most likely, and I didn't have a bike this time—oh, but there were all the retrieved bikes—I would have my choice. I smiled. If I played this right I could go back and forth every couple of days, retrieving bikes and leading refugees, especially if we got that bandit crew cleared out. Maybe that's where my next task lay. Could I get my bike back from Troy? How much did we owe her for the horses?

Raised voices caught my attention. The dumpy woman was harassing Rom; gradually I understood she was citing the benefits of trade with the City. Rom was attempting patience, but he stood stiffly, as if holding himself back. Astrid looked even more angry.

"We understand that you have made this choice," he said, slowly and carefully. "But we are not interested in it—and I don't feel it would do any good to re-open that subject right now."

"But you will end up needing our help when you run out of your own resources, and that's not right!" she argued, conveniently forgetting that it was they are refugees who had come to Ambridge.

Rom stared as if she had gone crazy, and fortunately the president stood up and began a pompous, meaning-free lecture that was pure politics, calming everybody down through boredom.

Eventually, they did agree to send two volunteers if they could get them, and to increase communication with Ambridge and Justin's group. I could tell this would also increase tensions, and wondered why it was so hard for people to get along except when they were threatened by the outside. But how well-connected was I, on ordinary days? Not that I would see any of them soon.

The meeting finally broke up, and Rom came over to us. "We're heading back in an hour," he told us. "Just as soon as the two new apprentices show up. They are also sending someone to help us with the radio set-up. Did you see anything in the mall worth trading for?"

We both must have winced because a cautious look came into his eye.

"There was almost too much to see any of it," I told him. "Maybe sometime I'll have more energy and focus to spare."

"Yeah—I'm hoping we get a few trades approved, so I'll get to come down a few more times."

We went upstairs to get our knapsacks. The moment the door closed, Ciera turned on me and I flinched before I could stop myself.

"Are you really planning to follow through with this?" she demanded, glaring at me.

"*Which* this? The trades, the surveillance?"

"*Us*! Are you getting cold feet now because we're such barbarians?"

"*Hold* a momentito! I never said you were barbarians—you're putting words in my mouth! And what about you?? You just ran off and left me in a panic in the middle of that market—are you gonna keep doing things like that?" We were standing face to face, arms akimbo and it felt like the moment just before a gang brawl broke out. "Why are we fighting??" I asked.

"Don't you know?" she asked impatiently.

"No—as far as I can tell, I said something that you took wrong and now you're convinced that somehow I'm backing out."

"Well, are you? Or are you making a commitment?"

"A commitment to *what*? In Ambridge, we'd been talking about getting to know each other—I really want to do that, and I wouldn't have taken you to see my friend if—" I paused struggling to put it into words. "He's all the family I have, dammit, and I'm willing to go back and meet your family, and find out more about you and your town, and even be blindfolded, dammit!" I was shouting now, but I didn't care. "But I'm not going to, if you keep jerking me around!"

"What are you talking about? *You're* the one who keeps acting skittish! And then jealous! Don't think I haven't seen you looking at me when I smile at other guys! You're like a dog in a manger!"

She spun away and started slamming clothes into her knapsack. I felt bludgeoned—if this was what a relationship was like, you could have it! I grabbed my knapsack and threw the few remaining bits into it. The air felt bruised and I was angry to see my hands were shaking.

"Why do you keep running hot then cold?" she demanded.

I refused to turn around. "You do the same—first you're all friendly, and then you're picking fights! I don't understand you!"

"I'm responding to you—don't you realize that you keep pulling back whenever we get close? Don't tell me you don't see that?"

I stared at the wall, racing through my memories of our conversations. Maybe it was true—maybe something in me hung back when things got intense. But was that so bad? Right now I would trade this sick feeling for a half a dozen fractures.

"Because it hurts!" I shouted.

"Love? No—loss, maybe…"

"All of it, all of it." I felt sick and I couldn't catch my breath. I hadn't hurt this much since I'd been slammed to the concrete by a falling wall. *Dammit!* I punched the window frame, and could feel something crack. The surge of pain up my arm pushed back at whatever was trying to tear me apart. This was too hard! When I could look at her again, she was crying.

"I thought I made you feel good—feel better," she murmured.

"Yes, yes! You do—I—I guess it's fear of losing you. That's worse."

"Worse than not loving?" She shook her head. "I don't think so. And *I've* lost people. You can't give up because you might lose."

"Why not? Why not stay off the roller coaster??"

"I don't know what a roller coaster is."

"It doesn't matter. I do love you—I think. Yes—I definitely do. And that's what hurts, and I don't know what to do about it."

She stared at me in silence, and my sick feeling increased. I could see where this was heading. Finally, she picked up her knapsack and in a very quiet voice said, "Well, when you figure out what to do about it, you can contact them in Ambridge and they know where to find me." She turned and walked out the door, letting it close quietly behind her.

I sagged against the wall, staring numbly for a while. I suddenly heard tires rattle on gravel, and a quick glance out the window confirmed the group was driving off. I staggered to the bed and sat. I told myself it was better—better to find this out now than after I was trapped in a town that I couldn't get out of. But I still loved her, and I still didn't know what to do about it.

31

Some time passed, and finally I roused myself and went downstairs. I went down the short passageway to the main Hall, and stood looking in. The alcoves were bustling as members did their daily chores; laughter and chatter floated across the room. It was hard not to feel it was mocking. A slim black woman walked toward me and I recognize Jalisa. I tried to muster a smile but couldn't. She took my arm and led me over to a small empty table with a benches.

"I heard what happened," she began, urging me to sit. "I'm sorry to hear, but I think maybe you are both just overwhelmed. I could tell you really liked each other, and I remember when this group first split off from the main one, five years ago. We got here, all excited at our new home, and then the fights broke out everywhere. Jared and I were snarling at each other, and just about every other couple were having problems. We finally had a group meeting and realized that we were all just overwhelmed by the change, and we had not been paying enough attention to our inner balance. What I'm trying to say is that I think you'll be okay—just give her a little time to calm down and maybe you spend a day or two resting—you really have been doing a lot, from what I hear."

She was watching me carefully and I tried to process what she was saying. It sounded like good advice, but it didn't soothe the knives inside. Part of me was screaming that I could *not* go through this pain *ever* again—it wasn't worth it, wasn't worth the good feelings, and the very best thing I could do was to just walk away. Another part was screaming I couldn't walk away from her—and ever be at peace again.

Jalisa was waiting for an answer. I shook myself and thanked her for the advice, hoping I sounded sincere enough.

"You can stay here a couple days, if you want. I know we can work that out," she said.

I thanked her again but said I would go stay with Justin and Zara. "I really appreciate your hospitality," I assured her, "and I hope this whole problem blows over and maybe your group gets some more trade out of it." I picked up my knapsack and headed through the back door.

It was late afternoon, and the shadows were getting longer. The streets smelled like sun-warmed stone with a bit of rancid garbage wafting up from somewhere. Fewer people were on the streets, and most of those ignored me. I headed toward Justin and Zara's, trying to frame an explanation: *just after we left your place, we had one fight after another...must've been something in the carrot cake, she just blew up...I guess you were right about refuseniks after all, Zara...*I found my feet had led me in another direction, and I was closer to the Wall than I had realized. I turned back, trying to pay attention, but sinking into morbid memories—remembering how green and stupid I was when I first met her, and how I thought she was... well, yes, a barbarian. And how she'd gone out of her way to bring me to a safe place. Grief clogged my throat and I squeezed my bruised hand to stop it. It was like a deep well of misery had suddenly overflowed since I met her—in the City, I was pretty happy, not really close to anyone but with enough companions to have a good time. Maybe I should go back there. Then I remembered the City's supply lines, and that I had no control whatsoever in there. This was not a safe time to be depending on the City's goodwill. No—it was probably better to stay outside and figure out what this war was about—make myself useful.

Once again, I found my legs had veered off and I was close to the strange old pub where I'd first met Tegson's group. I stopped still. What was wrong with me? I suddenly realized that I didn't want to face Justin and Zara right now—didn't want to try and explain when I was feeling so raw. I needed time to digest what had happened, and be able to tell the story with a better face. I'd be exhausted if I walked around for another couple of hours though—was there a park where I could just sit? If I wasn't too restless to sit.

"Hi Marty—I thought you'd be on your way back by now." Elontee's voice startled me—I almost jumped out of my skin. I turned and tried to smile. It ended up as a grimace.

"They've gone back," I told her. "I, uh, I stayed because I still don't know why the City sent me out, and I hope to get better information here." *Damn, I was smooth at lying!*

She looked at me carefully, nodded and said, "So you're busy now?"

"Not necessarily. Is there something I can do for you?"

"Well actually..." She was thoughtful. "We're going on a bit of an adventure tonight, and the way you helped us last time might come in handy again. Would you like to come inside and discuss it?" She gestured to the corner where the strange old pub loomed like a Gothic nightmare in flaking pink.

"Sure—as long as you don't think the General would object."

She smiled. "No, I think he was quite pleased with your performance last time."

I followed her to the corner, wondering dully if she knew about Teg. What was so secret about him? I could hardly ask Tegson to bring me back there a second time so quickly, nor could I face my friend's amusement at my fumbling this. We walked up the dirt-streaked concrete steps. Elontee looked around quickly, and seeing no one, opened the door and ushered me in.

It was just as dim as the last time, just as dry and airless. She lit two oil lamps over the bar and they glowed orangely. The place echoed like a vault as she walked around it and pulled a bottle and a couple of mugs from under the counter.

"This is vintage Scotch whiskey," she said, "at least 50 years old, and probably a lot more." She poured two generous helpings and I accepted gratefully. Hard liquor wasn't that plentiful, and I drank cautiously, remembering the burn the first couple of times I'd tried it. This was a lot smoother, going down warm, but not harshly.

"Tastes real good, thank you," I told her. "So what's up?"

"We found an encampment over the river, and at first we were just going to wipe it out—but they are in radio contact, so we've decided to step in more cautiously. We're going to surprise them tonight, capture them before they can signal home, and leave a handful of our group to keep sending false signals—and if we can get some information that way, all to the better. Are you up for it?" She grinned wickedly, and I could tell she enjoyed her job.

I thought back to the terror of the first expedition. Somehow the fear didn't bite as deep right now, and although I still had some resentment for Tegson's tricking me, I couldn't think of any reason offhand why I wouldn't go with them. Maybe one.

"I'm not as fit as you all—I wouldn't want to slow you down." I took a couple more swallows and was surprised to find the mug empty.

"This isn't about fit, it's about finesse," she assured me, refilling it. "We've got a team to get us across the river, and it's less than two miles from there. There's five of us, and you'd make six. I've always preferred even numbers. I can see you stumbling in on them, claiming to have just encountered some bandit group—hold their attention long enough for us to get in the back way." She watched me as she spoke, perhaps looking for signs of fear, but she wouldn't find any—I still felt numb.

I tried to picture walking in on a camp of soldiers—all of them armed, maybe hyper alert—probably a lot more dangerous than she was saying. But what the hell—I was a useless lump around here. If I could help Justin's group by making this raid work, it was a lot better than sitting around feeling sorry for myself. I told her yes.

"Is there any place to catch a nap, first? Frankly, I haven't had a full night's sleep in at least a week." And the scotch was making my head spin a little—best to sleep it off.

"There's a couple of rooms upstairs. We're gathering here tonight about 11—I could bring you late dinner." She pulled a thick candle from under the bar and used a long thin roll of paper to light it from a lamp.

"Sounds great." I followed her up some very dusty stairs, noting that very few footprints had scuffed them—would I be sleeping on dust? Not that it mattered. But the bedroom was surprisingly clean—obviously someone stayed here regularly. The bed had sheets and a green wool blanket, and the air wasn't nearly as dry and dusty as downstairs. Puzzled but grateful, I took the candle from her, set it carefully on the bedside table, and set my knapsack on the floor.

"I'll come get you later," she said as she closed the door behind herself. I realized I was still wearing Justin's armor—good thing I hadn't given it back. I didn't bother to undress, just blew out the candle, slid under the blanket and lay back. I wished the night closer; if sleep didn't come, this would be a nasty couple of hours. The scotch did its work, however, and I slid into a dark dreamless sleep.

* * *

When Elontee woke me, at first I had no idea where I was, then it came back—too much of it came back and I groaned, then apologized. My head was throbbing a little, and my mouth was dry, but she told me my dinner was downstairs and I could splash water on my face there too. I followed her closely, as the dark had deepened—was it really almost 11? I focused on not stumbling—she wouldn't take me along if I was clumsy.

Downstairs, several of the previous team were there, and a new member that she introduced as Marco. He was the radio expert, apparently—a slightly beer-bellied man about my age with thinning black hair. I ate some spicy, chewy beef stew at the bar, listening as she gave the team instructions.

"Desan, Chala and Haji—you will be circling around the back. Martin is going to get their attention up front, and Marco will have set up the white noise a few feet away. I'm guessing we will have no more than 15 minutes before somebody notices the radio's not getting through. We don't know if they have backup communication plans, so we can't risk them getting suspicious. Desan, you've been listening in for the past couple of days—do you know the schedule of their call-ins?"

"Got it—since not much is going on, they're not expecting a lot of info, which is good—we just need to keep up regular check-ins, and hopefully they will be sending us word before they move any troops forward." He grinned and flashed a bright set of teeth.

"Good. We've got the river patrol to escort us over," Elontee continued, "and Desan says it's less than two miles from there to the encampment. They might have sentries, but six of us should be able to slip past in any case. Any questions?"

There were none, so we got kitted up—she had found me a jumpsuit like theirs, which fit nicely over the armor. I was relieved to see none of the large guns, and when I asked, she explained that they could do too much damage to the radio equipment.

"Pistols and knives should do the job just fine," she said.

She handed me a knapsack that I suspected was lighter than the others, but I wasn't going to complain. I wondered briefly about leaving word with Justin where I was, but it wasn't worth the effort. No one would care that much if I vanished.

The hike down towards the river was similar to the first time—Chala, who was in front, kept a brisk pace, and soon we were at the wall under the highway. Elontee let us through, and on the other side used our single flashlight to make our way down past the warehouse where the plane slept, to a brushy area. I could hear the river murmuring beyond. It was scarcely a footpath leading down, but at the water's edge, in the flashlight's glare, I saw a flat raft-like boat and a half dozen figures beside it. I watched the others step down into a flat-bottomed gully between two rows of seats and I attempted to imitate their agile movements, cursing myself as I set the boat rocking, though I was surprised at how little it moved. The six other soldiers got in last, taking their places in the seats. I chuckled when I realized the soldiers were bicycle-paddling it across the river! There was no moon tonight, so the crossing was a series of blurs and shadows, with the boat's silent passage making barely a change in the night chorus of birds and frogs. Within a few minutes we were on the other side, and scrambling up a bank, brushing aside thick shrubs and slipping a bit on the muddy incline.

"If we're not back by dawn," Elontee told the boatman, "report to Aida and tell them we failed. But I feel sure we'll be back."

Desan took the lead, as we made our way slowly down a broken highway without lights, luckily finding few obstacles. My head still throbbed, but the exercise helped bring back some energy, as I stepped as quietly as possible. I had no idea what to expect, so I didn't even think about it—somehow it didn't seem that important. I would do my best, but in any case, the main group would be in the back door within a moment or two, and if I got shot—well... so be it. The night's chill breeze felt good on my face and the sighing and whispering of the shrubs around us was pleasant. My mood was almost peaceful, though slightly unreal.

The encampment was on a ridge, on the edge of an old suburb that seemed like rows of giant, half-collapsed plaster and cardboard boxes as we passed by them. We were moving slower, and despite myself, I was getting more tense. I didn't want to mess this up for them. Marco stopped us in a bare space and unslung his knapsack.

"This should be good for the interference pattern," he said. We left him setting up his equipment, and moved forward. Just the other side of the next house, Desan paused. Peering ahead, I could see the merest wedge of light about waist height ten feet away. *Must be a loose window shade*, I thought. Elontee brought me to the front and whispered, "The door is straight ahead. Count to twenty, so we have time to get around the back, then start to make some flailing noise, and call out for help. Be careful to keep your hands where they can see them—but why am I giving you advice? You know how to do this really well."

She patted me on the shoulder and they disappeared silently. I began my wait, slowly counting elephants as I had been taught for hide and seek. *One elephant, two elephant*—the Ambridge group would be fast asleep by now—*three elephant, four elephant, five elephant*—and hopefully Erma had convinced them that they needed to band together. *Six elephant, seven elephant*—

wonder what an elephant was?—*Eight elephant, nine elephant, ten elephant*—she was sleeping, completely unaware that I was facing death. *Eleven elephant, twelve elephant, thirteen elephant*—an unlucky number, or maybe unfairly scapegoated. *Fourteen elephant, fifteen elephant*—almost there—what was behind that front door? I began to move slowly forward, so I wouldn't have as far to run. *Sixteen elephant, seventeen elephant*—this was it—time to find out if Justin's armor worked—*eighteen elephant, nineteen elephant. Twenty*.

"Oh my God! Oh my God—let me in please, somebody help me!" I cried out in a querulous voice, stumbling forward and waving my hands. I reached the door just as someone opened it, and stepped back three paces, with my hands up, facing a double barrel shotgun, and behind it a very young, frightened freckle-faced redhead. "Please sir," I bleated, "you have to help me—there are bandits out on the roadway—they stole my bike. I got away just in time."

More soldiers crowded in behind him, scrutinizing me. I gulped for breath, not much of an act since my mouth was as dry as dust. Could I throw myself on that rifle when hell broke loose? Would the kid think to shoot me first and deal with danger later? I stepped back a half pace, and waved my hands slowly, trying to draw their attention.

"I don't know who you are, sir, but for God's sake, be kind to a traveler! I'm half dead, sir—" *was I laying it on too thick?* But most of these looked like boys, not real soldiers. Was that the click of a door? I talked faster, raising my pitch to try and cover any rustling. "I think maybe they're gone, but I saw them down along that highway." I turned and gestured behind me, and one of the soldiers shone a flashlight, as if that would have illuminated anything. And then my team struck.

A crash, a yelp, cut off. The young soldiers in the back turned and I dove at the boy with the rifle, ducking under the barrel and catching him in the ribs—we went down hard in the doorway. I heard shots—a woman's scream—the crash of furniture and crockery, then all my attention was captured by the redhead trying to strangle me. I set my thumb in his eye, thanking whatever God that he'd dropped the rifle. I pushed hard, and he screamed, then another explosion or gunbattle *pock-pock-pocked* nearby, and I felt a stabbing pain in my arm and my side. Gasping I lost my hold, but I saw the young soldier had been hit in the head—blood flowed from his temple, and his gaze clouded over, his arms grew limp.

Struggling to my knees, I stifled a groan and clutched my ribs with my forearm. It looked like we had won—I didn't see a single standing gray uniform. Chala and Haji were bending over a burly soldier, tying him hand and foot. Another lay trussed nearby. Desan was doubled over near a knocked-down table, his eyes white, almost rolled back in his head. I stumbled to him, pain shooting up my left leg, and tried to see where he was wounded.

"Let me see," I grunted, trying to pull his arm away. Blood gushed out, but it wasn't the bright arterial blood that signals a deadly wound. Why hadn't we brought a medic? Pain was causing a rush of adrenaline that set my teeth chattering. I called the others, and Chala rushed over with her knapsack, dumping it on the ground and fumbling for bandages. Desan tried and failed to bite back a groan as she pushed some padding into the wound and quickly wrapped his belly, tying it expertly.

"Elontee's dead." Chala's voice was flat, unemotional, but she also was shaking. "The first round got her—a lucky shot." She turned to me and examined my arm. "Shrapnel, I think," she said. "We can't stop and take it out now. Where else?"

"Leg and side, I think," I gasped, feeling a gray wall of unconsciousness heading toward me. "Any pain meds?"

Haji's hand appeared in front of my face with the pill, I opened my mouth obediently and he popped it in, then held a water bottle to my lips as I struggled to drink—Chala's bandaging sent waves of pain, but I was grateful for her competence. My side was merely a bruise—Justin's armor held an embedded wedge of metal that had scratched but not buried itself in my ribs. For a moment, the only thought I could spare was for myself—was this where it all ended? I'd been battered and bruised many times, but never shot—I kept seeing those torn apart bodies from the Haunt. What I could see didn't look huge, but God it hurt like hell! And seeing my blood leaking out onto my clothes felt unreal. Desan was lying on the floor and he looked bad. How would we manage to get him back? Or me? That two-mile hike was impossible. And Elontee, dead? I couldn't picture it—didn't want to picture it. Her wicked grin as she described the adventure, her calm certainty at the boat—surely they were mistaken! Chala finished binding my leg wound, and I staggered to my feet, using the knocked-over table as support.

"I think I'll need a crutch," I gasped.

Marco stumbled in the back door, his face white in terror. "Oh my God—she's dead!"

"We know," Chala said flatly. She seemed to have taken on the lead, and frankly I was glad of her calm, no matter how fake. *Now what?* "Desan can't stay here—Marco, would you stay with Haji, just till we can get someone out here tomorrow?" she asked. He was trembling, but he nodded, and she turned to me.

"If you give me something to lean on, I can walk out," I assured her. "But what would you do with—the body?"

"We can't take her back, not right now," she said. "We'll have to bury her temporarily, just something to keep her safe—" finally her calm collapsed and she turned away, trembling. Her grief finally broke through my numbness, and I wrapped my good arm around her shoulders from behind and hugged, feeling hot tears rolled down my face onto her neck. We stood for a moment in silence, then she broke away, wiping her tears and smiling weakly. I glanced down at Desan—would he make it? Would we have another corpse on our hands?

"Is there a cart? Something to help him?" I asked. Haji was setting up the tables again, and Marco fumbling with the radio equipment, some of which had fallen to the floor. It looked like three of the rebel soldiers were dead, and two tied securely. We couldn't get those home, either! But Chala had other ideas. She walked over to the hogtied soldiers.

"You're going to carry our comrade back, or I'm going to shoot you," she said, calmly. "If we get back safe, you'll be treated well, and probably traded back at some point. But if you don't help us now, you'll never make it. What do you say?"

They both nodded vehemently, and she held a pistol on them as Haji retied their wrists in front and removed their leg ropes. She ordered them to their feet, then marched them out back and I followed, leaning on tables and walls for support, hoping I wasn't imagining the pain easing slightly.

In the back corridor, Elontee's body lay twisted, half leaning on the wall. Her beautiful face was waxy, her eyes staring ahead at nothing—the corpse didn't look like her; just like the few other corpses I'd seen, it didn't look human somehow. The eyes, especially—like the glass eyes of dolls, or the dead eyes of fish on a platter. Whatever had been her was gone.

"I want you to carry her outside," Chala ordered, "I saw a place under the back window. Hurry up!"

The southern soldiers picked up the body and half-carried, half-dragged it outside. I leaned against the door frame, feeling sick, shaky and weak. As the soldiers put Elontee down and began to cover her body with tarps and stone, I looked around for something I could walk with. Nothing showed itself, so I stumbled back inside and in a small closet found a broom that I could tuck upside down under my armpit. I was grateful that it was my right arm and my left leg, otherwise I wasn't sure how I would have managed.

In the front room, Haji and Marco had dragged the other corpses out the front door and gotten the furniture restored. Haji was speaking into a headset, trying for a southern drawl as he reported all was well. When he got off, he cursed and muttered, "Desan is the one who's good at accents—you'd better send someone else soon, cause I don't know how long I can fool them."

Chala called to us to bring Desan and we went out back, Haji and Marco carrying him between them. It was awkward, and I really feared we wouldn't be able to do this. But Chala had fashioned a sling from a tarp and they placed Desan in it. The two young southerners fortunately seemed strong enough to carry him.

"I always wanted my own sedan chair," he joked, gasping. "And my own carriers. This is living!" Then he lay back and close his eyes; he may have passed out.

We started back through the suburbs, me in the lead with the flashlight and Chala behind with her gun trained on the rebels. I tried to pick the flattest, widest way, so the going was much, much slower than our approach. I desperately want to know what time it was—how far away was dawn? We seem to be crawling at a slug's pace. If we missed the rendezvous and the soldiers went back, was there any way at all to signal them? Would we be left on the riverbank, slowly bleeding to death? Trapped in the pain, I found that I really wanted to live, after all. Living meant there was a chance to try again, to make up for all my stupid mistakes. I focused on moving as quickly as I could, knowing I was the one who was slowing us down. I ignored the stabs of pain, hobbling along with my broom crutch and trying to follow the trail of broken twigs we had left coming up. Down on the highway, we made much better time, as I fought between pushing so hard I'd collapse and moving too slow to catch our ride. The shrubbery was beginning to reveal itself in a slow-spreading light and I hobbled faster—where was that riverbank??

32

Where that big broken alder is—turn left!" Chala called softly behind me. I almost flung myself down the bank, and the soldiers caught me as I stumbled. I yelped at the pain of impact, and babbled my gratitude. They helped me into the boat and set Desan carefully beside me, unconscious but still breathing. Chala got the captives in—they looked more like scared boys in borrowed uniforms—and she sat at the end, her pistol unwavering, her expression grim.

The ride across was a glitchy mu-vid, as I closed my eyes and tried not to puke with the pain. Did they have a hospital? Desan probably had a home to go to—where would I go? Was Tegson waiting to hear how this went? Without his lieutenant, did they know how to contact him? Justin would know. Would Justin take me in? The gray humming of blackout swept over me a couple times, but I was awake enough to sense the bump as we hit the other side.

The paddlers scrambled up and Chala sent one running. I didn't think I had the strength to get out of the boat, so I waited patiently until they carried Desan to the bank and two soldiers came back for me. With their help, I made it to shore; they lowered me onto the grass and I looked up at Chala.

"What now?" I asked her. My voice sounded weirdly thin and high-pitched.

"We've got help coming," she said, staring at the city, as if willing them to arrive. That was the last thing I heard before the gray humming took over and I passed out.

* * *

I woke in a bright room, in a soft bed with pale blue sheets, and in no pain. Surprised, I tried to get up on my elbow, but my muscles didn't want to cooperate, and I flopped back. I felt woozy, and wondered if someone had injected opium. Not that I had any objection. I looked to my right and saw a closed door—looked more like a house than a hospital. I glanced longingly at a tin mug on the table, but didn't have the strength to pick it up. I slipped back into sleep for another while. When I woke again, there was a woman by my bedside, examining my arm, the bandages loose on the bed.

"Welcome back," she said softly in a low throaty voice. "The good news is you didn't have fever, and nothing looks infected." She rewrapped the wound.

I asked for water, and she held the mug while I drank; it tasted better than any ale. Then I asked her where I was and how long I'd been out.

"You're in a safe place, and you've been out about five hours," she replied. "I'll tell them you're awake."

So I probably wouldn't be allowed to know the location. Another one of Tegson's tunnel houses. My thoughts were as weak as my muscles, and I couldn't quite put together a chain of thought, so I left it and just lay there looking up at the white ceiling. After a few moments, the door opened again and I heard the clank of metal as Teg awkwardly steered his walker through the doorway.

"Good afternoon, Marty—you're a glutton for adventures, did you know that?" He turned his walker around and dropped an attached ledge, then sat by my bed.

I smiled then winced, my cloudy thoughts reminding me of the past day. "I've lost her, Teg. Somehow I just... fucked up." Emotions welled, and I couldn't use pain to slow them. Tears leaked from under my eyelids and I turned my face away, ashamed.

"I heard some rumors of an argument," he replied, "and then you apparently dropped off the face of the earth. Did you know Justin and Zara have been looking all over for you? The colony sent word to you at their house, and they said that you had never arrived."

"I ran into Elontee as I was—she's dead, you know—Elontee?"

"Yes—we heard. It's tragic. That's the worst part of war, the deaths. But Desan looks like he'll pull through."

"I'm glad—I don't know what went wrong—"

"Maybe nothing—you can do everything right and still have people get killed."

"I guess. Am I at your house?"

"Yes—and I have to be careful what I wish for," he said with a short bark of a laugh, then explained, "You remember I hoped that you would be able to stay over a couple of days?"

I closed my eyes and smiled. "Well, I won't complain about that. There's so much I want to know." Then I remembered, and the despair hit again. "Though I don't know how much it will matter if—"

"I wouldn't give up on that too soon," Teg said. "Arguments are part of getting to know each other. I worry more about couples who never fight—I think they're still hiding parts of themselves from each other."

"Maybe—but I don't know if I can handle—" was I the only person who felt that much pain from an argument? "How do you tell the difference between the end of...everything...and just a spat?"

"Experience, I guess," Teg said. "And I've been told to let you sleep, so I'll leave you now, but I'll be back soon."

"I'm glad someone else knows where you live," I blurted, "The nurse, or doctor, whoever she is. I thought of that yesterday—what if something happened to Tegson—"

He winced and closed his eyes, and I cursed my tongue. But in a moment, he said calmly, "Yes, something could happen, especially with the risks he takes. That's why I'm hidden—did you figure that out?"

"No—I'd wondered but never remembered to ask."

"As crippled as I am, I'm not just a liability—I'm a danger. I'm sure he's made a few shitloads of enemies, and any one of them could torture me or kill me—but mostly they could use me as hostage."

"I guess it's been too long since I lived in the gangs. It would've been my first thought back then."

"Life's gotten a little better, fortunately—but there are always enemies."

"I think you could trust Justin and Zara," I said, "and I asked Ciera not to say anything—and I trust her... I trust her with that."

"I'll keep that in mind. Now sleep well and I'll talk to you later."

I lay back, slightly detached from the images floating through my mind. Those were some powerful meds. I saw the redheaded soldier's face, my thumb pressing into his eye, his agony and the feel of his hands around my throat. I saw Elontee's body, limp and inhuman, bereft of her personal spark. Justin and Zara floated up, and I felt a twinge of guilt at disappearing. Only yesterday I was feeling warmed by their joy at seeing me—how could I forget? Last night my mind had been twisted, the world seen from a weird slant. Not in my right mind. Seeing it all through a bubbly fog now, I vaguely wanted to find my right mind again. Maybe I'd never had it. With such odd thoughts, I drifted off to sleep.

* * *

I felt stronger when I woke next, able to sit and drink. Also needed to use the pot; hopefully it was under the bed. I didn't really want any assistance with that. I tried my sore leg and the stab of pain didn't keep me from standing. It was hard to bend, but I fished for the chamber pot and peed quickly in case the doctor/nurse was due back. Then I settled myself upright in bed. Most of the pain was still at bay—maybe this wouldn't keep me out of things for long.

The woman returned after a while, with a tray of food—a good-smelling stew, a glass of apple juice and some buttered bread.

"Glad to see you sitting up," she said.

"Thanks Doc—or nurse?"

"Medic. And Julia's the name," she smiled and helped me balance the tray—which had little unfolding legs—on my lap. I ate with gusto and she nodded approvingly. "Your wounds aren't serious of themselves, but you need to keep them clean and dry. Infection can come from anywhere. We don't have antibiotics out here, though I have some herbs on the wounds and I'll give you more to take later." She gave me another pain pill, and I took it gratefully.

I thought longingly of the City's meds—but were they any more than rumor? I'd never been sick enough to need them, and they could be as much of a lie as the satellites.

"Can I walk around?"

"Yes, if you don't overdo it. The more you rest, the faster you'll heal."

So after my meal, I asked for some clothes and refused her assistance in dressing, though I heeded her warning to go slow. Barefooted, I found my way down the hall to the living room, where Teg was reading in the armchair. He glanced up in surprise, and grabbed the chair's arms to lift himself, his blanket slipping down, but I told him to stay put.

"I can get to the couch, and I'll sit quietly there," I assured him.

"I'm glad you're feeling lively, but don't push it—I found that we don't heal nearly as fast as we get older." He sighed, adjusting his lap robe. "That's another one of the nasty secrets they don't tell us about getting old."

"The way I'm going, I'm not gonna make it that far."

"You didn't tell me you have a death wish."

"I don't, I think, but honestly—there are times where it doesn't seem like it's worth the effort to stay alive."

He had rested his book in his lap, now he stared at me quietly for a few minutes.

"And yet, did you notice that you still kept yourself alive?"

I looked at him, frowning. "Huh?"

"Life definitely has its shitty moments," he said, "and there were many times I wondered what it was for, but somehow, when it comes down to it, it always seems worth hanging around for a bit longer."

I remembered last night, how the pain flowing through me drove me back toward the boat, as if a part of me absolutely wanted to live, no matter what I thought I was thinking. That was a bit confusing, with all the pain meds, so I gave up on it.

"Teg, I need to know—how do I survive out here? I mean, do I have to become an apprentice or something? I'm sure there's not just some Human Assets department that hires people out here."

He laughed. "No—no Human Asses Department out here."

I thought about the differences between the City and these towns. *Laugh or cry?* "This is the fourth time I'm starting over, do you realize that?"

"Let's see—childhood, the slums, the City... and now this—yup. That's four times. And pray that it doesn't end up happening again." His sympathy was tinged with amusement.

I groaned. "No, don't tell me it's all going to completely change—let me get through this shift first."

"All right. I don't think you have to apprentice—in fact, I can think of several jobs you would be good at back—where I live."

"Thanks. But you said you'd be hanging around here for a while—how do I support myself *here*, when we don't know what's coming next?"

"Seems to me you've been pretty useful so far—that *does* count for something, you know."

I shifted on the couch, wincing at slight pain in my arm and leg. I must remember to thank Justin for his armor! "But I don't know *how* it counts—how do I know what they owe me, or what I owe them—how do we ever keep a good tally?"

"Out here, that doesn't matter quite so much," he told me. "I know in the City there are set prices for everything, and everyone feels free of debt if it hasn't been written down somewhere—but it doesn't work like that out here. We're all in each other's debt, all the time. And if we need to help someone, we do—and it all works out in the end. It may feel sloppy but it really works better."

"How can you call that working better? It sounds like a confused muddle."

"Only if you see debt and credit as the primary issue," he explained. "Out here, it's more important to grow friendships, to keep communities alive—it's not so much about what you personally own or accomplish, it's about how you belong, how you can be helpful."

"But that's what the City says—and that makes us peons," I protested.

"Because the City is *lying*—the rich bastards on top aren't doing anything for you, they're using words like patriotism and pride to get you to do their dirty work. Here, everyone's living on the same level, so we know if there are people cheating or giving lip service. And believe me, those people either shape up or they're gone." His voice was bitter and I wondered how many townsfolk he'd had to kick out.

"But Ciera's town—" I stumbled over her name, "they have prearranged deals of some kind, and I've seen how very formally they negotiate—and you have tokens or something that you count."

"Yes, there is a lot of that, especially for large deals. And between strangers. But people don't turn everything into dollars and cents. Often you're aware that you owe somebody, and you're looking for a chance to pay it back—but they are patient and you're patient, and eventually something comes up where you can even the score."

It felt very tricky to me. I knew I would at the very least have to make my own list so that I wouldn't risk forgetting. In fact, today I would ask for paper and pencil and get started on that. It might feel better to know.

"So you're saying that I might have enough credit to be able to stay out here for a bit, until I could figure out how I fit in?"

"Yes, certainly—you can stay *here* until you heal and find someplace, and that's for old time sake, and for the pleasure of chatting with you. And I'll bet your other friends know of arrangements that could be made. And in my opinion, you still have good credit left over from last night and that expedition to downtown Pittsburgh." Something in his tone of voice made me think his son had only recently given him the full story.

We were chatting about how this town differed from his current hometown when the tunnel door opened and Tegson walked in. He waved to me, and stepped aside—behind him Justin and Zara were climbing the stairs. My mouth dropped open and I glanced at Teg; he was smiling. Just like old times—he'd loved to surprise me, though back then they were mostly practical jokes.

My friends stepped inside, blinking a little, hesitating, confused. Tegson stepped behind them to the doorway, turned back and said, "Thanks again, Marty—I'll see you all in a little while. Things are busy."

Justin and Zara tensed, turning back as he closed the door, then turning to look at me and my friend. It took a moment, but I saw comprehension spread across their faces.

"So your friend really was alive," Zara said taking a step forward. She seemed tightly wound, and I wondered what Tegson had told them to get them here.

"Yes—that's where I was the morning after we went over the bridge," I explained. "I really couldn't believe it myself—but I knew the General looked familiar."

Teg began to rise awkwardly, but I stood and waved him to his seat. I limped to my friends, put my hand on their shoulders and apologized. "I am sorry—I don't know quite what came over me, but it was wrong to just vanish. And before I forget, Justin—your armor saved my life, I think. Please, have a seat on the couch, I can get us something to drink from the kitchen."

"No—I'll do it," Zara said, "just point me in the right direction. He said you were wounded pretty badly."

"Not that badly, but I'll accept," I said pointing out the kitchen door and limping back to the couch with Justin's help.

"I apologize that I cannot be a better host," Teg said, "but I am what I am. And I am Teg. Pleased to meet you."

"I'm Justin and that's Zara. We didn't even know that Teg had a father—here," Justin amended. He looked awkward, as if suspecting what it meant to find out.

"Well, Marty trusts you, so I will also," Teg said. "Though you will understand how dangerous it would be for some people to find out the General has a vulnerable family member."

"They won't find out from us!" Justin declared. He turned to me. "And I'm glad you're safe—I heard about—" he stopped. "I'm sorry."

I wasn't sure if he meant Ciera or Elontee, so I just nodded. Too awkward to discuss my personal life right now.

"What's the news outside?" I asked him. "Has anything happened?"

Zara came back in with a tray and some mugs. She set them down on the table and brought mine and Teg's. "I gave you water, Martin, because I'm guessing you're full of pain meds."

"We found out they're rebuilding the railroad as fast as possible," Justin said, "and apparently they want the ringleaders rounded up and brought to them ASAP. Teg—the General—thinks he can get most of the families off, but we have to find at least the ones they know about."

"Will that be hard?"

"I know at least a couple of them ran, but we're doing our best. Meanwhile, we got the radios working and we can even talk with Ambridge now. Makes it a lot faster, and we've set another meeting in two days, to show some goods and do some formal trading. And we sent a group up to deal with that detour from 65—try to clear the roadblock, or at the very least clear out any bandits."

"I can't imagine you'll clear all the danger," I replied. "That's a really long stretch of highway."

"True," Teg said. "If we're going to have more travel, we might have to have armed escort, or more regular patrols."

"A bit difficult, especially during this season, when we send all our extras to the fields," Justin replied. I could tell he was nervous, maybe wondering if my friend would be reporting these conversations to his son. And as much as I respected Teg, his son still seemed like a shark extraordinaire. It would take a lot to fully trust him.

"One bad bit of news," Zara said, "they've started blocking their signals inside, so we're gonna have to go in tomorrow and see what our contacts have discovered."

"I'll go!" I said immediately.

All three of them protested, but I kept insisting I was in better shape than they feared. I hoped it wasn't just the pain meds talking. But I suspected that neither Zara or Justin had enough experience of being a citizen. Especially now, it would be dangerous to try to fake it. Granted, I was probably on some watchlist or other, but I could get around that—with a bribe, if nothing else. I thought about that little certificate shop and wondered how much it would cost to get a new identity.

"Well, we'll wait till tomorrow, and see how you are," Teg said with finality. He changed the subject, asking Justin about his armor making—where he got the extra materials he sandwiched between the leather pieces.

"We found an old recycling warehouse," Justin explained, "and it had a lot of their old foil containers—lightweight, but with enough strength to slow down something coming through the leather."

"It certainly worked last night," I said and explained about the bit of shrapnel.

"We're all broke up about Elontee," Justin said, then sipped his drink to steady himself. "They've sent a crew over there, and we'll have a ceremony tomorrow. Have to be careful, of course—can't call attention to ourselves."

"She had a husband, but no children," Zara added. "Her parents are dead, but I think she had a sister and brother. And many friends, of course."

We were all silent for a moment. I remembered gang ceremonies for those killed in battle—the nighttime expeditions to "the catacombs", which were a sub-basement in an unused area. Citizens were cremated because there was no room for cemeteries anymore, but gang members were interred in concrete in the floor. I looked up at Teg, wondering if he remembered.

"Do you have—cemeteries here?" I asked.

"Something a bit more sophisticated than a basement," he replied; his quick smile told me he remembered well. "Most of us want our remains to go back to the earth, becoming fertilizer rather than toxic waste." He paused, as if about to launch into another lecture, but stopped himself.

"My son has discovered there is some army buildup," he said instead. "It looks like some of the northern planes are coming down to the old Jersey airport, and troops are being moved through South Jersey—as far as we can tell, they're focusing on Philly not Pittsburgh. We can't quite figure out why yet. Justin, that might be some of what you can find out—what's the rumor about where the battles will be."

"The hard part with that," I broke in, "is that citizens only hear what the City wants us to hear. I hadn't realized how good their lie machine was, but now I think we're the last to know."

"True," Zara said, "but out here I think the officials are a bit more open. They're not isolated in some tower, so a few of them leak information, especially if they don't approve."

"Those contacts are going to be important," Teg replied. "Luckily armies move slowly, and are fairly obvious. But I wouldn't rule out teams of saboteurs sent to make things difficult for DC or anyone aligned with it. DC is demanding more coal, wheat and chemicals for the return of the children," he added, "not that they put it that way. But under the formal language, it's clear they're going to push for more of what New York has."

"And if they don't get it?" Justin asked.

Teg shrugged. "Eventually, there would be war. Unless we can figure out a secondary supply line—say, an anonymous group that offers to trade DC what they want, having gotten it first from New York."

My jaw dropped, as I had a glimmering of what Tegson might be setting up. Would DC go for something like that? Would they allow New York to think they had given in, as long as they got the materials they needed? What a ploy! If New York caught on, we'd all be running flat out for Chicago. But it certainly fit Tegson's audacious attitude.

Teg questioned my friends about town politics, asking how the Council was handling recent pollution from coal and wood burning, and whether they were going to set limits on dangerous businesses within town limits. Again I felt overwhelmed—how would I ever get to know all the new rules?

Sooner than I expected, Tegson showed up to guide Justin and Zara home; I saw curiosity in his expression, and wondered if he resented others getting to know his father. Or did he consider this simply another channel for info?

Once they'd left, I felt fatigue wash over me, and as much as I wanted to chat, I told Teg I needed to rest again. "But I really do want to go in with them tomorrow," I told him, "the authorities are going to be more careful now and Justin didn't even know about Snitch Anonymous."

"We'll see," was all he would say.

* * *

The next morning, I felt much stronger. I refused the pain med Julia offered me, wanting to see how my body felt on its own. Teg and I had breakfast in the little kitchen—scrambled eggs, toast, a slice of natural ham. I wondered if Teg enjoyed city food at all. I was grateful my sleep had been without dreams, because waking and remembering the past few days was bad enough. But she had told me I should follow her if I figured things out—if she *meant* it, then it wasn't over. But I wasn't even close to figuring things out, whatever that entailed.

"Is Tegson really trying to set up a supply line that does an endrun around New York?"

Teg looked down at his plate; I wondered how much he really trusted me yet. Or maybe he wasn't sure of his son. "It's still very early," he replied. "We're just keeping our options open."

I remembered Ciera's rage when I mentioned options. Maybe you could never take the slum out of the slumster. "Does the town—the group, whatever—get to vote on something like that? It could be really dangerous."

He shifted uncomfortably. "That's a tough one. These groups are a real improvement over rule by the rich... but they take forever to decide things. That's one of the reasons cities turned their troops over to generals and such."

"Why is Tegson called 'the General'?"

"It's just an honorific. We don't have an army, but for years we used to call him 'general factotum'—that's a person who does a little bit of everything. And somehow it just kind of stuck." He grinned.

But that wasn't how the others saw it, I was sure. Did they believe there was an army hidden somewhere? Still too much to try and decipher.

"What about today?" I asked. "What do we absolutely need to find out?"

"We?" Teg grinned, then sighed. "But you're right—Justin doesn't have your experience, and Tegson is busy. Right now things are really critical; we can't afford to mess up. Are you sure you're up for it?"

I assured him I was; the twinges in my leg and arm wouldn't keep me from strolling around, although they might be crippling in a battle situation. I refused to think about one of those.

"All right then, Justin is going to contact one of our informants, a minor clerk in the chamber of commerce. We need to know if New York is really focused on Philly or if that's a bluff. It would be good to know how many they have conscripted—"

"I might be able to get that from my colleague at Commco—but she told me it was just sixteen to twenty-two-year-olds when I last texted her. They couldn't have finished training all those in two days."

"It might be too dangerous to contact her, not to mention they've blocked the signals, so your phone probably won't get through."

"That reminds me—Teg, *are* the satellites completely gone? Is the City really talking to Los Angeles?? Why would they fake that?"

He leaned back in his chair, sipping his coffee. "I've wondered about it; I doubt we'll know unless we find somebody in the upper echelon willing to talk. It's possible that one or two satellites are still functioning, so they might be catching a signal or two. But most of them would be dead by now. As to why they'd fake it—I think New York really wants to be in charge of whatever comeback this country makes, and one of the things you realize about power is the more you seem to have it, the more people will give it to you. So they will scramble to seem impregnable until they get to where they think they really are, if at all possible. But I'm not sure it is. Possible."

I thought about my colleagues—how many of them had any suspicion that it was fake? "What will happen to everyone living inside if they run out of supplies?" That was a dumb question, and I knew it, but part of me still didn't want to acknowledge what Ciera had been hammering at me the whole trip.

Teg shrugged. "First, the City will get more harsh and frantic in grabbing what it can reach. And then they'll start pushing people out—maybe sending them on volunteer salvage expeditions, or conscripting everybody who can toddle, limp, or crawl, and sending them toward the frontier, wherever it is. And then leaving them there. It happened in Russia, during a big war. Human nature seems to come up with the same lousy solutions time after time."

There was none of his usual amusement; this really bothered him.

Tegson poked his head in the room, startling me so that I spilled my coffee. "We're just about to go," he reported, "any last-minute instructions?"

"Yes—take Marty with you," his father said with a grin.

"Tegson's coming with us?" I bit my lip, hoping I didn't sound disappointed.

"Only as far as the first stop," Tegson replied. "Then I'm on my way further in. Seems they repaired the rail line."

"That colleague I mentioned—her name is Cheyenne Hanover. She works at Commco in DishService with me. She's hungering for a top spot and has her fingers in just about every scheme, so I'm sure she could fill you in on whatever is known over there. You can say you know me, if that will help. But I never was a player, so I doubt it will." That factoid didn't bother me as much as it used to. And maybe Tegson could help her and a few others out of danger.

"I'm not going that far this time, but good to know," he replied. "Now hurry up—I have a train to catch."

* * *

We used a different tunnel to get in, one that started in old tombs below a church, and ran a much longer distance, coming up inside what seemed to be an old transit station. Zara kept close by Justin, and I sensed she was there because she'd insisted. Letting him go off alone overnight had been too difficult, maybe. I began to understand what Ciera said about sending couples together. The transit station had boarded-up windows and the long wooden benches were thick with dust; apparently this place was still awaiting transformation into something new. Zara swept our footsteps away with a clump of wool on a stick; there were several hanging by the tunnel doorway and several more by the front door where we left, just another group of puzzling pre-Adjustment doodads if anyone poked their head in.

It was close to the noon hour, and groups of citizens were leaving office buildings, spreading out to the various cafés. A good time to be anonymous.

"Remember, if any one of us gets stopped," I said, "first thing to do is to walk away so they don't think we're together. Like we did at the hotel—walk up the block a bit and pretend to loiter, but don't immediately turn back. Give me a chance to think of something."

Tegson was a half block in front, leading us, and I took up the rear so I could watch for problems. We traveled about four blocks through the food and entertainment section, then Tegson paused to look at a theater poster. Justin and Zara caught up to him, casually turned to look for witnesses, and turned back to Tegson. Justin murmured something and Tegson swiftly ducked inside the theater. Justin and Zara kept moving and I followed, puzzled. I was starting to chafe at this "need to know" business. We stopped at a pizza place, already half full of lunchers. They queued up and I took my place four people behind them; I could see Justin looking casually around, then nodding without making eye contact. A short man in a stylish blue tunic—I refused to think of it as hospital garb—hunched over a salad in the corner. Our informant, apparently. As we picked up our pizzas and brought them to his table, my nerves were hyper alert, and I pretended to be fascinated by all of the stupid pictures on the wall, turning on my heel to glance all the way back behind us. Didn't seem like anyone was interested.

"Excuse me citizen, do you mind if we share your table?" Zara asked formally.

He gestured with apparent disinterest and returned to his salad. We sat and took several bites before Justin murmured, "Pitts or Philly?"

The man never looked at us as he muttered, "Philly—they think we're too far for DC to manage. They think it was an attempt to intimidate, to look bigger than they are." He grabbed his salad and drink and left without a backwards glance.

Justin leaned back, thoughtful. "Gives us space," he murmured. "Maybe they'll wear themselves out in Philly."

"I hope so," I responded. This pizza really was good—I would really miss synth-food. "At least it gives time for a backup plan."

We finished our meal—I looked longingly at the counter, wishing I could get another slice or two to go—and stepped out onto the sidewalk, going with the flow of pedestrians. The mild weather meant most people were strolling rather than hurrying back to their offices. Justin had mentioned he had to pick up something from Quince, so we headed towards the clothing section.

Suddenly a familiar slouch caught my eye coming out of a hardware shop—it was Geoff! I strode forward, caught up with my friends and murmured, "I just saw the guy who hijacked me. Walk around the block to the left, and I'll catch up with you. Be careful."

"*You* be careful!" Zara hissed as I sped past, crossed the street and hurried up the sidewalk until I was a step behind my erstwhile guide.

"Greetings, asshat," I said quietly. "Doing some more spying for the South? And don't even think of hollering—I'm completely legit here." He had no way of knowing I lied.

He jerked upright but didn't glance in my direction, and he kept walking. "Found your way home, did you?"

"Careful, tracker boy, I could turn you in for a reward. But I still want to know something—who contacted you first about me, and where?"

He was silent for the length of a block of old-fashioned storefronts painted in bright candy colors, the shiniest bits of pre-Adjustment crap hanging in the windows. Finally he said, "Someone I had helped out before—I'd found him an old friend—or an old enemy, I don't know or care—said there was someone who needed my services."

"Were they from Commco?"

"I met them in a back row of a very dark theater. It probably wasn't even the real contact, but in any case we wouldn't recognize each other again."

Too many people were too good at being anonymous, dammit. "Is the contract still open?"

He glanced over at me, as if tempted to lie. "No—this new stuff canceled all that," he said. "So you're free and clear, desk boy. Go back to your pixel pushing."

"Thank you, fuck you, and goodbye," I said and paused as if looking in the shop window. He kept going and at the end of the block turned right.

I crossed the street, and began to walk the other way, back toward my friends, who I could see two blocks down. I would have to be careful—walking up and down the same street a couple times often marked you as some kind of troublemaker. Without turning my head, I strained my peripheral vision and was grateful to see cameras only every other block. Either this place was just too unimportant or they had a damn good spy ring here. As Justin and Zara passed me, Justin casually dropped an old plastic pen on the sidewalk. *Good man!* I paused, bent down, picked it up and returned it to him, and we continued to stroll up the block.

"What did he say?" Zara asked.

"He's not being paid to kidnap me anymore, but he doesn't know who ordered it."

"That's the toughest thing about fighting the big guys," Justin commented. "We only get the barest scraps of information. I'll drop in quick to Quince's, and then we can go out."

I dropped back a bit and let him lead; I vaguely remembered the shop was three or four blocks north. Traffic was thinning out again as people went back to work, so we were more noticeable, but we couldn't hurry because that was noticeable too.

At the shop, Justin went in while Zara and I wandered, seemingly window-shopping, a little apart from each other; I watched the cameras and looked for Snitch Anonymous. We would have to get back soon, or risk looking like out-of-place workers. *Hurry up, Justin!* I watched a man on the other side of the street, as he paused to look in a window. I watched him glance at me twice, and then sidled over to Zara.

"Might be a tail," I muttered. "Best to go inside—stay with Justin." There was no time for more and I sidled down the street, pausing with my hand on a shop door as if to go inside, then shaking my head as if remembering something and walking more briskly, not looking back. I'd go around the block and be sure.

A moment later, a shadow loomed up from behind, and a deep voice said, "Josephus Martin Gearhart Barrister?"

Oh, shit.

33

I flinched but kept walking. The man followed and repeated my name, then said, "Excuse me citizen."

Then I turned and looked surprised. "Yes sir? Did you want me?"

"You are Josephus Martin Gearhart Barrister?"

I stepped back, astonished. "No sir. You have me mistaken." My tension would be easily explained away—no citizen wanted to be approached on the street by an authority.

"Facial recognition software has deemed that you are Josephus Martin Gearhart Barrister, and I need you to come along with me."

The man was slightly taller than me, wearing black, with black hair that looked artificial, hollow cheeks and that vulture stare that meant I was in trouble. I took a deep breath.

"With respect, sir, I am not sure who I am speaking with, and as a software technician, I can assure you that our facial recognition software is only semi-accurate at best. Can you show me the camera that identified me, sir?" I would have to give a false identity soon, but needed to find out if he had any way of checking it quickly. And it was true that recog software was shit. This was likely a bluff. Or a last kick from Geoff? Either way, I was in trouble.

Like most authorities, he looked shocked that I even questioned him. He frowned, hesitating. I couldn't give him time.

"As I'm sure you'll know, sir," I continued trumptroiding, "the penalties for false identification and arrest have been recently increased, and interception due to facial recognition software alone is no longer permitted." I forced a chuckle. "At the office, we joke that the old mugsoft cameras can usually tell if it's a male or female and the age within about 10 years. We got tired of going to court and being shot down, so we put in for the change in the law. You *are* familiar with that out here, aren't you?" My stance became more threatening. "Shall we go back to that camera? I could identify it by serial number, and let you know if it has the updated software."

Without waiting for him I walked back down the street, up toward the clothing store. Halfway there, I walked into the street and turned around slowly, looking up as if I was looking for the correct camera. That motion would certainly catch viewers' attention if anyone was watching, but I had to risk it. I pretended to find one, pointed at an alley and strode across the street. Realizing he had lost his momentum, he hurried after me.

"I can see the problem now," I called back, moving into the alley close to a grimy white videocam that most definitely wasn't a later model. I made as if to climb the jutting metal poles to reach it. The man caught up with me, stepping into the alley to take hold of my shoulder. I lashed backwards, jamming my elbow into his throat then grabbed and threw him to the ground. I clamped my hand over his mouth, rolled him face down and pressed on the neck artery point that I had learned as a last ditch trick—death or unconsciousness, always a dice-throw. My arm and leg throbbed but I ignored them, muffling a moan in the back of his jacket. After a moment, he slumped, and I dragged him by the coat along the alley, breathing thanks that there were a couple trash cans to hide him behind. Brushing myself down, I turned and limped out of the alley, forcing myself to stride across the street and toward the shop.

Justin and Zara were watching through the window and came out as I reached the shop. They had been smart enough to change clothes; Zara wore a strange hat that would prevent her face from being seen. Without speaking, I passed them and continued quickly down the street, feeling my heart trying to claw out of my chest. I shouldn't have put my friends in danger. I should've guessed there would be a watch on me—but I hadn't used a Pay Pad and had no clue they had mug-cog software out this far. *If* they did—it could have been a lucky collar. Well, if we got to the tunnel okay, this settled the question of whether I was going back to the apartment!

Twice I paused and looked in a window, so I could turn back to make sure my friends were following. Fortunately, no one else seemed interested, and we managed to reach the abandoned transit station. Zara almost forgot to wipe our footprints prints off as we hurried across the dusty floor toward the tunnel door. Once down the steps, with the door safely shut, I paused and took several deep breaths. Pain was zigzagging up my arm and leg, but not crippling—yet.

"I'm really sorry about that, Justin," I said. "I had no idea that would happen." I winced, thinking that wasn't exactly true, but pieces of it were.

"No problem," he said, patting me on the shoulder, "we're safely out of it, and we got the information we need—let's head home and you can rest again. You must be exhausted." Zara lit the lamp at the base of the stairs.

"You know—until you mentioned it, I'd almost forgotten…But it's all coming back to me now. Ow," I joked. I wasn't going to tell them the pain was definitely hollering for a med. We eased our pace as we headed through the tunnel and out through the church. Since none of us knew where Teg's house was, we'd agreed I go back to Justin and Zara's until he could send for me.

As we trudged down the street, I swore I could *feel* the lack of cameras, the lack of spies—walking shouldn't be a crime! It was like a layer of tension I hadn't even known I was carrying lifted. Sure, there were curious bystanders—but they didn't work for some black-ops department, and they wouldn't be paid to snitch us out. Just a couple blocks away, my would-be nabber was waking up, with any luck, or whoever sent him was realizing he was late. Somebody would be scrambling, reports would be fed into the system, and my name would pop up on various watch lists. Unless that efficiency also was a lie. Maybe New York wasn't as powerful as it pretended to be. And their power stopped at the Wall, in any case.

Back at the house, Zara made me lie on the couch as she made coffee. Justin brought out a blanket which he draped over me, and I protested they didn't have to fuss.

"This was all my fault—I ran afoul of the nasties somehow," I said.

"No—we all run that risk inside," Justin said, bringing over coffee and sitting near me. "I remember a close call I had about six years ago, before I got here. They were swearing I was someone else, and I had no way to prove I wasn't. That was a terrifying moment." But he seemed to enjoy telling it now. By the table, Zara frowned her dislike of war stories. I wondered how many times he'd worried the hell out of her.

"The Ambridge group should be down this afternoon," she said, changing the subject. "Siegfried, Rom and Astrid will be back, and someone called Pippin."

"Pippin?! Great! You'll like him," I enthused. Would he be bringing news of Ciera? Would the group have heard? But of course they would—look how fast Jalisa knew. I wondered what the group consensus was. Damn, it would be tough to live where everyone had an opinion about my love life.

I took a nap after that, and was awakened by my friends as they went out for the trade meeting.

"See if you can bring Pippin back—I'd like to talk with him," I said. My curiosity about the meeting wasn't as strong as my need to rest, so I let them go.

It was dinner time before they returned, with Pippin bringing up the rear, towering over petite Zara. He hailed me with enthusiasm and I moved to let him sit on the couch. Now that I could know, I was reluctant to find out—good news or disaster?

He didn't give me much time to worry. "Sounds like you two had a bust up," he said. "but from what I hear, she's telling the gals that you need to get your head on straight—and that's a sure sign she's left the door open." He smiled and tilted his head. "You're like that owl and the pussycat—not exactly the same background. It's gonna take some work. Have you been hurt?" It was like he just noticed.

I explained to him a bit about the expedition, how I had thrown myself into it just after our fight. "A stupid thing to do, I guess," I said. "When there's too much coming at me too fast, I just kind of flail."

"We all do," he replied. "we all do."

He was quiet for a minute and I wondered what memory had been dredged up. Justin and Zara were busy in the kitchen, and I was distracted, wondering how I would pay back all of the meals they had given me. Was it meal for meal? Or could I pay back in another way? How much was friendship, how much was trade? I sighed, and Pippin misread it.

"Come back with us and talk to her," he urged me. "Don't let it dangle too long. I know you like her." He grinned like a boy hiding a fast-fingered sack of cookies. "And she likes you—it's a good start, and worth finding out if you can push past the rest of it. We can't choose our starting points," he continued, "but it's up to us where we end up. And that's all I'll say." He slapped his hands on his thighs and nodded. Then he got up and went to the kitchen to help.

Over dinner, I found out that Ambridge had sent a patrol south of the river, and also into Ohio to explore for any signs of a new migration.

"With those strange accents, they'll have a hard time fitting in—that makes our job easier," Pippen said around a mouthful of turnips.

"I'm surprised they haven't thought of that," Justin commented. "If they come up here again, they had better have enough staying power. Any half-assed wave can wash over a beach."

I remembered the first time he'd said that—I had just met them, and was focused on getting information. He'd seemed like an old man, respected but no adventurer. It was funny how people looked different after you got to know them.

"And it looks like they're willing to trade for some of our glassware, pottery—" Zara said.

"And shoes! Don't forget shoes!" Justin cut in with a wink—obviously he meant armor.

"Justin—" I glanced over at Pippin, then continued, "if I wanted to stay here for a while—in town, I mean—how would I arrange it? I have no idea what my list of debts looks like now, and though Teg said I could stay with him for now, I might eventually want to set up something more... permanent." I glanced over at Pippin again. "After... a few things are settled, I mean."

They all grinned, apparently knowing exactly what I meant. I felt like a prize display fish! But I couldn't bring her back here if I didn't have a place for us. If by some miracle she still was interested, I wanted to show her I had something to offer.

"I think you're in credit territory, at this point," Justin replied, "and as for housing—we'll look into it. I'm sure there's something."

"Elontee's funeral is this evening, just after dark," Zara said. "Will you be able to come, Martin?"

"Absolutely. I owe it to her."

"I'm sure she'd understand if you—"

I shook my head firmly. There were some things you just had to do.

So as dusk thickened in the streets and alleys, we dropped Pippin off at the colony and kept heading northwest until we arrived at a hilly forested area. I was a little nervous about walking in the dark through such wilderness, but Justin and Zara proceeded as if it were daylight on the main street. At least the path was wide and well-defined.

"They go down to the dark, so we do it in dark," Zara explained.

"Also, we hide the bodies from the bone tribes," Justin added. He explained many desperate groups were digging up cemeteries to get bones for fertilizer. "Most fields are in pathetic shape."

It seemed a morbid way to deal with it. Eventually the path opened out into a clearing, and I saw at least 30 others gathered off to our right. When we joined them, I could see a deep hole had been dug, and a white-shrouded form lay on a pallet next to it, draped with a brilliant red cloth, with several clumps of daffodils, snowdrops and even branches of holly leaning against it.

I recognized many of the soldiers holding torches, standing stiffly at attention, a stance that brought back sharp memories of Grandma Barrister's memorial service. They stood at the corners of the bier, forming an honor guard, as others filed past, pausing a moment, some dropping flowers, some touching the body. We joined the queue and I gave silent thanks to the woman who had been so brave and zestful. Then I joined the mourners on the other side of the grave, as Chala stepped to the head of the corpse and began to speak quietly. She acknowledged Elontee's service to the community, and her value as a wife and friend. It was painful to hear her history, knowing that this young woman wouldn't have a chance to make any more.

"The General sends his profound regrets that he can't be here," Chala said. "But as we all know there are many urgent tasks right now."

The group murmured agreement. I looked around and didn't see Desan. *Must remember to ask about him.* His body could of been lying beside Elontee. Or mine. It suddenly hit me how close I'd come. She was younger than me, and already gone. I had no reason to believe I'd live to be Justin's age—or even Teg's. And what if I'd been crippled? Who'd take care of *me*? They couldn't ship me back to Long Island... Such gloomy thoughts weighed on me during the ceremony and burial, where we took turns shoveling dirt into the grave.

Julia the medic tapped me on the shoulder after it was over. "Teg sent me to get you," she said. I asked for a moment and found Chala in the group.

"Thanks again for getting us—the rest of us—back safe," I said, "and how is Desan? Do you know?"

"Mending slowly," she said. I saw tears sparkling on her cheeks. "Medic said the bullet missed major organs, but he'll be off his feet for months."

"I'll be staying in town." *True for most definitions of true.* "Let Justin or Aida know how he's doing, so I can hear. And maybe I can visit after a bit."

She nodded and I found Justin and Zara, thanked them, and followed Julia to the tunnels.

34

The first thing on my mind when I woke the next morning was whether to join the party going back to Ambridge that afternoon. On the one hand, I needed to know one way or the other; on the other hand, I needed something set up here in case I could talk her into joining me. The thought that it could have been me at that funeral nagged. If she was gonna occupy most of my waking thoughts, I wanted her near me. I'd promised Justin I would attend a town hall meeting today, and Teg wanted my opinion on it in any case. Apparently negotiations with the City had been successful, as long as the rebel leaders were turned over, and Asrah had sent word they had located the last one. So the ceremony and formal agreement—as much as any secret agreement could be formally acknowledged—was to take place around noon. I would have time to attend that and still join Pippin and the others for the trip back. I wished fervently for a few days of quiet, but *if wishes were horses, then beggars would ride* as my uncle used to say. Perhaps if I got to Justin's early, I could work out a housing arrangement with him—much as I loved visiting with Teg, it was awkward, to say the least, not knowing where I exactly was.

"Morning Marty, how are you feeling today?" Teg was frying up some eggs, leaning awkwardly against the counter, his walker just behind him.

"Almost healed," I lied, "and—I need to go back up to Ambridge today, for a bit. After the meeting."

"Gonna bring her back?"

"I hope. I still don't understand how I blew it, but like that part of me that knew I wanted to live, I guess there's a part that knows I need to be with her." I rubbed my beard; it still felt strange after a week. And what a week! No, almost two weeks—13 days, to be exact. I brought some plates to the table. "Teg, can I ask what your overall plan is? I mean—what will I be bringing her back to? That's fair to ask, isn't it?"

"More than fair. But hard to answer." He handed me the plate of eggs and maneuvered himself to the table. Coffee and mugs were already there. "It's not a plan so much as riding the curl—do you remember me telling you about the people who stood on boards and rode waves to the shore?"

"Yes, I didn't believe you then—and I'm not sure I believe you now." I grinned at him. "Skateboards are one thing, but riding on crashing waves? That's not possible."

"Didn't they ever show you any surfing movies? There used to be dozens of them. No matter. The idea is it takes a moment to moment adjustment to the situation—no amount of theory is gonna get you that skill. We've been practicing, if you want to call it that, on a small scale where I live, knowing that sooner or later the status quo would shift. There are so many variables that you can't plan for all of them, you just have to practice your best response."

"But how do you know it's the best response?" My head was spinning a bit—it was too early in the morning for philosophy.

"You start to recognize patterns, ways that things unfold given various combinations. For example—the City has a habit of making a big showy slap-down, and leaving it at that. So that's probably what they're gonna do this time. They'll show off the rebel leaders, hang them in some particularly gory fashion, and tell the populace that they've handled the problem."

I nodded. I understood that pattern. "But—how do you keep track of all the things you need to keep a town or city or country going? It's a little too late to find out that you've run out of something when it's gone."

"Excellent observation. And that's what happened to them—Before. Even if the flare hadn't happened, the system would've fallen apart. They were running out of oil, certain rare metals and fertilizer, among other things—and they kept pretending they weren't."

"Maybe they didn't realize it," I said. "I can't begin to think how you would keep track of every little thing and how it's connected."

"That's one reason your lady's town tries to keep things simple—the fewer things needed, the easier it is to see how they interact."

"Okay—that makes sense too. But *this* place seems a lot more complex. Weirdly, it almost seems more complex than the City."

"That's because the City has hidden most of the details. They deliberately keep you from knowing what it takes to run the place, because they don't want you interfering."

"We still vote on things, you know."

Teg started laughing so hard he almost choked on his breakfast. "Marty, you are so naïve! You never get to vote until they've already made the decision, set up the people they want in power, and arrange the ballot so that there really isn't much choice. And on the off chance the people vote wrong—who do you think counts the ballots?"

I felt my face get red; would I ever get past the vast number of things I didn't know?

"You still haven't really said what you're hoping to do," I replied. "Are you setting up another country? Will you try to get control over the East Coast eventually?"

He grew thoughtful. "In a nutshell, we want to have the freedom to set up this area in the best way we can, and to trade with whatever other cities or states are still viable. We realize that means we have to defend ourselves if they come after what we have—but we also know that the bigger an area gets, the more difficult it is to run. The only reason a country as big as the United States could even *exist* was because they had almost free energy. They could fly across the country in a couple hours, and they could talk instantaneously anywhere in the country—anywhere in the world! Because of oil. Oil gave them the ability to build the other power—nuclear plants and the solar plants, and the wind turbines. Ever seen pictures of those? It looked like they were trying to build all the way up to the moon! I heard it's been really hard finding people to climb up that high to dismantle them, even with all that valuable metal. Anyway—you can't have something that big without that kind of power, and it's gone. So we're hoping to set up this area so that it gives every person a decent life. That's harder than it sounds, but I think we're heading in the right direction. Does that answer your question?"

I sighed and turned my palm up. "I don't know—I don't think I have your gift for theory. I was thinking more in practical terms, like what kind of job I could get, whether or not there'd be a lot of crime, and how good the food supply was."

He reached over and patted me on the shoulder. "There's lots of work in this area, there's less crime than in the City, and as long as I have food, you'll have some."

Julia poked her head through the kitchen door and asked if I had time to have my wounds looked at. Afterward, she led me through the tunnel, as I tried to find familiar objects in the maze to guide me if necessary. There was a tension in the air as I came out in a familiar house and walked over to their place—emotion that was being suppressed, the passersby alternately anxious or fuming. Was this about the rebel roundup? Maybe some people were still either on the fence or feeling rebellious, and not everyone was happy about turning the ringleaders over to the City's tender mercies. I couldn't see any difference between those who were anxious and those who were angry—no ethnic clues or different dress. If the friction got more severe, it could be really tough to know allies from enemies in this town, I thought. I picked up my pace, and got to the house just as Justin was leaving.

"I wanted to drop by my workshop before we went," he said, "you haven't seen it yet, have you?"

I leaned inside to holler hello to Zara, then followed Justin along streets that were becoming more familiar. There was a bush at the end of their block just beginning to bloom pink, and around the corner, a little man with a face like a garden gnome sat on his stoop, whittling. We passed the warehouse and Zir was in the doorway—he waved and said his brother had already left for the meeting. We strolled through the food district and the metalworking, and finally he gestured to the left.

"Almost there," he said.

Justin's workshop was in the leather district, and the stench from tanning leather was sharp in the morning air. It was an ordinary storefront, but inside there was an amazing amount of light, and Justin pointed to the large light tube installed in the ceiling.

"Put that in myself," he said, "makes a huge difference and keeps me from going blind with the fine stitching." He showed me the work benches, one for cutting leather, one for stitching—wooden shoe lathes were lined up on a shelf behind the combination seat and angled workbench. The cut leather on the bench—tan, dark brown, black—were all vaguely shoe-shaped.

"Apprentices won't be here till this afternoon—they're from Ambridge, did you know? I'm letting them work on shoes first—once I get to know them, I'll teach them about the armor."

I nodded then switched to the subject that was more pressing. "I want to go back up with the group today, and I'd like to have some place ready to bring Ciera back, if she agrees. Though I'm probably being over-optimistic."

"A pessimist like you? Overly optimistic? I doubt it." He grinned to take the sting off. "I know women are really hard to figure out—there are times when I have no clue what sets Zara off. You just have to do your best, maybe apologize even if you don't know what you did—and just keep appreciating her. That's an old dog's advice."

"So you met Zara out here? How long—five years, you said, right?"

"That's right—five years ago I was really flailing—run out of the town I'd gotten to know, coming to this jumble of merchants and smugglers—you know about the smugglers, right?" He'd sat down at the stitching bench, absentmindedly turning a piece of leather in his hand.

I hadn't had much time to think about it, but of course smuggling would be part of the whole thing, so I nodded.

"So I met this saucy woman with a wonderful flair for gold and silver—I'd been sent to her because what I had been able to bring out of my town was mostly gold and silver, and I needed to trade it for a place to stay and some food. We got to talking, and found we both had the same passion for...well, I call it justice—for changing the City's obnoxious suction on its surroundings. She was cautious, but eventually told me about the group who was trying to make subtle changes, to get the City wanting enough goods that they would be willing to cut us some slack. She's a very brave woman, did you know that?"

"Yeah, I could tell—she keeps going, despite her fear."

"And she's been a messenger in some really dangerous situations—I hate even to think about them," he said. He rubbed his mustache furiously. "Last year we agreed we wouldn't go on missions without each other anymore—that's why she was so upset when I went with the General over the bridge into the Haunt. But what could I do? He's not exactly someone you say no to. I know you're closer to them—"

"Only to his father," I cut in, "I still don't totally trust Tegson. He's smart, and he's really skilled, but he also doesn't seem to care that he puts his assistants in mortal danger."

"Oh, I think he cares—but he really believes that the big picture is more important than one life. He's put his own on the line many times."

"I don't doubt that—I recognize a daredevil when I see one."

"Takes one to know one, I suspect," Justin said with a slight smile.

Me? A daredevil?? That was so far from true! I was shocked at the impression I'd given him.

"About the place to live—Zara is working on it today, so drop over after this meeting and she should have some details."

I thanked him profusely, and he gathered up a few things before we headed out to the meeting.

* * *

It was held in a building very close to the Wall portal—apparently City representatives would come through with some vehicle to transport the rebel leaders back inside. It was an old warehouse, cinderblock walls decorated with fading stylized letters that spelled out nothing legible. Inside, some metal support pillars had been fenced in with thick metal mesh to make holding pens. The faint smell of cattle and a few leftover turds indicated an auction house or similar. The pens were empty except for a group of six men hunched on wooden benches within one locked stall. I felt a pang of pity—the poor idiots probably had thought they were doing some good for their town, trying to get some power back. And now their fellow citizens had turned on them—but although idiocy wasn't a crime according to City statutes, sometimes it came very close—the rebels hadn't bothered to consult with their townsfolk and had completely overestimated their own abilities. That was fatal in the slums—and likely so in this case. I noticed there were no women or children in the building—so the families either had been forbidden to say goodbye, or had done it earlier. I was more used to slumlords dishing out punishment quickly. This felt cold, although I knew it was necessary.

Justin walked me over to Aida, Asrah and a group of five men and a woman whom I didn't recognize.

"Three of these are stand-ins. The rest of us will be in a back room, just in case. The 'negotiators' are skilled traders from local towns who we've paid to help—the City won't find them here often again," he said. I told him I thought that was wise.

It looked like they did a good job of picking the clichéd middle-class burghers, two slightly paunchy, one balding. Exactly what the City would expect to find in the boondocks. The noise of new arrivals made me turn, and I was startled to see Pippin walk through the door. He had a stranger with him, a sandy-haired man with a stub nose and a hangdog look. Pippin waved, more solemn than I'd ever seen him. He walked over to the locked pen and when it was opened, pushed the man inside. So—another ringleader, one from Ambridge?

"The meeting's taking place in a much nicer room next door," Justin told me, "once the terms are agreed on—and they're almost settled—a formal handover happens." He looked anxious, darting glances to the door and back to the pen. "I don't know what happened to the other," he murmured. He turned to me. "We were kinda hoping you would keep an eye on the meeting from the back room, just let us know if they're trying to pull anything sneaky. We have a one way mirror, a small one, installed—found it in a bank and we figure they won't think we're that sophisticated."

"They probably won't," I said, inwardly cringing at once again being considered an expert. Didn't they realize I was only a peon in there? It had become glass-clear to me that I knew next to nothing about what the City was really doing. "And you can almost guarantee they're gonna try to pull something sneaky—I'll try to figure out what it is."

At some unseen signal, the group of representatives headed toward a door in the far wall, and we followed, joining up with Pippin as we went through.

"Morning, Martin—are you heading back with us today?"

"Yes," I replied, "but I want to stop by Justin's and see about one thing after this meeting."

"Prime time," he replied. "We've got a few extra bikes to be brought back. Handy to have one more body." But his usual banter lacked joy. I could tell he was as bothered at this as I was.

We walked out of the warehouse, crossed a narrow alley and entered a nondescript building. At the end of a short hall, we filed into a tiny back office poorly lit by a tiny skylight. It would be cramped with all of us in here. I walked over and inspected the one way mirror. It was scratched up—I would have to be careful standing behind it so movement wouldn't give me away. But it would suffice. The room beyond was bigger, well lit, with an elegant sidetable that held a bowl of flowers, and upholstered chairs arranged in rows facing each other. The three actors went out to the front room, and after several minutes, they received a delegation of two smartly-dressed City representatives, who were flanked by four hefty bodyguards who stood on either side of the front door. The reps seated themselves. The formal body language, semi-bows and slow exchange of papers along with the poker-face expressions didn't make it easy for me to pick up much. *I wish they'd stop depending on me.* I wish I could read the documents. I strained to listen to their discussion, but too often it was obscured by the thick wall. I saw a City rep shake his head sharply, frowning, almost rageful. One of our reps stood and began to gesture, but both City reps glared and shook their heads *no*. Something was definitely wrong. Before I could step back and report, that rep came back to the office.

The man was dripping sweat like it was summer—he glanced back and forth, his shoulders hunched, then he looked helplessly at us. "I don't know why," he said, "but if we don't have eight leaders to turn over, they say the deal is off. I told him they were only seven, but he doesn't believe me." His stricken look matched ours, as we all realized what that meant.

"What happened to the other one??" Justin demanded.

A thin balding man spoke up. "We thought we had him, but this morning we found the house he'd been held in was broken into, and he was gone."

"Has anyone rounded up his family?"

"Gone too. I doubt we'll ever see them again."

"Maybe we could…bring out a...dead body?" someone suggested.

"Don't know if we can afford to take the chance," Justin said, his voice grating and dry. He looked 10 years older. He kept taking deep breaths, and I was panicky—was he going to offer himself?

"I'll go—if they have their numbers and they go away, that's good for everybody."

I swiveled and found it was Pippin speaking! "No…" I breathed, "no…they need you and...you're not a rebel! They'll find that out!"

"Oh, I'm sure I can make something up, maybe talk to the others," he said calmly. It was like he was suggesting running to the store.

I stared at him, my brain refusing to come up with any response. The others shifted uncomfortably, looking back and forth, but I could sense the relief on their faces and in their stance. *Let someone else go.*

"Pippin—you *can't*! You didn't have anything to do with this!" I finally blurted.

He gently led me into the hall and put his hand on my shoulder. "Sometimes, lad, the needs of the others are more important. I'm an old man, and if this keeps war away for another couple years, that's certainly better than anything an old man can do in those years."

I gripped his elbow and shook him a little. "But you don't know—this could fail and they'll come back for someone else!"

He smiled ruefully. "Sometimes you just have to take the risk—there are no ironclad guarantees. Hey, we're all red shirts, in the end. Even if it doesn't work, I'm satisfied that I tried. Tell Rom and Astrid—they'll know who to tell." He patted me on the shoulder and walked back to the group.

"Come on—let's go before they get impatient," he said.

I watched Pippin and the balding man head back out to the holding pen, my mind refusing to comprehend. The rep returned to the front room. *They'll reject him, he'll be back in a moment*, my mind kept repeating. Nobody was looking at anyone else, everyone caught in their own misery and guilt. I felt sick—I couldn't look through the one-way mirror. I stumbled out the back door, and puked in the alley. *He'll be back—he must.* I leaned against the door frame. What would I tell Ciera and the others? In the silence I could hear my own labored breathing as my thoughts flailed around, disconnected. Suddenly I heard the rattle of the cage cart they had brought to carry the prisoners through the Wall. The squeal and rumble as metal grated on metal sounded like the shriek of tortured victims. I stumbled to the front of the alley, sagged against the wall as I watched the horse-drawn cart follow the sleek black car carrying the reps and their bodyguards through the huge gates waiting to close ponderously behind them. Pippin's head and shoulders were clear through the bars until the doors swung shut.

35

He was one of the Survivors, one of the valuable people who could tell us how it used to be—wasted in the crushing maw of the military "intelligence." Only three days ago I was sorting clothes with him, hearing his memories of growing up with the machines, blithely ignorant of the upcoming chaos. I thought of him speaking calmly to the group, and helping me and Ciera—dammit, there wasn't anyone like him! I was brushing tears away, only half aware of them.

After a moment my gaze, which was aimed unseeing at the distance, gradually focused on a blond man walking up the street—Tegson coming to check that his plan was working. *Damn him! Damn him to the lowest hell!!* But it wasn't his fault—Pippin had chosen of his own free will—and I didn't understand why, but I knew it was true. It was no different than if he had jumped up and stopped a bullet. Only it seemed so much more...deliberate.

Tegson watched me as he walked up, cocking his head to the side in mute question. I had a sudden blaze of crazy panic and rebellion like when I leapt over Jamaica Joe and threw myself on little Ganga, taking the clubbing on my back and legs. *No!* No—I could *not* let this happen!

"Teg—General! We have an emergency!" I ran toward him. His expression didn't change except to be slightly more watchful. I quickly explained about Pippin, and almost grabbed his arm, but pulled back. "I know a way to get him out, a way that will keep them from coming after someone else. But I need your help."

"A cunning plan?" he asked quietly. "Do we get to see the famous Marty in action?" He was probably mocking, but I brushed it aside.

"I've done something similar before—I need to get to that shop that made the certificates—can you get me there again? I'll owe you."

He glanced past me and I turned, but we were still alone on the street. "It sounds dangerous," he said, as if he didn't fly a little plane held together with wire and spit, “It will risk an important team member—me. And you too,” he added.

I took a deep breath—this could be suicidal, but I was past caring. “Anything you want—name it—and I’ll pay it later. I know I can get us back out, and Pippin with us—but we *have* to hurry. The further in they get, the harder it will be.”

He watched me for a moment, the beginnings of a smile barely touching his lips. Then he gestured with his hand. “Lead on, MacDuff,” he said.

Confused, I pushed off all thoughts but the plan, leading him down the street that led to the tunnels.

“I don’t know the way from the tunnel to the shop, and besides they might not let me into the tunnel alone.” It occurred to me that I could take Justin instead, but Tegson could get out more easily if something happened. And part of me wanted a very dangerous man as my backup for this. The audacity of it made me tremble, so I pushed everything away except the next step.

Tegson easily got us through the gatekeeper and we ran down and through the tunnel, emerging carefully into the back room of the library, which was open today, forcing us to stroll through the two rooms and out the door.

“It’s five blocks, then a left, then right and three blocks,” Tegson murmured, strolling swiftly beside me, then dropping back, then overtaking me, as if he were taking in the sights. He seemed as comfortable inside as outside, and I wondered how many times he had made this trip.

I was probably walking faster than was prudent, but I knew that wagon was heading straight to the prison and we had to catch it before it got there. I watched the few cameras on their slow swivel, yes—they were set up as badly as some areas of the City.

“Slow for a moment,” I murmured, “then in a moment pick up your pace—and we’ll be in between cameras. They are aligned just badly enough to avoid being seen, if you get the right pace.”

“Interesting…” Tegson said, not turning his head toward the camera. I could almost believe he had mastered the body language that would ensure none of the auto-triggers would be set off; I hoped I was managing that.

We got to the shop and I rushed to the counter, grateful there was no one else there. The bushy-browed man, Mackey, looked at me suspiciously, glanced over my shoulder and twitched like he’d been hit with a live wire.

“What can I do for you, sir?” he purred.

"I need a certificate and a badge," I said, grabbing a blank piece of paper and a pen and sketching out what I needed. "I should have more than enough credit to get it." I put my hand on the pay pad and read him my bank balance—"will that be enough? I need it *immediately*." Would the pad trigger an alarm? I couldn't think about it.

He glanced from me to Tegson, who was lounging against a blanket shelf. Either the huge amount or my urgency got through to him—without saying anything he turned, grabbed his camera, snapped my picture and worked his little machine, and I jiggled from one foot to the other as the authorization took shape. In my mind, I was watching the wagon rattling down the streets, praying they'd be arrogant enough to slow it and show the dumb citizens the dangers of crossing the authorities. Finally, after an eternity, he handed me a slightly warm piece of paper and the plastic card etched with the supposedly un-reproducible official stamp and my face. With a few buttons, I transferred my entire balance to his account, hoping for his sake he routinely washed all transactions. I raced out of the shop, not checking to see if Tegson was after me.

I stopped and took a breath, trying to picture where to go—in a normal town, it would be down 10 blocks and over five. I glanced at the cameras, altered my pace and as fast as I could manage, headed toward the jail. The last thing I needed was an image of a man running down the street to come to the attention of whoever watched those infernal videos. On the other hand, the videos wouldn't matter if we got there too late.

"We have to keep moving," I said as Tegson stepped closer. I picked up my pace, clutching my card and striding like an official. The few citizens we encountered simply stepped aside. This must be how government officials felt—their power pushing forward ahead of them, leaving peons in the dust. The streets were emptying out again after the noon rush. I tensed as a pair of riders on sleek brown horses trotted by, their jackets standard police-issue, but they didn't even glance over.

I could see the bulk of the prison towering four stories over the area, and I craned to hear that weird wagon, catching my breath as the squeak and rattle finally came echoing down a side street. Glancing around, seeing no one, I broke into a dead run.

The cart was a block away from the prison; the reps' car was probably already at the hotel. I raced up, grabbed the reins of the horse and shoved my badge into the driver's face.

"Stop this crate, asswipe!" I shouted, "Open up the back—you nearly cost us vital information, you bit-brain!" I stepped back and unfolded the form, flashing it at him as I groused, "I don't know about you shit-for-brains—you keep trying to do intelligence, but you just don't have the gray cells. Hurry *up*!" I glared and hovered as the startled driver—a rumpled old man with gray tufts of hair sticking out like a half-blown dandelion—blinked a couple times, looked from me to Tegson, possibly picking up the General's dangerous aura, then slid off the seat and stumbled around to the back. I risked a glance at the prison; there seemed to be no porters waiting outside. But there were cameras on two corners and I knew we only had minutes.

"That one—*that* one! Get him out here!" I ordered, pointing at Pippin. The other prisoners had never looked up in the warehouse, so I wasn't in danger there. Pippin's jaw dropped, and he drew back—fortunately, a normal response under the circumstances.

"I'm...I'm not supposed to touch them, sir—I'm just the driver, sir. Only jailers can touch them, sir." He was trembling beside the back door.

"What I say *goes*, dumdroid! Look at this card! You get who I am? Now *move* it!"

The driver climbed in, putting keys into Pippin's manacles. I almost pushed him aside and did it myself, but that would be out of character. At this point I was shaking and had to hold my breath to prevent it from getting worse. I poured all of my panic into rage, letting years of habit work their magic.

"*Move* it, bastard! You think I'm doing this for my *health*?? I got a deadline and you're in my way! What's your operator code?" I realized I was making the driver fumble—slowing him down. I backed off, as he finally removed the chains and exited the cart, with my friend following.

"Thank you. Fine," I spat out, shoving the paper into the driver's shaking hand. "Lucky for you I caught you. Next time, *dammit*, call us and don't take this on your own *stupid* selves." I grabbed Pippin by both wrists, jerked them behind him, turned him so we both were at a bad angle to the cameras and pushed him along the street. "Let's go, Sonny boy," I told him. I didn't wait to see what Tegson was doing, just moved as fast as I could to the nearest corner, continuing the pretense for about two buildings, then dropping his wrists and grabbing his elbow. It'd taken maybe five minutes total. I think I staggered as the haze of panic finally broke through the anger—I could feel ringing in my ears.

"Quick—we have to get out of here really fast," I told Pippin, not daring to look in his face. I gulped breath, forced my emotions back into their box, willing myself into numbness until it was safe. I glanced back and Tegson was within three steps, grinning broadly.

"I think we have to risk walking together," I told him, "because I don't want to risk separating right now. Just try to look as normal as possible." That almost forced a giggle from me; we had to get somewhere safe before I broke down.

"I know a quicker way," Tegson said.

Of course he would know of other tunnels—I hadn't even thought of that. I nodded to my friend, then followed the General along new streets, going in the direction of the Wall, praying that the cameras weren't suddenly being aimed to find escapees. The walk back was a blur, but we must've done it right, because we got to the bricked-in line of buildings without incident. Tegson trotted up the steps of a rowhouse painted industrial gray, and led us inside.

"It's empty, it will be okay from here on," he said. Patting me on the shoulder, he added, "that was damn good work. And I don't say that often. You got a gift, Marty."

I was shaking too hard to answer, so I just nodded. I finally looked up at Pippin, feeling the tears well in my eyes. Brushing them away, I gripped his hand, and said, "I'm sorry, I... I think you're too important to the group to lose. They won't come back after us—the papers were official. You've just been 'disappeared' into black ops."

"Is that like the Men in Black?" Pippin asked. He was pale, and I thought I saw a few tears.

"Something like that," I said. It was still too raw for me to smile about, but the smiles would come later.

* * *

The meeting with the group was a blur—I was shaky with delayed panic, barely noting the surprise and exclamations of the others. Fortunately, Tegson's presence quashed any of their concerns about consequences. He reassured them I had taken care of it well. This would make me even more an expert in their eyes, but *c'est la guerre* as Uncle Rory would say. He murmured to me that he'd bring his father a report and let me head out early. As

Pippin turned to leave to the colony, I grabbed his elbow instinctively, then dropped it, slightly ashamed. I assured him I would be there within the hour to join the trip up. Justin and I were silent for most of the walk; I could tell he felt really guilty and I didn't know what to say.

"It was his choice, you realize," I said finally. "I know that."

"Yeah, but we were the ones who screwed up." His voice was bitter. "But we'll find out who was responsible, I promise."

"It...it occurred to me this morning that if the town splits over this, it would be really hard to know friends from enemies—that could get really messy. Maybe it's better to be united against the City and the south."

"Maybe," was all he said.

Our expressions as we walked through the door caused Zara to drop a plate on the table.

"What happened?? You both look like death!"

Justin hurried over and hugged her, and I assured her that things were fine "—it just got a little shaky for a while, but it worked out."

"Yeah—thanks to Martin again," Justin said. "He ran back inside after Pippin, who'd volunteered to be the last rebel leader after some asshole let Rodney get away!"

Zara looked at me from within the cradle of Justin's arms; her eyes wide. Several emotions flashed across her face, and she finally said, "I guess I can't really let you out of my sight for a minute—either of you!"

"I didn't go, and I wasn't in trouble—though I should've been," Justin said, still bitter.

"It's done, and it worked out okay—so let's forget about it." I said with false joviality. I'd have nightmares for a while. "Have you—have you found any room for me to rent, or however it works?"

"There's a brownstone on the next block," Zara said, slowly unwinding herself from Justin, "we've fixed it up a bit, though it still definitely needs more. The way things work around here," she explained, "is that all abandoned properties technically belong to the town, and so the Town Council has the right to award them to people for services, or in trade—sometimes just for fixing it up." She paused, watching me.

I was having a hard time catching her drift. "Are you saying a *house* might be available? But how would I pay for it? Nobody can afford to buy a single *room* in the City, let alone a whole brownstone."

"Well, maybe they have fewer vacancies," Justin said, "but we still have plenty, and we're always looking to attract good workers and good townsfolk. I can't speak for the Council, but after today…" He finally smiled. "And we'd be happy to cede our partial claim in favor of you two. Good neighbors are important."

I was dumbfounded—a whole house—just for us? And… somehow not costing me? That part was unbelievable, but there had been so many crazy things out here, maybe even *that* was true.

"We'll speak to Aida," Zara said, "if you're interested, that is. There are taxes that townsfolk pay—for specific projects and maintenance of the infrastructure we have, such as it is. But you'll be able to afford it. Ciera's expertise in solar would be useful here, and Justin always needs help, and so do many others, if your friend Teg doesn't already have plans for you."

I thought about Teg's invitation to live up north, eventually. But I wanted to stay here, where things seem to be coming together. And they could probably use me as a spy on the inside—Tegson had been impressed, apparently. I smiled.

"This is all too much, but I thank you, and if I'm not saying anything, it's just because..."

"We understand," Zara said, patting my hand. "We'll let you think about it. Would you like to look at it now?"

I nodded dumbly; all this was unreal, super bright like a mu-vid. We walked around the block to a rowhouse very similar to theirs, but on the end of a threesome. The bricks were chipped and rain-darkened; the door elegantly carved in arched and rectangular panels, with bleached red paint flaking over black. Inside, instead of their large open front room there was a tiny entry, with a door on the right and a narrow hall running back.

"We've taken care of the roof and any leaking windows, but we never got to opening up the ground floor," Justin commented, opening the door and showing me a square room with a large fireplace and graceful molding along the ceiling. The wood floor was scratched and unpolished, looking like that hotel where carpets had been removed and nail boards left. But there were windows on two sides and the room had such a graceful design I could immediately picture Ciera sitting there.

"Would she like this?" I turned and asked Zara. "You've met her—you probably know better than me."

She smiled and nodded. “Yes. That’s what made me think of this place—I think she would like it a lot.”

“The roof would work for solar panels,” Justin added.

I eagerly followed them through the rooms: the hall leading to a decent sized kitchen—twice Teg’s—and stairs leading up to bedrooms front and back with a tiny bathroom wedged between.

“We haven’t had much time to do what we were hoping: light tubes, fix the cracks and brighten it up with paint—well, paint’s been getting a bit expensive as the supplies disappear,” Zara apologized.

I looked out the back bedroom window onto a tiny yard of neglected dirt—but next door, neighbors had raised garden beds and even a small chicken coop. I watched a pair of hens circle the garden fence looking for ways to get at the new lettuce. Beyond the back fence, which would need repairing, the little alley that Justin and I had followed Tegson up on the first leg of that crazy overnight. I glanced up and saw the back windows of Justin and Zara’s across the way. That clinched it.

“I think it’s amazing,” I told her. “I couldn’t in my wildest imagination picture myself having a place this big and...elegant.”

Justin laughed. “It’s not elegant yet—but I know what you mean. We liked it for its bones, and I know it could be really beautiful place. With a lot of elbow grease.”

I was suddenly aware of the time and told them I needed to get to the colony. I asked them to convey my interest and thanks to Aida and the rest them. I raced to Buttercup Way, buoyed by images of sitting by the fire with Ciera, or watching her make dinner on the pink granite kitchen countertop.

I was out of breath when I arrived, and was happy to see the group clustered around an open wooden two-horse cart which held stolen e-cycles and bikes. Four e-cycles stood nearby, and community members were hoisting sacks and barrels into the cart. Siegfried, Rom and Astrid gave me extra wide grins, and Astrid added a big hug.

“You’re certainly *my* hero,” she whispered, then let me go.

Pippin was doing his best to act casual, but I suspected he was as bubbly as I felt. I couldn’t keep a grin off my face as we headed north, and even the gray skies threatening drizzle couldn’t dampen my mood.

36

We were traveling as fast as the horses could canter, each hungry for Ambridge in their own way. I short-circuited my increasing panic by glancing at the acres of empty buildings and crumbling but still salvageable materials—surely there was still enough we didn't need to go to war over it! Maybe it just needed more organization. But maybe Ciera was right about there being one or two items in short supply—something I wasn't seeing. I pondered all this as we whizzed through the deserted towns, keeping half an eye open for danger. I was too close to mess it up now.

It was astonishing how much of the rockfall had been cleared—there was enough room for us to go through single file, with Siegfried getting out and leading the skittery horses, the cart scraping the sides of the dirt mounds. A half-dozen workers were hauling rock and dirt off to the side, with a pair of armed guards keeping watch. They hailed us as we rode through, and we waved—then the road widened out and we picked up the pace again. In less than two hours we were in Ambridge.

The community looked different without the refugees—in the Hall, the long tables were re-arranged in the middle for dining, the chairs spaced around them. It was empty at this hour and our footsteps echoed as we crossed toward the kitchen. I realized I was holding my breath and let it out with a whoosh. *Where was she?*

Pippin inquired among the cooking staff, then turned back to me with a tragic look. My heart stuttered and I took two steps forward.

"She's gone back to her town," he said. For a moment all I felt was relief that nothing bad had happened. How was I going to be able to deal with this ever-present panic? How does somebody love and not walk on knives every moment??

"She must have left just after I did. Sorry, Martin."

I rubbed my face. "Is there some way to—follow her? Or get a message?"

A sturdy black woman no taller than Pippin's elbow turned from stirring a large pot and walked over. "That group has always been so secretive," she said, "they don't want us to know exactly where they are. Even relatives don't know. We always have to wait till they come back."

"Once we get more radios," Pippen said, leading me back to the Hall where we sat across from each other at an empty table, "maybe we'll be able to stay in contact."

"Will they want that?" I asked bitterly. Would I have to wait here for months?? Why didn't she wait? Hadley was probably trying to match her up with that damn carpenter right now. Maybe I could find Monica's again. "I mean, they *say* they want to be independent, so why would they want anyone to call them?"

Pippin rubbed the stubble on his chin; our day had been long enough to bring on a 5 o'clock shadow. "Maybe they won't—especially since you can sometimes locate people by their radios," he said. "On the other hand, if it were me, I'd take the risk. We've known for a long time that this plateau couldn't hold—we're moving into a different phase now, and we're *all* going to have to change."

We were interrupted by Rom walking in with Siegfried and Erma. She rushed to us, more agitated than I'd ever seen her. She stopped and looked us over as if searching for holes.

"Rom told me—Pippin, you fool—I'm so glad you're back!" She laughed but it turned into almost a sob. "I don't know what we'd do without you, you crazy old man! If you weren't my only first cousin, I disown you!" She sat next to him and leaned her head on his shoulder, closing her eyes.

Cousins. I'd forgotten there'd be so many relatives—just like my family's commune. She reached out without opening her eyes, felt across the table till she found my hand and squeezed it.

"Thank you, Martin—here's another thing we have to be grateful to you for. I hope we can pay you back."

"No need," I assured her. "I was as eager to get him back as you were."

"Well, I owe you. And the one thing I *can* do –" she opened her eyes and smiled at me, "is to tell you that Miz Ciera is planning to come back in a week—she is getting permission to become their representative out here, trying to convince them they need connection right now."

Pippen thumped the table. "Just like I said!" he crowed. "I knew that girl had her head on straight."

He grinned me in triumph, and I smiled weakly. So, maybe only a few days wait—but what if it didn't work? She had defied Hadley, but could she defy an entire town? What if they made her stay?

My gut was still in turmoil as I followed Pippin to one of the staff rooms, where he indicated the top bunk was empty. The tiny space was almost completely filled with stacked chests of drawers interspersed with bookshelves—what small bit of wall was visible around the ceiling was crammed with pre-Adjustment oddiments.

"I'm an old man—I've collected a few things in my time, I guess," he explained. "You can hang your knapsack on the bunk bed. I can empty a drawer if you need one."

I told him the knapsack would be fine. "If it's going to be a week, I might go back down and—arrange more things," I told him. "If you can be sure to tell her to wait, that is."

"Oh, I'll *tell* her—but she seems to be the type it's hard to tell anything." He was smiling but serious.

I nodded vehemently. "Yeah—I found that out several times. I'm not quite sure what to do about it."

He shrugged. "What works for me is just to tell those kind a' people what I plan to do, and let them decide for themselves. Of course, you have to be ready for anything."

He filled me in on the town meeting as we walked back through the kitchens and outside. Apparently there was still disagreement about the wisdom of the rebellion, "—even after it blew up like the Empire's Death Star!" he said with a snort, then sighed. "Looks like there's gonna be some push-pull for a while, and we're going have to be careful who we tell what. I hate when that happens."

"It's happened before?" We were walking across the commons where the rope makers had been. The sun was warm, and children were laughing, playing a game of carrying mostly-flat, lipped plastic circles on their heads. A small child dropped hers, and the water in it drenched her, to the hooting of the others.

"It's happened several times," he said, watching them. "Even though we all have the same general idea of sustainable, there's a lot of difference in details. It used to be called dissensus, but I call it a pain in the ass." He walked over to a child who was holding a circle, took it out of her hands turned it upside down and tossed it flat with a flick of his wrist—it spun like a top and flew across the grass. The children yelled and ran after it, their water-filled "hats" spilling everywhere. They tried to imitate his toss, but the plastic circles flopped and bounced; some cracked.

"They can't get the hang of frisbees," he chuckled. "I've tried to teach 'em, but they just don't get it."

He led the way across to a weather-stripped yellow clapboard bungalow and we stepped inside. The front room was heaped with broken plastic items, all shapes and colors, like the fringiest junk shop imaginable. At a central table under a light tube, two young men, obviously brothers, were snapping the plastic bits with pliers and retrieving the tiny metal hinges and screws buried inside.

"How's it going, dudes?" he asked them.

"We found a bunch of good gears, dunno if they're the right size," one of them said, pushing a heap of toothed silver circles toward him. Pippin picked them up and looked them over, then replaced them.

"Prime time," he said. "I'll be back to check again later."

As we left, he explained that some of the smaller tools they used required parts they couldn't find or make—so they were searching broken plastic toys and junk to see if anything else would work.

"Like I said, we're moving into a new phase—this war is just one sign of it. There's still shitloads of some stuff, but too many scary gaps."

"Justin's group might know where to get salt, in case that's a problem," I offered, "and I know Long Island has a couple desalination plants. Maybe the General can include that in the trade agreement."

He looked at me eagerly. "Yeah, it's one of the items that's nightmare. Salt's something that doesn't grow on trees. And there's plants that they used to have, that prevented diseases, but we can't grow 'em up here. Oranges and stuff. Spinach helps, but only in spring. And oranges tasted sooo good."

"Don't you have greenhouses?"

"Yeah—haven't you seen ours?" He changed course across the green and led me down a brick-cobbled road between a couple two-story brick buildings, past a dual wellhead—one old fashioned bucket-type and one solar pump side by side. This compound was larger than I'd realized, several blocks in each direction. Tucked against one of the barrier walls was a one and a half story glass shed of old wood-framed windows fitted together in an intricate patchwork. Pippin gestured toward it proudly. "This is where we try out plants, and raise some of the spices and herbs that we really need. Not big enough for those orange trees, or coffee plants, and that's a bummer."

"They have factories in New Jersey that manufacture some of those vitamins—I think they're called that—but now that I know the City has been lying, I wonder if the pills have anything in them."

"It was that way Before, you know, "he said. "They were selling pills of all kinds, and they kept finding out they were full of sawdust or even worse crap. But people kept buying." He shook his head in disgust.

"Pippin—how good are the patrols around here?" The thought had been bothering me the whole ride up. "I mean—Ciera and her friends were riding around as if it was as safe as the City, or as if their guns would stop an ambush. But there are no town walls—except this place—and the forests could be full of bandits, and what about those slavers that act like they're singers?"

"Well, it's like this—we have a group of ten towns on both sides of the Beaver, stretching from the middle of what used to be Ohio, with Ambridge on the eastern edge. That keeps that area relatively safe. We've trained up some good trackers, given them the best horses, or sometimes bikes. They investigate all reports of theft, damage, violence—and they have the right to deal with the villains as they see fit. And frankly, we don't have money for prisons." His expression was a mix of grief and anger. "Of course, there are some towns in between that we haven't quite convinced to come over to the Force." He chuckled, then continued. "They benefit from our watchdogs and we think sometimes they look the other way if slavers come through. But those blueshirts know not to run into us, and real strangers aren't all that common—there's a *lot* of wilderness to travel through to get to our area, and as far as we can tell, out west of Ohio is pretty dang empty. One or two folk came through a couple years back, and said the middle of the country was just flattened by drought—almost a desert."

"How... how big is the country? I mean—I've seen maps but...until I came out here..."

He laughed. "I know what you mean—it's hard to wrap your mind around the distances. And when you think people used to commute across the entire country, sometimes twice a week. It just feels like another world."

We were both silent for a minute, contemplating it. Teg had told me stories about Imperial Rome and the Dark Ages that followed its collapse, but those were like the stories of gods and fairies. This was *real*, close to home—whenever a mysterious piece of the old civilization cropped up, it was a peekhole into a time and place we would never comprehend. Even Pippin couldn't explain it to us. Why had *everything* been wrapped in incredibly detailed color pictures? Why had nobody thought about the dangers of putting all their information on magic machines that could just die?

"One of our patrols sent word there was a group lurking in the forest over near Economy, " Pippen said. "We're putting one of the best teams on it today."

I suddenly remembered about Jontee, the ringleader Aida had mentioned several days ago. "It could be a group from the Mall—I'd heard some of them headed this way when they found out the Southerners had withdrawn. They could be dangerous."

Pippin snorted. "Seems like a bunch of incompetents to me," he said. "But I'll let the patrol know. In fact—do you want to walk down with me to the Town Hall?"

I accepted eagerly, hoping for clues to how this all worked. He left word at the gate and we toiled up the gently sloping streets toward a rise that overlooked the river. Again, the pattern of shop-cluster and empty-area struck me, and I asked Pippin about it.

"Yeah—it might have been smarter to push everything together," he said, "but it was really hard to shake off the whole ownership thing after the Chaos. People got caught up with the idea of staying where they always had, maybe family moved in near them, and then they realized they were too far apart to protect each other. By then things were pretty bad and so they just circled the wagons wherever they were. The colony retreated behind their brick walls, and there are two other colonies in town that formed about the same time, using the old high school, and a mini mall. You can almost see one if you look down that street," he said, pointing. I looked along blocks of shops and homes, colored cloth flags gaily indicated *open for business*, but I didn't see anything that looked like the colony.

"And we still don't have enough people to fill in all the blank spaces, but we keep 'em from collapsing, and from hiding black hats. There were a couple of decades of Wild West around here," he continued, "before the treaty and people settling down to make do and trade. They say there's places where the Dark Side won, but in our area, like I said, we make sure folks are pretty safe. Here we are."

We were in front of a building of tan brick, with fully glassed arched windows; *Town Council* was painted on a board that hung just above the door.

Pippin ushered me in and was hailed from all sides—apparently his escapade had already been noised around. I let him deal with the excitement as I glanced around the room. Most striking was a map that took up half of one wall, behind a mostly unscratched sheet of glass. Markings on the glass—red circles, green squares, blue or yellow lines in between—seemed like updating. In the center of the room, a pair of light tubes carried illumination down to four large tables. Stacks of paper alternated with what looked like wood-framed chalk or wax tablets; I wondered how much paper they could access out here. A squawk and static directed my attention to the corner where a radio was set up—very similar to the Army box I'd seen. How many radios did the town have and did they share with the commune? Not enough, apparently, since Erma was so eager for more. A young black man sat in front of it, listening to the *tappetty tap* that I now knew was Morse code. I wandered closer and my attention was caught by three long lists tacked to the wall near the map. I read "Current Needs," "Trade Surplus/Salvage," "Infrastructure." I scanned the lists—they *were* looking for salt, also small gears, as Pippin had mentioned, and wire, broccoli seeds and canvas sacks.

"Broccoli seeds?" I murmured.

A young woman looked up and said, "Two years ago, we had a bad crop failure. We've been trying to rebuild our supplies ever since, especially of resilient strains," she said.

"So this is where you organize the town?" I asked her, but before she had a chance to answer, Pippen pulled me over to introduce me to four women and a couple men—the town leaders, who fussed over me as the author of his escape. Most of them were about my age, far younger than my friend. He finally got them to shift to the topic of security, and let me repeat what I knew about Jontee supposedly going west from the Mall.

Reluctantly, I added, "They might have some really—fancy—guns. I've seen some that fired really fast."

"Semi-automatics?" Pippin asked, startled. "That would be evil." It looked like about half the group knew what he meant and the others were puzzled. Feeling like the Snake in the Garden, I described the guns and their abilities as best I could.

"If you had a pencil and something to sketch on, I could draw you a picture." A young man with cropped black hair pushed a piece of paper and sharpened pencil toward me.

"He's really good at drawing," Pippin commented, looking over my shoulder as I sketched. "Looks like AK-47s."

I pushed the picture back and said, "I don't think any armor you have would work against this. You'll just have to catch them by surprise, before they catch you. Or duck behind stone or steel."

"Forewarned is forearmed," one woman said. "I'll put the word out."

They gave me a tour of the room, confirming that the marks on the glass were settlements. I peered closely, with a vague sense of where Ciera and I had traveled, trying to figure out where her town might be. I saw two small lakes that might fit her description, but they were far apart and it would take me weeks to check them out, if I could even get that far. It wasn't time yet, but how the hell should I know when to stop waiting and start panicking?

The Council members showed me pictures of the town before the Chaos, tucked away in drawers to prevent light fade. The buildings looked similar, but the people—they were wild! Clothing stranger than anything I'd seen even in Madison, and colors impossibly bright and clashing... maybe what I thought was Adjustment Shock was really the way they used to live! I'd never have been able to concentrate with all the color, and words painted and hanging *everywhere*. How did people ever pay attention?

On the infrastructure list, I noticed "solar laser forge" and asked about it. Pippin told me it was an experimental project using a small satellite dish and a bunch of broken mirror. "We found the instructions in an old book, and it says you can make light strong enough to melt metal. Once we found a couple of Fresnel lenses, we decided it was worth trying. But I guess the measurements are tricky—" he looked at a slim woman whose no-nonsense stance marked her as an engineer- type. She nodded.

"We have to catch the maximum amount of light and funnel it directly to one point on the lens," she said, "so that the focused light is concentrated on a single area. We've burned through wood so far—so I think we're gonna do it eventually." She nodded again, with satisfaction; not a smiling type.

My stomach growled—we must be getting close to dinner. Pippin thanked the group and we returned to the colony. The evening meal was animated and upbeat, as if we weren't on the brink of war. Would I ever get used to that? I still sat out the various games and dances of the evening, but I laughed more and cheered on the most creative. *Some* things were starting to feel familiar.

Fortunately for my nerves, my attention over the next two days was taken up with constructing a security post along Highway 65 about a third of the way toward the mall. Town and colony volunteers teamed up to construct an outpost in an old water tower—building a platform below the tank, adding a little hut and furnishing it with supplies for several weeks. The trio of teen boys who were to stay guard were given a precious pair of binoculars and promised a radio handset as soon as new ones were made. Until then, they had two rifles and a signaling bow with pitch-dipped arrows to fire in case of danger. The view from the platform reminded me of the bridge, and I was grateful I wouldn't be spending *my* time staring down. They couldn't see into the forested areas, but they had an excellent view up and down Hwy. 65 from Ambridge to the rockfall.

As we were finishing that, word came over the radio that another group of about ten carts and bikes had been rounded up down at the mall, so I volunteered to go with a group to fetch them. The plan was to put bikes on each of four carts and ride one back, so the four young men with me rode double on the way down. They hollered and waved at the kids in the tower, who waved a bright blue flag at them as we passed. I thought about that Fresnel laser idea—if they could make that work and mount one up at the tower, it could be a nasty weapon in the right circumstances. Then I caught myself—did I want City tactics out this far? My parents had said *the best defense is a good offense*, but that was probably what got us to this mess.

The carts had been rounded up in the warehouse/cattle shed where the rebel leaders had been held; seeing it again brought a shudder, and I didn't stay long, letting the group arrange the return trip as I hurried over to Justin's workshop. He'd been waiting for me and had a large heavy canvas package on the table.

"Five armored jackets, various sizes," he reported. "Part of the swap, but perhaps not as public."

I assured him I would keep them covered and hand them over to Erma. I explained how Ciera had gone back, and that even if she succeeded I didn't know whether she would feel tied to Ambridge.

"Well, we obviously would prefer you down here, but now that the road is getting more use, you wouldn't be far away," he replied.

"I know—but always I hate being in the back where I can't see what's coming," I confessed. "I get antsy when I don't know what's in store."

"Don't we all," he chuckled. "This feels like the eye of a hurricane—have you ever been through that?"

"Once, when I was a child—it was really scary. Where everything suddenly gets still, but you know the rest of the storm is just a few miles away."

"Yep. This storm's gonna break open a huge can of worms, if I can mix my metaphors," he said with a grin. "But sometimes when it's iffy like this, we can change things for the better. And if they're really focusing on Philly, we've got time to make the best defense possible. Teg—Tegson, I mean—has gone into the City to find out as much as he can—I don't envy him that, but we'll find out and maybe even influence what's gonna happen."

"That's why I want to be here!" I said. "I've *got* to convince her that this is the best place. Can we... can we get some furniture for the house?"

So we spent the next couple hours pulling together a few pieces—a dining table and chairs, some kitchen equipment, and a comfortable bed. We borrowed one of the Ambridge carts and hauled the stuff over to the new place. It still looked empty, but Zara promised she would add a few nice touches before I got back.

"And we just got word—the young lady in question has arrived at Ambridge and is wondering where the hell you got to." She grinned.

A zap of something like strong electricity shook me. I chivvied the youngsters who were loading the carts and we pushed ourselves out of there within the next hour, heading back with recovered vehicles, a few extra trades and the armored vests tucked in one of the carts. The weather was strange—sun was shining through a gentle rain, that surprising spring combination. There was even the slightest hint of a rainbow, though I was focusing mostly on possible attack. As usual, the closer I got to a goal, the more superstitious I got. But finally, Ambridge and the colony were in sight. The boys were creating a parade, waving to the townsfolk as if they were returning veterans, so I raced ahead on my bike.

I ditched it by the entrance and flat out ran to the Hall. She was standing by the door to the kitchen, chatting with Erma. I raced across it and did what I should have done the last time—grabbed her and kissed her vigorously. She needed to know my doubts were gone.

When we broke apart, Erma was struggling to keep a straight face. "Good to see you again, Martin," she said. "I was just telling Ciera about some of your adventures."

"You've been back inside twice??" Ciera demanded. Her eyes were wide, and she was frowning.

"Had to," I told her. "But I'm hoping it's the last time for a while."

She seemed disappointed. "So it'll be dangerous in there for you now?"

"Unless I can become someone else—but that's not impossible. But what about you?"

She tried to look casual but her smile gave her away. "It took a while, but I convinced them that somebody at least needs to be on top of what's going on. And also, there *is* a precedent—our town members do marry away on occasion, and stay connected." She looked at me from under her long lashes, but I simply smiled.

"Well, that's settled then," I replied. Had I just proposed? Probably—but I'd try to do it a bit more romantically that evening. "And what about that carpenter?"

She snorted. "I told him Gilda who works in the bakery was really hot for his body."

Erma turned aside and her shoulders shook. I assumed she had to keep up her presidential demeanor, but any cousin of Pippin's would have to have a good sense of humor. She waved us off.

Ciera brought me to the room they had given her, and we had a chance to really greet each other. After a while, I tried to explain why I had been so ambivalent, tried to tell her about the fear that seem to knock me sideways every time I thought about us.

Ciera shushed me gently and said, "Pippin told me you're like a Survivor. Only in the next generation. He said some families never recovered from the Chaos—they pass the scar down."

Bless you, Pippin. It made sense, though again I didn't know what to do about it. "Did he say there was any hope?" I asked. An attempted chuckle turned into a groan.

She cuddled me harder. "He seems to manage," she said, "maybe he'll have some tips."

"Also—" It felt like there were too many—what did Teg call them?—variables. "I know things are going to be bungee-jumping for a while, but I'm sure that I want to be with you out here." I thought about Pippin's advice on not telling her what to do. "I'm going to be needed in the Mall for... a while, and I have something to show you down there, if you wouldn't mind a trip back."

"I have to set up an arrangement with Erma about communications—but then, yes. And I'm sorry I got so upset on our tour. It's hard to sort out what's temptation, and what's just a different way of life. But I'm beginning to think... my town... is wrong to keep us away from it. It doesn't make it easier to resist—it made it harder."

"Pippin was talking about dissensus—about differing opinions and what a pain they are," I said. "But I'm seeing that you *have* to have different people trying different things because we've lost the instruction manual to our world and have to switchup until we figure out what works. *I* sure didn't have it right. If I hadn't volunteered for that stupid job, I'd be stuck inside the City right now, totally clueless until the famine hit."

She squeezed my waist. "I've gotten chills several times this week, thinking about how we stumbled on each other and how we could've missed. Do you believe in Fate? Stories used to tell of something called kismet."

"I dunno. Mostly I try not to think about it. That stuff's way too big. I've spent my whole life worried about survival, and unless I could eat it, drink it or sleep in it, it didn't matter to me." I stroked her hair, thinking how much bigger my world had become. "Now my surviving has widened out to include the survival of a couple towns and several people." I kissed her nose. "Including—no, especially—you."

The next day I was frankly hovering as she worked with Erma to arrange a series of relay riders and info-drops that would ensure regular news to and from the lake town. Apparently her friends Lio and Matty had agreed to travel to a meeting point at least twice a week while things were unsettled. Radios would be discussed, but were not yet agreed to. I tried not to be impatient, tried not to think only of myself, but my excitement built along with my panic. What if she didn't want to stay? What if she didn't like the place?? I supposed I could make do somewhere here in Ambridge, but I already had such a craving for pink and synth-cafe that I'd be constantly cycling back and forth, and what if I couldn't afford the fuel? *Just let me find out one way or the other,* I prayed.

It felt like forever, but just after lunch we were ready to head down, accompanied by Rom and Astrid on another run to trade and pick up more precious radio equipment. Using the new radio set-up, I'd told Justin and Zara we were on our way. Without a cart, we could move faster and I pointed out the new security tower as we passed. We made it in less than two hours, and I waved goodbye to the others as I led Ciera toward our street, improbably called Warlo.

I fumbled with the key as I opened the door. Keeping Ciera on the porch, I hurriedly looked inside. Zara had put up new-ish curtains, pinned them back and carefully angled several polished tin sheets to reflect light around the almost empty rooms. The furniture only seemed to make the house bigger and more empty, but she'd put some pretty jars on the mantelpiece. I sniffed dried lavender and rosemary; a nice touch. I took a deep breath, opened the door again and stepped aside.

"This way," I said, ushering her into the square entry hall; the door to the right was propped open and sun streamed through the windows.

She stepped inside and looked around, then glanced at me suspiciously.

"What am I supposed to be looking at?"

"Um...our new home?" I watched her expression closely—maybe I should have warned her. She stared at me in confusion, then turned slowly, poked her head into the side room, then walked down the hall to the kitchen, glancing up the staircase, then back at me.

"What—all of it??" Her footsteps echoed as she returned.

"It's ours if we want it," I said, searching her face for clues. "The town owns these places and it's ours to fix up—there's two bedrooms upstairs, and a bathroom—though that doesn't work. I think the roof could hold a solar panel, though," I said enticingly.

She still looked suspicious; did she think I was joking? She walked down the hall and poked her head in the kitchen again. She called back, "That stove won't work. But there's room for an ice box." She came back in the hall, then stepped out the back door. "No space for vegetables."

"But look what they did in the yard next door—a lot in a small space. Even chickens. And both of us will be busy working. Not as much time for gardens." I joined her by the back door; my gut was roiling.

She came back in, looking stunned, as if it had finally sunk in. "Really? *All* of this?" I saw tears in her eyes.

I hugged her and whispered, "Yes, all of it. *If* you want to stay here in town. I know it's farther away from Evansville, and there's not enough nature, but—don't you want to know what's happening? You can still be representative here, especially with the radios. And we'd have plenty of room here for visitors. Maybe it's dangerous, living close to an edge, but it's more exciting."

She looked up at me and smiled. "You make things exciting no matter where you are," she said. *Was that a joke?* "And yes—I *do* want to know what's going to happen next."

"This doesn't have to be forever—but I think we could learn a lot here."

She hugged me tighter. "I think so too."

"First thing we'll have to do is get a tunnel installed," I said. We broke down into helpless laughter, leaning on each other until it passed.

* * *

Our handfasting was held at the Ambridge colony a month later—Pippin stood beside me and I met her three sisters and another brother, though it was Hadley she chose to bring her down the aisle. He almost mustered a smile. It was a large ceremony, with a dozen coming up from the Mall, and another dozen from her town, and all the colony members. Teg sat in the front row, anonymous, disguised to avoid any resemblance to his famous son, who was back from the City and off flying some mission.

We had another small spat during the reception—something about my wandering off with the guys when I was supposed to cut the cake. Inevitable, I suppose, and quickly mended. I'd have to get used to it. Like living with a firecracker. But I couldn't think of anybody else that I wanted beside me as the next phase unfurled. I'd started out as blind as that poor Adjustment-shocked old man, and I still had a lot learning to do. And hopefully a few things to share.

ABOUT THE AUTHOR

Catherine McGuire is a writer and artist with a deep concern for the earth and the living beings residing there. She uses her creativity to speak to the many deep concerns facing us all today and into the future. Her poetry book, *Elegy for the 21st Century,* was published by FutureCycle in 2016 and her two children's SF novels published by TSR in the 1980's. She lives in Sweet Home, Oregon on a mini homestead, with chickens, rabbits and bees. Find her at www.cathymcguire.com.

CPSIA information can be obtained
at www.ICGtesting.com
Printed in the USA
FSHW011252291018
53383FS

9 781945 810046